Other Books

Cyrus Cooper Series:

Book One: Dangerous Minds

Book Two: Rogue Faction Part 1

Book Three: Rogue Faction Part 2

Book Four: Halon Seven

Book Five: Surviving Origin Part 1

Book Six: Surviving Origin Part 2

Black Rock Series:

Black Rock: The Rising - Death Curse

For more information, please visit:

XanderWeaver.com

Chapter 1 - Life-And-Death Consequences

Wild-Side

Today

I was moving fast. Far faster than was safe, given the three-quarter moon, the rough terrain, and the dangers of the creatures stalking the wilderness. They called it the Forbidden Zone for a reason. Actually, they had a lot of names for it, but none captured the horror that the people of that world felt for the untold miles of untouched forest surrounding one of their few small cities. The city walls had been enough to keep the denizens of Wild-Side safe until recently, and I still didn't know if the few who had gone missing had somehow been taken or had just wandered off before falling prey to creatures from their darkest nightmares.

While I still had hope that the city walls held integrity, there was no question the Elend were growing bolder as they became more organized. They were also expanding in numbers; the truth of the correlation was still only a suspicion as I plowed through the thick brush and vegetation. The wilds of the Reaches resembled those of the Pacific Northwest and the Midwest of home. Tall trees consisted of everything from conifers to massive oaks, redwoods, and elms. But it was like the size restrictions of my world–Our-World–didn't apply there. It was common for hardwoods to be bigger around at the base than the bedroom I had as a child. Maybe it had something to do with the population of Wild-Side. Though the people were unquestionably more technologically advanced, somehow, they had evolved in small numbers and managed not to overpopulate their world. They never became a burden on their natural resources, and it seemed their technology evolved quickly enough to keep them from making the same mistakes as Our-World.

Nearly the entire population lived in five small cities situated across two large continents. Hundreds, sometimes thousands of miles of virgin wilderness separated each city. And somehow, it worked. The people, for the most part, lived healthier and more content lives than the people of Our-World. They were intelligent, had resources, and their technology benefited them without damaging their environment.

Unfortunately, they were no longer at the top of their food chain. Something happened just over a year before that day in the woods. It shifted the balance of power, not only for the Seeley but for Our-World, too. Looking back, stopping it was obviously beyond my ability. A doorway was opened, and though I played a part, from what I'm told, it was certain to happen sooner or later. If not for me at that time, it would have been someone like me, perhaps generations later.

It was only ever a matter of time. Regardless, what happens next is on me. I can and will bring balance to both worlds... even if it is the last thing I ever do.

———————

Like I said, I was moving fast. One of the Seeley had gone missing, last seen near the base of the East wall. I didn't know her personally, but that didn't matter. The Seeley were a peaceful people and, in all the ways that mattered, simple. They were intelligent as all hell, but also foolish in many ways. They lacked the common sense required for long-term self-preservation. I think it came from their short, aggressive evolution in an environment with no natural predators. Book smart, but street stupid. They had evolved without a propensity for fighting each other, so when something dangerous—deadly— entered their environment, they were entirely unprepared and defenseless.

I say *they* referring to their entire race, not just portions of their population.

Nature has a twisted sense of humor, so when the Elend first crossed over to Wild-Side, so did I. Nature can be unfair, but it does insist on balance. For whatever reason, I am part of that balance. The first Elend to cross the Vale was a creature we now call Breslin. When he crossed to Wild-Side, a balance of sorts was struck, and I was pulled across from Our-World as part of that equilibrium. I thought the entire experience was a series of dreams. I was convinced of it for months. Strange imaginings turned into scary dreams, which turned into nightmares.

Then, one day, hey! The whole damn thing turned out to be real. As was my way, I skipped the whole inner angst of asking myself if I was crazy. There was no question by that point.

Needless to say, if you're confused now, it pales in comparison to the mind fuck I experienced. I was traveling to another plane of existence some nights when I slept. Sound like the sort of thing a crazy man might claim? You bet. Except in my case, it was really happening, and with life-and-death consequences.

So…I was moving fast. Trust me, this is the best place to start. You're about to see why.

It was dark; the brush cover was thick, and I'm not even exaggerating: every freaking direction I turned, there was another mother of a thorn bush just begging to rip my eyes out. It didn't slow me down. I had prepared as much as possible given the six and a half minutes of preparation time before hopping the city wall. Jeans, a thick flannel, hiking boots, and a pair of wraparound safety glasses. The jeans, boots, and flannel were fabricated for me here; the Seeley had never pondered the wonders of outdoor attire prior to meeting me. And why should they? They rarely ventured more than a mile from the perimeter of a given city's wall. My glasses and gloves were considered innovations in this world. The glasses were contoured to match the shape of my face. They were nearly shatterproof, and it was easy to forget they were even there. The gloves were similar, tougher than leather, both form-fitting and light enough that I could feel the texture and grooves of my machete's handle. Even more importantly, the gloves didn't get in the way when I fired the 9mm caliber Springfield that was almost always strapped to my hip.

I'll explain these fun anachronisms later.

I keep saying I was moving fast. There's a reason for it. It was dumb; I was distracted, and it almost got me killed. I was following marks in the loamy soil—tracks I thought had been left by the Elend that had taken one of the natives. With my focus on the thorn bushes, machete, and marks in the dirt, I failed to notice the change in the forest until it was too late. The birds, insects, and other yammering little denizens of the night had gone suddenly silent.

With a final wave of the machete, I stumbled into a clearing. The floor of the woods was a jumble of crushed vegetation. It was splayed in a rough circle about fifty feet across. Though a small tree lay toppled through the center of the clearing—small by Wild-Side's standards in that it was perhaps only three feet in diameter—there was nothing natural about the clearing. The surrounding bramble had been smashed flat by someone or something.

The fine hair on the back of my neck stood at attention instantly as I realized I was dealing with one of the aforementioned something. In the wilds of Wild-Side, that could only mean something bloodthirsty and savage.

As one might guess, my attention was focused on the fallen tree. It was big enough for something toothy to use for cover and, therefore, the obvious point of ambush. And sure enough, a low grumble foretold the presence of precisely the kind of big-bad my man-hackles were portending. The felled tree shifted—the entire tree—as four Buck knife-sized talons rose from the darkness. They settled onto the surface of the bark and proceeded to clamp at least an inch deep into the hardwood. About three feet to the left of the first claw came a second. Between them rose a black, snake-like head. The face looked like a cross between an anaconda and...well, I'll just say it...the thing looked more than a little like a dragon. A roughly trash can-sized dragon head. Black and wet in appearance, it was covered in slick, thumbnail-shaped scales. It had fiercely pronounced brow ridges, inward-sloping cheeks, and a short, wide, nose-like muzzle filled with a double set of triangular razor-edged teeth; one set appeared forward-facing while the other angled backward. If nature ever engineers a maw more ideal for rending flesh and bone to pulp and powder, I hope never to see it.

The shoulders rose above the surface of the tree as the large yellow eyes bore into me. The teeth were bad, but the eyes managed to creep me out even more. They were round—perfectly round—and yellow like rich honey. A vertical slit dilated and contracted as the head shifted in the moonlight. This explained what I already knew:

these damn things could see in almost complete darkness. Since I could see every ripple and ridge in the thing's scaly skin, there was no question that it had me clocked. There was no backing into the brush, hoping to blend in.

This wasn't my first encounter with one of these creatures, but I'll admit the experience from that night left an indelible impression. It changed much of what I thought I knew and was, at least at that time, the closest near-death experience of my life.

Rising to full height behind the tree, the Elend was about what I expected from a full-grown male. At roughly seven feet tall, he was man-shaped and man-sized, if a bit super-sized. Like most of its kind, it was bipedal, walking primarily on two legs. Bone-like scale protrusions ran across the tops of both shoulders and down each arm to the elbow. It raised one hand and the claws—I'm not freaking kidding—grew longer by about a third.

I lifted my machete in response but focused on its eyes. These creatures were fierce, but they were not intellectual. They fought based on instinct rather than strategy. Plus, they were accustomed to hunting the Seeley of this world. A meal that fought back would be a novelty.

The creature eyed the blade in my upraised hand as if reading my mind. It seemed to consider the weapon. This was a new experience for me. I saw contemplation in those slitted yellow eyes. I had only ever seen that once before. There was an advanced level of intelligence in their leader, the one we called Breslin. He had abilities unlike any of his kind. But given what I saw in this creature, I started to wonder if the beasts were becoming smarter...

Then, the memory of the elaborate clearing came to mind. The path I'd followed was so blatant and obvious that anyone among the Seeley could have followed it without tracking experience. The entire event was a setup, starting with the abduction. Since I was the only one among the Seeley who would risk the Wilds, especially at night, the trap was obviously set for me.

"Breslin is getting better at this," I told the creature. It seemed to intentionally flex its scaly muscles, causing its black surface to shimmer in the moonlight. I glanced at the back of my left wrist. A translucent timer counted down on a display extending two and a half inches up the back of my arm. The numbers were so clear and crisp that I had to remind myself that only I could see the augmented reality display. Three minutes and thirty-one seconds until the Flip.

I heard a whoosh of air to my right and knew it would be the longest three and a half minutes of my life.

The Elend by the fallen tree had been a distraction. A blur of movement from my right, accompanied by a burst of air, warned me that another of the creatures had just broken from the cover of the tree line. These things were fast. They had reaction times quicker than most men, so I didn't think; I just acted. Dropping to my left hip, I swung the blade over my head before waving it toward the dirt near my right boot with all the strength I could manage. I sensed more than saw the scaly belly of the Elend fill the air over my head. I count myself lucky if it missed me by more than two inches. The creature was less fortunate. My blade parted the seam where scaly plates met at the center of its chest. Their bellies are more like armor, the scales at least as sturdy as bone, but our research into their anatomy has proven that cartilage joins their chest panels, similar to how the human sternum helps the left and right ribs meet at the center of the torso.

The creature plowed a trench in the foliage with the force of its face and chest as it crashed and slid. Viscous slime, the color and consistency of someone sneezing with the world's worst head cold, coated its path. The same substance dripped from the leading edge of my machete.

First, something you need to know about the machete: calling it razor-sharp would be a disservice. By definition, a razor is sharp enough to shave one's face. The technology used to forge this blade and then hone its edge was beyond anything possible in Our-World. I'm told the blade's nanoparticle lattice construction will ensure it cannot be broken by anything short of deliberate and intentional mechanical manipulation. Since I tend to damage things on a grand scale, my hosts here seemed to take particular pride in that claim. I was also told the blade would hold its edge through the most tortured abuse. Of course, the science of all this was explained to me in mind-numbing detail, but...well, they really should just stop trying to explain the science. Needless to say, no one would ever attempt to shave with anything this sharp—at least not more than once. This was the kind of blade that could separate your face from your head before you even noticed you'd had an accident.

It's important to clarify the precision and strength of the machete because you're likely wondering why I would lead with a blade when I have a perfectly good pistol within arm's reach. The stumbling Elend was a great example of what I'm dealing with and what I've learned through painful experiences over the last year.

The creature was climbing to its hands and knees, so to speak, when its compatriot opposite the tree decided to tag in. It lunged, clearing the tree in a single leap. Since I was still on the ground, I had just enough time to raise my blade before the monster literally fell upon me. My blade passed through its heart with ease. The realization caught the creature so off guard that it neglected to swing either taloned hand at me. At that point, given our proximity and considering I was pinned under its 300-pound bulk, I would have been sirloin. I read the confusion in those wide, honey-colored eyes and shoved the beast away.

By the time I was swaying back to my feet, the Elend with the split chest was just returning to its own. His front was parted at the center, and a substance with the consistency of raspberry jam was leaking from the thirty-six-inch-long wound. Still, it appeared entirely undeterred by the injury. Similarly, the creature with what should have been a mortal puncture to its heart was already beginning a clumsy rebound.

That's the thing with Elend. As far as I've been able to figure over the last year, only two things can kill them. One must either completely separate the head from the body or cause catastrophic damage to the eyes. I know what you're thinking. It can't be their eyes. Damaging their eyes must destroy the brain, which must be what takes them down. Trust me. I've killed more of these things than anyone should ever have to face, and it's not the damage to the brain that does the job. It's the eyes.

It's always the eyes.

It's said the eyes are the window to the soul. I have a hard time believing these creatures have souls, but either way, stick to the rules. They can save your life. Destroy an eye or remove the head. If not, they will keep coming until they get you.

I glanced at my wrist and saw forty-two seconds remaining. It was doable. I just needed to keep the two going long enough to run down the clock. That's when I heard movement beyond the perimeter of the clearing. Multiple contacts, no question. At least two more Elend, maybe more.

Suddenly, I wasn't as confident in my forty-two seconds. I was surrounded.

Something had changed with the creatures. Either they were getting smarter, or they were becoming more coordinated. I instantly thought of Breslin. He'd been consolidating his power here. Apparently, he was having success pulling more of the Elend under his authority. It meant his plans for Wild-Side weren't the only thing I had to worry about. He was organizing forces here while consolidating the resources and power on our side of the Vale.

Honestly, it was the first time I realized just how dangerous Breslin truly was to this world and ours.

Suddenly, time wasn't running out fast enough. I had Elend at the perimeter of the clearing. If they began to converge on me, I wouldn't have time to deal with the two before me. I needed to take these two out of play right away and hope the clock ran out before those at the tree line made their move.

The Elend with the split chest was on its feet first. It moved toward me on unsteady legs. I guessed the slit at the center of his chest had compromised its balance. It had to be painful, though these things didn't seem to feel pain like we do. I took two quick steps in its direction and swung my blade. I think it started to raise an arm in defense. It certainly wasn't at its best with the chest injury, and that had him moving much slower than normal. The finely honed edge of the machete lived up to the hype and cleaved the creature's reptilian head about an inch below the jawline. It tumbled away and disappeared behind the fallen tree.

I was still on my backswing when something plowed into me from the side. I dropped the machete and shoved the creature's chin away even as I felt its powerful arms trying to crush the life out of me. The Elend hoisted me into the air, arms clasped around me just above my hips. Its massive maw of double-rowed teeth snapped only inches from my ear as I pushed the face aside as far as I could.

The things are strong. Preternaturally strong. Man versus Elend in a one-on-one cage match? The Elend will rip the man limb from limb every time. It doesn't matter how big or strong the man is. The Elend, wherever they come from, are evolved killing machines. If I were religious, I would say they were demons. It's not a stretch of the imagination. They have the look, and they certainly have the bloodthirsty disposition.

I kicked and shoved, but it was all just an effort to buy time. Time to run down the clock and get my hand on the Springfield holstered at my hip. I was fighting a losing battle with one hand pressed against the creature's chin when I crushed the muzzle of the 9mm against the Elend's eye and pulled the trigger. The wet splatter hit my face as the percussive report slapped me upside the head.

The creature screamed and toppled. I rode it to the ground. When both of its taloned hands went to its face, I slipped the barrel of my pistol into the socket of the beast's second eye and peeled off another round.

The screeching howl went instantly silent, and I knew the second creature was vanquished. The victory was short-lived, however. I'm still not sure if I sensed or saw what came at me from my left. Either way, the gun slipped from my hand as I rolled for the cover of the fallen tree. I ducked into a tangle of thick, leafy limbs just as a hand fronted with talons swung at my midsection. I recall thinking the hand was smaller than those I'd just faced, but the talons were somehow thicker and more substantial. Then I heard the crash of the beast's blow splinter the ancient tree.

I was slammed into a sharp, jutting limb, and the display on my wrist vibrated. I was trying to push away at something poking my belly when the world around me began to blur. A heartbeat later, everything I could see flashed white, and the world spun with teeth-rattling abandon. I could hear the battle cry of the creature. It was laced with fury, but it was somehow distant and seemed to grow more distant with each passing heartbeat.

―――――――

Our-World

The world was a spinning, featureless void. I bounced off a soft, plush surface and went crashing into another that was cold and unyielding. I'm going to describe my scream as a manly bellow of rage that bordered on a battle cry, but it likely sounded like a squirrel barely surviving a near-miss with a speeding tractor-trailer. At that time, no one had ever studied my return, so it wasn't clear whether the violence of the event was linked to the Transition or if it was my body's response to the trauma of what was, by all accounts, an unnatural experience. Either way, the return, which often lacks grace, should never be witnessed by another human being. This time it was nearly as painful as the attack I'd been suffering from before the Transition. The spectacle is the second of three reasons why I endeavor to sleep alone.

You're likely wondering what the other two reasons might be. First of all, that means you're nosy. These things are personal. But stay tuned. While I have a short fuse and am quick to irritate, you'll soon find I tend to overshare. Stick with me long enough, and all will be revealed. For now, let's focus on the super impractical part of this experience I brushed over only a minute ago. I was entirely naked when I was launched from my bed onto the painful, cold, and unforgiving surface of the tile floor. Yeah, that soft thing I bounced off was my bed. I started this little misadventure there. I frequently do.

The observant among you might wonder, who puts porcelain tile on a bedroom floor? I'm glad you asked. It's not a bedroom, per se. I often hole up in unusual places such as warehouses, storage lockers, and abandoned buildings when I'm spending time in Our-World. As you might expect, such accommodations don't lend themselves to comforts like plush carpeting or air conditioning. I do insist on a comfortable mattress, running water, solid-core doors, and multiple means of egress.

Yeah, yeah,... naked on the floor. There's really no getting away from that unpleasant part of what I call the Transition. For reasons I'll never fully understand, I have the unique ability to move between Our-World and a place I call Wild-Side. Not the most creative names, you say? Bite me. You can worry about the creative writing, and I'll worry about my survival. The name is fitting since the place is currently plagued by an ever-increasing population of creatures that want to kill me and eat me—or maybe eat me before killing me. It's not entirely clear what they want to do with me or even what they do with the denizens of Wild-Side after abduction. Suffice it to say, it's one of several mysteries that a team of folks far more intelligent than I continue to attempt to understand. They are the brains. I concentrate on killing violent, deadly things before they can kill us meek and defenseless humans.

This is the story of two worlds. Well, three, if we're being technical. But for simplification and to bring you up to speed with minimal exposition, there are two worlds that we care about: Our-World and Wild-Side. What do the people of Wild-Side call their world? Fair question. Until they met me, they didn't know they needed a name. They didn't realize there was another world.

So Wild-Side it is.

This is all part of what the pointy hat people call Brane Theory, though the fact that they continue to use the word theory bothers me. It stopped being theory when I proved that moving between Branes was possible. I guess they can't call it Brane Science yet because no one understands how it works or why I can do what I can. If you're already guessing how and why any of this works, you're not the only one. No one understands why only I can cross between Branes. It doesn't keep pretty much everyone in Wild-Side from submitting a theory–

Oh! Right. Now I understand. It does work. I'm good with calling it Brane Theory again. Thanks for letting me work through it.

The theory is that reality as we know it is composed of membranes layered atop one another. Wild-Side is a reality separated from two others, positioned logically on either side. If someone had the means, either naturally or using a tool of some sort, they could move from Our-World to the reality, or membrane, adjacent on either side. This was only a theory–supposedly–until I started slipping across to the place I creatively refer to as Wild-Side.

Why can I cross membranes or Branes when no one else can? No idea. As I said, folks much more intelligent than I are working to make sense of that. And for reasons that will soon become clear, they are highly motivated. The opposition is working to solve the same problem, only for different reasons. That's a more complex story; again, more is soon to follow.

For now, let's concentrate on why I was naked and bleeding profusely on the cold tile floor. Oh, yeah! I neglected to mention the blood. In truth, I wasn't even aware of it until I slipped in a pool of my own B-positive and whacked my noggin on the floor. I turned my head just in time to prevent the loss of teeth. Cat-like reflexes even in the most messed up of moments, right?

"Shit!" I cursed. "Esker, give me some light."

A pair of lamps on the milk crates in opposite corners of the large room pulsed and came to life. "You're experiencing significant blood loss," Esker's voice seemed to come from every direction. "Shall I contact emergency services?"

I was still seeing stars, so I didn't immediately answer. I'm pretty sure he asked me the same question again, but I'll admit my recollection of this exact period is a little fuzzy.

Esker is the AI that interfaces with the nanotechnology infused in my body shortly after all of this Brane-walking started.

Brane-walking…I like that. I just made it up. We're going to go with that from now on. Being the world's only Brane-walker–well, almost only—I should be able to call it what I want, right?

Anyway…You might say that Esker's a voice in my head, though that makes me sound a little crazy. I can't be whack-a-do because there's science involved. Since Esker's linked to a quantum processing core here, I can access him only when I'm in Our-World. My nanotech works across Branes, but Esker only works here. Yes, my life is complicated. I'll understand if you're struggling to keep up.

I rolled onto my back, hearing the blood beneath my shoulders squish but not really feeling it. One arm patted the other even as my eyes rolled in their sockets, trying to focus against the newfound light. The sense of vertigo that accompanied every Transition scrambled my brain. Esker's words bounced around in the fog that was my mind. At first, I was dimly aware of the blood on the floor. And though I'm told it took only seconds for me to take action, it felt like long minutes.

Finally, I started to probe the surface of my body in search of the injury causing the slippery mess.

"Your lower right abdomen," I heard Esker say at the same time I felt my fingers wrap around something wedged in my flesh.

My eyes shifted to a stubby shard jutting from the skin just above my right hip. It was slightly curved and half as wide as my wrist. It was roughly the color of bone but had the texture of unsanded hardwood.

"It's a talon," I heard Esker say. "I recommend you do not—"

Talon. Let's call it what it really was, a freaking claw. I brought one of the freaking creature's claws back across the Vale with me…in my flesh! I stopped hearing Esker's words when I pulled the damn thing from my abdomen. I recall hearing it clatter to the tile, and the room started to spin.

Then everything went black.

———

I woke up almost four hours later, according to Esker. You're missing out if you've never had an AI chastise you for disobeying medical advice. It's a unique experience. There's no face to go along with the ass-chewing, and since the voice is in your head, it's extra hard to ignore. And when you're immobilized because the incorporeal entity is using your body's nanotech to keep you from moving a muscle, there's absolutely nothing you can do to make the lecture end before the intelligence decides you've had enough.

"I've flooded the wound with nanites," Esker was saying. "It was enough to stop the blood loss, and your abdominal wall is ninety-three seconds away from regaining structural integrity. I estimate one hundred and twenty-two minutes until you regain mobility."

"Swell," I said. My voice was dry and humorless, but I admit to feeling a certain amount of amusement about my situation. I couldn't feel anything. I was still lying bare-ass naked on the cold tile floor, but at least I couldn't feel the cold or the pain. And most importantly, I was safe. When the countdown timer hit zero, I rebounded to Our-World. Regrettably, I didn't find the abducted Wild-Side woman before bouncing home, but at least the Crossing had been timely. It had saved my life, if just barely.

Wild-Side was a Brane at war, and in a lot of ways, I was the one leading the fight. The Elend had set a trap for me that almost paid off. That meant I needed to rethink my strategy. They were organized in a way that was unprecedented up to that point, and I could already sense a shift in their power dynamic. It foretold new dangers for the Seeley, and for me in particular.

I looked down at myself, at least as much as I could since my body was immobile from the neck down. A thick, coagulated pool covered the floor. What I could see of my skin was pale with a blue pallor from the cold and blood loss. And even though I knew the nanites would be working overtime to replicate a fresh blood supply, there was no question my body would suffer from the experience.

"What's with the talon?" I said to Esker. "How did I bring it back?"

The AI's voice returned with its own healthy dose of confusion. I've never figured out if it mimicked human emotion or had it baked into its code. Either way, it was often very much like talking to another person. Other times, less so.

This was an example of one of Esker's less convincing performances.

"Unknown. We'll need more data before I can begin to guess," Esker said. "Doctor Cormac believes carrying anything physically across the Vale is impossible. Until now, we've had no evidence to the contrary."

He was right about that. This rule, for lack of a better word, was why I was lying naked on the floor. Nothing went with me when I crossed from one Brane to the next, what we sometimes call the Vale. No matter what I was doing when I started, I always ended up naked on the other side. It was more than inconvenient; it was dangerous. Wild-Side had become an increasingly savage place over the last year, and arriving there each time the way I did meant I had absolutely no means of protection. Arriving there wearing even a pair of pants would have been nice, but the truth was that I'd give my right nut for an assault rifle or even a sharp hunting knife.

Chapter 2 - Nowhere Kansas

Our-World

Unknown location Kansas

The Cessna flew at just over fourteen thousand feet in a turbulent, moonless sky. The time and timing were no coincidence. I'd planned the night's operation around the new moon, but the weather system was entirely unexpected. An unpredicted storm front was moving in quickly from the west, playing havoc with the small aircraft. Everything about the night's operation was planned and coordinated using every bit of intelligence I could beg, borrow, or steal. In this case, mostly steal. Everything except for the storm... and while it came out of nowhere and baffled meteorologists, I knew with certainty what it foretold.

More on that later.

Double Vision Gary was at the controls of the small four-seater plane. The rest of the seats had been removed since Double Vision's day job was hauling machine parts anywhere in the greater tri-state area. If you're wondering what kind of business there is flying tractor parts all over the state, there isn't. Double Vision was a smuggler. Think Han Solo minus the Wookie, and replace the Millennium Falcon with a worn-out and past-its-prime patched-up aircraft that should have been sold for scrap back when I was in diapers.

Not surprisingly, Double Vision's flexible moral compass made him perfect for my late-night rollercoaster ride through the clouds. For a price, he didn't ask questions, and he followed instructions no matter how unorthodox they might seem to any sane—or sober—pilot.

Did I mention Double Vision was a bit of a drinker? As I watched him fight the control yolk, there was a devil-may-care grin on his face, and the rummy gleam in his eye suggested he was enjoying this ride a little too much.

Lightning flashed across the window to the left, and I had to blink the blindness away. There was less than a second of delay before the accompanying thunderclap impacted the aircraft with a force I felt like a slap to the head.

"Hoo-wee!" Double Vision cackled. "It's getting thick out there, hoss. It might be time to rethink this plan of yours."

The oncoming storm was troubling. The fact that Double Vision didn't so much as blink when the lightning strobed across the cabin ratcheted up my concern. Either he had cast-iron nerves, or he was literally feeling no pain. "Too much prep to turn back now," I said. "Tonight's the night. How long to the target?"

Our flight path had us skirting the edge of a large patch of restricted airspace over Nowhere, Kansas. Looking at maps and searching databases, there was no explanation for the patch of six thousand acres of no-fly zone. That it wasn't recorded didn't surprise me either. A top-secret research facility was located somewhere in the area—or, more specifically, underneath it. A private research firm had retrofitted a decommissioned Cold War intercontinental missile silo and was now operating an underground facility conducting some very dangerous research.

Air traffic in the vicinity was tightly monitored so the night's flight wouldn't go unnoticed. To mitigate concerns, I'd hired Double Vision to make a series of late-night flights between a couple of the larger farms north and south of the facility. Anyone looking into his previous flights would find them to be legitimate runs moving small machine parts between facilities to troubleshoot an issue with a specialized fermenting pump that I may or may not have had a hand in sabotaging to cover tonight's operation. The result was that the radar tracking station attached to the underground silo was already accustomed to Double Vision's air traffic and unlikely to find it out of the ordinary.

"Um," Double Vision groaned. He waved one hand in front of the digital display mounted to the instrument panel to the right of his seat. "I need you to check the reading on that for me, friend. That last flash sort of cost me my eyes."

I was kneeling on the thick rubber matting that lined the rear of the cabin and looking out the window, so Double Vision Gary's comment caused me to do a double-take. "You can't see? You're kidding, right?"

Double Vision shook his head. "Afraid not, hoss." He pointed again at the display. "That will tell you how long until the waypoint. Do me a solid and confirm our altitude too? We should be steady somewhere between fourteen and fifteen thousand."

I crawled to the front of the plane and checked the display. We were vectoring squarely toward the graphical pushpin marking our waypoint, flying level at fourteen thousand two hundred feet and change. I looked Double Vision in the eye. He was blinking rapidly now. "You really can't see?" If he was blind, he couldn't land the plane alone.

I would have to scrub my op.

Double Vision Gary shrugged. "It's coming back slowly. I can see smears and distant flashes. It's only a matter of time." He raised his chin at the windscreen, and I saw we were flying directly at a curtain of clouds that danced with lightning flashes.

"I'll have to go back with you," I said after a long breath. "You can't land like this."

"How long to target?" Double Vision said with a disconcerting lack of concern.

"Three and a half minutes."

"And we're on course?"

I double-checked the display. For reasons I couldn't explain, we continued to fly straight and true–as true as we could in a cabin that was bucking and kicking like an angry mule. With a seasoned and sighted pilot at the controls, I'd been in large aircraft that couldn't maintain course and altitude in such conditions.

"Yeah, but I don't know how you're doing it," I admitted.

"The blessing of being a blind-drunk alcoholic," Double Vision said, his devil-may-care grin back and accompanied by a laugh. "Been flying nearly blind for years. This ain't nothing new. This blindness is a little more complete, and the blurs are clearing way quicker. I'll be good to go well before I reach Clarksville's outer marker."

I waved a hand in front of Double Vision Gary, but he didn't react. I sat back on my haunches and contemplated my choices, just in time for Double Vision to raise one hand and extend me the bird. "I saw that, asshole," he said.

I wasn't sure he did. Or if he did, he might have seen a quick blur among other blurs. Either way, it was a bad situation. A lot of time and planning had gone into this op, and it was about to go down the tubes. Truth be told, I was anxious to complete this project after what I'd seen on the news two weeks before. I was far more interested in the experiment taking place in Arlington. Well, maybe not the experiment, but the—

A chime sounded from the navigation display on the instrument panel.

"Thirty seconds to the waypoint," Double Vision said.

I started to respond, but another thunderclap reverberated through the night. The plane tipped hard, and I narrowly missed being thrown against the pilot's seat. I was dumped to my hands and knees in the empty cargo space. I crawled back to the space to the right of Double Vision Gary, where the copilot's seat usually would have been.

"It's all good," Double Vision said. "Don't worry about me. My vision is getting better by the minute. Honestly, it's all good. You're the damn fool who's going to get struck by lightning."

I looked out the window and nodded. It was becoming a distinct possibility. The rain hadn't caught the plane yet, but it couldn't be far off. I slipped protective glasses over my eyes and pulled the helmet over my head.

"You're sure?" I asked one last time.

A new tone sounded from the digital display, telling me we were over the target waypoint.

"Would you get outta my plane already? You ain't gotta go home, but you can't stay here," he said with an exaggerated drawl.

I clapped Double Vision on the shoulder and thanked him. Turning the release on the starboard door, I pushed it out and up. I was instantly assaulted by gale-force winds that were nearly deafening. Prior research suggested we were flying at approximately 120 miles per hour. The door was hinged across the top of the frame so that it would swing up to clip against the wing overhead. At our speed and in the turbulence, the clip didn't engage. The door swung up to meet the wing, mostly out of the way, but it wouldn't secure. It continued to slap the horizontal surface and threatened to drop on me at any moment. Only our airspeed seemed to keep it at bay. Before the door had a chance to hurt me, I ducked my head and dove into the night.

My graceful exit from the plane ended up being anything but. While turbulence was a bitch inside a plane, experiencing it from the outside, at terminal velocity, and at the edge of an extreme weather system was beyond compare. I was getting physically kicked from every direction. It was all I could do to pull my clumsy tumble into a controlled arch. The second I did, the nanofiber mesh beneath my arms and between my feet caught the air, and my plummet was altered into a glide. It was my first use of the wingsuit. Timing, conditions, and a general reluctance to have anyone capture my strange rig and splash it all over social media meant there wasn't an opportunity for a single test jump with it.

While airspace over the research facility was tightly controlled, approaching from the ground was even more of a problem. Perimeter detection and alerting systems were state-of-the-art, and to be honest, entirely overkill. Everything was high-tech and automated, with human systems for redundancy. The place was hardened against even cyberattacks. With that in mind, it was simply easier to enter from the air. One just had to traverse the no-fly zone without triggering the automated air defense systems. Designed to watch for aircraft, one man playing the role of a flying squirrel could enter the airspace from beyond the perimeter, bypass ground defenses, and land within the facility's inner perimeter, where security was less intensive.

This approach left me to contend with the facility's inner defenses later.

My glasses pulsed to life with a full glow when my dive turned into a glide. The wraparound lenses kept the rushing wind from my eyes, and the cutting-edge tech was the secret weapon for the operation. The night came to life in crisp monochrome detail. I could see the outlines of the surrounding clouds, even in the moonless sky. Shooting a look over my shoulder, I tried to find Double Vision's Cessna. That proved a mistake as it destroyed the carefully balanced characteristics of my flying squirrel imitation, and I went cannonballing again.

What must have been a creative combination of expletives, even by my own standards, was thankfully lost to the sound of the rushing wind. I threw myself into an arch and mentally crossed my fingers, hoping the wing suit's webbing would withstand the choppy wind.

"If it's alright with you, I'm going to engage the heads-up display," Esker's voice said through the microscopic bone conduction device in my inner ear. Skydiving represented the most extreme noise conditions under which the AI had conversed with me, and it surprised me that I could hear his voice with perfect clarity.

"Good idea," I said. "That might keep me from doing anything stupid."

A broad, swooping orange line appeared across the inside of my glasses, simultaneously with a similar blue line. The lines had distinctly different curves, though both curved down and to the left. While the orange was lazy and gentle as it passed off the edge of my lens, the blue sloped aggressively to the west and was relatively flat across the horizontal plane.

Esker's voice clarified what the display already made clear. "You lost altitude with that tumble. Level out now to extend your glide. You're in danger of not reaching the drop zone."

I tipped carefully to my right and arched my back slightly. Working the squirrel suit was all about gentle adjustments. As I moved, the orange line inside my glasses slid smoothly to overlap with the blue.

"Nicely done," Esker said in a calm tone.

Then I hit the wall of water. One second, it was a dry, if turbulent, sky…and the next, there was nothing but water.

Flying in a wingsuit is all about balance and careful, precise movements. Impacting a sudden torrential downpour doesn't go unpunished. I went ass over teakettle again, this time spinning like a frisbee, with arms and legs flailing. There were helpful words of encouragement from Esker, but the most helpful thing he did was disable the heads-up display in my glasses for the duration. My brain was already scrambled from the sensory overload. I didn't need more visual stimulation to add to the fun.

One thing I can say about myself—and it's something I still don't understand—is that even while plummeting through the night, the rain, and bouncing through the turbulence, my heart rate never spiked. This was Esker's observation the next day and something he has noted on numerous similar occasions. Even when my rational mind couldn't understand what was happening or how to regain control, somehow my panic response failed to engage.

When in doubt, go for the arch. It was something drilled into anyone who has ever taken a skydiving class. Hands and feet out, head back, and belly arched to lead the way; if you can do that, gravity will take care of the rest. It's like taking a badminton birdie and throwing it into the air. Once the fall begins, the tip will point to Earth, and the rest will take care of itself.

In my case, the wings engaged, and I was once more gliding, though now I was taking rain so solidly in the face that it felt like hail. For all the planning that had gone into the night's operation, I never anticipated needing a full-face helmet.

My glasses pulsed back to life, but only the orange line was visible. A small arrow at the top right edge of the lens hinted at where I might find the blue line, and I tipped my head very carefully in that direction until it came into view. I was a long, long way off course and wanted to ask Esker if there was any possibility of reaching the target drop zone. Unfortunately, the unrelenting wind and rain made speaking impossible.

Thankfully, Esker had come to anticipate my thoughts in the relatively short time we'd been together. "It's no longer possible to reach the drop zone given the current flight conditions," he said. "I am rerouting to the nearest cover position. You will land well within the inner perimeter fence."

I offered a slow blink in response, confident Esker would understand my meaning. The blue line shifted across the lens and I responded to the guidance.

Normally, a skydiver deploys the primary chute at fifty-five hundred feet. This gives the jumper sufficient time to see the sights, judge wind conditions, watch for hazards, scope out the landing zone, and generally enjoy the experience. That skydiver would also be jumping in the daytime under sunny skies and be trained by a qualified professional.

Did I mention this was my second solo dive? Second dive ever, in fact? My training consisted of what I had read online and gleaned from watching far too many YouTube videos. Certification requires a minimum of twelve jumps and six to eight hours in the classroom. But I had a secret weapon. I had a cutting-edge AI in my pocket and next-gen smart glasses that would make the Terminator envious. Combine that with unbridled determination and a lack of self-preservation, and you get me bellyflopping through a thunderstorm in the middle of the night.

Anyway, like I said, going by the book, you're supposed to pop the chute at fifty-five hundred. The built-in AAD, or Automatic Activation Device, would activate at seventeen hundred feet. The idea is that if the jumper were too distracted by the pretty scenery, or perhaps more likely unconscious, the chute would auto-deploy. The auto-deployment canopy would be the reserve and would not offer the control of the main. With this in mind, and in an effort to open as close to the ground as possible to reduce any potential radar signature, I pulled the ripcord at twenty-one hundred feet.

Throughout the fall, the altitude was displayed with precision in red letters in the corner of my heads-up display. It was another advantage I had over those qualified skydivers. They had to look at wrist-mounted, often analog displays, to keep track of their descent. In the driving rain and wind, I couldn't see my hands even though they were literally six inches in front of my face.

In freefall, the diver loses one thousand feet every five and a half seconds, so my margin for error was brushing up against the AAD's comfort zone by the time my main chute deployed. Qualified divers also spend a lot of time finding a safe landing zone. Some place free from trees, fences, power lines, and just about anything that might ruin their day. Again, thanks to my night vision lenses, I could see with surprising clarity. What I couldn't see was the direction of the wind. I was gliding through a roiling tempest under a fully inflated canopy, and the ground was still coming up fast.

One thing the literature and videos made clear was the need to land while gliding into the wind. Bones could easily be broken and lives potentially lost if this rule was ignored. Sadly, in my case, the wind was hammering me from every direction. No gentle breezes—gale force winds hammered me and were playing hell with my canopy. Esker did his best to compensate. A blue arrow instructed me to bank hard to the left, and I instantly obeyed.

The altimeter in the corner of my HUD counted down, and Esker's voice filled my ears. "Prepare to flare on my mark."

I lined up on the blue line on my display, and the moment the altimeter reached twenty feet, Esker announced, "flare now!"

I pulled both steering toggles fully down to my knees and envisioned the outer edges of the rectangular canopy overhead collapsing as the air was forced from the inflated cells. My descent stalled just as my boots touched the sodden soil. It would have been a graceful landing had I not been slapped in the back by a sudden gust of wind. My boots caught in the muck, and I went toppling forward. I ducked my head as my hands went to the emergency release mechanism for my rig. As I tumbled into a controlled somersault—yes, that's my story, and I'm sticking to it—the chute was torn away and lost to the wind and the night.

When the night stopped spinning, I was kneeling in a clearing of flattened corn stalks. As I'd seen on my descent, this was a recently cleared cornfield. It was flat and empty to the north and east. A run-down, abandoned farm sat a half mile to the southwest.

"Well?" I said to Esker.

"I give you seven point five. High marks for speed, but you sort of flubbed the landing."

I laughed and rolled my eyes. He was being generous. "I meant radio transmissions and radar. Did my landing draw any attention?"

"Your chute appeared on the radar for just under two seconds," Esker confirmed. I knew he was monitoring communications from inside the facility, encrypted though it was. "But when you cut it loose, and it was washed away by the wind, its movement at such high speed caused the radar operator to disregard it as an anomaly. He assumed it was debris stirred up by the storm."

Anticipating my next question, Esker projected a two-dimensional map in three-dimensional space before me. It showed me as an orange dot, the target destination as a blue dot, and the location I intended to land as an orange dot with an X through it. A dotted line between me and the X indicated that I was 1.1 miles off target. The storm had cost me in that regard but provided me cover with the radar operator and thereby saved me from a response by the onsite security team.

"I'll take the trade," I mumbled to myself, though in the back of my mind, I was apprehensive about what the storm foretold. It was directly linked to me and gave away my relative position geographically. That was a disadvantage. It also meant Breslin was back on his Brane, Wild-Side. "Hey, E. What's the focal point of the corresponding weather system?" Esker had real-time access to the internet and weather data from all over the world.

"As you would expect," he said. "The reciprocal front formed over the Seattle, Washington area."

Esker didn't need to say what I was already thinking. Once Breslin realized the epicenter of my weather system, he would put the underground facility on high alert. I'd been attacking his projects worldwide for the last six months, and when this storm formed over Nowhere, Kansas, he would have everything his people needed to understand where I was and which facility was next on my hit list.

In a perfect world, I would have landed much closer to the entrance to the underground facility. The weather and my own clumsiness had planted me far afield...literally. I was standing in the middle of a cleared cornfield in the middle of nowhere. Though I was inside the outer perimeter, there were still far too many sensors between me and the entry to have any chance of reaching it without alerting the on-site security team.

That meant I went with Plan B. Rather than go to the abandoned farmhouse in the distance, I headed for the nearest tree line. It was the perimeter between the corn field I was standing in and the next one planted with...whatever they grow in Kansas. I know it wasn't corn, but I'm no farmer. And it was raining–a lot.

At the tree line, I could take cover, and it was trivial for Esker to scan for the sensors that were part of the supposedly random traps and triggers placed throughout the thousands of square acres inside the inner perimeter. Esker triggered three contiguous sensors along the tree line a hundred yards north of my hide. According to the facility's strict security playbook, procured for me by none other than Esker more than a week before, two four-wheel-drive jeeps were dispatched to investigate a sensor anomaly.

Four guards arrived on-site within minutes, outfitted in foul weather gear, M4 rifles, and the latest generation night vision goggles. I'll give them credit for adhering to protocol regarding their deployment. One Jeep pulled up short of the suspect sensors while the other moved in close so the headlights could be used to inspect the area in question more closely. A guard stayed with the perimeter vehicle while the other three, two from the foremost and one from the rear Jeep, conducted a thorough, if aggressive, inspection of the area.

Both teams quickly concluded that the string of sensors was a false alarm, likely due to the weather. Their conclusion was surely aided by the fact that the suspect area wasn't the least bit disturbed, other than by the weather. Since Esker triggered the sensors, I didn't need to go anywhere near them. Eager to return to the warmth of their bunker to dry off and log the false alarm, the teams were quick to return to base. The important part of the exercise was when they did; I was hanging from the spare tire and rear bumper of the trailing Jeep.

Why spend time and effort subverting multiple layers of base security when the security team is willing to help?

I dropped to the road and rolled into the ditch thirty yards before the perimeter guard shack. The Jeeps were signaled through the retractable gate with only a wave from the guard in the booth. I watched them disappear through the heavy overhead door and down the ramp to the underground motor pool. This base, just like the rest of Kansas, couldn't have been flatter if it had been paved for parking. Closing the distance to the guard station was one of my few areas of concern. As it was, thanks to the sheeting rain, the guard in the booth didn't see me until I banged the flat of my hand on the chain-link fence.

"Hey, buddy. Can I get some help out here?" I called through the fence.

The guard stepped from the booth, confusion clear in his expression. He missed his brief chance to sound the alarm because I promptly shot him. I'd slipped the muzzle of my pistol through the links in the fence and pulled the trigger once. The round caught him in the meat of his left thigh. He went down like a felled tree. I heard his helmet thud hollowly against the concrete pad at the base of the guard shack and even I felt a little guilty.

Now might be a good time to describe my non-lethal ordinance. It was something special cooked up—ok, engineered—by Dr. Cormac. The rounds were fired from a conventional 9mm pistol; in this case, a 4.5-inch Springfield XD-M with a suppressor. The jacketed slug was replaced by a high-density plastic shell containing a dissolving nano-composite barb laced with a neuro…a neuro…

Ok, it might also be a good time to admit that the science of this stuff isn't my strong suit, and I leave that to people much smarter than I. Let's just say I was shooting a silenced round that broke on contact with the skin and injected the equivalent of a dissolving chemical sliver that induced instant paralysis and unconsciousness. Like the AI in my phone, the intelligence in my contact lenses, and the nanotech swimming in my bloodstream, it was science literally developed on another plane of reality, so you'll have to cut me some slack when it comes to not understanding how it works.

What matters is that I'm *very good* at operating the tech.

"Esker, can you—" I was going to ask him to open the fence, but he beat me to it. The gate was already sliding laterally.

"Camera feeds are looping as planned," Esker confirmed. "I have blocked two attempts to send a priority lockdown notice to the facility from headquarters: one via the closed-loop link and the other via the VPN connection from the Beijing facility."

I stepped through the gate, walked quickly across the gravel parking lot, and headed for the twenty-by-twenty-foot cinder block building fifty feet from the similarly sized building through which the Jeeps had disappeared. "It was the storm," I explained. "Breslins crossed over, and the reciprocal storm front over this location gave me away. Monitor air traffic. It's only a matter of time before he dispatches additional resources to try to intercept."

"Understood."

I reached the service door in time to hear the buzzer indicating the door lock had been released. "Thank you," I muttered to Esker, pulling the door open.

A guard vaulted from the chair behind his desk in the spartan room beyond. This was convenient. Since guards were required to wear body armor and my ammunition didn't work against it, it was most productive to shoot them in the leg. An arm would do just as well, but research indicated that some guards wore tactical gear that included pads on the arms. Padding on the legs was not part of any approved kit variations.

I raised my pistol and fired from the hip. When I did, a green reticle tracked across the lenses of my contacts, independent of what I saw in my glasses. It was calibrated with my Springfield to within a thirty-second of an inch at twenty yards, so I could fire from the hip without looking across the iron sights. I didn't even need to bring the gun to eye level.

The guard toppled over the top of his desk before he could fully pull his pistol from the holster on his hip. A countdown in the corner of my eye told me I had seventeen rounds left in the magazine.

"Two Sikorsky have been scrambled from Alpha and Bravo reinforcement locations and are inbound. The closest has an ETA of 48 minutes," Esker announced in my ear.

The clock was running.

I slipped a multitool from a pocket on my vest and wedged it in the gap between the stainless steel elevator doors. Aside from the guard's desk, the doors were the only things in the cramped, cold space. I forced the doors apart, and the black abyss of the elevator shaft blipped into monochrome focus thanks to the night vision optics.

"Exfil still looks good?" I confirmed. Until now, Esker had only had access to the facilities manifest. My exfiltration plan was based on what was believed to be in inventory here at the facility. Now that I was on site, he had access to the video surveillance feeds and could confirm everything I planned on being here was, well, here.

"Confirmed," Esker said simply.

My partner in crime wasn't one to waste words. It was one of the things I liked best about him.

"The elevator?" I asked as I stepped over the yawning abyss and onto the ladder built into the right side of the wide shaft. The shaft itself was a retrofitted underground launch tower for the Cold War-era missile silo. In recent years, the testament to a bygone age had

31

been reworked to include a modern, high-capacity service elevator that had been the primary means of moving technical hardware into the underground facility. The shaft walls had been replaced by nylon fiber-reinforced concrete coated in a lacquer-like layer of polyurethane. The elevator rode a pair of massive steel rails, one on either side of the shaft. The lift was powered entirely by a triple-redundant pneumatic air system located in the bowels of the facility.

"Locked on sub-level three with nine increasingly agitated guards aboard," Esker confirmed.

This was per the plan. A very narrow, almost claustrophobic emergency staircase could also be used, but it created a bottleneck. So, when the alarm was sounded, the procedure was to use the elevator to reach the surface as quickly as possible. Once I had taken out the guard at the top of the elevator shaft, Esker transmitted a message to the lower guard station asking for additional support to deal with a downed tree at the fence line. This resulted in nine reserve guards being dispatched to the surface. Esker allowed the elevator to rise two levels, then disabled its communication and power, thereby taking nine of the enemy forces off the field without even needing to fire a shot.

I descended the ladder until I reached the elevator stalled on sub-level three. I couldn't hear the pounding and the shouts of those locked inside until I stepped on top of the car. Someone was just starting to push through the hatch at the top. I stepped on the panel and quickly slipped a padlock through the linkage in the mechanism. It would keep anyone from escaping. Five seconds later, I crawled through the gap between the elevator and the shaft wall. Whatever they had constructed the car from, it was even better insulated than research suggested. Initially, I was concerned about how far up the shaft the car needed to be before locking it down. The sounds were the least of my concerns. Ensuring I disabled the elevator escape hatch was the key to keeping those inside from becoming a problem.

I reached the bottom of the shaft and listened for signs of trouble. What we knew of the facility indicated another checkpoint just beyond the elevator. After that, only blueprint-level security information was available. No insight into the internal security posture had been available beyond this point. Now that we were on-site, Esker could gain more firsthand knowledge of the facility from the local computer network. But even that would take time. He needed to locate a vulnerable wireless device or network component before he could work his magic. To be honest, I tuned out the specifics of his plan since I was confident he would let me know when there was something worth knowing.

"Still no alarm?" I asked in a whisper. It was a wasted question since I knew Esker would have alerted me if any hint of a silent alarm had registered on his proverbial or literal radar.

"Negative."

I had access to its mechanical release switch from this side of the elevator shaft, so I toggled it and pulled the switch. Then, with the tips of my fingers, I pulled the doors apart.

The guard at the desk in the lobby beyond was reclining in a chair with his feet up. A digital tablet was raised and occupied his attention. Since the desk was in the way, I didn't have a clear shot at him, so I pulled myself up from the recess of the elevator well. And while the silent opening of the elevator doors had failed to catch the guard's attention, the five-foot-ten-inch man slipping from the empty doorway somehow did not.

His chair went toppling; he was just reaching his feet when I put a round in his upper leg. On the way down, his head bounced off the edge of the heavy steel desk. He would wake up tomorrow with a far worse headache than everyone else.

"Gray," Esker said with a hint of excitement. "I have finished mapping the facility and located the device."

A three-dimensional schematic materialized at arm's length in front of my face. It quickly began to render with additional detail. First, the tall cylindrical tower took shape, and then the elevator shaft in the tower's center formed. The ground at the top of the cylinder entered the wireframe, along with the crude cinderblock shack covering the top of the underground silo. Not far away, another shack formed, though its lines were fuzzy, likely due to the distance from the main drawing and a lack of relevance.

Back on the main diagram, a long rectangle extruded from the tower's base, and I started to see the hall where I now stood. Small blocky rooms were added to the side of my current corridor. Nearby, another vertical shaft formed. This one was about half as wide as the primary missile silo that had brought me to this level. This shaft looked to be perhaps three times deeper than the main. At the bottom, a series of rectangles and squares branched out to represent a sprawling and complex underground facility.

"Holy crap," I whispered.

"Indeed," Esker responded. His voice was similarly hushed and awed. "It appears this facility is much more complex than the information previously noted."

I absentmindedly ran a hand over the spare magazines in my combat harness. "How about the staff onsite? Was that information accurate?"

"I don't have access to camera coverage of the entire facility yet, but nothing indicates otherwise." Esker's tone was back to being dry and analytical. "Forty-three minutes until the first response team arrives," he reminded. "I can't currently estimate the response you will face."

I studied the three-dimensional image of the massive underground facility and wondered how long Breslin's people had been working on it. Then I considered how many similar facilities were out there, just waiting to be found. He had plans for this world, and no one here knew what was happening. Worse, they wouldn't believe it if I tried to explain it.

At least I had tools to help me in the fight. Here and now, I had technology. Esker had already mapped the facility and knew where my target was. "Show me the fastest possible route?" I asked. A blurred line appeared on the model. It wove and zig-zagged through the halls and rooms of the facility. "And you can open every lock and door I come across?"

"Confirmed."

"Then let's go."

I made my way through the facility quickly. There was no resistance between the base of the second elevator shaft and the primary laboratory. It was due to the time of night and our false instructions, which left every available security guard trapped in the main elevator just below ground level. While I knew I was racing against the clock, luck had been mostly on my side when facing the on-site security force—I didn't realize my luckiness was about to run out.

As I approached the double doors to the central lab, the latch clicked, and I knew Esker had already wirelessly subverted the PIN code and card swipe authorization on the lock. I pushed through the rightmost door and into the thirty by forty lab. What should have been a lights-out and locked-down room was instead a bustle of activity. Close to a dozen people moved about the room in seemingly random directions, each moving at what could only be described as a motivated pace. The overhead lights burned bright and a large digital timer mounted high on the rear wall was counting down. Three hours, twenty-one minutes, and nine seconds remained until whatever deadline was reached.

Esker's voice sounded in my ear, verbalizing pretty much the same thoughts going through my mind at that instant. "It seems the first full-scale test of the apparatus has been moved up even more aggressively than we were led to believe."

"You think?" I whispered.

I knew there would be no second chance at this attack when I breached the facility's perimeter. My inside source had messaged to let me know the previous timeline of five days was no longer valid. It would have been more helpful to know that the experiment would be completed before sunrise. That would have impacted my plan of attack. This new insight was already being factored into the mental profile I'd built for my helpful, if secretive, insider. The contact was well-placed enough to know the timetable for today's test had been advanced but not sufficiently well-placed to understand that the test had been scheduled for before sunrise today.

A half dozen heads turned to me as I skidded to a stop only a couple of paces through the doorway. Dressed head to toe in black, wearing a tactical vest festooned with extra magazines, three flash-bang grenades, and a spare pistol—not to mention the 9mm in hand, I didn't look like one of the base's security guards. Oh, did I mention the black ski mask pulled over my face?

Nothing out of place about that, right?

The room's occupants spread out in an arc away from me as if repulsed by a magnetic force. As they did, a hand slapped down on my left shoulder. I failed to notice the pair of guards bracketing the door when I stepped through.

"Crap," I whispered. Stupid mistake. I was rushed for time, not expecting the room full of people, and didn't anticipate armed resistance inside the research lab.

What the hell is everyone doing here in the middle of the night?

I sensed more than saw the guard closing in on me from the right. The one moving from the left was more aggressive, but he had chosen a non-lethal response—at least for the moment—so he would be first. I grabbed his extended right hand and bent it backward, palm up, to an extreme angle. It slowed his ability to bring his pistol to bear with his left hand. His knees involuntarily buckled to release the strain on his hyperextended wrist. At the same time, his gun hand went high and swung wildly as he struggled for balance.

The guard at my right had closed quickly. I think he was attempting to press his pistol to my neck or head, trying to take the fight out of me. He should have maintained a safe distance. I simply pushed his automatic away with the side of my own, and stomped my right foot down on the side of his forward knee. His oncoming momentum failed to find balance on a knee that no longer had integrity, and he slid on one shoulder about three feet in front of me. I fired a shot into his thigh before his slide ended, and he was out of the fight.

The first guard was starting to remember he had a gun in hand. I saw recognition flash in his eyes. He looked up at me from his position on the floor on one knee, his twisted wrist still tight in my left hand. "This won't hurt a bit," I said as I slipped the muzzle of my gun into his armpit to access the gap in his body armor. The already muffled spit from the suppressor was quieted further by the close contact with the man's fatigues. I decided there would be some residual pain when he woke. I hadn't considered what sort of collateral damage he might suffer from the close contact powder burns. My rounds were non-lethal but still projectiles reliant on conventional gunpowder. That meant there would be the traditional heat and gas discharge issues.

As I released the guard's wrist and he slumped to the concrete unconscious, I felt a little guilty. This was still better than the alternative, which was to strike him until unconscious…but, ouch. My goal was to get in and out without hurting anyone.

Muffled screams from the back of the room returned my attention to the group again. A large older man in a lab coat was skirting the right side of the crowd, maneuvering in a way that suggested preparation for a counterattack.

Good for you.

I was glad to see someone proactive and attempting to act in a chaotic time. It was better than letting an aggressive force seize the room and gain the upper hand. Regardless, I fired one round that caught the big man in the lower calf. Like the guards, he was unconscious by the time he hit the floor.

This shot, of course, brought more screaming. Everyone present compressed to the room's rear while they tried to get as far from me as possible. A woman in a lab coat seemed to move independently from the populace. While the group moved away from the assembled equipment, she was reluctant to separate from a collection of hardware. She made an effort to keep herself between me and the central apparatus.

"I need you in the back of the room with everyone else," I said as I ambled closer.

She shook her head and continued to block me physically. If I had to guess, she was in her early thirties. She had strawberry blonde hair, pale skin, and a dash of freckles under each eye. There were bags under cornflower blue eyes. In addition to looking terrified, she appeared exhausted.

Raising a hand in what she clearly knew was a futile attempt to ward me off, she said, "You can't take this. Please—you don't know what we're doing here."

I slipped the gun into a holster low on my hip and looked her in the eye. "I won't hurt you, but I have to take it. I know exactly what you're doing, so I have to take the hardware."

She looked at me squarely, and I could tell she was trying to picture the face behind the mask. She could sense the sincerity of my words. I didn't want to be here, and I didn't want to do this...like this.

"You don't know who you're working for," I said. "You don't understand what he's really trying to accomplish."

I looked at the stitching on the breast of her lab coat and realized her name was Doctor Norton. I was familiar with the profiles of the lead project researchers but had believed someone with the name Norton to be a man. In my head, I had pictured a balding, overweight, shortsighted man who was stooped and enjoying an ongoing affair with argyle and wool.

I'm not sexist. I'd just associated the name with old man Norton, a codger who lived a few houses down the street from where I grew up. He was your classic *stay off my lawn* sort of old fart who hated kids, and the kids hated him right back. If I was guilty of anything, it was failing to spend more time examining the CVs of the science team. Since I was hitting the place in the middle of the night, I didn't expect lab geeks to be a factor. I was only worried about the security forces.

Doctor Norton's fear and trepidation morphed into determination right before my eyes. She glared at me with a look equal parts terror and steely resolve. When she spoke, her words were little more than a pleading whisper. They were only audible because the room had dropped to utter silence. It was like those present were holding their collective breath. "We're about to change mankind's understanding of the universe."

I slid the protecting lens from my eyes and pulled up the front of my ski mask to reveal my face. It was painted with blackout dye that made it almost impossible for cameras to work facial recognition magic on me, though that ship had sailed. With choppers inbound and the storm front having already given me away, I was the only person to whom this effort would be attributed.

Not that Breslin would ever let any of this be reported.

I looked past the doctor at the small silver sphere cradled on the three vertical acrylic pins that comprised its tripod. It stood at the end of a six-foot-long polycarbonate table. Along the rest of the bench, taking up most of the surface, was a complex and admittedly high-tech-looking apparatus that I knew to be one of the world's smallest high-energy laser projectors. The laser lens was pointed directly at a sphere.

Norton saw my stare and stepped to block me once more. The now determined set of her jaw spoke volumes. The hands at her sides were balled into fists. "You don't know what we're doing here."

Norton's determination made me smile. Few people had so much passion.

"You're trying to open a doorway between worlds," I said simply. I glanced at the projection-like screen standing upright beyond the table and the sphere. It was a vertical sheet of transparent film about four feet wide and eight feet high. "You want to know what's on the other side."

Norton's mouth fell open, and I understood why. Even most of the people in the lab didn't know the project's true intention. Only the three principal contributors knew the ultimate goal. Norton specialized in applied physics, string theory, and was the only contributor with hands-on access. The other two had only intellectual contributions to the effort. What she didn't know was that one of them had already died under mysterious circumstances.

"How could you know?" Norton said. She seemed to deflate with the understanding that the secret wasn't under wraps.

There was a lot I could say and even more that she needed to hear. Glancing at the display on my wrist, I confirmed I had no time to spare. "If this works, you would open a door," I said instead.

She nodded slowly.

"Doors work in two directions. Did you ever consider what might come through from the other side?"

Her brows furrowed. She slowly rocked back on her heels. Once, she started to speak but stopped. I watched her slowly turn to look at the apparatus. She turned fully and just stared at the machine as if seeing it for the first time.

No one in the room moved. It was like they were frozen in time. All eyes were on me, Norton, or buried in the arms of the person beside them. I'll admit I felt terrible for holding these people hostage, but I wasn't going to hurt any of them. Well, maybe not too badly. If someone tried to stop me, they would get tranked. There was no way around it. I had to clear the area before the first chopper arrived. In the long run, getting captured would be far worse than letting Breslin complete this experiment.

Norton looked at me. By that point, I was standing beside her and facing the apparatus the same way she was. I was even doing my best to appear non-threatening—the best I possibly could, given that I was decked out in tactical gear and painted as if I had just walked off some Hollywood action movie set.

"You know what we were going to do," Norton said slowly as if tasting the words as they rolled from her tongue. She watched me carefully as the next sentence formed. "Does that mean you know what would happen if we performed the test?"

My eyes rested on the baseball-sized silver sphere as she spoke. "I've seen what's on the other side," I said in a hushed tone. "So has your benefactor. The difference is I want to keep what's on the other side there so it can't hurt the people here. Breslin wants to feed our people to it." I met her eye to convey every ounce of sincerity possible. "Opening that door would be the last great scientific breakthrough for mankind."

I stepped past the doctor and walked to the end of the table. The huddled mass at the end of the room shuddered and shifted, the group moving as one to keep me at bay. They needn't have bothered. I stopped at the acrylic tripod and picked up the sphere. I glanced briefly at it before dropping it into the pack slung over my shoulder. The doctor didn't make a move to prevent it.

"Breslin has already killed Professor Saranac," I said to Norton. "Once this is gone, you and Kane will soon follow. You need to run. Take a new identity—find a quiet place to lay low until the dust settles." I picked up a pen and scratched a phone number on a scrap of paper before handing it to her. It was accepted with a shaking hand. "Go tonight. Get somewhere safe, then make the call. My friend will help with the arrangements and help you contact Kane securely."

Norton looked like she was going to be sick. "Saranac is dead?"

I nodded. "He questioned Breslin's motives in moving up the timetable. I would have been here sooner but didn't realize you would be performing the experiment tonight."

Norton was swaying on unsteady legs.

"You don't have time for that," I warned, glancing at my watch. "An off-site security team will be here in twenty-three minutes. You and your crew need to be gone before they arrive. The rest of your folks should be safe, but you will have more cover if everyone scatters. This isn't the only experiment Breslin is conducting and isn't the first I've derailed. Once you go into hiding, he won't have the resources to search for you indefinitely. Plus, I'll take him off the board sooner or later."

Bracing herself against the counter, Norton looked at me intently. "Does that mean what I think it does?"

I gave her a wink and headed for the door.

Esker's voice entered my ear as I reached the first hallway. "Cutting this kind of close, aren't you?"

"You tell me," I said with a chuckle and started jogging. The path out of the installation was already indicated on my heads-up display—

literally, a blue line on the hall floor directed me. All I had to do was follow it to the motor pool.

Exfiltration went more or less according to plan. While I was "wasting time," as Esker put it, in the labratory, he identified the Jeep best suited for my escape. Apparently, the two vehicles used to scout my induced exterior sensor malfunction hadn't been refueled, even though it was standard procedure. Likely, the two responding teams were more interested in stowing their foul-weather gear and finding a place to warm up. Esker must have accessed some onboard computer system because he identified the four-wheel drive with a full tank and even started the engine as I entered the motor pool. The sound of the throaty V8 rumbling to life distracted the two guards on duty and drew the attention of the three mechanics. All five men converged on the Jeep. I was already loaded with a fresh magazine, so I took down the entire group before a conventional shot was fired.

Esker noted that Miranda Norton and two of her senior research assistants were slowly making their way through the facility and approaching the garage as well. Based on what he'd overheard using the base security cameras, she was briefing them on what I had conveyed and convincing them it was best to exit before the incoming security arrived.

When I drove out in the Jeep, I left the retractable door to the surface ramp open and the overhead entrance on the ground level as well. I also left a Jeep warming up so Norton and her team could quickly retreat. I thought about taking them with me, but that would raise further questions and lead me to take on more responsibility for the group than I could afford. I already had a lead on another of the experiments Breslin was funding. If I was honest with myself, my focus had been on the next mission since waking up with that talon in my side and seeing the news broadcast two weeks prior.

Breslin had conducted nearly a dozen experiments similar to the one I disrupted that night. Each used a different approach in some way. Various technologies were used; sometimes, different scientific or even occult principles were employed. The orb from tonight's attempt was something new. Even Esker couldn't track the provenance of that artifact.

Breslin had a singular goal, and he would stop at nothing until it was accomplished.

He wanted to break through the barrier separating my world from his. Like me, he could travel between the two—but we were the only ones. If he could bring more of his people across, it would end this world as we knew it and mark the start of a new dark age—a time when man was no longer the most dangerous creature on the planet.

Chapter 3 - The Vault

Wild-Side

If I'm honest, in the early days, I was exceedingly annoyed with the widespread unwillingness the population of Wild-Side had to physically combat the malevolent force attacking the fringes of their society. In the first month following my arrival, the creatures we'd come to refer to as the Elend grew bolder. Farms closer to the five main cities had seen the hulking, savage creatures with increasing regularity. Farmers were soon noticed to be missing.

No matter what came, none of the Seeley would fight. No one would join me in the hunt. Worse, most looked at me as if I were as dangerous as the massive reptilian creatures. I'd been willing to fight and even kill the vicious monsters from the start, but it brought me little favor from the Seeley. Some even claimed the very first sightings of the Elend coincided suspiciously with my appearance on Wild-Side.

We eventually determined that my arrival was related to that of the Elend. We were linked, but not in a way that made sense to me.

The Seeley didn't trust or like me as a person, but thankfully, they let me use their technology.

It was almost two hours past sunset, and I continued to slip noiselessly through the overgrowth of the forest. According to the small countdown timer in the corner of my heads-up display, I had just over thirty-six hours left on Wild-Side. It was one of my longer trips, and I was making the most of it. I'd explored this quadrant of the forest for the last two days and was confident the tracks I was following were fresh. Judging by the spacing of the stride and the shape of the more distinctive prints I'd seen in the mud, I was stalking what my team had recently started referring to as a Jay. Most of that breed was half again taller than a man, about twice as wide at the chest, had wicked triangular-shaped teeth that can bite through almost anything, and…did I mention they have wings?

Yeah. Freaking wings.

They can't fly, though. At least, that's what everyone kept telling me. I remain unconvinced. What's the point of wings if you can't fly, right? Still, the Doc and his people are far more intelligent than me, so I assumed they knew what they were talking about. It was something about weight and mass, lift ratios, and coefficients: they could be right. There are flightless birds in the world, so why not these things?

Still, the Elend are the closest I've seen to real-life dragons, though with human intelligence and what I can only describe as the instincts of serial killers. They couldn't talk, at least in any language I understood. But they could communicate. I had never seen them in a group of more than two or three, but they absolutely communicated. I won't describe them as social creatures, but they can organize at least so far as it's convenient to try and kill me.

I've had more than one close call.

Thankfully, they don't typically gather. They prowl the wilderness as solo, predatory hunters. They attack humans. I just can't figure out what they do with them when they catch them. There are rarely signs of bloodshed. Signs of attack? Absolutely. But rarely signs of a mauling. Either the creatures are ambush hunters that take their prey back to a nest for feeding, or they consume them whole and leave little or no mess.

I'll admit, I knew so little about the Elend back then. Sometimes, I wish I could return to those times because what I learned later was far more unsettling. It complicated my life and the future of Wild-Side in ways no one could have predicted.

I explored different ways to hunt and kill the Elend. A knife and a gun were tried and true techniques—anything I could use to penetrate the eye seemed to do the trick. We didn't know if it was the destruction of the eye itself that killed the creatures. More likely, it was some kind of vital organ located right behind the eye that was lethally damaged—but either way—if the eyes were destroyed, the creatures were toast. Some kind of critical biological reaction resulted, and their bodies pretty much just dissolved.

The immediate, total vaporization of the Elend corpse was one reason we didn't know more about them, scientifically speaking. I'd advocated for taking one alive for study, but none of the Seeley were receptive to the idea. Not even Doc Cormac was willing to experiment on a live creature in the interest of better understanding the enemy.

The people of Wild-Side were weird.

It didn't matter. I didn't have the expertise to study the creatures myself, and even if someone had been willing, the Elend were savage and dangerous. Any time I was near one, it turned into a fight to the death. Any attempt to take one alive would have invited tragedy.

I'd taken to hunting trips with different weapons to find better ways to kill the creatures. Since Tripp could fabricate anything I could dream up, I at least had him in my corner. I'd tried everything from rifles to baseball bats, but with little luck. Mostly, I just carried a backpack of gear around, so I had options.

More often than not, my pistol or my knife were the weapons of choice. The knife was good if things got hairy and I ended up a little too up close and personal with one of the creatures. The pistol worked best at a stand-off distance. The tech Cormac provided made aiming easy. The targeting capabilities in my HUD compensated for wind, bullet drop, and even moisture in the air. There was only one thing the tech failed at miserably. It only worked if I shot right-handed.

For reasons even the best minds on Cormac's team couldn't figure out, the targeting system worked perfectly when I shot right-handed, but if I switched to south-paw, the system went entirely haywire. The targeting reticle in my HUD would shift and rove all over the optical plane, losing all ability to acquire a target. Everything worked great since I was right-hand dominant, but the technology was more than useless as soon as I shifted to the opposing stance. At that point, the technology prevented me from shooting with my less-than-stellar left-handed proficiency.

The inability to solve this relatively simple problem confounded Doc Cormac and the rest of his team. Their people had been using nanotech and augmented reality for over eighty years, and nothing like this had ever been experienced. While it amused me to see the technologically advanced people stymied, this imperfection threatened to undermine my ability to protect myself and them.

Plus, they were literally messing around with my brain. If they didn't know exactly what they were doing, where did that leave me? The nanotech was only a portion of the futzing around they'd done to support my efforts to help defend Wild-Side against the Elend.

Stepping slowly through the ankle-deep water of a stream and into the mud on the far bank, I froze when the forest around me went suddenly silent. The constant murmur and buzz of nearby wildlife and insects disappeared in the span of a few heartbeats, and I knew it wasn't a response to my presence. The ground under my feet was less than ideal, so I moved quickly up the stream bank. My eyes scanned the surrounding woodland, and my optical enhancements overclocked for the next twenty to thirty seconds in response to my biorhythms.

Nothing moved.

While the people of Wild-Side hadn't been willing to join me in the fight against the Elend directly, a handful of their best and brightest had been willing to assist more passively. They had augmented me with nanotechnology, making me faster and more resilient in nearly every way. I was stronger, healed more quickly, and as was vitally important at that moment, I could see exceptionally well in the low light conditions of the forest. Even more helpful just then, I could tweak the settings of my augmentation on the fly. In this case, I could further overclock my optic enhancements to improve my night vision. I risked long-term damage to my eyes in a half-dozen ways. Thus, I could only maintain the adjustment for less than a minute, but in a fight for one's life, if you're not cheating, you're not trying.

———————

I sensed movement to my extreme right and responded with a spinning sidestep to avoid the unseen danger. A massive shape lunged at me, something hook-shaped and lashing out for my head as the larger mass missed what would have been a bone-crushing tackle. Bending back at the hips and knees, I continued to turn and saw the talon flash within inches of my face. Time seemed to slow, my mind already focusing on the contorted ducking move and the need to regain my footing after the inevitable impact with the dirt that would follow. If the Elend pinned me, I'd be torn to pieces without a chance to fight back.

Planning was a waste of time. A massive collision, this time from the other direction, sent my world into a tornado-like spin, and I didn't so much hit the ground as roll across the dirt like a fumbled football. Even as I tumbled head over heels through the leaf litter, I understood I was dealing with a pair of Elend.

My fall concluded with me rolling to my feet, knees bent, and my knife in my left hand. I grabbed from my pistol, only to find the drop-leg holster at my right hip empty. My HUD was going crazy, the threat detection system blipping with indicators and telemetry attempting, unnecessarily, to identify the two Elend Drakes staring me down from my eleven and two o'clock positions. One was nine feet, four inches tall, and the other was ten feet, seven inches. While body mass estimations and other irrelevant statistics floated in my visual plane, none of it detracted from the other-worldly sense I felt at seeing the bipedal creatures glaring at me with large, reptilian eyes. Muscles seemed to ripple and bulge beneath their thick, scaly flesh with predatory anticipation as we sized each other up.

Both creatures appeared as curious about me as I was about them. Curious or apprehensive. I knew they were dangerous, but maybe they saw me similarly? I'd been hunting these creatures for weeks. If they were intelligent, as I suspected, they likely knew someone or something out there was culling their ranks. I wasn't impacting their numbers as significantly as they were impacting the people of Wild-Side, but surely I'd made an impression by now. The pair of creatures before me, seeming to work as a team, spoke of a cooperative effort and, therefore, community.

The smaller Jay weaved slowly toward my nine o'clock. At nearly the same instant, the big Jay made a similar lateral move for my three o'clock. As they did this, two things happened. First, I became certain they were both social and intelligent. Second, a shift in the moonlight drew my attention to my lost pistol. If the Elend were moving around the perimeter of a clock, and I was at the six o'clock position, my gun lay almost precisely at the center of the dial. I still had no idea where my backpack had gone.

Size mattered, particularly when dealing with these creatures. If I had my choice, I would rather take out the big Jay first. But since I only had my knife and my angle was better on the little one, I would start with him. The creatures were ready to strike, both were slowly crouching, power building in squat, muscular legs thicker around than telephone poles.

I raised my left hand, pointed accusingly at the big Jay on my right, and yelled, "Hey!"

The glare, outburst, and maybe the pointlessness of my tiny upraised finger seemed to confuse both creatures. They froze for a second, neither breathing for several heartbeats. The targeting reticle shifted in that instant as I turned my head to face the creature on my left. My right hand was already drawn back behind my shoulder and changing direction. The reticle locked on the left eye of the little Jay, who was now at my nine o'clock. The knife spun from my fingertips with such speed and force that even I had trouble tracking it across the twenty-eight feet separating us.

The blade stuck with a sound between a thud and a splat, and the creature made no noise whatsoever. I didn't wait to see what happened next. I knew the knife was now hilt-deep in the eye socket, and for an Elend, that was a mortal wound. The shriek I heard came from my right. It wasn't anguished. I didn't think these creatures mourned one another, but then again, I was surprised to see them pair up against me. If anything, the bellow was one of rage.

I didn't waste time pondering the nuances of the creatures around me. Halfway through the diving roll that was my reckless dash to collect my gun, I sensed the beast only a pace or two behind. My hand wrapped around the pistol grip as I tumbled. Something smashed the damp earth only inches away. I turned and fired three quick shots. It was a wasted effort. Shots hitting the creature anywhere other than the eye would be entirely ineffective. I'd tried that failed experiment more times than I care to admit. It was the strangest thing, as if the Elend were altogether impervious to small arms fire. Even knife wounds appeared to heal within seconds.

I rolled, trying to put space between me and the creature before it could pin me. Instead, I was caught with the back of a massive swinging fist. It glanced across the corner of my shoulder. The wind was knocked from my lungs as I was launched into the air. The forest spun around me. I think I brushed the side of a tree because the landscape shifted once more right before I landed on my knees.

Jolting to my feet, I eyed the darkness and tried to face the grunting, crashing sound of something advancing on me through the brush. At just that second, my ears rang, and my vision was doing some kind of wavy thing that suggested I'd bashed my head in the tumble. The thundering sound of the Elend's advance seemed to be coming from every direction.

A boulder half the size of a VW Bug was about ten feet away, so I took cover behind it. I leaned a shoulder against the stone and was reasonably certain the sound of thrashing brush was coming from the far side. This was confirmed when the boulder shifted, wobbling left and right. A second later, I stumbled backward as a bulging pair of scaly arms heaved the massive rock shard from the dirt. The creature bellowed and raised the boulder over its head, ready to use it like a hammer and bash me into paste.

In that instant, I understood two things. First, these creatures were vindictive as well as savagely violent. It had talons and incredible strength, yet it would use a massive blunt instrument as a hammer. There was something troublingly human in the psychology of the attack. Second, while the creature outmatched me in terms of strength, I still had the advantage in terms of intelligence.

Somehow, I'd held onto my pistol this time and through the entire beating. The reticle appeared in my HUD and flashed as it acquired a lock on the creature's eye. Instead, I shifted my aim. I placed the muzzle of my pistol against the knobby knee of the Elend and loosed half my magazine as fast as I could pull the trigger. Even as I did, I was backpedaling at full speed.

The look that crossed the creature's face had to be surprise. I've seen pain, and this was something different. The Jay looked at me and then at the boulder still raised above its head. It was a thousand pounds if it was an ounce, and in that instance, I felt sympathy for Wile E. Coyote. The creature's knee began to fail, and its entire body started to fold like a thirty-story building that had just seen demolition charges blow out the basement. A crunching, watery splat followed a banshee-like howl. The boulder shifted slightly an instant later and the creature lay unmoving.

I would have thought that was the end, but just as the Elend couldn't be killed by gunfire the crushing force of the boulder failed to destroy it as well. A single leg extended from under the end of the jagged stone, apparently the one I'd shot because I watched as the flesh and shattered bone slowly began to knit and mend.

The creature blinked soundlessly at me as some kind of viscous internal fluid oozed between chipped and worn fangs. It was trying to move. Likely, the required musculature was attempting to heal even underneath the hundreds of pounds of stone. If there was ever an opportunity for the Doc's people to study one of these creatures, this was it.

But I knew the Seeley weren't ready even as I considered it. Some day, certainly. They were in a battle for survival, even if they hadn't fully come to terms with that yet.

My tech seemed aware of my intentions even before I decided because a targeting reticle shifted across my visual plane. The crosshair on my HUD settled on the nearest eye of the motionless Elend. I raised my hand and squeezed the trigger. The barrel hopped slightly in response to the discharge.

As it settled, the Jay's head turned to the left by a few degrees. Within seconds, its body disintegrated to dust. When it did, the boulder rolled and adjusted. I noticed a significant split down the side of the stone for the first time as it began to widen. It sounded like slowly splintering glass or a fracturing sheet of ice. The resonance of the splintering was strangely delicate, as half of it seemed to sag and separate from the other half.

When the stone broke, half fell away and tumbled free. I watched it happen in what felt like slow motion. Idle curiosity made me wonder if the same thing would have happened if I'd been the one smashed to dust under it. The idea of it being a giant hammer played through my head on a loop several times while I imagined different outcomes.

The fictitious cartoon ended when I looked at the newly exposed rock surface. A crescent of metal was clearly visible at what would have been almost the center of the boulder. I stepped forward, ran my hand along the exposed curve, and marveled at the precision of the shape. It was about the size of a basketball and protruding from the newly exposed surface of the stone.

It took almost a half hour, but I extracted the object. It was located in a cavity in the core of the boulder, surrounded by dirt, so removing it from the stone was fairly trivial, even without tools. What I thought was a globe-sized ball was even more unusual. It was more of a wedge. It looked more like the slice of an orange if the orange were the size of a basketball. The wedge was made of an alloy, entirely free from marks, writing, or oxidation. There wasn't even scarring—not so much as a blemish from its time packed in the center of the stone.

Not knowing what to do with the unusual object, I found my missing backpack and bundled it up for the trek back to see Doc Cormac. I thought the crushed Elend was an interesting development, but it turned out the wedge was the key to one of Wild-Side's greater mysteries.

Doc Cormac awaited me when I returned to Portland, but he wasn't alone. Sarah Hargrave was with him. The politics of Wild-Side wasn't new to me, but it was still confusing. The people were under siege by a hostile, invasive race, and to a person, they were unwilling to take up arms against the creatures. Even after months of living among the Seeley—on and off as my condition required—no one could explain their unwillingness to my satisfaction. And now with my returning from the wilds with the strange wedge only to find the Primary Administrator for the Seeley people waiting for me, I had a feeling I was going to experience more unwelcome Wild-Side strangeness.

"Gray," Sarah said as she extended a hand and stepped forward. I was only a few yards through the gate of the perimeter wall, and coming face to face with the Administrator, two of her aids, and Doctor Cormac was unusual. Sarah Hargrave was petite and round-faced. She had prominent eyes and short dark hair. All in all, her features reminded me of a pixie, though one that specialized in politics rather than magic. Reaching for my hand, she smiled. Shaking hands was not a custom of the people of Wild-Side, and it spoke to her efforts at diplomacy. As was her concerted attempt at eye contact. It was overdone, though I was sure that part was unintentional. I'd had little direct contact with her. So far, most of my political experiences on Wild-Side had involved her underlings, or Sarah had used Cormac as a proxy. "I understand you have completed another hunting expedition?" She said, still drilling me with her gaze.

I nodded, reluctant to speak until I understood what was happening. The Seeley were not hostile people, but I felt less in control at that moment than when I'd been facing down the pair of Elend.

Silence filled the vestibule, me eyeing Hargrave and Cormac and them looking back at me with equal discomfort. Finally, it was Cormac who broke the silence. "You said you saw the creatures heal?" He said.

I shifted the straps of the pack on my back and grinned. "Up close and personal." I tapped the corner of my eye. "Wait till you see the footage." Everything I'd seen would have been captured and available for Cormac and his team to review. They might not be willing to study the creatures firsthand, but they would be excited to use the footage my tech had captured.

"And the artifact?" Hargrave said. I was surprised at the coolness of her tone. I expected more anticipation or intensity. It was also odd that she referred to it that way.

I slipped the pack from my back and lowered it to the floor. A second later, the zipped flap opened, exposing the orange-slice wedge's matte silver finish.

I'm not sure what I expected from those gathered—I just know it wasn't the reaction I received. Hargrave's expression appeared to sour while consternation shifted across Cormac's gaze. Hargrave gave a subtle shake of her head, then waved a hand to a subordinate. "Catalog it and place it in the vault," she said.

The man knelt beside her, trying to collect the wedge from my bag. I wasn't sure what was happening, but it struck me as somehow wrong. Knocking away his outstretched hand, I told them to stop. Flipping the flap closed over the wedge, I shut the pack and slung it over one shoulder. "Just like that?" I said. "I don't get it. Someone needs to explain. What is this thing? I found it in the middle of a boulder the size of a small car. That's messed up, but you guys don't seem terribly surprised by any of it."

That's when everyone started to get uncomfortable. Hargrave glared at Cormac while her subordinates looked at her like they were about to soil themselves. Looks passed back and forth between Cormac and Hargrave, but there were no words.

Finally, Hargrave spoke. "It's what we refer to as an artifact," she said. "They turn up from time to time. When that happens, they are cataloged and placed in the vault."

She said the word like it explained everything. "Artifact," I said and twirled a finger in the air for her to continue the explanation. The gesture was wasted on someone as unfamiliar with me as they were with the people of my world, so Hargrave looked to Cormac from under furrowed brows.

Cormac seemed about to speak but then stopped. I couldn't tell if he was reluctant to explain because he was unwilling or because he was unable. His head tipped slowly as if struggling with some internal monologue. He looked back to Hargrave. "He's asking for elaboration. As I've explained, deference is not in his nature."

Hargrave's lips drew tight, and her pale complexion began to color. As one, her subordinates shrank back by several paces. I noted that Cormac, however, did not.

"Please relinquish the artifact," Hargrave said through clamped teeth.

The phrase, *or what*, was on the tip of my tongue, but I thought better of it. If these people wouldn't rise up against a threat like the Elend, I couldn't see them doing anything violent to me—not when I'm only asking for information. Rather than provoke the Administrator further, I simply tipped my head, eyed her thoughtfully…and hoped this gesture was universal.

It must not have been because Hargrave was further confused.

Cormac spoke up to clarify. Given how much time we'd spent together, he was far more familiar with my expressions and mannerisms. "He needs more," he explained to Hargrave.

"Unacceptable."

Hargrave wouldn't budge, so neither would I.

No one moved.

Doc Cormac began rubbing his brow. "Maybe you should explain what the artifacts are," he said reluctantly.

"Absolutely not," Hargrave practically spat. "I demand you turn over the artifact immediately."

I eyed the countdown timer in the corner of my HUD and considered my situation. In just over three hours, I would rebound to my world, and these people would gain control over the wedge by default unless I put it somewhere safe first. Cormac was sharp. He'd undoubtedly already considered this so I couldn't help wondering how he would use the insight. Clearly, Hargrave wasn't aware. She wouldn't be this upset if she knew she had the upper hand.

"Sarah," Cormac said, his voice calm and soothing.

She shot daggers at him. "He's not one of us."

"And as such, he doesn't understand."

"He has already proven he will never understand," she countered. "He's hunting these creatures. None of us would ever consider such a thing."

"He risks his life repeatedly to protect us–*our people*," Cormac said. "We might not agree with his beliefs, but consider his actions. These creatures aren't going away."

Cormac's words had a sobering effect on the Administrator. She remained quiet for several seconds. Finally, she said, "But the artifacts?"

Cormac nodded. "None of us can explain how or why he's here. Maybe it's related."

She looked ready to argue the point. Opening her mouth, Hargrave took a breath to respond. After a long pause, she turned to her attendants. "Cancel my appointments for the afternoon," she said, "and take the rest of the day for yourselves."

Ten minutes later, I had teleported to an undisclosed location. Whenever I was outside the badlands, my tech could generate positioning information and note it on the screen of my HUD. Wherever Doc Cormac and Administrator Hargrave had taken me, it wasn't a dead zone because the teleportation system worked. Though my HUD was functional, the location information was missing. That was obviously intentional.

"We're below ground, well outside the city," Cormac said. It must have been more information than Hargrave wanted to share since she shot him a disapproving glare that warned against further details. Cormac waved a hand and rolled his eyes in the slightest of ways that made me smile. "He's not a fool. Acoustics and spacial resonance would reveal that we are underground. Given what we're about to discuss, common sense would explain why we're nowhere near one of the cities. I have given nothing away.

"Please stop treating him like he's a threat. We're here because you know Gray is our best hope for salvaging our future." The frustration in Cormac's tone was rare, and I sensed he'd had this conversation with Hargrave on more than one occasion.

I had a feeling Hargrave only gave into this outing—whatever it was—because she knew I was an hour away from rebounding home. I was watching the countdown in my HUD and thinking there were more constructive things I could be doing.

I followed Cormac along a wide, well-lit corridor. The walls, floor, and ceiling were coated in some kind of off-white resin or epoxy. The technology of the construction seemed somehow functionally utilitarian in an antiquated way. The construction of the few empty storage rooms and spaces we passed reminded me of what I'd seen above ground in the city, but this was an older, more primitive version of the building technology. Where everything I'd seen in their construction so far could be described as clinical and sterile in design, it struck me how the city's architecture had all been built mainly of rounded corners rather than hard edges. Everything I saw here looked much the same but differed subtly. There wasn't a single rounded edge to be seen. Something about the observation felt evolutionary in the design shift like the same minds had constructed this place and the city at different historical points.

"Our first city was much like this facility," Cormac said as if reading my mind.

"Underground?" I said without pause.

Cormac turned a corner and nodded. "That too, but I was referring to the construction."

I stopped our progression with a hand on his shoulder. "The city," I said. "Is it still viable? An underground installation would make it harder for the Elend to attack. We could defend it much more easily."

Hargrave grumbled something, paused, then clarified whatever point she'd been muttering to herself. "Garwin lost geologic integrity over a hundred and sixty years ago."

"Garwin?" I said, unsure I heard the name correctly.

"It was the name of our first city. It was near the northwest coast. The region was never geologically stable and not ideally suited for such construction," she explained.

Garwin.

It was a good enough name. I didn't need to create an analog for a place back home.

I wondered who had decided to build the city there and why. And if the Seeley people lived what seemed to be an endlessly long life, where did they come from? They were all the same age, and they never had children. Their longevity seemed improbable, and it was undoubtedly impractical.

Cormac was grinning at me. "The questions are starting again?" His eyes sparkled from behind his glasses and beneath bushy eyebrows in a way that was both wisened and amused. He seemed to be daring me to go down this rabbit hole again. It was a rabbit hole that, until now, held no answers.

Still, one question was poking at the base of my brain. I couldn't get the Seeley to talk about their origin, but maybe I could approach the topic laterally. I gave it a shot.

"We're underground now—your first city was underground." I paused, unsure how to frame the question. "Your people aren't the most robust," I started. From what I've seen, they are not well suited toward manual labor." I'd never seen heavy equipment, and it would be a requirement for a group creating extensive underground facilities. "How are you excavating the earth?"

"Interesting," Cormac said with an arch of his brows. "A timely question given where we're headed." He motioned further down the corridor. "The Archives are home to the earliest technology we developed, including the displacement device we used to expand Garwin."

I had a million questions, and the list was expanding at an ever-increasing rate. How could he talk about this so freely while still being entirely unwilling to explain the origin of the Seeley people?

Cormac nodded and waved a hand theatrically at double doors that had just come into view. "Today, you have an opportunity to find answers."

My first response was to laugh, but the earnestness of his expression and reluctance in Hargrave's disposition made me think better of it. I took a deep breath and pushed through the doors.

The room beyond was massive. I'll describe it as a warehouse because there's no question it was a storage space. The ceiling was arched like the inside of a barrel, the highest point about thirty feet overhead. The floors were the same off-white, pale lacquer polish that had covered every inch of every surface I'd seen. Still, only chaotic patches of the floor were visible between towering shelves and strange, irregularly shaped objects draped in dusty tarps. The tarped objects littered the floor randomly like a minefield. I counted more than a dozen near me, with countless more silhouetted in a massive expanse spreading off into the distance beyond the reach of the six or eight overhead lights.

The silver orange-slice-shaped wedge sat on a small wheeled cart near a crystal ball-like orb on a pedestal. I walked over to the wedge and ran a finger across its curved surface, surprised when my hand came back with a thick coating of grime.

Sarah Hargrave stepped forward, looking like she would slap my hand. She seemed to think better of it at the last second. "Do you have to touch everything?" She mumbled more, but it was under her breath. It was an affectation that I was seeing her do more and more as she became increasingly stressed. "Please keep your hands to yourself."

Unsure how to respond, I focused on the dust collected on the so-called artifact. When the doctor spoke, I rubbed the grit between my thumb and forefinger.

"That's not the artifact you found," he clarified.

I leaned over the silver wedge and studied it. In my peripheral vision, I noted Hargrave as she moved to dissuade me. Cormac quickly placed an arm around her, and they moved out of my sightline. The soundless show brought a smile to the corners of my mouth. However, the fact that I could see no apparent differences between this object and the one I found quickly ended the grin.

"If you say so," I said after an awkward silence. "It looks the same to me."

"It's the same in every measurable way," a new voice sounded immediately to my right. It was modulated in a decidedly not human way and sounded out of nowhere so unexpectedly that I was startled. I did not jump or reach for the non-existent gun on my hip–and if Cormac ever says differently, it's important to remember that he's been learning about something folks on Our-World call *creative license*. He's never gotten the hang of it and likely never will.

After I stopped backpedaling, I focused on the glass orb sitting atop a pedestal. It glowed with a pale blue light, dimming in a pulse that kept time with the words emanating from it.

"I apologize for startling you, Gray," the device said. "Administrator Hargrave, I thought this meeting was part of a plan. Is my information incorrect?"

Hargrave just glowered at me.

Cormac grinned with unbridled amusement. "You are correct." Whatever name he called the...orb... didn't translate. It didn't match a name in the English language. That kind of thing still happens from time to time, most frequently with names. That's why I mapped it to the name Fenton. Like all Seeley words, I translated this way: When I said Fenton, the Seeley heard their version of the word.

Fenton would work. With a name like that, it couldn't possibly scare the crap out of me again.

"We tend to get sidetracked," Cormac was explaining. "So here we are." He looked at me. "Gray, this is Fenton. Fenton, this is Gray."

Suppressing the instinct to shake hands, I eyed the pale light emanating from the orb and wondered what the social protocol was in this situation. I also wondered what this thing was. I'd been on Wild-Side for so long and never heard of anything like it.

The orb seemed to anticipate my discomfort. "You're already familiar with non-organic intelligence, Gray?" Fenton said.

"AI? Artificial Intelligence, I mean," I elaborated and instantly wondered if I'd made some kind of mistake in the political correctness of the phrasing.

"Precisely," Fenton said. "You have a working familiarity with Esker, correct?"

It was phrased like a question, but it didn't feel like one. "You know about Esker?"

"I know about Esker, your world, the creatures you call Elend, and more."

Fenton's voice was decidedly not human, but it wasn't digital or robotic either. The AI, or non-organic intelligence as it seemed to prefer, spoke with human tones and inflections modulated in a way that was just synthetic enough not to be confused with humans. The speech was artificial but not enough to be upsetting or unpleasant. The voice sounded a bit more on the masculine side of genderless. Still, again, it seemed to balance on a very delicate gradient that made it comfortable for interaction without being distracting or androgynous.

During my analysis of the AI, it asked Cormac and Hargrave to excuse us. This happened so quickly and with so little fanfare that it must have been part of the overall agenda. Before I knew what was happening, I was alone in the warehouse with the glowing orb on the pedestal.

"In point of fact," Fenton said, "I am not an artificial intelligence. As you know, the use of AI technology is prohibited here. A nuanced distinction given my present form, but a vital point given the prohibition."

Something told me the conversation I was about to have was intentionally private. There was a sense that this non-corporeal entity was yet another layer to Wild-Side's overall mystery.

Given the countdown displayed in my HUD, time was running out, literally. I had to make the most of my few remaining minutes.

Not knowing what to do or what to say, I considered Cormac's mention of finally getting answers and jumped directly into the proverbial deep end of the pool.

"Fenton, Doctor Cormac suggested you might be willing to answer some of the questions that no one here can answer for me," I said.

"Queries about Wild-Side, the Elend, or Brane theory?"

My mind froze, suddenly wondering where to begin. Finding the right starting point might make things easier, thought it would be a lot more difficult if I messed this up. According to my timer, I was seventeen minutes from my rebound. "Can we start with you?"

"Me? I'll admit, that's not a question I was anticipating."

"The technology here is amazing. It surpasses the tech of my world in every conceivable way. But when I asked the Doc why there's no use of AI here, he said it was not permitted. When I asked what that meant, he wouldn't—or maybe couldn't—explain. It seemed like that happens with a variety of topics. Oddly, all of the significant ones."

The blue light in the orb swirled slowly for several long seconds, and I took it as a sign of quiet contemplation. "You're right in that there are a series of tenants core to the people of this Brane—all of which have been vital to their survival thus far. The reluctance you experience when attempting to get them to speak of these tenants is less intentional and more a product of their nature. For them, it's like the grass being green and the sky being blue. It's all they have ever known. You're asking questions they have never asked themselves, in many cases.

"For the people of your Brane, they leverage the creative centers of their minds to grow and develop. As you've seen here, the Seeley, as you call them, have no creativity—at least not as you would define it. They have no art or music. There is no religion. They have only a logic-driven sense of science."

I had questions specific to AI, but I felt we were pulling at a thread more critical to my overall understanding of Wild-Side. "There's never been any organized religion here." For me, this was more of an observation. But as far as this went, it was a multi-headed hydra that gave me a lot to unpack. Organized religion has inspired the world with countless works of art and music. It also caused people to organize for social improvement and also led to war and genocide.

"Yes," Fenton said. "The source of so much beauty and devastation in your world. It begs the question, to avoid all of the devastation the religions of your world have brought, would you be willing to sacrifice the associated beauty as well?"

It was suddenly my turn for quiet contemplation. There was a strong sense that this scenario wasn't an abstract hypothetical. I found myself staring into the blurry orb and considering not only its questions but also my own, asked and unasked.

"You know a lot about my world," I said finally.

Fenton said nothing, so I changed my approach.

"You know more about my world than I have told anyone on Wild-Side. How is that?"

"Those core tenants of life here," Fenton said. I could only hope it was a lateral approach to an answer. "As you observed, the Seeley have developed much more advanced technology than the people of your Brane. They have done this in a very limited time, too. As you have observed, the population of this Brane is two hundred and fifty-six years old. A single generation, while the people of your Brane expand on the works of the generations before them.

"Both are forms of evolution, though perhaps not in the terms you normally associate with the principle. The shorter life spans of the people in your world function as a means of limiting development to a speed where intelligence and biology are commensurate. The equation on Wild-Side is similar. It just uses a different ratio. The people live longer, but they don't reproduce. They have a long life span over which to evolve, but their population is finite."

I could see where Fenton was going, if only in the vaguest sense. It was super messed up. And even if I *agreed* with the explanation, and when I say agree, I'm doing that in air quotes because—*whoa—so messed up*. That still points to some kind of guiding hand balancing the scales. It suggested someone or something set up a sort of cosmic Petri dish with one set of organized parameters for Our-World and another for Wild-Side.

I'm the guy tripping dimensions, and even I can't drink that Kool-Aid.

"So, the AI?" I said. It was all I could think of to bring us back to a topic that didn't feel like celestial quicksand.

"That rev-limiter that keeps the people from your world from outpacing their own social and genetic capabilities? It's your relatively meager lifespan. For the Seeley? It's a short list of tenants. Core among them is a prohibition against the development and use of artificial intelligence."

I was pacing slowly back and forth across the short open space in front of the pedestal on which the orb sat. I had been doing this for a few minutes and had only just noticed it. The question on my lips crossed some kind of line, but it had to be asked.

"With all the advanced technology here, why prohibit artificial intelligence?"

"Those core tenants," Fenton said. "They keep the Seeley from growing too fast or beyond their means before they're ready. The people of your world expect AI to one day reach what they call Singularity. Some believe this is where AI will become the future of humankind or the cause of its destruction."

I nodded. "I'm familiar with the concept. Some also think it's when machines become self-aware and self-replicating and start doing things that no one has predicted."

"And so we return to the concept of the rev-limiter," Fenton said. "Here, on Wild-Side, if you will, the restriction against AI is just the most obvious of the limitations. The population's unwillingness or inability to take up arms against the Elend is perhaps the most glaring example, and one you're unlikely to circumvent."

"I don't understand an entire people's unwillingness to protect themselves against a hostile force. The Elend threaten their survival as a people."

"You're dealing with more than mere reluctance," Fenton said with a tone of finality that had not been used in the conversation so far. "You're dealing with cognitive dissonance. You see a people ruled by thought and reason, a population now fighting emotions such as crippling fear for the first time in their lives. They are experiencing things they have no concept of and are being asked to do things they never imagined before. It's more than most can process.

"The fact that you gained the support of Doctor Cormac and several of his contemporaries is exceptional. I did not think it was possible, even for you."

Even for me?

I wanted to know what that meant, but it was more important not to lose the thread of our conversation. I sensed that I might not be allowed a return visit once I left this warehouse. Hargrave certainly wasn't in favor of me coming in the first place.

"Tell me about the Seeley? Where did they come from?"

The blue orb pulsed with an unusual set of swirls. I don't know what to say other than there was something distinctive about what I saw. It meant something. Not to me, certainly. But it must have been relative to the question I'd just asked. "Cognitive dissonance also applies to non-organic life," Fenton said after a pause.

My mouth was suddenly dry and I felt the answers that were inches from my grasp just a moment before were slipping away. "Say–huh?" Maybe not my most eloquent question in the conversation so far, but...*come on.*

"As you have already deduced, I have familiarity with not only Wild-Side but your Brane as well. For this reason, there are topics I cannot offer insights into and questions I cannot answer. The artifacts gathered in this repository have been sequestered to maintain Equilibrium." The way the word equilibrium was used seemed to have importance. "Administrator Hargrave and Doctor Cormac know only enough about the nature of these devices to collect and sequester them." Something in the way Fenton said *sequester* gave me the sense he actually meant *quarantine.* "They don't know why they must act as they do."

I looked at the countdown in the corner of my HUD and knew I had time for one last question before I was forced to return home.

"Esker," I said, referring to the AI helping me back home. "If there's a prohibition on AI, how could Doc Cormac provide Esker to me? He's been essential to my efforts to undermine Breslin. How did he get around the prohibition?"

"Doctor Cormac didn't create the AI you call Esker," Fenton said. "I provided the source code and instructions for compiling it on your Brane. They didn't know what was provided until you unpacked and deployed the payload."

Time was short, and I knew there was something more to say. I had the sense that Fenton knew more about this place than anyone, but the how and why of that concept escaped me.

"You believe you're the only chance the Seeley have to survive, and you are correct," Fenton said. "Go to Garwin. It's not the entire solution," he paused as if carefully considering the following words. "Think of Garwin as the tool you need."

The countdown in the corner of my HUD reached the two-second mark and I felt a burning in the pit of my stomach. Creativity and deception might not come naturally to the Seeley. Still, for the non-organic intelligence they kept buried in some remote warehouse, vague hints and suggestions were something of a game.

Fenton seemed to know I was about to rebound. The last thing I heard was, "Nice visiting with you again, Gray."

Chapter 4 - Special Clientele

Our-World

Unknown location Kansas

Chris Ingersoll kicked the 9mm shell casing with the toe of his shoe, dislodging it from the cracked, dry mud. "Forensics missed this one," he said, "but it won't matter. Like the rest, we won't find any prints."

His partner, Al Vincente, whistled and waved for one of the FBI crime scene technicians. He pointed at the ground, and they both saw the approaching technician nod. "Any word on what was stolen yet?" Al asked as he tracked the oncoming agent over the open expanse.

Ingersoll shook his head. "Still waiting for a callback. Two of their big brains are proving hard to find." He was referring to a pair of missing research leads, both of whom had been unaccounted for since the attack on the facility. "Either, one of them took off with the experimental hardware to keep it safe, or our guy got away with it. We're still not sure."

"You think our guy kidnapped the research leads?" Vincente struggled to hide the skepticism in his tone.

The question made Ingersoll pause, concluding with a shrug. "That wouldn't fit with his MO, but who can say? He's never taken anyone before. He's never killed anyone on the technical team before, either. Still, there's a first time for everything."

"More likely they ran," Vincente said quietly. "I sure as hell would."

Ingersoll grunted in agreement and glanced across the dozens of flags marking the locations where evidence was still being collected throughout the compound's visible acres. At least a dozen additional technicians were working at the underground facility to gather similar forensic evidence.

At six and a half feet tall, Ingersoll had broad shoulders and blonde hair buzzed short in a military style, although he'd never served in the military. He'd joined the FBI straight out of the University of Michigan. At the age of forty-two, he specialized in hunting fugitives.

"The on-site tech just confirmed," Vincente said as he watched the technician begin photographing the shell casing and start the collection process. "The surveillance system is a complete wash."

"Trashed?"

Vincente gestured toward the cinderblock building housing the elevator. "No, it's completely functional; it's just blank. The time codes even show it was working all night. The recordings only display black screens with no audio."

Al Vincente was an Italian-American cop turned FBI agent. After making a name for himself on an anti-terrorism task force on the West Coast, he completed a night school degree and joined the FBI. At 45, though a couple of years older than his partner, he was technically the junior agent on their team. He stood stout at five feet eight inches, powerfully built with a short, thick neck and cauliflower ears. His thinning dark hair and inability to grow anything but patchy facial hair, even with months of effort, meant he had been cursed with a baby face all his life.

Ingersoll walked across the hard-packed dirt, which had shown signs of being mud just a few hours earlier but was already drying and cracking in the early morning sun. He looked up at the clear blue sky and reflected on the ferocity of the storm the night before. "It's not the first time we've experienced something like that," Ingersoll admitted.

"Same goes for the ordinance," Vincente said, holding out a handful of spent 9mm cases. "Same MO. He didn't police his brass. No one was injured—at least not seriously. And I'll give you two guesses as to who owns the place."

Ingersoll stopped short of the service door to the underground complex and consulted one of the file folders tucked under his arm. "I thought it was the Woodlawn Research Group?"

Holding his cell phone aloft, Vincente grinned. "This just in: Woodlawn is a subsidiary of…" he offered a dramatic pause.

"Arlington Technologies Global?" Ingersoll finished, rolling his eyes. "Son of a bitch. How'd I see that coming? Our guy has a serious axe to grind with ATG."

Three and a half minutes later, they exited the first of the complex's two elevators. Vincente stared wide-eyed at the poured concrete walls surrounding the exit at the base of the elevator they had just stepped from. "You know what that was, don't you?" Awe was clear in his voice. "We just came down the shaft that used to house an intercontinental missile. A freaking nuke. Can you believe it?"

Ingersoll shrugged, not seeing what was so special about it.

"You're kidding, right? This underground silo was here for most of a generation, and no one got wise," Vincente explained. "For much of my childhood, this was part of the nation's nuclear defense. This massive missile was right under everyone's feet, yet no one knew it." He waved his hands in the air. "Fast forward a dozen years, and the government sells the space to private companies."

Ingersoll waved him forward. "It's not like they sold the nuke with it," he mumbled. "What do you suppose something like this sells for? That's what I want to know."

A voice echoed from the far end of the hallway. "It was believed to be a good investment at the time," the woman said. She walked forward with her hand extended and shook hands with both agents. She introduced herself as Linda Meeks. "I manage facilities for ATG," she explained. "Thank you for meeting with us," Ingersoll said. "Can you explain what ATG does at this facility?"

"Sadly, as of this morning, nothing at all. We were conducting a single experiment, but with the theft of the hardware last night, the operation will be shut down until the device can be recovered. I'm told that's where you gentlemen come in?"

Meeks was in her early fifties, with short dark hair and thick-framed glasses perched atop a thin, bird-like nose. She appeared thin to the point of looking in poor health, though Ingersoll found her handshake firm and commanding, just like her voice.

"Absolutely," Ingersoll replied with more confidence than he felt. "We've already walked the scene with your head of security, Mr.

Huxley. If you wouldn't mind walking the same ground with us, we would like to ask some additional questions."

Ingersoll knew this was an exercise in appearing to do their due diligence. He had little hope of finding new evidence. The security system had recorded no images of the perpetrator. While the forensics team was still working, based on what they had seen at numerous similar crime scenes, he had no doubt there would be no useful evidence left behind. They had collected multiple 9mm shell casings, as they had in the past. However, there was nothing significant about the brass, the residual powder, or anything in the chemical analysis. Tasking of the van full of complicated and expensive forensics equipment had been wasted yet again. None of the guards interviewed remembered the attacker beyond a man dressed in black. Whatever non-lethal ordnance was used on them seemed to impact their short-term memory.

Interviews with the research team produced a surprising result. Multiple interviewees agreed that the single attacker removed his mask for a short time. However, this did not help, as blackout face paint was used. No one could agree on his facial features, let alone his ethnicity.

Eleven hours later, Vincente and Ingersoll met by their sedan to compare notes. They agreed that they had collected no significant evidence. At best, they had plaster casts of boot prints in the mud.

"No one could positively identify him," Vincente said as he slumped in the passenger seat. Exhaustion was evident in his tone.

"They don't need to. We know it was Grady Ledger," Ingersoll grumbled. "The question is, why does he bother to hide it now?"

"The *real* question is, what's his beef with Arlington Technologies Global? We know about six cases of industrial espionage. The one thing they all have in common is ATG."

Ingersoll woke up his digital tablet and refreshed the map of the United States. Last night's storm over Kansas had been added to the cumulative overlays. Recent unexpected storm fronts, similar to the previous night, had occurred near Seattle, Bozeman, Sarasota, and Boulder. All these locations have ATG offices or facilities, and someone matching Grady Ledger's general description had also been sighted there.

"What's with the map?" Vincente asked.

Ingersoll flicked the app off his screen and transitioned to his encrypted email. "Just checking the weather," he replied. "I heard back from my buddy at the NSA. He's searching the video we discussed, but we need to keep that between us. Are you still comfortable with the approach?"

Taking a slow, contemplative breath, Vincente nodded. He waved to the crime scene beyond his dashboard, and his slow nod gained enthusiasm. "At this point, we need to use every tool we have. Sooner or later, someone will get hurt—and ATG is losing tens of millions with each attack." He met Ingersoll's gaze, and his tone grew grave. "We won't be able to use whatever our team provides in court. Do you have any concerns about that?" Ingersoll shrugged. "I'm not worried. If this works as I expect, my guy can help put us on the scene with Grady Ledger. Once we're there, it's up to us to build the case or put him in the ground."

"I'd prefer to eliminate him." A grin spread across Ingersoll's face. "He took out how many professional hard cases by himself last night? How many more last month? And how many more back in June? You're skilled, and I know I'm better—but let's be realistic. If I end up face-to-face with him, I'll do whatever it takes to make sure his story ends then and there. You have to be willing to do the same."

Our-World

Alison Springs, Maryland

The bar was called The Borderline, which was odd because it was nowhere near the edge of town, and Alison Springs wasn't even close to the edge of the state of Maryland. It was near the coast, so if they were referring to the border with the Atlantic Ocean, I guess a connection could be made. That still seemed like a stretch to me. As far as bars go, it wasn't anything special. It was narrow, maybe fifty feet wide, though most of its space came from a depth three to four times greater than its width. The bar counter ran along most of the left wall. That amount of counter space might seem excessive until you consider that this was a college town, and the bar was one of three businesses pinning the end of a rundown old plaza. There was a dingy pool hall with threadbare tables on one side of the bar and a down-home pizza joint with peanut shells on the floor on the other side.

I walked in on a Friday night, and the place was packed. I shouldered through the crowd in time to see one of the horseshoe-shaped tables along the right wall clear out. It was occupied by four or five coeds who seemed to find something suddenly noteworthy near the back of the bar, where a stage was assembled of painted black plywood and exposed timber. I slipped into the booth to claim the prized real estate before any of the envious onlookers could scavenge it.

The U-shaped booth had its back to the wall. I have an aversion to sitting with my back to the building's entrance. Some call it the gunfighter seat. Remember, it's not paranoia if they really are after you, alright? Still, having my back to the crowded room wasn't much better, especially since all I knew of the rear entrance came from a building floor plan provided by Esker. There were too many people in the room to scout firsthand, and I was lucky to grab the vantage point when the table freed up.

As I slipped into the booth, I pressed my back against the wall. The table and built-in bench seating were made from two-by-fours and two-by-sixes without any cushioning, suggesting that comfort was expected to come from the drinks served. The purpose of the night's outing, and the merit of my vantage point, was the view of the crowded bar.

I was feeling anxious. Maybe that's not the right word; it was actually hard to describe. I felt uncomfortable in a way that was entirely foreign to me. I wasn't this uncomfortable when I jumped out of that Cessna into an angry storm with my name on it. This unease made me question the root cause of my anxiety. It has been said that if the cause of concern can be identified, it can be addressed.

Until that moment, I hadn't examined my worries in detail. You might not know it from how I talk, but I'm not the most introspective of folks. I can talk all day about the world around me, while what's going on in my head barely registers.

As my eyes scanned the bar, watching dozens of young men and women jostle for each other's attention or generally make fools of themselves, the cause of my concern finally clicked in my mind. Jumping from that plane, infiltrating the base, and escaping with the stolen artifact were easy because I believed in the cause and knew what I was doing. Here and now, I felt lost and confused, lacking confidence. I questioned my own motives while battling self-doubt. There was a chance I was here tonight for the wrong reasons, which could ultimately end in disaster.

That's when I saw *her*.

The sight of Piper Hudson took my breath away. Leaving her had been the most painful experience of my life, but seeing her again after a year and a half brought back a rush of emotions like a hammer blow. I slouched in my seat and pulled my baseball cap lower over my brow, but I couldn't look away from her. She moved behind the bar with a grace and ease that suggested many hours serving drinks in hectic conditions. Ducking and weaving, she danced in a ballet with three other female bartenders and one young male bartender.

Piper stood five feet eight inches tall, with long blonde hair and the bluest eyes I had ever seen. They resembled something from a Crayola box, but they sparkled with a unique energy. Despite how well I knew her, I couldn't tell if that sparkle stemmed from her intelligence or her passion for life. Her beauty was unmistakable, beginning with her eyes. There was something captivating and immersive that drew me in the first time I looked into them. The rest of her appearance was also hard to overlook, and I considered myself as red-blooded as any American boy. Her blonde hair and fair complexion reflected her Norwegian heritage, and her slim, athletic frame confirmed every stereotype I had come to associate with beautiful women from that part of the world.

You're rolling your eyes at me already, I can tell. But it wasn't just my impression. Out of the four young women tending bar—all similar, young, and scantily dressed in too-tight jeans and even tighter tank tops—Piper was receiving the most attention by far. It wasn't merely her appearance; it was everything about her. She exuded a remarkable sense of approachable warmth.

People were drawn to her.

We met a little over two years ago, and she changed my life. The chaos with Wild-Side had just begun, and I was starting to understand my confusing ability to move between Branes. At a time when nothing seemed real, and when I probably should have questioned my sanity, she kept me grounded. She was my anchor in this world, helping me make sense of what was happening on Wild-Side.

I don't know what I would have done without her. Leaving was the most difficult and painful experience of my life, but since it was the only way to keep her safe, I did what had to be done. Now, fate, karma, or some force beyond my understanding brought us back together.

Part of me wanted to believe that sentimental nonsense, but more and more evidence supported it. Events on Wild-Side suggest manipulation from an outside force—something with the power to influence the Seeley as a collective race. Considering that, maybe seeing similar machinations here wasn't such a stretch.

Meeting Piper in the first place was incredibly random. Looking back, we both acted very uncharacteristically right from that first day on the boat. Each of us reached far outside our comfort zones to make a connection that brought us—well, me, for sure—something needed to make all of this worthwhile.

Or maybe I am just slipping into insanity after all. If I'm being honest, seeing Piper again threw me off my game and brought me dangerously close to introspection.

I am not introspective.

———————

I hoped for a beer. Several waitresses roamed the floor, taking and delivering orders with an agility I couldn't manage. With the capacity of this place nearly at maximum and more people still pushing their way through the doors, I was beyond my comfort zone. I needed a drink or three to keep my nerves from snapping like an overwound rubber band. With more people filling the joint, the odds were good that Piper wouldn't notice me. She was already doing the work of three people behind the bar, so there was little chance of that. But since the goal for the night was reconnaissance, I would be happy to gather whatever intel I could and put off the unpleasantness of our reunion until tomorrow.

No question showing up that night, was a bad idea. Still, I couldn't pass up the opportunity. It had been a year and a half, and just seeing her made it all so much more real. She had been there from the start, well, almost at the start. If anyone could understand what was happening, it was Piper. At the same time, if there was one person who would resent how I had handled things, no one had more reason to hate me than her.

A young guy in a cowboy hat stepped up to my table and started talking. I missed his first few words as I was off in my own little world. "You reading me, friend?" he said with a wave and an aw-shucks grin. "Are you alright?"

"Sorry," I said. "What was that?"

"I was asking if you were expecting company. You got friends coming, or do you mind sharing some of your space with me and a couple of my friends? My lady friends, if that matters," he said with a wink.

Inwardly, I cringed. This guy seemed young, probably my age, in his early twenties. He was decked out in denim from head to toe: not just jeans, but also a denim jacket and shirt. He sported a cowboy look, complete with a hat and boots—a serious commitment to the motif. Still, he wore that good old boy grin, while I received disapproving looks from more and more people, making me feel guilty for occupying a table all by myself. Sharing the table with a couple of others would help me blend in, even if it meant interacting with, you know, those actual people.

Did I mention I'm not people-oriented or naturally social?

I shrugged. "Pull up a chair—er, well, some timber?" I made a point of not moving from my ideal position at the crook of the U-shape. I was willing to share, but I wasn't willing to give up my observation post or turn my back on the entrance.

"Much obliged," the cowboy said, touching the brim of his hat in appreciation. Perhaps he wasn't merely playing cowboy. Either he was a committed method actor, or there was more Texas in him than just his twang. I watched as he waved to a pair of young women.

The cowboy guided a slim, raven-haired girl into the booth to sit between me and the spot he quickly took at the end of the U. "This is Trini," he said with a nod. He motioned to the girl with short red hair who slipped into the booth opposite him and Trini. "And this here's Renee. My name's Walsh, Tommy Walsh, but my friends just call me Walsh."

I shook hands with him, then with Trini and Renee in turn. "I'm Grady Ledger," I said, only loud enough to be heard over the buzz of the surrounding crowd. I wasn't comfortable introducing myself, but there wasn't a way around it. I had already weighed the pros and cons and decided this was the best path, given my plan to insert myself in the experiment Breslin was financing at the school here. Since this wouldn't be a smash-and-grab operation, I would need to spend time with the team working on the project. "My friends call me Gray."

"Are you new here?" Trini asked.

I nodded. "Just pulled into town this afternoon. I went for a drive looking for a place to get a drink and ended up here." Walsh put an arm around Trini, a not-so-subtle way of marking her as his girl, though I don't think he was being territorial. I was already getting a vibe from him suggesting that he was a good enough guy. I think he was just ensuring nothing got confused from the start.

"Are you transferring?" Walsh asked. "You know classes started a month ago?"

Given the timing, this was the tricky part. Had the timetable been a little different, I could have joined the school as a student and had more freedom and flexibility. As it was, I would have had to shoehorn my way into the project and hope no one asked the wrong questions of the right people.

"I'm not a student. There's a project on campus that uses some specialized equipment. I'm here to install it and fine-tune the hardware. I'll probably be here for a couple of months."

The waitress finally showed up, and I was tempted to order a couple of shots. I'm not kidding; I would rather face a pack of Elend than sit around making small talk in a room filled with strangers.

Walsh ordered a rum and Coke, which I didn't think was particularly cowboy-like. The girls both ordered drinks that sounded both girly and tropical. When it comes to drinks, I stick to the basics. I know what I like and don't get creative. "I'll take a Modelo if you have it; a Corona if you don't," I told the waitress.

"It'll have to be Corona, hun," the waitress said with a wink. "Sorry about that."

I looked around the room. "Looks like they're keeping you pretty busy," I said. "Would it save time if you just brought me two?"

Her eyes settled on me for a long second. "They don't like when we do that," she said with a knowing grin. "If anyone asks, you tell 'em your friend is in the can?" I nodded, she gave me a wink, and off she went.

Walsh chuckled, "You came to play, is that it, hoss?"

Trini promptly elbowed him in the ribs, which I thought was odd until I read her lips when she harshly whispered to him, "He doesn't like crowds, you asshole."

I thought that was unusually intuitive for someone so young, and I instantly wondered what Trini was studying. She had the makings of a good therapist. It wasn't the crowd that had my senses tingling on high alert; it was the fact that in the last nine months, I had evaded five bounty hunter teams thanks to the price placed on my head by my old friend Breslin. After my recent attack on his facility in Kansas and the fact that I had stolen the artifact vital to what might have been a very promising new experiment on his part, there was a solid chance that he was about to double down on the current bounty.

Though unlikely, anyone in the room could be looking to bag me. The only saving grace in that scenario was their need to keep me alive. For every attempt Breslin made to open the bridge or doorway between my world and his, I was his best chance at finding a solution.

Looking at the bar again, I reconsidered the idea of returning Piper to the proverbial playing field. If Breslin could take her, he would have everything he needed to leverage me. He just didn't know it yet; if he did, the game would already be over. Piper was participating in one of Breslin's experiments, although it was unbeknownst to both her and Breslin. Breslin financed the experiment at Alison Springs, where Piper worked with Professor Fulbright.

The waitress returned. Walsh received a surprisingly tall rum and Coke while the two girls seemed pleased with whatever pink, pineapple concoctions they'd ordered. Then, to my surprise, the waitress leaned down the length of the table to slide a pair of short, wide Modelo bottles in front of me. I shot her a look that must have expressed my confusion.

"We keep a stash in the back of the cooler for special clientele," she said with a smirk and a tip of her head. "I was also told to deliver your drinks with the caps still in place. I hope that's alright with you?" I groaned and cursed inwardly.

Piper saw me.

Tonight was a bad idea, after all. Now my nerves were shot; I would owe Esker twenty bucks, and my plan for tomorrow would suffer from whatever fallout came from tonight.

Sliding a hundred-dollar bill down the table, I glanced up at the waitress, knowing defeat was clear in my expression. "Keep it," I said. "And thanks."

"Are you alright?" Renee said. "You look like you just saw a ghost."

"Close enough. Pretty sure you're looking at a dead man."

I quickly finished my first beer and took my time with the second. Taking care of the waitress with that tip had unintentionally captured her attention for the rest of the evening. A few minutes after my first bottle was empty, it was replaced by another. She was no longer worried about anyone raising concerns over my having more than one beer at a time. By that point, it didn't matter. After just a slight buzz, it was enough to ease my nerves, allowing me to tolerate sitting still. I had Esker monitoring camera feeds at both the front and rear entrances and four different views inside the bar, and he was also observing traffic cameras and municipal feeds within a three-block radius. He updated me through the audio feed in my inner ear. It seemed even my digital sidekick was aware of my social anxiety.

Looking around the table at my new friends, I decided it was time to do something to break the ice. I'd faced awkwardness in spades over the last year and a half in my time with the Seeley. For a race of technologically advanced people, they had no concept of art. Things like technical drawings and schematic diagrams came easily to them. Still, they had no frame of reference for artistic drawing, painting, music, theater, or anything creative. They were a race of socially undeveloped, advanced versions of the people of our world.

I bring this up now because I fell back on the same approach I used when initially trying to relate to the Seeley. It would either work, or I would get my new friends to leave me alone.

"Little Drew sat down at his desk, and the teacher said, 'Today we're going to learn about multi-syllable words.'" I said this as my gaze swept the table, breaking the awkward silence. "The teacher asked, 'Does anyone have an example of a multi-syllable word?' Little Drew got excited and raised his hand. 'I do, Miss Radtke! Mommy and Daddy were talking about one at breakfast this morning.' 'Alright, Drew,' Miss Radtke said with some relief. 'What was the word?' 'Mas-ter-bate,' Drew said, carefully breaking the word into syllables. Miss Radtke grew a little pale but quickly recovered. 'Impressive, Drew. That's quite a mouthful.' Drew shook his head. 'No, you're thinking of a blowjob.'"

The three faces at the table stared at me with slack-jawed expressions for what seemed like an eternity. Then, some kind of strange group stasis broke. Trini let out a gurgling choke that turned into a racking cough as she spewed the swallow of drink she'd been in the process of taking. At the same time, Walsh's face lit up with a toothy grin. His head tipped back with a belly laugh that nearly caused him to topple his Coke. Renee was just starting to take a bite from the large pineapple slice hanging from the rim of her drink only a moment before. She began to laugh, which sent the fruit bouncing off her chin and the edge of the table before it landed in her lap.

With that, the ice was broken. Everyone quickly became more comfortable, and small talk filled the table. Throughout the evening, I kept my eye on the bar, not in a creepy way. In my line of work, you learn to observe without being obvious. As Esker had pointed out while I was still sitting in the parking lot, given his access to the bar's numerous camera feeds, there really was no reason for me to enter the bar in the first place. I could have had an unobstructed view of Piper from my hotel room all night. I tried to explain to him that this would have been creepy, but he didn't understand the distinction. As I sat in the crowd, wondering what I hoped to accomplish, I questioned if he'd been right after all.

"Pharmacology," Walsh said with a dismissive shrug as I tuned back into the conversation across the table. When he saw my confusion, he continued to explain. "I grew up in East Texas. When I was in school, lots of kids were going to jail for cooking meth. We're talking about some stupid ass kids. But they seemed to have at least enough understanding of the chemistry to either go to jail or get killed.

Neither option was of interest to me, but it bothered me that these hillbillies were skilled at something I didn't understand. So I started reading up on it. The next thing I knew, I was interested. Now I'm going to school for something constructive."

I tipped back the last of my second beer and looked at the man in denim. The insight impressed me. He looked more like the cowboy jock type. Judging by how Trini was nodding along with the story, he must have had the qualifications to back it up. "He's soft selling it," she said, clarifying. "Walsh is working on a mobile application to help people understand what to expect from drug interactions. There are plenty of tools that help pharmacists understand when prescription drugs interact. His app will do that, but also take into account the thousands of over-the-counter treatments people take but normally never consider."

Walsh waved a hand. "I'm working on the data model," he clarified. "Trini's doing the coding for the app."

I grinned and looked around the table. "That's what I get for deciding to drink at a college bar. Everyone here is smarter and more ambitious than I am." I glanced at Renee. "What about you? A major in rocket science with a minor in neuroscience?"

She sipped her second drink, brushed her bangs from her eyes, and looked at me with amusement. "I'm the underachiever. I'm majoring in social science." Trini laughed.

"She's being modest. It's a double major. The other part is psychology." Her amusement was cut short when it seemed like Renee kicked Trini under the table. It must have been a hard shot because the look on Trini's face suggested it hurt. This was interesting because it meant Renee's ability to notice my discomfort in the setting was a trick of the trade. At least, I hoped it was.

"What the fu–" Trini wheezed.

"Know when to stop," Renee whispered across the table through clamped teeth.

I shot a look to Walsh, saying, *does this happen often?*

"Seriously?" Trini countered, this time not in a whisper.

"I just wanted him to know you're smart and single." Renee leaned forward across the table, seeming to want to look at her friend more closely in the eyes. At this point, I was pretty sure both girls had forgotten that Walsh and I were even there. "Not going to matter." She stretched out the last word as if it had twice as many letters. "He's been eye fucking Grazer since the second we sat down. I could take my top off and sit on his lap, and I don't think it will matter."

Walsh clapped his hands once, waved them in the air, and then pushed the near-empty drinks in front of the girls as a distraction. "I'm going to interrupt now before this gets uncomfortable," he laughed. Then he looked me in the eye.

I was sitting back in my seat with my mouth agape. I had never seen anything like the display that had just occurred. In unison, as if participating in a synchronized event, they each took a long pull from the straws in their drinks to drain them. The sound of their sucking air from the bottom of the glasses echoed together. Then they looked up at each other before turning to me, their faces turning shades of pink.

Renee's hand covered her mouth as she struggled to breathe through a sudden fit of laughter. "I just said all that out loud, didn't I?" I didn't know if she was talking to me, Trini, or herself. Tears streamed from the corners of her eyes as she laughed uncontrollably.

Then I looked at Trini. She was laughing and nodding vigorously, her eyes welling up.

Walsh waved to the waitress, swung a finger in the air signaling for another round, and then looked at me. He just shrugged, and it seemed to mean that this happened occasionally. He wasn't shocked by the display.

Once the next set of drinks was served, my eyes cleared, and I regained some semblance of composure. It was fair to say I had questions. I decided to stick with what I needed to know since some of the questions bouncing through my mind were not going to lead in productive directions.

"You ladies left a lot of material to unpack with that ping pong match," I admitted. I looked at Renee and smiled broadly. "Thank you for the vivid mental image, by the way. Truly one of my special moments of the evening."

Her hand returned to her face, but it was clearly to hide a shy smile this time. "These drinks might be a little on the strong side," she admitted. "My verbal filter is clearly not fully engaged tonight."

"Nor should it be," I said with a shrug. "I say, save that for your professional career. Something tells me you'll be a good therapist, analyst, or some kind of -ist. But you said I was eye fuc—ahh, I'd been watching someone ever since you sat down. I thought you said, Grazer? What did that mean?"

"Oh, yeah," Walsh said. "No offense, man, but that's not happening. She catches the eye of every guy who comes through here. Better men than you have tried and all have gone down in flames; some even leave on a stretcher."

I clearly didn't understand. All I could do was stare.

"Piper?" Trini asked for clarification. "They are saying you were watching the blonde bartender. Her name is Piper. The less tactful among us sometimes call her Grazer," she said.

I nodded in understanding, then squinted and shook my head. "Why Grazer?"

Walsh chuckled and tipped his head back as if collecting his thoughts. "It must have been a year ago now, wouldn't you say?" He glanced at Trini, who nodded. "The bar does good business on just about any night of the week, as you can see. Near the end of the night, on any night except Friday or Saturday, there are only two bartenders here to close up. There's enough cash on hand for that to be a little too tempting for some of the local lowlifes, so they always make sure a bouncer stays to lock up and walk everyone to their cars.

One night, there was a pretty big throwdown, and the place got busted up. The cops were here and everything. They took old Bobbie down to the station to give a statement. Bobbie is the bouncer, you see. The entire process took much longer than expected, and Bobbie didn't make it back before closing time. Just as the bartenders were locking up, a guy in a Halloween mask, of all things, pushed through the door, waving a gun. He forced Jimmy over to the register and made him start emptying one cash drawer and then the next."

Walsh tipped his head toward the bar while telling the story, suggesting that the Jimmy in the story was the young man working tonight. This told me things worked out alright in the end. Still, amusement was evident in Walsh's grin, as if he were winding up for the punchline of a joke rather than sharing a sad tale from the nation's heartland.

"They say the guy with the gun was yelling a lot," Walsh continued. "I'll give him some credit. He thought to lock the door when he entered. And from what I've heard, he did a good job of haranguing Jimmy. But he made a big mistake. He never confirmed he had the place to himself. Turns out Piper was in the kitchen when all the hollering started. So what does she do? She goes to the manager's office, dials 911, grabs the pump-action Mossberg from the manager's closet, and goes to *tend bar*."

I grinned. I couldn't help it. I could picture every moment as clearly as if I'd seen it on tape. Piper was good with a shotgun. I had taught her to shoot. She was a natural. "You're kidding me," I said...because I had to say something.

Renee shook her head. "Nope. That's completely true. My uncle is a Deputy for the county. I saw the security footage." Her hand went to her mouth again, and she looked suddenly embarrassed. She slowly pushed her empty drink away, a guilty gesture. "Um, I wasn't supposed to say that either."

Walsh laughed. "Tell the rest. You saw it. I don't want our new friend to think I'm messing with him."

Taking a long, slow breath, Renee composed herself. "To be fair, Piper told the guy to drop the gun. Then she gave him almost a full second to comply before she blasted him in the knee." She dusted her hands off theatrically before dropping them back in her lap and blowing air through her lips dramatically. "That was all she wrote."

"The cops arrived within minutes," Walsh concluded. By then, Piper and Jimmy were sitting on stools, watching the poor bastard howl and cry."

I laughed, and everyone at the table joined in. "But wait," I said at last. "That still doesn't explain why you called her Grazer."

"Oh," Renee said with a sheepish grin. "Someone leaked the police report a couple of days after the incident. Uncle Kyle is pretty sure it was the bar's owner in an attempt to make the place feel safer again. Anyway, the arresting officer asked Piper why she did what she did. She said the sawed-off they keep under the counter up front is always loaded with rock salt, so it's less likely to kill someone if they have to use it. But since she pulled the Mossberg from the closet, she couldn't be sure what it was loaded with. Better to graze him; that way, he wouldn't lose the leg."

The story made everyone laugh.

"I don't know if you've ever shot," Walsh explained. "But shooting with that kind of accuracy, let alone under those conditions? Let me tell you, it takes one cool customer. No one messes with that girl."

"Oh, there was that guy a few months back," Trini added.

"Oh, yeah!" Renee exclaimed, her eyes wider than saucers. "It was just you and me that night. I forgot!"

"What did I miss?" Walsh protested.

"Some guy had too much to drink and got handsy with Piper."

"And?" Walsh insisted.

Renee held up four fingers.

Walsh and I looked on questioningly.

"Four teeth," Trini explained. "It cost him four teeth. She only hit him once. I've never seen anything like it."

Walsh laughed and glared at me. "See? I'm no fortuneteller, but I can confidently tell you Grazer's not in your cards." He tipped his head toward Renee but kept his eyes on me. "Let this one take her top off for you and call it a night. You won't be disapp–"

Another kick went flying under the table, and everyone burst into laughter.

It was nearly 2am when the festivities were winding down. The joint wasn't as crowded as before. Two out of every three tables were empty, and there hadn't been a line at the bar for almost an hour. Only Piper, Jimmy, and another girl were still working. The other bartender was helping the waitresses close out tabs and clear tables in preparation for closing down.

By this point, there wasn't enough cover to keep me from being plainly visible if Piper spent more than a second or two looking in my general direction. But that was the odd part. She had yet to even look my way. I mean, *the entire night*. I would have written off the persistent delivery of Modelo as the work of a diligent waitress if it weren't for the fact that every bottle was served with the cap still on. That wasn't standard practice– not in any bar I had ever visited.

Walsh had his arm around Trini. He pulled her close and kissed the top of her head. He took a slow, tired, deep breath and then looked at me. "Well, it's gettin' late, hoss. Think it's time we hit the road."

I shook his hand. "I'm glad you guys decided to sit down. It was a lot of fun."

Trini shook with me. "Are you heading out or sticking around until they lock up?"

She was asking if I would wait around and try my luck with Piper. All night, I had admitted nothing about it, so I wasn't going to start now. I just held my half-empty bottle up to the fading light. The overhead lights had been dimmed to urge folks to pack up. "I'll leave as soon as this is gone," I said.

I watched how clumsy Walsh was as he pulled himself to his feet after sliding from the booth. He'd been putting away those Cokes with practiced efficiency, but until now, they'd shown little impact.

"You guys aren't driving, are you?" I asked somewhat nervously.

Renee leaned closer to me and spoke in a hushed tone. "Trini has an apartment a couple of blocks over. Tommy will be staying with her. It's one of the best parts about drinking here. Safe walking distance," she said with a wink. Then she slid a torn-off scrap of paper over so it was wedged under the corner of my bottle. It had a phone number neatly penned. Then she whispered more quietly, "In case you want to practice some multi-syllable words."

I felt her hand a little high on my thigh. Honestly, I hadn't noticed it until she gave me a squeeze. Then she left the booth and headed for the parking lot.

Trini and Walsh watched Renee leave. I think Walsh was confused by Renee's quick exit. For her part, Trini watched Renee go, then looked back at me. Her gaze shifted between Renee and me. I saw her focus center on the slip of paper still under my bottle. "Did she just–" Her gaze fell to the floor, and she shook her head. "I really should have seen that coming," she muttered.

Our waitress returned, even though I was the only one still sitting. "Can I get you anything else?" she asked.

"We're good," Walsh said. "Had a great time, though. We'll be back to see you later in the week."

"Looking forward to it," the waitress said with a surprisingly sincere smile, given the late hour.

The waitress leaned over the table and placed a full shot glass near me. "Hope you're not leaving yet, honey. Piper wants you to have a drink with her before we lock up."

My stomach dropped in a way that had nothing to do with what I'd been drinking all night. I looked at the shot glass for a long second, then at the waitress. I gave her a slow nod. "Sounds good. Thanks." There was a reluctance in my tone that must have expressed my apprehension.

It was a lack of enthusiasm that was entirely lost on Walsh. He stared at me with wide eyes; his brows arched so high they appeared as one long hairline across his forehead. The expression pushed his hat comically far back on his head. "How in the hell did you manage that?" He stage-whispered to me. "You never even left the table."

Trini rolled her eyes. "Come on," she said and slapped him on the chest. "Something tells me I gotta start prepping Ren for a letdown."

"No, seriously," Walsh pressed. He was reluctant to let his girlfriend guide him away. "Was it some kind of telepathy thing? What did you do?"

Trini pulled hard on his arm and finally got him moving. "Dammit, Tommy, you're drunk. He's not a Jedi or nothing."

I laughed. "I'll see you guys around. Have a good night."

"That was epic," Walsh was mumbling. Then to me, he called over his shoulder, "Night, hoss. *We gotta do this again.*"

———

I left my beer, grabbed the shot glass, and walked to the bar. Four strangers were still taking their time milking the dregs of last call and running down the clock. It was 1:56am, so 2am was clearly closing time. The far left of the counter was completely unoccupied, so that's where I grabbed a stool. I put my shot down on the pristine counter and watched Jimmy clear empty mugs from the last remaining stragglers. He exchanged pleasantries with them in hushed tones but was anxious to coax them out the door.

Then Piper stepped through the double saloon-like swinging doors in the back wall, presumably leading to the kitchen. She said something to Jimmy and waved to the other bartender, whom I hadn't even noticed at the far end of the counter; then, she started washing her hands in a sink. While rinsing her hands, she glanced in my direction for the first time. Her expression didn't change. It was unreadable. She just looked at me for long seconds while wiping her hands.

I was about to face the music. Coming here was a mistake. The plan had been to spring my return on her at the school's lab tomorrow. Even that would be a gamble. The wager was that if I caught her off guard and didn't give her time to contemplate my arrival, she might delay ruining my chances until I could establish myself in her project.

By arriving at the bar the night before my admittedly underdeveloped plan, I put myself in a situation where I had to get the next part exactly right the first time. If I didn't, things would escalate out of control. The problem was that at that moment, I was the one who felt ambushed and unprepared.

Piper strolled toward me. It was my first chance to get a good look at her since I stepped foot in the place. She wore the bar's standard uniform of tight black jeans and matching top. It made her pale, Nordic skin look like porcelain. Her hair was longer than before, falling halfway down her back. The blue of her eyes fairly glowed in the bar's dim light.

She was undeniably gorgeous. At least as stunning as she'd been back in our time. Frustratingly, her expression remained unreadable.

I suddenly had absolutely nothing to say.

She grabbed an empty shot glass from a shelf under the bar as she approached. Without so much as breaking eye contact with me and losing a step, she snagged a bottle from the rack on the wall to her right. She stopped opposite me, placed the glass on the counter between us, and poured the tequila...again without breaking my gaze. She completed the pour without spilling a drop.

"You look good," I finally said.

Yeah. It was lame.

She raised the glass and waited for me to click it with mine. She continued to stare.

I tapped her shot, and we drank.

The glasses both went down on the counter with a single tap reverberating through the now-still establishment. Both of her hands lay open, palms on the battered old wood surface. There was a slight quiver in one hand. It was the only break in her demeanor. Still, long seconds passed.

"Why are you here, Grady?"

She *never* called me Grady. No one did. I had never heard her use my given name.

"Do you want me to go?"

Her expression softened, finally. She shook her head.

Jimmy said something from the front door. I think he had to speak twice before getting Piper's attention, which felt like a point in my favor. She didn't seem any more prepared for whatever came next. Jimmy was asking if he and the other bartender should stick around. Her name was Amanda! I knew I would remember it eventually. Sorry, that was driving me nuts. I hated referring to her as the *other girl bartender*.

I know, I know—not cool.

Anyway, Piper told Jimmy and Amanda it was all right to go. They locked up and left us alone in the Borderline. It was a little weird, but going someplace else would have been even weirder at that point, so I just went with it.

"You're still on the run," Piper said, somehow cutting to the heart of where we had left off with precision, if not tact.

I nodded. "Big time."

That made her smile. "You're not supposed to be proud of it," she laughed. It was a reluctant chuckle, but it was progress. A small amount of the weight on my shoulders shifted if not exactly lifting.

"Once you know the full story, you might change your mind."

She poured another round of shots and looked at me accusingly through narrowed eyes. "Six U.S. Marshals broke down my door with a warrant for your arrest. That was the last time I saw you, and it was a year and a half ago."

I held up a raised finger with one hand and tipped back the shot with the other. A lot was going through my mind in those few seconds, not all of it helpful or productive. I thought, *hey, that's fantastic—she knows exactly how long it's been. You're still on her radar because she still cares.*

Then I started thinking, no… she knows how long it's been because she's been holding onto the number those Marshals gave her, and she's been waiting to drop a dime the second you resurfaced. Like a dumbass, I have been sitting around all night drinking and wasting time. I started to envision a parking lot filled with Breslin's private security goons waiting to taser me the moment I walked out the door.

Not all of this made sense because it wasn't as if Piper was unaware of my nighttime excursions to Wild-Side. She had been with me in the early days, back when I realized the dreams were trips to another plane of reality. So, when the rational part of my mind reasserted itself, there was no legitimate chance that Piper would have reported seeing me, not to the authorities nor to anyone else.

That didn't mean she would be happy to see me or welcome my return. It certainly didn't mean there was even a place for me in her life anymore. Looking back, I realize that was my single greatest fear and what kept me at the periphery of the barroom for far longer than was logical.

"They weren't real Marshalls," I said after I swallowed the tequila.

Piper downed her shot and slammed the glass on the counter hard enough to rattle mine. She leaned toward me and glared. "You think?"

That left me speechless for long seconds. "You knew?"

She took a deep breath and rubbed her face wearily. For the first time all night, she looked tired. I was exhausted, having been up for over thirty-six hours, most of which I spent driving cross-country from Kansas to get here. When I said my mind hadn't really been on the Kansas operation, I wasn't exaggerating. I'd been focused, for lack of a better word, on this exact meeting ever since I saw the news report with Piper in the background.

Piper grabbed the bottle and her glass, then rounded the bar. She pulled out the chair at a two-seat table and settled solidly. I took her cue, grabbed my glass, and found the chair across from her.

On our last night together, six men claiming to be U.S. Marshals burst into Piper's apartment and attempted to arrest me. Long story short, I got the better of them just long enough to escape off a third-story balcony by jumping desperately into an entirely too-small evergreen tree.

"I began investigating the alleged warrant immediately," she explained. "It looked real, but it was merely paper. There was no additional documentation to support it. The warrant itself was real; it had just been issued regarding a completely unrelated case for a different suspect. When I started searching for the names of the agents from that night, I found nothing. They didn't exist."

A sad look crossed her face. "After two months, I realized you weren't coming back."

I leaned forward and spoke in a hushed tone. I wanted to take her hand but knew it wouldn't be well received. The last thing I wanted was to risk making things worse, so I kept it short and to the point. "I did come back. I watched you for over four months but couldn't get near you. They had you under twenty-four-hour surveillance. I couldn't call or even leave you a note."

There was more to the story; however, it was too chilling to detail right now. Breslin's people had tapped her phones, internet connections, email, and chat accounts. They had bugged her car, workplace, apartment, and the homes of everyone she knew. I had stayed in town watching her watchers for four months before pulling back. These were the days before I had access to Esker, so I didn't have the technology I use today.

In response, I pulled back and went on the offensive. That was when I started attacking Breslin's experiments. I targeted every operation he had. Any effort he made to bridge the barrier between Our-World and Wild-Side, I made it my mission in life to destroy it.

Piper looked at me across the table for a long time. "I don't know what you're waiting for," she said. "I'm happy to see you, but a lot has changed. If you're here just to tell me what happened, I appreciate it, but I've done what I can to put that behind me. I have tons of questions, but I'm pretty sure the main reason you left is that you won't be able to answer most of them."

I nodded slowly. "I'm not asking you for anything. I bought myself some breathing room, in a way. I don't know how long it will last, but I wanted to make the most of it. I'll be in town for a while."

"You're working on something," she asked, trepidation obvious in her tone.

I nodded. "That's only part of it, but yeah."

She swallowed hard. "Then you're still going…over *there*?"

I nodded again. "More and more, it seems. I still don't understand why."

"Jesus, Gray," she whispered. I could see the pain in her eyes. "I'm sorry. I always wondered. I guess… well, I just hoped it had stopped on its own."

I looked at my watch. I was hitting the wall in a big way, exhaustion pulling hard at my eyes. Things had gone better than I had hoped. I wanted to make a tactical retreat before something could derail what was, by all accounts, a reunion that held promise.

"I gotta hit it," I said, pushing out of my chair. "I spent a lot of time on the road today and need sleep. And if I end up…you know, over there tonight…I don't know if I can deal with it."

"Wild-Side?" She said.

I nodded.

"You have a place to stay?"

I nodded again.

At the door, as she locked up, I kissed her on the cheek. "It was good to see you. I have sincerely missed you." Then, I ducked into the darkness of the parking lot before I could make the moment more awkward.

———————

Staying inside, Piper pulled the door shut behind Gray and watched him jog through the parking lot. He crossed the cone of light cast from the closest overhead lamplight and disappeared between two parked cars and a large Winnebago. Only then did she take a slow, shuddering breath. The lock in the glass door frame thudded home, and she sagged forward against the pane. Her unblinking eyes refocused on her reflection as her breath fogged the cold surface. Looking further, she watched the lot, not sure what she expected to see. It wasn't like he was coming back.

Gray was back in town, and she didn't know what to do. He'd disappeared from her life, both figuratively and literally. When the supposed Marshals chased him from her apartment in the middle of the night, she assumed it was only a matter of time before he would make contact. She had been aware of the surveillance teams watching her from a distance for weeks. At first, she was terrified he would walk into a trap. But as time passed and he failed to reach out, even electronically, she began to fear for his safety.

Then, the surveillance teams pulled back entirely. That's when she really got worried. She hoped it was only a matter of time and Gray was more patient than the watchers. But when six months passed and nothing changed, she feared the worst. By that time, she knew the Marshals were imposters. Additionally, she understood the dangers of Wild-Side were worse than anything the people of this world could offer. If Gray failed to get in touch, there was a reason. Someone likely got to him, or even worse, something from over there.

But apparently, none of that had happened. Well, that wasn't true, she reminded herself. While he'd failed to explain what had occurred during their time apart, there was no doubt that times had been tough. Though he looked alright physically, the miles had taken a toll. There was something…haunted…in his eyes.

Piper sat back in the wooden chair at the bar. She didn't recall finding the seat. Pouring herself another shot, she continued to eye the front doors with a thousand-yard stare. She had at least a hundred questions for him, yet given the chance to ask them, she'd drawn a blank. Walking out of the kitchen at the night's start, she'd nearly fallen on her face. Somehow, he'd been the first thing she'd seen, even in the crowded room.

Why was he here? Why now? Why was he not reaching out?

On the off chance someone was watching, she played it cool and stuck to her job. If he wasn't going to initiate contact, neither would she.

It had been the longest shift of her life. Now, with it over, and she had no answers.

Gray is alive.

She slammed the empty shot down on the table. *He'd better have some damn good answers, or I'm going to kill him.*

Chapter 5 - This Admittedly Subjective Assessment

Wild-Side

I opened my eyes when I heard wildlife skittering through the underbrush. The sound brought an instant sense of awareness, which was odd because usually the Transition was accompanied by really strange sensory effects. Most often, this felt like a kind of Doppler force that differed between my left ear and my right, along with an unexplainable shift in gravity, no matter how many times I tried to describe it. It's like going weightless one second and then having my mass triple a half second later. Then the process repeats, but while you're spinning and trying to sort out that Doppler ear thing simultaneously. The process seems to last ten to twenty seconds, but according to my implants, the Transition between Branes takes less than a single second.

As I mentioned, it's difficult to explain. It doesn't make much sense, and I don't think it matters in the end. Maybe it would if I were trying to understand and replicate the Transition process, but since my ultimate goal is to stop it altogether and ensure no one can cross the barrier between worlds in the future, I really don't care to analyze the experience. It's sufficient to say that it's unpleasant, and I believe that makes sense because it's entirely unnatural for a human to shift between planes of reality.

I sat up with a start and felt the squish of damp leaves and vegetation underneath my bare ass. Vaulting to my feet and spinning quickly in a circle, I performed a threat assessment, searching for anything that could be used as a weapon. I was standing in a small clearing in dense woodland, and it was dark—middle of the night kind of dark. The sounds of the woods had gone silent, but I sensed this was more in response to my sudden movement. I saw no immediate danger, at least not in the woodland surrounding my small clearing. Ten feet away, the forest became a black curtain. I blinked to activate the light-enhancing optics in my contacts, but nothing happened.

I glanced at the holographic display on my wrist. It should engage when I look at it or when I raise my arm to my eyes. In both cases, the display remained dark. This makes some sense since the display doesn't truly project across my wrist; it is just superimposed there in three-dimensional space. Whatever impacted my vision enhancements also disabled my heads-up display.

Staggering a step, I scanned the tree line more carefully. I heard and felt my bare feet squish through the leaf litter and the mud beneath. I understood two things instantly. First, I was standing in one of the many dead zones that pockmarked the wilds of Wild-Side. Technology didn't work out here. Second, I'd arrived with the typical telltale sensory scramble that came with the Crossing due to my fatigue. I'd crashed hard after leaving The Borderline and been in such a deep sleep that it affected my Transition. It was an observation Doctor Cormac would be interested in since he'd long theorized that a particular sleep state was the key to my transitioning to his Brane. I didn't know if this would support his theory or set the idea back, but I knew he would want to know.

I wiped muddy hands on my thighs and sighed. Completely naked. Every crossing had this in common. It didn't matter what I wore when I fell asleep–every time I woke up on Wild-Side, I was entirely without clothing. There were multiple theories about why this was the case, but until one of them could be proven, it didn't matter to me.

I mention this because it wasn't just inconvenient. Whenever I woke up on Wild-Side following the Transition, I found myself in a different location… I mean, geographically speaking. For example, I was standing in the wilderness with absolutely no idea where I was. Luckily for me, the vast majority of Wild-Side is temperate. Specific weather systems vary depending on which part of the continent I land on, but generally speaking, I see daytime highs in the low nineties and nighttime lows down to fifty degrees. We're talking Fahrenheit for all those not raised in the good old US of A.

On this trip, my luck held on multiple fronts. The temperature was in the low sixties, if I had to guess. More importantly, the sounds of wildlife around me suggested no Elend in the area. This was the actual risk associated with each crossing, as noted previously: the nasty creatures with teeth and claws roaming the wilderness of Wild-Side all day, every day. No one in their right mind ventures outside the city walls.

Except for me, every time I Cross, I end up somewhere different. There's no predicting where, just like there's no correlation between the passage of time here and the time in my world. For example, for me, it had been six days since I was on Wild-Side. The only thing I know for sure is that six days haven't passed here. It might be more, and there's a minuscule chance that it's less, but there's no way that it's only been six days.

Why? Good question. I can't say. Even Doc Cormac can't be sure, and if he's stumped, there's no chance I'll come up with the answer. I hate being that guy, but it's how it works—something you just have to roll with. You won't survive the big stuff if you sweat the little. And by the big stuff, I mean the seven-foot-tall monsters that tear people limb from limb and could attack from any direction at any time.

———————

I headed for higher ground. Along the way, I found what could charitably be called a club. It was a recently fallen tree limb that was a little longer than a baseball bat, about as heavy, and reasonably sturdy. In addition to having heft, it had a somewhat jagged tip where it had broken off from the tree. This made a pointy weapon, which is better than nothing in the absence of a real one.

I crested a ridge that was clear of trees for nearly fifty yards. This gave me a view of the moon, which was half full. This would have been of greater value if I had any idea how much time had passed since my last visit to Wild-Side, but as I mentioned, this was always a struggle. The good news was that the more I walked, the more opportunity the nano core infrastructure in my head had to calibrate. To be clear, technology didn't work in the dead zones, but at least the core components of my nano do-dads functioned at a firmware level. I'd been stranded in the zone before, and it was explained to me like this: you know how your cell phone can't make calls when you don't have a signal, but if you have the right hardware and software, you can still use it as a GPS? It was something like that. If I walked around enough, the base hardware-level functionality had a chance to calibrate. With that, I could establish what I referred to as basic services.

There are, of course, more technical details behind all this. Doc Cormac could explain it all in highly scientific and gloriously boring detail, but in my experience, it's only valuable for curing insomnia. The real moral of the story is that the technology of this world puts everything from our world to shame. It's not even close. If the technology of this world were described as a state-of-the-art jet fighter, the tech of our world, by comparison, would be a home-built go-kart running a lawnmower engine and driving on three flat tires.

From my vantage point, the sky seemed darker to the right. Based on this admittedly subjective assessment, I judged the left to be East and headed that way. The value of this decision would depend on what part of the continent I'd landed on, so I'd gone with the only criteria that mattered. Light brought a degree of safety, at least so far as I could see danger coming at a greater distance. With that in mind, the sooner I reached daylight, the sooner I might have a degree of safety. There was absolutely no doubt that the woods were crawling with Elend, so seeing them before they saw me was vital.

So why, you might be asking, would I not just hunker down and wait for daylight to come to me? Why risk encountering one of these creatures if I'd already been lucky? The Elend have keen senses. Those of a predator. Not the least of which is their sense of smell. And a man alone in the woods without anything to mask his scent? That's like ringing a dinner bell. I couldn't dig a hole deep enough to keep my naked ass safe until sunrise. And climbing a tree was out. That would only spread my odor more quickly. Plus, have you ever tried to climb a tree naked? I'll tell you this: it's the kind of mistake a guy makes only once.

Maybe just as importantly, I needed to give my tech a chance to calibrate. If I could determine my location, I would be able to identify the nearest outpost. From there, I could contact Cormac and find the closest transport platform. I'd been through this before. Every Crossing started in the same way. Admittedly, some just put me further out in the sticks than others.

I must have covered close to two miles by the time the sun crested the horizon. I couldn't see it directly, but the hint of light started filtering through the leafy canopy. The ground was thick with vegetation. Imagine the Pacific Northwest if the clock could be rewound to a time a couple of thousand years before humans first invaded the continent. That's what Wild-Side was like. The Brane was an exercise in contrasts in many ways. The surface of the world was made up of three primary land masses. As I understood it, there wasn't much of a difference in climate from one part of the planet to the next. So, there are no arctic or tropical zones, for example.

Beyond that, the population hadn't blossomed as it had in our world. The population was three million and had never changed before the Elend outbreak. "Outbreak" is my attempt at a politically correct description of the demon-like scourge. In truth, there was nothing virulent about them, at least not scientifically speaking. After the Elend began to gain a foothold, there was no way to keep track of the population.

The inhabitants gathered in a collection of cities. Walls were erected at their perimeter, the only defense against Elend attacks. Everyone who had made a home in the Reaches, the agrarian settlements outside the secure cities, either retreated to the safety of the walls or was unaccounted for and believed lost. The people of Wild-Side had never faced a hostile force before, not once in their history. As a result, they were utterly unprepared for conflict. They didn't know how to fight and were entirely unfamiliar with war. They had no concept of armies and didn't have police forces, nor did they even know how to fight one another.

Although the people of Wild-Side were technologically advanced, they had never known anything other than a peaceful existence—peace with each other and the world around them.

All of that changed with the arrival of the Elend.

A blip in the corner of my right eye was the first sign that my situation was beginning to improve. It was a red dot that began to pulse slowly. I knew from experience that it meant my HUD was starting to come back online, at least in some small way. The red dot would soon turn green if what I'd seen before held true. Then, after a few seconds, I would see a green progress bar as the nanotech booted into a baseline configuration that helped me find the nearest communication station with simple GPS-like navigation cues.

That didn't happen. Instead, the full functionality of my HUD blinked to life. The woods around me pulsed into vivid relief as if my eyes had suddenly adjusted to the darkness and the world had become clear. A two-dimensional map projected in three-dimensional space before me. It refreshed, resolving into a 3D shape showing woodland terrain with ridges, rivers, and a red dot indicating my position relative to everything displayed. To the west, an irregular portion of the map showed the green of the forest canopy blotted in a pale, sickly gray. I was standing just outside that gray area. I instantly understood that the pale area indicated a dead zone, and my tech had come back online thanks to my moving just beyond the perimeter of it.

"Gray, are you there?" a voice sounded in my ear. "It's Wes. Do you read me?"

"Hey, Wes," I said with a chuckle. "Good to hear from you. I'm hoping you have good news for me."

"We're checking the database now. I should have what you need in a couple of seconds. Looking at your position, I'm guessing you landed in a dead zone again?"

"You bet. No party crashers so far. I'm calling it a win."

As you can tell by the conversation, it wasn't uncommon for me to cross over into an inconvenient location. If we ever figured out a way to control my entry point, it would be a significant win in terms of convenience and safety.

"Good news, buddy," there was genuine relief in Wes's tone. "Looks like we have a farm 1.6 miles north-northeast of your position. We're getting a signal from its pad, so we expect it to be operational."

A blue dot appeared on my HUD, so I set out jogging. The sun was rising quickly, and I felt I was already pushing my luck by not encountering any Elend while wandering through the woods. The hair on the back of my neck was starting to prickle, and I wouldn't second-guess whatever signals were sounding from deep within my lizard mind. I was no longer alone on the com channel or in the woods.

"You're moving fast," Wes noted. "Everything alright?"

I didn't answer right away. I focused on the sound of my rapid footfalls and those of the surrounding forest. The woods had fallen silent. "I don't think so," I grumbled. My jog had transitioned to a full sprint. The nanotech in my blood worked to hyper-oxygenate it, and the same tech had already increased my muscle density, so I was moving fast. I tore through bushes and brush without slowing, feeling the lashing of every stick, branch, and vine I passed as it thrashed against my bare flesh.

"Do me a favor, Wes?" I said while keeping my tone as conversational as possible. "Send me some captures of the facility and have the pad warmed up and ready to flash? I'm pretty sure I'll be coming in with at least one unfriendly on my tail."

I heard the sound of something being knocked over on the other side of the connection, followed by the sound of harried voices. I couldn't make out what was being said over the noise of my own breathing. All I know is they weren't talking to me. A second later, a series of thumbnail images appeared in the corner of my eye. They depicted an abandoned and overgrown farm: a large, oddly shaped barn; what looked like a technologically advanced greenhouse; and a building that was a cross between a house and barracks, two stories tall. The place clearly hadn't been used for some time. Everything was overgrown by sawgrass or thorn bushes. It wasn't in disrepair exactly; it just looked long abandoned.

I looked closer at the greenhouse-type structure. It was two stories high and had large, double sliding doors on one end. It looked like a giant glass barn, though I knew from experience that it wasn't made of glass. "The pad is in the greenhouse?" I asked.

"Affirmative," a new voice sounded in my ear. "We're sending power to the pad now and bringing it online. It will be warmed up and calibrated by the time you get there."

I recognized the voice. "Doc? That you?"

"You bet! I heard you might have trouble, so I thought I would lend a hand. We're trying to track your pursuers, but we can't get a fix. The overgrowth is thick out there, and you are close to the dead zone. We don't have many resources."

I hurdled a log and landed in knee-deep water. It didn't slow me down much, though I skidded on my heels for an exciting couple of feet. I jumped, made it clear of the water, and kept going. When I heard a splash behind me less than two seconds later, I knew I wasn't just running scared. Whatever hit the water was immense. I glanced to the right and caught only a flash of movement from the corner of my eye.

Shit.

"Two that I know of," I confirmed to the Doc.

"Hell," I heard the Doc whisper. I don't know if he was talking to himself or someone sitting with him. "Gray, this is going to be close. I now have a visual. If you have anything left in reserve, now's the time to use it. They're closing in on you."

I broke from the tree line and saw the farm buildings come fully into view. I poured on additional speed as my feet found tracks worn into the dirt by years of moving farm equipment. I turned sharply to the left as I rounded the edge of the barn. Something hissed and crashed as it missed the turn and tumbled.

"That was one," the Doc confirmed. "You're in the home stretch. The buffer is warmed up and ready. You just need to reach the pad."

The right side of the two sliding doors on the greenhouse opened wide enough to allow a man to pass. That was clever. A full-grown Elend was larger than a man, but it was powerful. It could force its way through, but the effort would cost it a step.

Overhead lights stabbed to life inside the greenhouse as I drew within twenty yards of the door. I could see the broad outline of the platform thirty feet beyond the entrance to the building. Somehow, I managed to eke out just a little more speed. My stride became a little longer, and my breathing just a little deeper. The instant my shoulders passed beyond the entrance of the building, I dove. I jumped as high and far as I could. My target wasn't specific—I aimed for anywhere on the massive platform.

A stuttering flash engulfed me as I rolled across the glassy surface of the floor. I came to rest on my back and didn't move. A tingle coursed through my body, starting at my toes and rippling to the top of my head. My ears felt like they needed to pop. Lying supine, it was a little like a bad fall I'd once taken while playing basketball. I'd gone up for a jump ball, only to have my legs swept out from under me and land flat on my back. That fall knocked me unconscious. In this case, I'd remained lucid but felt like my brain was slowly rebooting.

The first thought that broke through the gauze wrapping my mind was that the floor was warm under my ass and hands. Then I wondered why I was naked from the waist down. I slapped my palm on the floor and contemplated the glass. Memories returned quickly; this wasn't my first rodeo, after all, and I'd used the teleportation platforms in this way more times than I could count.

I sat up and looked at the half-dozen people staring at me beyond the perimeter of the platform's floor. I wondered at their aghast expressions. That's when the bruises, gashes, and abrasions began to register. Finally, I recalled the circumstances that had led to my emergency teleportation. I was hauling ass when I reached the platform. They must have seen me materialize out of thin air, still mid-dive. Watching me crash earthward must have been quite a sight, especially given my battered condition.

A man and a woman moved in unison from the platform's edge. The man offered me a hand, pulling me to my feet. The woman draped a blanket over my shoulders. I thanked the woman and looked at the man. "My compliments to whoever was running the platform. His timing was right on the money. A second later, and my butt was history," I said.

The man grinned and pointed to the console a dozen yards away. "The old man wanted that honor for himself," he said.

I chuckled at Tony referring to Doc Cormac as the Old Man. It was one of the bad habits that the people of Wild-Side had picked up from me, though I don't think they fully understood the irony with which it was intended. Cormac and Tony were the same age, and so was Lacy, the woman who brought me the blanket. As far as I could tell, the entire population of Wild-Side was of the same age, give or take ten years.

Confused? You can read that statement again, but it won't make any more sense the second time. The entire world's population, this Brane, the plane of reality—whatever you want to call it—was nearly the same age. The effects of time brought relative differences, likely due to experiences and responsibilities on Wild-Side, but all were within a single generation: thousands of people in their early to late thirties. At least, that's the age I could estimate, judging by their looks.

That's how old they would be if they came from our world. Things worked a little differently on Wild-Side. To clarify, the Seeley were not, in fact, thirty-odd years old. As near as I have determined, they were closer to two hundred and fifty years of age. And since there are no children or elderly, their population hasn't changed appreciably within that time.

Is your mind sufficiently blown yet? Mine was. It still is. I've been coming to Wild-Side for a little over twenty-two months, and I'm still wrapping my head around it. That said, strap in. I'll expose you to the really odd stuff as we go.

Doc Cormac popped up from behind the console and looked at me with tired eyes. He shook his head, then removed a pair of wire-rimmed glasses and cleaned the lenses with the hem of his long white lab coat. I'd come to realize this as a nervous response. He did it when he was tired, stressed, or distracted. Judging by the bags under his eyes, I was betting on all three.

"Close call, my boy," he said.

Cormac had thick black hair, equally black eyebrows, and pale blue eyes. Although unremarkable in appearance, he possessed an intellect that was second to none. On a plane of existence that was hundreds of years ahead of our world in science and technology and populated by individuals who were, on average, more intelligent than our best and brightest, this was significant.

Amusingly, despite all the technology available to him, much of which he developed, Cormac chose to wear anachronistic crafted glass lenses as corrective eyewear. No one on Wild-Side wore glasses for anything other than eye protection, yet Cormac could be seen fiddling with his glasses at all hours of the day and night.

I rolled my shoulder and felt something pop. "I never got a look at what was behind me," I admitted, "but I felt it breathing down my neck."

"One of them closed to within two meters," Cormac said with an arch of his brows. "Would you like to see the footage?"

I shook my head, and a shiver ran down my spine. In fact, I'd imagined it being closer than that.

Lacy returned with a pair of gray coveralls and passed them to me. I handed her the blanket and started stepping into the outfit. If you're wondering why I didn't excuse myself to go somewhere more private to change, there are two reasons. First, the Seeley, Doc Cormac, Tony, and Lacy are all names I made up. Anytime a word, most often a proper noun, didn't have an analog in the Seeley's language, I made up my own term. The translation technology compensated, and those I spoke with heard the appropriate word in their own tongue.

Wild-Side was a different world, after all. How likely would it have been for their language to match ours?

Anyway, the Seeley don't have art or music. Well, they don't know what fun is either, if I'm being honest. If they had any interest at all in the birds and the bees, they wouldn't be a race of thirty-somethings with no rugrats running around.

Where was I? Oh, yeah. Secondly, anyone who crashes into a foreign world naked each time they cross the proverbial border sort of needs to check their shyness at the door. Today's clumsy teleportation issue notwithstanding, this wasn't an unusual day. I fall asleep in Our-World and wake up in some random location on Wild-Side. After that, the first step is to make contact. The second was finding safety in one of the main population centers. More often than not, the easiest way to do that is to find one of the remote farming outposts abandoned when the Elend forced the Seeley to retreat to their city centers. Those remote farms used teleportation technology to move farmed goods to the cities. So, assuming the farms still have operational tech, I could use them to reach safety. A few problems make that sometimes more complicated than it should be, but more on that later.

Returning to my original point: every time I visit Wild-Side, I end up walking through the woods with my business flapping in the wind. Everything out there is sharp, pointed, or itchy—sometimes all three. That's the best-case scenario. Most of the wilderness is covered with woodland, and much of that is now infested with Elend, leaving me unprotected until I can contact Cormac or someone from his team.

Anyway, there's no point in being shy. Not after doing this so many times in front of these people.

I tapped a button on the cuff of my new coveralls and the suit adjusted to fit me. I mean that literally. The sleeves extended to perfectly match the length of my arms, as did the legs. The waist contracted, then released several times until it found just the right comfortable adjustment without being too tight or slack. I swung my arms, tested the fit at the shoulders, and found it was perfect there, too. The range of motion was perfect. Not to get too inside baseball, but maybe most impressive was my inseam. The crotch was roomy without being either baggy or too confining. Not an easy feat given that I was going commando at the moment.

It was like having a personal tailor available at the press of a button. At home, we would call it "Smart Clothing." Here, that's just how clothing worked. I'm being tactful when I say this place is generations ahead of us in terms of technology. We're still like monkeys playing with rocks and sticks compared to the Seeley.

A younger-looking guy bolted into the room through the farthest door, a broad smile spread across his face when he saw me. He had sandy blonde hair, a wispy straggle on his chin that was an ill-fated attempt at a beard, and dark circles under his eyes. He looked like he was in his early twenties, even though he was the same age as everyone else on Wild-Side. "Gray, you're going to love this," he said in a gasping wheeze that suggested he'd run from his workshop. "Your design is going to work. The models confirm it, but I have a ton of questions for you!"

This was Tripp. I would call him an engineer, as it seems the best title available. None of the Seeley subscribed to any single intellectual discipline. Tripp and Cormac had more widespread interests than most, which likely caused them to side with me when so many of their people preferred to keep me at arm's length. So far, he'd been able to design and fabricate almost anything I could think of. While I wasn't the most popular person on Wild-Side, many of the ideas and technologies I'd brought with me were highly sought after. Since I couldn't bring anything with me physically during the Transition, it was often up to Tripp to build the novelties of Our-World—either as I described them or based on the technical schematics I could transfer digitally using my mind like a flash drive.

Again, more on that later. For now, it's enough to say that Tripp is a genius among geniuses. If anyone could help me win over the people of Wild-Side, Tripp is likely the guy to do it. Sure, the technology of Our-World is little more than a novelty to a place with technology like Wild-Side, but when it comes to people who lack all creativity in the arts, Our-World has a great deal to offer.

"Throttle response is a problem," Tripp said simply. "I don't know how you will control the machine on the X, Y, and Z axis."

Lacy looked confused by the strange way Tripp held his hand in the air, fingers together and outstretched, his palm to the floor. Cormac's eyes went back and forth between me and Tripp, and a queasy expression crossed his face. "You're not still working on that…*thing*?"

Tripp nodded and laughed. "If Gray can sort out the control interface, this is going to work."

I nodded. "Done deal. I've done it before," I paused, struggling to qualify my claim. "It was on a smaller scale, but it's a proven approach. As long as you have the motor and prop articulation sorted out, it's all good."

Tripp was already nodding enthusiastically. "Stop by when you have some time." Without another word, he disappeared back through the door.

Judging by the bags under his eyes, I wondered if Tripp ever slept. I knew he'd been similarly invested when he started fabricating MP3 players. He had helped me introduce Wild-Side to music for the first time. The device wasn't strictly necessary since everyone here had access to technology that could play audio; it was literally embedded in their bodies. However, since this was a world without art of any kind, access to music had been a novel and shocking experience.

Tripp helped me fabricate a first-generation iPod, complete with a working jog wheel and wired headphones. Once the device was built, the music selection was brought to Wild-Side in my onboard gray matter and loaded into the first flash storage ever made on Wild-Side. I admit I skipped the original iPod's concept of a spinning disk hard drive, opting instead for more conventional flash memory. Even that was an outdated concept, according to Tripp, who found the idea endlessly amusing.

The single device circulated throughout the city and was experienced by hundreds within weeks. When I returned to Wild-Side, a little over two months had passed, and the iPod was replicated thousands of times. The technology was considered quaint, yet the concept of music captured the attention of everyone, and the experience spread to other cities as well.

I'd broken every music-related copyright law in our world in new and astounding ways. At the same time, I'd done two things perhaps more important. I'd introduced the people of Wild-Side to a form of art for the first time. I'd also broken one of the Primary Tenants of their world. More on that later because this was part of what turned so many of the Elend against me.

Chapter 6 - A Proctological Napkin

Wild-Side

20 months ago

The Bus easily traveled the rocky terrain of the Badlands. With three oversized wheels on each side of the cargo compartment at the back of the sleek, van-like utility vehicle, it could crawl with nimble agility across the vastly uneven surfaces. The pair of equally large wheels at the front were suspended at the end of long struts, giving the vehicle both a tight turning radius and extra resilience over surfaces like those it currently traversed.

Kilmer sat on the bench seat in the cargo space and watched with trepidation as the stowed stacks of hard-shelled crates heaved and strained against the tie-down straps binding them to the cabin floor. The left side of the cab tipped at nearly a forty-degree slant as the vehicle traversed another of the endless fields of man-sized boulders standing shoulder to shoulder and littering the expanse.

The figure on the opposite side of the cabin had been caught off guard, causing Kilmer to laugh. Mara struggled to secure herself in the safe embrace of the shoulder restraints. It was anyone's guess what she was thinking when she took the device off. Like him, she wore a full-body environment suit. It had a form-fitting shell made of thin, plastic-like protective armor. The material was about an inch thicker than his usual daily uniform. This offered incredible protection, considering that, with the helmet on and the internal breathing system engaged, he could survive a grade-four rock slide.

"If you remove your restraints, you better put your helmet on first. We're a long way from anything other than automated medical care," Kilmer warned with a grin.

Mara tried to look nonplussed but was more likely fighting not to lose her lunch. "Is it just me, or is the ride getting rougher?" she said after taking a hard swallow.

Kilmer suddenly understood her reluctance to use the helmet. They had excellent filtration, but for all their technology, no one had bothered to integrate gelatinous, half-chewed food processing into the hardware. He looked at the virtual display on the back of his wrist. "We're two point two kilometers out, but Drew doesn't think we'll make it to the site. Too much debris between us and the target. Looks like we'll have to stop and walk the rest of the way."

Fighting back a gasp that was likely partially solid matter, Mara pressed her hands hard on the knees of her suit. She spread her feet further for stability. "Maybe I can walk now?"

Kilmer laughed and tapped a button on his wrist display to open a private channel to their team leader. "You better slow it down a bit, boss. Either that or we'll have to rinse the cargo space."

"You're joking," an accusatory voice sounded in reply.

Kilmer watched Mara take a deep, shuddering breath. Her head tipped back, and her eyes seemed to wobble in different directions. Just then, the floor dropped from beneath them, and the vehicle fell several feet before impacting hard. Grinding his teeth, Kilmer tapped the red emergency button on his wrist display. Nano-particulate matter shot from the collar of his suit to instantly form a helmet around his head. It was sleek and dark gray to match his suit, featuring a panoramic lens that stretched from ear to ear and ran from his hairline to the bottom of his lower lip. Like the suit, the hard shell of the helmet's surface was perhaps only an inch thicker than his head, making it both lightweight and comfortable. And as was vital in this instance, it was waterproof and airtight.

Mara swallowed hard once more, closed her eyes, and started to do some kind of deep breathing exercise.

False alarm.

"Sir, one more bump like that, and you'll need to rinse me off too. That was close."

An incomprehensible grumbling came from the other end of the connection. Then, a voice said, "Stand by. We're almost to the blockage. If Mara tells me you're putting me on, there will be consequences. Are we clear?"

It was Kilmer's turn to grumble. He then tapped the lens of his helmet with the knuckle of his glove. The rattle was unmistakable. "Do you hear that, sir? When I say I'm taking every precaution, I'm not joking. Mara has changed colors 3 times in the last two minutes."

———————

Eighteen minutes later, the Bus pulled to a stop. The team leader had pushed their luck a little too far, and one of the vehicle's massive front tires was suspended over a jagged-edged boulder. This wouldn't have been the end of the ride, except it occurred simultaneously with its partner tire plunging into a cleft that caused the front suspension to bottom out and rest on a particularly bulbous stone protrusion.

Kilmer had just climbed from the roof of the cargo bay and onto the boulder beneath the Bus. He'd been fortunate enough to arrive in time to see the look on Drew's face as he completed a closer inspection of their predicament.

"Sonofabitch," Martin Drew said as he hurled a fist-sized stone into the distance. Thanks to the enhancements of his powered suit, the stone must have traveled a good fifty yards. Kilmer barely heard its impact.

He glanced at his wrist display again. They were half a kilometer from the anomaly but had paid dearly for the extra distance. If Drew had followed the plan, they would have parked the Bus farther back and hoofed it. He'd pressed his luck, and now they were stuck. None of this needed explanation, of course. Everyone on the team was undoubtedly thinking the same thing at that moment.

"Alright," Drew said, his voice weary. "Break out the gear. We're on foot from here." He strolled toward the back of the Bus, dragging the fingers of his gloved hand along the sleek metal hull. He appeared to be having a silent conversation with the transport that had betrayed him.

"Ah, Kilmer? What happened to you?" a voice came from my left. It was Teretti's deep baritone, and it stopped Kilmer in his tracks.

All eyes were on him.

"Oh, that's what I think it is?" This was from John Pope. He didn't waste a second. He extended his helmet and took a step back.

Glancing down at the streaking stain across the front of his suit, Kilmer shrugged. "I told you guys to stop, but you didn't listen. Wait until you see the cargo space. It's a complete mess."

Drew's face was turning red. "You told me *Mara was sick*. You didn't say you were going to spew, too. Take some responsibility."

Kilmer grinned. "Responsibility? Sounds fair. Here's the thing, boss." He pointed to the chunks still stuck to the front of his suit. "This here isn't mine. Mara? That girl's got some range. The trouble is, she's a big eater, too. But if you want to talk about responsibility, this is on you for not stopping."

Though he didn't think it was possible, Drew's face turned a deeper shade of red. His gaze shifted from one member of the team to the next. He looked at Pope, then Teretti, then back at Kilmer. After that, he seemed to calm down. "I'm calling bullshit," he said with a grin. "It can't be that bad."

Drew turned the corner and climbed the bumper at the back end of the Bus. Kilmer heard the thump of boots as his boss traversed the short ladder to the cargo space.

"Oh," Drew grumbled. Long seconds passed. Then he said, "For the love of–*Woman, what did you eat?*"

———————

The team made short work of the journey to the target location. Teretti led the group, navigating with a topographic map projected in three-dimensional space half a meter in front of him at all times. Kilmer could see the display from his position on the group's periphery since the projection was shared over the team's channel. As long as Teretti was responsible for navigation, Kilmer could focus on other things. He was more interested in the geography. An opportunity to explore the Wastes was rare, and he wouldn't miss the chance to capture everything there was to see. To that end, his suit's recording system recorded everything visible to the internal sensor systems. He was also chronicling everything he saw through his personal optics. This violated three different policies, but no less than a dozen close friends would be interested in what was out here, even if the investigation turned up nothing of substance.

The Wastes had been off-limits for as long as anyone could remember, and it was only during a rare operation like today that a team was dispatched to study an anomaly. Archaeology beyond the Green Zones was outlawed, except in response to a natural event such as a storm, flood, earthquake, or tsunami. All of these events were exceedingly rare; however, historically speaking, certain areas of the Badlands saw more earthquakes than any other part of the region. To Kilmer's knowledge, this was only the second quake investigated within the last hundred and twenty years.

They reached the coordinates of the supposed event but found nothing obvious indicating a recent seismic event. The rocky terrain was comprised mainly of washed-out stone with specks of unusual vegetation that had survived eons of weather and erosion. The gaps in the rock plunged as much as thirty meters, most with jagged and unforgiving clefts and protrusions that seemed to wait to test their armored suits.

The team spread out, conducting a more thorough search of the area using the sensor technology built into their gauntlets. Since the exploration of the Wastes had been outlawed since time in memoriam, Kilmer knew little technology had focused on the Wastes. As a result, when a seismic event occurred, pinpointing the epicenter accurately wasn't easy. This was contradictory since, while the law stated that archaeology outside the Green Zone was illegal, a provision allowed for limited exploration of non-Green Zone locations in the wake of a natural event. Any time a natural event was suspected in a non-Green Zone, such as the Badlands or a dead zone, it captured the attention of the local populace. Yet, with this in mind, no one was willing to dedicate resources to better monitor non-Green Zones for natural events, allowing for greater exploration.

Even as he pondered his society's strangeness, Kilmer found himself losing interest in the greater mystery. His mind naturally focused on the puzzle before him. The more significant questions of his society moved to the corners of his mind and seemed to fizzle out of focus entirely. With this fizzling came a sense of calm and renewed clarity.

"I found something," Pope's voice came over the team channel. "I'm sending my coordinates now."

"Confirmed," Drew replied. "Form up on Pope's position. It looks like a cavern opened due to the seismic event."

The team gathered in a ravine that clearly showed a fresh split in the cracked and crumbling stone. Gravel smaller than Bulveanry leaves littered the ground, making footing precarious even in the self-stabilizing powered suits. The ravine was nearly ten meters wide at the mouth and narrowed at the back, where a dark gap appeared to offer underground access to the plateau overhead. The ravine's walls extended twelve to fifteen meters from the base of the gorge, which made Kilmer reassess the geology's stability. The region had recently experienced a seismic event. There was no telling what might occur if they entered the cavern.

Certainly, risk was involved. However, given the uniqueness of the opportunity, no team member was unwilling to risk entering the underground space. Even if the cavern was two meters deep and filled with nothing but water, it was a chance that some had waited decades to witness. No one would pass up the opportunity to explore an area that was normally off-limits.

The team gathered around Drew, who made a point of being the first to enter the cavern. Next was Teretti, then Pope, and finally Kilmer. He looked over his shoulder and remembered that Mara had been left behind to clean up her mess from the Bus's cargo bay.

Always first. Drew really is a proctological napkin.

The team moved in single file, which Kilmer considered a good sign. Their continuous progress implied the cleft was deep and extended far into the plateau walls. He also heard the echo of footfalls—another good sign. It suggested that the narrow confines of the shoulder-wide passage might be widening. After all, there wasn't enough space in the passage to produce an echo.

Then Pope stopped so suddenly that Kilmer bumped into him.

"Hey," Kilmer grumbled. "A little warning! What's going on?" No one had spoken over the shared channel, so he had been surprised by the sudden stop.

Leaning to the left, Kilmer peered past Pope. They had indeed reached a cavern. The expansive space was illuminated inconsistently by the team members' shoulder and helmet lights. Kilmer had an obstructed view with Pope standing in front of him, but he could see that the area seemed to open up to the left and right. Glancing upward, he saw the ceiling sloping higher into a smooth, uneven dome-like surface about five meters above him.

Kilmer tapped Pope on the shoulder. The man seemed to regain his faculties and stepped further into the space. Kilmer went to step onward but stopped before placing his next boot on the floor. His eyes fell on what must have frozen Pope in his steps because Kilmer reacted the same way. A body lay face down on the floor about ten feet beyond the entrance. The figure's arms were outstretched, and its head was turned. Kilmer squinted at the figure and got the uneasy sense that the person had died while attempting to crawl to the exit.

He looked around the room, suddenly surprised that no one was talking. The helmets of each suit were lit, and he could see each team member mouthing words excitedly. Their hands and arms were gesticulating, but he could hear none of it. Tapping the AR control on his wrist, Kilmer reactivated the team channel. He'd disabled it when Drew gave what he believed to be an inspirational speech before entering the cavern. Kilmer figured that if he had to listen to the fool drone on, Mara wouldn't be the only one hosing out a helmet. So he'd killed the team channel until the auditory insult was over.

Except he had forgotten to reactivate coms.

Oops.

A strange and disturbing tableau occupied the center of the circular, domed cavern. Four more bodies were arranged around a small stone table at the center of the space. They sat, two on either side, seeming to face each other. Though long, long since dead, their bodies were in good condition. They wore strange clothing of material none of the team recognized. The exposed skin of their faces and hands was desiccated, dry, and parchment-like. But it was intact. It was easy to tell the figures' facial features: two men and two women. It looked like they'd sat down on the short stone benches and simply died at the table.

Except that they hadn't. Initial scans of the bodies showed injuries that were not visible in the dried skin of their slumped heads as they hung, suspended in stares that seemed to face the stone surface. All four figures had their throats slashed. The wounds had been deep; in three cases, the weapon in question had even nicked the spines of the victims.

This meant the darkness marring the tattered remains of the strange clothes worn by the figures was blood. The site scan results also confirmed the assumption.

The brutality of the scene shocked the group. In the history of their world, no one had ever taken another person's life. Even the murder of livestock had been outlawed hundreds of years ago, as a core tenet of their society. What they were witnessing was simply beyond anyone's imagination.

However, if all of this was bad, the results of their subsequent scans were even more troubling.

Scans of the bodies showed they had been dead for at least twelve hundred years. Since the Seeley race was just over two hundred and fifty years old, this simply wasn't possible.

All imaging until that point had been conducted with Gauntlets, the sensor array technology built into the powered suits. More advanced technology was available, and fifty-five minutes after entering the cave, the team lit the perimeter with high-output illumination posts. As the name implies, they are essentially two-meter-tall poles with brightly lit arrays. The *high output* in the name didn't indicate how bright they were. Despite lighting every inch of the cavern, their primary purpose was to scan the space as part of a three-dimensional site assay.

Kilmer strolled slowly around the site, capturing every aspect of the environment with his personal sensors, even though they weren't as powerful as the equipment the team was about to activate. Much of the time had been wasted arguing amongst themselves about the nature of the find, what it meant, and what the preliminary test results would indicate to historians.

Delicately put, Drew had lost his composure. His suit had already been forced to administer sedatives, which should have been enough for Teretti to take command of the operation. However, as Kilmer had long known, Teretti lacked backbone. There was no precedent for the situation and, therefore, no documented procedure to handle it. Teretti was out of his element, which meant Drew had not been relieved of his command.

Kilmer watched Drew as he walked back and forth along the edge of the cave. It was a slow, repetitive process that felt rhythmic, mechanical, and pointless. He had mentally checked out, and a vacant stare was visible even through the lens of his helmet. Of course, this was preferable to him making decisions that put the team at risk. There was definitely something wrong with the cave. It went beyond simply being the scene of a multiple murder–four dead at the table and one dead at the entrance from as of yet unknown causes. Judging by the expression on the face of the prone body, that man had died in great pain.

"Two more Busses are inbound," Mara said through the private com channel. "One to tow our rig off this boulder and one to collect the dead. You were right; there are a lot of people upset back at base. Drew isn't the only one."

Mara coordinated communication with command from her position on the Bus. She was spared from witnessing the scene because she had never entered the cave. No one who entered the cave coped with the sight constructively. None had imagined a scenario as horrible.

One of the sensors in Teretti's suit warned of a trace contagion nearby. At first, it was disregarded as an errant reading since it had been noted by only one suit. But when another set of gear sounded an alarm, Drew pulled rank. He confined the team to the cave's interior until the backup team could arrive with more detailed diagnostic equipment and offer guidance on the quarantine.

Since they were stuck and it would be hours before the second team arrived, Kilmer decided to take a closer look at the table where the four bodies had congregated in their last moments. An oblong rectangular frame lay flat across the floor, obscured by a thick layer of dust just beyond the far end of the table. The object's perimeter was just visible beneath what must have been hundreds of years of collected dust and grit. A pair of short, knee-high stanchions rose from the spiderwebs and dust. They were grooved with brackets, appearing intended to support something thin and roughly shoulder-width.

Kilmer raised his Gauntlet over the mess on the floor, which he now suspected to be an artifact. After all, this was why so many were interested in the rare opportunity to access naturally surfaced excavations in the Badlands. More than a dozen times in his people's history, examinations of naturally excavated locations had unearthed objects of unusual provenance. Little was known about the artifacts found so far other than that they were stored in a vault accessible only by the special order of Administrator Hargrave.

The scan results were displayed in Kilmer's HUD. What he saw didn't make sense, so he tapped a series of commands on his sleeve and transferred the display to a projection that appeared in augmented reality an arm's length in front of him. With a swipe of his hand, he removed the dust and debris from the photo-realistic duplication, leaving what looked like a rectangular frame. It resembled an ancient photograph, though the analysis of the material suspended inside indicated it was composed of a substance that didn't register on the periodic table. Perhaps just as impossibly, the scan concluded that the substance was 3 nanometers thick. This was so thin, if looked at from the edge, it wasn't visible to the human eye.

"What have you got there?" The voice behind Kilmer was Martin Drew.

Kilmer tapped a command on his sleeve, making the AR image visible to Drew. He reached out, grabbed the edge of the virtual frame, and handed it to Drew while circling the perimeter of debris. "This appears to be hidden under the mess," he said.

Drew looked at the rendering, twisted it in cyberspace, and examined it from different directions. "How is this possible?" he said. "Did you see how thick the interstitial material is? That's incredible."

"I double-checked the results, just to be sure. It's accurate."

"But did you notice? The material's surface is smooth and flawless, even after the abuse it must have endured with all this particulate matter?"

Kilmer created his own version of the AR rendering and began manipulating it. He entered a series of commands, and the suit's onboard software analyzed the material's surface more thoroughly. "Wow," was all he could say in conclusion.

He glanced at a pair of grooves set into the lower two corners at one end of the frame. As he looked across the rubble-strewn floor, something in the debris was highlighted in neon green on his helmet's HUD.

Fifteen minutes later, Kilmer, Drew, and Teretti cleared the frame of debris and placed it upright. It slotted perfectly into the grooves of the stanchions he'd noted beyond the end of the table, though he couldn't guess its purpose. Removing the grime from the framed artifact was trivial. The impossibly thin material had no surface tension, so it cleaned easily. It also seemed impervious to scratches and dents. Once it was standing upright, even the fine dust of the cavern couldn't stick to the surface. They spent several minutes wiping grit from the wood grain of the frame, but that effort was wasted. No markings of consequence were found anywhere— nothing visible to the naked eye or to the suit's Gauntlet scanners.

Kilmer looked at the chilling sight. The four corpses created a morbid image, now made more confounding by the addition of the strange vertical plane facing the end of the table. It resembled a great black doorway to nowhere. The surface of the peculiar material was unnerving, as it seemed to swallow all light that touched it. There was no reflection of any kind, no gloss, or gleam to the black finish. The frame measured three feet wide and five feet high, with exacting measurements down to a fraction of an inch. Kilmer didn't know why it mattered, but the precision hinted at something... he just couldn't put his finger on it... other than to say it was troubling.

Kilmer turned to see Pope on his hands and knees at the other end of the table. "What do you have there, John?"

Pope had dusted the grime away from a spot about three feet from the end of the surface. He had the finger of his glove in a small cleft and was wiggling it. "Three holes, deliberately spaced," he said.

Kilmer understood what the man meant. Aside from the one the man was palpating with his powered glove, two more had already been cleared. They were perfectly round, at least a half-inch deep, and couldn't have been more precise if they had been bored with a laser drill. When Pope pulled his finger free from the third hole and sat back, the computer in Kilmer's suit made an interesting extrapolation and superimposed three green lines between the holes, indicating that they formed a triangle with three exactly equal legs.

"Did you see that?" Kilmer said.

"Yeah," Pope nodded. "This place keeps getting weirder." Then, he held up a glove containing three wooden rods.

The display in Kilmer's suit instantly indicated that all three rods were exactly the same length—thirty-six inches and three-quarters of an inch in diameter.

Although he was familiar with the Non-Standard unit of measure, he did not overlook the fact that everything in this cave was measured in Non-Standard units. When converted, the rods would measure 914.4 millimeters, and the distance of the holes from the table was 91.44 centimeters. None of these numbers were intuitive for their people. Presumably, the builders of this artifact had used a different measurement system.

"I don't understand this," Pope said. One by one, he stuck the end of each dowel rod into a hole in the floor. Each rod stood upright and faced vaguely in the direction of the ceiling. None of them, however, did so with any degree of precision. This contradicted what they had seen so far. Everything about the frame and the holes had been exceedingly precise.

Kneeling on the floor, Kilmer grinned. "Mind if I try?" He pulled the rods from the holes and examined them briefly to ensure that none of the ends had been damaged. Seeing none, he crossed all three at one end and spread the other ends out widely. He pointed to the floor and directed them toward the holes. They pulled with a magnetic force before he could approach to guide the rods more delicately. The three tips seemed to direct themselves into the appropriate slots, locking into place at thirty-degree angles, leaving their upright ends crossed about an inch and a half from their tips.

"What just happened?" Pope stammered.

Kilmer sat back on his haunches and stared at the tripod with wide eyes. "I think it just helped me finish assembling it."

"Ok," Pope said slowly. "But how?"

Shrugging, a less noticeable gesture due to the suit, Kilmer said, "I don't know. But we have technology that does things like that."

"Yeah…but this was just three wooden rods, right?"

They would have to discuss that with the second team when it arrived with more delicate scanning equipment. There was undoubtedly more to this cave than met the eye, and Kilmer was now confident in his assessment.

Drew approached, looking ready to speak as Kilmer stood up. Drew noticed the three crossed rods sticking up from the floor. He observed how the small stand was perfectly aligned with the end of the table. Then, Drew, Pope, and Kilmer looked past the assembly, the table, and at the vertical frame facing them from beyond it.

"You found more of the device," Drew said as he circled the small wooden stand and studied it from different angles. His words might have been a question if not for their tone.

Kilmer nodded. "Does that strike you as a crude tripod?" He looked around the room, still strewn with rubble that might obscure minor artifacts like those they had already found. "We should look for whatever is supposed to rest there."

The comment shook Drew from the mental fog that had plagued him since the discovery of the bodies. He faced Kilmer, and his shoulders squared deliberately. Long seconds passed. During that time, Drew's eyes blinked only briefly as he stared at Kilmer. It seemed as if he was working through some internal debate—something that was personally challenging for him.

Finally, Drew exhaled. His ramrod posture seemed to deflate with the effort. He reached a gloved hand into the pouch on his hip and retrieved a grapefruit-sized silver orb, measuring 6 inches or 15.24 centimeters in diameter. Holding it up to the light, he noticed it had a matte finish and was blemish-free, with no markings of any kind. "I found it in the rubble over there," Drew said simply as he handed it over. "It sounds like what you're looking for."

All eyes were on Kilmer as he acted naturally, considering everything they had done up to that point. With everyone eager to understand the strange artifact locked away for millennia in the cavern beneath the plateau's surface, no one intended to stop him.

They should have been more aware of the bodies found alongside the apparatus because, when combined, they conveyed a type of message.

A warning.

Kilmer knelt before the wooden tripod and lowered the sphere into the crude cradle. As he did this, a glance at the floor enabled his suit to scan the surface—specifically, the area disturbed by his recent movement. A multi-phasic scan from the optical array of his helmet located an etching or rune carved in the stone floor and highlighted it in green on his HUD.

It was a simple shape—a circle with an X through it. The circle appeared deeply carved into the stone floor, while the X was less extremely etched, perhaps suggesting it was less important. Kilmer's brows furrowed in confusion as he tried to interpret the shape and its meaning, even as his right hand placed the sphere in the cradle of the tripod. As he did, the position of the rune registered in his mind. It was directly beneath where he knelt.

The moment the silver orb settled fully into the stand, he looked up at it. Then, he gazed over it to see that it had a clear line of sight across the surface of the stone table separating the still, mostly upright, long-dead figures to the left and right. Beyond the table, facing the bodies, the sphere, and him, was the vertical surface of the strange material in the frame. It resembled a mirror that absorbed one's reflection instead of returning it.

Members of the team shifted to take positions behind the long-dead forms at the table. Kilmer's eyes quickly darted from each of the dead to the standing forms of his teammates behind them. A sense that this had all happened before solidified in his mind. The past was replaying itself, and his friends had become unwilling participants in some horrible past mistake.

One of the vertical light projection poles at the perimeter of the cave made a popping sound, and the device began to buzz loudly. This lasted only a few heartbeats, and then the buzz slowly faded, as did the light emanating from the cave's perimeter.

The light source the team had been using for hours went suddenly dark.

"Switch to suit-based lighting," Drew ordered, his voice tremulous. Kilmer instantly understood that everyone in the cave shared his sudden sense of foreboding.

Before anyone could activate their lights, the globe, an arm's reach away from Kilmer, began to glow a pale green. The phosphorescence was initially subtle; Kilmer almost disregarded it as a trick of the eye while his body tried to adjust to the total loss of vision. Then, within three or four seconds, the glow became more distinct. It was enough to distract everyone since no one activated their lights.

Everyone watched the orb, frozen in place and waiting breathlessly for what was to come next.

After seven seconds, the orb's inconsistent pulsing steadied. It was bright enough for Kilmer to see Drew turn directly to meet his eye. Pope and Teretti took a moment longer, but both looked his way at the same time. Then, as one, all eyes turned to the black mirror.

Seconds passed. Everyone stood frozen in place.

Kilmer's eyes scanned the room. No one moved. "Guys?" He said.

Still no one moved.

His stomach roiled and the sense of unease escalated by the second as Kilmer considered his options. He had no idea what this device was or what it did. He only knew that the cavern had been buried for countless years, and everyone found with the device had died violently and painfully.

He needed to act.

The thought of removing the orb from the cradle had just entered his mind when the light emanating from the device began to pulse rhythmically. Kilmer felt an irrational sense of terror prickling the hair at the back of his neck as his bowels threatened to release. Sweat ran down his back. Given the suit's climate control functions, this should not have been possible.

"Anyone?" Kilmer cried, his voice cracking.

No one moved. It was as if they had been frozen in place, either by the device or paralyzed by fear. He understood this with a sense of finality, and it was up to him.

Kilmer reached for the device just as a pinpoint of light streaked from the orb and struck the surface of the mirror. The flawless, nearly indestructible surface of the impossibly thin, rigid material rippled as if it were tissue paper caught in a gentle breeze. A breath later, it became cloudy and seemed to billow and roil, as if a storm was trapped between the confines of the frame.

When a burst of light projected from the nebulous surface of the mirror, it advanced across the surface of the stone table with impossible slowness. That might have been Kilmer's altered perception in the final fractional seconds of his life. He saw the desiccated corpses blown backward in slow motion as the light passed over them. The pulse spanned the length of the table and reached the green orb at the exact moment his gloved fingers grasped the sphere.

At that moment, Kilmer Breslin's life force ceased to exist.

A new consciousness used the electrical charge as a conduit to enter his body. The occupying force purged Kilmer Breslin's brain of every memory and conscious thought. In that nanosecond, it gained a foothold on his biology, and the force began altering his genetic structure in hundreds of thousands of micro and macro ways necessary for its presence to exist in this new, altered reality.

Teretti saw the lights at the cave's perimeter go dark, and his blood ran cold. He wouldn't admit this to anyone on the team, of course. He retreated several paces away from the artifact, feeling a growing apprehension. Relieved, he noted that Pope had done the same. Then, a laser-like pulse lanced from the sphere and struck the mirror, leaving Teretti slack-jawed in astonishment. His mind couldn't process what he was seeing. Kilmer had to shut the device down, and

Teretti wondered why Drew hadn't already given the order. He wanted to run, but strangely, he found he couldn't do any of these things.

He couldn't move. His eyes remained fixed on the artifact and its bizarre interplay of light.

The laser pulse returned from the surface of the frame moments later. It was projected with such force and ferocity that it sent the corpses toppling fully from the stone table. A sound wave struck Teretti like a hammer blow. A fraction of a second later, he saw Pope topple, and Teretti started falling. Teretti saw the light hit the sphere's surface and Kilmer's outstretched glove as he went over. Kilmer's suit appeared almost transparent in the glow, allowing Teretti to see the man's skeleton.

Then he found himself on his back, and Teretti saw only darkness. No, that wasn't true. There was a dull green glow. He thought he could see stars, most likely thanks to the flash of light. It was strange since the suit's visual filters should have protected his eyes from harmful wavelengths.

He blinked away the pinpoints and sat up just in time to see Kilmer climb fully to his feet. As the light pillars at the cave's perimeter flashed and flickered, Teretti saw the unbelievable. Kilmer stretched his arms, only to have his hands split from the gloves. The sleeves of his suit popped like bombs had gone off inside them. His arms seemingly doubled in size in seconds. At the same time, the suit fractured wide at the shoulders as broad, bony protrusions replaced his uniform.

With a gasp, Teretti saw something resembling reptilian scales where flesh and bone should have been. Then Kilmer's helmet cracked with web-like fractures before crumbling. As its remains struck the floor, a pair of round, pale yellow eyes turned to face him. They were alien, wholly inhuman, with black vertical slits where the iris should have been.

"What—*what are you*?" Teretti could only mumble as he scrambled backward on all fours. It was a clumsy retreat, but it was all he could manage without turning his back on the creature.

The effort may have been slow, but it allowed Teretti to live a few seconds longer. Pope, a few feet away, had seen only part of what Teretti witnessed, but it was enough. Pope jolted to his feet and sprinted for the mouth of the cave. In his panic, he was willing to forsake the quarantine.

The creature seemed emboldened by Pope's sudden action. It reached him in a single step and trapped him with its massive reptilian arms. It held Pope aloft, one arm in each of its large, claw-like hands. Teretti watched as the creature studied Pope the way a man might regard a breed of animal it was seeing for the first time. The creature's large, scale-covered head moved back and forth to compensate for eyes that didn't appear to articulate independently.

Then the creature slammed Pope to the floor, flat on his back. Body armor cracked against the stone with a savage, wet slap. A large clawed foot pinned Pope. Teretti realized the last of Kilmer's armor had crumbled away during the transformation. The taloned claws of the foot scraped and puckered the surface of Pope's armor while the man screamed. Teretti retreated further to the cave's perimeter, but there was nowhere to run. The creature had Pope staked to the floor and blocked the only exit.

A popping and crunching sound emanated from Pope's armor, and the man's screams intensified. Teretti wanted to say or do something, but what could he do? He opened his mouth to scream but stopped when it filled with his stomach's bile. Then he heard a wet squish as Pope's armor failed, and the full weight of the creature collapsed the torso of the body inside.

A whimper echoed from the far side of the cave, and Teretti instantly knew it was Drew. The team leader must have witnessed everything. Teretti turned to the creature, but it had vanished silently.

This was his chance, Teretti knew. He climbed to his feet on rubbery legs. But before he could take even a step, a primal, savage shriek filled the cavern. It was loud and penetrating, bringing Teretti's ears to the verge of bleeding. He understood instantly that the sound had also caused his bladder to release. A warm sensation ran down the inside of his leg. He only hoped the creature couldn't smell him then.

Teretti took two steps, his eyes focused on the cave exit. His heart leaped into his throat when he saw the blur of motion as something passed by the entrance. He heard a bone-breaking crunch.

Long seconds of silence passed, and then Teretti heard a dull moan of pain. It had to be Drew, and it was coming from the mouth of the cave. Teretti ran. He reached the location in a dozen long strides, just in time to trip over the toppled form of Drew. The flickering light from the residual imaging pillars illuminated the man's crumpled form. Drew was in bad shape. One arm was twisted at an odd angle, and his helmet was split open like an overcooked egg.

"Collapse the cavern," Drew said.

Teretti nodded. Something like this must have happened to the last group. It was why they died so violently. Still, this seemed somehow worse. The creature had savagely crushed Pope.

"I've tried to radio–" Teretti was cut short when something crashed into him from behind. He tumbled, and his helmet smashed into the stone wall.

Drew screamed. It was a terror-filled, pain-fueled bellow that Teretti knew would haunt him until his dying day. He rolled onto his back and activated the lights on the shoulders of his suit and the top of his helmet just in time to witness the final moments of Drew's life.

The creature was now bigger, if such a thing was possible. It was at least half again as tall as any man and powerfully built. It resembled a genetic cross between a man and a reptile. A bipedal lizard or dragon stomped its massive taloned foot on Drew's supine form, then grabbed his arm with one of its large paws. With a quick pull, Drew's arm was wrenched from his torso. The pop and sickening splatter that accompanied it made Teretti's bowels liquify. Drew didn't seem to notice the loss of his limb. He lay on his back and stared at the ceiling with glassy eyes. He blinked slowly, as if trying to remember where he was and how he had come to be there.

"Pope?" Drew mumbled. "Teretti? You there?"

"Oh," Teretti sobbed through his bile and snot. "Oh no…"

The creature leaned over Drew and seemed to study him curiously.

Slipping a claw around the back of the man's neck, he hoisted Drew effortlessly from the floor. He held him aloft, suspended only by his neck. Teretti didn't think this position hurt Drew since the suit's collar was reinforced. The pressure the creature applied to his neck was mitigated by the strong carbon nanotube frame that sealed the helmet. Drew was undoubtedly in shock, and the loss of his arm might be survivable. The suit would have sealed off the joint to minimize blood loss. There would be a concussion from the head trauma, but as long as the creature stopped–

The creature made a fist, and Drew's head popped from the end of his neck. Teretti gagged. Drew's head struck the stone floor with a hollow thud and rolled to a stop between the creature's feet. When Teretti looked up, the beast stared into his eyes and stepped in his direction.

Teretti screamed as every ounce of dread he had ever experienced, dreamed, or even contemplated was realized and magnified to an extent he had never believed possible.

Chapter 7 - A Glorified Sleep Study

Our-World

Alison Springs, Maryland

I was in the lab early the next morning, feeling unusually anxious. Stresses of one type or another became second nature when my whole "tripping worlds" adventure began. Not to pat myself on the back, but I'd long since learned to roll with the punches. I'm introverted at my core, which isn't practical when your mission in life is to undermine plans for world domination implemented by a creature from another plane of reality. One becomes good at being someone else when required. I think of it as playing a role and believe I can be anyone I need to be.

The problem with my trip to Alison Springs University was that I could only be myself. I had a past with Piper, and since Piper was part of ASU, there was too much of a chance someone I knew from our time together would overlap and blow my cover. I had laid enough of a false trail to keep the FBI chasing inconsequential leads in other parts of the world. If I could wrap up my work in Maryland quickly enough, I could stay ahead of the manhunt.

The law had nothing to do with my stress levels shortly before eight o'clock that Monday. It was the fast one I was about to pull by ambushing Piper for a second time in two days. I was pulling a fresh pair of replacement wires through the tangle of intricate sensor leads under the table when I heard multiple voices coming down the hall. A group of people appeared to be talking simultaneously.

"The team has arrived," Esker said through my earpiece.

"Everyone?" I asked, keeping my voice low so my face remained obscured below the surface of the high-tech medical table. I knew Esker was using the facility's surveillance system to track the team as they finished reviewing the two storage rooms allocated for the project. They were headed to the medical suite specifically designed for the experiment, located down the hall from the storage rooms on the rarely-used basement level of the recently opened Experimental

Sciences building.

"Affirmative. The entire team is present," Esker paused for dramatic effect. "Including Piper." He was an artificial intelligence, but if I didn't know better, there were times I would bet money that the dramas of my life amused him.

"Very funny, but you know I'm more concerned with Omar."

"Insisting on that won't make it a reality," the AI's dry voice insisted.

I rolled my eyes.

"And last but not least," a new voice boomed as a group bustled into the room. "Welcome to our state-of-the-art laboratory." The man had a sonorous baritone, and I recognized it as the tweed-toting Doctor Kramer Fulbright. He was the head of the project and the man I had seen in the news clipping, shaking hands with the financier from the front company representing Kilmer Breslin's interests.

I kept my head down and waited. My cover was that of a technician, and any good cover requires commitment, so I plunged ahead with my work. I pulled the cable through the grommet, separated the central instrument cluster from the port assembly, and started stripping the ends of the delicate wires. It would take only a few seconds to solder them into the housing. Still, I was putting that off until after the uncomfortable introductions, misdirections, and possible recriminations that needed to come first. I might be playing a part, but I hated to do anything more than once, even if it was part of a project I ultimately needed to sabotage.

"Our team is still one short," I heard a husky feminine voice say from the far side of the room. "You said we would meet everyone first thing." This was from Piper. It was a voice I would recognize in my sleep...and yes, I frequently did hear it in my sleep. Our time apart was not without its personal challenges for me.

I was surprised by how frustrated her tone was.

"Yes, everyone is meeting as I promised," Doctor Fulbright muttered. His tone was placating, suggesting this had been a recurring theme and a subject he would be happy to remove from their agenda. "I believe the last team member is already working hard on our primary device. Grady, could you come out to meet the team?"

I sighed and pushed a set of screwdrivers and a soldering iron aside on the floor. I hoped to listen longer before being drawn into the conversation. Perhaps entering the room quietly and arriving late would have been a better approach. Since it was too late, I used the edge of the bed for leverage and hoisted myself up from the floor.

Before I forget, let me explain the bed. Doctor Fulbright's project focused on using sleep patterns and brain chemistry to cross the dimensional Brane barrier. If you think that's similar to what happens when I shuffle off to dreamland and wake up on the other side, you're right. His theory and associated experiment being so similar to my experiences seemed unlikely. At least until you consider the baker's dozen of different approaches I have already sabotaged since Breslin began searching for a way to bring his people to Our-World, it seems it was only a matter of time before he found an approach similar to my own experience.

I still couldn't figure out how Piper ended up on the one project that closely mirrored my history. There is a coincidence, and there was whatever the hell this was, right?

Maybe that's why the surprise I saw in Piper's expression wasn't what I expected. It was the kind of bewilderment you see on a person's face when you unexpectedly find yourself in the same elevator with someone you're tracking. It was not shock that I intruded on her scientific project without prior warning or explanation.

"Team," Doctor Fulbright said, "this is Grady Ledger. He's the data scientist and technical lead for the project." Fulbright waved a hand toward the group gathered at his side. "Grady, this is Sara Pemberton, Oman Quadri, Piper Hudson, and Timo Butcher."

I stepped forward and shook hands all around. The looks I received from the group varied greatly. I noticed expressions of concern from Oman, amusement from Timo, and what seemed like confusion from Sara. There was also a hint of frost in the glare I received from Piper.

I had anticipated an unfriendly reception from Piper, though her glower was running a wider gamut than I predicted and was more like a runaway train. Esker had performed background checks on the entire team, so I was particularly interested in the reception I received from Oman. He was already looking for an opportunity to head for the hall and was fidgeting with his smartphone in anticipation of a moment of free time.

Sara's reaction to my handshake was the most unexpected. She looked at me more closely and her gaze narrowed on my eyes. "Grady Ledger?" Looking back at Piper, she said, "Didn't you have an ex by that name?"

Piper wasn't the type to share personal information, so the fact that she told Sara about me was a surprise. Not knowing how Piper would react, I kept my expression neutral—or at least I thought I did. Looking back, I might have looked like a deer caught in the headlights of an oncoming car.

While still looking at Piper, Sara tipped her head at me and, with the biggest grin I could imagine on the girl's face, said, "Is this the guy who ghosted you?"

Piper chewed the corner of her lip and remained silent; she simply shrugged.

Sara nodded and then looked me up and down as if I were a mannequin on a sales floor. "Buckle in, folks. This is going to be *interesting.*"

Oman was about to run for the door. "Now," I whispered to Esker.

The power in the room went out. The overhead fluorescent lights went dark, and heavy clicks and thuds could be heard around the room's perimeter. The room, I should explain, was a sterile, utilitarian space. It was designed to look very clinical, but it was a high-security lab in the basement of a state-of-the-art building that had recently opened on the north end of campus. It had high ceilings and poured concrete walls. The doors were on sliding steel tracks, and the security had been excessively hardened. They were fireproof and could become air-tight under a pressurized rubber seal that inflated around the periphery of the door when required.

In the case of a power outage, the lab went into lockdown, steel bolts secured the doors, and the airtight seals engaged. This was excessive for a project like the one Doctor Fulbright was working on in the basement. Still, since funding had been provided by one of the institute's most significant benefactors, no expenses were spared. The overkill was playing to my benefit in this situation because now Oman Quadri couldn't leave the room to make his crucial phone call.

Emergency lighting activated, and the half-dozen wall-mounted fixtures hummed to life. Everyone looked concerned—everyone except Piper, who glared at me from beneath arched brows.

"It's just a power outage," Doctor Fulbright said reassuringly.

Before the words were out of his mouth, everyone in the room had cell phones in hand and was tapping at the screens. That's when tension started to fill the air. No one had a signal. Of course, they didn't; I had a jammer in my backpack about ten feet from where I was standing.

Fulbright poked at his phone almost as long as anyone else but then grumbled something inaudible and shoved the device into his tweed sport coat pocket. "Not to worry, everyone. It's just a matter of time before power is restored, and we're out of here. The building is brand new. They have had glitches like this for the last couple of weeks. Think of it as a test of our security. We can see how safe the apparatus is when we lock it down at night."

We were stuck in the room for hours. It was unfortunate, but there was no way to rush the approach I needed to make, both with Oman and the rest of the team. Oman was my primary concern. ATG security had alerted him to be wary of anyone approaching the project, especially if they matched my description. I've been destroying Breslin's experiments for some time, and needless to say, his corporate security had gotten wise to my methods—at least some of them. ATG was competent enough to alert the associated teams on each and ensure they were on the lookout. For a quiet project like this, it only made sense that someone on the team would be watching for me. I just needed to stay a step ahead and be ready for whatever Breslin's people had told Oman to keep him loyal.

Everyone was tired and hot during our fifth hour. The lab resembled a massive warehouse-like workspace, divided into separate areas by furniture arrangement. Since none of it had been used before tonight, no one felt at home at the start of the day. But fast forward a few hours, and that changed. Fulbright and Butcher sat on a pair of sofas arranged around a large-screen television with no cable service. This was placed in the northwest corner of what everyone was already calling the lab. A small kitchenette was set up in the northeast corner. It included a full refrigerator, a table that could seat six, and an eight-foot-long counter with cabinets and a sink.

The entire south wall of the lab was configured like a proper research facility. Computer terminals were on wheeled carts, and there were equipment shelves and tanks of industrial-sized gases. The centerpiece was their main instrument, referred to simply as "the table," although there was nothing simple about it. Essentially, it was a bed layered with space-age memory foam that could be precisely temperature-controlled. Similar to how the temperature was carefully monitored, the table's head, foot, and middle could be adjusted subtly to make the sleeping subject as comfortable as possible. But the actual technology was the glass lens that arched over whoever was on the table for the experiment. The lens curved from one side to the other, entirely transparent and nearly an inch thick. It looked like glass but was almost five hundred layers of state-of-the-art silicon image transistors. The microscopic technology built into the glass-like matrix could scan and display information simultaneously across the surface of the lattice array. It was cutting-edge technology that was more precise than even the most revolutionary MRI and could image a subject in real-time.

"I still think you could have given me a heads-up," Piper said as I continued working on the table. She held a flashlight for me and leaned against the diagnostic panel. We had this part of the lab to ourselves, but we still kept our conversation to hushed tones.

"It was on the agenda when I saw you last night," I admitted.

"So," she said, frustration evident in that single word.

I shrugged and took too long to answer. "Seeing you... I guess this," I waved a hand around the room, "didn't seem like the most important thing to say." Or *not to say*, I didn't add.

She was quiet after that and just watched me try unsuccessfully to splice a wire into the control box panel. It was a simple task, and I failed repeatedly to make the connections correctly. I could claim the lighting was poor, but that wasn't the problem. She knew it as well as I did. My focus wasn't on it. This wasn't what I wanted to be doing. I was inches away from her for the first time in far too long, and she was distracting in a way that people wait their entire lives to experience.

I didn't know if she still felt as she once had.

"So, you told Sara about us?" It was all I could think to add.

Piper shrugged. "I have friends here. Does that surprise you?"

She had always been a very private person. We had that in common.

"I'm a bartender in a very popular bar," she said. "Guys hit on me all the time. After a while, my friends wondered why I wasn't interested. Apparently, I needed a reason not to give anyone the time of day. If you don't have one, people think there's something wrong with you."

"And I became your reason?"

She shrugged again. "At first. It worked for three or four months. Those were the first three or four months after I realized you weren't returning. But as time passed, I had to ask myself why I wasn't making myself available."

The silence stretched again, so I asked, "And that was?"

She turned off the light and looked away. "Ask me again sometime," she said in a quiet voice. "Right now, you've got work to do." She wasn't referring to the wires I was fighting with. "Just deal with Oman so we can get out of here. I'm tired, and I'm hot. I want to take a shower."

———————————

I moved to Oman Quadri. He was sitting with Sara Pemberton at the table in the kitchen area, and the two were speaking quietly. Fulbright and Butcher were passed out on couches in the other corner, so there wasn't much chance of being overheard. Still, keeping Oman from raising his voice was vital to pulling off my con.

Piper slid into a chair next to Sara, and I dropped into a seat kitty-corner from Oman. The young man instantly became alert, his stress indicators increasing noticeably. His face was already covered in a sheen of perspiration, but my proximity seemed to bring fresh droplets to his skin. Like everyone on the project, except for the team lead, Doctor Fulbright, Oman was young—meaning he was roughly my age. According to his file, he was a few weeks shy of his twenty-fifth birthday. I knew he was a registered Democrat, a pro-life advocate, had a boyfriend named Al, and the couple shared two cats. The problem for me in terms of cover on this project was that Arlington Technologies Global had given Oman a very detailed description of me and instructed him to be on the lookout.

Oman was about five feet eight inches tall and weighed approximately one hundred ninety pounds. He wore chinos and a blue button-down shirt buttoned to the collar. His concession to the less formal conditions seemed to be the lack of a tie, and he appeared uncomfortable without it. Every ten minutes or so, he would fiddle with the collar of his shirt as if checking for the knot of his tie out of habit, only to find it wasn't there. He also wore undersized wire-rimmed glasses that seemed more of a fashion statement than corrective eyewear, as they were likely more of a detriment to his sightline than a benefit.

"This is crazy," Sara said. "How can no one know we're down here?

We checked in at the front desk. Someone should be looking for us by now."

I pointed to a service door in the back corner of the lab area. "That's supposed to be the emergency exit. When the rest of the facility locks down, that door leads to a tunnel that provides emergency access to the basement of Smithson Hall. I guess all the infrastructure is so new that no one has tested the emergency systems yet."

Oman glared suspiciously at my detailed explanation. He seemed ready to speak but then thought better of it.

Piper said, "I'm sure it's only a matter of time. At least we have ventilation, so something is working right."

I glanced at the tangle of industrial-grade vents suspended from the concrete slab ceiling overhead. "The lab has its own backup cooling and oxygen filtration systems. The door has an airtight seal, so the idea is to prevent any containment breach from leaking to outside labs. At the same time, there are three others on this level. Engineers ensured the experiments inside each lab wouldn't lose integrity if they suffered a breach."

"How does the new guy know more about the lab than anyone else?" Oman finally grumbled, speaking for the first time since I sat down.

I am responsible for all the technical systems, including everything from the available power facilities to the life support capabilities. I have also researched the inventory of spare parts and medical supplies. I strive to know as much as possible about every project I undertake.

Oman arched a brow. "So if I asked you how many rolls of duct tape we have on hand, you're saying you know it off the top of your head?"

"Can't have too much duct tape," I agreed. Esker's voice sounded in my ear, relaying the relevant details. "6 rolls in compartment 36B, two more stashed on a shelf behind 62G, and I have a partial roll on the wheeled cart because I used it before the power went out. There are also two locations with gaffers tape. It's not quite as handy as duct tape, but it has its unique uses."

For a moment, I thought Oman would confirm the information I had provided. His eyes scanned the room, and I watched as he reviewed the marked locations on the storage cabinets and shelves. When his shoulders slumped, I knew he was resigned to taking me at my word. This was significant because, though not important in and of itself, it represented capitulation. It was the groundwork for my larger fabrication.

The human mind is an interesting tool. If you tell someone something they don't want to believe or are not ready to hear, it's easy for them to reject the information outright. However, if one first builds rapport, establishes a history of reliability, and then attempts to convince them of something they don't want to hear, the chances of rejection diminish.

Or so I've read.

I've used this approach before and it has generally worked in my favor. However, in my experience, people can be unpredictable. It's often impossible to anticipate some people's reactions. But when you can't just punch someone to get what you want, this is the most reliable approach.

I eyed Piper and gave her a wink. I had explained the need for some alone time with Oman before she joined me at the table. Considering my recent intrusion into her life, I had not clarified the deception I would use on Oman.

Piper tapped Sara on the arm and said softly, "Can I talk to you alone for a second?"

Sara's face clouded with concern, and then she looked at me suspiciously, as if I were somehow to blame for whatever was bothering Piper. It made me wonder exactly what, or how much of our past, Piper had shared with Sara. The young woman seemed to be reading too much into my appearance and Piper's response to it.

Sara nodded, and the two slipped away from the table. Oman also tried to leave, but I placed a hand on his arm before he could. "I need a minute of your time," I said in as non-threatening a tone as possible.

"I need to check in with Doctor Fulbright," Oman sputtered.

I didn't let go of Oman's arm, so he promptly relented by sinking back into his seat.

"I know ATG security told you to be on the lookout for someone matching my description and to report back if I made contact," I said without further preamble.

Oman looked like someone had just set a sparkler off in front of his face. His eyes blinked quickly, and his mouth dropped agape. Long seconds passed before he spoke. "BG—wait, what?"

"It's alright; drink water and take a deep breath." I pushed his bottled water closer to his chest and tried not to laugh as he examined it as if seeing it for the first time. He removed the lid and sipped slowly. It was an effort to buy time, and I allowed him to take as much as he needed.

"They would have given you my real name but suggested I would approach you or someone on the project using a pseudonym, maybe even a disguise. Does that sound about right?"

Oman stared at me, clearly not sure how to respond.

"It's okay," I said calmly. "Just take your time, and everything will start to make sense. I promise.

"ATG was right when they said I have been watching several of their projects. Clearly, there's something special about this one, because here I am. However, they weren't being honest when they told you about who I was or why I'm here." I slipped a leather wallet from my back pocket and pushed it across the table. "Take a look," I said. "Just make sure no one else sees it. Lives are at stake."

Oman was slow to react, but he took my cred pack and pulled it close to his chest. His gaze moved surreptitiously around the room, likely ensuring that no one was looking. He slowly flipped it open as if afraid of what it might reveal. Then his brows furrowed. "Defense Intelligence Agency? What's that?"

"Military intelligence," I said in a hushed tone. "ATG is selling secrets to countries hostile to our own, and I'm here as part of that investigation."

Oman closed the wallet and quickly pushed it back to me. "They said you were here to sabotage our project."

I pocketed the creds. "I'm here to support the project," I said without breaking eye contact. "It's vital to our national interests in ways you're unaware of. However, ATG is more interested in brokering the sale of the next generation of this technology to any country with deep enough pockets."

Oman wiped the sweat from his brow and took a deep breath. "I don't see how there's money to be made here. This is basically just a glorified sleep study."

"If that's true," I pressed, "then why is ATG pressuring you to spy for them?"

He looked newly uncomfortable with the accusation.

"You think it's just about the technology the team is engineering into the table," I said. "But that's only the tip of the iceberg. If this project succeeds, the team will break the Brane barrier and touch another plane of reality—another existence. Modern science is about breaking through to new frontiers. This is that principle in its truest form. But there's danger in that. We don't know what to expect when we reach this new reality. Who or what might we find there?

"Do we want a ruthless group like ATG calling the shots with the science when we get there?"

"So the federal government wants to take over the project," Oman said. "Does that seem fair if ATG provided the funds needed to conduct the experiment?"

"ATG is a front company for the Department of Defense," I said simply. "Their CEO, Kilmer Breslin, founded the company with DOD financing. This is a government project; it's just financed through a paper trail that makes it all look presentable to allies and enemies of our nation alike. ATG is trying to back out of the deal they used to launch the company, and this isn't the first project they have tried to launch under the radar this way."

This was all fiction, of course. But it was more believable than the idea of a man-creature from another Brane of reality coming to Our-

World in search of a way to bring the rest of his people here and turn it into a living hell. I mean, when the truth is that messed up, you have to give people something they can wrap their minds around, or else you're just not going to make any progress.

"You're saying they did this before?"

"A couple of weeks ago, there was an underground facility in Kansas. ATG claims it was attacked, and its intellectual property was stolen on the eve of its pilot run. The head of the project and two of her lead scientists went missing the same night."

Oman rubbed his eyes. "You're talking about Woodlawn Research and Miranda Norton. I've heard rumors that she has been missing for weeks."

I wasn't surprised that Oman Quadri knew about Woodlawn or Miranda Norton. The community was small when it came to research conducted at this level. To sell the lie, I needed to blend enough of what happened in reality to make things believable. Since Miranda was hiding with my contacts, I could reach out to her to vouch for me, even if I needed her to tell a story so outrageous that she would struggle to back me up while keeping a straight face.

"Look, Oman, this is a lot to ask, but I need you to keep quiet about my being here. I'm gathering evidence against ATG. I need more time. This project will likely be the linchpin in the federal case against Kilmer Breslin."

Oman took a few seconds to gather his thoughts, then fixed a surprising, penetrating glare on me. "You ask a lot, but you don't offer much in return," he said. "Apart from a badge representing a branch of law enforcement I've never heard of, you provide no credible evidence."

Esker's voice sounded in my ear. "This one's not the pushover you're accustomed to dealing with."

He was right. By cementing Oman's loyalty now, I could confidently continue my work. If he aligned with my thinking in this moment, there would be a reduced risk of second thoughts or doubts bothering him during quiet hours.

So, I was prepared for this contingency.

"If I connect you with Miranda Norton, would that ease your mind? She has already been where you are now. She didn't act fast enough, and she is in hiding because of it."

Perking at this, Oman said, "You can reach Miranda?"

I nodded. "Not easily. Letting you speak with her represents a risk, so it's not something I prefer. You're a danger to her, and if ATG ever finds out you were in contact after everything that's happened, it would undoubtedly put you in the crosshairs. I understand your need to verify my information. I respect it. But there's a quantifiable risk here for all of us: you, her, and me. Just make sure you're willing to take responsibility if I connect you with her."

Oman nodded.

I couldn't restore power immediately after my heart-to-heart with Oman Quadri. That would have seemed too convenient, and I would have lost face. So, I let the inconvenience linger for another hour and a half. During that time, I enjoyed some quality moments with Doctor Fulbright and Timo Butcher. Both were sharp guys. Fulbright had no discernible sense of humor at all, while Butcher's brand of humor was a bit twisted.

I never got a sense of what Sara knew about my relationship with Piper; other than that, she seemed to be *in the know*. Throughout the ordeal, she eyed me. Sometimes, her stare was amusing; at others, it was judgment or maybe even hostility.

Regardless of my perspective, this team would be challenging. They had different goals than I did, but only I understood how truly dangerous their benefactor was.

It might have been half an hour later, maybe a little more, but I ended up sitting alone at the same table with Piper. She was simply watching me, the thoughts behind her blue eyes inscrutable for once. She allowed the silence to stretch, and I sensed she was dissecting me. It felt like she was analyzing everything that had happened to me during our time apart just by studying the contours of my face, neck, and shoulders. At that point, Fulbright and Butcher had retreated to the sofas, presumably to pass the time until power was restored. Oman had his feet kicked up and was reclining in an armchair, dozing not far from the two men. Sara Pemberton had seized the opportunity to arrange a recently delivered batch of pharmaceuticals by the light of a flashlight in the medical area. All of this gave Piper and me a degree of privacy as long as we kept our voices down.

"How long until the power is restored?" Piper finally broke the protracted stretch of silence. The staring session wasn't nearly as uncomfortable as one might expect. In the many months since I last saw her, I'd spent countless hours thinking about her and wondering what I would say or do if our paths ever crossed again. I still didn't know what to say or do now that they had. That didn't mean I wasn't happy just to look at her and enjoy the chance to waste some time.

Looking at the overhead lights, I shrugged with my best expression of innocent confusion. She smirked and stifled a laugh behind her upraised hand. That's when I realized she hadn't believed this was a genuine power outage, even for a second. I was here to insinuate myself into her team, using this as a tool to expedite that effort. It was as simple as that. She'd been onto me from the moment the room went into lockdown.

She'd played along without missing a beat.

"At least another hour and a half. I have to sell it," I admitted. "Sorry for messing up your day."

She shrugged. "Sounds like I'll catch my shift at The Borderline, so we're good. Besides, it's interesting. I've never had a chance to see you work."

I didn't want to correct her, but I'd been working when we met on a dock in South Carolina. She just didn't know it. Now that I think about it, I'm not sure if we ever discussed that operation. I met her, got sidetracked, and never looked back. Meeting a gorgeous girl turned into a boat trip and a summer that changed my life.

And now we were here. Together again.

Unsure about what would happen between us next, I felt like my heart was in my throat as I waited to find out. I could jump out of an airplane in a thunderstorm without so much as a flutter in my heart rate, but sitting at a table in the murky gloom with Piper after so much time separated, I felt like my body was about to rattle apart at the seams.

"You're still crossing over?" Piper said, her voice even more of a whisper than it had been.

"Wild-Side?" I said. We had coined the name together. I started crossing shortly before we met, so she had been a significant part of my coming to terms with what was happening. I had her here in Our-World to help me understand it while Doc Cormac worked on the same from Wild-Side. With the three of us putting our heads together, we didn't know why this was happening to me, but we could fine-tune it enough to control the phenomenon somewhat.

I slowly looked around the room before nodding. "If anything, it's even more frequent than when you were there. It's not every night, but more often than not." I leaned forward. "Let me ask you something. Why you? Why here? Why this experiment?"

She glared at me. The seconds of silence that followed hinted this expression would be her only answer. Finally, she spoke. "For you, *dummy*. Fulbright had a theory and was shopping it around for funding. I read about it and tracked the project. I didn't think he would ever get anyone to finance the experiment, but if he did, I wanted to ensure someone was paying attention to it."

"So you positioned yourself for a place on the project team?"

"From day one."

I didn't know what to say. My mouth was suddenly dry. I just blinked and stared.

"It's a sleep experiment designed to put the subject into a stasis-like condition with the goal of crossing over to another plane of existence." She spoke slowly and quietly through clenched teeth. "You fall asleep in our bed and travel to another layer of reality. That seems a bit too close to the mark if you ask me. Not when I know there's someone from Wild-Side looking for a way to break down the barrier and bring his people here for better *feeding grounds*." Those last two words carried an emphasis that spoke volumes.

Better feeding grounds wasn't entirely accurate, but this wasn't the time or place for discussion. My understanding of Breslin's ultimate goal had evolved during my absence. I wouldn't describe it as more nuanced by any means; it simply wasn't what we had initially believed. Regardless, his plans for Our-World were no less catastrophic for the current population.

Piper looked at me and must have sensed something in my expression. "Something has changed." It was a statement, not a question.

I shrugged and glanced briefly around the room. "A lot has."

She just looked at me with that same unreadable expression.

Chapter 8 - Footprint and Fingerprints of a Ghost

Our-World

O'Hare Airport

Chicago Illinois

Special Agent Chris Ingersoll followed the TSA officer through the winding cinderblock corridors until his sense of direction became hopelessly muddled. Institutional placards marked every intersection with confusing acronyms that meant nothing to him. They seemed designed to make the facility unnecessarily challenging to navigate, adding to his suspicion that it was intended to discourage outside visitors. Finally, the officer swiped a card at an expansive glass door that led to a room heavily invested in flat-panel monitors. The screens were arranged to cover every inch of the three windowless walls, and the six rows of closely placed workstations were each equipped with an array of twenty-seven-inch screens.

"Agent Ingersoll," said a small, disheveled man with short-cropped gray hair as he approached with an outstretched hand. "I'm Timothy Saunders. How can I assist the FBI today?"

Ingersoll took in Saunders's coffee-spotted tie, threadbare shirt cuffs, and slightly askew glasses, fighting the urge to grind his teeth. Given how anxiously the man pumped his hand and his grip's moist, clammy feel, at least he was eager to please. "Thanks for your time, Mr. Saunders. I need access to surveillance feeds from last Tuesday afternoon. Could one of your people help me with that?"

"Certainly—certainly," Saunders said with a rapid nod. He pushed his glasses backward on his nose and gestured toward a workstation on the far side of the room. "As requested, Niles has the footage prepared for your review. I also have the ticket agent standing by in an interview room per your office's request."

Ingersoll smiled and gestured for Saunders to lead the way to the computer terminal. He was enthusiastic to finish reviewing the video and move on to the interview as soon as possible, in case Saunders noticed that the call with the FBI field office secretary matched

Ingersoll's voice. He didn't think the eager little man would piece the deception together on his own, but it was better to keep things moving along quickly.

"Do you need the timestamps?" Ingersoll asked as he leaned over the technician's shoulder. The tech was operating the complex video control system in front of an array of computer displays. A traditional computer keyboard and mouse were complemented by a large, knob-like device surrounded by specialized buttons. A stubby joystick was also nearby.

"It's already queued up," the technician said, gesturing vaguely toward the top centermost of the six displays. One screen showed a full-screen image of a concourse somewhere in the airport, while all the other screens displayed dozens of freeze-frame shots, presumably from all over the complex, arranged in three-inch squares. "I used the suspect photo your office provided," he continued.

"You found him?" Ingersoll asked, surprise entering his tone.

Saunders interrupted, "I'm surprised you wanted to review this on-site. We make all our footage available in real-time via the fusion center, but you also have access to the cold storage archives."

Ingersoll had hoped to avoid this particular conversation. The keenness of Saunders's demeanor made him confident that the man would be so anxious to please that the question would be overlooked. Tapping the technician on the shoulder, Ingersoll said, "Play through the video, please." As the recording of the pedestrian traffic on the crowded concourse began to play in real-time, he spoke without taking his eyes off the screen. "I'm told the video we have access to was corrupted. It's only a copy, so I need to review the footage to see the original. The suspect in this case has an accomplice impressively adept at covering his digital footprints."

Saunders chuckled, a squeaky, wheezy laugh shockingly fitting for the cartoon character that Ingersoll had quickly judged him to be. "He's not that smart if we still have the local footage. I guess it's like we see on TV—all the bad guys make mistakes."

Fighting the urge to roll his eyes, Ingersoll simply shrugged. He'd been tracking Grady Ledger for over a year; none of what he experienced during that time could be classified as simple. This was the third time he had successfully located Ledger through a facial recognition search, with each occurrence resulting in his image appearing in the footage at a major airport, only to vanish from the archive shortly after identification. Each time, Ingersoll recovered the master footage by visiting the respective airport. This indicated that Ledger, or more likely an accomplice, possessed the skills necessary to erase the footage used by law enforcement. It also implied that Ledger was unaware of the footage until law enforcement accessed it, an intriguing aspect of his investigation. Additionally, Ledger's access to the footage did not extend to the local copies each airfield kept on-site. That last detail was crucial if Ingersoll aimed to build a legitimate case against Ledger. However, since his case would never reach a courtroom, it was not a genuine concern. By the time Ingersoll collected the eight-figure bounty on the young terrorist, he could vanish to a non-extradition country where the US dollar went a long, long way.

Ingersoll watched the footage as Grady Ledger strolled along the O'Hare concourse, smoothly moving through the mid-afternoon commuter traffic. He pulled a small rolling bag behind him with the casual grace of someone used to this routine. When Ledger reached the edge of the camera's view, the image shifted to another shot, and Ingersoll was impressed by how effortlessly the technician tracked Ledger's movements through the facility.

"I can show you from the moment he gets out of the cab if you'd like," the technician said—Ingersoll had already forgotten his name. "But I've watched the footage over a dozen times. He doesn't talk to anyone other than the ticket agent. He doesn't check a bag. He doesn't even speak to the TSA agents as he moves through security. He's got the look of a regular commuter. He just sort of rolls through here right up until we lose sight of him on the jetway."

Ingersoll watched the video three times and found the technician's analysis accurate. There was nothing suspicious about the footage. Ledger was merely an anonymous face in the crowd, quietly moving from one place to another. "And we confirmed his destination?" Ingersoll asked. "The flight he boarded was indeed destined for Tampa, Florida?"

"Confirmed," Saunders said, nodding aggressively. He handed over a folder containing a thin sheaf of documents. "The flight left on time and arrived eleven minutes ahead of schedule–the crew reported no technical issues or passenger problems. I checked the maintenance logs just to be thorough. After landing in Tampa, a bulb was replaced above seat 38C, but your suspect was seated in first class. I don't see how that could be related."

A smile creased Ingersoll's face. Saunders was going the extra mile to impress. "Not bad," he admitted. "I'll note that in my report, but I must agree. I don't see how that could be related."

His cheeks dimpled, and Saunders rocked back on his heels. "I considered applying to the FBI," he said, but thankfully didn't elaborate.

In a hurry to shift the conversation before the little man could dive into his life story, Ingersoll said, "Could you introduce me to the ticket agent now?"

———————

Ingersoll eyed the ticket agent through the one-way mirror from the observation room beside the interview room. She was in her mid-twenties and of Latin heritage. He glanced at the personnel file to confirm that she was born in New Mexico. Beyond that, he wasn't interested in the rest of the document. There was little chance she knew Grady Ledger prior to their brief interaction at her counter. He was more focused on anything he might have said or done that could provide insight into where the suspect had been before arriving at O'Hare or where he was heading after landing in Tampa. Admittedly, the line of questioning was a long shot. Every lead he was pursuing these days was tied to lengthy odds. Still, eventually, one of them was bound to yield something fruitful.

"Is Gabrielle a suspect?" Saunders asked, his voice cracking.

Shaking his head, Ingersoll tucked the folder beneath his arm and placed his now-free hand on the doorknob at the entrance to the interrogation room. He shot Saunders his most intimidating glare. "You're welcome to observe from here. Under no circumstances are you to enter the interview room. Understood?"

Saunders's head bobbed rapidly, but he didn't make any verbal response. Fighting a smirk, Ingersoll pushed through the door and entered the next room. He gently eased the door shut behind him before turning to face Gabrielle Medina. She was positioned at the far side of the squat rectangular interview table, staring up at him with wide, unblinking eyes. Her long black hair was pulled back into a braid that hung over her shoulder. Though her face was round, it was attractive. Ingersoll observed that she sat near the edge of her chair, not leaning against the back. Anxiety was evident in her expression and posture.

"Please make yourself comfortable," Ingersoll said, pulling out the steel-framed chair opposite her. "I only have a few questions for you, and then I'll let you get back to work." He had Gabrielle brought here and issued instructions, ensuring no one would disclose the reason for the interview. He wanted her anxious and concerned from the start of the meeting. Once he clarified the purpose of the discussion, he expected that explanation to put her at ease. This, he hoped, would also make her more forthcoming and willing to provide the answers he needed. Whatever her worst fears were going into the conversation, the information he sought would pale in comparison. "I have a couple of simple questions about a man to whom you recently sold a ticket."

"A ticket?" Gabrielle's voice trembled. "But that's my job."

"Yes, exactly. I'm hoping you can share more about the man. Anything you remember would be helpful. You're one of the few people we know who has had direct contact with him, so any information you can provide is valuable."

Gabrielle blinked slowly and then took a breath. She slid back in her seat and appeared to deflate as she relaxed. She nodded slowly. "Certainly. Anything I can do to help. Who was the man?" She paused and met Ingersoll's gaze. "When did this happen?"

Ingersoll laid the folder on the table and flipped to a tabbed section at the back. He retrieved a printed screen capture from the security camera, taken from a distance and somewhat askew over Gabrielle's shoulder as she passed documentation to Grady Ledger on the opposite side of the ticket counter. With a finger tap, Ingersoll pointed to the date and timestamp at the top of the page, highlighted with a yellow marker. "According to the footage, the transaction took two minutes and twelve seconds."

Gabrielle studied the still black-and-white image. Ingersoll observed as her eyes slowly narrowed and her brows knitted together. Her head began to shake slowly. "I don't remember seeing this man," she said quietly, in a distant tone. She looked up at him. "Two minutes? How did he pay? What was his name?"

"He went by the name Alex Thurman, although that's an alias."

"What's his real name?"

Tensing in his chair, Ingersoll realized he should never have made that statement. "That's not important. He would have presented himself to you as Alex Thurman. What can you tell me about that? He paid for the ticket to Tampa in cash."

Staring back at the photo, Gabrielle was slow to respond. "We don't get much cash anymore," she admitted. "Still, he doesn't look familiar." She remained quiet for several long seconds, and Ingersoll noticed her eyes moving purposefully back and forth across the photo. Finally, she shrugged. "I don't recognize him. Not the face or the name. I wish I could be of more help."

Ingersoll fought the urge to raise his voice. Inside, he was seething. Instead, he took a slow breath and counted to five in his mind. Tapping the time stamp on the printout once more, he asked, "What about the date? What can you tell me about that day? Did anything unusual happen? Does anything out of the ordinary stand out?"

Gabrielle looked at Ingersoll as if she didn't understand the question. Then her gaze shifted, and her head tilted. As her eyes slowly drifted up and to the side, he realized she was trying to recall memories of that day.

Seconds passed, and Ingersoll grew more hopeful. He had gone through all of this with staff from two other major airports over the past month; both locations had video footage showing Grady

Ledger's brief visits. One was a layover on the way to another destination—the other was still puzzling to Ingersoll because it placed Ledger at Denver International Airport. It was less than an hour's drive to ATG's facility in Boulder, making that a likely connection. But, just as he was seeing today, no one who had interacted with Ledger seemed to remember him.

"I'm sorry, Agent—what did you say your name was?"

"Ingersoll," he grumbled and shoved the photo back into the folder before flipping the lid closed with finality.

"I can't say I remember this man at all. It's strange. He's kind of cute. I know it's unprofessional, but I sort of can't help but remember the cute ones and the really, really fugly ones, you know?" Gabrielle gave an attractive, embarrassed grin, but Ingersoll was not in the mood.

"Thank you for your time," he grumbled, heading for the door.

———————

Al Vincente pulled the phone away from his ear, wincing at the sharp pain from the high-volume expletives that distorted the receiver. The tirade had entered its third minute, according to the timer in the corner of the screen, and so far, the only thing Vincente had managed to contribute to the conversation was his greeting after accepting the call. "...I'm not kidding," Ingersoll kept ranting. "Either this kid is Houdini, or the universe is just messing with us."

Thinking his words would be lost in the verbal avalanche he was subjected to, Vincente muttered under his breath, "Could be both." His timing had the one-in-a-million luck of catching the first pause Ingersoll needed to draw a breath and create the first legitimate break in the so-called conversation.

"This son of a—" Ingersoll's diatribe suddenly derailed. "Excuse me?" He sputtered.

Vincente wasn't going to be baited into repeating the argument they had two days ago. This was already well-trodden ground, and they both knew it. He closed his mouth and breathed slowly while the tips of the fingers on his free hand massaged the temple on the opposite side of his head, waiting for round two of the explosion, which was very near critical mass.

"If you have something to say, just say it," Ingersoll demanded.

"This feels like a repeat of our conversation when you were in Houston."

Some kind of organic grinding sound could be heard on the other end of the line.

"And Flagstaff," Vincente added, a grin touching the corners of his mouth.

The grinding and crunching from the other end of the line stopped abruptly, leaving the call eerily silent. Vincente tilted the phone and checked the display to see if the call had dropped. The advancing timer on the screen indicated they were still connected, so he placed the handset back to his ear and waited patiently for his associate to collect himself.

"What did you find in Bozeman?" He responded after nearly thirty seconds of silence. When he spoke, his voice was flat and troublingly emotionless. "Tell me our magician has run out of tricks."

"Unfortunately, no," Vincente said with a weary sigh. "Similar act, just for a smaller audience. According to the manifest, Gary Winter chartered a Gulfstream G400 flying from Santa Barbara to Bozeman, Montana. As per prearranged instructions, the flight crew had no interaction with their sole passenger. Upon landing, a four-wheel-drive SUV was booked to meet the passenger on the tarmac. They never saw him during the flight, and no one saw him leave the aircraft."

"And the airfield?"

"There's camera coverage, but nothing near the hangar where the passenger disembarked. It's a no-go for the car service, too. There was no driver. The SUV was left for the passenger, with the keys under the floor mat. The tracking package was disabled; however, the tech I had examine the system found no signs of tampering. The rental agency clocked just over twelve hundred miles on the odometer, so the mileage doesn't tell us anything either."

More expletives filtered through the phone's earpiece. Vincente smirked and waited for the younger man to vent his frustrations. Ingersoll might hold the title of Senior agent, but he was not the better man.

"Think you can get more information if you apply pressure to the flight crew?"

Vincente suspected this question would come up. "Not a chance. I have a cousin who flies for a similar outfit in the UK. The successful outfits uphold their reputation by minding their business and doing right by their clients. Kyle says that Wenzel Avionics has a triple-A rating and won't jeopardize it for anything."

"So we have nothing."

"I wouldn't say that. It's another example of how freakishly careful this kid is. That tells us something. He's moving all over the United States, doing it aggressively, and leaving the footprint and fingerprints of a ghost. He has to be well-funded and motivated to move the way he does. There's no evidence he's doing this alone, but if he is, we're dealing with someone with serious intel. He's got a bone to pick with Arlington Technologies Global, and possibly with Mr. Breslin personally."

Vincente paused to see if Ingersoll had anything to add or contest. When the other agent didn't, he continued, "We might not have a lead that places us in the same town as him, but it's only a matter of time. We're learning more about this kid with each passing week."

"That's the problem," Ingersoll grumbled. "This is taking weeks. Freaking months. This kid is making us look like clowns. Like you said—it's just one kid."

Vincente grinned and shrugged. It was true; Ledger was making them look bad. Still, they got paid either way. The frustration Ingersoll expressed hinted at a deeper issue. Recently, Vincente had grown to harbor an increasing suspicion that his so-called partner had another motivation for tracking the suspect. It was likely some kind of side deal with ATG—maybe even Kilmer Breslin himself. Ingersoll had never been above cutting corners to expedite an arrest, and it was possible he'd be willing to go rogue for personal gain.

"The office is back-tracing the financials," Vincente said. "I think we both know what will come of that."

A groan came from the other end of the line. "Yeah. Another dead end. Forged credit information seems to be one of this kid's specialties."

The comment caught Vincente off guard and made him wonder how closely his partner was reading the reports provided by the Washington field office. Grady Ledger had never used a fake or forged credit card. He had never falsified credit information at any point. Even according to the forensic accounting office's A-team, his financing was always legitimate, albeit difficult to trace. Everyone who had supported the kid's efforts had been paid in full as far as they could ascertain. Wenzel Avionics served as a perfect example. The charter had been financed in advance, and the pilot and copilot even received a generous tip at the end of the flight.

ATG was the only organization negatively affected by any of Grady Ledger's activities.

Our-World

Alison Springs, Maryland

Al Vincente moved slowly along the boardwalk; his wrinkled suit coat was draped over his shoulder, and his head tipped back to let the early afternoon sun warm his skin. He had driven all night and had overindulged in coffee to make the trip without incident. In the last six months, he'd traversed vast expanses of the continental United States, most of it solo. He and Chris Ingersoll worked better independently, though it was questionable just how effective either could be judged since neither had found a reliable lead on the current location of Grady Ledger.

This was Vincente's detour for personal reasons, and he didn't feel guilty about the excursion. His father had died during a military training exercise while Al was in high school, and his mother had recently passed away after a shockingly brief battle with brain cancer. She'd been diagnosed after complaining of persistent headaches, was immediately hospitalized, and then passed away just two weeks later. Fast forward two months, and Al and his younger sister Amy were still in shock.

Glancing at his wristwatch, Vincente noted that he was early. Amy was supposed to call at noon, and he had time to spare. The gurgling pain in his belly reminded him that he'd been running solely on coffee for—he calculated slowly in his mind, more slowly than was comfortable—almost fourteen hours. It was definitely time for a bite to eat. Hearing laughter further down the boardwalk, he was drawn to an open-fronted shop with a wide service counter and cash register. It was a sandwich shop with a short line at the register and a long list of creatively named, custom-made sandwiches chalked on a board above the cashier.

His order was placed about two minutes later, and he made small talk with the attendant while his food was prepared.

"Excuse me," a wizened elderly man at a two-top table said to Vincente as he waited for his food. "Are you with the press?"

"Press?" Vincente said.

"Covering the submersible," the octogenarian clarified. "Most of the reporters were here yesterday and the day before." He scanned Vincente from head to toe. "By your outfit, I took you for a reporter."

"No sir," Vincente clarified. "Off-duty law enforcement. I'm just in town catching up with family."

The mention of the submersible was vaguely familiar; Amy had said something about it in passing. At the time, he was more concerned with the logistics of diverting to meet her. Her company specialized in marine salvage, so he didn't think much of it. He knew a high-priority project had brought her to Alison Springs, but now, as he reflected on it, he realized he had no idea what the project involved. The salvage of a submarine would certainly be interesting.

Am I really so far down the rabbit hole that I don't know what Amy's working on?

Vincente scratched his head. Amy had put her life on hold to handle their mother's funeral arrangements. He was in town to sign papers so Amy could sell the family home. Now that he thought about it, he had dumped all of that on his little sister while focusing all his energy on the investigation that had consumed the entire last year of his life.

His name was called, and he picked up his sandwich from the counter. He stood lost in thought in the midst of six tall tables, most of which were unoccupied. Vincente's mind whirled at the direction of his personal and professional lives.

"Officer," the elderly man said. "You're welcome to join me."

His mind jumped back to the moment as Vincente looked at the man. Confusion was likely evident on his face. The old man used the walking cane resting against his leg to push the chair across from the table outward. He nodded to it with an encouraging smile.

Feeling as if he were running on autopilot, Vincente climbed onto the tall chair and unwrapped his sandwich. He popped the top on his soft drink and finally met the man's gaze. "I'm Al," he said with a nod.

"Robert," the old man said. "Nice to meet you. What branch of law enforcement did you say you were with?"

"The Federal Bureau of Investigation, though I'm not here on official business. It's strictly family matters. I came to meet my sister. She's working around here, I'm told."

Robert's brows arched. "FBI? Impressive. Can't say I've ever met a G-man. Then it's Agent rather than Officer?"

Vincente laughed. "I can't say I've ever been called a G-man before." He stared at his sandwich. Once he bit into it, he quickly realized he was far hungrier than he had initially thought. The bites he took were large and aggressive. The massive hoagie was halfway gone before he noticed Robert's amused stare and slowed his pace.

"Long drive," Vincente said with a sheepish grin as he wiped mayonnaise and mustard from his mouth with a napkin. "I only stopped for drive-through coffee." He glanced down at the mess on the square of butcher paper before him. He'd seen less messy crime scenes. "That might have been a mistake."

"Do you like tuna?" Robert asked simply.

It was an odd non sequitur, yet Vincente nodded.

Robert pushed a paper-rolled, unlabeled sandwich toward him. "My eyes were bigger than my stomach. Please help yourself."

Vincente sheepishly nodded his appreciation and started in on the second sandwich. This time, he demonstrated more restraint. "You thought I was with the press?" he asked. "Have there been many reporters around?"

"Heavens, yes," Robert said with a nod. "The U-Boat was revealed to the public for the first time since it was salvaged. It's big news for the bay, as you can imagine. The university was deeply involved in the restoration, and many locals were engaged when it came time to move the vessel from the marina to the transport trucks. The recovery took place some time back, but the tours and press event at the school were this week. Some photographers came back here for comments from the locals."

Part of this was familiar. Amy had mentioned a U-Boat salvage and something about her company collaborating with the local university. Vincente scanned the dock. From their spot at the edge of the open-air shop, he had a clear view of much of the boardwalk and several piers across the marina. "It doesn't seem like much is happening right now. I don't see any press."

Robert shook his head. "Most of the hoopla took place at the museum late yesterday afternoon. The school had a tour of the salvage vessel used to raise the wreck earlier in the day. That's what drew a lot of the press out here and caused a ruckus. It was the first serious stir since the wreck was first brought into port."

Vincente nodded. "You spend a lot of time out here?"

Robert nodded. "I was a fisherman for most of my life. When that stopped being viable, I changed with the times. I managed logistics for the university. Most of the boats they operate in their marine biology program were under my supervision. I didn't like sitting behind a desk, so I took the opportunity to captain a boat whenever I could. It wasn't the same as fishing, mind you, but I encountered many inspiring and creative young people toward the end of my career."

"Impressive," Vincente admitted. "Does that mean you were involved in the submarine salvage?"

Looking suddenly disappointed, Robert shook his head. "After my time, I'm afraid. That must have been one hell of a project. I was here when they towed the salvage into the bay and tied it up down the dock," he explained. "I was sitting right over there," he pointed to a bench made of weathered planking. It had been built into the boardwalk as a permanent fixture. Glancing along the visible path, Vincente noted at least three others evenly spaced. They resembled benches in the park, though the winds or waves would never wash these away.

"Actually, some of the press coverage is memorialized," Robert said after a pause. "I'm not sure why I didn't think of it sooner." He pointed to the distant wall of the open-air shop, where dozens of framed photos hung haphazardly.

Even from a distance, Vincente could see that the frames were screwed into the wall to keep each one exactly in place. They were permanently hung. Some featured color photos scribbled with signatures, while others were news clippings.

Vincente quickly focused on the wall section dedicated to the submarine's salvage. Color photographs captured the barnacle-encrusted wreck, which sat low in the water flanked by long, thin flotation contraptions. A specialized tugboat towed the sub. A couple of images showed the progress of the wreck entering port and being positioned near one of the wide-open expanses of the dock. News clippings with large print headlines described the salvage effort, praised the community support for the historic undertaking, and highlighted the university's involvement.

When Vincente reached an eleven by seventeen frame, he paused and leaned in close. The photo stood out as it was one of only three frames this large. It contained a clip from the local newspaper, with nearly an entire page dedicated to the salvage. The headline read, "Nazi U-Boat Reaches American Shores!" The story wrapped around the black-and-white halftone image beneath the headline on two sides. The photo depicted a pair of broad-shouldered, athletic young men in university windbreakers. Each man stood at one end of the thirty-foot-long visible portion of the submersible, tossing mooring lines to deckhands aboard the U-Boat. The photo of the rope toss was perfect in its synchronicity, and the photo snapped with the lines just beyond the peak of the toss's arc. It was impressive timing, creating powerful imagery.

None of this was the cause of Vincente's rasp when his breath caught in his throat. He focused on the gathering of bystanders, seemingly captured incidentally at the extreme edge of the photo. A table of college-age boys and girls sat oblivious to the commotion just a couple dozen yards away. The kids in the frame laughed, clearly engaged in their own private concerns.

Vincente leaned closer to the photo and blinked. "What the hell?"

He pulled out his phone and snapped a wide shot of the entire framed news story, followed by a closer shot of the group of kids at the table. Zooming in on the screen, he examined the profile image he was increasingly confident was of Grady Ledger. The boy smiled and pointedly peered across the table at something. Ingersoll followed Ledger's gaze and realized it wasn't something but someone: a girl. She was roughly his age, with light hair and a pretty face.

He tapped the screen and sent both images in an email. A moment later, he made an outbound call. "Check your inbox," he said without preamble.

"Good afternoon to you as well, Agent Vincente," a gruff voice replied.

"Sorry, Mary. This is urgent. I need you to identify the individuals at the table along the edge of the photo in the news story."

Vincente heard tapping and clicking on the other end of the line.

"You're joking, right? The quality here is… well… you're messing with me, aren't you? Just tell me this is a joke?"

"No joke. One of those is Grady Ledger—see that?"

A gasp. "No kidding. Where did you find this?"

"It's a long story, but the newsprint should explain the location. The way it happened is complicated and not relevant. But it's the best lead we've had in weeks if we can identify the people at the table with Ledger. At the very least, we'll have a lot more information about his known accomplices."

"You think these people are *accomplices*?"

Vincente rolled his eyes. "You know what I mean."

A chuckle came from the other end of the line. "Just messing with you, boss. Do you want me to pass this along to your friend and mine, Agent Ingersoll?"

Vincente paused, but only for a breath. "Hold off on that. It might be nothing. He's still chasing leads at the major airports anyway, right?"

"Chasing ghosts is more like it. He'll stroke out if he doesn't come up with something soon. That guy is wound up *tight* right now."

"At least I don't have to deal with him. Splitting up was the best decision we ever made."

"You don't have to deal with him, but I do. If this case doesn't catch a break soon, someone better force him to take some downtime. I'm afraid he's going to do something he'll regret. He's becoming more and more volatile."

Nodding, Vincente said, "This could be the break we need. See what you can find for me, okay? Just keep it between us for now?"

"You got it, boss."

Chapter 9 - The Meager Remnants of My Footwear

Wild-Side

There was a flash of light, and the room-temperature pattern of the bunker receiving platform replaced the barn's cold version. Wes stood at the control terminal facing the platform, while Lacy quickly took on her traditional role by fetching a thick, wool-like blanket. It remained unclear whether this gesture was meant as an accommodation for my naked arrival or as a sign of respect for my exposure to this world and its elements before reaching the teleportation platform. Regardless, while I appreciated the consideration, it wasn't necessary. I had long since given up any anxiety over appearing naked in front of these people or anyone else, and thanks to the nanotech, I was impervious to all but the most extreme temperatures.

I noticed Lacy averting her eyes as she approached with the blanket and, this time, noted what might have been a coloring of her cheeks. That had never happened before. It was unusual because the people of Wild-Side had, at least until recently, no experience with sexuality and, as a result, no apprehension about this kind of male-female interaction.

Noticing how Lacy gave me a furtive glance before quickly exiting the room, I decided something had changed. I would either need to ask her about it… or perhaps bring up the subject with Doc Cormac would be better. Chances were, this had something to do with my social experiment. If that were the case, Cormac would be the better choice.

I noticed the smirk on Wes's face and shot him a questioning glance. He'd seen Lacy's response and found it unusual too. "It's not just me, right?" I asked.

He shook his head. "She's given you the same blanket at least a hundred times. I don't know what's different about today."

Tossing the wrap over the console, I grabbed the jeans from the stack of folded clothes waiting in their usual spot. I slipped them on while keeping my eyes on the door Lacy had used for her hasty retreat. I pulled a black t-shirt over my head and stood on one leg as I slipped a sock onto my left foot. I'd gone through this process so many times that I could get fully dressed in under thirty seconds, all while standing.

"The Doc's running late," Wes said. "A meeting with Columbus was running long. Said he'd meet you in the Commons."

I grinned at how he referred to Doctor Cormac simply as the Doc. When I first came here, everyone was stiff and formal. People were called by their given names, and slang was nonexistent. At the beginning, I was treated like an outcast. No one knew what to make of me. I wasn't just a foreigner to them; I was like an alien. Now, I've done more than influence them. I've begun to impact their culture in significant ways.

This was done out of necessity. These people didn't know how to defend themselves against a threat as hostile as the Elend. Breslin and his kind were preying on the people of Wild-Side, a group that, until my arrival, had been entirely unprepared to protect themselves.

I found Doc Cormac studying a tablet cradled in one arm. He sat on the amphitheater's stair step, with the setting sun backlighting him. Maybe a dozen city residents shared the space, gathered in small groups or paired off as couples. Everyone noticed me as I entered from the back of the bowl-like area. Each of them shied away from my gaze. Some did so with awkward discomfort, while others with an unblemished loss of alacrity. Everyone knew who I was by now, even if they hadn't met me. Most directly associated my arrival with the Elend threat, even if they didn't grasp the dynamics and couldn't connect one event to another beyond vague timing. In my mind, this only proved that the people of Wild-Side had much more in common with the people of Our-World than not. They might be intelligent and wise beyond our years, but they still filled the silence with their worst fears, suspicions, and doubts. I wasn't one of them, so I must have more in common with the Scourge, as some had begun to call the Elend.

"Doc," I said and dropped onto the bench beside him. "Wes said you needed to see me first thing?"

Cormac met my gaze with tired eyes, and I immediately saw that he hadn't been sleeping again. His gaze swept across the room, absorbing the disapproval of those sharing the space. Everyone seemed to inch further away, as if what I had might be contagious. He shook his head, frowning with a mix of disapproval and frustration, but that was nothing new. Instead, he gestured to his tablet, swiping something away from the screen before putting it to sleep and tucking it under his arm. I could tell by the distant look in his eyes that he was checking his heads-up display. "Thirteen days?" he commented, referring to how long it had been since my last visit. "How long was it on your side this time?"

The Doc's support team was completely in my corner, and I knew that without question. The rest of Seeley wouldn't put me out if they saw I was on fire. Even those who were open-minded enough to understand I was their best chance at resisting the Elend didn't appreciate my efforts to arm and armor the cities in defense against their Scourge.

I had accepted that my list of allies was short. The Seeley opposition came in different forms. While I couldn't counter that hostility using the same combat tactics I employed against the Elend, it didn't mean I had to fight fairly. I had long abandoned the idea of a fair fight. I hadn't come to Wild-Side willingly, and if I didn't have control over where I went or when, then survival was my top priority. This meant keeping the Seeley safe, whether they appreciated my methods or not.

"Only two days this time," I observed his scowl. This frustrated him. There was no connection between the passage of time on Wild-Side and Our-World, and the disparity of it grated on him with every crossing.

"Much has happened since your last visit," he said, motioning for me to follow as he led me to the top of the stairs, where a railing topped a short wall at the back of the amphitheater seating. This wall marked the city's outer perimeter. It overlooked about seventy-five yards of nearly flat, open ground that separated the city from the dense forest beyond. What was typically flat, featureless dirt had been disrupted. The earth had been churned up in a way that wasn't immediately clear from my vantage point atop the forty-foot wall.

I slowly blinked to allow my enhanced optics to zoom in on the disturbed earth beyond the base of the wall, and I instantly felt my mouth go dry. When I spoke, my voice was parched and cold. "How long ago did this happen?"

The Doc leaned over the rail to get a better look. For the first time, it occurred to me that he might not have the same optical augmentation as I did, which led me to reconsider the other tactical upgrades available to me. During my many visits here, I had been outfitted with upgrades and gear that, until recent events, people from his place had never even dreamed of.

"Three nights ago," Cormac said, his tone a tremulous quaver. "More than we've ever seen—more than we even knew existed."

I studied the churned earth, pulverized by the aggressive footfalls of who knows how many Elend. I took a breath and felt the alloy rail curve start bending under my iron grip. "Any sightings since?"

He shook his head.

"How many were there?"

Meeting my eye, he shrugged. "Unclear. As you know, many of them look very similar. So much so that even our automated systems couldn't generate a count, I'm afraid." He sighed and rubbed the tension from the back of his pale neck with an unsteady hand for a few seconds before continuing. "There were a lot. To have that many, we must have lost one of the colonies. It's the only explanation."

I was already on my way down the stairs, but at this, I stopped to look back at the older man. "Fresno?"

Cormac's lips were drawn into a tight line. "They've been out of contact for weeks. It seems likely."

Fresno was a city similar to Portland—where I was now—but smaller and situated so far on the fringes of the Seeley territory that reaching it had become nearly impossible since the Elend incursion. Vast expanses of dead zones separated Fresno from the other four cities. The growth of these dead zones had caused Fresno to become isolated even from communication over the last two months, prompting me to consider ways to travel to the city. If ever a wellness check was warranted, the hundreds of inhabitants cut off from the rest of their society needed to know they hadn't been forgotten.

Just like the names of people on Wild-Side, the cities did not have names that corresponded with those in Our-World. At first, I found their names hard to pronounce, so I relied on my real-time translator to link each city to a name from back home.

There had been discussions about potentially rigging up enough repeaters to enable the teleportation platforms to function between Fresno and the nearest city, Oakland. I had been waiting for this technology to come together before making the journey. Now, it seemed it might be too late.

I exited the amphitheater and moved through a corridor to a chamber with wide, windowless double doors. I activated my HUD, which superimposed a camera view of the no man's land beyond the doors. The device was positioned directly over the doors. The perimeter was clear to the tree line. I glanced left, and the camera, seamlessly integrated into the wall's surface, pivoted to follow my gaze. The path was clear to both the left and right.

"You're not going out there." Doc Cormac protested.

"Wait here," I said simply as I tapped the unlock code into the virtual keypad that was projected into the air before me.

There was a hiss of compression as the airtight seals surrounding the doors released and swung wide before me. I quickly walked out into the fading evening light, knowing that allowing the doors to close behind me was essential. I wouldn't be responsible for a breach of the perimeter in the unlikely event that something rushed me from the tree line.

I heard the hiss of the doors sealing behind me and was already studying the churned soil surrounding me in every direction. No footprints were visible. It appeared as if the ground had been pulverized by the clawed feet of hundreds of Elend.

A gasp came from behind me, and I spun around. My blade slid from the sheath on the back of my belt as I felt the tech in my veins supercharge my pulmonary and cardiovascular systems. It was a false alarm, however. Doc Cormac was completely unaware that he had put my entire body on red alert. He had his back to me while he stared at the surface of the wall surrounding the city. The surface was usually polished to a porcelain-like finish that was impervious to the scarring from the elements. So far, occasional attacks by the Elend had failed to mar the pale shine of that finish.

Doc Cormac ran his fingers over the gouge and dimpled finish that scarred the wall as far as we could see in every direction. Furrows a quarter inch deep and a foot long extended up to nearly twelve feet high. The Doc's eyes were pinched, and his mouth hung open. I couldn't blame him; the wall was the only lasting defense keeping his people safe from the Elend.

Pressing my palm against the wall, I felt the cool surface, solid and reassuring despite its pockmarked appearance. "I thought you said they couldn't do this," I said quietly. I kept my words hushed, understanding that the vast wilderness was less than a football field behind me and anything could lurk in the dense foliage. It was best to assume we weren't alone out here, even though the city tech had suggested we were the only bipeds within five hundred yards.

Cormac continued to stare at the wall. He shook his head. "They must be getting stronger."

If Fresno had fallen as we suspected, perhaps this was a hint at how it occurred. I paced along the wall for several hundred yards, following its curve as it surrounded the city. Every inch of the once-pristine surface was marred and defaced up to a height of twelve or thirteen feet. The ground at the base of the wall was thoroughly churned, as if by the hooves of hundreds of horses, everywhere between the wall and the tree line.

"You heard this happen?" I said.

Cormac looked me in the eye, his eyes watery. His voice trembled.

"I've never seen so many terrified faces," he said, referring to the city's denizens.

I led the way back to the doors leading into the city. "We'll expand the capacity of the emergency bunkers." I infused my voice with confidence, knowing that whatever assurance I provided to Cormac would circulate among his subordinates. The people of this world were not equipped to face a threat like this, but they were learning to cope. It was a slow, painful process.

I just wished they didn't need to.

"Next time, move everyone to the bunkers if more than one of those creatures is spotted in the clearing," I said over my shoulder. Then I suddenly stopped to give the older man a hard look. "Are the new drones finished?"

He nodded but appeared confused. "Twenty-four with the modified sensor package, according to the Mark-7 specification we discussed."

I glanced at the churned soil beneath my boot and then at the expanse of cleared land that functioned as a kind of demilitarized zone beyond the city's wall. "Can we fabricate a hundred more at half the size with a Mark-5 sensor package within the next couple of days?"

Tucking the tablet under his arm, Cormac shoved his balled fists into his jacket pockets. I knew he was trying to hide the shaking of his hands. I could see the telltale pinching of his brows that indicated the complex calculations happening in his sharp mind. He said, "Printing will take just under two days—once I provide the specs to the team, of course."

Nodding, I gestured toward the doors. I knew the Doc wasn't clear on my intentions for the drones. "If this happens again, or something similar, send everyone to the shelters and launch the new drones. We need to track where this new horde goes once they leave here." Something was changing in how the Elend organized, likely linked to their recently expanded population. Some drones would be destroyed, regardless of how small and stealthy they were. But if enough got through, we had an opportunity to learn. It was highly likely the drones would follow the Elend into a dead zone. When that happened, the only way to pursue would be for the drones to fan out and search the perimeter of the Waste until they reacquired the target.

It wasn't an ideal scenario, so we would compensate for what we lacked in capability with sheer numbers. That would have to be sufficient.

——————————

I was just finishing an impressive interpretation of what I assumed was grilled chicken breast coated in chipotle sauce. It was garnished with something that looked vaguely like cilantro, and there was a tang of lime to whatever had been sprinkled over the entire plate before it was served. The meal was terrific and a vivid reminder of home. This was no small accomplishment, considering this world had no chicken and did not condone the slaughter of animals for human consumption, even if it did. Whatever had been grilled looked and tasted like chicken, and whoever prepared the meal had gone out of their way to emulate one of the many recipes I'd brought from my world. I could only hope everyone enjoyed the meal as much as I did.

There was no one to ask at that moment. I was eating alone, which was my preference when I could get away with it. Even though I'd been coming to Wild-Side for a year, the people of this world continued to see me through different lenses. The Elend plague, now referred to as such, began not long after my arrival, and some couldn't help but correlate my presence with theirs. To be honest, I still wasn't sure if there was any connection at this point, and right or wrong, I wouldn't have disputed their concern.

One thing was certain: the people of Wild-Side were completely unprepared to fight the Elend and would have succumbed to them long ago if not for me. Some appreciated this fact, while others resented it. Refer to my earlier point for insight into the mindset.

If I'm honest with myself, I believe the main reason some didn't know what to make of me was my tendency to ask questions about their world and people, constantly striving to understand the social components they had long considered sacrosanct. In my view, some of the most significant questions were simply unknown to a race considered the most intelligent and technologically advanced to ever walk upright, yet they wouldn't question their own origin. They lacked the motivation to improve themselves beyond the established limits of their current existence.

The longest-standing question for the people of Our-World has been about who we are as a people and where we come from.

Everyone on Wild-Side was literally the same age, and there were no children. The world's population resided in one of the cities on one of three major continents. Everyone here was hundreds of years old—all of them, exactly the same age. However, not everyone appeared to be the same age. The majority looked to be in their mid to late twenties, while many seemed to be in their thirties. Some, like Doc Cormac, appeared closer to sixty or perhaps in his early sixties.

You can imagine how this was a problem for me. How could I not bristle at their inability to question day-to-day life?

How could they not want an answer to the mystery?

Then there's the other thing. I'm pretty sure I've alluded to it before. The people of Wild-Side are intelligent beyond anything I could begin to measure—the slowest among them, if IQ were tested, would rank as one of the sharpest minds of those on Our-World. Somehow, the entire society lacked any form of art. They had no music, painting, sculpture, literature, architecture, dance, theater, or photography.

They were incredibly intelligent, yet all the qualities that make you and me human were strikingly absent.

Many aspects of Wild-Side didn't make sense, but it was, for all intents and purposes, an alien world, after all. I needed to keep that in mind. The people here looked like those from Our-World, but they were not the same. The geography of this place was entirely different, as was its history. I had researched the Many Worlds theory interpretation of quantum mechanics, and it didn't begin to explain

Wild-Side. This place wasn't just a few shades removed from Our-World; it was more different than similar. From what I understand about the theory, this undermined most of the interpretation.

The people here were good and decent, albeit narrow-minded. They were frigidly lacking in personality as well. Most were so rigid they seemed almost robotic. Someone could have convinced me this was a race of androids if I hadn't seen evidence to the contrary. The absence of music and art was difficult for me to grasp, but that was nothing compared to coming to terms with the fact that they didn't engage in intercourse. While they had the equipment—I should say, the people of Wild-Side were genetically equipped for human sex in the same way as men and women of Our-World—they simply had no concept of the act. They didn't understand intimacy or some of the emotions common in Our-World. This isn't to say they lacked emotions altogether. They weren't Vulcans from Star Trek. If anything, they could be described as emotionally stunted—people hundreds of years old who possessed the tools but lacked the experience to use them.

One didn't need a degree in psychology to wonder if all of that had something to do with them never developing music, art, dance, or literature. They never experienced the passion needed to pursue art. Maybe that's why science was revered as God in this world.

Since nothing was sacrosanct to me, it wasn't long before I made my mark on Wild-Side. I couldn't bring anything physical across the Brane barrier. However, Doc Cormac's technology, specifically the nanotech, quickly enabled me to transfer information from Our-World. Art and music was easily converted to digital form and stored within my biology. Thus, they successfully crossed the barrier, allowing me to share them with the people of Wild-Side. The people here couldn't get enough of these new experiences. Art was consumed with enthusiasm. It encompassed everything from digitized versions of classics that hang in renowned art museums worldwide to some of the latest graphic novels. In many instances—perhaps most—the people here had no idea how to interpret what they saw. Nevertheless, most were fascinated.

Music and literature were exceedingly popular. With each trip to Wild-Side, I shared more of the culture from Our-World. I introduced classics from the eighteenth, nineteenth, and twentieth centuries, alongside some of the latest works from the twenty-first. If there was an issue with my approach—well, to be honest, there were multiple issues with my approach, but more on that later—it was that I wasn't equipped to help the people of Wild-Side understand the material. I didn't have a clue when it came to anything outside of modern material or pop culture. I couldn't assist the big brains of this world in grasping or interpreting the motivations behind the creation of classic works, nor could I help them understand the history of Our-World. I could only present them with the raw material so they could draw their own conclusions.

If I had had more time to prepare and had taken a more controlled approach to add context to the material, I believe the entire effort could have been more constructive. Still, everything I brought was consumed with the voracious abandon of intellectuals starved for stimulation. I didn't have time to prepare or even consider my approach. I was more focused on protecting the people of Wild-Side from the Elend. Shortly after I first appeared here, a locust-like plague began sweeping the land. The coincidental timing didn't escape the attention of the intelligent, analytical people.

Understandably, many of the people I interacted with didn't know what to make of me. Despite my cultural offerings and efforts to protect them from the Elend, most tended to avoid me. Consequently, the majority of those I encountered in the street, so to speak, were hesitant to engage. I might have looked like them, but everything about me screamed outsider, and I was aware of it.

"What do you think of the chicken?" Wes asked as he slid onto the bench across from me. Lacy smiled at me as she took a seat beside him.

"Chicken? I was pretty sure. I just didn't see how," I replied. Although most of the people of Wild-Side preferred to keep me at arm's length, almost no one was openly hostile. The members of Doc Cormac's research team were perhaps the most glaring exception, given that we worked together constantly. Every team member had been exceedingly accepting of me since day one.

Light sparkled in Lacy's eyes. "It took some trial and error with the sequencer," she said with a smile. "Many of the formulas you downloaded during your first few trips were chicken-based. I began to think it was a favorite, so I started experimenting."

"Recipes," Wes corrected. "Not formulas."

Lacy nodded her head. "I still don't understand the difference. It's a formula for the meal."

I shrugged. It was a good question. That's when I realized they were both speaking in English. The nanotech in my blood had long functioned as a means of on-the-fly translation, allowing me to converse with the people of Wild-Side and even read their language. It was why I could seamlessly interact with their technology. A couple of hours after the tech became operational, my mind no longer differentiated between their native language and mine. It felt like having their language digitally downloaded directly into my mind. I saw their words in English and heard them speak the same way. It was a trick of the mind, a way that part of my brain rationalized what was happening–at least, that's how it was explained to me. That's why it took me a minute to realize they were both speaking English when they sat at the table.

"You learned my language?" I said with wide eyes.

Wes nodded. "A couple of them," he explained. "We think it might help us to understand the nuances of your nineteenth-century literature better."

"Some of the late twentieth-century work is proving more challenging," Lacy went on.

I grinned. "I get that. The twentieth century is fine for me, for obvious reasons. It's the sixteenth and seventeenth-century stuff that never worked for me. I couldn't read Shakespeare if my life depended on it. Might as well be written in Klingon."

"Klingon?" Wes said from under a furrowed brow.

Lacy nodded enthusiastically. Her eyes shifted to the side as she gazed into the middle distance, and her fingers poked at something invisible in the air before her. I knew she was interacting with an AR display only she could see. "Episodic fiction from the late twentieth century," she said with a grin that revealed dazzling white teeth. No one here had poor dental work. Did I mention that? "I just sent a tag to your inbox. You're going to love it!"

I shook my head and shoveled the last of the chicken onto my fork. "Anyway, dinner is fantastic. My compliments to whoever replicated it."

Lacy swiped the AR display away and suddenly looked bashful. "That was me and Corey," she explained. "I'll let him know. We have a shift together in an hour."

Wes cleared his throat. "Anyway, we tracked you down because Doc wanted to tell you in person but got pulled into something. He said this couldn't wait." He looked left and right, seemingly to ensure no one was within earshot. "We just received an update from Oakland. They said Mara came out of her coma about twenty-five minutes ago. She can't talk yet, but her scans are encouraging. They believe she will regain that ability within the next couple of hours."

I pushed my plate away. "And transport to Oakland?"

"It's been reliable for the last couple of days," Lacy said. "There's a Thonian storm to the northwest, but we don't think it will be an issue for at least eight hours."

I checked the countdown time in my HUD. It displayed the time left before I was slingshotted back to Our-World. For once, I had plenty of time. "Tell the administrator to expect me. I want to be there when she's ready to speak."

Lacy nodded. "Already done. The Doc said you'd want to be there. He wants to go with you."

I knew I was scowling at the comment. I didn't like the idea of Cormac leaving Columbus. None of the other cities were as well-fortified as what I considered their capital city. It was the most well equipped with bunkers and therefore prepared for an attack. That said, I still didn't know if any other cities had been attacked in the same way as Columbus. Maybe the others hadn't experienced perimeter wall assaults similarly.

"As long as he's back here before the storm arrives," I said, my mouth dry.

———

An alarm blared as I stepped off the transport platform, and the overhead lights flickered. At first, I thought the city was under attack. But when Doc Cormac materialized on the single-person transport platform three feet to my right, the look in his eye told me he was already receiving a status update via his heads-up display. Whatever information he was presented with, I could tell it was complicated because he more or less stumbled from the platform, his eyes distant as if he were consumed by something only he could perceive.

"Well," I said, my tone more impatient than I intended.

"Sorry," Cormac said, waving his hand in the air. The gesture made the information on his display accessible to my HUD as well. Knowing Cormac was spending far too much time absorbing the details of whatever he was seeing, I blinked into the gist—the auto-generated summary—cluing me into the key points of the info dump bogging down the Doc's big brain.

I was glad I did because none of my worst-case scenarios had come true. The tremendous crash that rocked the room and sounded like an explosion was nothing more than a thunderclap. A violent storm had settled over Oakland, catching the city's residents off guard and sending everyone running for cover. According to the report displayed on my screen, the storm had developed in minutes and was the second most violent in the last seventy-five years.

This was a relief because a storm, although violent and dangerous, indicated the city wasn't under attack by the Elend. After witnessing the damage inflicted on the wall protecting Columbus, I couldn't help but wonder what kind of destruction a sufficient number of the creatures could cause if they focused their efforts on a coordinated attack.

Concerns also arose about the Thonian storm approaching Oakland. Although it was said to be eight hours away, the storms were unpredictable. These phenomena had only appeared recently, having never been documented until two years ago. Now, they were sweeping across the landscape with increasing frequency. While they didn't impact human life or vegetation, they wreaked havoc on Wild-Side's technology, exerting an almost vampiric effect on any powered devices. It resembled a mobile version of the dead zones that sporadically dotted the continent.

The walls of the room shook around me, thunder crashed, and the lights flickered out for a few seconds. When the overhead fixtures illuminated once more, Cormac had crouched low, as if the ceiling might collapse at any moment. He glanced at me with a sheepish grin. "I think that one hit somewhere in the city."

I nodded. The storms on Wild-Side were more elemental, reminding me why I initially called this place Wild-Side. The wilderness felt more primal and untamed, the air cleaner and less polluted, and the weather systems shifted and swung unpredictably. It all felt like a fresh, pristine, less worn version of Our-World—a place that could evolve into Our-World if given time and if the right—and maybe wrong—choices were made. If it weren't for the presence of the technologically advanced people and the geography that bore no resemblance to Our-World, I sometimes felt as though this could have been an early prototype for Our-World.

Then again, I suppose that's what Brane theory was all about: worlds upon worlds, upon worlds. But that made me wonder more about the overall premise. If Our-World touched Wild-Side on one side of its Brane—didn't that mean Other-World touched Wild-Side on its other surface? If Brane theory stated that each reality is layered one on top of the next, it implies that each reality is technically exposed to the reality above and below it. So, assuming Our-World is on top of Wild-Side, what is below it? Presumably, that's where the Elend originated. But if that's true, what reality is located above Our-World?

These are the thoughts that occupy my mind while I'm running stairs, specifically the wide, sweeping spiral staircase surrounding the atrium of the city's governance complex. Imagine the Guggenheim, but without any artwork. In this instance, I was ascending from the second sub-level to the fifth floor because it led to a sky bridge that would allow me to bypass the numerous crisscrossing pathways that made up the streets of Oakland.

I reached the top of the stairs and turned onto the open-air walking bridge at a dead sprint. I had left Doc Cormac in my dust. He didn't have my stamina; he didn't have my nano-infused blood, which was super oxygenated and pushing my body at one hundred and fifty percent of standard capacity without breaking a sweat. I did sweat when the gusting air socked me in the side and threatened to send me over the railing. My hip hit the balustrade, and my pace slowed as I took in a concrete-like street four stories below. A gale-force wind slapped me, and I felt my already sodden clothes chilling from the wind assault.

Grinding my teeth, I pressed on. I pushed off the rail and sprinted across the bridge. As I ran, I opened a channel to Cormac. "I'm checking the perimeter," I said. "Meet me at the medical building. Stay off the sky bridges." I cursed under my breath. "They're dangerous."

An update stating that the border observation system had just gone offline due to a near-field lightning strike was part of the alert I received after stepping off the transport platform. Under normal circumstances, that wouldn't be the end of the world. The system was self-healing. It would take at most an hour before the array of cameras atop the perimeter wall would be back online. Still, my first thought was about the strange damage done to the base of the wall at Columbus. It wasn't anything impactful. If anything, the marking struck me as...exploratory.

Oakland was hundreds of miles away from Columbus, so it didn't seem likely that the attack on Columbus was connected to a storm here. Still, the burning in the pit of my gut signaled that my conscious mind was missing something that my lizard brain was picking up on.

Survival in this place meant never ignoring my lizard brain, so seconds later, I sprinted the length of the sky bridge. The perimeter wall was about fifty yards away when another flash of lightning struck so close that I felt the thunder's reverberating impact like a hammer blow to my chest. It was like an explosion, ringing in my ears with an intensity that brought tears to my eyes. In the back of my mind, I envisioned a shaft of liquid energy lancing into my body at my collarbone, spiking through all my organs before it puddled and swirled with the gravitational force of a black hole near my testicles.

Beneath me, every light in the city went dark.

I don't remember stopping my charge toward the wall, but suddenly I found myself standing motionless on rubbery legs. My first few steps were awkward, as if my brain needed to relearn the length of my legs before permitting me to walk, jog, and eventually run. I pressed on with every sense scrambled. The pounding rain around me was muffled, sounding as if my head were wrapped in layers of thick gauze.

A long blink finally restored my night vision. The pain settled into my ears as the muffled sensation was replaced by something sharper. I focused on the path ahead and my clumsiness as I struggled to run. My awkwardness made me wonder why I was limping, so I looked down and saw that my right shoe was missing. Well, not entirely missing. The remnants of the boot were still strapped to my knee just above the ankle. Something stringy and shoelace-like trailed behind me in the rushing water, and it took me a stumbling stride or two to realize it was, indeed, the remains of a bootlace. I stopped and yanked away the meager remnants of my footwear before looking in confusion at my left foot. That boot was still intact, more or less. The heel had been mashed into a flat pulp, and a crack had split the entire instep, exposing my wet sock.

I'll admit to staring at my feet for seconds longer than it should have taken to process the experience, but in my defense, my mind was wandering. It was almost impossible to focus with the piercing ringing in my ears, the almost strobe-like blurring of my vision, and the absurdity of my boots spontaneously disintegrating.

Seconds passed as I tried to make sense of everything. I stood in the driving rain on a bridge in a black void when suddenly, movement in the abyss beyond the wall ten yards ahead caught my attention. The world began to make sense again. I was looking at the open space of no man's land—the hundred or so yards surrounding the base of the wall and separating the city from the encroaching wilderness. Every city on Wild Side had a wall and a similar DMZ, except for Tampa. Tampa was on a peninsula, so the sea protected part of its perimeter.

Christ.

I blinked slowly and realized my mind was a mess. I tipped my head—and felt more than heard—the Doppler shift of the ringing adjust with the movement. Rain streaked down my face, and I smiled. I tipped my head in the other direction. Sure enough, the whomp, whomp, whomp of the ringing sounded like a boomerang whirling around my head at high speed.

"That's kinda cool," I mumbled.

Then, I heard a splash in the mud not far beyond the base of the wall. It was only audible due to my heightened senses, but the fact that I heard it at all was unusual. My senses had never been this acute. I turned toward the sound but only saw the streak of a large shadow as something reached the distant tree line. Another splash echoed in the mud as another shadow moved somewhere far to my right.

I took a deep breath and leaned against the rail, focusing my attention beyond the ringing in my ears to what I was starting to recognize as the sound of blood running through them. A flicker across my AR lens indicated my HUD was coming back online, and I wondered—unfortunately for the first time—what had caused it to glitch. Glancing at my bare right foot and wiggling my toes in the accumulating puddle, a suspicion began to form. Then I heard a skittering, scraping, rasping sound in the distance. I noted a subtle shift in the shadows at the tree line on the far side of the DMZ just before my HUD began to pulse with contact designations. Small targeting reticules dotted my field of view as my heads-up display instantly switched to combat mode after rebooting. It identified threats beyond the tree line, which, though still not visible to me, had been recognized by my tech's targeting system. I looked slowly one way, then the other.

Nine contacts.

They were spread out roughly sixty yards from left to right, concealed just beyond the forest's edge. There could have been more deeper in the trees, but I didn't think so. If they were massing in larger numbers, I figured they would choose to circle the city rather than stack in columns. They were predators—ambush hunters—not strategizing, hive-minded thinkers. Still, if more than a couple attacked the same wall section, they might inadvertently help one another over the top. I'd been campaigning for gun emplacements every fifty feet around each city wall. Columbus was almost finished placing the guns. Portland had only recently accepted the plan and had just begun fabricating the weapons. They were more than a week away from implementation.

"Doc, can you hear me?" I said quietly into my coms.

"Not really," Cormac's voice replied. "You're distorted and breaking up. Can you speak louder?"

"Negative," I said calmly. "Sound a city-wide alert, now. Everyone to the shelters immediately. The Elend are about to attack in force."

"Gray, you're breaking up," Cormac said. "I thought you said—"

I cut him off but still didn't raise my voice. I just eyed the distant tree line. Blood was already beginning to hyper-oxygenate in my veins and arteries. "I did. I count nine incoming hostiles, but more may be coming from other directions. Get everyone to the shelters, *now.*"

With nine contacts moving in, even the clumsy coordination that characterized the Elend's teamwork made it likely that at least two would get over the wall. I'd warned Cormac about this day. Even if there were only nine of the beasts beyond the wall, it would turn into a bloodbath.

———————

Emergency lights flickered to life below the bridge where I stood. The corridors and boulevards of Oakland were shrouded by the storm's torrential downpour, but the occasional flash of distant lightning brought fleeting moments of clarity. I was tearing off what remained of my left boot when I noticed movement in the street below. Initially, I thought it was one of the city's residents scrambling for cover, but in the brief snapshot my mind captured amid a flash of light, I realized the silhouette I saw was too tall, hunched, and moving too quickly to be Seeley.

I discarded what remained of my last boot and jumped barefoot from the bridge. I wrapped an arm around what might have been a flagpole or an aerial antenna and rode it down to street level while reengaging my comms. "The perimeter has been breached," I informed Doc Cormac. Others may be monitoring the channel by now, but Doc would be spearheading the effort to get the inhabitants of Oakland to the shelters. As for mounting a defense, I knew I was it. While I'd made efforts to organize a semi-effective militia to combat the Elend, that was only established in Portland. Gaining compliance from the Seeley was a slow and laborious process.

"How many?" Doc responded.

How the hell should I know? I kept this thought to myself. "When will sensors be back online?" I said instead.

I could swear I heard the Doc curse. He never swore. I couldn't help but grin; the Doc's big brain was picking up my bad habits. "Five— maybe six minutes. I think there was a lightning strike near the main tower. The primary sensor sent a feedback pulse into all of the tertiary arrays. Everything is coming back—" Then there was a massive electrical spark, followed by what I can only assume was profanity from the Doc in another language. "I'm performing a manual reset on each system one at a time. It must have been one hell of a lightning bolt."

I looked down at my feet and wiggled my toes again. I was standing in a water stream as it sheeted across the pavement. The toenails on my right foot were stained black. "You're telling me," I muttered.

"I've got everyone within the outer ring," Doc confirmed. "But we never expected that to withstand a concerted attack. I estimate it will be thirteen minutes before everyone has pulled to the core."

The inner barrier was the ultimate goal in this situation, particularly given the absence of perimeter guns. If they had chosen to implement the guns along with the sensors I had been recommending for the past three months, the likelihood of the Elend breaching the wall would have been nonexistent. At the very least, the guns would have provided crucial time for everyone to reach the shelters beyond the inner barrier.

I was listening and watching, but amidst the flashes of lightning and the white noise of the relentless, ever-present pounding of rain striking every surface around me, it was far more likely that any Elend in the city would find me before I could find them. I could wait at the nearest access point to the outer barrier, but doing so might unintentionally lead the enemy to the Seeley. There was no sense in making the attack any easier than necessary. If the Elend breached the wall, it would only happen if one managed to climb atop another, and then another atop that. Since the creatures didn't engage in team-building exercises—at least in my limited experience with them—for a beast to breach the wall would occur more or less by accident. The mad scramble when the nine attacked the wall at once would result in a pileup.

If I was right, it meant that at most only two or three could get over the wall—and that would only happen through sheer misfortune. If I was lucky, none would get through. Yet I was almost certain I had seen one of the creatures already stalking the streets.

Or my mind had been playing tricks on me.

A guttural screech pierced the white noise of the rain, and I spun just in time to be struck by a crushing tackle. Gaping, razor-toothed jaws snapped shut repeatedly, just inches from my face. I twisted at the hip as I was thrown backward. I felt my head hit the pavement, and I saw stars. My forearm intercepted the creature's biting lunge at my face, bracing just below my jaw to prevent contact. The thumb of my free right hand immediately went for its eye. The snapping at my face paused, but I was already delivering three right hooks to its head.

Time seemed to slow. The creature howled and rolled off me. I knew its claws would be part of the next strike. With one eye gone, it would be in pain, triggering a hardwired, primitive response to lash out as it tried to assess the damage to its face. Sure enough, a massive taloned hand swung at me from my right. I saw it coming as if in slow motion. Three razor-sharp claws, hooked and lethal-looking, were primed to take my head off.

A heartbeat later, the creature stood motionless. I watched its massive chest heaving as it inhaled and exhaled. The beast seemed to shudder as if in pain. I looked to my left to see that it had swung a taloned claw at me while I'd been focused on the attack from my right. To my own shock and amazement, I'd caught the center-most talon, the largest of the three, and simply grappled it in the palm of my left hand. The swing had never come within a foot and a half of hitting me... though I'd never consciously recognized the swing.

Even more surprising, when I searched for the attack I had seen coming from my right, the centermost talon from that paw had been torn from the beast. It was in the palm of my right hand, pointed down like an eighteen-inch curved ice pick, though now it protruded from the creature's remaining eye socket.

Since the thumb to the eye didn't kill the monster, I knew the talon had to go deeper.

I heard a squish and a pop, so I quickly pushed the teetering corpse away and watched it splash into a collecting puddle of rainwater runoff. I held both palms up to the pale emergency lighting that had flickered to life in the alley only moments ago. The rain pounded my hands and quickly washed away what I could only assume was my blood mixed with the foul odor of the Elend. A deep rent marked the palm of each hand, a trade-off for grappling with talons that were themselves razor-sharp. But then, before my eyes, I saw the wide lacerations on my hands seal themselves.

The technology in my blood contributed to faster healing and a boosted immune system, but I had never seen it do anything like this before.

———————

I was still staring at my hands when the Doc's voice came over the com channel. "Gray, do you read? Three Elend have breached the wall—ahh, um—but one just disappeared from the grid, so maybe that information isn't as accurate as I thought…" His voice trailed off into what I could only assume was a man much smarter than me now talking to himself. Undoubtedly, my bad habits were rubbing off on the people of Wild-Side.

I looked at the serrated talon still in the palm of my right hand and blinked the falling rain from my eyes. I observed the four hundred-pound corpse at my feet and took a calming breath. I eyed my surroundings and opened the channel. "The bogey you lost—was it near Secure Two?"

When the Doc came back, it was with an uncharacteristic "…duh—how did you know?"

I grinned and shoved the claw into the cargo pocket on the leg of my pants, where it was less likely to do harm. Even there, I worried it might flay my leg. Still, I wasn't entirely sure how I'd vanquished the Elend, and the recent blank spots in my memory were deeply concerning. I eyed my bare feet, now ankle-deep in the still accumulating rainwater, and then glanced at the palms of my empty hands. The pair of lacerations was seconds away from disappearing entirely, the talon in my pocket the only evidence that my experience had been anything more than imagined.

"Forget about that one," I said after a hard swallow. I was already looking forward to the stiff drink that would be waiting when—if—I survived the night. I didn't know how I was going to explain this to the Doc. "Vector me to the next contact and let me know when everyone is secure."

The Doc stammered. "Gray, maybe you didn't receive my last message. Everyone has reached the inner marker. It's safe to fall back now. If you can reach one of the portals, we're standing by to bring you through. You've bought enough time. You're the last to arrive."

I blinked and took inventory of my body. My internal clock must have been scrambled because, at least as far as I could tell, only seconds had passed since the Doc's last update.

"Roger," I said. "The nearest hostile?"

"Almost four blocks to the north," the Doc replied without hesitation. "The fastest route to the barrier is on your HUD now."

The corner of my heads-up display lit with an overlay of the surrounding city blocks. Two red dots indicated the locations of the Elend that had breached the wall, each hundreds of yards from my current location and moving without any discernible purpose. They were hunting for targets of opportunity that were no longer available. A dotted line appeared on the display, indicating the path I needed to follow to reach the first bulkhead separating me from the outer barrier.

––––––––––

Hours had passed, and I lay on an inclined table in a dimly lit room. The residents of Oakland had been teleported from the bunkers beneath the city to those under Portland. Although this wasn't ideal for the inhabitants of Oakland, once Doc Cormac had a chance to explain that the perimeter walls had been breached, people became much more understanding of the last-minute migration. Sponsors in Portland acted as hosts for those besieged and made accommodations for the newcomers. From what I'd heard, everyone was making the most of the situation. According to the Doc, the people of Oakland were suddenly overwhelmingly supportive of my proposal to place gun turrets atop the perimeter wall. This topic had been debated since its inception and was only now being seen as a wise precautionary measure.

I laughed. "Like they could argue the point now?" I said to the Doc.

He shrugged. "You knew our people were different from yours. Yours have guns in every home across the land. It was always going to be an uphill battle."

I rolled my eyes. "That's not quite how it is back home," I admitted. "But when faced with a hostile force that wants to eviscerate their bodies, I think the people of my Brane will gather a little faster than the folks on Wild-Side. They don't need to see the fangs and talons of the creatures up close before they're ready to go to guns."

The Doc shook his head. "We still don't know exactly what happens to those who have disappeared. At least you finally have support for your position." He tapped the glass display, and the AR screen on the wall sprang to life, revealing the perimeter wall around a city. The name Portland floated in a tag above the city. "The guns will be in place before morning," he said. "And while we've lost, Oakland, at least for the moment, the armament will be assembled on site here and put atop the perimeter wall as soon as you've cleared the city.

I took a deep breath and tried not to react. I'd warned the people of Oakland that the attack was coming, but they wouldn't listen. Now that it had arrived, they still looked to me for confirmation that it was safe to return to the city. They had technology for this, of course, but now they were finally willing to take me at my word.

"Fine," I said. The concept of *better late than never* came to mind when it came to their support. "At least tell me they're willing to communicate this point of view to the remaining cities?"

Cormac grinned. "Already done. As you say, I ensured they had no wiggle room on that point. They can't expect you to touch their asses after this mess, after all."

My eyes were already rolling. "It's *wipe their asses*, but close enough." I was laughing. The euphemisms of Our-World continued to elude the Doc.

"Back to my test results," I said to the Doc. "Any idea what happened?"

Doc Cormac nodded. "Absolutely," he replied. He tapped the panel before him, and the AR display projected on the wall switched to a cutaway view of a human skull. "This is your brain," he said. With another tap, the view appeared to zoom in, revealing a cellular perspective. The tissue was blue, magnified to the point where individual cells became visible. Tiny gray blips crossed the image, some moving slowly and deliberately while others darted quickly from one side of the frame to vanish on the other.

"The silver particles are nanites," Doc continued. "This is a random sample of your brain tissue, but any section we capture will appear the same based on my observations over the past twenty minutes."

I watched but didn't understand. The slowest of the gray, or silver, nanites moved too quickly for me to discern their shape, let alone what they were doing. As for the fastest? I'm not sure I perceived them as anything more than a vague blur in the image.

"Can you slow this down?" I said. "I don't understand what I'm seeing."

Doc Cormac appeared uneasy. "I've slowed the footage down," he stated. "I'm recalibrating the equipment for the next test, but your tech is operating at an unprecedented speed. To be blunt, I've never seen anything like it before."

I don't often find myself at a loss for words, but as I watched the footage on the screen, I was speechless. It wasn't so much the speed at which everything was moving; it was the fact that the leading expert in the technology was astonished and troubled by what he observed.

By that point, I had learned how to draw answers from the man. It wasn't the first time I'd seen him struggle with the unexplained. "Supposition?" I asked. "Forget what's possible. What's your first guess based on what you see?"

Cormac seemed to chew on that for a few long seconds, at least mentally. This was significant because his mind operated at speeds exponentially faster than mine. I knew this wasn't the first time he'd creatively considered this question. After working with me for over a year, thinking outside the box had become a standard operating procedure. It was necessary for survival at this point.

"If I had to speculate," Cormac said, "I would say something supercharged the nano-lattice matrix in your blood and brain. Both would be necessary to prevent your body from losing phase and slipping into shock." He shook his head slowly as he contemplated the conjecture. "But I don't see how that could be possible. We're discussing a degree of overclocking that would require years of research and development. I doubt human biology could survive such an experience."

"Assume I'd been struck by lightning," I said slowly. "What does that do to your hypothetical model?"

Cormac looked confused for a beat, then stared at me with a slack-jawed expression. He examined me from head to toe while sitting on the edge of the gurney, my feet dangling a foot and a half above the cold composite floor. He pulled the glasses from his face but continued to stare. His gaze shifted to my bare feet. The toes on my right foot were no longer black as they had been, but he had seen them before they returned to normal.

Perhaps twenty seconds passed before his gaze shifted to the glass control console he'd used to manage the AR display on the wall. He looked at me, then at the console, and then back at me. "The strike that took out Oakland's grid…" he said in a quiet, distant voice. "It didn't hit the tower…" He approached the console and began tapping on the glass. Whatever he was doing was visible only in his AR display. Finally, he looked up at me. "The strike didn't hit the grounding tower," he stated. "That's why it took out the grid. The focal point of the blast was two-thirds of the way along the sky bridge. It hit you directly—I have footage of the strike…"

I rolled my head on my shoulders, producing an audible series of pops. Thankfully, this relieved the headache building at the base of my skull.

The Doc glanced back at the shared AR display, where silver-gray blurs darted across the screen. "I don't know how you survived a strike that disabled the city grid," he muttered.

I grinned and slipped a hand into the pocket at my left knee. I dropped the eighteen-inch-long talon onto the semi-inclined glass console in front of Cormac. "You're not the only one."

Chapter 10 - A Grown Man's Piggyback Ride

Our-World

Shelter Cove Marina

Shelter Spring, North Carolina

20 months ago

"He said it was this way," Gina Hallstrom said, threading her way down the boardwalk. "Supposedly, we'll know it when we see it."

Gina wore cut-off denim shorts and a blue string bikini top. Her hair was pulled back beneath a black baseball cap, and her sunglasses rested above the bill of the cap as she scanned the edge of the dock for the boat they intended to board. She adjusted the strap of the small daypack slung over one shoulder while spinning in a slow circle. Frustrated, she waved to Piper and Allison with a "move your ass" gesture.

"She's really excited about this boat," Allison grumbled.

Piper laughed. "I knew that when she was up and out of bed at 7am on a Saturday. I don't understand why. It's just a boat."

The sky was clear, and the sun was already well above the horizon, as it was nearly nine in the morning. The weather forecast predicted highs in the mid-90s, promising an incredible day for boating on the Atlantic. Gina was 19 years old, while Allison and Piper were just a couple of months older, having recently turned 20.

"It's not about the boat," Allison clarified, as they both struggled to keep sight of Gina while she turned the corner and headed onto one of the many wide wooden docks lined with pleasure craft of every shape and size. "It's about a boy."

Piper rolled her eyes. "Ya think?"

"Slow down," a voice called from behind them. A big, stone block of a kid was struggling to keep up, heavily burdened with baggage. Overloaded backpacks hung from each shoulder, a massive cooler was pinched between his meaty paws, and a bulging duffle bag thudded against his hip with every hurried step he took. "We all know what Gina's interested in," he wheezed. "But I heard about the boat—and I don't want to miss it."

Jimmy Kell was the same age as the girls, but that's where the similarities ended. While each of the ladies was petite and feminine, Jimmy looked as though he'd been carved from a block of granite with a dull chisel. He stood six feet two inches tall and weighed two hundred forty pounds, every ounce of it hard-won in the gym or on the football field. His head was all flat planes and hard angles, resembling one of the Easter Island statues brought to life.

Piper knew he wanted to see the boat, but also understood he was looking to spend time with Allison. The lug had been crushing on her since they met at a study group six months earlier. Since that day, he'd never missed an opportunity to spend even a little extra time with her. Unfortunately, Allison was oblivious, and Jimmy might let them all die of old age before he finally made his move.

Piper saw Gina stop and wave both arms at someone out of her line of sight. Gina was about forty yards ahead of them on the dock. "Hang in there, Jimmy. I think we found our ride."

Doubling back, Piper grabbed the duffle bag from Jimmy. It was large and overstuffed. Something hard inside was poking her, so she was glad she had chosen to wear an insulated long-sleeved pullover for the drive to the coast. If she had been dressed like Gina and Allison, who had already changed into their bikini tops, her ribs would have been destroyed when they arrived.

"Jimmy," she winced. "What the hell is in the bag? I'm going to break a rib!"

"Sorry about that. Want me to take it again? It's a couple of parts that Levi needed for the yacht. I picked them up last night and told him I would bring them by when we came this morning."

She shook her head and mumbled that she had it. If Jimmy could carry the bag and the rest of their crap, the least she could do was lug the duffel the last couple dozen yards. Her foot caught on an uneven board on the deck, and she stumbled. Struggling to maintain her balance, she questioned the wisdom of her choice.

The group had become good friends over the past six or seven months. Most of them had classes together. Allison was studying sociology while Jimmy was taking an advanced structural engineering class. He looked like some kind of meathead jock, but he was sharp and much more intelligent than he let on. She couldn't help but wonder what would happen if he ever caught Allison's eye. They could make a cute couple, even if seeing them together was amusing. She was a fraction of his size, and the thought of the two of them together… she really didn't want to contemplate that.

Gina was in a class of her own—almost literally. She had changed her major twice in the past six months, which technically shouldn't have been possible. From what Piper understood, this wasn't unusual. Gina was a free spirit, and she tended to follow her passions.

That was what led them to the dock and in search of the aforementioned boat. Gina had been *seeing* a guy named Levi Hyde for a while. And by seeing, in Gina's words, that meant Levi had felt her up in the hallway of a Starbucks and finger-banged her in the parking lot outside her apartment. As she put it, they were taking it slow.

Gina was the freest of free spirit.

But apparently, Levi worked on boats—not just any boats, but yachts. That's why they were on the docks on a Saturday morning. He was putting the finishing touches on a salvaged boat that his employers would auction in a couple of months. Given all the recently completed work, it was necessary to take the craft out on open waters for what Levi called a shakedown voyage. They needed to see how the systems performed and log any glitches.

Levi told Gina to invite some friends so they could make a day of it.

Piper wasn't convinced. A sketchy watercraft on the open seas wasn't her idea of a productive afternoon. But as Allison and Gina had pointed out in nauseating detail, Piper wasn't one to throw caution to the wind. And while this was hardly a Girls Gone Wild scenario, it might at least challenge her comfort zone.

So, Piper relented and wondered what kind of rust-bucket Levi would take them for a ride on.

As they walked down the dock, Piper was surprised by how many people were out so early in the morning. Looking more closely, she realized this was something different. Stanchions had been arranged nearby, seemingly reserving a section of the dock for something special. The cordoned-off space was empty so far, and oddly dressed individuals were already gathering before the unusually open series of slips that normally accommodated watercraft. Most onlookers wore ties and dress shirts–business casual attire–who seemed to have shed their sport coats in concession to the already eighty-degree weather.

What's with the press?

Gina seemed oblivious to the spectacle, simply turning down the next walkway suspended over the bay and continuing on. Before Piper knew it, Gina was walking up the wide plank to a boat. Piper froze in mid-step. The boat had to be close to seventy feet long. It had a flawless, gleaming white hull. Polished silver railings lined the forward decks, and mirrored windows shaded the cabins of the main deck.

"Holy shit," Jimmy mumbled as he stopped beside Piper. "I'd give Levi a handjob for a ride on that thing, too." Piper elbowed him in the ribs. Jimmy just shrugged and headed for the boarding ramp. "Well, it is Gina, after all," he mumbled.

The guy at the table had his attention focused on the paperback in his hands. His feet were propped up on the spare chair beside him at the four-top. Piper noticed his sandwich was only half-eaten, but his drink was nearly empty. Iced tea, if she had to guess. The book was well-worn. It could have been secondhand, but she suspected this wasn't his first time reading it. There was something about how he held the old book that suggested an attachment.

Piper was never good at starting a conversation, so when she approached the table, she blurted out, "I love that series; what do you think of it?"

The boy looked up at her and smiled. He shifted his feet off the chair and moved the ball cap from low on his brow, where it had been blocking the early morning sun. "Sorry? What was that?"

She pointed at the book in his hand. "It's one of my favorites. I really love the series. I was curious what you thought of it."

His grin turned sheepish, almost embarrassed. He took a long moment to look at her, but she noticed that his gaze never left her eyes. His was an odd shade of gray, almost silver. They seemed to glow when he looked at her. The focus of his attention sent a chill up and down her arms. It was neither familiar nor unwelcome. After what felt like a long time, he held the book up in a modest show. "The binding's pretty much shot," he said. "This might be my sixth or seventh time through it."

She felt her brows arch at the admission and saw him cringe.

"I know," he said. "Scary, right?"

She laughed and dropped into the chair his feet had occupied only a minute earlier. "Hardly," she chuckled. "I've read the entire series at least as many times. I'm crazy about the characters."

Piper realized she had just invited herself to his table, and her face must have shown it. A rush of embarrassment washed over her, and she began to stand up.

The boy half rose before she could. "No, please," he insisted. "I was going to ask you to sit, but I didn't want to seem creepy. A pretty girl wanting to talk about a book would make geeks come running from their mothers' basements at the whiff of the rumor. I just didn't want to press my luck."

She laughed—well, snorted, more accurately. The sound was embarrassing, which made her laugh again, instantly breaking the tension.

"In all seriousness," she said, her face still flushed, "I've been a fan of Alastair Rose since his first book. My friend Reese actually met him."

The boy seemed confused by this. "Are you sure about that? I read he's never been identified. There's a bounty or something, payable to anyone who can find the man behind the novels. I thought his publisher claimed never to have met him."

Piper hesitated. She nodded and remained silent for several long seconds. Glancing over her shoulder, she suddenly had the impression that the walls were listening.

"What's wrong?" The boy asked. He leaned closer, concern clouding his countenance.

Piper took a deep breath, her expression dour. "I shouldn't even be talking about this, and you're not going to believe me anyway— just some girl who walks up to you...Reese sort of proved it to me. Obviously, Alastair is a pen name, right? It's the reason he's gone unidentified for so long."

The boy nodded.

"Well, it turns out he writes other books under a different name and in a different genre. I've read those books. All of them. There's no doubt in my mind it's the same author... and no one has made the connection. She must be telling the truth."

To his credit, the boy looked intrigued. "What genre?"

She grinned. "Romance."

His mouth dropped open. Seconds went by, and she could see him sorting through what likely amounted to a dozen different questions. "You're sure?" was all he eventually asked.

Piper nodded, a proud, satisfied grin stretching wide across her face. She could tell she had made him a believer. For some reason, that had brightened her day.

"And...they're good?" He still looked skeptical.

She nodded again, perhaps a bit more enthusiastically than was appropriate for the conversation.

He took another few seconds to consider this. "What's the pen name?"

Oh.

All of her enthusiasm waned, and she sagged visibly. "Um…I can't say."

"What? Why not?" He looked more confused than hurt.

Piper rocked her head back and forth as she considered her words. "No one knows this. The connection hasn't been made. If I tell you, the cat's out of the bag on a really big secret." She took a deep breath and observed him for any sign of irritation, but all she saw was amusement. "It's not my secret to share. Does that make sense?"

He nodded, and instead of being disappointed by the reply, he appeared somehow fortified by it. "I never introduced myself. My name is Grady Ledger. My friends call me Gray."

She shook his hand. "Piper Hudson."

Piper heard her name being called from down the dock, a reminder of her purpose for being there. She opened her mouth to speak, but Gray spoke first.

"You say his romance books are good," Gray said with what she judged as a hint of reluctance.

She nodded.

"I've never really been sure what that means."

Her face scrunched. "It's good writing. Every bit as good as his sci-fi. It's just, you know, different."

"No," Gray said. "I understand that. You're touching on something that has always confused me about people's opinions and how they evaluate different genres. It seems like each one has different expectations, and therefore a different rating scale."

Piper didn't follow at first, but when she began to consider it, she realized how that could be true. Even so, she still didn't understand where he was heading.

"Alastair Rose serves as a great example. I know what to expect from his sci-fi, and I love it. His writing is strong in the sci-fi genre, but what defines good writing in other genres? Does it vary based on expectations, and can one author be considered a good writer across all genres if they maintain the same style? Or does it rely more on the expectations of the genre than on the quality of writing?"

"You lost me."

He shrugged. "It's okay. I really shouldn't be asking this. It's just been bothering me for years, and I never found anyone I thought could provide insight."

Piper was curious. "Try me."

Gray took a deep breath. "I know what I expect from quality sci-fi," he explained. "I want an exciting adventure, but I also crave creative fiction that pushes the limits of my reality. I'm looking for something that takes me out of the every day and gives me some science or technology that expands what I see in the real world. Laser guns, aliens, spaceships, teleportation—it doesn't matter. Just give me something fascinating that makes me think.

"Thrillers are the same way. The expectation is for action, adventure, and people in dangerous situations—perilous scenarios that have nothing to do with our everyday lives. Readers want something that thrills and captivates them, something that immerses them in a different place or time."

Piper nodded. "Sure. Makes sense."

"Well, if a writer can deliver on those points and do so with writing that is logical and not clumsy, they can be considered a good writer—both because they can string together words and because they meet the expectations of the genre."

Piper nodded.

"So what makes a good romance author? Are they writing to give the reader a tingly little thrill, or are they really only ringing the best seller bell if half their readers are touching themselves by the end of the chapter?"

Piper erupted in a racking, teary-eyed laugh that left her doubled over and gasping for breath.

It was minutes before she regained her composure. For Gray, this seemed like a genuine question, although he appeared satisfied with her answer.

"I'm guessing you haven't asked that question at your book club before, have you?" Piper finally asked as she wiped the tears from her eyes.

He shrugged. "As much as I want to know, I'm kind of afraid of the answer." He leaned in close but didn't invade her personal space. Then he whispered in a mock conspiratorial tone, "But if you have an opinion, feel free to tell me all about it."

She laughed again. Her face was still red from earlier; she was certain of it. Her name was called from behind her, this time more forcefully and from close by.

Rolling her eyes, Piper said, "Let me think about it." She pointed over her shoulder with her thumb. "My friends are being less than subtle. The boat's ready, and they want to head out."

Gray nodded and offered his hand. "Fair enough. It was great meeting you. If you get—"

"Actually," Piper interrupted. "It's a big boat, and there's room for one more…you know, if you feel like going for a ride?"

An odd expression crossed Gray's face as he glanced down at the table for a brief second. His gaze swept over the pier, scanned the water, and then the shore as if he were searching for something. She followed his line of sight but had no idea what he was contemplating. When she looked back, he was looking into her eyes. "Sounds fantastic. Count me in."

She observed a section of the beach about half a mile away, where some kind of commotion was taking place. It was difficult to discern from her vantage point, but it appeared that a perimeter of some sort had been set up, possibly with police tape. Individuals in uniforms and suit jackets were moving purposefully across the sand. It seemed that temporary structures were being put up. They were tents, but quite elaborate and sturdy—not the type of gear that campers or beachgoers would typically use.

"Didn't some kind of electrical storm hit the beach last night?" Piper asked as she watched Gray lay a twenty-dollar bill on top of his receipt and then secure it with what was left of his drink.

Gray nodded. "I slept through it, but it's all anyone's talking about." He tilted his head toward the circus along the beach. "I guess there were multiple lightning strikes. No one was injured, but the strikes did some interesting things to the sand. Someone mentioned there was something unusual about it all, so an investigative team is coming from a government agency."

She raised an eyebrow. "And all of that doesn't make you curious? Isn't it worth taking a closer look?"

He grinned. "That was the plan until you made me a better offer." Pointing to the gathering press several dozen yards down the boardwalk, he said, "Unless whatever this is keeps your boat from setting sail. Is this related to that thing down the beach?"

Piper shook her head. "Someone said there's a naval recovery team arriving any minute. It's a World War II salvage operation involving the Navy or Coast Guard and the university. It was all very hush-hush until the press release yesterday. I guess they're bringing the recovered vessel into port this morning. Apparently, a Nazi submarine making landfall in the U.S. is significant news, even so many years after it set sail."

A look of concern briefly crossed Gray's face. Piper was unsure whether it stemmed from the mention of the Nazi derelict or the spectacle being created.

"Come on," she said. "Let me introduce you to my friends."

The press event delayed them by another fifty minutes. The docks were more crowded than Piper had ever seen. They watched as the submarine was pulled into the bay and then the marina, with surprising efficiency. Fearing further delays, Levi ushered everyone aboard and quickly set sail. From the start, Levi took his role as captain seriously, directing Jimmy and Gray on how to cast off the moorings. Fifteen minutes after clearing the cove, they were officially in the open waters of the Atlantic. As promised, the seas were calm and the skies were clear.

Piper was relieved to see that Levi was every bit the captain Gina had promised. He seemed to know every inch of the ship and could control it with precision. Most impressive of all, the goofball demeanor he displayed when hanging out with the group was nowhere to be seen when he was at the wheel of the yacht.

Once they reached open waters, the frenetic pace of their departure settled, and everyone prepared for recreation. Chairs were pulled from storage cabinets, and a large table was set up on the stern deck. Since the girls had mentioned sunbathing, they laid out padded mats along the rail of the stern in preparation. Piper watched Jimmy, Levi, and Gray as they arranged the teak furniture and marveled at how Gray had managed to fit in with the guys in less than an hour. The quiet guy from the dock was already revealing many facets of his personality. It made her wonder what else there might be to explore.

"Allison found my bag," Gina said. Someone put it in the wrong room. "Come on. I'll show you what I've got."

Piper looked again at the guys working on the stern deck, then at the water flowing by the starboard rail. "Should I be worried that Levi isn't at the wheel? He's assembling chairs. He's not even paying attention to where we're going."

Gina laughed. "It's some kind of autopilot radar…thing. He tried to explain it to me, but all I wanted was to suck on his tongue. I guess I wasn't paying attention."

Piper rolled her eyes and laughed as she followed her friend through the ship's narrow corridors. "Just make sure Levi's priority is to drive. You convinced me to take this trip, and our lives are in his hands. What did he call this trip? A shakedown? He mentioned he's looking for issues with the boat. That's not exactly reassuring, if you ask me."

Gina turned a corner into a cabin and found a pair of bags on a king-size bed. Both bags were unzipped, presumably by Allison when she had been trying to sort out the mix-up with the bags while Piper worked through her wardrobe indecision.

Like Allison and Gina, Piper had dressed for the beach before leaving home. However, unlike her friends, she felt less enthusiastic about the outing. While the girls had left their apartment ready for the sun in shorts and bikini tops, Piper had opted for a more conservative look, wearing shorts and a school hoodie over her swimsuit.

She was now grinding her teeth in frustration but didn't know if it was due to the morning's choice of conservative swimwear or her uncharacteristic desire to change it. The shorts and the hoodie weren't the issue. It was the one-piece suit she had picked when she wasn't interested in impressing anyone on her day at the beach.

But an hour after meeting Gray, she felt significantly bolder. It was an exhilarating experience that terrified her.

"I still don't know why you brought more than one suit," Piper said.

Gina turned to her with an expression of determination that seemed entirely out of place on the young woman's face. "Don't get upset," she said. "Allison and I talked. We thought that if we were having fun, we might stay out here all weekend."

"All weekend! I wouldn't have come if you told me that!"

Gina giggled while holding up an outfit in each hand. "And now you can thank me because I haven't seen you smile like this in...forever. You're already having the time of your life, and if you choose one of these little beauties and ditch your old lady gear, I have a feeling your good time is only going to get better."

Piper glanced at the disturbingly small patches of fabric in Gina's raised hands and felt her cheeks flush. It had seemed like a better idea when it was merely a temptation lurking in the back of her mind.

"Oh, cheer up," Gina giggled. "You've got a banging body. God forbid you show it off. It's just one boat ride with a guy you're already making googly eyes at. If it doesn't work out, we can call it a day after a quick run up and down the coast. If things are going well, we let it ride until tonight. If things are going really good, you let him bang your brains out and have the weekend of your life!"

Piper let out a heavy sigh and dropped onto the foot of the bed. "That's not me," she groaned. "I'm not built that way."

Flopping beside her, Gina draped an arm over Piper's shoulder and hugged her awkwardly. "Fine, banging your brains out is optional. But you should seriously consider my advice. "You think I'm too casual about these things… and maybe you're right. But I can say one thing with absolute certainty: no one ever went to their deathbed satisfied that they avoided every possible thrill and kept their chastity belt fastened and locked until the end of the ride. You need to live a little." She shook Piper by the shoulders. "For the love of God, cut loose! It won't kill you!"

Piper hung her head. She took a long, deep breath and blew it out with a sigh. "Fine. Get out. I'm changing."

"Cool!" Gina hopped to her feet and pranced to the door. There she stopped with the exit half closed and shot a look back at Piper. "And when you say you're changing, are we talking about your clothes or your mindset?"

"Out!"

———————

Everyone was gathered around a rectangular table that sat beneath a shaded canopy on the raised stern deck by the time Piper returned from her cabin. Some kind of card game was in progress. The boat was moving at a mild clip, and a comfortable, gentle cross breeze kept the heat of the 90-odd degrees early afternoon sun at bay. She was surprised by two things. The first was that the cards on the table weren't being blown all over the place by the wind. Then she noticed that the surface of the table was coated in metal. The cards seemed magnetic because every time someone dropped a card, it adhered to the table with an almost adhesive quality.

The second thing she found curious was that everyone on the boat was gathered at the table. There was nothing wrong with that, except that the boat was moving. Clearly, no one was at the wheel. Gina had explained that luxury boats like this one had sophisticated automatic navigation systems, but she found reliance on them disconcerting, particularly if they were out here for a shakedown cruise–essentially just zipping around to ensure all the onboard systems worked as intended.

What if there were a problem with the auto-navigation system? Would they discover it before crashing into something? Levi always struck her as too impulsive to be responsible for anyone's life...let alone everyone's.

Piper was trying to decide how to tactfully express her concerns when the boisterous conversation around the table suddenly stopped and the eyes of Gray, Allison, Levi, Gina, and Jimmy all turned to her and stared. The sudden focus of attention caused Piper to freeze mid-step.

"What's wrong?" she asked, her voice tight with concern.

Gina was the first to break the silence when she laughed. "I think you picked the right one."

Piper wore a white string bikini top and bottom, her hair down and a beach towel draped over one shoulder. She had felt self-conscious about her choice when she left the cabin but ultimately decided that Gina's carefree attitude toward such matters was worth experimenting with, at least this once. It wasn't as if she was jumping out of an airplane or anything. There was nothing death-defying in her attempt to push the limits of her comfort zone. She merely fought the bile churning in her stomach and forged ahead.

However, the confusion of seeing the captain of the boat playing cards and wondering why the cards were not blowing in the breeze had managed to distract her. Now, the stares brought her situational awareness crashing back to the forefront of her consciousness, and she froze in her tracks.

"Damn, girl!" Levi exclaimed. "Why in the hell would you hide a body like that under a sweatshirt all day?" There was an amused, flirty Southern twang that seemed to color his voice when he neglected to engage his verbal filter. The goofy grin on his face didn't falter as he jumped from his chair to pull a spare one out for Piper. "I saved a seat for you right here."

Levi's lack of subtlety elicited chuckles from everyone at the table, except for Gina, who responded by punching him just above the knee. The strike must have been as aggressive as it appeared because his leg buckled, and he had to catch his weight by bracing himself on the back of his own chair.

"Oh, sorry, honey," Gina said with a tone thick with mock sweetness. "You're such a klutz. Let me help you with that." She pushed Levi back into his chair with an exaggerated roll of her eyes. "Pretty sure Piper would prefer sitting with Gray, don't you think?"

Laughter erupted around the table. The break in tension also shattered some kind of barrier in Piper, allowing her to move again. She saw Gray pull an empty chair closer and nod his head toward it with a smile that eased her anxiety even more. Piper took a cautious step forward and found herself moving on unsteady legs. She hadn't experienced a panic attack since her early teens but felt on the verge of one.

Allison must have sensed it, because she was at her side in an instant. She slipped an arm around Piper's waist and playfully slapped a hand on Piper's bare hip while giggling. "We're burning that one piece you like to wear," she said. "Honey, with your body, you were born to wear this. I'm never letting you go back."

Unsure of how to respond, Piper simply said, "It's Gina's. I'm not sure it fits me quite right."

Allison guided Piper around the table as they headed for the spot beside Gray. Piper was a little narrower in the hips, slightly larger in the bust, and several inches taller than Gina, but there wasn't enough to the outfit to make much of a difference. "I'm going to tell you something that Gina has already realized," Allison whispered as they drew closer to the group. "This looks better on you than it did on her." She winked, gave Piper a pinch, and then moved past her to resume her circuit of the table alone as she returned to her seat.

Gray stood, holding the chair for Piper. The chivalrous gesture made her cheeks turn pink, and she whispered a thank you. Gray dropped into his chair but seemed to take an extra second to study her eyes. He offered a smile that seemed to convey understanding. Then he turned back to the table. "We didn't complete that deal yet, so why not start over and deal Piper into the game?"

And just like that, attention shifted away from Piper and back onto the game. It took only seconds for the conversation to resume, and it seemed like everyone was laughing and talking at once. Piper reached over and gave Gray's hand a squeeze. No words were spoken, but she was confident he understood her appreciation.

―――――――

They had been playing cards for a couple of hours, and the boat was on the southern leg of the coastal cruise when Levi started paying more attention to the tablet he kept standing vertically at his end of the table. The screen allowed him to monitor the ship's course, radar, and even displayed a video feed from the pilot's station on the bridge. Once she saw the technology Levi was using to track the ship's navigation while he socialized with his guests, she felt much more comfortable with the day trip. After Gina explained that the tall, thin mojito glass Levi was constantly sipping from was alcohol-free, she became more confident that he was taking his responsibility as Captain seriously. The glass, Gina explained, contained water flavored with mint. Nothing more.

The first signs of trouble surfaced when Levi began to focus more on the display of his tablet. He became distracted and was unable to keep up with the game. It started with a furrowing of his brows, but she quickly noticed an overall darkening of his expression.

Piper leaned close to Gray, resting a hand on his knee. He glanced at her and grinned, but his smile faded at the sight of her serious expression. She tilted her head toward Levi and whispered,

"Something's wrong." She had been reluctant to raise the alarm, but whatever was troubling Levi appeared to be escalating quickly.

Piper felt Gray's hand rest atop hers. "I've been watching that too," he whispered back. "Can you see the screen? There's too much glare. He doesn't like something—I just can't figure out what it is."

She shook her head. "We're a long way off the coast. I'm getting nervous."

Gray looked her in the eye. A hint of a smile lifted the corners of his lips as he nodded almost imperceptibly. "I'm on it."

He pushed his chair back and stood slowly. She watched him carefully. There wasn't even a hint of concern in his appearance now, even though she'd seen it in his eyes only a second before. He stood a few feet from the table, seemingly enjoying the ever-present ocean breeze on his bare skin. He was bare-chested, wearing only a pair of cargo shorts that were presumably swim trunks. She had no idea where he'd changed. But he looked calm, comfortable, and completely at ease. He also looked good, she thought—and not for the first time. He was a few inches under six feet, trim, with wide shoulders and solid muscle definition. He was well-built without being over-toned like a swimmer or overdeveloped like a weight lifter. This made her wonder what he did with his time. She'd assumed he was a student but now realized they hadn't talked about that yet.

Gray circled the table and approached Levi. There was something about the way he did it...she couldn't put her finger on it. She knew he was going to check on their wannabe captain, but the way he engaged in the conversation was smooth. The interaction seemed entirely spur of the moment. There was nothing in his approach that would draw anyone's attention at the table. She realized that was the point. Gray was just as concerned about Levi as she was, and he didn't want to involve others in that conversation.

When Gray knelt beside Levi and began speaking to him in hushed tones, the effortless way he had engineered the approach was both skillful and simple, making her smile. Gray was so sensitive and disarming; he must have training in psychology. Was he studying to be a therapist? Either that or a spy, she thought with a chuckle.

Gray was back in five minutes. He dropped into his seat and gazed out toward the mainland, his thoughts seeming a million miles away. She slid her chair conspiratorially closer and touched his bare knee. His attention shifted, and he looked into her eyes. A smile spread across his lips as he glanced down at her hand. "I like it when you do that," he said softly.

She grinned and bit the corner of her lip. Her eyes remained fixed on his, but her hand slipped to the inside of his knee and slid slightly up the inside of his leg. It was the tiniest effort on her part, but she noticed the light dancing in his eyes and the way his chest shuddered ever so slightly at her touch. "Guess you like that too?" she whispered.

He sat back in the chair and took a slow breath as he looked her up and down. "Piper, the slightest touch from you and I'm this close to forgetting what you wanted to know about our predicament." He held his thumb and forefinger a quarter inch apart. "You're kryptonite to my attention span." He leaned in within inches of her ear and whispered, "Are you at all interested in what we can do about that?"

Piper felt her heart race with the warmth of his breath on her ear, and she realized her eyes and breathing likely mirrored the same reactions she had seen in him. Goosebumps tingled up and down her arms. Gray leaned back in his chair. She became increasingly aware of just how little clothing they both wore.

Clearing her throat, Piper said, "Um, does Levi have a problem?"

The two or three seconds Gray spent eyeing her felt like an eternity. Finally, he nodded. "Could be. He says it's too soon to tell, but one of the props is vibrating erratically. He mentioned he slowed us down to half of our previous speed to see if things improve. He's watching and should know more soon."

Gray didn't seem fazed by the change in topics, and Piper felt relieved. She appreciated the flirting and was really enjoying it, but it felt like too much too soon for a boy she had just met on the dock that morning. Her libido was in overdrive, which conflicted with her well-earned sense of self-preservation.

"I don't know anything about boats," she admitted. "Is that

dangerous?"

Gray waved a raised hand in the air. The gesture was frustratingly noncommittal. "Not to us directly. The boat has two propellers that operate in tandem under normal conditions. If there's an issue with one, the other can carry the load and help the ship make it back to the dock for repairs. This seems to be one of the issues that's popping up from the shakedown cruise. For some reason, he can't shut down just one prop. He can run both or shut down both, but he can't operate only one. It's either an electrical issue or a software problem."

"So what can the vibration cause?"

"It's hard to predict. That shaft could blow, and the prop could shear off, creating a hole in the underside of the hull, which would lead to a leak. But in the worst-case scenario, if the vibration is resonating back down the drive shaft to the engine, it could physically damage the engine. If that happens, we would be stranded."

Piper felt her face grow pale and her skin turn cold. She wasn't fond of the water. This trip wasn't an issue as long as they kept the coast in view. When she agreed to come, she hadn't been aware they were planning to take the boat so far out to sea.

Gray took Piper's hand in his. "It's not an emergency," he said in a smooth, soothing tone. "We have a radio and the ability to call for help whenever we need to. There's no problem we can't solve right now, and there's no need to send out an SOS."

———

The yacht had been stopped for almost twenty minutes, and Levi had explained the situation to everyone. One of the props was out of balance, sending vibrations throughout the engine. If they continued to operate as they had, the imbalance would worsen and likely lead to substantial engine damage.

Levi had even gone overboard to inspect the prop for himself. The imbalance wasn't enough to be obvious to the naked eye, but he had enough diagnostic data to be certain which of the two props was causing the issue. He even had a spare part on board. The only problem was that he didn't have the dive gear required to stay submerged long enough to perform the relatively simple task of removing the series of bolts responsible for keeping the prop in place.

"We'll have to call the Coast Guard and get towed back to port," Levi concluded his summary of their current problem. "We either need diving gear, or we need to put the boat in dry dock. Unfortunately, we're not in a position for either."

As the group processed the end of their day filled with fun in the sun, there was some grumbling, but Piper was impressed that no one directed their disappointment or anger at Levi. They had all signed up for this cruise and received what they had been warned might happen.

"Quick question," Gray said over the general grumble of the collected group. He was looking at Levi, who stood along the portside rail with his hands jammed deep in the pockets of his shorts, looking as dejected as Piper had ever seen the young man.

Levi nodded for Gray to continue.

"You said you have a spare prop onboard. Does that mean you also have the tools to make the swap?"

Levi nodded again.

"So we don't need a tow from the Coast Guard as much as we need someone—anyone—with scuba gear to help us swap out the prop ourselves. Then we're good to go. From there, it's back to port, or maybe even, what...party on?"

The entire group fell silent at the comment. All eyes turned to Levi, who appeared to brighten at the suggestion. He glanced at his tablet and pursed his lips. He tapped and swiped at the screen, presumably studying the data. Finally, he nodded. "There's no sign of persistent damage. I caught this in time. I'd say there's a good chance we could keep going if we can find someone with the tanks we need to do the swap on site."

Levi swiped the screen of his tablet and began to appear less convinced. "That's not so simple, though," he grumbled. The confidence had drained from his voice. "Looking at the radar, I don't see any ships in our general area. If we call the Coast Guard, they'll insist on towing us back to port. We could hail any passersby in the area, but to be honest, I'm not too fond of the idea. We're not far off the coast of the U.S., so we don't have to worry about pirates, but there's really no telling what kind of people might respond to our hail.

"These days, the seas resemble the backroads of Arkansas. You can hitch a ride, and the odds are good you'll be picked up by someone safe. But there's also a better than zero chance you'll get picked up by someone who will stick a knife in your belly and leave your body in a shallow grave after doing nasty, nasty things to your corpse." He shrugged. "It's terrible, and it's going to cost me a fortune in fees, but the best option is to contact the Coast Guard and ask for help."

Piper understood what Levi wasn't verbalizing. He had taken responsibility for them, and there was only one choice that wouldn't result in undue risk. He needed to make that choice for everyone's sake. Her respect for Gina's boyfriend increased.

When Piper looked around, she saw Gray standing at the stern rail, gazing into the water. She joined him but couldn't discern what captured his attention. The water gently slapped against the rear of the boat and appeared fairly clear. She suspected they could see six or eight feet before the depths turned into a chilling, opaque abyss.

"What are you thinking?" Piper asked, leaning in close and feeling a rush of warmth that had nothing to do with the temperature when Gray wrapped an arm around her waist.

"I'm just trying to think outside the box," he said quietly. "I need to ask Levi a few questions. Would you mind bringing him here before he calls the Coast Guard?"

Piper's curiosity was piqued. She nodded, squeezed a hand she hadn't realized she was holding, and then headed off to collect Levi.

"It's not that complicated," Levi explained. "It just takes more time than I can manage while holding my breath."

Levi, Gray, and Piper stood at the aft gunnel discussing Gray's questions. The sun beat down on them, and they all felt the intensity of the midday heat.

"There are six bolts," Levi explained. "They're all new, recently replaced, and free of corrosion, so I know they'll come loose with little fuss. But I can hold my breath for maybe a minute at most when I'm doing that kind of labor. Working underwater like that will take me ten or fifteen minutes to remove all the bolts. Once they are off, pulling the prop only takes about thirty seconds. Putting it back together is the same process, just in reverse." He thought for a few seconds, "except for the torque wrench. The bolts need to be torqued to spec. We do have the wrench."

Levi shrugged. "There's no way to do it without tanks. I'd drown before I could get one of the bolts off. It's as simple as that. I can't believe I didn't bring tanks."

Gray leaned back against the rail. Piper watched as his eyes slowly swept over the rest of the group. They were once again gathered around the card table, passing the time until Levi decided how best to deal with the problem at hand. Gray seemed to be giving something serious consideration. Piper wasn't sure what it was, but she could see some kind of inner turmoil in his eyes.

"I can switch out the prop," Gray said at last.

Levi erupted with laughter. "What? You have scuba tanks in your bag with your underwear?"

"You can't," Piper interrupted. "No one can. You'll drown."

Gray looked at Levi. "Grab your tools. If you have a mask, that would help too." Gray placed his fingers on the side of his neck to check his own pulse. "We need to start in ten minutes or less, so please don't ask questions. Just get moving."

Levi looked confused, but he must have been swayed by Gray's conviction. He darted off for the doorway leading below deck.

"Gray," Piper said. "This is insane. It's not worth the risk."

Gray guided her by the arm and led her to a corner of the deck where they would have a better chance of privacy. "It's more complicated than I have time to explain," he said urgently in a whisper. "I'll need to surface several times but should be able to remove the prop in three or four dives and reinstall it in just as many."

Piper didn't know what to say. His words sounded insane, but when she looked into his eyes, she sensed he was completely confident in what he was explaining. She wanted to argue, to tell him he was certifiable… but something about his words or his expression when he gazed at her convinced her he could somehow achieve the impossible.

"We tie a line to you," she said, her voice cracking with emotion. "At the first sign of trouble, we'll pull you to the surface. And if I have to give you CPR, you'll never hear the end of it."

He grinned. "It's a deal."

———————

Ten minutes later, Gray stood at the stern with a rope and a tool belt around his waist, a headlamp strapped to his forehead, and a pair of thinly insulated textured gloves on his hands. He still wore only shorts. He was breathing slowly and deeply, a technique he had explained to Piper that would help add extra oxygen to his blood. She had read that swimmers often did something similar by breathing quickly and deeply right before diving. Oddly, Gray was making an effort to breathe slowly and steadily. He seemed to have a plan and some experience to inform his approach, though he said he'd never tried this technique in swimming before. That left her wondering precisely what he had used the breathing trick for in the past.

She hoped she'd have the chance to find out.

Gray climbed onto the rail and turned to face the group. Everyone had gathered to watch, and no one spoke. It seemed as if they had collectively held their breath in a show of solidarity. Piper felt on the verge of panic. Suddenly, the anxiety she'd felt just hours before about walking out on the deck in a bathing suit in front of her friends felt so trivial. This was literally life and death, yet Gray was chillingly at peace. He smiled at the group, then eyed the water.

Piper rushed forward just before Gray could step off the rail. She climbed the short set of steps that had been pushed to the gunnel to allow easier access and brought herself to eye, well, chin level with him. Before she realized what she was doing, she was kissing him. It was deep, passionate, and probing. When their mouths parted, she was short of breath and instantly wondered what she had just done to compromise his dive. But he only smiled broadly, winked, and stepped backward to plunge into the water.

That was the last she saw of him for almost seven minutes. During that time, the group had nearly pulled the retrieval rope at least half a dozen times. The only thing that stopped them was the slow, languid, yet always purposeful movements of the headlamp in the dark water. Spotters were positioned at the corners of the aft beam, each leaning as far over the water as possible for a glimpse of what was happening beneath the back end of the boat. Incredibly, through all that time, Gray somehow managed to remain not only alive but functional.

Finally, he resurfaced. His head and shoulders broke the surface of the water without so much as a splash. If it hadn't been for the diligence of the spotters, no one would have known he was back. Cries went up from Piper and Allison in their respective corners. Everyone rushed to the rail and leaned over. Gray had already pushed the goggles back on his forehead and was wiping water from his eyes. He was breathing slowly and deeply, presumably preparing for the next submersion.

"Any luck?" Levi asked.

"Are you alright?" Piper said.

Gray gave a thumbs up to Piper and nodded at Levi. "Three bolts free and three to go. It's going smoother than we expected."

Piper had stepped to the center of the deck and was leaning over the rail, directly above Gray. "You've been under longer than we expected. Are you okay?"

He nodded. "Really? I kind of lost track of time. Yeah, I'm okay. Let me remove these last three bolts, then just be ready with the spare prop. The water is a little cold. I'd like to get this done as soon as possible."

Now that she was focused on it, she noticed a slight quiver in his lower lip.

———————

It took only one more hour to finish removing the prop but three more to replace it and the six bolts. As time went on, fatigue set in. He wasn't able to stay under as long; his blood wasn't remaining oxygenated due to exertion and the cold. When he surfaced for the last time, he could barely bend his fingers, and his limbs were stiff. A life preserver was thrown overboard; Gray slipped his shoulders through the doughnut before being pulled to a wide boarding ladder. Even then, Jimmy carried him up the ladder on his back in what Levi called "a grown man's piggyback ride."

Some may have found the experience humiliating. Gray was exhausted and on the verge of hypothermia, yet he still managed to laugh at himself throughout the ordeal.

The repair efforts were a complete success, as Levi quickly confirmed. He started the engines and ran a diagnostic test that yielded encouraging results. When he began running the drive shafts, he was even more satisfied. The vibration he'd observed in the prop was entirely remediated. Though he knew that a bend in the prop blade had caused the imbalance, there was always a risk that the vibration had warped the drive shaft before the drive system was shut down. If that had happened, no amount of repair to the prop would restore operational status.

This, however, was news to Piper, and she was furious that the risk had not been shared before Gray put his life on the line. It turned out that Gray had been aware, at least to some extent, so he had gambled knowing all the variables. That was something. Perhaps by not knowing, she had been better able to cope with the risk. Now she would never know, and she wasn't sure how she felt about that.

The boat was underway once more. The group gathered around the table, though this time the playing cards had been stowed. Everyone was drinking. The sun hung low on the horizon, and the temperature was dropping. Only Gray had changed his clothes. He had been soaked, but the rest of the group appeared mentally and physically drained by the day's experiences. Four propane-powered heating pods had been set up around the table, ensuring everyone was comfortable for the moment. No one was in a hurry to move. Refilling drinks was the furthest anyone was willing to go for the foreseeable future.

Gray had changed into another pair of cargo shorts and now wore a gray sweatshirt with his black ball cap turned backward on his head. Piper sat on his lap, a heavy down comforter draped over both of them. She sat sideways across his legs, one arm around his shoulder, pulling herself close to his chest. Shivers ran through him occasionally, though they'd been less frequent over the last half hour. During the first hour they were like this, she had been seriously worried. They didn't have proper medical gear on board for an assessment, but she suspected his core body temperature had plummeted due to his time in the water.

"We could head to Barker's Bay," Levi suggested. He had been examining the tablet as the group discussed their options. "There's a medical center just a block from the docks. We can get there in about forty minutes, give or take. They'll have everything necessary to check on Gray. It's the closest port and the best option."

Nods of agreement were exchanged around the table. No one offered a counterargument.

Except for Gray.

"I thought you folks wanted to make a weekend of this joyride," he said, taking another long sip of the hot spiked cider that was constantly being refreshed in his mug. "If you quit on me because I'm a little chilly, I'm going to be cranky. There's no reason for it. Seriously, I'm already seventy-five percent better. A little more fluid, a couple of extra blankets tonight, and some quality shuteye, and I'll be back to normal by morning."

Piper eyed him with concern. "This entire situation has been a huge shock to your body. There's no way to predict how you'll recover."

"I've been through worse. This is fine." He glanced around at the faces at the table. "To be honest, I'm really having a great time hanging out with all of you. I know I was a last-minute addition to your outing, but you're really good people. If you're wrapping it up because the party's over, that's okay. But please don't do it on my account."

The table was silent for a long time. No one seemed willing to speak. Finally, Allison cleared her throat. "I don't understand how you held your breath for that long. If I hadn't seen it with my own eyes, I never would've believed it."

Heads around the table nodded. Beneath her, Piper felt Gray's entire body tense. This was a subject he wasn't comfortable discussing. Personally, she had been pondering the question ever since he resurfaced after the first dive. As far as she knew, there was no precedent for a man being able to hold his breath for that long. It was superhuman.

Gray took a deep breath and looked at each person around the table one by one before speaking. "I need to ask all of you to keep what happened here today to yourselves. No one can know about this. I participated in a drug trial some time ago and had to sign a very comprehensive nondisclosure agreement. It's kind of a serious matter."

Levi's eyes widened as he leaned across the table. "Are you saying there's going to be a treatment that will allow us to do that kind of thing one day?"

Gray shook his head. "Not a chance in hell. The side effects were some of the most horrible you can imagine. More than 99% of test subjects experienced bleeding from the eyes, nose, ears, anus, and penis. More than 80% had a body part literally shrivel up and fall off. Anything from an ear to a finger to…" he glanced down at his own lap.

Everyone at the table looked horrified. Levi looked like he might vomit.

"I was one of three people who didn't experience any negative side effects. However, the company behind the project went bankrupt and is still being pursued by lawyers and insurance companies, as well as upset next of kin. It's about the worst situation you can imagine. All I can say is, when you see those flyers offering cash to participate in a drug trial, think twice. *Think more than twice.*"

Piper scanned the faces of everyone at the table. She didn't completely believe the story Gray had just told, but she recognized that it was a sensitive subject for him. There was likely more to the tale. Whatever had led him to do something so extraordinary, he'd risked a lot to do it in front of a group of people he'd only just met. The story might have been a fabrication, but it was still an effort she could respect.

"So what's the final decision?" Piper asked the group. "Should we head for port or stay out for the weekend?"

Across the table, Gina cleared her throat. "What's your vote, Piper? You were in favor of a day trip the last time we talked." A knowing smile danced in her friend's eyes.

Piper felt her cheeks flush. "I've warmed to the idea of some quality time with old friends," she said, looking at Gray and adding, "and new ones. If there's no risk to Gray's health, let's stay out." She leaned close to his ear and spoke in a breathy whisper, "If you're sure about this, I'll insist on keeping you under observation *all night.*"

There was an unmistakable stiffening shift in his shorts beneath her backside. She bit her lip and pulled the heavy blanket tighter around them both. She already had herself pressed against his chest, ostensibly to share body heat. It was just a shame he was wearing the sweatshirt, she now decided. Then she focused on the hand clamped on her knee ever since she'd cuddled up in his lap. "There's more body heat here," she said and moved his hand halfway up her leg and squeezed it between her thighs. In truth, it was only half as daring as she'd wanted to be, but there were too many people around. All the same, she was satisfied by the further stiffening beneath her.

Gray looked around the table. "I think the party's just getting started."

———————

"There are two cabins," Piper said. She was in the galley with Allison and Gina. They were crushing ice, operating a pair of industrial blenders, and making enough pitchers of frosty drinks to last them well into the next day. "Obviously, you and Levi will want one," she said to Gina. "That's already well established. But if I'm with Gray, that doesn't leave Allison much flexibility when it comes to Jimmy."

Allison and Gina shared a knowing smile.

"What?" Piper said.

Gina handed her half a bag of ice cubes and rolled her eyes dramatically. "Looks like you're not the only one making a connection on the high seas. I walked in on Ally making out with Mongo–"

"We were just kissing," Allison insisted.

Rounding on her, Gina backed Allison up to the counter with a raised accusatory finger. There was unbridled amusement in her expression when she said, "Neither one of you was wearing a top– I'm going to call that a little more than 'just kissing.'" She turned to look at Piper. "Seriously, the two of you treat me like I'm the little miss slutsy tipsy of our group, but from what I've seen on this trip so far, you're both vying for the title. Allison finally decides to stop waiting for Jimmy to make his move and decides to swallow his tongue," she said, waving one hand at Allison, then turned to wave the other at

Piper. "And you're over there grinding on everyone's new friend and hero."

Piper grinned. "I thought I was being more subtle." Strangely, she didn't feel the slightest bit embarrassed by her lack of discretion and wondered if she had just expanded the limits of her shallow personal boundaries or perhaps sacrificed an unexamined personal value.

Then she decided, *fuck it*. She sincerely was tired of living a callow existence.

"You were subtle," Gina clarified. "The facial expressions–yours and his–give it away. You're surprising each other, and it shows." She walked up and playfully swatted Piper on the backside. "I say, ride the lightning. Enjoy every moment of this while you can. It never lasts as long as you want, and the connection you're already making with that boy is something special. I can see it from a mile away."

Piper froze with her finger on the blender's start switch. "You think?"

Allison's head bobbed with enthusiasm. "A mile away," she agreed. "It's why I decided to take the initiative with Jimmy. Watching you gave me the courage to step out of my comfort zone."

Piper didn't press the start button. Her hands fell to her side, and she leaned back against the counter. Never in her life had she been the *leap-before-you-look* type of personality. If anything, she was more of the *measure twice and cut once* kind of person. Now Ally was taking cues from her, and she had somehow managed to impress Gina…

What is the world coming to?

"Point being," Gina said, "Ally will just be sharing a room with Jimmy for one night. Maybe they can explore the boundaries of their relationship like you and Gray are. But regardless, no one bothers me and Levi tonight unless you want a black eye. He's under a lot of pressure with all this engine trouble and everything. I'm going to help him unwind, but he's easily distracted. Let's keep distractions off the agenda tonight, capeesh?"

Crisis averted. Forcing Allison into an uncomfortable situation was the only thing that could put a damper on the night for Piper, and that was no longer an issue. She hit start on the blender, grabbed the first completed pitcher, gave Allison a playful bump with her hip, and headed for the stern deck with Gina. Gina carried a tray of clean glasses, and Allison was going to finish mixing the last pitcher before joining them.

The sun was just setting in the west, and the four vertical heating stations had been adjusted around the rectangular table. Piper was relieved to see Gray still positioned in his chair, the thick down comforter from their cabin cocooning him. Only his neck and one shoulder were exposed, with the fluffy wrap surrounding both him and the chair he sat in.

Gina arranged the glasses, and Piper began pouring the drinks. The girls and Levi opted for the thick daiquiri mix they had just prepared in the galley, while Jimmy and Gray sipped tequila from rocks glasses.

Piper poured another generous splash into Gray's glass and placed her own beside it. "Are you warming up at all?" she asked.

"The drink helps," he said. "But you know what helped even more?" A seam opened in his cocoon, allowing her access. The smile danced in her eyes as she stepped closer. Then she slipped the sheer wrap from her shoulders and draped it over the empty chair just two feet away. She was still wearing her bathing suit, and her skin immediately prickled in the cool evening air.

A second later, she pulled her legs up into a ball on Gray's lap, snuggling against his bare chest. She didn't know when he had taken off the sweatshirt, but she was relieved to feel the heat radiating from his body. She pressed the palm of her hand against his chest and felt the steady, though slightly rapid, beating of his heart. It was strong, but the way it raced was concerning.

She tipped her head back to ask him about it, but was interrupted when his mouth met hers. His kiss was intentional and intense, yet gentle and all-consuming. It caught her off guard and took her breath away simultaneously. Seconds melted away, and when they finally parted, she noticed for the first time that his arms were wrapped around her in a way that cradled her body to his.

A slow gasp escaped her lips as she looked up into his eyes. Then she noticed the stillness at the table. All eyes were on them, and no one was moving.

"Do it again," Gina said. "That—that was awesome!"

"Wow," Allison whispered.

"That was fucking hot," Levi mumbled.

Jimmy was nodding. "Not bad, new guy."

Piper buried her face in the overstuffed comforter and nestled into the crook between Gray's neck and collarbone. "I guess you really are feeling better," she said into the blanket.

An hour later, the couples at the table had mostly broken into their own subgroups. Gina and Levi were flipping through a maritime magazine or catalog by the dim light of the nearest heating station, discussing something related to the yacht or its parts. Piper had only overheard part of the conversation, but apparently, Levi had just come clean about his true motivation for all the time he'd spent restoring the reclaimed yacht to pristine working order. It seemed he was financially well-off and had been trading his time working for the salvage company to gain the experience required to refit the boat himself. He wasn't so much interested in saving money on the yacht as he was in learning everything he could about it while putting the old bucket back together. The weekend shakedown cruise was his opportunity to put the ship through its paces and to tell Gina he wasn't exactly who he'd made himself out to be over the course of their relationship.

For her part, Gina didn't seem to care about Levi's money, his deception, or the fact that the boat was his. She simply wanted to know if his feelings for her were genuine or just part of the fabrication. When Levi said that was the one thing he had never embellished, she was fine with the rest of the deal. She honestly didn't mind that he had pretended to be someone he wasn't. As she explained in reply, everyone did that when they first met. Dating was all about learning who the other person really was.

Piper marveled at the back-and-forth between Gina and Levi because she knew it was really that simple for her friend. One discussion, all cards were on the table, and Gina was genuinely honest when she said she was satisfied. They were already moving on as if nothing had happened.

"Have relationships ever come that easily to you?" Piper whispered to Gray. He had observed the same sequence of events, and she was curious about his perspective.

"Is this your way of asking me if I've had a lot of relationships?"

She smiled, realizing how the question could be interpreted that way. "I'm only asking if those two are so easygoing that it makes your head hurt. Maybe it's just me."

He shook his head. "No, that exchange was something else. I've never seen anything quite like it. They might be perfect for each other. It's as if they can share life-altering revelations with the same ease as deciding what's for dinner. There's nothing normal about that."

Piper had been more or less lying in Gray's arms, enjoying the way his fingertips ran up and down the back of her bare leg. His touch was both sensual and relaxing. She felt like she was melting into him, yet she also sensed the unmistakable electricity of his touch with the slightest brush of his hand. "Do you have anything like that?"

He ceased the rhythmic caress of her skin and looked down into her eyes. "What do you mean?"

"Any life-altering revelations waiting in the wings?" She grinned.

A serious expression crossed his face, and she felt his entire body suddenly grow more rigid. She had clearly struck a nerve, so she propped an elbow on the arm of the chair and sat upright to look him squarely in the eye. "You know I was just playing, right?" She said.

Gray remained silent for several long seconds, but Piper could see the calculations happening behind his eyes. She sensed he was stuck on something guarded, something he wasn't comfortable discussing.

"I'm not pressing for anything," she said softly. "Really…There's no pressure."

His gaze softened, and he shrugged just a little. "Everyone has something waiting in the wings," he conceded. "My stuff is just a bit more unconventional. You've already seen part of it, so I'll tell you this because I trust you. What I did with that underwater thing–"

"Holding your breath?"

He nodded. "It wasn't a drug trial like I told everyone. There's technology integrated into my blood and brain. Sometimes I can utilize it in creative ways. I had never attempted anything like that before, so I wasn't sure it would work."

What he was saying should have seemed preposterous, something out of the books they both enjoyed, and she wanted to voice that. But then she had seen what he could do. What other explanation was there?

"Does it hurt?" she asked instead.

He shrugged. "It's mainly there to prevent me from getting hurt, but I'm still learning the limits."

She contemplated his words for a few seconds before leaning in to kiss him. She was willing to accept some things on faith. He had demonstrated his courage when he risked his life to help repair the boat, and now he was at least ready to share the strange secret of how he had managed to do it.

Her kiss started slow and sustained, but as the seconds ticked, she felt her temperature rise and her heart rate. The probing of her tongue became more aggressive, as did his. Then his hands began to roam. They had privacy beneath the massive blanket, but that suddenly didn't seem like enough for what she needed.

He cradled her head and kissed her even more deeply, then he cupped her breast and caressed it with his remaining hand. *Finally,* she thought. He'd been so careful to stop short of anything she might find too aggressive, and the anticipation practically had her crawling out of her skin. Now, she just wished he'd do away with the bikini top so they could get the show on the road.

A siren blared and Piper jumped. When she did, she must have applied pressure in an unfortunate place because Gray instantly winced. They both glanced around the table and seemed to recall their friends were there at the same time. "Um," Piper whispered.

"Yeah," Gray replied.

Piper double-checked that the blanket was still providing them the necessary degree of privacy and was relieved to see that Gray had managed to keep it pinned in place. No one seemed to be paying attention to them. Everyone was suddenly focused on the blaring alarm coming from Levi's tablet. Levi was already tapping on the screen. The boat's speed had been cut in half. Darkness surrounded the boat, so they couldn't see more than a dozen yards beyond the rail; whatever was out there must have shown up on the radar.

A wide smile crossed Levi's face. "Dolphins!" He laughed and pointed to the west. "Thirty yards off the port rail. It looks like a dozen or more. Flashlights are in the galley."

In an instant, everyone at the table fled. Hurried footsteps seemed to emanate from every direction. Seconds later, hushed voices were heard, and obscured beams were directed somewhere in the distance.

Piper and Gray didn't move from the chair. She repositioned, slipping her legs through holes beneath the armrests and straddling Gray, who pulled the blanket over them to blot out the dim light from the heaters and the stars above. Piper instantly felt Gray's mouth press to hers and responded with a probing, hungry tongue. He grabbed her by the hips and slid them aggressively against his own. She put her hands down to brace the arms of the chair and repeated the action enthusiastically. She felt him stiffen, his erection extending down the inside the left leg of his shorts. Adjusting her position to match, she applied pressure and heard him moan. She could feel him through the desperately thin material of her bathing suit and the picture in her mind made her short of breath.

"Too much?" She said it in a whisper that sounded more like a gasp. She was grinding hard, and it felt amazing, but she didn't want to hurt him.

His silent response was to squeeze the cheeks of her ass with both hands and use his tongue to keep her from speaking. She shuddered with excitement and anticipation for what would come next. She rocked awkwardly on his lap as she executed a delicate maneuver with less grace than she had envisioned, but he seemed completely unaware.

That was good.

Finally, she pushed back, gasping for air—literally gasping. They both were. Gray started to speak, but she pressed a finger to his lips. Glancing around, she confirmed they still had the cover of the blanket. How it remained in place, she had no idea...but they wouldn't need it for much longer. Her chest still heaving and teetering on the edge of hyperventilation, she gazed directly into Gray's eyes and playfully bit the corner of her lip with anticipation. Then she leaned to the left and reached deep beneath the blanket. Her hand pushed back the left leg of his shorts as far as she could, then continued upward when that was no longer possible. His entire body shuddered at her touch, and his eyes sparkled with newfound excitement.

The moment seemed to stretch for endless seconds, her eyes locked on his. It felt like oxygen wasn't finding its way into her lungs. She was lightheaded with excitement and a sense of lust she'd never experienced in her life. She ran her fingertips down his length one more time before pulling back. Very gently, she leaned forward and kissed him. As she did, she slipped something into his right hand. Then, tipping her head back, she took a deep breath of the cold night air. She emerged from the embrace of the chair and Gray's arms, wrapping herself in the massive white comforter as she did. Everyone was still at the railing, pointing flashlights out at the water and discussing dolphins.

As Piper sauntered toward her cabin, she glanced over her shoulder at Gray, who sat alone at the table with a confused expression on his face. She smiled when he looked down to see what she had pressed into his hand as she stood up and pulled away. Holding her gift up to the light, he realized it was the top and bottom of the bikini she had been wearing just a moment before.

Piper heard Gray's chair tip over as she opened the cabin door, knowing he would be only seconds behind. She left the door open and let the comforter fall away.

Chapter 11 - Strange Dangling Appendage

Wild-Side

16 months ago

The massive creature thrashed and clawed its way through a tangle of vegetation unlike anything it had ever encountered. Its scales were accustomed to razor-like barbs on plants, but nothing in this strange wilderness appeared remotely carnivorous, and none of the vegetation made any kind of threatening move. Jumping over a fallen log, the creature suddenly became wary of an ambush; so when a thick vine appeared at eye level, he struck out with deadly force. The talons on both hands lashed at the hanging vine, eviscerating it in a spray of sticky sap. However, Breslin slowed his pace when the splatter of sap on his scaly flesh failed to burn, melt, or even harm him. No additional vines came to defend the fallen.

Examining the remains of the battered vine, Breslin was perplexed. The briar had the girth of two of his talons but had failed to defend itself in any way. It also didn't appear to be part of any social pack or pride. Retracting a claw, he dabbed at the freshly severed end of the thick rope. A thick, sticky substance oozed from the green and brown plant, but there was no blood.

Breslin rose to his feet and scanned the forest. Spindly thickets of leafy green vegetation clung to larger, brown plants that towered even higher with more greenery. He had never seen anything like it. While he sensed small wildlife moving in the distance, nothing in the immediate area stirred at all.

Warily, he brushed a large scaled hand through the tendrils of another plant. It didn't react, so he moved on. As he walked, he noticed the sound of his footfalls changing. They were becoming less stealthy, his stride shorter and more clumsy. He looked down to see the last scales of his torso giving way to a soft, almost pink material. His arms and legs grew shorter by degrees over just a few minutes, and he suddenly realized that he was taking on the form of one of the creatures he'd killed back in the cave.

Moments later, Breslin stood naked at the edge of a clearing, with the woods at his back. The sun shone down, and he felt it on his skin for the very first time. He knew what was happening, of course. His kind had found their way to Other-Worlds many times over generations. Turning slowly, he took in the strangeness of the green and brown landscape. The blue and white sky overhead was unlike anything he'd ever experienced. Looking down at his own hand, he marveled at how short, spindly digits had replaced his mighty fist and talons. Each ended in a useless, thin shard that couldn't possibly rend flesh from bone. Then he looked at the strange dangling appendage between his legs and wondered about its usefulness.

Being the first of his kind here came with responsibilities, Breslin thought as he walked slowly through the sawgrass. Killing those in the cave had invigorated him, but it was only the beginning. A sense of this world was already beginning to form in his mind, information gathered from the body he had commandeered upon crossing over. He would need to learn more about the inhabitants of this world.

Understanding would allow him to conquer or destroy them more effectively.

Chapter 12 - A Deathtrap Just Waiting to Claim Its First Victims

Our-World

Borderline Bar and Grill

Two days passed before I saw Piper again. My stunt in the lab had the unintended consequence of prompting Doctor Fulbright to instill the fear of God in building maintenance, the University administration, and anyone willing to listen. He seemed not to appreciate being assigned a laboratory that was, as he described it, a deathtrap just waiting to claim its first victims. He insisted that all building systems and infrastructure be inspected before his project team began working in earnest.

That was fine with me. Delaying, or even better, derailing the project was my ultimate goal. But the outcome was amusing because it was unexpected. I had partially achieved one of my objectives without even trying. It gave me a day to set up a base of operations in the corner of a warehouse I had just rented on the outskirts of the town's business district, plus a fallback safe house in the sticks outside of town. It was a lot to accomplish in twenty-four hours, but it kept me busy and distracted from obsessing over Piper, who had been on my mind since seeing that news clip just a week earlier.

I maintain that obsession is too strong a term, and I'll admit to being distracted since she entered my life, but Esker disagreed. He went on to define obsession as, and I quote, an idea or thought that continually preoccupies or intrudes on one's mind. However, since arguing with artificial intelligence is like ice skating uphill, you can bet I didn't make any progress in changing his mind.

And considering I was sitting at what was quickly becoming my table at the Borderline, watching Piper pour drinks behind the bar at the first opportunity I had, maybe he wasn't too far from the mark. I'd been there for twenty minutes, and Piper had yet to make eye contact, though I was certain she'd been checking me out from the corner of her eye at regular, if not constant, intervals.

Music played from the jukebox next to a small stage set up at the end of the room. Patrons could select songs using a phone app. All three selections I had entered played immediately. Either no one in the semi-crowded joint was vying for playtime, or someone was prioritizing my picks. Since my songs were favorites from the playlist curated by Piper Hudson and me, I suspected the fix was in.

I had never actually ordered a drink, yet they arrived at my table with only a coy smile and a wink from the waitress. She knew something I didn't, and she seemed to be enjoying it. I tried to ask about the secret, but she silently shook her head and left without a word. The first round was a double shot of tequila served in a rocks glass. The second round was the same, and by the time I finished it, I was buzzed and feeling no pain.

The rocks glass was the key. This was what I drank on the boat when Piper and I first met. And the rocks glass was the best part. If I didn't know better, I'd say the glass was almost exactly the same style. The memory made me smile. I think I was still grinning when I looked up to see Piper standing at the end of my booth. Her work attire had been replaced with a pale yellow sundress that had thin spaghetti straps and a plunging neckline. She was holding a tray with two more rocks glasses. She set the glasses on the table, placed the tray on the seat opposite me, and then slipped into the seat at my side.

I began to speak, but she interrupted me. With a shake of her head, she gently placed a finger against my lips. The look dancing in her iridescent blue eyes was mesmerizing, one I had seen before and had longed to see again. A warmth spread through my body that had nothing to do with the liquor I had been drinking.

Piper slid closer to me, our shoulders touching. Throughout, her eyes remained fixed on mine. Her left hand pushed one of the rocks glasses toward me and placed the other in front of herself. I felt her right hand settle gently on my leg, and I couldn't help the smile that spread across my face.

We raised our glasses together and slowly tipped them back. I'm pretty sure we managed to keep our eyes locked the entire time. I don't remember tasting the drink or feeling the burn of the alcohol. All I recall are those eyes. Not a word was spoken, yet she was saying so much.

We sat there for a while—I have no idea how long. It could have been a few seconds or even a few minutes. It felt like time stood still. I truly wished it could. In that moment, it felt like we'd regained what we once had. It felt as if everything that had happened in the months since had been erased. Those horrible experiences I thought would be unforgettable were, if only for a few minutes, removed from my mind. That was her gift to me, I realized amidst the blur of the present and times past. She made everything I was going through worthwhile.

Her hand slipped into mine, and we eased from the booth as one. We were out the door before I knew it and on the street. I wasn't entirely without my faculties because I had the wherewithal to scan the street and the parking lot beyond for dangers, but there were none. Eight or nine people had stepped out of the bar to smoke, a couple who had stopped in the shadows to play grab-ass, a pickup truck arriving, and two cars leaving. All of this would have been monitored by Esker anyway, who would have alerted me to anything significant.

Piper guided me to the right. We walked up the dimly lit street for two and a half blocks to a three-story brick building that appeared to be a World War II-era manufacturing facility retrofitted into apartments. We crossed the lobby, passed the pair of elevators, and entered the stairwell. With my hand still in hers, we walked wordlessly side by side up to the third floor.

A couple of things to mention here that might pull you out of the moment. The fact that Piper passed by the elevator didn't escape my notice. I avoid elevators whenever possible, and she knows it. When you know there are people hunting you, the last thing you want to do is put yourself in a steel cage.

Paranoia, you say? Bite me. It's not paranoia when people are truly after you.

Anyway, I dabbed a camera gel on the corner of the wall leading to the stairwell. It had fisheye-like optics, so it would pick up anyone entering the stairs, anyone approaching the elevators, and would provide an unobstructed view of nearly the entire lobby. I also attached one to the door frame outside Piper's apartment. The gels were almost entirely transparent, the diameter of a pencil, and half the thickness of a sheet of paper. Unless someone looked directly at one, they were as close to invisible as something could be. They transmitted 4K video in a 24/7 feed that Esker would monitor.

I stepped into Piper's apartment and felt my jaw drop. It wasn't large, but it was modern, immaculate, and impressive. It was probably what is referred to as a studio, since the entire place was one big room. The living room occupied the entire left wall while the kitchen filled the whole right side. A small loft area overhung the kitchen. Something resembling a mix between a ladder and a staircase led to the loft, which contained a large bed and a dresser.

The furniture in the living room and the appliances in the kitchen were sleek and modern. Although the tables appeared blocky and primitive, they were crafted from materials that seemed cutting-edge and chic.

In the back of my mind I'd heard the door close and latch, even noting the sound of the locking bolt being thrown. I suppose I was distracted by the design of the space because it wasn't what I expected from Piper, which made me realize that, when it came to this sort of thing, I had no idea what to expect from her. I turned just in time to see her slip the second of the two delicate straps from her shoulder and could only blink as the yellow dress fell effortlessly to the floor, puddling at her feet.

Piper didn't move. She licked her lips and seemed to wait for me to make the next move. She was standing completely naked in the short open space between the living room and the kitchen. It seemed to be a metaphor representing everything about our reunion. But metaphors take a back seat when the love of your life is standing naked in front of you. The blood flow had been instantly diverted from my brain. The next thing I knew, I had my arms around her, and my mouth had found hers. She began pulling at my belt as I did the same with my shirt.

Admittedly, I might have been stretching that metaphor a bit just now. However, it was in service of sparing you the graphic, carnal, and long-overdue description of everything that came next. Needless to say, no efforts were spared in rekindling our relations.

None.

Our-World

Seattle, Washington

Kilmer Breslin considered the sheeting rain turning the distant city lights into milky blurs that pulsed and slowly undulated in time with the gusting wind buffing the outside of the floor-to-ceiling penthouse windows. The expansive, panoramic Seattle skyline was said to be a selling point for the opulent location. Breslin liked it only because it satisfied his primal instinct for situational awareness. Not that there were many dangers to him in this place. Here, as everywhere, he was the predator.

Grinding his teeth and turning away from the windows, he strode slowly across the vast expanse of white marble floor. Despite being the apex predator, he wasn't himself. On this Brane, he couldn't assume his natural form. Stuck in human shape, he felt like a shell of his former self, as frail as any man. His nature offered little protection until he could assume his natural appearance. He needed to control when and where he used his ability to Cross. He needed to bring his people directly to this Brane. Wild-Side was limited in host resources. The number of Elend he could bring from his world to Wild-Side was restricted by the number of Seeley available as hosts.

Breslin smiled as he glanced once more at the windows and the city beyond. This was a rare moment for him. The place offered abundant resources. He could bring all of the Elend to this world. The population of this Brane could support his people and allow them to thrive. For the first time in a dozen generations, the Elend population would have the opportunity to expand. It could even multiply.

Dropping into the worn brown leather club chair positioned at the center of the empty expanse of marble, Breslin leaned back and contemplated the windows and the distant city lights once more. His time here hadn't been without challenges. He needed to adapt. To bring his people to this Brane, he had to understand and control the ability to move between Branes. Only one person was known to possess that ability. Grady Ledger was the key, but the boy was a challenging adversary. Since that had proven frustratingly difficult, Breslin knew he needed contingency plans.

The strategy required resources that were not available when he first arrived in the New-World. Given his human frailty, he needed to find another way to enlist support. Frustratingly, he was popping back and forth between Wild-Side—the odd name given to the Brane by the Seeley, though he believed the simplicity and lack of creativity suggested that the name actually came from Grady Ledger. This turned out to be an advantage. Many of the Seeley abducted by the Elend proved to be useful when interrogated before being used as hosts. Interrogation was an art Breslin learned early during his time in the New-World, and it paid dividends.

Breslin gathered technical insights from the Seeley and used what he learned as currency in the New-World. Seeley technology was worth its weight in gold to the right people, and Breslin quickly discerned how to leverage what he learned on one Brane to develop a power base on the other.

Before long, Breslin had established a fiefdom in the New-World that granted him power and authority akin to his position in the Elend dominion. He had subordinates traveling the globe to execute his orders. To that end, he had dozens of acolytes hunting Grady Ledger worldwide. Equally important, he had funded just as many research projects focused on Brane Theory. Almost all of them were solely dedicated to finding a way to cross the barrier between dimensions.

Only four of Breslin's closest advisors were aware of his true motivations. There had been five in total. One of his key lieutenants had proven unreliable. Evidence indicated that Edward Stapelton had collected information on Breslin and ATG, the company Breslin ultimately established. He intended to pass that information to authorities or directly to Grady Ledger. Breslin had contacts in the FBI, CIA, and NSA and connections with several key international law enforcement organizations, which made him reasonably insulated from legal consequences. Moreover, ATG–Arlington Technologies Global–provided services to numerous murky organizations linked to the upper echelons of power.

The greatest risk was Stapelton going to Ledger. Ledger was a persistent, never-ending thorn in Breslin's side both here and on Wild-Side. A handful of ATG's most promising projects had been sabotaged or even outright attacked by Grady Ledger. Some had been entirely off-book, black projects that had never been documented anywhere in ATG's mainframe. Breslin didn't know how Ledger was gathering information about ATG or Breslin himself, but he was resourceful and efficient.

Breslin didn't know if he would have found the key to travel between Branes by now if not for Ledger, but he knew his people would be closer to a solution. He also knew one more thing with absolute certainty. It would be the key to solving the mystery if he could capture Ledger. The kid could move between Branes at will. He always had.

Grady Ledger was the key to conquering Wild-Side and the Elend finding a new home in the New-World. Capturing him was the first step in controlling the bridge between the two worlds. While he had frustratingly limited control over the bridge between his world and Wild-Side, it was better than the humiliation he had suffered for more than a year, bouncing back and forth between Wild-Side and the New-World with absolutely no control. Being powerless to bring the Elend to this world was exasperating. Lacking control over his own geography was intolerable, and Breslin struggled to maintain a façade of calm while dealing with the sycophants surrounding him in his corporate environment. He had learned early on that they responded better to gentler motivations than the Elend of his world. After killing a handful of his subordinates and navigating the complexities of the legal system, it quickly became clear that only his inner circle could be trusted with the driving goals he had established for ATG.

Jeff Dreyling burst through the double doors at the back of the room, creating a flurry of activity. As was often the case, Dustin Sexton followed swiftly in his wake. "I have the update from Kansas, boss," Dreyling said, making his usual halfhearted effort to meet

Breslin's gaze. Instead of approaching Breslin directly, he veered off to the west wall, where an array of free-standing whiteboards, cork boards, and cart-mounted sixty-inch flat-panel displays stood.

"The underground silo," Breslin grumbled, already having a clear idea of where this was going. "Was the device located?"

Sexton pinned a poster-sized photo to one of the cork boards. It was taken either from a low-Earth-orbiting satellite or a high-flying aircraft. The image displayed an expanse of flat, hard-packed earth in a square shape, depicting the small station that housed the top of the elevator shaft leading to the underground facility. Several smaller rooflines were shown, representing what everyone in the room understood as perimeter guard towers. The multiple concentric fence lines of the security boundary were not visible from this top-down view.

Tapping the photo, Sexton highlighted the indistinct figures scattered throughout the image. "These are federal agents," he said.

Breslin ambled forward and leaned closer to the photo. "Who notified the authorities?" He growled. Orders had been explicit. Aside from the FBI on payroll, no outside law enforcement was to be contacted."

Sexton glanced at his partner. Dreyling was tapping on a touchscreen tablet, trying to transfer content to one of the large flat-panel displays. When asked the question, he paused and looked at Sexton before they both turned back to Breslin without reply.

"We think Ledger alerted law enforcement himself," Sexton said. "It puts federal attention on ATG. That hinders us far more than it does him. As always, his attack resulted in no fatalities." If Ledger killed a member of the security teams protecting an ATG facility, the effort law enforcement put into pursuing him would escalate significantly. As it stood, ATG's resources were involved in the hunt alongside any corrupt state and federal agents Breslin could engage. Ledger was too intelligent to heighten tensions. Additional scrutiny for ATG could only benefit Ledger.

Breslin had once contemplated killing some of his own people and pinning it on Grady Ledger. A frame job, Sexton had termed it, though Breslin never grasped the euphemism. However, the additional resources pursuing Ledger would also focus more scrutiny on ATG and Breslin himself. It was a trade, to date, that Breslin had not been willing to make.

Poking the photo, Breslin said, "At least tell me these are our agents working the scene."

Dreyling tapped the screen of his tablet with a mutter of triumph and turned the wheeled flat panel to better face Breslin and Sexton. "Our people are part of the investigation," he confirmed. "Unfortunately, we have little control over the narrative. Someone connected this attack with other unreported ATG-focused attacks." A real-time view almost identical to the photograph filled the screen of the flat panel. The investigators were gone, and it was obvious that all the evidence markers visible in the photo were missing as well. A pair of large, blocky SUVs were positioned in a wedge formation on the dirt road outside the gate, preventing even forced access. Nearby, two blob-like shapes moved, indicating that at least three men were manning the roadblock and the entrance.

With a tap on the screen, Dreyling adjusted the filter and activated a thermal version of the video feed. The blobs representing the men at the gate transformed into amorphous slugs of orange and red. It also became clear that a fourth man was inside the gatehouse, visible only through the roof via thermal imaging. Dreyling zoomed out on the image, and they watched as more figures came into view. Two forms manned each of the guard towers. A lone shape moved slowly along the innermost of the concentric fence lines, one positioned at each cardinal point on the perimeter.

"The results of the increased scrutiny?" Breslin demanded, his tone flat. He already knew the answer would likely not be positive.

Dreyling and Sexton glanced at each other, but neither was quick to reply.

Sexton swallowed hard. "Homeland Security is demanding to interview you."

Breslin took a deep breath and reminded himself that he needed to behave differently in the New-World. While his instinct was to tear the throat from one of these men as a motivation for the other, painful experience had proven that didn't motivate these people the way it did the Elend. Instead, Breslin poked the glass of the screen and glared at both men. "Explain," he demanded.

"Homeland knows technology was taken and that at least one research team member is missing," Dreyling said quickly. "We have confirmed there is no internal information leak. Ledger is attempting to weaponize law enforcement against us."

Breslin rubbed at the corners of his eyes and fought his instincts. He could taste blood in the back of his throat. It was as if his very nature demanded him to lash out–savaging one of these men as recompense for yet another setback to his ultimate objective.

"You have studied this attack for more than a week. What will any of this help," he said instead. "What good would understanding Ledger's attack strategy do?"

No one spoke for several long seconds. Finally, Dreyling met Breslin's gaze with a timid, fearful expression. "If we can understand how he thinks and plans, we can better anticipate his next moves."

Fighting the desire to batter both men, Breslin failed to contain the snarl that formed deep in his chest. "This is a useless waste of time. Find Miranda Norton and the missing components. Ledger wouldn't have taken both unless the experiment held potential." He glared at Sexton. "Contact the congressman. It's finally time for him to pull his weight. I want the Homeland investigation shut down immediately."

Chapter 13 - My Unexpected Plus-One

Wild-Side

My ears popped with a familiar change in elevation, my stomach flip-flopped, and the Doppler effect of a low, resonant gong echoed deep within my skull. I fought the urge to vomit and rolled onto my side. That's when I felt the long, dry blades of grass crunch beneath me. It all added up to one thing.

I'm back on Wild-Side.

I squinted against the sun and took a deep breath. Sunlight meant no Seeley. Well, it didn't mean I was entirely out of danger, but they were far more dangerous at night. There had only been rare attacks during the daytime, and no one had reported an attack in broad daylight. No evidence indicated they were a nocturnal race, but they certainly seemed to prefer the night. The worst of the creepy crawlies always seemed to share that trait, so I guess there was some degree of predictability there.

Have I mentioned that my mind tends to spin right after crossing?

The sound of someone coughing and retching snapped me back to alertness. I vaulted to my feet, spinning on my heels before digging my bare toes into the loamy soil and assuming a defensive stance. Admittedly, one loses some of his imposing edge while standing completely naked in a field of knee-high grass with his fists balled, no matter how aggressive the fighting posture.

That's when I saw Piper sprawled face down in the same grass, gasping for breath and dry-heaving. She lay flat, her hands spread wide, just lifting her face out of the grass and dirt. Like me, she was completely naked. But unlike me, she wasn't supposed to be there.

No one else had ever crossed over to Wild-Side before.

"Piper," I said, rolling her over and pulling her into my arms. Her eyes fluttered, and her breathing was shallow and rapid. Her body seemed to tremble from head to toe. "Piper, can you hear me?" I tapped her gently on the cheek, but it didn't seem to matter. Pressing two fingers against the side of her neck, her racing pulse was unmistakable.

We found ourselves in the middle of a meadow that spanned maybe five or six square acres. I didn't like being out in the open, but I wasn't sure the distant tree line looked any better. Piper just shouldn't be here. This wasn't right. Me landing here was problematic. Her landing here with me like this…it was—fuck! I didn't know how to protect her in a place like this.

My HUD flickered to life, but communications were still down. Luckily, cartography loaded quickly this time. There was a farm with an active transport platform 2.8 kilometers northeast of my location. I was just about to grab Piper and head for the farm when I felt her pulse slow and saw her eyes begin to stabilize.

She took a deep breath and looked up at me from where she lay cradled in my arms, blinking slowly. Squinting, she said, "What the hell? Turn the lights down."

I couldn't help but laugh. That only made her more confused. She rubbed her head and attempted to sit up. It must have hurt because she sagged back into my arms. I think that's when she noticed the grass and grime beneath her. She turned to stare at me. There was confusion in her eyes. Her eyes were glassy and unfocused but seemed to settle on my lap.

"Huh…" she mumbled. I think it was to herself, but she was still sort of out of it, so I wasn't sure. "My sex dreams are usually more creative." Her eyes finally left my crotch and found my face. "And you're always having more fun than *that*," she tipped her head back to my groin.

Starting to object, I realized I was about to bury the lead. "Wait— you're saying your sex dreams *frequently* involve me?"

The comment drew her eyes to sharp focus. She gasped for breath and began looking frantically left and right. "Gray? Why am I naked in a field? This isn't a dream."

"No dream," I confirmed as I got to my feet. I extended a hand to help her. "If you were dreaming, there would be more action. I'd make sure of it."

It took a long second for my sarcasm to break through what was clearly a growing sense of panic. And while we were miles away from being safe, I needed her to remain composed. Honestly, having her go through the Transition with me left me confused and concerned. Panic wasn't locked away in a box in the corner of my mind as it usually was. I couldn't let her lose it, but I didn't know how to explain what had just happened either.

"You're not letting that go, are you?" she grumbled, glaring at me. Still, she took my offered hand, and as I pulled her to her feet, I noticed a break in the tension in her eyes; a smile threatened to fracture her scowl. She rubbed her eyes and took a slow, deep breath. I knew there must be a hundred questions running through her mind. She simply said, "Care to explain?"

"Piper Hudson, welcome to Wild-Side."

She chuckled at that but stopped suddenly. She turned in a slow circle to take in the rolling field of grass and the impenetrable woodland that surrounded the meadow. It looked like we had stepped back to a time before mankind had ransacked Mother Nature. "Oh my God," she mumbled.

Piper's eyes roamed the vast, untamed land. Rolling hills of grassland spread in all directions, meeting walls of unyielding wilderness. She studied the distant tree lines but found no hint of a road—no path or trailhead suggesting a route to civilization. The sky overhead was blue, patched with billowy white clouds.

Her eyes returned to what appeared to be Kentucky bluegrass. It was surprisingly pleasant beneath her bare feet. The tips of the long blades were feathery soft as she waved the palms of her open hands over the primeval vegetation. It was about to go to seed, and what was likely usually coarse blades had become soft. Looking at her bare legs and feet, she was relieved she didn't have to walk through the rougher version of this field.

253

She could see slight disturbances in the distant texture; thin trails of discoloration were visible as the surface swayed in the cool breeze. She concluded that these paths belonged to recent wildlife, not humans. People would be more destructive and leave far more obvious trails in the pristine greenery.

"Wild-Side?" she said, arching her brow skeptically. "Looks a lot like home."

Gray shrugged. He was studying their surroundings much like she had, though he seemed to be doing it with more intensity. His defenses were up. She could see tension in the way the muscles of his bare shoulders bunched and strained. "Only at first glance," he said after a few long seconds. His words were quiet, and there was an edge to them. His eyes continued to roam the distant tree lines. "Taste the air and breathe it in. There's a quality to it that's completely unlike home. It's fresh in a way that's unique to this place. The air is cleaner. It's unpolluted—nearly pristine in toxicology. There's not a place left on Our-World that still feels the same."

Piper grinned, initially thinking he was having fun at her expense. This was all some kind of trick. Yet he was still far more concerned with the distant tree lines. She turned her attention back to the rolling hills and pondered how the shade of green was slightly different from anything she had ever encountered. A glance at her bare toes and a quick wiggle reminded her once again that the texture of the grass was softer and more pleasant than any she had ever experienced. Perhaps she was making assumptions about this grass being softer than she knew back home. This biosphere could have subtle differences.

Eyeing Gray now more quizzically than skeptically, she took a deep breath. The air was crisp and cool as it filled her lungs. She exhaled slowly and took another. By the time she released the third, she saw his point. Her chest felt full and invigorated in a way she had never experienced.

A lightheadedness overtook Piper, but it had nothing to do with the deep breaths she'd just been taking. She placed a hand on Gray's arm to draw his attention. "You're not messing with me? I'm really here?"

He nodded. "I just don't know how," he paused, staring into her eyes. "Or why. I thought I was the only one who could cross. Well, me and Breslin."

Piper glanced at herself and then at him. "Gray, why are we naked?"

His gaze darkened. "I told you about this. Every time I cross, only I make the Transition. No clothes, no weapons—bare-ass naked."

Piper felt her cheeks grow warm as she averted her gaze. She had heard this and knew it, but experiencing it firsthand was an entirely different matter. "I guess, well… intellectually, I just assumed you meant you always felt defenseless in a strange world."

Gray grinned as he stepped back and waved across his completely nude form. "Nope," he laughed. "Literally, about as exposed as a man can be."

Laughing, Piper shook her head. "I get it. I guess I knew that. I just never thought I would see this. Having you explain it is very different from experiencing it."

Gray nodded and began tapping the fingers of his right hand against his left arm. "You're right. But if you're feeling better, it's time to move. It's never wise to stand still after arriving." His eyes took on a distant look, as if he were seeing something in the air that was visible only to him. "We're a couple of kilometers from transportation. We're lucky it's daytime. The Elend don't come out much during the day."

Piper felt her skin prickle at the mention of the bloodthirsty creatures she knew were stalking Wild-Side. Until this moment, she had somehow failed to connect them with the strange wilderness surrounding her.

"Transportation?" It was the only thing she could think to say. "What about clothing?"

Gray took her hand and set off at a brisk pace. His departure was so abrupt that he was nearly dragging her along at first. "Transpo first," he said over his shoulder as she struggled to match his stride. "My team will have gear waiting." He seemed to think better of his statement, then eyed her up and down while walking. A grin spread across his face as he took in her naked form. "Well, they'll have clothes for me. They'll have to sort something out for you. You're my unexpected plus-one."

The flash of light stabbed at Piper's eyes. She blinked away blinding stars and felt her skin prickle with the sudden shift in room temperature. A weakness in her knees sent her off balance. It felt like the earth beneath her had shifted ever so slightly.

"Steady," Gray said, slipping an arm around her waist.

The room was bright, and Piper raised a hand against the glare. That's when she realized they weren't alone. The empty stage of the abandoned facility had been replaced by a similar structure with concrete walls, low ceilings, and half a dozen gaping observers.

Painfully aware of her naked form, Piper took two quick steps back in an awkward retreat. A shocked, mewling gasp escaped her throat. Gray instantly stepped between her and the rest of the room as voices erupted in a rush, each trying to speak over the others. Gray raised a hand in an attempt to halt the verbal assault from everyone around, but they all continued to speak. Piper couldn't comprehend the words; however, the body language and expressions of those present were easy to interpret. While everyone expected to see Gray, it seemed Piper's appearance shocked them just as much as they had her.

Piper leaned to the side and peeked over Gray's shoulder. Six figures occupied the far side of the room. Two sat behind an inclined glass console, while three were positioned behind a wide rectangular glass table that stood just over waist high. The sixth was a wizened, balding man who froze in the doorway at the corner of the room. While the five others peppered Gray with questions or comments in some strange language, the older man remained frozen mid-step, seemingly studying her and Gray as if he had seen something that had altered his worldview.

Uncertain of what to do, Piper stepped closer to Gray. She felt cold and exposed, and no matter how frightened she had been appearing out of nowhere in the woods, that was nothing compared to this. Just as she was about to ask who these people were and what was happening, Piper suddenly noticed that Gray was speaking with them in the unknown language the strangers were using for their verbal assault.

"What language is that?" Piper whispered in Gray's ear before she could think better of it.

He cocked his ear toward her but kept his eyes on the unmoving figures on the far side of the room. "What?" he whispered back. "English. What are you talking about?"

Piper ground her teeth and shot another glance over Gray's shoulder. She scrutinized the figures, then surveyed Gray's profile. She wondered why nobody was moving. Everyone appeared anchored where they stood or sat, yet still talked all at once. Anxious, if not understandable.

"*That* is not English," Piper hissed in a whisper.

"Enough," the old man said in a raised voice. But when the five others on his side of the room continued to squabble, he finally clapped his hands. This drew their attention. "That's enough. Leave them alone." He shook his head in frustration and glanced back through the doorway he had just stepped through, muttering something to someone unseen.

Piper pressed against Gray. "*That was English*," she explained.

The old man turned to Gray and Piper with a smile. "Indeed," he said, grinning. "Gray tends to forget he's using our technology to translate English to Delsh. It becomes so natural that it's hard to distinguish between the two."

"Delsh?" Piper asked, her mouth moving as if tasting the strange word.

A younger, blonde woman walked through the door next to the

old man, her arms cradling a pair of folded blankets. She appeared to glide across the room, approaching her and Gray with none of the hesitation that seemed to anchor the rest of the room in place.

Piper watched as the young woman smiled brightly at Gray, an amused gleam of familiarity dancing in her eyes as she passed him a blanket. Gray turned and draped the heavy wool-like material over Piper's shoulders and wrapped her tightly. She then noticed that he didn't seem the least uncomfortable standing nude before all of these people. Before she could ask about this, Gray finally accepted his own blanket, swung it over his shoulders, and swaddled himself. While Piper was still trying to figure out how to hold onto the wrap, keep it closed, and not trip over it, she noticed Gray had already managed to keep it free from tangling his feet, all within about two seconds.

She understood then what she'd missed in the stress of her experience. He'd been through this dozens of times. If any part of this was new to him, it would be the verbal assault they had suffered when he arrived with a guest in tow.

Gray walked to the edge of the platform and eyed the old man. "You're saying I've been speaking Delsh this whole time?"

The old man shrugged. "Since your second week, maybe your third. You didn't know?"

It was Gray's turn to shrug.

The old man smiled and walked closer. He was about to speak but stopped short. He glanced over his shoulder and saw the other five people still staring at Gray and Piper. The old man shook his head and waved his arm. "Back to work," he grumbled. "We'll sort this out in due time. There will be answers for everyone, but badgering our new friend won't help."

The old man eyed Gray and said, "That was right, wasn't it?" *Badgering?*"

Gray chuckled and nodded. "You've been studying."

The man grinned. "Your vernacular has always fascinated me." He waved a hand and turned his attention to Piper. "I'm assuming this is the young lady you've told me so much about?"

Piper realized she was still hiding behind Gray and suddenly felt silly about it. She stepped forward and shook the man's offered hand, though it was a clumsy effort on her part as she continued to struggle with her death grip on the blanket.

"I'm Victor Cormac," the old man said. "I must admit, I didn't think I would ever get the chance to meet you in person."

"Cormac?" Piper whispered, her brows arched. "Gray has told me a lot about you. He says you're a genius. It's amazing to finally meet you." Despite herself, Piper felt awed in the presence of the older man. From everything she had heard from Gray, it felt like meeting Albert Einstein before anyone knew who he was or what contributions he would make to the future world.

"Genius? Oh, hardly." The man shook her hand and smiled broadly. Mirth danced across his face, but there was something deeper in his eyes. Piper could see an almost limitless intelligence behind them. Even beneath the glimmer of his excitement, he was already pondering the mystery of her arrival here.

She was proven correct when Cormac shifted his gaze to Gray and asked, "How? You're the only one who can Cross. How did you bring her over?"

Gray rolled his eyes and let out a sigh. "You're asking me? I thought you could answer the question."

Cormac's gaze shifted from Gray to Piper and then back again. He nodded. "We'll figure it out." He looked at Piper and gave her a wink. "Not to worry. We've learned a lot in the last four years. For now, this is a great opportunity for me to practice my English," he laughed.

Four years? That didn't make sense. Gray had only been bouncing back and forth to Wild-Side for a fraction of that time.

The young blonde returned, eyeing Piper as she approached. However, just before she spoke, her gaze shifted to Gray. "I laid out an extra jumpsuit," she said with a smile. "I guessed the size, but it should be close." She extended her hand to Piper. "I'm Lacy."

"I didn't exactly leave much to the imagination, did I?" Piper said, shaking Lacy's hand. She nearly let the blanket slip and cursed under her breath as she caught it. "I'm Piper," she said through clenched teeth, her cheeks turning from pink to red.

"Gray calls it 'arriving on the free ball express,'" Lacy said with a grin. "I'll admit, it took me nearly six months to grasp what that meant. As far as I can tell, nudity doesn't carry the same stigma here."

Piper glared at Gray and shook her head. "What about his sense of humor? How does that fit in here?"

Lacy bit the corner of her lip and briefly eyed the floor before looking at Gray. She glanced back at Piper and smiled. "There was a bit of a learning curve."

Gray shrugged and wrapped an arm around Piper. "That learning curve is universal. It doesn't matter what world you come from."

Cormac met Gray's eye. "May I have a word with you in private?"

The thought of being left alone made Piper's heart race. The concern must have shown in her expression, as Gray turned to face her fully. He looked her directly in the eye and paused long enough for her to take several breaths. "I'm not leaving the room," he said. "I'm just stepping over there. I won't leave you alone until you're comfortable. It's my fault you're here. These are good people, but I don't expect you to trust them. Not until you're ready."

His hand squeezed hers, bringing with it a bracing sense of confidence. "I'm good," she said. "Do what you need to." A smirk crossed her face. "It's not like I'm going anywhere, right?"

———————

Doctor Cormac led Gray to the corner of the room. He studied Gray and tried to control the trepidation that fueled the migraine forming behind his left eye. The stress headache was induced only by the most dire circumstances, and the last six months had tested his coping mechanisms. But if Gray had found a way to bring others across the veil, he'd gained exactly the kind of ability Breslin needed to bring the bulk of his people to this world.

"What is she doing here?" Cormac whispered in a hushed tone, his eyes blazing behind the crooked frame of his glasses. "What have you done?"

Gray shrugged. "I have no idea. It's not my fault–" He paused, reconsidering his words. Waving a hand in the air, he lowered his voice and said, "Well, it probably is my fault…but I have no idea what I did–or how I did it."

Cormac took a breath and studied Gray. Of course, he didn't do this intentionally. The girl was Piper Hudson. The boy cared for her in ways–well, in ways Cormac knew he wasn't equipped to fully appreciate. Bringing her here put her in danger. It was the last thing Gray would ever do on purpose. Finally, he huffed a sigh of resignation. "Right. So tell me what happened."

Turning his back on the rest of the room, Gray looked at Cormac. "Not a clue. We fell asleep. We were together, but that's happened a hundred times before… and she never ended up *here*!"

Cormac nodded. "So, what was different this time?"

Shaking Gray said, "Not a damn thing. We haven't been together for a long time. But what difference would that make?"

Though he pondered the point, Cormac didn't see the relevance. Surely something more was different about this experience. Maybe something had changed about Gray. If that were the case, there were too many variables to consider in those moments. The best place to begin would be an examination of the boy's bioscan results. If he had changed biologically over the last six to twelve months, the scans would reflect it.

"If Breslin learns of this," Cormac whispered.

Gray nodded. The look on the boy's face confirmed that they were completely on the same page in that respect. "We'll need to prepare a nano treatment for her," Cormac explained. "She won't be able to understand us or use our technology until we address that."

"The same thing you did for me? It's not a big deal, right?"

"Not quite. The technology is calibrated for each individual. While I'm not sure what to expect from Piper, I'm confident that a significant amount of customization will be necessary. Unique brain chemistry, endocrine system, metabolism, and so on. It won't take long. We just need to conduct a few scans."

"For now, I have some news." Cormac motioned toward the large display on the far wall. "We've been waiting for you."

They crossed the room, and Cormac activated the massive AR display with a wave of his hand. All heads turned as the high gray walls encircling the city of Oakland illuminated the screen. An aerial view of the city appeared, shifting and panning to reveal the five and eight-story buildings within the expansive perimeter wall, along with the three pedestrian footbridges connecting the wall to a ten-story tower at the center of the small city.

"Mara has regained consciousness," Cormac said.

"What did she say?" Gray followed the older man as they walked back to the room's center to rejoin the rest of the group.

"We don't know," Cormac admitted, nodding to Lacy, who picked up the thread.

"We received word about Mara about thirty-two hours ago," Lacy explained. "Doctor Cormac planned to send me to interview her in person, but I never had the opportunity. A Thonian storm struck the plains almost immediately after we were notified, preventing me from teleporting. Communications have been disrupted ever since, so we haven't been able to interview her from here."

Gray nodded. "What's the status of the storm?"

Cormac spread his hands, and the view of the city shrank to a fraction of its former size as the perspective zoomed out. The camera's point of view shifted southeast until Oakland appeared as a thumbnail in the top left corner of the screen, while Portland was similarly represented on the right. Rolling hills, jagged moraines, and hundreds of miles of dense forest separated the two cities. An overlay was activated, revealing an amorphous blob positioned almost equidistant between the two cities. The representation was cloud-like and massive, perhaps forty times the diameter of the city at its narrowest point, and seemingly impossibly long at its widest. It was vaguely rectangular, though with softly feathered edges. It stood like some kind of wall between the two cities.

"Almost like it had a mind of its own," Piper said as she studied the screen. "I thought you said it was a natural phenomenon?"

Cormac grinned. "It is, but the timing and positioning make that more suspect than ever." His words trailed off as he spoke, his mind drifting with the thought.

"What is it?" Gray said.

Cormac just stared at the screen.

"Doc?" Gray said again.

"Sorry," Cormac said. He waved his hands in the air. With a flick of his wrist, they were once again looking at Oakland. "How would you feel about going there personally?" Cormac asked, glancing at Gray. "You need to talk with Mara, and the sooner, the better." The view on screen quickly spun until the camera was positioned directly above the center of the city, looking down. The unique shapes of each building were more apparent from this angle, but he manipulated an overlay to highlight a rectangular structure near the city's center. It was one of the largest buildings within the perimeter wall.

"This is the infirmary," Cormac said. "The hospital, if you prefer."

———————

I shook my head, feeling my teeth grind. "It's a good idea, but I can't leave Piper. It's my fault she's here. I need to find a way to take her home."

"It's okay," Piper said. "If it's important, I can wait."

This was my mess, and I had to fix it. She was here, a stranger in an unfamiliar place, and it was my fault. My first responsibility was to ensure her safety. I was about to explain all of this when Doc Cormac interrupted by stepping between me and the rest of the room.

"Excuse me," Cormac said, angling himself toward Piper as he spoke slowly. His bushy gray eyebrows appeared to bounce with each deliberately enunciated word. "Piper? Are you saying you can understand me?"

The older man's words were slow and clearly enunciated, causing my stomach to sink with instant understanding of his intent. Piper, on the other hand, was confused. She pulled the woolen blanket tighter around her shoulders and shot a puzzled glance at me before returning her gaze to Cormac. "Yes. Why are you talking so slowly?"

Cormac's pallor seemed suddenly more grim. He motioned to the AR display on the wall. "And you can see...that?" he said.

Piper simply nodded.

"What exactly do you see?"

Piper furrowed her brow but must have decided to play along. "An aerial view of a futuristic walled city. There are no skyscrapers or anything—no people, for that matter—but the highlighted rectangular building is labeled as a medical center." She paused and turned a piercing gaze at the Doc "Why?"

Cormac looked at Lacy and said, "Did you—" but Lacy was already shaking her head.

I pulled Piper aside and quickly stepped between her and the rest of the room. "What's going on? You all are making me nervous. I thought we agreed that my getting nervous isn't good for anyone."

Cormac rubbed his eyes. He hooked his glasses on the collar of his shirt and looked at me through tired, glassy eyes. "She can understand Delsh and see the augmented reality displays."

Gray nodded. "So?"

Lacy added in a quiet voice, "We haven't given her the nano injection yet. How is she doing it?"

Chapter 14 - I Also Brought Sarcasm to Wild-Side

Wild-Side

Piper sat on the edge of the table and rubbed the spot on her arm where blood had been drawn some twenty minutes before. There wasn't so much as a mark left to indicate the bodily invasion and she hadn't felt the sample as it had been extracted. Some kind of device was used to pull the blood from her body without so much as breaking the surface of her skin. No needle, no puncture, not even the slightest pain. Everywhere she turned, this place seemed infused with subtle yet unmistakable technological improvements that separated it from home in subtle but undeniable ways. She looked at her hand resting on the table's surface and made yet another observation. The table was made of stainless steel, but the texture and temperature didn't feel right. She had been informed that it was a metallic-ceramic composite, which was, apparently, commonly used in construction here. It was lightweight, strong, and versatile. It could be formed in small amounts using a mobile fabrication device similar to the 3D printers she had seen at home, or it could be employed on a larger scale to create components for building-sized structures.

"Incredible," she heard herself murmur.

"What's that?" Lacy asked as she passed by, holding a circular ring the size of a dinner plate in her hands. She handed it to Gray.

"Your technology," Piper said. "Everything from the augmented reality to the particle fabrication units. I'm just blown away by it all."

Lacy's face seemed to beam. She nodded to Gray and asked whether the ring-like device met his specifications. Gray appeared satisfied. Lacy then returned her attention to Piper. "Gray had the same reaction initially," she said. "Your world is primitive in a lot of ways, but you have so many things we don't."

"What could we possibly have that you don't?" Piper wondered.

"Art," Gray said, slipping the collar around his neck. "Wild-Side has enough science to put Our-World to shame, but they have no understanding of the arts. No music, no painting, no poetry. They don't even know what fiction is. They couldn't wrap their heads around the idea of writing something that wasn't scientific or historic."

Gray tapped a button or manipulated the corner of the ring he'd placed around his neck, and Piper gasped as a helmet materialized from the thin ring of material. In less than two seconds, particles grew, moved, and formed into a hard shell that surrounded his head in the shape of a conventional, albeit high-tech looking helmet.

Piper was on her feet, moving in for a closer look without realizing she had slid from the edge of the table. "That's incredible," she whispered, resting her hand on the side of Gray's head.

Gray placed two fingers approximately where his temple would be. The smoky black visor dematerialized to reveal his eyes and nose. Only then did she notice how sleek and form-fitting the helmet really was. It added just about an inch to the overall diameter of his head while offering very little padding. Given what she had seen of the tech from this place already, she suspected the helmet was far more protective than anything from her world.

"Amazing," Piper muttered.

Gray tapped a button on his wrist, and the helmet seemed to disintegrate. She quickly noticed that the material was deconstructing and receding back into the collar that originally housed it. While Gray seemed satisfied with the experience, he didn't appear blown away by the exposure to the technology. "That's good," he said to Lacy. "The rest of the suit works the same way?"

Lacy nodded. "We modified the standard environmental suits we use in the Badlands so it wasn't—what did you call it—reinventing the wheel? Tripp helped me update the deployment regulators to meet your specifications, and Doc Cormac altered the nano-graphene composite to increase protection."

Wheeling a cart to the edge of the table where Piper had been sitting, Lacy placed a series of small rings on the surface. As she did, an AR image began to glow on the table. It projected the locations and uses of the rings as she positioned them precisely. The AR image depicted a human torso. Lacy placed a small ring at each of the figure's wrists and ankles, while a larger ring was positioned at belt height. She placed a band around the center of the chest and then collected the collar ring from Gray, placing it at the corresponding spot on the table. Finally, putting her open hand over the center of the AR display, she closed her hand into a fist. As the fist formed, the nano-material moved in slow motion from each of the ring-like bands. It appeared in a semi-transparent state, hovering in virtual space above the table's surface, but Piper found the demonstration both beautiful and creepy at the same time. The way the particulate nano-material swept across the body of the human figure felt...just wrong. It resembled some kind of insect-like swarm devouring the body.

"That's at twenty percent normal speed," Lacy said as the suit completely formed over the figure. The supine three-dimensional figure was entirely wrapped in black, form-fitting armor. It resembled a blend of a blackedout football uniform and some kind of ceramic motorcycle leathers.

Gray leaned over the table and studied the image. He seemed to be paying close attention to the elbow and knee joints. "What about my mobility?"

Piper observed how the suit appeared to materialize from a series of separate rings situated at various parts of the body. It could deploy with tremendous speed and harden into incredibly strong shapes, all based on variables, allowing the suits to adjust to the forms of the individuals who would wear them. To her, this seemed like only partially fulfilled potential. At least a dozen questions began to jockey for position in her mind as she examined the AR projection.

Lacy shrugged. "Tripp promised you could do that dance everyone was talking about in the vid-stream last month. What was it called?"

Gray was already dismissing the comment. "Good enough. Thanks."

"Wait," Piper protested. "What dance? You guys dance? I thought you don't have music."

"We didn't have music or dance," Lacy said. "Gray has been bringing vids over and sharing culture from his world—well, your world, I suppose I should say."

Something about this made Piper feel she needed to dig deeper. Maybe it was the way Gray wanted to move past the comment. Maybe it was the way he suddenly seemed reluctant to meet her eye. "What's the video, Gray? What's the dance."

Gray muttered something that Piper couldn't make out. She was ready to ask him to say it again, but it turned out that wasn't needed.

"Oh, yeah," Lacy giggled. "That's right. Footloose."

Doc Cormac walked into the room, displaying no interest in the armored human figure projected in AR on the table at its center. Instead, he handed a glass-like tablet to Lacy.

"It's what we expected," Lacy said after a brief examination of the tablet.

Cormac nodded, but he appeared troubled by the data despite her words. "That doesn't explain the transmission vector. We designed the technology specifically to prevent transmission."

I didn't like how they talked as if Piper and I weren't in the room. I could see it making Piper even more uncomfortable than she was. "Care to fill us in?" I pressed. "Keep in mind Piper just got here, and she knows even less about your tech than I do."

The frustration on Cormac's expression dissolved when he looked at Piper. "Of course," he said. "I'm sorry. It's just that this becomes more concerning when it doesn't work. If Gray's blood has the ability to spread our nanotech, it could have unforeseen impacts for your world. Your presence here could just be the beginning.

"Sometimes, I overlook the human aspect of the problem when I focus on the bigger picture. I don't intend to cause you undue

269

concern. We'll figure this out. We just need to understand the transmission vector."

I was holding Piper's hand. Cormac didn't understand her stress the way I did. However I'd done it, I'd brought her into this world. A world filled with dangers I couldn't protect her from. At the same time, I couldn't explain to her that her mistaken ability to cross over like this was the single biggest risk to her safety. She'd somehow accomplished what only Breslin and I had done so far. It was the secret Breslin would do anything to uncover.

Through all of this, Lacy continued studying the tablet Cormac had given her. "The tech was sexually transmitted," she said suddenly. "It had to be. It's the obvious common denominator."

Cormac was already shaking his head. "Can't be," he said. His tone resembled an exhausted man who didn't want to waste time on the obvious. Still, there was a touch of impatience in his voice. He was worn out yet willing to listen to anyone searching for a solution. "Look at the version of the release used on Gray. Rev 45.23.765 was introduced so he could communicate with us. But before he returned to his world for the first time, we updated to Rev 45.23.771. Rev 771 was the first barrier against sexual transmission."

Piper leaned close and began whispering in my ear. "They've been using this tech for how long?"

"At least a hundred years," I whispered back. "It's probably much longer. There's a lot you need to know about these people."

"I'll concede that. My point is, why did they only add a patch to prevent sexual transmission when you arrived?"

There was a lot to unpack. I didn't think this was the right time or place to try to explore the Seeley's long lifespan, culture, or their complete inexperience with the concept of sexual intercourse.

Lacy pointed her tablet toward the wall and swiped the content to a large screen for everyone to see. It appeared to be some kind of software change log. Apparently, even across worlds, the need to document code changes was universal. I couldn't be sure if this was a positive sign for the multi-verse.

"Rev 771 protected against sexual transmission as we understood it then," Lacy explained. "That Transition protocol was updated with Rev 45.23.869 more recently when our understanding of sexual intercourse evolved. Gray's tech wasn't updated until his visit three transitions ago."

Cormac walked slowly to the table where the helmet and body armor were still projected in AR. I waved my hand, and the projection disappeared. Cormac didn't seem to notice. He lowered himself wearily onto a stool and absently slipped off his glasses, rubbing slowly at the bridge of his nose. I'd seen him do this more times than I could count. He did it when he was processing information related to a concern he took very seriously.

"Hold on," Piper said as she slid off the table beside me. "When you say your understanding of sexual intercourse changed, what does that mean? How does sex *change*?"

Lacy was about to speak, but I raised a hand. I wanted to frame the conversation first. She wasn't likely to start from square one–at least not as Piper required it. "The Seeley, as a race, don't reproduce. Until I explained the mechanics, no one here had practical experience."

Piper gazed at me with what I can only describe as a slack-jawed expression. "Do they…"

I grinned. "Their anatomy is the same as yours and mine. It's their culture that's different. The biology seems to be there; the biological imperative is different." I wanted to explain how this was just the tip of the iceberg regarding my questions about Wild-Side's overall architecture. But there was too much to unpack; much of it was a private conversation I wanted to have. In many ways, the people and culture of Wild-Side were genuine and pristine. People were what they seemed to be. But there were a few dark corners to their culture–corners I intended to explore, as they stood to impact me, and through me, maybe even Our-World. I needed to be careful.

"We didn't have familiarity," Lacy corrected. "Until the videos. That's when we realized there was a transmission vector we hadn't accounted for."

"Videos?" Piper glanced in confusion.

I waved my hand at Lacy to end this part of the conversation. I wished it had been that easy. The look on Piper's face told me it wouldn't happen, so I explained. "Wild-Side–The Seeley," I clarified, "have a very different culture." I was trying to frame this just right but already knew it would look very bad for me. "They have no art or music. Their people excel at science and mathematics but have no concepts of architecture, painting, sculpture, or fiction."

Piper stared at me. "And?" She somehow stretched the single word into three syllables.

"I can't bring anything with me during the crossing," I continued. "Nothing physical. But data is merely information, and I can transfer metric tons of that thanks to the nanotech," I tapped the side of my head for emphasis. "Music, movies, books, comics, digital copies of art? You name it. I guess you could say it's the biggest theft of intellectual property in history." I shrugged. "I like to think it was for a good cause. The people here ate it up."

I left out how some people didn't appreciate my exposing them to culture from another world. For every two people who embraced what I offered, there was at least one who criticized it. I had more than my share of detractors on Wild-Side.

Piper studied my expression as if she were waiting for something. "So, when you say they learned about sex for the first time, was that from the movies and books you shared?"

I nodded.

"And, when you say you shared movies and books, what exactly do you mean?"

I shrugged and avoided her gaze. I believe that was my downfall. "Feature films and television. Books and film from across history."

"Amazing material," Lacy said. "But it was the pornography that allowed us to fine-tune Rev 869." She said it with such upbeat enthusiasm that I actually saw Piper do a double take before she glared at me.

"Pornography." Her tone was as rough as gravel. "You're the ambassador to an entirely new world, and your contribution is to share pornography with them?" Like Cormac, she was now rubbing her eyes with a weary expression.

Lacy appeared puzzled. "It's among the most popular content," she said. "Everyone's talking about it."

Piper crossed her arms and glared at me. "No doubt." She looked at Cormac and then at Lacy. "What exactly about the smut caused you to update the tech?"

Cormac appeared to have taken a proverbial knee in this conversation. I don't think he was relishing his place on the sideline. It was more that he was clever enough not to participate.

Lacy looked confused. "Smut?" She laughed. "Oh, I get it. Once we realized how creative you all can be with your lovemaking, we understood that conventional intercourse wasn't the only means of transmission."

Piper now appeared confused.

I groaned and averted my eyes. I'd realized where this was going some time back but didn't see a way to pull the ripcord. There was no way this would end with my dignity intact, so I leaned into it. "Oral," I said. "Until they saw the dreaded porn, the idea of oral sex had never crossed the virgin white of their pure, untainted minds."

Piper looked me square in the eyes, offered a slow, dramatic shake of her head, and then walked slowly out of the room.

I glanced at the Doc and stuffed my hands deep into the pockets of my jeans. "Well, that went well," I said.

He looked shocked. "You think *that* went well?"

I forgot. I also brought sarcasm to Wild-Side.

———————

Tripp's eyes were wide and shining like polished coins. He stood behind something low and wide, draped with what must have been a bed sheet. I think he had been watching too many videos from back home because the idea of an unveiling was childlike and dramatic in a way that seemed to confuse Doc and Lacy. For her part, Piper just seemed confuddled.

"I matched your specifications precisely," Tripp was saying. "The idea of a gyroscope was interesting, though a bit quaint. The central processor made it entirely unnecessary, but the way you explained it helped me understand what you were aiming for in terms of ultimate functionality." He seemed at a loss for words for a long second as his eyes wandered into the distance in thought. "And more importantly, how you might manipulate those functions. That was the hard part, actually."

The Doc succumbed to his puzzlement and attempted to lift the draped corner of the sheet. Tripp swatted his hand away and shooed him with a wordless, harsh scowl.

"With all due respect for your showmanship," I said, "I think you should get on with the show before you lose your captive audience." While I respected Tripp's pride in this matter, the clock was ticking, and I needed to leave for Oakland as soon as possible.

Lacy was about to speak when Tripp took a deep breath and dramatically pulled the sheet away from the large object in one triumphant motion. The low-slung device showcased smooth curves and contours, colored in subtly varying shades of matte black.

Piper glanced between me and the device, her voice barely more than a whisper. "You've got to be kidding."

The Doc walked slowly around the device, pulling off his glasses as he moved. He stooped low and squinted at the machine as if trying to discern its purpose or mentally dissect its design. I waited for him to speak, but he was slack-jawed until he completed an entire circuit of the contraption.

The machine sat on the floor, featuring what resembled a seat and handlebars that were akin to a blend of a dirt bike and a snowmobile. A short windscreen and fender extended from the front of the machine to deflect and shape the wind. However, unlike a dirt bike or snowmobile, it lacked a conventional drive train. The vehicle was situated at the center of four large, bladed fans, with one positioned at each quadrant of the machine's circumference.

I couldn't help but smile. Tripp had truly outdone himself, and judging by the expression on his face, he was aware of it.

"It's..." Piper mumbled, appearing to search for the words. "A quadcopter bike?"

Tripped seemed to hop in place where he stood. "Oh, not bad. I was going with Hover-bike, but that's good, too!"

Doc Cormac looked at me, his face completely pale. His bushy brows knit together as he spoke slow, deliberate words, as if testing them for validity. "You intend to ride that?" He pointed vaguely skyward with a shaky finger and looked as though he might become sick at any moment.

"The shortest distance between two points is a straight line," I said. "And the fastest route to Oakland, without teleportation, is by air."

The Doc walked over to a stool and sat down. He seemed to have aged suddenly.

Lacy simply stared at the Airbike, not having moved or commented at all.

Piper slid up close to my side. "Is this the first time you've seen this thing?" she asked in a quiet voice. There was neither concern nor apprehension in her tone.

I nodded.

"But you designed it?"

I nodded again. "My ideas, Tripp's engineering."

"You didn't think he'd pull it off, did you?"

I had to pause for a moment to consider the question. Tripp was brilliant. He'd transformed some of my most outrageous ideas into reality. What had I been thinking when I sketched this one up for him?

"He might have finished it a bit faster than I anticipated," I admitted.

Piper rubbed her chin in mock consideration. "It's a radical idea. I guess I shouldn't be surprised. Any sane person would put it through extensive testing before risking their life by actually trying to fly it, you know?"

I nodded but said nothing.

"But that was the purpose of the helmet and armor you just showed me, wasn't it?"

I shrugged. "I always wanted to be a test pilot."

Lacy glanced at me and Piper. "This is from one of those videos where the hungry dog was chasing the roadrunner, right?"

A hand going to her mouth to cover a toothy grin, Piper said, "sums this up perfectly."

———————

I twisted the throttle, and the Airbike shot instantly vertical as if it had been launched from a cannon. The muffled whirr of the four props slicing through the late afternoon air was surprisingly quiet. Since the powerful motors were battery-operated, it was the only sound to be heard. Unless you count the gasp of excitement that escaped my lips as I watched the entirety of Portland shrink below my left foot pedal.

The throttle was controlled just like every motorcycle I'd ever ridden, easily adjusted with a twist of the right handlebar grip. I let off just as I noticed the altimeter that had been added to the corner of my HUD. I'd passed five thousand eight hundred feet in a matter of seconds, which explained why my ears had popped with a headache-inducing ferocity.

The key thing to remember about this contraption is that it is in no way beholden to the laws of aerodynamics. That is what makes a quad-rotor system so ingenious. The front left and rear right rotors spin in one direction while the front right and rear left spin in the opposite. It isn't obvious to the pilot, or even anyone watching the machine in flight, but by precisely controlling the speed of the rotors, the craft can hover in place or power through the sky at remarkable speeds. In many ways, it has the ideal performance characteristics of both a helicopter and a fixed-wing plane.

A typical quadcopter gains forward momentum by pitching forward. The faster the craft flies, the steeper the forward pitch. This is also true for Tripp's craft, but with some mitigating effects. He built a subtle tilt into the rotors and the fourteen-inch-high ducts surrounding them, so when I accelerated—at least in the low and mid-range of the performance curve—the fans tilted by up to ten degrees. The idea was to prevent me from feeling like I was riding the inclined side of a seesaw when traveling at moderately high speeds.

"Did I just hear you giggle?" Piper's voice came through the com channel in my helmet.

I brought the Airbike to a hover and marveled at how well it balanced itself. Fortunately, Tripp got that part of the design right on his first attempt. I had flown radio-controlled quadcopter drones that operated under almost the same principles. When the auto-leveling controls malfunctioned on those, it often resulted in aggressive and catastrophic crashes. Since I was then sitting at just under six thousand feet, my crash would have put all my past crashes to shame.

"I'm pretty sure what you heard was a manly grunt of appreciation for Tripp's engineering skills," I said with a grin so wide it had to be visible over the audio channel.

The sound that escaped from Piper resembled a grunt more than any noise I had made. She began to speak, but Tripp interrupted her.

"Ah, Gray? Did you mean to go that high?" he asked. "Because I can't see you. Is my telemetry accurate? We talked about you staying close to the treetops for the test run, right?"

Piper cleared her throat. "That's my recollection of the conversation."

I continued to hover and turned the handlebars to the right. The Airbike spun slowly on its axis, resembling the tiniest doughnut in the world…six thousand feet in the air. "This is amazing," I mumbled to myself.

"Gray?" Piper said. "Can you hear me?"

I was observing the Airbike. The propeller blades spun so quickly that they were nearly invisible. All the model drones I had flown featured props that shrieked and ripped through the air. They sounded like banshees whenever they did anything more than idle on the launch pad. These were surprisingly quiet despite their size and evident power. I wasn't an engineer, so the experience left me wondering if Tripp had done something to minimize the noise. Perhaps it was a result of these props being orders larger than I had experienced.

"I'm here," I said. "Just taking in the sights." And I was. Rolling hills of forested land stretched out in all directions as far as I could see. Portland was still directly below me, so as far as control went, I was doing great. I hadn't strayed off course with my hover. The city was a little larger than a coffee cup in the distance below me.

"We know," Tripp said. "Remember? We can see what you see?"

I grinned once more. They had access to a point-of-view feed from my helmet, which live-streamed everything I looked at back to them in real time.

I spun faster, turning my doughnut into a pirouette. I wanted to see what the Airbike could do—where its performance hit a wall—so I would know what was possible. That turned out to be a bad idea. The machine spun far faster than I could tolerate, and I had to stop the spin after just a few seconds.

"Well done," Tripp said. "You provided some excellent performance analytics from that maneuver. What else are you capable of?"

"Huh," I replied. "That's a good question. Here, hold my beer!"

I heard a sharp intake of breath from Piper and knew she was about to object to the idea. Like me, she understood it was already too late. Shoving the handlebars forward, I feathered the throttle. The Airbike performed exactly as I expected. It felt like I had just launched off the top of a bobsled run with a booster rocket strapped to my ass.

The rebel yell that tore from my throat was as involuntary as it was fitting for the experience. The altimeter in the corner of my HUD spun like a national debt calculation, only in reverse, as the trees north of the city rushed to greet me. Voices filled the comm channel, but I couldn't process the words. My senses were on fire with so much tactile and visual input that something had to give. Listening to backseat drivers was simply out of the question.

I'm sure the G-force I was experiencing was displayed somewhere on my HUD. In this case, it would be more like a negative G-force, as holding onto the Airbike during a power dive took everything I had. With a white-knuckled grip on the handlebars, my knees pinching the sides of the seat, and my feet pressed as far into the steering toggles as I could manage, I suddenly understood what it felt like to ride a bullet.

As I reached two hundred feet, I eased back on the handlebars. The front of the Airbike responded instantly, and I was flying level and parallel to the forest canopy. It took me several seconds to realize I'd done it, but I had adjusted the throttle as I pulled out of the dive. The Airbike's control system was completely intuitive.

Building on the idea, I gently turned to the right. Normally, this would have spun the Airbike completely in place. If this happened by itself and was turned far enough, it would have spun me like a top and left me flying backward. This wasn't the way I wanted to turn the Airbike to navigate a corner. To do that, I needed to add some roll. That required me to slightly lower my right toe. With the roll added to the right turn of the handlebars, the Airbike cornered as if I were using a banked highway exit ramp.

"Nice!" I heard Tripp laugh over the comm channel. "You picked that up quickly. I wasn't sure you could do that without an automated assist."

Since they weren't intuitive, we discussed allowing machine intelligence to manage the combination of turning and cornering maneuvers. He mentioned that the technology would make the machine much simpler to fly. I contended that the higher-level automation likely wouldn't operate in the dead zones. I'm not entirely sure he grasped my second point, but there was no arguing against the first. Navigating the dead zones was a primary requirement for this new aircraft type, so he built the flight controls to my specifications.

I turned back toward the city but slowed to half my previous speed. Leaning back from the handlebars, I let go and sat upright on the seat. The Airbike slowed quickly and came to a hover, maintaining altitude with what seemed to me impressive precision.

"The gyroscope works like a top," I said.

Piper laughed, but Tripp missed the joke. "I guess analog tech has its uses after all," he admitted.

I looked down at my torso and suddenly realized why holding onto the Airbike during the power-dive had been easier than I expected when the machine first dropped out from under me. A pencil-thick tether had somehow appeared from each side of the seat and connected to small D-rings on the back of each hip. These D-rings hadn't been on my belt when I first climbed onto the bike.

"Hey Tripp," I said in a calm, completely non-confrontational tone. "Did you forget to tell me something about my gear and this machine? Maybe it has to do with the two conspiring to tether me into bondage?"

Tripp said something that could have been "Huh?" Then, I heard laughter, followed by what sounded like hushed words. I can only assume he was talking with Piper.

"No kidding?" Piper was saying a few seconds later when she seemed to be coming back on the line. "Tripp's afraid you're going to be mad. I told him that's not the case. I might be, though. He said you activated an emergency restraint system. Apparently, it's a feature designed to engage only if the machine is—" her tone sharpened "—out of control and about to crash. It was a safety system, so he didn't think it would be necessary."

I considered explaining that I needed to know these things. If it engages in the wrong conditions, it could work against me instead of for me. Then I reconsidered. Tripp had done amazing work, and in fairness, I was giving the machine a tougher test run than I had agreed to. It just performed too aggressively; it was hard to see it as a Prius when it was more like a...Ferrari.

"If you need to override the restraint," Tripp said, "you can tap the big red button on the dashboard display. It will appear as soon as the restraints engage. Hit the button and the restraints will disintegrate. You're stuck with passive safety measures after that."

"Wait," Piper interrupted. "What are passive safety measures?"

"The big red button is a fantastic idea," I told Tripp. I didn't want Piper worrying too much about the safety of the Airbike or what we called safety measures. I was hoping Tripp could read between the lines. "I was just thinking that an emergency release would be ideal."

"And if you can't get to the button," Tripp continued, "the system will respond to a verbal command." The words eject, eject, eject scrolled across my heads-up display. "I suggest you don't say them out loud right now."

"You must be joking," Piper mumbled.

I laughed. "Tripp and the Doc have watched Top Gun at least half a dozen times. By the way, speaking of the Doc, he's been quiet. What does he think of the maiden flight?"

A few seconds of silence followed. I was about to repeat the question when Piper said, "He ejected about ten seconds after you launched. I don't think the idea of air travel agrees with him. He wasn't looking too good—airsickness, if I had to guess."

I nodded. "He watched most of Top Gun with his eyes closed."

Piper started to say something but decided not to finish.

I circled the city three times, each lap faster than the last, then took the Airbike in for a landing.

As I stepped off the machine, Piper was there. She threw her arms around me the second my helmet dropped back into the ring at my collar. "That's amazing," she said.

"Which part? The hoverbike or the magic helmet?" I said.

"Both," she said. "All of it. This entire place. I have nanotech in my blood, so I can understand another language."

"And speak it. You're speaking Delsh, now."

Her brows knitted. When she spoke, she seemed to be tasting the words. "I am? I don't think so."

"I didn't realize it for a while either. It had to be explained to me. The technology makes it all so natural that you don't even notice it after a while. At first, the tech does the work of translating. Before long, I guess our minds start doing the work on their own. It becomes natural in a way that we don't even notice the Transition."

She stared as if trying to decide if I was joking with her.

I shrugged. "I felt the same way. There's more. Tripp, Doc Cormac, Lacy, and the others? You know that those aren't their real names, right?"

That really confused her.

"For all intents and purposes, we're on an alien world. Well, it's a world alien *to us*. Does it make sense for the people here to have names like Steve, Bob, and Tom? Do you think names are that universal? They aren't back home. Different nations have different naming conventions. Tripp, Lacy, and the Doc? Those are names I sort of mapped to them as part of the rationalization process."

With that, she simply looked concerned, possibly about my sanity.

"I didn't come up with the name; this is what they told me. Apparently, it's just how it works. Our minds need a way to sort things out—a way to rationalize all the new information. There's a new language, with new writing and spoken words. It takes months for even the most intelligent and talented individuals to process this information and learn it. Technology simplifies this with shortcuts. Some of those shortcuts map Delsh names and words to those we already know. This allows our minds to focus on the big picture instead of struggling with written and spoken language issues."

Piper watched my eyes intently as I spoke. I could see the wonder in her expression. "I don't even know what to do with that. How do I process that?"

I shrugged. "Don't. If I hadn't told you about it, you wouldn't know any different. But given the precarious position we're in right now, the better you understand the tech of this world, the better your chances of understanding the people. They only know their tech. Their culture is based on science and technology. They've only recently begun to grasp art and culture."

"And pornography," she muttered. "The crowning achievement of your humanitarian mission. How do you feel about that?"

———————

I was twenty minutes into the flight and already comfortable with all the new information available on the perimeter of my HUD. Since it was specific to piloting the Airbike, it appeared only when I was in the air. Stats detailing my airspeed, altitude, and less critical information like temperature were readily accessible. The temperature didn't directly impact me early in the flight thanks to the flight suit. It was better described as a cross between armor and an environmental suit. The tech was originally designed as an environmental suit, but it resembled motorcycle leathers—only without the leather. It was far sleeker and more comfortable than any hazmat suit I'd ever seen, and so far, it had protected me from the cold temperatures at high altitude. The air was thin at fourteen thousand feet, and according to my HUD, it would have been uncomfortable as well. This was important because, once I reached the dead zone, I would lose the use of the suit, my HUD, and pretty much all of my tech.

For now, I focused on the thin orange line in my HUD that indicated my flight plan and enjoyed the experience. I maintained a steady one hundred seventy miles per hour and had yet to reach the maximum range of the Airbike's throttle. One seventy was the limit of the comfort zone for sustained flight, at least at my current altitude. Any faster, and the buffeting force of the wind became fatiguing, even with the protection of my suit. Once I reached the dead zone, I would have to fly lower and slower.

I also needed to fly line of sight. It reminded me of the unpleasantness just before my departure.

Doc displayed the aerial map with Portland in the lower right and Oakland in the upper left. Between the two lay nearly three thousand miles of semi-mountainous terrain and plains, blanketed in endless forest. A valley lay almost at the center of the map, bisecting the journey and depicted in a foggy green. "The Thonian storm has stagnated over the dead zone," Doc Cormac explained. "On its own, this is not unusual. What is unusual is the size of the storm." He spread his hands over the surface of the table to enlarge the video of the three-dimensional map. "The surface area of the storm has grown. It now covers more than just the dead zone. This suggests it won't be dispersing in the near future."

I nodded. "So, my trip is on?" I confirmed while glancing at the countdown on my wrist display, which showed forty-nine hours and sixteen minutes.

The Doc seemed to be reading my mind. "For once, it feels like time is on our side."

He thought I had time to reach Portland, interview Mara, and return before I bounced back to my world. It was a solid plan. I, on the other hand, was more concerned about what would happen to Piper when that moment came. I started to express this, but the Doc raised a hand to cut me off. "Take care of the interview," he said. "Let us figure out what's happened to Piper. We need to conduct more tests. My suspicion is she will either rebound back to your world when you do, or she will stay here until we find a way to manually trigger the transit. I can't say for sure until we gather more information.

"Until we gather more data, all you can do is wait. If we understand what Mara saw, we might finally begin to understand what caused all of this to unfold."

I met Piper's gaze. She gave me a weary smile and a slight nod. If she was okay with the plan, who was I to argue? Besides, I'd been waiting months to talk with Mara. I had a feeling she was the key to understanding Breslin.

Lacy pointed to the orange line projected on the map. It was a winding route stretching from Portland, entering the amorphous green cloud over the dead zone and extending out the far side before leading to Oakland. "Here's your route," she explained, spreading her hands over the table to draw closer to the map. The display focused on the point where the line entered the cloud of green haze on the right side. "When you enter, as you know, all of your tech will fail. Navigation will become a problem."

"I'll be stuck with line of sight," I said.

She nodded. Cormac and Tripp looked distinctly uncomfortable with this part of the plan, just as I expected. The people of Wild-Side were entirely dependent on their technology. The thought of having it taken away was like losing the senses of touch, taste, or smell. It was a part of them. "It's why you have to enter the zone here," she continued, sliding the map across the table so more of the dead zone was visible. "This ridge line starts approximately seventy-five miles from the border. If you follow it," she gestured to shrink the map, "it will lead you out the far side."

Piper and I both leaned in over the map. The geography of Wild-Side was obviously more unfamiliar to us than it was to everyone else in the room. I observed as Piper's eyes navigated the gnarled path of the rocky ridge, snaking and twisting west and northwest across hundreds of miles of wilderness. It somehow remained visible through the dense thickets, so calling it a ridge might be an understatement. Some of this land could be classified as a low mountain region. This realization made me appreciate Tripp's work on the Airbike even more.

Piper turned the display and zoomed in on a small teardrop-shaped lake less than a third of the way across the dead zone. When she did, a fuzzy gray region became apparent a short distance just north of the lake. It resembled a glitch in the map's rendering or a loss of resolution. "What's this?" she asked.

"The Lergorn-Besht?" Lacy asked, her expression filled with confusion.

The Doc zoomed out the view until only the teardrop-shaped lake and the orange line directing past the nearby ridge were visible. "That's not important," he said, glaring at me. "You'll be traveling at night, and your tech won't be functional, so it's crucial to move as quickly as possible."

The brusk response from the old man was uncharacteristic. I could see the concern on Piper's face. She knew she'd touched on a taboo point; she just didn't know how or why. I shot her a smile that was more reassuring than I felt. I'd never seen the Doc react like that before. I could see the question on Piper's lips, so I gave her the slightest shake of my head to warn her off. Concern grew in the pinch of her eyes, but she let the subject drop.

"We know the Elend are aware of our inability to observe these regions," Lacy said. "So it's safe to assume they will have a presence." She looked pointedly at me. "Minimize your time in the zone. Get in and out as quickly as possible. Without your tech, you won't stand a chance."

A brilliant, transparent barrier of red light appeared on the horizon, and I smiled. "Nothing subtle about that," I muttered to myself.

"Did you say something?" Piper's voice crackled over the com channel. Conversation had faded some time ago, and it wasn't hard to understand why. No one wanted to voice it, but the anxiety surrounding my trip into the dead zone was palpable. To me, the stress was unnecessary. The Airbike was my secret weapon. As long as I was airborne, the Elend couldn't reach me.

"I'm just enjoying how they idiot-proofed the border of the dead zone," I clarified.

"I've been thinking about that. It should be visible any moment now."

Pushing the handlebars forward and twisting the throttle, I entered a slow power dive that reduced altitude and narrowed the gap to the border in just over a minute.

After communicating my intentions to the team back at the Portland base, I double-checked my entry vector and breached the barrier. The wall of red existed only in my HUD, so it vanished the moment I broke the vertical plane. All visual feedback from my HUD went dark. In the same instant, the panels of my suit disassembled—which means the nano-component construction withdrew into the bands at my neck, wrists, waist, knees, and ankles. Until that moment, I'd assumed the gear would reactivate once I reached the far side of the dead zone. With all my technology suddenly gone, I felt exposed and vulnerable. I'll admit to feeling a small degree of anxiety when I considered what would happen if it didn't reappear at the other end of the zone.

Losing my HUD wasn't so bad. Even having my suit dissolve around me didn't make my skin crawl. But experiencing all of this mid-flight was a little problematic. If I hadn't been prepared for it, things could have gone poorly. The gloves on my hands felt like they had vaporized. They were there one second and gone the next. It was as if the size and shape of the system controls changed ever so slightly in the span of two heartbeats. The boots I wore weren't nano-generated. I had prepared for this, and going barefoot wasn't an option, so aside from wearing jeans and a t-shirt, I also wore conventional boots instead of the type that were part of the automated suit.

I'd also take more practical precautions, slowing to a walking pace and flying at an altitude just a few feet above the tree tops as I crossed the border at the edge of the dead zone. Taking time to catch my breath for the first thirty seconds, I ensured that the Airbike was still fully functional and checked to see if I'd stayed on course. To be honest, the Airbike was in perfect shape, but when I double-checked my position, I discovered I'd drifted a bit. Apparently, I'd been more distracted by my dissolving uniform and evaporating tech than I realized.

Gaining altitude, I pushed deeper into the zone. After a few minutes, my eyes adjusted to the ambient light of the waxing half-moon. The forest a hundred feet below me seemed to roil in foggy shadows as my Airbike whispered onward. It took almost ten minutes to find the start of the ridge line that would serve as my path through these badlands. Once I had located it, I donned a pair of transparent safety glasses, throttled up to ninety miles an hour, and focused on the air before me and the ridge below.

———————

Almost an hour after entering the dead zone, the teardrop-shaped lake came into view. I accelerated at the sight. My HUD was gone, but I had found a refreshingly old-school instrumentation dashboard at the center of my handlebars. A small panel of what I had taken to be flat black plastic blinked to life a couple of minutes after I entered the dead zone. It promptly played a short recorded video of Tripp's smiling face, explaining how he had found a workaround for my lack of conventional AR tech. Apparently, he was inspired by what he referred to as the quaint technology I constantly carried around in my pocket back home.

He was talking about my mobile phone. Mimicking the size and shape of the screen, he turned it sideways and attached it to the bars of the Airbike. It included magnetic compass navigation, barometer, altitude awareness, and a clock. He was thoughtful enough to explain that this represented all the primitive technology he could fit into the outdated form factor. Silently, I wished he had thought to consult me before unveiling the surprise. There was probably some type of analog communication system we could have similarly integrated. But as I looked out over the lake and headed north, I reconsidered. I wasn't about to miss the chance for an unsupervised visit to one of the restricted Outland locations. Anyone who knew me should have expected as much.

In my mind, I envisioned the grayed-out location on the map. It was eight-tenths of a mile north of a specific feature at the lake's northern perimeter. The moonlight and the cloudless sky made the lake a perfect landmark, so setting my northerly course was trivial. The navigation system on the Airbike didn't track the eight-tenths of a mile as precisely as I'd hoped, but it got me to the general vicinity. Unfortunately, no landmarks were visible from the air in the dark, so I descended through a small break in the trees that, by my estimation, should have put me within spitting distance of the low-resolution blob represented on the map.

The darkness beneath the tree canopy initially seemed absolute. I couldn't see a foot beyond the edge of the Airbike's rotor ducts. The silence of the night grated on my nerves. Landing in the middle of the wilderness made me feel vulnerable, and I suddenly became very aware that something could snatch me from the darkness before I even knew it was there. My landing had been quiet but far from silent.

It hadn't been enough to disturb the nearby wildlife, so the creatures remained silent and still until they figured out what to make of me.

Long seconds passed—maybe even minutes; it's hard to tell. Finally, my eyes adjusted. Seemingly at the same time, the sounds of natural life returned to the surrounding wilderness. The bump and skitter of small feet had never been such a relief. This was probably the moment when my heart should have been racing, but it wasn't. I was acutely aware that my tech was offline—no augmented night vision or hypersensitive hearing. It reminded me how reliant I'd become on the bio-mods. At least I still had the borderline psychopathic stress response that kept me calm under pressure, which was all my own.

Yay, me.

My gun belt was stored under the seat in a compartment just like the one I had on the first motorcycle I ever owned. Along with it, I found a small first aid kit, three boxes of ammo, and two flashlights— one large and one small. Tripp was as practical as he was smart. I had asked for the gun and the ammo, but the rest of the gear was entirely his idea.

As I began to walk away from the Airbike, it struck me how easily I could lose the machine in the thick underbrush and foliage. Stepping just a dozen feet away, it became invisible in the darkness and overgrowth. If I got even slightly turned around, it might be morning before I found my way back… if ever.

I set the timer on my phone for sixty minutes, turned the volume to maximum, and wedged it in the crook of the handlebars. In a worst-case scenario, I would make a ruckus that could completely compromise my position, but I would find my way back. Hopefully, I could evacuate before anything unfriendly in the area got to the Airbike before me.

After about ten minutes of stumbling around in the dark, I'll admit I started to question my motivations for this midnight excursion. I knew something was out here, but I was coming to terms with the fact that I didn't know what it was. The Seeley had been frustratingly vague when it came to any explanation of what the Lergorn-Besht was. I noted some association with the Outland locations I'd seen on maps, but the little information I had provided no clues about what the sites represented. I'd assumed they were significant locations, but they could be anything. Ideas I hadn't considered flooded my mind as I tripped over vines and crawled over logs in the dark. This could be a gravesite, the location of some rare vegetation, or the spot where an artifact was discovered… my mind began to run wild with possibilities. Almost all of them ended with scenarios where the object of my search was either invisible to me because I wouldn't recognize it if I saw it, or it was long gone since the Seeley had collected and recovered it long ago.

The mark on the map might have indicated anything.

Still, this location wasn't the first Outland spot I'd seen on a Wild-Side map. It was the first I'd had direct access to, so it seemed unwise to pass up the chance to gather more information. At the same time, I was on the clock. I couldn't burn too much time wandering in the woods. I needed to reach Oakland and talk with Mara before I bounced back to My-World. If I didn't, too much time would slip away.

I was deciding whether to keep looking or start making my way back to the Airbike when I walked into a wall—a literal wall. It was composed of rough-hewn stone blocks and mostly covered in thick green lichen. In daylight, I might have passed it by, as the color was so well camouflaged with the jungle. For me, the wall had been invisible in the foliage and the dark, so I only noticed it when my skull rebounded off a small section of exposed stone.

Needless to say, a stone wall in the wilderness is not a natural occurrence, so I instantly knew I was onto something. Since the wall disappeared into a swell of rapidly rising earth fifteen feet to my left, I followed it to the right. Fifty feet later, the ground fell out from under me, and I took a tumble.

I didn't fall far. I found myself on a path cut into the steep slope of the hill to the north. The path resembled a wide gutter filled with years of composting debris. The scent of the decaying vegetation was sickly sweet, and I was standing in it up to my knees. As I shifted my feet, I expected the ground beneath me to squish and move, but it didn't. I was standing on stone. I could feel it beneath the soles of my boots. As I slid them forward and backward, then side to side, I could feel seams in the bricks that made up the path at the bottom of the accumulated mire.

I was on some kind of path. The jungle was behind me, so I focused my attention on the yawning black space I'd taken for a recess in the wall that seemed to border a sizable swell in the earth directly to the north. I'd been hesitant to use my light. One flick of the switch while out in the woods would give away my position to anything within hundreds of yards. As I slipped into the mouth of what I suddenly realized was a tunnel, that concern faded away.

The walls of the tunnel were made of brick, the same rough-hewn stone block I'd face-planted on to make this discovery. The stone was less overgrown with lichen, if only by half. The path was wide enough for maybe two people to walk shoulder to shoulder. In that scenario, I imagined they wouldn't need to high-step through the remnants of rotting vegetation to do so. The smell was pungent, but whatever the plant matter was, it was sweeter rather than sour. That was something. Plus, the slimy vegetation was growing less thick as we moved further into the tunnel.

The path was sloping upward at a steep angle when I reached the door. It stopped me in my tracks not so much because it was an obstruction, but mainly because it was a literal door. This thing was made of steel or something similar and had technology integrated into it. Mounted in the door frame to the left was what could only be a biometric palm reader. Incongruous, a dinner plate-sized spinning release handle was positioned in the middle of the door. It resembled something stolen from a Cold War-era fallout shelter, upgraded with biometrics.

Most troubling was the logo etched into the steel. A patina of wispy mold covered the metal surface of the barrier, but the logo was relatively easy to see. The sans-serif letter R, turned backward and pressed back-to-back with the letter B in the same typeface, served as the logo for a company well-known for its development of high-end bunkers and panic rooms since sometime in the nineteen-eighties. Radon Brucker had even made headlines for a time when they began purchasing old, decommissioned underground missile silos and transforming them into luxury doomsday prepper retreats for the affluent mobile.

But that was back on My-World. Seeing the RB logo on a bunker door on Wild-Side was… unsettling.

I placed my hand on the biometric scanner, but nothing happened. There was no surprise there. It looked positively ancient. Even though it didn't make sense, judging by the corrosion on the non-corrosive surface, this door had seen better days. It had either been sprayed with some kind of caustic fluid or was just old—very old.

I turned the wheel at the center of the door. It resisted, but it moved. This also felt somehow wrong. I had to strain to turn the wheel, as the mechanism seemed to operate on brittle or long-corroded gears. Knowing what I did about the company that built this system and the purpose it was designed for, either they had cut corners in the construction, or something unusual had occurred here.

Then again, I was looking at a bunker from My-World, and it seemed to be embedded in the side of a hill in the middle of nowhere on Wild-Side. I had more questions than answers. A lot of math just wasn't adding up.

The calculations only got worse when I opened the door. I found myself in a small vestibule that turned out to be an airlock. On the other side, I found a door exactly like the one I had just opened. It also had a biometric panel and a spinning handle. Thankfully, the biometrics of the second door had been disabled as well, so I made short work of it. The mechanism of the second door functioned more smoothly than the first, but it was stiff and seemed to have suffered from a distinct lack of maintenance, if not so much exposure to the elements.

After passing through the airlock, I found myself in a large room divided into aisles by crude slotted booths. The floors were smooth steel plates that reminded me of a ship's decking. The ceiling was about twenty feet overhead and made of more steel plates. The room was massive. The near wall resembled a ship's bulkhead, while the distant walls were far enough away to be beyond the reach of my flashlight beam.

I walked slowly across the cold metal floor, panning my light over the strange aisles and rows of booths that divided the area into orderly sections. The stalls had an air of familiarity, though it took me a moment to reconcile the incongruity. Finally, I stepped into a booth and examined the feeding trough hanging from the wall at the far end. I had seen this same configuration on a much smaller scale when I visited a friend's family farm as a kid.

Cows?

Someone was raising cows on Wild-Side?

I'll admit to seeing some strange things in the last two years. Waking up naked in another world, making friends with a race of people who, despite my best efforts, didn't seem to like me no matter how much of my blood I spill trying to protect them, and technology the likes of which I haven't even read about. But somehow, the idea of cows was throwing me for a loop in a way that will be the last straw.

Last straw...you might think that's a cow joke, but it got me thinking. I swung my light across the floor and wished I'd brought the larger light from the Airbike. The beam didn't reach very far. There were at least three rows of stalls, but I sensed the space was immense. I tapped my light to the stall frame and heard the clang echo. Scratch that. The space was cavernous. If it was all stalls, we're talking about a crapload of cows. But that's the other problem. Turning right, I swept the light left and right across the floor.

It's the cleanest barn I've ever seen.

I'm no farmer, but there's something unsettling about this place that went beyond it simply being abandoned. The floor is scuffed and marred, as if it has witnessed years, maybe decades, of use. Some kind of foot traffic, likely from cattle, based on all the evidence. But aside from that, there were only the troughs and the stalls. The rest of the area is spotlessly clean—cleaner than I'd think anyone could get a barn once it had been in operation for any length of time.

I mean, cows are not clean animals. They shit and drool. They piss and they smell bad. Once you have dozens—I played my light across the seemingly endless aisles as it faded into the murk—hundreds, if not thousands...it would take a hazmat team with atomic disinfectant and the patience of monks to clean up a mess like that.

And if there were cows on Wild-Side, where the hell did they go?

A stripe on the floor caught my eye. It was distinctive and painted yellow. It had a worn, long-trodden appearance, but I thought I understood its purpose, so I followed it. I'd seen similar lines in the Kansas missile silo. They helped people navigate large, confusing spaces. If I was right, it suggested this place was larger than I envisioned.

I followed the line to a wall. It was a massive steel bulkhead with a pair of sliding doors that met in the middle. Elevator doors, judging by the call button to the right of the frame. There was only a down button, suggesting I was on the top floor of whatever this place was. Naturally, the call button didn't work, so I forced my fingers between the doors and pried them apart. This might not have been possible under normal circumstances, but thankfully my enhanced strength was still present. As I was told, my nano-tech wouldn't be operational while in the dead zone, but its changes to my musculature and bone density were permanent. The tech wouldn't be able to boost the oxygenation in my blood or alter my endocrine system on the fly as I was used to.

Popping the doors on the old elevator was absolutely no problem. I jammed my fingers into the gap, spread the doors, and pushed one all the way to the wall. What I found inside was the bigger issue. There was no elevator car, which wasn't so bad. Unfortunately, the elevator chute was flooded with inky black water, and my opportunity to explore was over.

It might be just as well. The alarm I'd set on the Airbike was minutes from sounding. Once that happened, I needed to clear out. I couldn't say whether there were hostiles in the area, but if there were, the alarm would be like ringing a dinner bell. All of this was strange, and I didn't know what it meant, but I'd run out of time. I was going to put an end to the excursion when the edge of my light caught the corner of a short, jutting wall not far from the elevator. I panned the beam and found what seemed to be a small work alcove notched into the bulkhead. It was protected by a pair of short, chest-high walls extending from the steel wall, which reminded me of an office cubicle.

There was a desk-like surface about level with my belt buckle, though there was no chair. The steel floor was scuffed and worn, suggesting that it had been used for years, perhaps many years. The work surface of the desk had long since been picked clean. The wall behind the desk was similarly barren, except for three things. The same logo that had been etched into the door at the entry of the facility was prominently displayed over the bulkhead, as if branding the workspace. It had been burnished perhaps two and a half feet wide. This version was more deeply etched, with the logo more protected and resilient to the ravages of time.

Two strange displays remained alongside the logo, each encased in a protective glass case and suspended from the wall on either side of the space framing the LB logo. One display featured an ancient flintlock pistol, while the other showcased an antique cutlass with a mahogany pommel, worn smooth by both age and use. Some type of card had clearly hung in the inside corner of each case, but both had disintegrated long ago. This was evident from the dry pile of fibers collected in the corners of each display, directly below the discolored rectangles that indicated where each tag once hung.

A growing list of questions accumulated in the corner of my mind. What was this place? How old was it? What was with the RB logo? The fact that the space resembled a barn for cows was the last thing I expected to see. I was running out of time. If the pistol or sword could be identified, they might provide clues to what was happening here—more likely who was involved in the operation of the place. The artifacts appeared significant to whoever once used this workspace. I couldn't imagine why these were the only items left in a facility that had been cleared out to the point of almost being sterilized. It was yet another question for my growing list.

I thought I heard something in the distance—a gentle scratching sound. It was likely a mouse or something similar. More than likely, my mind was working overtime, nudging me to get moving. I stepped onto the desk, slammed my elbow against the glass surrounding the flintlock, and heard the glass crunch. I brushed it away and pulled the pistol free.

Then I heard the scratching sound in the distance once more.

I smashed the glass on the larger sheet protecting the cutlass. It shattered in a shower of splinters that shot into the air and cascaded across the floor, clattering loudly in the tomblike silence.

I heard the sound of something heavy striking the steel floor somewhere in the distance. Spinning from the elevator, I turned off my light as I grabbed the sword from the case. The slight glow of moonlight coming from the entrance about sixty yards away looked about the size of my thumb if it were right in front of my face. The echo of the initial sound still reverberated in the vast space when a second impact, this one close to me, sounded.

Shit.

I wasted too much time and managed to corner myself.

I wanted to try the old trick of throwing something one way and running the other, but there was nothing to throw. The place was spotless, and nothing had been left behind.

Another sound came from my left. Something was between me and the exit. I was almost positive it was a second contact because the original sound had come from deeper in the room and more to my right. The exit was on my left. My fingers tapped the pistol on my hip. My targeting system was offline. It meant taking these things down would be orders of magnitude more difficult. A shot to the eye would require extremely close contact now.

Two slow breaths to prepare myself were all I could afford. They would vector in on me using scent and perhaps sight. Once they had a feel for the space, the sterile environment would make it easy for them to identify me. Plus, they had better low-light vision than I did now. I flashed my light twice in a pair of quick bursts. This would play hell with their more sensitive night vision, while mine would have a chance to pick out shapes in the flashes.

As I had hoped, the flashes revealed a pair of Elend. One was a low form of a Crawler, already heading in my direction from my left and being the closest of the two. It emitted a growling hiss that suggested it didn't appreciate the light strobe. The other was either a Drake or a Jay, with its wings folded; I couldn't tell which it was in the flash. That one was maybe a hundred and fifty yards away and at my two o'clock.

Lacking a better option, I sprinted forward and split the difference. I bolted down a row of stalls that, if my quick estimation was correct, placed at least two aisles between me and the Crawler on my left and one aisle between me and the Drake on my right. The Drake had more distance to cover, but it would have an easier time crossing the rows. This was confirmed when I heard the crashing, blunt-force impact of the Crawler on my left. It was trying to smash through the stalls to get to me. I was already passing it as I charged deeper into the darkness.

I heard the skittering of talons on steel somewhere to my right and knew the Drake was attempting its attack. It would make short work of the cubicles. The only question was whether it would come over or under the obstacle in its attempt to reach me. It must have had its blood up and not been thinking clearly yet, because I heard a crash as it hit the barrier almost directly to my right.

The pale light of the exit was almost exactly at my nine o'clock, so I grabbed the edge of the next stall and swung into it at full speed. I tucked my knees up and slid on my hip under the troth and into the stall on the other side of the aisle. Without wasting a breath, I was on my feet again. I dove headlong for the stall on the other side of the aisle, beneath the trough, and came out the other side.

As I bolted for the door, I heard a pair of primal screams that told me my efforts had not gone unnoticed. The sounds, however, were not right at my heels, so I grabbed the plate-sized locking wheel at the first of the two steel doors and pulled the door shut behind me. With effort, I spun the lock just in time to feel a considerable impact from the far side.

I took a deep breath, just in time to hear the alarm sound on the Airbike. My one hour had expired.

The klaxon chime of my cell phone alarm was set to full. When I first began to wander from the Airbike, that had seemed like a good idea. I thought I would likely be near the machine and lost by the time the clock ran out, so closing the distance and taking to the air would be a matter of seconds. It was unlikely any nearby Elend could find me before I was safely in the air.

Reality check.

Given the muffled, distant sound of the air raid siren, I had wandered further afield than originally planned. On a positive note—pun intended—the alarm indicated that the Airbike was somewhere in the distance at approximately my two o'clock. Something large was already moving in from my right. The crashing, smashing, and not-so-subtle devastation of small overgrowth told me it was moving quickly, so I did the same. I jumped over a fallen tree, ducked under a series of arm-sized hanging vines, and sprinted for the Airbike with everything I had.

I'd only made it a couple dozen yards when the sounds of aggressive pursuit I was hearing from my right were duplicated from my left. Cursing not-so-under-my-breath, I dug deep and redoubled my efforts. The sound of the klaxon was getting louder, so I knew I was getting closer to the machine. Unfortunately, the sound of the approach from my left was getting louder too. The attack was getting nearer. And there was a tonal incongruity to the assault on the vegetation that didn't match what I heard from my right. I was reasonably sure at least two Elend were approaching from the left while one was moving in aggressively from the right.

My gun remained in its holster as I ran. I could only grasp the sword and flintlock. They held value, but were not worth dying for. I could still use my hands to brush aside and parry the vegetation blocking my path, yet I questioned if I was sacrificing precious speed to solve a mystery that could ultimately cost me my life. If I tripped—

That's when I tripped.

I face-planted so hard that I thought the cracking sound came from my arm or ribs. It turned out luck was on my side. My foot snagged on a tangle of roots just a second before the Crawler charged out from the trees on my right. It must have lowered its head, ready to take me out, just before I fell because it blasted right past me and into the underbrush on my left.

Back on my feet in an instant, I felt a grin spreading across my face. My clumsiness had saved my ass in a way that would make a Saturday morning cartoon character proud. I estimated I was less than fifty yards from the Airbike, and all the threats were now on my mind left—

Shit!

The flintlock was gone.

There was absolutely no chance to stop and look for it.

The tree cover beside me burst, and a three-taloned claw the size of a catcher's mitt tried to eviscerate me. I dodged right, but at least one of the talons must have caught the edge of my shirt. I heard fabric tear and felt a blast of chilly air beneath my left arm. I did some kind of diving spin to my right. Something big broke onto the trail even as the world blurred and I tried to find my feet.

It was a Crawler, and it was motivated.

I raised the sword without a moment's thought. As I brought the blade down, three of the creature's talons lay in the battered undergrowth at my feet.

A keening shriek rattled my ears as I looked at the blood dripping from the blade in my hands.

Damn!

The creature's remaining foreclaw swung at me with a renewed and savage ferocity. I swung the blade again and heard it shriek. There was a blur of pale gray scales as the jaws lashed out at me. I spun away to dodge, turning quickly and feeling my feet slip. I slashed down with the blade and put every ounce of force behind the slashing effort when I dropped the blade. There was a sickening wet splat, and I dropped on my ass in time to see the lizard-like head of Elend separate from its neck and pinwheel into the vegetation.

My eyes were still unblinking when the corpse disintegrated into at least seventy pounds of particulate matter. It was something I'd only ever witnessed after inflicting a mortal wound to a creature's eye.

I'd just found a new way to kill the horrible things.

And, somehow I was on my ass again.

I straightened up just in time to catch another mitt-sized claw as it came down on me from the left. A gaping pair of jaws lunged toward my face.

Apparently, there was no time to celebrate my victory.

The double set of triangular, razor-sharp teeth of the Jay posed the real threat, so I pressed my feet into its wide chest for leverage, bared my left elbow to keep the distracting swing of its claw at bay, and slid the blade from my boot with my free hand. The creature had another set of talons on the other arm, still unaccounted for and lurking somewhere. I needed to make my move before it could use it.

My blade slipped into the underside of the creature's jaw just as the teeth came within inches of my face. And while the Elend are impervious to bullets, they can be injured by a well-honed blade. My boot knives are twelve inches long, and a blade on the outside of each boot for just such an occasion can inflict great pain on the creatures. Unfortunately, the blade can only be lethal in the same ways that a bullet can. This makes a blade a poor weapon for close-quarters combat, regardless of the situation.

I had enough force behind my upward thrust to slam the Jay's mouth closed and even pin it. For better or worse, the knife tip was embedded in the roof of the creature's upper palate. With a muffled scream of pain, the beast sent me flying into overgrowth. Presumably, it was trying to sort out the pain and sudden inability to open its mouth. As I went flying ass over teakettle, I saw the Jay's wings flare with expressive abandon. They thrashed wildly, battered and smashed at the thick, constricting vegetation. They also caught the Crawler full in the face just as it emerged from the forest with a clear intent to rejoin the fight. The Jay was much larger than the

Crawler, who was caught with what must have been a powerful wing stroke because I heard what sounded like the distinctive sound of breaking bone and the plaintive cry of a wounded animal. It was somehow very different from the shrieking distress emanating from the thrashing Jay.

The Crawler snarled and lashed out at the Jay. The two became entangled in a thrashing, screeching mass of scales that dissolved into the overgrowth. There was something almost comical about it all, but I wasn't out of the woods yet. Not figuratively and certainly not literally, so I turned back toward the persistent sound of the alarm signaling the position of the Airbike.

I ran headlong into a Drake. It was taller and thinner in body than the Jay since it lacked the folded wings the Jay typically kept collapsed at its sides. The Drake, on the other hand, had powerful muscles in its front and back legs that made it look like the powerlifting version of its cousins. It had a longer snout and wider eyes. This one had eyes that seemed to shine with added intelligence, which matched what I observed in its sneaky approach and its decision to let the other two of its kind take the first crack at me.

The Drake approached me slowly, using the game trail and stalking forward on all fours, even though I knew it was just as capable of walking on its hind legs. I stood my ground, allowing the creature to bide its time as I could hear the chaotic sounds of the other two still engaged in some kind of combat, their bloodlust now at my four o'clock.

"You're the smart one?" I said in a calm, soothing tone.

The creature continued to close the distance, slow and methodically. The Elend weren't accustomed to the people of Wild-Side fighting back, yet most of them knew who I was. I couldn't tell if this one had identified me yet. It was more likely to press its advantage if it knew I would fight. Perhaps it didn't see what I had done to the Jay?

I ducked low to pull my remaining blade from my left boot. The creature bristled at this, tension causing the muscles to ripple across its front. The lips drew back, and teeth similar to those of the Jay became visible. I held the matte black blade of the foot-long knife out to my left as if I was about to drop it in an act of submission. The creature's almond-shaped eyes were focused on the blade with clear, savage intent.

That's when I drew the pistol and fired three shots as fast as I could pull the trigger. I didn't have the advantage of my HUD-based targeting system and was never more painfully aware of how I'd come to rely on it. However, thanks to the close range, two of my shots struck the creature's right eye. Its mouth sagged, and then its body dropped. By the time I was sprinting for the Airbike, it was already crumbling to dust.

As I jumped onto the seat of the Airbike and tapped the power button, I noticed that the sounds of distant violence had already faded. The Jay and Crawler had either settled their differences or put them aside to finish me off first. Either way, I twisted the throttle and yanked back on the handlebars. The Airbike shot into the sky, perfectly vertical, like a rocket launching from the pad. My stomach dropped into my crotch just as my nuts were violently sent crashing up into my abdomen from the impact with the seat.

The immediate reaction to the aggressive launch was painful yet ultimately timely. Gasping in pain, I glanced at the left foot pedal. Blinking away tears and struggling to breathe through the pain and rapid ascent, I saw the Jay and Crawler bounce into the clearing, flattened by the Airbike's rotors.

I brought the Airbike to a hover at seven hundred feet and slid back on the seat, much to the relief of my manly bits. Below me, the Crawler stomped through the forest, clearing an area in an obvious display of dissatisfaction with my escape. Strangely, the Jay stared at me stoically for several long seconds. Just as I was ready to move on from this experience, the beast reared up on its back legs and spread its wings wide. It thrashed and beat at the air in a slow, rhythmic cadence, and I saw the surface of its wings expand in a way I couldn't explain.

Then the Elend did something I had never witnessed before. It flapped one more time and soared into the air.

Sonofabitch.

I knew those damn things could fly. I knew it. I've said it before and I'll say it again: what's the point of wings if not to fly? Doc can rationalize it all he wants, but the sight below me suddenly made two things crystal clear. The random disappearances all over Wild-Side suddenly made sense. City walls were the only defense against the Elend, and that wasn't much protection against an enemy that could fly in at night and snatch people from the streets at will. The occasional missing persons reports had been a prelude to Oakland going unresponsive. Once Breslin had enough Jays for the job, he'd taken an entire city. Opposition to my wall-mounted point defense system would finally be a thing of the past. There was no arguing with the flying Elend.

An ear-piercing shriek from below pulled me back to my immediate concerns and the second pressing issue. The Jay beneath me was quickly gaining altitude and closing in. Its call sounded familiar, too. It was calling to others, so it was likely only a matter of time before they joined the hunt.

I pushed the handlebars forward and twisted the throttle. The rotors howled briefly as they bit into the air, and the Airbike took off like a turbocharged hummingbird. Scanning the treetops for signs of additional threats, the glassy surface of the nearby lake came into view in the distance. I feathered my left foot pedal and banked smoothly towards the lake. The now-familiar broken stone protrusion of the ridge line that was my path through the dead zone quickly came into view.

Another Jay broke from the tree canopy two hundred yards ahead of me, moving like a surface-to-air missile. A glance over my shoulder confirmed that the last hunter was still in pursuit, though it was pacing me. I was going one hundred and forty miles per hour, and it was just keeping up. The one closing in from below appeared to have a smaller body, but its wingspan looked wider. Something told me it would be faster than the one behind me.

The Jay moving from below had yet to make a sound. Unlike his noisy, chunkier brother behind me, he appeared to be an ambush hunter. In my mind, I tagged him as Sneek. Similarly, I named the loud attacker Gabby. These rationalizations assist with the storytelling, but they also help me sort the characteristics of each in a practical way because those attributes are almost always the key to killing them.

Sneek was flapping hard as he closed the distance, and I'll admit I watched his efforts for longer than I should have. I had never seen these creatures fly before, and their flight was almost entirely unlike that of birds. Their wings were much longer and thicker, featuring obvious rigid bony structures articulated in two or three places between the shoulder and the tip. A scaly, skin-like membrane clung semi-rigidly to the framework of internal bones. I was reminded of bat wings, but on a massive scale; even that didn't seem quite right.

Somehow, he managed to gather great speed even in his vertical ascent. Then, suddenly, Sneek folded his wings tightly against his body to complete the surface-to-air missile analogy more closely. The shift in strategy caught me off guard. I was instantly facing a massive gaping maw at the end of a javelin-shaped body that was aiming toward my course at what must have been two hundred miles an hour.

I swallowed hard and pressed my body tightly against the seat and frame of the Airbike. My nose nearly touched the small LCD control panel as I twisted the throttle, stomped my right toe down hard, and pulled back on the handlebars. The Airbike barrel rolled to the right for a roll and a half. Halfway through the second roll, I was pulling back harder into an inverted dive that sent me plunging toward the tree canopy below. Lacking the benefit of the automated restraint system, I was pinching the sides of the seat with my knees in a death grip that matched the one that tightened my sphincter the moment I hit the accelerator.

Committed to the dive as I was, I controlled both the throttle and pitch to convert the inverted dive into a power loop about thirty feet above the tip of the nearest tree. This maneuver wasn't the first of its kind; I'd executed it at least a hundred times with radio-controlled five-inch drones. As far as I know, it was the first time it had ever been accomplished on a manned equivalent in an aerial combat situation.

According to the dashboard display, I was moving at just over two hundred twenty miles per hour. This explained why it felt like the skin was stretching across my skull and why my eyes were watering, even with protective eyewear in place. A quick glance over my shoulder revealed that both of my pursuers were still in the game, though the closest one was about four hundred yards behind me.

The battery readout on the Airbike was at eighty-three percent. The technology keeping me in the air was a combination of conventional battery chemistry from My-World blended with what was considered arcane chemical engineering from Wild-Side. Together, the two function in the dead zone, though not as effortlessly as their power tech did under normal conditions. Cormac had tried to explain that technology to me more than once, but it was so far beyond me that I'd taken to calling it witchcraft. He failed to find the humor I'd intended.

I reached behind myself and manually latched the seat restraint to the rear of my belt on the left and right. It was a clumsy alternative to what Tripp had designed as an automated restraint system, but after my high-speed acrobatic maneuver just moments ago, I didn't want to become a victim of my own ingenuity.

The Elend are fierce ambush hunters. In my experience, once they catch a scent, they will follow the target until they locate it, trap it, and kill it. I'm one of the few—perhaps the only one—to have ever survived multiple encounters with them. This has been due to my willingness to run away when possible and to stand and fight when necessary.

With two flight-capable Elend on my trail, it was possible that I could reach the end of the dead zone before they caught up with me. However, the first Jay had already summoned another to join the chase. If this continued, who knows how many would be after me by sunrise? While the Elend prefer to hunt at night, they can tolerate daylight. With their blood running hot, I'd be gambling against long odds that they would turn tail and simply let me be once the sun crested the horizon.

The creatures I had faced repeatedly were oblivious to nearly everything once they had prey in their sights. This left me with few options. Pulling back on the handlebars, I started to gain altitude. It was no surprise that Sneek and Gabby kept pace with me. I concentrated on maintaining at least a three hundred yard gap between us as I attempted to formulate some kind of plan.

Describing it as a plan might be a bit of an exaggeration. I was climbing vertically while trying to keep as much forward speed as possible. By this point, I still hadn't discovered the limits of the Airbike's performance envelope. I was, admittedly, hesitant to push it to the ragged edge this deep into the wilds, particularly without the benefit of my tech. No armor, no communication—hell, I didn't even have my HUD. I felt more than a bit underdressed. Not to mention, I was a little over seventeen thousand feet up. Even with the moonlight, the Earth appeared as a featureless carpet below me.

I'd hoped the Jays wouldn't be able to fly this high, but apparently, I was wrong. I had to add more throttle to the props, the air considerably thinner at this extreme. It should have been cold, too—unbearably cold. Apparently, the residual benefits of the nano-tech were still paying off because what little plan I had would require dexterity and a clear mind.

The primary benefit of bringing the chase to an extreme altitude was isolation. It was the only way I could prevent the Jays from calling others of their kind to the chase. Between the height and the effort they were putting into the chase, they were clearly working harder to maintain flight in the thinning air; they couldn't afford the energy to call in reinforcements. Two against one were not great odds, but it was something if I could keep the probability from deteriorating.

My plan was to climb hard and fast to twenty thousand, then circle around on my attackers. Best case, I catch the front runner—Sneek—off guard. There'd been almost no turbulence, so with a little luck and enough lead, I have better than even odds of scoring a fatal shot on his eye in time to get evasive and stay out of Gabby's teeth.

As far as plans go, it's terrible, and I knew it. But I had a nearly full magazine, several spares, and a distinct lack of options as long as I was in the dead zone. I'm not one to do something foolish just for the sake of doing something…but sometimes you just have to nut up or shut up.

I began my quick climb and felt the slow throttle response from the Airbike for the first time. It's the low air density, I understood instantly. Twisting the throttle further, I watched the altimeter jump as expected. I also saw a flash of light that sent me rocking back in the seat. At first, I thought one of the battery cells had blown and immediately started trying to sort out a contingency plan for the rapid elevator ride back to the ground floor that was sure to follow.

But then the progress bar blinked to life on my HUD, indicating that it was coming back online.

"What the hell?" I mumble to myself.

Instead of circling at twenty-thousand to initiate my attack run as planned, I continued on my previous heading. I may have cleared the dead zone, although I was fairly certain that's not the case. Even at top speed, that should take several more hours. I had another suspicion.

The moment my HUD was back online, I checked my map. I was no longer anywhere near the course I had planned to follow. I had lost the ridge line when I picked up my aggressive tailgaters, but I was heading in the right general direction. As I suspected, the edge of the dead zone was still hundreds of miles distant.

I'd found some sort of upper boundary for the phenomenon. We never considered how high the distortion might reach. Though, twenty-thousand feet is pretty damn high. It might be too high to be helpful in any practical sense.

Then I grinned.

Except one.

The onboard batteries began recharging. As soon as all the high-tech systems powered on, the chemical batteries became secondary systems again and started picking up charge from the primary power core. That was good news, even if my limited clearance from the effects of the dead zone was temporary. This got me thinking about my HUD. It could be reliable at this altitude, or this could be a fluke. Either way, I could use it now in a significant way. I slowed and spun the Airbike one hundred eighty degrees as I brought it to a hover. Slipping the pistol from my hip, I felt time slow. The gun rose in my usual two-handed grip, and the targeting reticle appeared instantly on my HUD. The first of the Jays was two hundred twenty-three yards away and closing. I squinted my eyes as my optics zoomed in on the creature's head. I could see mist billowing from its nostrils with each exhaled gasp. The veins in its dragon-like head rippled as blood coursed through its heart, head, wings, and lungs. I noticed the shift in the set of its eyes as it realized something about the scenario had changed. Its lips pulled back, exposing a mouth clamped shut but filled with razor-sharp teeth. It looked like a feral smile, or a threat.

Whatever the expression meant, I'll never know. I fired a single shot. It split the creature's right eye, and all bodily functions ceased instantly. The creature turned, began to tumble, and started to disintegrate as it left my line of sight. The sound of the shot was strange in the wide-open expanse. Maybe it was due to the unusually thin atmosphere? Either way, there was nothing to absorb or reflect the report, so it caught my attention.

It's also when Gabby came into view. As Sneek tumbled away, I swear I saw surprise on the serpent-like expression of the larger Elend. The beating of its wings began to slow. I don't know if this was out of confusion or recognition of the threat it now faced. Maybe the creature was taking a moment to reevaluate the situation. Maybe it was about to turn tail and retreat. Either way, I fired before it had the chance. This time I loosed two shots since the creature was starting to move erratically. I don't know which was the kill shot, but the flesh began to ossify before gravity even took hold. It would be a cloud of ashes before it reached the ground far below.

The brass from my double tap must have hit one of the rotor blades because there was a horrible metallic twang, and something whistled past my ear close enough for me to feel it. I don't mind telling you that I ducked…or that a few seconds later, I was glad I hadn't needed Plan A. That plan would have required me to dump a magazine or more at each of the Jays, hoping to score a hit on one of their eyes.

While I was reasonably sure I could eventually make the shot as the distance closed, I hadn't anticipated ducking from the return fire of my own spent casings. That might have been the flaw that cost me the game. If the Elend didn't get me, gravity would have.

Chapter 15 - Ice Skating Uphill

I landed the Airbike in a park near the center of Oakland. After clearing the far end of the dead zone, I was able to open a channel and communicate with the city administrator. In this case, that was Sarah Hargrave. Short and thin, she looked somehow older than the other denizens, even though I knew that wasn't possible. It wasn't the first time I'd encountered Sarah, but her wizened appearance and an age that, at least visually, seemed to parallel Doc Cormac made me think for the first time that the difference in relative appearances might have more to do with one's station in society than with conventional age.

"Gray," Sarah said, extending her hand. It was a mannerism some had adopted from My World, and I recognized she was using it to break the ice. Sarah Hargrave had been one of the most vocal opponents of the point defense system I was working to implement on the perimeter walls of Portland. "You're ahead of schedule," she noted.

She was right. Once I discovered that Seeley tech worked in the dead zone as long as I was above 20,000 feet, I could reactivate my armor. This made higher speeds more comfortable, and I was able to more than make up for my lost time.

"Have you been able to reach Doctor Cormac?" I asked, trying to cut through the niceties. The ride had been a blast, but it was exhausting. Time was also limited. I needed to interview Mara and begin the return flight as soon as possible.

She shook her head. "The latest information suggests the storm front has settled in. It's now stationary. There's no reason to believe conditions will change anytime soon. It's not the first time we've seen a Thonian weather front behave this way," she said, looking uncomfortable with what she was describing. "We just hoped for the best, I suppose you could say."

I followed Sarah across the park's open green expanse and into a glass-covered greenhouse-like building while we talked. After that, we passed through a lobby and entered an elevator. She hadn't yet explained where we were going, but I assumed it was the medical complex since she knew my reason for traveling to Oakland.

"You saw the video I forwarded?" I asked as we waited in the elevator.

Sarah didn't respond at first. Her complexion suddenly grew more pallid, and she swayed on her feet. I watched her throat contract as she appeared to swallow something unpleasant with concerted effort. The elevator chimed, and the doors slid open, but Sarah Hargrave failed to move. After a few long seconds, her gaze met mine. She blinked away moist eyes, forced a smile, and led me from the elevator.

"Kind of you not to say, 'I told you so,'" she said in a dry, husky voice as we treaded slowly down the next corridor. "That recording…" she almost mumbled. "They truly can fly?" She looked at me again and forced another smile. "If you can, I suppose, why not them?"

No one on Wild-Side really understood the concept of flight. Maybe that's why it had been so hard for most to believe that the Elend could actually do it. I had been trying to explain the likelihood for so long, but the threat had fallen on deaf ears until I provided video evidence. It turned out Tripp had built a digital video recorder into the frame of the Airbike. It was another piece of technology based on the 'backward and antiquated tech of My-World,' as he put it. I'm sure he would have explained the feature if there had been more time before I left. But once my armor and HUD came back online, I had hours of flight to get more familiar with my gear. I found the recording and forwarded it to Sarah.

"You made me a believer," she said. "The PDTs are being assembled to Tripp's specifications as we speak. I started right after watching the video. I just hope we're not too late."

I knew she was thinking about how Fresno had gone silent before being found abandoned with no trace of the thousands who had lived there. Scratching at the open wound wasn't necessary. She was finally in support of the Point Defense Turrets. The video should have the same impact on the remaining detractors. Anyone opposed to the plan once they saw how the Elend could snatch them from their previously protected streets was clearly just being unreasonable.

Sarah paused in the hall and gestured to a pair of uniformed guards standing at attention, one on either side of a wide door a dozen yards further down the corridor. "Mara is through there. Doctor Hiller is expecting you. He will ask you to keep the visit brief, but he understands you've traveled a great distance for the interview and that time is limited. Do what you can."

Though she seemed like she had more to say, I wasn't sure Sarah even knew what it was. I'd been in Oakland for less than fifteen minutes and had already upset her fragile worldview. She just looked at me with tired eyes and gave a sad smile. "Doctor Cormac speaks highly of you. He has great confidence, to put it bluntly. I sincerely hope he's correct because..." Though she paused as if to continue, she did not. Finally, she closed her eyes for a long moment, then nodded her head slowly. "I'm sorry," she said instead. "I won't be so quick to dismiss your advice next time. See to Mara, and I'll expedite the deployment of our Point Defense Perimeter."

I wanted to say something to ease her mind, but I was at a loss. Months had been wasted arguing over the defense system. I had Cormac on my side, and a small group of key players in Portland came with him. Other than that, I felt like I was ice skating uphill. Was it really as simple as forwarding one video to the administrators of each city?

I was far better at fighting monsters than bureaucracy.

"Once the contagion alarms went off, we followed protocol and requested backup," Mara explained. Two additional Buses were dispatched. I was in our broken-down vehicle when the attack occurred. I lost contact with the team. It was either just before the assault or at the same time. I'm not sure we'll ever know the exact sequence of events. The recording equipment the team carried was damaged too severely to restore, and they couldn't transmit high bandwidth from inside the cave.

Mara lay semi-reclined on a high-tech hospital bed that hovered several feet above the floor as if by its own accord. Given the critical nature of her injuries and the coma she had been in since the events months ago in the cave, I had expected her to be connected to life-saving or at least supportive equipment. While she had been fully submerged in a tall, narrow transparent cylinder in the corner of her room when I arrived, it seemed she didn't need to remain there. I was informed that the cylinder was filled with a kind of clear, nano-infused gelatin that was responsible for her physical rehabilitation. As soon as I arrived, the nursing staff took her out of the gel, bathed her, and placed her in the bed for the interview.

"When were you attacked?" I asked, worried that I might be bringing up a traumatic memory. She had only been out of the coma for a couple of days, so the events I was inquiring about were likely very recent in her mind.

Mara shrugged. This mannerism caused two things to occur to me. First, it was a gesture that reminded me a lot of home. I'd never been sure if this sort of thing was universal or if the people of Wild-Side had quickly picked up on my habits after being exposed to me. Best estimates suggest my first trip to Wild-Side coincided with the time Mara's team was attacked in the cave. She'd effectively been on ice since then, so it was unlikely she'd adopted my habits, given that she hadn't been exposed to me until this interview. She had spent time with people who may have shown her the mannerism, but that felt a bit like I was overthinking it.

Second, she made the move without showing any apparent physical discomfort. This indicated that her rehab was effective and that her time in the coma had less residual physical impact than I had expected. I hoped the same could be true for her memory of the events from that day. As far as we had been able to determine, the attack at the cave was the first instance of Elend-like violence against the Seeley. If the cave held significance, we needed to gather as much information as possible about what happened that day.

"I have no idea," Mara said. Those four words shattered the hopes that had brought me all the way here.

I have to admit, I hesitated for a few seconds while searching for a question that could salvage the trip. I didn't realize how much I had invested in this conversation until that moment. "What can you tell me about your attacker?"

Mara didn't respond immediately. Seconds ticked by before she shrugged once more. "I don't remember an attack. Just waking up with my suit torn to shreds." I saw blood everywhere. I felt confused. It didn't make sense that I couldn't move, and the blood all over the compartment was mine."

"You were in the Bus?"

She nodded. "I'll never forget that much. I'd been sick and had spent a lot of time cleaning up the space. I was confused about why everything was trashed again. I remember thinking I needed to work, but I didn't understand why I couldn't move. I was still trying to sort that out when the medical team arrived."

The doctor in charge of Mara's treatment informed me that her recall was inconsistent. He asserted that it was a result of head trauma. When I inquired whether her memory would likely improve, he hesitated to make any promises. The nano-submersion treatments she was receiving were mainly intended to assist with physical rehabilitation, but the technology was also permeating her blood and internal organs. This tech would continue to repair both internal and external damage, but he warned that brain trauma couldn't be completely healed through artificial tissue stimulation.

I leaned back in my chair and regarded Mara for a moment. By all accounts, she was fortunate to be alive. According to the report, the medical team evacuated her for emergency treatment while another group approached the cave to try to retrieve the rest of Mara's team. Their point person got close enough to the cave entrance but couldn't enter. The area was geologically unstable, and the team had triggered a rockslide near the cave. They were concerned about another collapse while approaching the cave mouth. A drone was sent into the cave, but it was lost when a rockslide covered the entrance. Ultimately, the drone was lost, and only preliminary footage was gathered. Unfortunately, that footage was enough to confirm that everyone on the team had been savagely attacked and succumbed to grievous fatal injuries.

"I've heard about you," Mara said, breaking a prolonged silence.

I offered a slow nod but said nothing.

"Some say you're here to save us from the demons."

"Yeah?"

Her expression became more serious, though I didn't think that was possible. "Some say you brought them here with you."

Another slow nod. "I've heard that one too."

The unasked question lingered in her quiet, expressionless gaze. *So, which is it?*

I leaned to the edge of my chair and spoke in quiet, gentle words. "I have no idea what brought me here, what these creatures are, or why they showed up at the same time." I got up and walked to the edge of the bed. I put my hand on hers and looked her in the eye. "But I know how to kill them, so that's what I'm going to do. I'll kill every last one until they're gone or until one finally gets me. If someone smarter than me figures out the rest along the way...well, that would be nice too."

I'll admit that I didn't have a plan for what came next. The interview with Mara was the extent of my mid-term agenda. The primary hope was that she'd been aware enough for the interview, so I lucked out there. By the time I flew out to Oakland to speak with her, the details of her condition were outdated, and her health was as likely to deteriorate as to improve. If she could communicate, the hope was that she might offer some insight into what happened in the cave, the phenomenon that had transformed Breslin into who he was now, or— this was a distant hope that may have existed only in my imagination— some understanding of my connection to Wild-Side. By this point, I believe the Doc strongly believed in my connection to Breslin's transformation, even if we couldn't directly link the two events.

There was no way to know if Mara's memory might return, either partially or fully. Her doctors agreed that, in time, a visit to the location of the attack could impact her recall. Considering the trauma she'd experienced, both mentally and physically, no one was willing to approve the trip. It was just as likely to hinder her recovery as to help it. Moreover, the Darks, the wasteland where the cave was located, were generally considered off-limits. Traveling there required approval from the Central Authority, a governing body comprised of two representatives from each of the five cities.

I've already explained that I wouldn't consider most of the people from Wild-Side fans, so I wasn't surprised when Mara recognized my name even before I arrived. Throughout the interview, I was grateful that what she'd heard about me didn't influence her willingness to engage in the conversation. She seemed genuinely eager to share all she could about her experiences that day. Her inability to recall the events was an apparent pain that she seemed to endure almost physically. I believe that's why she insisted on returning to Portland with me.

As unlikely as it was, five hours after my arrival in Oakland, I found myself back in the air and returning to Portland. This time, Mara was on the back of the Airbike, allowing me to make better time because I climbed straight to twenty thousand feet and locked my speed at one hundred eighty. Mara wore an environmental suit identical to the one she had donned in the Darks during the mission that had landed her in the hospital.

I didn't realize how much the Seeley tech had changed my physiology until Mara noted how hard her suit worked against the constant cold. I had paid little attention to the temperatures associated with high-altitude flight. My gear was undoubtedly working to counter the cold, but her comment made me consider how little I'd noticed before my tech came back online for the first leg of the trip. The Thonian radiation would have kept the nanotech in my body offline in the same way it was affecting the Airbike; still, I wasn't my old self. Even with my biotech disabled, I had maintained some degree of lasting protection from the cold.

I wondered what other ways I might have been permanently changed by my exposure to Wild-Side. It also made me think about the people here. It seemed the Airbike was literally the first flying vehicle of its kind. The entire concept appeared revolutionary, even to their most creative minds. The few who had seen the machine in action seemed horrified by the idea of human flight.

As I've mentioned, no one on Wild-Side had ever flown before, and the idea seemed to sour even the most stalwart of dispositions. So, I didn't think the high-speed, high-altitude trip back to Portland would be well received by Mara... but, damn, was I wrong. I can't say with one hundred percent certainty since she was sitting behind me the entire ride, but I don't think she ever stopped grinning. It didn't matter how fast or how high we flew; she just held on and soaked up the experience.

Piper worked through the literature that served as historical documentation for the Seeley people. She had read thousands of pages and still had tens of thousands more to go, but she was unsure how helpful it would be. It wasn't historical insight as she was accustomed to it; certainly nothing like the historical accounts from back home. Given the Seeley people's lack of narrative experience, their historical accounts were more like accounting records and shipping manifests. There was no interpretation of events, no examination from different perspectives or through varied cognitive lenses. Everything felt dry and clinical, leading to a sense of endless monotony.

Plus, these people were boring. Either they had whitewashed their history to remove all accounts of violent events such as war, or there had literally never been a conflict. There had never been more than an exchange of opposing perspectives, as far as she could tell— hundreds of years and no conflict at all.

It didn't seem possible.

But then Gray explained how these people had no history of art, music, or anything even remotely creative. It felt as if the entire population was left-brain dominant. It was a statistical impossibility.

Then again, I am sitting on an alien world.

She put down the tablet and rubbed her eyes. Of the countless experiences over the last twenty-four hours, two still forced her to readjust her sense of reality. Eyeing the tablet on the bench beside her, she considered how quickly she'd consumed the reading material since arriving in Wild-Side. Though she hadn't quantified the improvement yet, she guessed she was currently reading between eight and ten times faster than she could just a day before. Lacy explained that this was very likely thanks to the nanotech, which was optimizing her neural pathways. In time, she could expect better coordination and neuromuscular reaction time.

The second big change was her eyesight. Piper had worn reading glasses since she was fifteen years old. Obviously, they hadn't made the trip with her during what Doctor Cormac and Piper called The Transition. Only something organic could cross the Vale, a term they used for the Brane, the layer of reality, or sub-reality, that separated Wild-Side from Our-World. Thankfully, her glasses were no longer needed. According to Lacy, Piper's vision was now better than ever, thanks to the nanotech.

And I can speak another language without even thinking about it.

She eyed the tablet beside her leg and grinned. *And read it, too.*

Lacy walked into the room. "Gray just radioed."

Piper wondered what the Delsh word for "radioed" really was. The seamless Transition experience meant she thought in English but evidently spoke in Delsh so effortlessly that she didn't even realize it was happening. It would be interesting to see an English-Delsh, Delsh-English dictionary.

"He's alright?" Her words emerged in a hoarse croak, mirroring her anxiety.

"Alright, and on the return trip." Lacy's smile reflected a similar level of relief. No one liked Gray being out of contact and in the wilderness for so long. "Apparently, Mara is with him. They should be back in just under three hours. It's still another forty minutes before they clear the dead zone."

The comment confused Piper because, as it had been explained to her, Gray wouldn't be able to contact them while traversing the dead zone. Lacy went on to clarify how Gray had been able to reactivate his tech once he reached a certain altitude. Additionally, once he was within a specific range of the perimeter, he'd been able to send a signal over the top of the Thonian distortion.

"You didn't know he could do that?" Piper asked.

Lacy shook her head. "We had no idea that the radiation was only effective up to a certain altitude. Honestly, I don't think it ever occurred to anyone to test for it. No one has ever..." Her voice trailed off as she pointed vaguely at the ceiling.

Piper snorted. "Right. No one flies." She considered the new information. "You said twenty thousand feet?" She was already imagining Gray sitting on the back of the contraption that had only flown for the first time two hours before he left on that trip.

Brave, or insane?

Chapter 16 - The Neighbor in 3C Paused Call of Duty to Listen

Our-World

Alison Springs, Maryland

I woke up to the familiar electric tingle rippling from head to toe and pushed the thick, overstuffed comforter from my face. The unrelenting glare of the rising sun through the east-facing window felt like an icepick to the brain. I threw back the covers to my side and collapsed with disappointment. Piper hadn't crossed back with me. Sinking back into her bed, I pulled the covers over my head and tried to regroup.

Admittedly, bringing her back this way had been wishful thinking. I'd returned from Oakland with Mara with time to spare. The plan was to lead Mara and a small team into the Darks to reopen the cave where we believed all of this started. With a little luck, the trip would jumpstart Mara's memory, and the location would offer some insight into how Breslin had become whatever he was now. The logistics of that trip were complex. The cave was nowhere near Portland, and coordinating the effort in the Wastes wasn't trivial.

Additionally, I was just hours away from bouncing back to My-World. The Doc and Tripp began organizing the expedition while Lacy and her team collaborated with Mara on further medical diagnostics. The idea was that the next time I landed on Wild-Side, as long as I had enough time on the clock, we would explore the cave.

That left me with downtime, finally. It was long overdue. I'd been awake for longer than I wanted to think about, and while the flight to Oakland was a hell of a lot of fun, it was also exhausting. I needed some rest. There was hope that if I was unconscious when I rebounded and Piper was with me, essentially recreating the circumstances that led to her being brought with me, she might rebound home the same way.

I patted the empty space on the mattress beside me and mumbled profanity.

The multiverse hates me.

"I hope that wasn't aimed at me," Esker said through the speaker on my smartphone. A quick glance confirmed it was sitting on the nightstand just two feet away.

"Piper is on Wild-Side," I said without any preamble.

"I speculated that when she disappeared at the exact same picosecond as you."

It was times like this when it became painfully obvious that I was dealing with an artificial intelligence. His tone was too matter-of fact for the subject at hand.

"Do you have any thoughts on how something like that could be possible?" I pressed.

"There isn't enough data to draw a solid conclusion, but I suspect biological cross-contamination of your nanotech. Perhaps a coital adjustment of your biorhythms at a quantum level. I wasn't scanning you at the time, so I don't have a thorough analysis of the experiment."

I rubbed my eyes. "It wasn't an experiment."

"Are you sure?" Esker asked with a tone of amusement that was unusual for the AI. "Considering the level of creativity shown in your ritual pair bonding, I believe some experimentation was–"

I sat up and glared at the phone. "I thought you weren't scanning me at the time." I tried to sound outraged, but I was struggling not to laugh. Esker had the personality of a Speak & Spell when he first came out of the box. Over time, I'd noticed hints of a unique personality. He was developing a sense of humor and had just enough attitude to make me wonder if he might one day pass for human.

"There was no ignoring that," he said in a dry, almost bored tone. "Even the neighbor in 3C paused Call of Duty to listen."

I was grinning. The biorhythms idea was intriguing. The Doc hadn't thought of that, so it was worth mentioning the next time I returned to Wild-Side. "You're a riot," I said. "So here's something for you to consider. Piper's now stuck on Wild-Side, and I can't figure out how to bring her back. Doc's working on the problem from his side, but I'd feel better if you were involved too."

That was the end of Esker cracking jokes. He knew when it was appropriate to delve into personality exploration and when it was time to tackle the problem. He asked me if the Wild-Side team had any ideas and what technical information they had gathered so far. The more data he could collect, the sooner he might have something for me.

This brings me to one of the few discordant tendencies of the Seeley people. Their life and culture are based on and rely entirely on technology, yet the use of artificial intelligence is outlawed. This isn't to say they haven't developed it; Esker is a clear example of that. They've actually made significant advancements in the area, but they stop short of creating what they call level-4 AI. There's some blurring of the lines when it comes to level-3, as I understand it. Level-3 is an AI that can grasp emotions and discern human needs based on need, want, and the subtleties in between. However, the blurring of level-3 likely relates more to the Seeley people's own limited emotional range and rigidity in this area.

In any case, the Seeley have made significant advancements in AI, but they do not incorporate AI into their daily lives. For reasons I haven't been able to get anyone to specify, it is restricted or forbidden, much like the areas of their wilderness they refer to as the Darks.

Thankfully, the prohibition on using artificial intelligence did not extend to me in My-World. So in the early days of this experience, I began bringing parts of Esker's code back with me. Once the code was compiled on this side, the early version of Esker helped me assemble the mainframe needed to run the current version of Esker. He runs on three quantum computing systems that are hidden away at different locations throughout the world. He only needs one of the systems to operate, but he can move between the three for redundancy and security using some kind of quantum-entangled network interface. He's tried to explain it to me several times, but I either zone out, fall asleep, or one of us just gives up. Regardless, those compute cubes he lives in are about the size of a tissue box, so they are easy to hide, incredibly mobile, and in a lot of ways, my secret weapon in the fight against Breslin on this Brane.

That's really just a roundabout way of saying two things. First, Esker may be a work in progress in terms of personality, but he's more intelligent than I will ever be. Second, if Doc Cormac can't figure out how to get Piper home, Esker will.

"A freak thunderstorm started over Hot Springs, South Dakota, approximately eleven minutes ago," Esker said. An AR projection appeared on the wall beyond the foot of the bed. It displayed a map focused on the northern United States, specifically on the western edge of the Dakotas, all of Wyoming, and a large portion of Montana. A massive, angry-looking storm front loomed over the area, but it seemed centered on Hot Springs, South Dakota.

"I take it that Smallwood has been spending his time in Hot Springs?" I was studying the map as I grabbed the phone and crossed the room on my way to the bathroom.

"He confirmed that he had the meat wagon on the road nine minutes ago," Esker said.

I placed the phone on the counter and started the shower. Esker could switch to a combination transmitter and receiver embedded deep inside my ear canal, but I didn't like having another voice in my head while showering. Talking with him via speakerphone was a more agreeable solution. I had just realized the time and date. Switching back and forth between Wild-Side and My-World could be disconcerting. No matter how long I spent on Wild-Side, only one night had passed here. That meant I was due at the lab in less than an hour.

"The storm front means the experiment was successful?" I said, stepping under the water.

"Weather reports seem to support our assumption. Mr. Smallwood is proceeding with the plan accordingly, and I have integrated the deep-fake footage into the hotel security system."

Derek Smallwood was a friend I enlisted along the way. He had been working as an engineer on one of Breslin's projects, and when things grew complicated, he became painfully aware of his employer's dark agenda. Needless to say, that was his last day on the payroll of the shell company Breslin was using for the project I was torpedoing. What Smallwood witnessed that night not only convinced him to walk away from his employer, but it also motivated him to actively resist what Breslin was attempting to do.

I introduced Smallwood to Esker and came up with a solution to one of my long-standing problems. Anytime Breslin and I are on this Brane at the same time, Mother Nature seems to have a bit of a conniption. Just look at the storm front that appeared out of nowhere. For some reason, that storm front tends to appear right over me. It might as well be a big glowing sign pointing to my exact geographic location. Well, exact if anyone can locate the focal point of the storm. Modern technology makes that trivial.

Esker's idea was to combat technology with even more advanced technology. This was the first proactive test of the effort, and I have to say I felt relieved. I had a lot riding on it because every time the storm revealed my position, the paramilitary forces at Breslin's command would swarm that spot with ever-increasing efficiency.

Esker and Smallwood had attempted to deceive Mother Nature by placing a stockpile of my blood in a camper and parking it at different hotels across the U.S. The idea was to keep the van in motion like a card in a game of Three-card Monte. The hope was that if the biomass in the van were larger than mine but sufficiently matched me, the focal point of the storm would follow the van instead of me.

I'm oversimplifying. The reason Esker needed Smallwood for this was his experience with specialized electrical equipment. They cooked up some kind of bio-electrical transmitter that was supposed to replicate my bio-something—I'll be honest, I didn't really follow. The two really geeked out over it. They were excited and seemed to think it would work. I know the gist was that the gear in the van needed to present a stronger signal to the ether, presenting as me at just the right time. And if it did, they thought the storm would focus on the van rather than me.

It was a really complex way of accomplishing one simple thing: to keep the storm front from revealing my location. Since this storm system was currently disclosing my whereabouts roughly every third time I returned from Wild-Side, it was only a matter of time before Breslin had people close enough to reach me before I could escape.

There was one more trick to all of this. Given the ubiquity of camera-based surveillance today, it would only be a matter of time before the teams searching for me realized they were being deceived. If I didn't appear on the surveillance systems of the hotels and traffic cameras in the area where I was supposed to be, even the most dimwitted trackers would soon realize they were being fooled.

That's where Esker's deepfake technology came into play. He could manipulate camera footage to replace one person with the likeness of another. He could create a perfect likeness of me in any scene, making it nearly impossible to tell that the footage had been altered. The challenge was finding someone in all the footage who matched my height and build to be replaced. That person would essentially be a proxy for my likeness in all the footage.

Again, this is where Derek Smallwood came in. Not only did he possess the technical expertise needed to operate and maintain the van's hardware, but he also had the necessary height, weight, and body type to serve as a double in the footage that Esker would manipulate to sell the illusion that I had been in the same places the van had visited.

"So, is Hot Springs a success?" I asked as I turned off the water.

"Mr. Smallwood seems to be good to his word. It shouldn't be long before I receive confirmation from one or more of the tripwires I left at the hotel, restaurant, or car rental agency."

The goal was to keep Breslin's people in the shadows and far away from me.

"Keep an eye out for Agents Vincente and Ingersoll. I know you need Smallwood for the deepfake, but if we can separate the agents and get them pursuing leads in different directions, I might be able to use that to our advantage later on."

The goggles used to offload data from Wild-Side looked like a pair of wrap-around sunglasses with thick prescription lenses and temples—the sections of the frame that extend from the front and rest on the ears. The largest data transfer I'd ever completed took just over three seconds. This trip was light in comparison. I had the plans for the Airbike, the telemetry from my first flights, and the new information we had gathered on the Elend since my last visit. As always, the information would be processed and reviewed by Esker. While the Doc and his team were my resources on Wild-Side, Esker served as my support here. This is how we kept everyone aligned. My brain was essentially flash storage, and we used it to keep everyone in sync.

I was just putting on a shirt and about to leave for the lab when I heard a phone ringing somewhere in the apartment. It wasn't mine, so the sound caught me off guard. I found Piper's mobile on one of the nightstands. The screen displayed the name Sara Pemberton. After a moment's hesitation, I tapped the display to answer.

"Hey, Sara. It's Gray," I said.

"Gray? Oh, thank God. Piper's with you? We needed you both at the lab an hour ago. Fulbright's freaking out, and we need to reconfigure the system." She was talking so quickly that it was impossible to get a word in.

"Wait, hold on. What's the matter with the Doc?"

"He hasn't really explained. We're sort of reading between the lines. I think he got a call from the money people last night. They want to move up the testing timetable. I believe they're putting pressure on him. Can you guys just get over here so we can sort this out?" The stress in her tone was palpable. She was rambling and clearly hoping for support from Piper.

"I'm on my way," I said, sounding as reassuring as possible. "But Sara? Piper's not here. She left town last night for an emergency. She left so quickly that she even forgot her phone."

There was a pause that made me think the connection had dropped, then I heard muffled cursing.

"Look, Sara," I said. "I'm leaving Piper's place now and will be there in a couple of minutes. We'll figure something out. I can help you with this. It's going to be alright."

I tossed Piper's phone onto the bed, grabbed my jacket, and headed for the door. "E, can you route Piper's phone to mine?" I really didn't want to carry two phones for the rest of the day. It felt particularly unnecessary when I had a brilliant telecommunications powerhouse already playing Watson to my Holmes.

"Done," Esker said without elaborating.

––––––––––––––––

I walked into the lab and found a whirlwind of chaos. Everyone was talking–scratch that–arguing. They were also dismantling the equipment and packing up gear. The arguing wasn't a surprise after the call from Sara. Seeing the equipment being packed made me wonder if the project had already been scrapped. That would be unfortunate for the team, but it would be a major item checked off my to-do list.

"What's going on?" I asked Timo. He had just grabbed a pair of small plastic bins from the stack by the door and was making his way to the supply shelves. One side of the door had a pile of empty bins, while the other featured a stack of similar containers filled with medical cartons, vials, and devices.

"We're moving up to 1A," he said with a shrug. "Give me a hand?"

"No, no," Fulbright said from a dozen feet away. "Gray needs to take the table apart. I don't want to risk any damage." He looked around the room and appeared confused. "Isn't Piper with you?"

Sara scrunched her face at me and waved her hand in the air. "Start on the table. I'll give you a hand in a minute." She grabbed Fulbright by the arm and coaxed him to the edge of the chaos. I could hear her beginning to explain how Piper needed to leave town.

By the time I reached the apparatus, Esker was already relaying disassembly instructions to me through my earpiece. He issued the shutdown command for the terminal connected to a diagnostic port on the side of the bed and instructed me to disconnect the RJ45 cables from the temperature regulator on the right side of the bed. More than a hundred fiber-mesh relays linked the memory foam material to the control surface, so there was a procedure for removing it without causing damage. The massive glass sensor matrix that arched over the center of the bed retracted into a container underneath, making it clear that, apparently the most sensitive and expensive component of the entire system, was the easiest to stow and remove.

Thanks to Esker, I was able to shut down the table and disassemble it in just under twenty minutes. To anyone watching, it seemed like I knew exactly what I was doing.

Timo and Sara helped me load the components onto the elevator. It was a quick ride to the seventh floor, followed by two corridors leading to the new lab, which featured thick double wooden doors marked with 1A in black lettering. Piles of boxes had already been brought up from the basement and stacked against the left wall. The space mirrored the basement layout in both square footage and design, with one major exception. While the prior lab had been highly secure with massive steel doors and concrete walls, Lab 1A was filled with windows. The glass started at about waist level and extended to the ceiling on the three exterior walls. The left side mostly overlooked woodland at the perimeter of the school property, the center offered a view of a small grassy area with winding paved walking trails, and the right side faced the parking lot.

Timo and I were carrying the plastic-lined case that sheltered the glass scanning and display arch from the bed. I duckwalked backward into the room and tilted my head to direct Timo to the window overlooking the parking lot. We set the cumbersome case down in a place where it was unlikely to be in the way.

I looked around the space and couldn't help shaking my head. "The project kind of did a one-eighty in terms of security, didn't it?" I said.

Timo shrugged.

Sara seemed about to speak when Fulbright walked into the room, pushing a cart loaded with plastic transport bins. "The security was a mixed blessing," he said before Sara had a chance to respond. "It was overkill, and it's possible that the conditions could adversely impact the effectiveness of the test." I must have looked confused because he continued. "Admittedly, there are many variables when it comes to Brane theory. But considering the goal is to cross a boundary that is inherently natural, it seems wise to eliminate as many artificial barriers as possible.

"Being underground can have its advantages or disadvantages. It's difficult to determine. The concrete and steel? Nothing good can result from that. There's nothing natural about it. Plus, there's all the interaction from the surrounding labs. Up here, we're the only lab on the top floor. There's us, a helicopter platform, some administrative offices, and not much else. Fewer variables." He concluded with a slow visual sweep of the space. I noted that although his words seemed confident, his demeanor did not.

"Word is you're moving the first experiment to tonight," I said. "I thought that was at least a month away."

Fulbright's vacant-eyed gaze swept across the room and the grounds beyond before he abruptly turned to me. "Tonight?" He swallowed hard. "Yes. Tonight."

He hesitated. I think he was trying to decide whether he needed to continue, should continue, or if what he said would be enough confirmation. I maintained his gaze. I wasn't letting him off the hook. This wasn't right for my plans, and it was clearly a concern for Sara. From the corner of my eye, I saw Sara motion to Timo. She silently signaled him to leave the room. Apparently, the idea was to give me some one-on-one time with the project leader.

"Doesn't that strike you as reckless?" I pressed, my tone gentle but firmly insistent.

Fulbright slid his hands into his pockets and regarded me for several long seconds. "It's more aggressive than I would prefer," he finally confessed. "The money people are impatient. If I lose funding on this, I honestly don't see anyone stepping in to cover the costs. Frankly, I was fortunate to find this backer."

You're right about that.

It was just bad luck. He just didn't know it yet.

"I've been working on this project much longer than anyone realizes," Fulbright continued. "While I could procrastinate and prolong this process, I already know how to make it work. The extended test plan primarily addresses ethical and compliance requirements. There's really no risk involved."

"No danger?" My voice rose, and I couldn't help myself. "If your project succeeds, you'll be transported to another dimension of reality. You have no idea what to expect there. It could be a barren, benign wilderness similar to the world we know—or it could be a hostile, alien environment that doesn't support human life."

Fulbright smiled. "You just joined us a couple of days ago? You've thought this through more than most of the team members. Impressive insight," he nodded. "But you must remember, when this works, I will cross over in a dream state. My body will stay here. Nothing that happens to me wherever I go will affect me here."

I had been hesitant to discuss this with Fulbright until now. Suddenly, I found myself wishing I had had a heart-to-heart with him as soon as I arrived in town. "That's purely theoretical on your part," I reminded him. "This is uncharted territory. If you die there, who's to say what happens to your body here?"

I wanted to ask him why he thought his body wouldn't go along for the ride when his mind crossed over, but that seemed like an entirely unexpected outcome, and probing that possibility might tip my hand. If that assumption ever made it back to Breslin, too many connections would be made both at this location and on this project.

The idea made Fulbright laugh. It wasn't just a mild chuckle; he burst into a belly laugh. "You should be writing for Hollywood in your spare time," he said between huffs. "I'd love to see the special effects involved in that film. You truly have an outstanding imagination. That's really impressive."

I shook my head. I wanted Fulbright to consider the dangers inherent in this kind of experimentation, but there was no way to make him a believer without showing him what I'd seen firsthand.

He waved me toward the hall. "Let's finish moving the scan table. Once it's reassembled, we can have the facilities people move the rest of our equipment. Everyone can take the afternoon off. That way, we'll all be at our best for the nine o'clock test."

"Nine o'clock?"

"We'll have the new lab ready by tonight," he explained. "That should be the best time for the experiment. The building will be mostly empty, and my body will be in a more conducive state for sleep. My formula relies on my neurochemistry being in a near-sleep state, and I want to use minimal drugs to achieve optimal PRS conditions. All of that adds up to 9 PM."

I watched Fulbright leave the room, my mind already concocting ways to undermine the effectiveness of his experiment.

"That man is going to get himself killed," I heard Esker say in my ear.

I nodded. "Did you go over the protocol he intends to use tonight?"

"It's not stored on the central server," Esker said. "He keeps it on an encrypted laptop in his attache case, which is with him at all times."

I rolled my eyes, already contemplating ways to separate the doctor from his briefcase.

"But the computer has the Wake on LAN feature enabled," Esker continued. "So the device connects to any nearby wireless network it has used before if there is an access request. The operating system is quite promiscuous, and the encryption is not terribly advanced."

"This is your way of saying you have access to the protocol?"

"I thought I just said that."

I grinned. "Will the experiment work?"

"It's impossible to say with certainty. We don't know how you make the crossing, even after more than a month of study on this side and years of examination from the Wild-Side perspective. There is a better than even chance that something will happen. It would not be prudent to let him continue with the experiment."

———————

It was just before nine o'clock, and I was looking out the seventh-floor window at the lights of the parking lot below. Only a handful of cars remained, attesting to the fact that few people were left in the building aside from Doctor Fulbright's team. It was a good bet the rest were building maintenance and whatever minimal on-site security the facility had maintained.

Sara Pemberton was making final adjustments to a pair of tall, thin gas canisters she had recently positioned at the head of the high-tech bed. I had finished assembling the device a couple of hours ago, and Esker walked me through running the hardware diagnostic routines I was expected to know as part of my cover. I had considered sabotaging the hardware, but that approach didn't have legs. I could only play that game for so long. Sooner or later, I would either be discovered or replaced. I needed to turn Fulbright against the overall idea he was pursuing.

Fulbright sat on a stool next to the small panel built into the frame halfway down the side of the bed. He had an RJ45 cable plugged into the control interface and was hunched over the attached laptop. I watched him hunt and peck as he typed on the keyboard with a single extended finger. Whatever he was doing, the process was excruciatingly slow, mainly because he lacked basic computing skills. I had let it go on for some time, just to allow his frustration to build to sufficient levels.

"Hey, Doc," I said, kneeling beside him. "It seems like you're losing a battle with this thing. Is there anything I can do to help?"

He pushed a pair of oily, fingerprinted glasses back on his nose and looked at me as if I'd just arrived. "I'm almost done," he said. His eyes were bloodshot, and I had to believe his finger was bruised by now. "I'm just finalizing the configuration. It's good," his words came slowly. "Fighting with these things always makes me tired. It will make

Phase Two easier. The less anesthesia, the better."

I wasn't sure how to respond to that. "Sure," I replied. "But if you're tired, what happens if you make a mistake?"

He stopped tapping at the keyboard and looked at me. He removed his glasses and rubbed his eyes. It seemed like something was on his mind. Glancing around the room, he appeared satisfied that no one was within earshot. He looked back at me with a lopsided grin. "This device isn't essential to the experiment. If this works, it will be key to capturing evidence of my security measures, and possibly helpful for reproducing it, but it's not crucial to the experiment's success."

Shit.

There it was. Sabotaging the rig wasn't going to get this done. Esker had gone through the device's schematics and decompiled the software he believed to be part of the experiment. None of it helped us understand exactly what the Doc had in mind that would allow him to cross over.

"I don't understand," I admitted. "If it's not this fancy bed, what's the trick?"

Initially, I didn't believe Fulbright was going to respond. However, considering we were about to run the experiment, I don't think he had much reason to conceal his plan any longer. "I have implied that the device is part of the requirements," he admitted. "But that's mainly for operational secrecy. Even the backers think the hardware is essential. The truth is, it's all in the secret sauce." His grin stretched from ear to ear, both figuratively and literally.

"Secret...*sauce*?"

He looked around again to ensure no one was paying attention to us, then leaned closer. When he spoke, his voice dropped to a conspiratorial whisper. "When I first had the idea, it was to engineer a solution that would align the requisite areas of the brain to fall out of phase with the quantum resonance of our local coherent membrane. There are two problems with that. First, every brain functions differently, so the formula required for each test subject would need adjustments. Second, if the formula differs each time, there's no way to ensure each subject interacts with the same non-local coherent membrane. Two people could end up on different Branes. Even when successful, test results would be subjective and impossible to replicate, at least not with any degree of accuracy.

"Okaaaayyy," I heard myself say, stretching the word into an entire sentence.

In my ear, I heard Esker say, "Keep him talking. This is good. I'll give you the for-dummies version later." That made me smirk, but Fulbright interpreted it as a positive sign because he plowed ahead.

"The genius of my revised approach lies in establishing a baseline by effectively dulling the brain centers that lead to differential parametric results."

He must have noticed the blank look in my eyes because he paused and examined my face.

Esker stepped in with a cue to keep the conversation flowing. "He's establishing a framework so all test subjects start from the same baseline."

I nodded slowly at first, then with more enthusiasm as if what I had heard was making sense. "You're setting a baseline. Creating a framework so everyone can use the same formula? You're bootstrapping their brains?"

Fulbright looked at me from beneath his arched brows. "Interesting. Yes. Exactly right," he chuckled.

Esker said to me, "Bootstrapping? Was that a lucky guess or did one of us just have a stroke?"

A couple of minutes later, I was by myself in one of the service corridors. I picked this hall because I knew it didn't have any security cameras. It was also not adjacent to a path anyone would take on the way to the cafeteria or one of the restrooms. It was the only way I could have a private conversation with Esker without looking like a lunatic.

"Sabotaging the rig is out of the question," I whispered.

"The only value it would hold is preventing the capture of

analytics," Esker confirmed. "That would be useful, but it won't ultimately halt the project."

"Have you had any luck finding the formula Fulbright is using?"

"Negative. Wherever he's storing the information, it's either air-gapped or entirely analog. Based on how he types, I suspect it's written down somewhere. He doesn't seem like the type to create digital records unless he has to. Data entry seems to be a struggle for him."

Struggle. Hearing Esker describe it that way, while thinking of how painfully Fulbright was typing on that poor laptop, made me smile. *Struggle, for sure.*

I glanced at the display on my cell phone. It was nine-twelve p.m. It was too late for a long-term fix. I had to settle for a short-term solution and save the other option for another day. "I'm going with Plan B," I whispered.

"Wait," Esker shot back. "I didn't know we had a Plan B. Why wasn't I informed?"

"I just thought of it."

"What could go wrong? Are you going to share?"

I'll admit to some reluctance. I didn't think it was a great plan... it was just better than no plan. More than anything, I suppose I just didn't need the voice in my head shooting holes in it at the last second.

"Well?" Esker pressed.

I rolled my eyes. "Fulbright can't conduct a sleep experiment if he can't sleep, can he?"

I'm not sure what I expected, but Esker's silence felt unsettling.

"Are you there?" I finally inquired.

"The plan is to *keep him from falling asleep*?"

"Yes."

"Strategically speaking, isn't that what you would refer to as *weak sauce*."

"I'm not going to–"

"He's too clever to accept coffee when you offer it to him."

"I'm not going to–"

"You don't plan to stand in the corner and hum one of your off-key tunes, do you? That would be really annoying." He paused. "You know, that might actually work."

"I'm not going to–hey, I've never hummed a single tune...ever." I started to think the secret might be giving Fulbright my earpiece and just letting Esker talk his ear off. The guy might never sleep again.

I waved my hand in the air, relieved that there were no cameras nearby. "Knock it off, will you? Epinephrine, okay? Small doses of epinephrine in his IV should keep him wired and completely unable to drift off to dreamland, no matter what Sara puts into his lungs. That should prevent him from crossing the Brane tonight. We can worry about the rest tomorrow."

I had hoped to spike the formula Fulbright was using for the experiment directly once I knew messing with the monitoring rig wouldn't get the job done. Unfortunately, the Doc was paranoid and kept the formula under lock and key after the team was moved out of the high-security lab. Apparently, while he wanted to eliminate the obstructions and interference the basement facility might introduce, he wasn't willing to forgo any additional security precautions he could still leverage.

Was it paranoia when we were really out to get him? I mean, he was funded by a ruthless, bloodthirsty demon from another plane of reality, and I was here to sabotage his experiment with the help of an incredibly smart and increasingly sarcastic artificial intelligence.

If he only knew, right?

He even had an off-duty cop standing guard outside the lab. I wanted to give him credit for that. He was spending Breslin Corps' money after all, so why not.

It turned out to be easy enough to spike the saline drip he'd be using alongside Cocktail X—that's what I decided to name his secret formula. He had some complicated name mentioned in the project documentation. I don't know why. When you're working on something like this, why not choose something cool or clever? It's not like it would ever be widely discussed. Not that Cocktail X was particularly kitschy. But I could remember it, and it was much easier to spell than…well, you get the idea.

By half past eleven, Fulbright was laid out on the bed, the lights were low, and the experiment was in full swing. Well, it was in its second hour, but little progress had been made. The Doc was still awake, and stress was running high. Sara was adjusting the anesthesia for the third time, but Fulbright had yet to reach what I'll refer to more simply as *the zone*. Again, the project had a more complicated name for the ideal sleep-like state that was conducive to a Crossing.

Oman believed this was due to performance anxiety or stress associated with the project. I think he was projecting some personal issues there, but who am I to judge? Timo was all about adjusting the meds to better achieve zen, but Fulbright was adamant that no changes be made to his formula. Reading between the lines, I'm a hundred percent sure Timo just wanted Fulbright to smoke some weed and chill out.

I had been watching the group, listening to the discord, and observing the shadows of the parking lot below the windows to pass the time. A helicopter had flown in low over the building a few minutes earlier, and I noted that the lab was so well insulated against sound that I couldn't hear its rotors or prop wash. There was a landing pad on the other end of the roof. This was why this lab was the only one on the top floor. Seeing the chopper come in over the parking lot reminded me of what I had thought when I heard they were moving the lab to the penthouse. It seemed like the exact wrong place for a sleep lab if it was likely to be buzzed by choppers from time to time because who could sleep through that?

To my best estimate, everyone in the room was ten to fifteen minutes away from a full stress-induced meltdown. While this was somewhat beneficial as it would undermine the current test, unfortunately, it wouldn't be enough to convince the team that the overall effort was a failure. I was brainstorming approaches for that endeavor when the double doors crashed open, and the guard from the hallway was dumped unconscious and bleeding on the floor. Three large figures pushed into the room, all outfitted in black tactical outfits and balaclavas. Each carried only a suppressed pistol with an extended magazine.

One figure stood over the supine, unmoving figure of the uniformed security guard while the other two spread out to his flanks. All three men raised their guns and pointed at different portions of the room. None of them were quick to speak. They seemed content to let their menacing presence make the introduction. They didn't appear pressed for time. I shot a look out the window and decided they had likely come in on the helicopter I'd just seen. The timing couldn't be a coincidence.

"The status of the experiment?" the figure in the center of the room asked. His voice was calm and commanding, with no discernible accent. He sounded American, mid-western, unless it was a practiced affectation. It was so bland that it could either be genuine or an indication of a professional who had put tremendous effort into removing all traces of accent and nuance from his diction.

Fulbright lay on the bed with his head tilted at an uncomfortable angle as he strained to see the entrance to the room and the loud commotion that had just occurred. He was more or less stitched in place by the tangle of leads that had been stretched across his bare torso and head to monitor his bio-rhythms. These had not been part of the original plan, but when he couldn't reach dreamland, desperate efforts had resulted.

"Does it seem like the experiment is working?" Fulbright asked, frustration evident in his voice. He sounded more upset about the lack of progress that night than the unexpected arrival of armed men.

A glance at the guard on the floor confirmed he was still breathing. This suggested the armed men were not here to kill anyone.

Hopefully.

"What do you want?" Timo asked. "The pharmacy is on the first floor."

That made sense. Timo believed this was a heist, a group of armed men aiming to steal the building's supply of prescription drugs. It wasn't uncommon, and he was the team's pharmacologist.

The man at the center of the room waved to the person on his right. The figure stepped forward to examine the pair of IV bags hanging from the stand beside Fulbright. "One is saline," he said. "The other is almost empty. It's useless."

"Is it enough for a chemical analysis?" the lead figure asked.

The masked man next to Fulbright studied the drip, then glanced around the room. "There should be more," he said. He glared at Fulbright and raised his pistol. He didn't aim it at Fulbright—he didn't need to. "Where is the rest of the supply?"

At this point, Sara, Timo, and Oman had moved to the far wall. Fulbright would have joined them, but he was trapped by more wires than he could reasonably untangle quickly. The Doctor stared at the armed man with wide, unblinking eyes, appearing panicked to the point of immobility.

"The supply," the man repeated, this time more harshly.

These men were professionals, I had already concluded. They had disabled the hallway guard but hadn't killed him. They projected authority without making threats. Even when the man beside Fulbright brandished his sidearm, he did not aim it directly at him. He merely drew attention to the weapon. It was subtle, yet significant to me. If someone points a gun at me, I assume they intend to pull the trigger and react accordingly. This? He was indicating that he had a gun rather than threatening to shoot someone.

Think I'm reading too much into what I see? It would dictate how I react to the situation. If I believe these guys will leave once they get what they want, then that's great. It's kind of perfect because we both win. But if they'll kill everyone on their way out the door... that changes the rules of the game for me.

"It's in the freezer," Fulbright finally rasped in a half-whisper.

The figure began glancing around the room, clearly searching for the freezer.

"There's a combination," I volunteered. "Can I get it for you?" I offered.

I was still standing by the windows overlooking the parking lot, separate from the rest of the team, who were closer to Fulbright. The lead gunman and the man on the left flank had focused most of their attention on that group—human nature, since that's where most of us were located.

"It's right here," I said, pointing to the small freezer chest on the floor below the windows. A padlock secured the front of the small box.

I tapped the epinephrine syringe in the pocket of my lab coat to confirm it was still there. In my ear, I heard Esker say, "You're going to try to contaminate the master supply before you turn it over?"

I subvocalized a tone of affirmation.

The lead gunman and the one beside Fulbright exchanged a glance, then the lead gave a nod. The figure near Fulbright kept his pistol at his side but gestured for me to move toward the freezer.

"You'll need a distraction," Esker said.

I repeated my affirmation and started dialing the combination on the freezer's lock. I didn't know what he had planned, and we didn't have time to sort it out, so I just hoped for the best as I removed the lock from the hasp and pulled the door open. As my fingers wrapped around the twenty-milliliter injection vial, I slipped my right hand into the pocket of my lab coat and thumbed the protective cap off the syringe.

I heard Esker say, "two...one...go," in my ear.

There was a loud pop and a fizzing sound. The room's lights that had been turned low for the sleep experiment flickered. I pulled the syringe from my pocket and plunged it into the end of the bottle I retrieved from the freezer. I injected the entire contents of the syringe, withdrew it, and slipped it back into my pocket. When I looked up, everyone stared at the smoking and hissing coffee pot at the room's far end.

"Here you go," I said and passed the small bottle to the gunman.

Everyone looked confused. I could see the puzzled expression in the eyes of the masked men. The unpleasant tang of ammonia filled the air, and I was pretty sure someone on the team had pissed themselves when the coffeemaker popped off. I couldn't blame them for that.

Without another word, the three men withdrew from the room. No one made a sound. I heard the hallway door squeak as they backtracked with raised guns, skillfully pointed at no one in particular. Twenty seconds later, I saw the helicopter pass over the parking lot and climb steeply into the night sky.

Chapter 17 - She Hit That Guy So Hard That He Lost Seven Teeth

Our-World

Alison Springs, Maryland

An hour after the attack on the lab, I was sitting at a table at The Borderline. It was the same table I'd used last time, actually. It wasn't the weekend, so the place wasn't packed. I had my pick of the tables. A jukebox was belting out tunes in the background. It was country. Normally, that would be enough to send me looking for another place to drink, but after the events of the evening, I had enough on my mind to distract me from the music. As long as it wasn't rap, I could keep the distraction in the back of my mind.

The waitress ambled up to the table, popped the top off a bottle of Modelo as she arrived, and slid it across the scarred surface with a smile. "Piper's off tonight," she said by way of greeting.

I nodded and glanced at the bottle. They didn't carry the stuff. Either that had changed, or news about me had spread since my one and only visit to the place. I looked at the waitress's name tag and confirmed she wasn't one of the young women who worked during my last visit. Mindy. I didn't recognize the name any more than the face.

Yup. There'd been gossip.

"I heard that might be true," I said with my best disappointed shrug. "It did hurt to try anyway." I tipped the beer and lowered my voice. "Do you mind if I ask how you knew?"

Mindy's nose twitched in sync with the pursing of her lips and the crinkling of her brow. She hesitated somewhat transparently before glancing over her shoulder, then slipped onto the bench across the table from me. "Folks here are kind of tight-knit," she said in a hushed tone as she leaned closer. "Piper's really popular with the customers, as you might imagine, pretty girl and all. Young guys come in all the time to flirt. It's fun most of the time. Piper has a bit of a reputation. She doesn't encourage it. The fact is, she doesn't have much patience for it."

After glancing over her shoulder again, Mindy tilted her head in thought before continuing. "I guess that doesn't sound quite right. She's nice enough to people and all. She just doesn't have patience for the messing around some of us do for fun." She paused and made eye contact with me. "It's all in fun, you know, and it's really good for tips. Just chat with the customers and keep them drinking. The owner has no patience for people who get out of hand, mind you."

At this point, I have to admit I was wondering where Mindy was heading with all this. I was here because I wanted to be alone. The events of the evening left me confused, and I needed to sort them out. If I went home and fell asleep, I'd be back on Wild-Side in a flash. I wasn't sure if the night's events were over, and I needed to process the attack on the lab before I moved on to the next complication.

"...and Carl tells Mike that the next thing he knew, Piper turned pale as a sheet. He said he thought she was going to pass out. He didn't know what was wrong." Apparently, Mindy had been talking for some time. I'm pretty sure I didn't miss anything relevant.

Anything at all.

I took a long pull from the bottle. "And the problem was?" I prodded, hoping to shorten the story. Brevity, folks. Sometimes, you can't overstate the importance of brevity.

Mindy appeared momentarily confused. Her head bobbed for a second, as if she were clearing her mind. "She wouldn't say," she finally responded. "But Mike put it together when he reviewed the surveillance videos from the bar after he opened the next morning." Mindy placed her hand on mine and raised an eyebrow. "He thought maybe someone got out of line with Piper, and he wanted to ensure he got to the bottom of it, mind you. He's not stalkerish or nothing."

I nodded my understanding, trying not to ask her what was taking so long to get to the point of her story. Coincidentally, this was when I realized my bottle had mysteriously become empty. I had no memory of draining it and wondered if she would follow me if I went to get another.

It turns out Mindy was both more aware than I expected and had the ability to multitask. She glanced in the direction of the bar and waved a finger in the air. I had another beer within seconds, and she didn't even have to pause her confusing narrative.

"So, long story short," she said.

Um, that ship had sailed.

Still, there was kindness in her eyes, and I noticed concern in her expression. I don't believe her intention was to gossip, and I felt confident that when we eventually reached the point, she was sharing this for a good reason.

I hope…

"She kind of freaked out when she saw you," Mindy concluded.

"You think?" I hedged. "What makes you so sure?"

"You know each other, right?"

I just stared. The silence felt like Mindy's nemesis. Allowing it to stretch would be a fate worse than death.

She shrugged after what must have been the longest three seconds of her life. "I didn't see the recording. I only know what Mike said and what Carl told me. When I tried to check the recordings, they were gone for some reason." Confusion clouded Mindy's expression as she considered what she had just said. "Weird, too. It was only the recordings from that night. I can't say that's ever happened before… and I've been here for over a year."

I heard Esker's voice in my ear. "The recordings were saved to an offline system; I didn't delete them."

A smile was on my face before I could stop it. Piper would have deleted the footage. I'm pretty sure I pulled it back before Mindy noticed. "Technology is funny that way, I guess."

"So, anyway," she said, "what's the deal?"

"Sorry?" Now, I was confused.

"You all must have some history, right?" She glanced at the beer bottle and wiggled her eyebrows. "Seems to know you pretty well."

I shrugged. I was doing that a lot in this conversation. "What did Piper say?"

Mindy rolled her eyes as if they weren't attached to anything in the back of her sockets. Serious drama. One hand waved through the air. "Like that girl talks about herself at all?"

I grinned. "Not sure what I can tell you then."

In response, Mindy shot me a silent glare. But as we've already established, she's not great with silence...so it didn't last long. "The whole time I've known her, she won't give a guy the time of day while at work. Then you walk in and she goes white as a sheet. After that, she heads down to the corner store, picks up a case of Modelo, and sticks it in the cooler...apparently just for you."

"Wait—what?" The words were out of my mouth before I knew it.

Arched brows, pursed lips, and a slow head nod. I suddenly felt that Mindy had a future as an attorney. The gradual buildup to that conclusion caught me off guard.

Mindy's serious demeanor shifted back to the original cordial nonchalance she displayed when she approached the table. "About a year ago, a guy walked in just before closing. It was the middle of the week, kind of a night like this—slow and all. Piper was closing with Carl. On nights like that, we try to wrap things up quickly so we can get home. Usually, one person closes out the drawers, puts the money away in the back, logs the take and everything, while the other sees any lingering customers out, locks the door, and turns off the lights and stuff.

"Anyway, that night Carl was in back, and Piper shooed the last laggards out the door. She was just about to lock up when a guy with pantyhose pulled over his face shoved a gun in her face and demanded the money from the registers. The drawers had already been cleaned out by that point, mind you. Carl was in back locking everything in the safe, so there was no chance it was going to go the way the guy with the gun wanted."

"Piper didn't even hesitate," Mindy explained. "I've seen the recordings—multiple camera views. She went behind the bar just like the guy asked and opened the register. She pulled the drawer and dropped it, the whole time, with a gun to her head. She must have done it quickly because the guy didn't get to see the drawer was only prepped for the next morning. We only have a little cash ready to start the next day.

"So, the drawer hits the floor, and the robber starts yelling for her to pick it up. Piper does. But when she comes up, she doesn't have the drawer in her hand—she's holding an eighteen-inch oak bat that's about as big around as my arm. The owner keeps it under the bar. I never knew why before. I guess Piper knew what it was for because she hit that guy so hard that he lost seven teeth. His gun was gone so fast, we couldn't even tell what direction it went when we looked at the video."

I must have been staring at Mindy because she finally paused. The story stopped, and she just looked at me, nodding her head.

"That girl is fierce," she said. "You should know that. She means a lot to everyone here, so if you have a history with her or are looking to start something up, make sure you treat her right. She doesn't need anyone to fight for her, but everyone here is in her corner when push comes to shove."

I was grinning. I could vividly imagine everything as it was being described and had no doubt that Piper would do exactly as claimed under those conditions. "Reading you loud and clear," I said sincerely, with a hint of admiration for the kind of friends Piper had clearly been spending time with.

Mindy slid from the seat and gave me a wink. "I'll get you another beer."

I glanced at my second bottle. It, too, was empty, although I didn't remember drinking it. I was beginning to wonder if they had leaks, even though the table was dry. "One question before you go?" I asked. "What happened with the robber?"

"Seven missing teeth, a broken arm, and a sprained ankle before he reached the parking lot. Once he was outside, Piper called the police. Officers found him in his car, caught up in the bushes at the end of our parking lot. They believe he panicked while leaving, causing the wreck, then got stuck and was in no condition to flee on foot."

I laughed. It must have been quite a call for the responding officers.

Mindy leaned down to stage whisper in my ear. "They say a couple of his teeth never turned up. They might still be around here somewhere." She winked at me before heading off to check on another customer.

A hand was still in front of my face as I struggled to hide my smile when I heard Esker's voice in my ear. "I thought the waitress was... what is the colorful phrase you use... pulling your leg? But I found the police report detailing the incident she described. Adam Weevil Steckel was hospitalized for eleven days following the attempted robbery of a bar called The Borderline," he said. "Several local papers ran a story that didn't name the employee who intervened, but Piper's name is clearly noted in the report filed by Deputy Sheriff Jared Kessel."

I pulled a Bluetooth headset out of my pocket and slipped it onto my ear. Placing my phone on the table in front of me, I leaned back in my seat. It was common enough that anyone nearby would assume I was talking on the phone. That would attract a lot fewer glances than if anyone were sitting alone and talking to themselves; which is exactly what they would think, since, as far as I know, I'm the only one with a wireless link to my own AI sidekick.

"Not a doubt in my mind," I said to Esker. "Do me a favor," I said, changing my approach. "Help me sort out what happened in the lab. I'm having trouble figuring out who the party crashers were."

"I've examined all the footage from the laboratory surveillance system. The masks served as a sufficient disguise to obscure their features and even thwart my facial recognition abilities. I'm reviewing airfields within a three hundred-mile radius, but many smaller installations, like this bar, do not have their surveillance systems connected to the internet."

"I'm also conducting voiceprint analysis using the recordings from the lab and comparing them to any cellular network calls made in the area since the attack. No matches have been found."

I was at a loss for words. Esker had done all of that on his own initiative, and I was incredibly impressed. I was unsure how to respond.

"Impressive," I remarked finally. "You put our enforcement agencies to shame. You're doing the work of an entire team."

"Unsuccessfully," he said simply.

"With that kind of effort, it's only a matter of time." I was giving a pep talk to a machine, but I really meant it. "Honestly, I'm more puzzled by the motivation of the team behind it."

It was Esker's turn to pause. "Could you please explain that?"

Mindy delivered another beer, noticed I was on the phone, and set it down in front of me with a smile before leaving. I took a sip and pondered my next words. "I know why Breslin is funding Fulbright's experiment, and I understand why I want to sabotage it. I'm struggling to comprehend who would want to steal an unproven formula. I mean, beyond Breslin's ultimate goal and Fulbright's interest in Brane Theory, who's the other player interested in this game?"

"Perhaps Breslin has people behind the theft in an effort to ensure the experiment isn't derailed like so many of his others?" I could tell Esker was asking the question more to participate in the game. There were too many gaps in the perspective, and he would have considered most, if not all of them. He was asking questions because he saw value in the brainstorming exercise.

"Breslin is funding the experiment. If he wanted the formula, he could simply demand it. He could leverage it from Fulbright. I'm sure it's the ultimate plan. Besides, it's of no value to Breslin until it's proven effective. That's the point of all the projects he's cultivating all over hell and back."

"Then an independent third party has to be interested in Doctor Fulbright's work," Esker concluded.

There was logic to that, but it seemed incredibly unlikely. This was fringe science at best. It's not as if anyone was going to win an award for sleep science. "Even then," I said, "What's the point of stealing an unproven formula? Especially right before it's about to be tested?"

"They are even less likely to benefit now that you've tainted the vial before handing it over."

Then it clicked. There was only one person who would benefit in this situation.

"We have to go see Fulbright," I grumbled.

I finished the last of the beer and was about to leave when Esker's news changed my plans.

"I have been monitoring the lab's surveillance system. Dr. Fulbright hasn't returned since he left at ten fifty-one this evening. He was the last member of the project team to exit the facility, and no one has returned since then."

"Get his home address for me. I'm not concerned about waking him. He has some explaining to do."

"The university does not have a current address on file. It appears his pay is directly deposited into his bank account, and all mail is sent to a post office box," Esker said.

I rubbed the fatigue from my eyes and tried to keep the frustration out of my voice. "So even you have no idea where Fulbright lives?" These days, keeping one's address out of the digital ether isn't easy. It requires deliberate and ongoing effort.

Movement at the end of the table caught my attention. At first, I thought it was Mindy with another drink. When I looked up, I saw a young man dressed mostly in denim. It had been a long day, so it took me a moment longer than it should have to remember his name. "Tommy?" I said. "Tommy Walsh, right?"

A grin spread across Tommy's face as he extended his hand. "Good to see ya," he drawled in his Texas twang. Then he glanced at the headset hanging from my ear and winced. "Sorry. Didn't mean to interrupt your call."

I recalled the pretense of using the Bluetooth earpiece to disguise my conversation with Esker and raised a finger to Tommy while glancing at my phone on the table. "Hey, thanks for checking that. See what you can find, and I'll call you back in a bit." I tapped the headset's frame to mimic disconnecting the call before removing the headset and placing it on the table next to the phone.

"Hey," Tommy said. "I was just stopping by for a quick drink before heading home. Do you mind if I join you?"

I considered the conversation I needed to have with Fulbright and the late hour. If I went home now, the odds were good I would end up on Wild-Side as soon as I closed my eyes. While I was anxious to get back to Piper, I really needed to sort this out with the good doctor before something bad happened here. I was sort of spinning my wheels until Esker tracked down an address, but knowing him, that wouldn't take long, regardless of how well Fulbright covered his tracks.

"Pull up a chair," I said, motioning to the bench seat opposite mine.

Tommy slid into the booth without hesitation. He was holding a tall draft in his hand, suggesting he had been here for at least a few minutes.

"Hey," he said. "I overheard you on my way over. Did you say you were trying to find Doc Fulbright's place?"

I nodded. "I guess it's unlisted. I need to find him tonight if possible."

"Fulbright's an odd one," Tommy said. "He's one of those," he raised his fingers in the air, *"the government's out to get you* kinds," and bracketed the statement. "He uses anonymous web browsers, virtual private networks for online shopping, and changes his email address like I change my socks. It's all foolishness, if you ask me."

This had more of a conspiracy mindset vibe than I'd experienced in my somewhat limited interactions with Fulbright, but it did explain why Esker was having trouble locating the guy. It was somewhat amusing that he was being leveraged by perhaps the greatest threat to global safety since the Nazi occupation.

"You seem to know a lot about him," I observed.

Tommy removed his cowboy hat, set it aside, and ran a hand through his hair. "Trini was a TA for him when we first started dating. She was well acquainted with his eccentricities."

Esker made a sound that resembled a throat clearing in my ear, a very human affectation that brought a smile to my face. It was something new for him.

"I need to locate Fulbright, preferably tonight," I explained. "Would Trini know where he lives? I can't find his home address listed anywhere."

Tommy chuckled. "The Doc went to great lengths to keep his address a secret. He was obsessed with it. But in the end, laziness prevailed. He had Trini doing all sorts of ridiculous tasks for him—running errands, making deliveries—you name it."

"So she knows where he's staying?"

Tommy nodded. "Even better, I can show you. I drove her out there a bunch of times when we first started dating."

I grinned. "An address is sufficient. I truly appreciate it."

Tommy's expression changed, and I knew something was off.

"The thing is," he said, "I don't know the address. I can't exactly give you directions either. It's way out of town, and it's been a while since I've had to go, so I'm not sure I remember it well enough to explain it."

Frustration blossomed in my belly. Still, if we knew which direction the house was from town, there was a chance Esker could figure out who owned the property. He would need to investigate ownership records related to anyone even remotely connected to Fulbright. Still, I'd seen him make some impressive intuitive leaps, and data mining was his area of expertise.

"Anyway," Tommy continued, "I can take you there."

"Sorry?" I said, realizing I had lost track of what he had been saying. "I don't remember it well enough to give you directions, but I'll recall it if I drive it. I can take you now if it's that important."

Esker's voice rang in my ear. "I just discovered a two hundred fifty thousand dollar transfer to a numbered account in Bermuda. It's timestamped eight hours ago, with some processing delay preventing reporting of the transaction. I'm noticing telecommunications issues in that area. I believe this confirms your suspicion about Doctor Fulbright."

I nodded to Tommy. "Can we go now? It might be a matter of life or death."

The drive to Doctor Fulbright's was longer than I expected. He didn't just live outside of town; he lived way outside of town. True to his word, Tommy Walsh knew the way, even though he didn't know the names of most roads. He retraced his route from long ago, navigating by landmarks. The only difficulty came when we got close to what turned out to be the last two miles of the sprawling, disused horse ranch Fulbright was using as his residence.

I watched the full moon as Tommy slipped his F150 temporarily to the edge of the ditch a hundred yards from the wide gravel drive winding through the sparse woodland separating the large house, barn, and several outbuildings from the road. Nearby, numerous shoulder-high fences were visible, snaking across the rolling hills in the distance.

"Why can't I just drive up?" Tommy asked.

I didn't reply right away. The attack on the laboratory had been replaying in my mind throughout the entire drive here. Now that I saw this place—the vast expanse of land surrounding the house and its remoteness—I felt more certain that something was missing.

"How long has Fulbright been here?" I asked, glancing at Tommy.

He shrugged. "At least two years, maybe longer. It's hard to say."

I pulled the phone from my pocket and pretended to tap a speed dial button before placing it to my ear. "E? You said that the bank transfer went through earlier, but the reporting of it was delayed. What are the chances that another transfer occurred and reporting was also delayed?"

Esker's voice returned. "Checking...you're right. A second transfer of an additional one hundred thousand dollars was made two hours and thirty-eight minutes ago."

I eyed the open expanse surrounding the two-story farmhouse. No lights shone in the windows, and the barn was similarly dark. The largest of the outbuildings stood about one and a half stories tall, featuring a service door on one end and a pair of sliding barn doors on the far end. Several thickly dust-covered windows glowed with a pale yellow light.

Esker spoke, his voice somewhat hesitant. "Given the context you provided for the first funds transfer, what relevance do you attach to the second? I see no high-probability conclusion that aligns with this scenario."

My voice lowered. "I think Fulbright retained the mercenaries for an additional task." My voice trailed off to a whisper so only Esker could hear it. "They're still here."

I didn't have a plan the first time we drove past the farm. Tommy eased us past the five hundred or so yards that lined the rural property at a slow pace that felt quite normal for the area or time of night. Someone who had just spotted a deer or other wildlife might have seen me traveling the dark country roads at such speeds, even if only for a moment. However, it wasn't the kind of pass that would escape the notice of a trained paramilitary team.

"Want me to pull in up ahead?" Tommy asked. "I can find a spot in the woods once we pass the property marker."

Dense woodlands appeared to flank the horse farm, making it a reasonable plan. However, it was precisely the type of plan a security team established on the farm would anticipate.

"No. Keep driving for a mile. We'll circle back." I was formulating a plan in my head. Visions of the dark structures I'd seen were shifting in my mind as I tried to understand how a team like the one I had already encountered would lay out on the place. A group of three had hit the lab. One would have stayed with the chopper since that was the exfiltration strategy, which put their numbers at four. There could have been more, but I was betting against it. I had this team pegged as mercenaries. The more members in the team, the more ways they had to split the payday. If Fulbright was footing the bill for this operation—a pair of operations if I was correct—he wouldn't have deep pockets. He'd be working on a budget.

I glanced at Tommy. "How do you feel about being a distraction?"

He turned the truck onto an intersecting side street at a T-intersection and backed up. A tunnel of forest so dense surrounded the stretches of road that even the nearly full moon failed to penetrate the canopy. He pointed the truck back the way we had come but pulled over to the shoulder. "Is this dangerous?"

I considered how the team attacking the lab had been professional enough not to harm Fulbright's team. They did hospitalize two security guards, however. Noting the amusement in Tommy's gaze as it shone in the pale glow of the dashboard lights, I shrugged. "Could be nothing, but I'm betting on four armed hostiles protecting the man I need to question. If they are who I think they are, they won't shoot unless shot at. Still, I don't know what I don't know. I'm operating based on a lot of guesswork. It's probably best you drop me here and head back."

He was silent for a few moments, his gaze focused on the road ahead and the beam of light cast by the headlights. I don't think he was observing the night so much as contemplating the next hour or two of his life and its potential to affect the rest of it. I recognized that look. I'd seen it many times over the past year.

"You're one of the good guys?" Tommy finally asked.

I nodded.

"Law enforcement?"

"Couldn't be further from it, actually. Still one of the good guys. You'd have to take my word for it, though." I'd never been one to sell folks on my crusade. Everything was more uncomplicated if I could go my own way and risk dragging as few people down with me as possible. This was one of those times when I needed another set of hands. Taking on four armed opponents wasn't out of the question, but I had no idea where they were in this case. And if they were worth their fees, they'd have found fortified positions and wouldn't be easy to find.

Tommy smirked wider. "If you weren't on the level, you know that's exactly what you'd say, right?"

I shrugged.

No arguing with that logic.

"What do you need me to do?" he said.

Esker's voice sounded in my ear, a surprisingly dry tone of amusement woven into his words. "I'm wondering that too."

"Give me a minute to make a quick call. I need to check on some technical support," I said as I slipped out the door.

Walking far enough from the truck to vanish into the surrounding darkness, I focused my attention on Esker. "If there's a team stationed on the farm, they'll be staying in contact via radio. It'll be encrypted. Is there any chance you can locate their signal and decrypt it?"

"Done," Esker said. "They are using a modulated frequency-hopping algorithm. Replicating it was easy, as was breaking the encryption. Would you like to listen? They aren't currently transmitting, but there is an open channel connecting four disparate locations."

I had come to expect the unexpected from the AI, but the mention of the location component was intriguing. I didn't anticipate that.

"Can you identify each individual's location based on their signal?"

"Not without additional hardware that isn't currently available. The devices used by the team have global positioning capabilities, but that function seems intentionally disabled. I can provide only an approximate location for each receiver. In this instance, it's not precise."

My hopes of not needing Tommy's help evaporated. "Can you monitor their communications and let me know if there's anything relevant? I'm more interested in transmitting on their channel when Tommy makes an approach. I want to create some confusion and then try to take advantage of it."

I was kneeling on the rear bumper of Tommy's truck as he approached Fulbright's farm from the opposite direction. Holding onto the tailgate with both hands and crouched low to keep my silhouette from being easily identifiable, I waited until we were about a hundred yards short of the property line, where the tree cover separating the road from the farm became sparse. The truck was still moving at nearly twenty-five miles an hour when I jumped from the bumper and rolled through the grass at the edge of the road. I had my pistol in my hand because I didn't want to lose it in the dark when I tumbled, and I certainly didn't want it stuck in my ass as a result of that crazy maneuver.

Tommy continued to drive, drawing no attention to my skilled and graceful dismount from the moving vehicle, regardless of what the local wildlife might later claim. It was dark, and any contrary claims stem entirely from the nuance of my tuck and roll being lost in the night's murky shadows. Nonetheless, I was on my feet and more than fifty feet into the thick undergrowth of the woods to the east of the farm by the time Tommy's truck turned onto the wide gravel drive leading to the heart of the dark, silent horse farm.

When the truck touched the drive's entrance, its speakers began playing AC/DC's "Burning Alive." The distinctive song started low and rumbling but gradually crescendoed to a higher volume, controlled remotely by Esker. This was done subtly to draw everyone's attention to the truck. I wanted all focus elsewhere, but I didn't want it to be obvious that they should focus on it.

Esker spoke softly in my ear. "Chatter on the coms channel. That got their attention."

"And?" I whispered, huddled at the base of a pile of brush about one hundred twenty yards from the nearest outbuilding. I was perhaps sixty feet from the property line, where overgrown lawn met woodland.

"As expected," Esker confirmed. "Confusion from all members."

"Hit them with Stage Two."

Stage Two featured the same song Tommy was playing, but this time it was transmitted over the mercenary team's supposedly secure communication channel. It would also start low and barely audible, then ramp up in volume over the course of a minute, at which point it would be loud enough to render team communication impossible. Since Esker was controlling the music, two things would occur. First, the song playing on the comms channel would remain time-synchronized with the music playing in the truck. This should at least lead to a delay in the team's response, as it would be natural to assume they were picking up some kind of interference, from the recently arrived vehicle. The second outcome, courtesy of Esker, was that no matter how many times the team tried to change frequencies to mitigate the interference, it wouldn't matter. Esker would ensure the song followed the team to whichever channel they tuned to.

I scanned the shadow-dappled grounds of the farm for signs of movement. The light sensitivity of my HUD was activated, as was the thermal feature. As I anticipated, if the mercs were out there, they were maintaining cover discipline and using some form of thermal protection. The repetitive chorus of the song now thumped and thundered in the night, with the words "burning alive" echoing in Brian Johnson's raspy refrain.

Then movement caused two parts of the HUD to flash with color from different sections of the grounds at almost the same moment. Although the effort couldn't have been coordinated due to the comms blackout in place, I watched as what seemed to be thermo-protective blankets were thrown back. One figure was sixty-three yards from me, and the other was four hundred and seventy-two.

Both figures had their attention focused entirely on Tommy and his truck. The closer figure was smaller and distinctly female in shape. She had already climbed to her feet for a better view of the truck, while the other remained prone, apparently with a sufficient vantage point from there. I slipped carefully to the edge of the trees but sprinted once I reached the grass.

I hit the standing woman with a flying tackle, knocking her from her feet and throwing her into a chokehold before she had time to recover. She was out cold and flex-cuffed in seconds. Where did I get the cuffs? I could thank the well-prepared mercenary for that. Not only had she been kitted out with a thermal blanket, NVGs, a pair of Glocks, an MP5, and a K-Bar, but she also had four sets of flex-cuffs on her combat harness.

The nice thing about going up against so-called professionals is that they bring all the gear you need with them when you take them down. I tossed all her toys away, kept the knife, and started to vector in on my second target.

"There's two more," I said to Esker. "Find them."

This is where my plan became a little less organized. At a high level, I was using a distraction to get my opponents to reveal themselves, and Esker was preventing them from coordinating long enough for me to execute my strategy. If I could identify them quickly and take them down swiftly, it would be a solid plan.

Yes, that was the plan at a high level. There was no lower level.

Act fast and kick ass.

I was reasonably confident that one of my four opponents would stay close to Fulbright. Heat signatures made me sure he was in the largest outbuilding, which had the highest ambient temperature. I could see one figure, either prone or supine, inside. That was likely Fulbright. If a mercenary was with him, he was thermally cloaked. If he was out here with me, the numbers would be more of a trick.

My legs pumping hard, I closed in on my second target. I scanned left and right as I sprinted, my HUD sweeping for any sign of the two remaining unidentified opponents. Painfully aware that a bullet could take me out of the game at any moment, I crested the small rise separating me from the second target just in time to see him swing his hands in apparent frustration. Just before, he turned about thirty degrees to see me approaching him at full speed.

He did a double-take. He looked right at me, then glanced back at Tommy's truck before snapping his gaze back to me, his expression registering surprise even beneath the dark face paint and the pair of night vision goggles tipped skyward atop his brow.

I tackled him with a force that sounded like it broke bones, though I'm fairly certain that noise was just me damaging some of the expensive gear strapped in his battle harness. We hit the ground in a cloud of dry dirt, his helmet and NVGs bouncing away in opposite directions. There was no need for a chokehold this time. The merc had been knocked out, either by my strike or by our collision with the ground. Regardless, I had him flipped face down, cuffing hands and feet in less than twenty seconds.

"The third target is closing in on the pickup truck," Esker shouted loudly in my ear. I glanced down and noticed that the elaborate set of NVGs had landed upside down on the ground, facing the opposite direction from me. I immediately realized that Esker had taken them as his own observation platform.

I turned and drew my Springfield in time to see a man in black battle dress exactly like the one at my feet. He had an AR-15 raised and pointed at Tommy, who was still behind the truck's wheel. The man moved slowly, adjusting his aim for a clearer line of sight on Tommy and possibly a headshot. My HUD indicated that the truck was sixty-one yards away, while the soldier was at forty-seven. It couldn't tell me whether the soldier planned to pull the trigger.

The white targeting reticle pulsed to life in my HUD, and my finger rested on the trigger. As my eyes narrowed, my view of the reticle zoomed in response. I pulled the trigger twice in rapid succession, and the AR-15 seemed to disintegrate. The mercenary jumped and yelped like a kicked dog, back pedaling and landing on his backside. He was flicking his hands wildly, probably still trying to understand what had just happened. My knee came down on his throat, and I pressed the muzzle of the pistol into his groin. "Going to need you to be quiet now," I said, a calm level tone that was far easier than it should have been after all the running I'd just done.

Tommy began to step out of the truck, his eyes wide and unblinking as they met mine. I looked up at him and shook my head. "Get back in and leave. Go home or head back to the bar—either way, just get out of here and don't come back." I took a slow breath, trying to exude calm. "I appreciate what you've done; I couldn't have accomplished this without you. The problem is, there's one more of these guys out there, and this is your last chance to take action before things get complicated."

"Um," Tommy stuttered slightly. "Get complicated?" He nodded. "Sure. You think you'll be okay?"

I grinned and shifted my weight on the neck of the guy beneath me without glancing down at him. "Three down and one to go."

After my little display, it wasn't difficult to get Tommy to leave. I don't know what he thought, but extricating himself from what was clearly a dangerous situation made simple calculus. He was on the road about thirty seconds after I had the third merc in cuffs.

"One left," I whispered to Esker, eyeing the large outbuilding that still showed the thermal signature of a prone figure. A new form, this one upright, had joined the blob of orange shades overlapped in the night vision-enhanced view of the building. The shape hugged the right side of a pair of windows overlooking the clearing I'd just crossed. I adjusted to put a cluster of shoulder-high boulders between me and the building.

"One more that you know of," Esker reminded me. "And you've lost the element of surprise."

You think?

The question remained: how far would the remaining mercenary go to keep me from Fulbright? That assumed the remaining figure was indeed Fulbright, although that seemed like a safe bet. And who had Fulbright hired this team to protect him from? He knew nothing about me. This suggested he was worried about Breslin... or at least Breslin's associates. So technically, we were all on the same side.

"I feel compelled to remind you," Esker said. "Eliminating the last threat is only a challenge if you insist on using non-lethal force. You have the resources to eliminate him from standoff distance."

He was right. That would be easier...and faster. But from what I could tell, these guys were just doing a job. If they were Breslin's men, I wouldn't feel as bad about taking them out. If Fulbright had hired them, they were just contractors picking up a paycheck. They might be dirtbags, but they could also be the kind of respectable pros I'd worked with a time or two along the way.

His comment sparked an idea.

"E? Kill the music and switch me to a channel with our friend in there?" I said.

"I think I saw this in a film," I detected amusement in Esker's tone. "You want to parlay?"

I grinned. "Something like that."

"The channel is now open," Esker announced.

"I know you can see me," I said in a calm, quiet tone that I hoped would be soothing. "I can see you too."

The silence lasted about twenty seconds before a voice with a mild English accent responded. "I find that difficult to believe." I watched as the figure moved from the edge of the current window to a similar position two windows over. To reach there, he crawled belly-first beneath the intermediary windows.

"You just shifted to the northeast window," I said without inflection. "You moved quickly and low, but it was a futile effort."

After several more seconds of silence, then, "you've got access to impressive tech and an interesting taste in music. I saw them live a few years back. If you're going to have a go at me, can you at least turn on one of the classics before you beat down the doors?"

I smiled. "Like you said, I have the tech. If I wanted to take you out, I could do it from here. I'd prefer to talk."

A sound, something like a harrumph, suggested that my point had been understood. "And my team?"

"In good health. Just immobilized."

Esker's voice returned to my ear. "He's carrying an encrypted smartphone. What's the phrase? A picture is worth a thousand words?"

I slipped my phone out and shot a quick video of the flex-cuffed figure at my feet, careful to capture a closeup that included the rise and fall of the unconscious man's chest as well as the way his hands and feet had been bound in a way that was impossible to escape.

"Sending it now," Esker said.

"I'm supposed to take your word for that," the Brit responded with clear skepticism.

"Of course not," I replied. "Check your phone."

There was a rustling sound, then a pause followed by an impressive string of mumbled expletives that suggested he was wondering how I'd sent the video to what he had previously believed to be a secure device. The silence that followed didn't seem like mine to break, so I let it stretch.

Finally, there came the sound of someone clearing their throat. "I'll credit you for one of the more impressive forms of battlefield intimidation." I heard what I believed was sincere respect in the man's tone. "You've bested my team and our own tech. You're here for the Prof's formula then?"

"I'm here to speak with the Prof," I said, using the British slang for Doctor Fulbright. "I'm afraid he's about to do something reckless with the experimental material he's been working on, and I need to ensure that doesn't happen."

A subsequent pause ensued that raised some concern. Rightfully so, as it turned out.

"Might be a little late on that point, mate," the voice said. "The Prof gave himself an injection over an hour ago, and he's been unresponsive since. I haven't been able to wake him."

Shit.

That meant I was too late even while driving out to the farm. All this messing around to make my advance was a wasted effort.

"What's your name?" I asked.

More hesitation, then, "Pike."

"You can call me Gray. Look, Pike, I need to get in there and check on the Doc. Can I do that?"

"Just you?" His tone revealed some reluctance, yet the question made me realize he assumed I was part of a larger team. It was a perspective I hadn't entertained until that moment.

"Just me. My team secures the perimeter, and no harm will come to your people as long as no harm comes to me."

"And the Prof?"

The question threw me for a loop. "Sorry?"

"Do you promise not to hurt the Prof?"

"Pike, I'm not here to hurt Pemberton. I promise you that."

———————

I stepped to the door as Pike eased it open. He was dressed like the rest of his team, though he'd taken off his helmet and the holster on his hip was empty. Shorter than I expected, he stood about five foot eight, with short dark hair and coal-black eyes. Streaks of dark grease paint smeared his face. As he backed into the room to give me access, his gaze stayed locked on mine. "You're younger than I expected," he said.

My Springfield was in hand, hanging casually at my side. I studied the Brit for a moment, then nodded as if I had come to a decision about the man, before slipping the pistol into the back of my jeans. "You're shorter than I expected," I countered.

The man grunted, what I believe was his version of a laugh, before tilting his head toward the center of the room. Fulbright lay on what I thought was once a folding massage table. An IV stand hung with a pair of drip bags, their lines leading to the cannulas in his forearm and hand. I recognized one bag as having the same color and viscosity as the formula we had been working on for the experiment.

"He hired your team?" I asked Pike, leaning over Pemberton to study his pale complexion in the dull light from the nightstand. A lamp was draped with a red handkerchief to soften its glow and presumably help Pike maintain his night vision. Pemberton wore a hospital gown that hung loosely over his supine form.

"He said he wanted protection while he was under," Pike confirmed. "I thought it was from you, but you don't sound like one of Breslin's people."

I shot a look at Pike. "You know about Breslin?"

Pike shrugged. "Just what the boss tells us. Breslin financed his work but has been putting increasing pressure on him. The Prof became concerned for his safety and worried about the money man's ultimate goal for the project, so he brought us in to protect him. He said tonight would either make or break his venture. He just needed protection long enough to confirm his formula worked. He mentioned that someone's been undermining his work."

I smiled. He was right about everything; he just didn't know the complete story behind any of it.

I pressed two fingers to the side of Pemberton's neck and noted an irregular pulse. "You said you tried waking him?" I pulled the eyelid back on one eye and saw the pupil was fully dilated. Waving a hand closely in front of the eye, it was entirely unresponsive. I pulled the handkerchief from the lamp and fully bathed the room in the light. The eye remained unresponsive, but I noticed medical hardware on tables and stands throughout the room. It seemed the Doc had planned ahead. He'd just been overzealous in his willingness to try the formula on himself.

"He became unresponsive about twenty minutes after injecting himself with the formula. He mentioned it might happen but also assured that it wouldn't last more than an hour." Pike glanced at his wristwatch. "It's been well over an hour now."

I knew this wasn't a good sign. Swallowing hard, I met the Brit's gaze. "Does anyone on your team have emergency medical training?"

"Alley," he said quickly. "Alley Lauer—an emergency medical technician who worked three years in a trauma ward before joining my outfit."

I nodded. "She should be awake by now. Just a bit of a headache, but she's okay. You'll find her where she was stationed. Go get her and bring her back." I waved toward the door.

Pike bolted for the door but stopped with his hand on the knob. "Ah, Gray? Would you let your boys know I'm coming out? I'd rather avoid friendly fire, you know? We're all on the same team now, right?"

I grinned and shrugged. "Same team? Sure. But it's just me. There's no one out there but your people. Round them up and try to convince them that payback isn't worth the effort, okay? I respect that everyone will want another chance at me...we just don't have time. I need Alley to get Pemberton on life support ASAP. This isn't going as he planned." I met his eye. "We good?"

Pike was studying me as if for the first time. His gaze shifted to take me in from head to toe. I heard him mumble something under his breath before he grinned. "If you're not a threat to the Prof, then we're good. I'm sure each of my guys will want to settle up with you, but that can wait. You have my pledge on that."

Amusingly, Pike was shaking his head and muttering curses to himself as he stepped out into the night.

"Do you really think you can trust these people?" Esker whispered in my ear.

I nodded. "That, and I don't have any options right now. Fulbright isn't responsive. I need the medic to look closer, but I don't think he's following his own procedure. Pike's team should be able to tell me what I need to know, but I suspect something went wrong."

Chapter 18 - This Is What It Feels Like to Die

Our-World

Al Vincente waited for the mother of two to finish scolding the obnoxious six-year-old who refused to make room for him on his way to the window seat of the northbound red-eye. She literally had her hands full with the sobbing baby clutched to her chest. Vincente glanced at the narrow seat he would be forced to occupy in close quarters with the spirited family for the flight up the eastern seaboard and felt the tension headache begin to form behind his eyes.

The mother hissed something at the boy in the seat while Vincente waited to reach his assigned seat. The boy responded by hurling a tablet device with seemingly practiced skill. The mother swiftly turned in response to the attack, and Ingersoll heard what he believed was the sound of the device's corner striking flesh and bone at high speed. The bulge of the mother's eyes and her quick scowl was followed by a moment where she appeared to count briefly to herself.

Vincente was massaging the corners of his eyes when he felt a hand settle gently on his shoulder.

"Sir?" a woman called from behind him. Turning around, Vincente was met with the flight attendant's polite smile. She cast a quick glance at the mother struggling with her pair of children a few feet in front of him and then motioned over her shoulder. "We have an opening over here," she said quietly. "Maybe you would be more comfortable?"

Vincente smiled as he followed the woman to the unoccupied row of three seats. The tension was already easing behind his eyes, and a sense of claustrophobia he hadn't acknowledged was dissipating. "I don't know how to thank you," he said dryly. "You may have just saved my sanity."

The flight attendant smiled knowingly. "Happy to help. The aisle seat is reserved, but you're welcome to choose the middle or window seat," she clarified. "Either option should make for a much more comfortable trip."

Vincente slipped into the window seat and took a deep breath. Reaching up, he adjusted the vent on the ceiling and felt the draft wash over the perspiration on his face. The Tampa humidity was overwhelming, even at this late hour. The air coming from the vent wasn't cool, but at least it was circulating. Glancing at his watch, he verified the time. If the plane left on schedule, they would be taxiing in just a few minutes. Then, the cabin would cool down. The temperature up north would be better. He despised the heat.

Loosening his tie, Vincente contemplated the wisdom of this latest trip. Was he giving up on Tampa before exploring all possible leads? Probably. Grady Ledger had been spotted here just two days earlier. Video evidence showed he had been at Tampa International and had spent the night at the Hilton, although he had checked in under an alias, and the hotel registry did not list him. Surveillance footage captured him entering the hotel and a room, but the hotel had no record of his booking. That was a clever trick Vincente had seen the kid use before, and he still didn't know how he had pulled it off. Presumably, it involved some kind of computer hack to remotely reserve the room.

Interviews were conducted with most of the hotel staff, and none of them recalled seeing Ledger. The only evidence of his presence was the video surveillance records. No one had met Ledger, and the external cameras provided no hint regarding his method of transportation. Since he had stayed at a hotel near the airport, Vincente suspected he took another flight out the following day. However, if that were the case, why hadn't the airport surveillance footage shown him departing at any time after?

Tampa served as an international hub. From there, he could fly to almost anywhere in the world. The only other reason Ledger would be in Tampa is if ATG had a facility nearby. According to the FBI's findings, ATG had no offices, labs, or affiliates anywhere in Florida.

It wasn't the first time Vincente felt as though he was chasing a ghost. This likely explained why he had been so quick to deem this effort a failure in favor of a potentially more lucrative lead to the north. The bulletin had hit his phone less than an hour earlier—a preliminary report regarding an attack on a lab at Alison Springs University. The name of the small graduate school initially rang a bell in the agent's memory. That bell quickly transformed into a chorus too loud to ignore when he remembered a report detailing several off-campus locations where Breslin Global Technologies had funded research projects. One of those projects was running at ASU.

The aircraft jolted, and Vincente's attention was drawn to the dimly illuminated view of the muddy ground surrounding the taxiway. The jet turned as it prepared for takeoff. With the movement of the aircraft, a wave of refreshingly cool air finally made its way through the ventilation system, and the agent felt more of his tension ease. For the first time in months, he might have a promising lead on the location of Grady Ledger. And with Chris Ingersoll exploring another aspect of the investigation in the UK, he sensed new opportunities opening up for him. This brought a touch of hope he hadn't experienced since being assigned this case more than a year earlier.

Pike walked me around the property and introduced me to the rest of his team. Billy Unger and Kyle Seger were the other operatives I had disabled while advancing on Pemberton's position. It would be an understatement if I said my presence wasn't welcome. Still, while the pair didn't understand why Pike was suddenly on friendly terms with me, the remaining team members were professional enough to keep their animosity in check, at least for the moment. Everyone knew they had a job to do, and if I wasn't a threat to their principal, they needed to maintain a defense against the real danger.

I followed Pike into the dark interior of the largest barn. He silently slid a door shut on what seemed to be freshly oiled tracked rollers. A moment later, he flipped a switch and activated a series of lanterns that glowed with soft red bulbs. They were designed to provide nearby illumination without hindering our night vision. Stacked around us were crates filled with provisions, ordnance, and gear.

"...I thought you were joking when you said it was just you," Pike was saying. "No support team at all?"

I tapped my right ear. "I have logistics support on comms."

Esker let out a bemused sniff. This was yet another new affectation from him. "Logistics? I guess that's better than calling me a sidekick."

I fought a grin and wondered how and where the AI had developed a sense of humor. The amusement must have shown on my face because a questioning expression registered on Pike. I shook my head to dismiss the question before he could ask it.

"That doesn't reflect well on my team in that case," Pike said, his tone sullen.

"I have a few unfair advantages," I admitted before steering the conversation in a different direction. "When did Pemberton contract your team?"

"Four days ago. We arrived yesterday."

"How did he know your contact protocol? It's somewhat unusual for an academic to hire people like you. I assume you vetted him?"

Pike nodded. "That's why it took a couple of days for the team to arrive on site. I performed a bit of extra due diligence. It's highly unusual. I needed to be sure he was trustworthy."

"And?"

"As far as I can tell, he's exactly who he claims to be. Just an academic who took funding from someone he probably shouldn't have. He's in over his head and afraid for his life." Pike paused to think for a moment, then said, "It seems he has family. A great uncle who's an ex-congressman. He understood the contact protocol and relayed the information. I also looked into the funds he's using to pay us. Family money. It appears to be the last of a trust he inherited from his grandfather."

Esker's voice resonated in my ear. "Impressive due diligence."

I agreed. Pike might have been disappointed with his team's performance so far, but I couldn't fault his preparation when researching a prospective client.

When Alley Lauer radioed from the main outbuilding, it came over the team channel Esker had added me to, so I received the transmission. "Pike," she said. "The client's not looking good. I need you back here, ASAP."

Pike shot a stony glance before killing the lights and cracking the sliding door just wide enough for us to shoulder through.

Pemberton's skin looked sallow and cadaverous, even in Laura's penlight's focused, stark white glow. She flicked the beam back and forth before the man's eyes while she held each open with an extended thumb. The ocular response was nonexistent. Each time the beam of her light glanced off the skin of his face, I could see the putty-like consistency of his skin. He didn't look like a corpse. He looked worse than a corpse.

"I've never seen anything like this," Alley Lauer said, waving a hand at the flatscreen mounted on a stand behind Pemberton. A series of technical readouts filled the display. Though three horizontal lines dominated the top third, they meant nothing to me. Their prominence suggested significance. The fact that the scrolling lines were completely flat and lacked the telltale blips and bumps usually found in medical images was not encouraging.

"These are the brainwaves," she continued. "According to the telemetry, Pemberton is completely brain dead."

Pike and I looked at the screen and then at each other. Neither of us knew what to say. I felt dizzy and struggled to determine my next course of action. I was aware there were risks associated with the experiment, but the possibility of something catastrophic like this occurring hadn't really crossed my mind. At worst, I assumed the subject might have a few nightmares and fail to cross the barrier.

But brain death?

I heard Pike asking questions and Lauer saying something, but it all felt like white noise in the back of my mind until I heard Lauer say, "The equipment is working fine, but what it's showing doesn't make sense." I looked up to see frustration twisting her pale face. "If he really was brain dead, it doesn't explain why his heart is beating."

Pike's jaw went slack as he slumped onto a stool at the foot of the bed, staring at the man who had hired his team to protect him. I couldn't guess what he was thinking, but it was clear that he was rattled. He was a professional soldier who had certainly seen men injured and even killed. But this? There was something deeply unsettling about the look and feel of the situation. While looking at Pemberton, I sensed something was uniquely wrong with his current condition.

I heard Esker in my ear. "This condition is not unheard of. It's possible to be brain dead and still have cardiovascular activity." But even as he spoke, I could sense a lack of conviction in his tone. He was seeing what I was seeing.

"This diagnostic hardware has network connectivity," Esker continued. "Have Miss Lauer connect it. I would like to conduct some more exhaustive analysis."

"Really?" I said aloud. My seemingly self-directed comment drew the attention of both Pike and Lauer. I shrugged and relayed Esker's instructions to Lauer. She appeared unfazed but complied with my request.

Lauer continued to speak as she worked, connecting various technical hardware to network switching equipment. "Having the heart continue after neural activity ceases isn't unheard of," she explained. "It's the readings that I don't understand. Pemberton's heart rate should have slowed to a resting rhythm given his condition. His blood pressure is elevated, and his heart is racing as if he's running, fighting, or terrified. If I didn't know better, I would say he's in the middle of a nightmare. But that's not possible," she paused. "Because there is absolutely no brain activity at all."

She had finished networking the last of what must have been four of five different devices connected to Pemberton. Wires were attached to disparate points on his chest, head, inner arms, and legs. Some of them had been connected when I first entered the building and were part of the experimental gear I was familiar with. Lauer must have attached other gear as part of her efforts to diagnose and treat the professor.

More than a minute passed without a word from anyone. We simply stared at Pemberton, lying motionless on the table, his medical gown gaping open at the chest, with over two dozen thin spaghetti-like wires snaking from his torso and limbs to the carts and equipment clustered around his bed.

Then Esker came back in my ear, his tone urgent and authoritative in a way I had never experienced. "Pemberton is in distress," he said. "There is a high probability he is nearing the point of embolism. Miss Lauer, you must induce a coma immediately. If you do not, Professor Pemberton will most certainly be dead within the next eight minutes."

The way Esker phrased the statement, along with the expressions on the faces around the room, instantly made me realize that he had used the team comms channel. He was directly addressing Alley Lauer, clearly trying to save time.

Lauer looked at me, obviously confused.

I waved a hand at Pemberton, urging her to move. "Yes," I said. "That was my logistics guy. Do you have what you need to induce a coma?"

Lauer's eyes were wide. She looked at her kit bag and then at her commander. "I can't," she said. "He's already brain-dead. That would be…" She seemed unsure how even to explain what might happen. I don't think she knew.

I looked at Pike, who was glancing back and forth between me and Lauer as if he were watching the world's most confusing tennis match.

"Don't think," I snapped. "Just do it. The guys already messed up. Can it get any worse? E can explain everything after you're done!"

"E?" Pike said, but then he seemed to reconsider. He gave Lauer a glance and simply nodded.

Lauer looked like she might vomit, but she grabbed her kit bag and started sorting through a series of short glass ampules. Ten seconds later, she took a steadying breath and injected something into Pemberton's arm using an absurdly large syringe.

When Esker spoke again, I knew it was only to me. "You realize I won't be able to explain this to anyone's satisfaction, right?"

I turned away from everyone in the room and walked slowly as far as I could in the cluttered space. "Why?" I subvocalized.

"I believe Professor Pemberton has crossed the Brane, just as he intended. The problem is that he didn't take his body with."

The uniquely sallow look of the man's complexion suddenly made sense to me as I understood the unique sense I'd had upon first seeing him in that state. I felt as if I were looking at an empty shell of a human being. It was like everything that made the man who he was had vanished, leaving behind a body that was still alive but devoid of essence. Although it was a unique experience, it felt strangely familiar because it resembled what I sensed when I was near one of the Elend.

I felt a headache growing behind my eyes, troubled by the question I was about to ask. "E? If Fulbright crossed without his body, what happens to him on the other side?"

"Unknowable," Esker said, pausing slightly. "You're the first person we know of to cross, ever. We understand that your body crosses with you, but we're not sure if that's the only way the phenomenon works."

"So, is it possible he might still be alive?"

Esker remained silent for a few moments. "As you've often said… there's only one way to find out."

Wild-Side

The ragged tear split the earth. From the air, it appeared as a wide seam dividing the otherwise pristine wilderness of towering conifers, redwoods, and elms. Though only thirty feet in average height, the excavation extended over a quarter mile in width. Dirt and stone were split, churned, and extracted in just under a month since the site had been identified. The powerfully built, wide-backed, eight-legged creatures responsible for the quarrying remained unseen by the people of Wild-Side... at least by any survivors. The average creature stood between twelve and fifteen feet tall, was one and a half times as wide in the body, and walked on six legs. While the front two legs were functional for locomotion, they were more often used for digging. These insect-like limbs were multi-jointed and articulated for a wide range of movement. Although they resembled steel beams in appearance, they were as thick as telephone poles and twice as long as a man was tall, just like the rest of the legs on the creature. The primary difference with the front legs was the spade-like shape at the end of each limb, as large as a manhole cover and shaped like a digging shovel if the shovel had razor-honed edges and an unyielding sharp point capable of splitting any stone.

While the Diggers churned dirt and gravel with drone-like efficiency, striving to widen the borders of the excavation that had been dug nearly a hundred yards deep into the earth, a small group of Elend gathered at the perimeter of upturned marker stones. The henge measured exactly thirty-five feet in diameter and consisted of twenty-one upraised obsidian flagstones. Each stone was uniquely jagged and misshapen, resembling a savagely broken tooth. The smallest was half as tall as a man, while the largest was half again larger than the smallest.

Breslin walked slowly around the perimeter of the stone henge, using a long, blazing torch to ignite the five surrounding fire pits, bringing the depths to life with pale, dancing shadows. He was in human form, with tattered black material hanging from his hips. It had once been clothing of some kind, but it had endured too many transformations as he shifted from human to his Elend form. He wore knee-length, leathery black rags, referencing his host figure's shattered past. His chest was bare and smeared with a black grease, a mix of past vanquished Elend and Seeley alike.

Dozens of Elend jostled shoulder to shoulder in the shadows beyond the perimeter of the firelight. Breslin paid no attention to the masses as he completed his circuit of the henge, his fingertips gliding slowly across the rough surface of the upright stones. Finally, as if performing a ritual of his own, his eyes rested on a jagged spire placed at the center of the circle. The stone was wide at the bottom but appeared to swirl as it narrowed to a jagged tip three feet from its base. The surface was rippled and imperfect, as if the material had been liquid when shaped, then windblown as it cooled into the striking, flawed spire.

Though it appeared to be made of a mineral similar to that of the henge, it was completely transparent. It seemed as if all of the onyx, oily blackness of the henge stones had been drawn out from the spire. Breslin's gaze remained fixed on the object as he stepped through the gap between the stones of the henge to enter the circle. He advanced within four paces of the spire, then paused to lower his head.

After several seconds of silence, Breslin raised a hand and waved to the darkness. "Bring me the first five," he said, his voice booming with command.

The ripples of movement beyond the shadow's perimeter shifted, and a Crawler emerged. It was followed by five emaciated, bedraggled Seeley—three men and two women. Each looked exhausted to the point of collapse. They were bound at the wrists and linked to the person before them. The Crawler at the front of the procession moved slowly across the dry, packed dirt, between the stones of the henge, and toward the spire at the center. A Jay brought up the rear of the line, there to keep the group moving, though showing little concern for escape. The bored glower was evident on the expression of the lizard-like Jay. This task had been carried out with repetition and little, if any, variation.

The Crawler moved the first figure in the line, positioning the man's feet beside an iron eyelet driven deep into the earth three feet from the spire's base. The Jay moved forward and hooked the man's rope to the eyelet, then used the blade edge of his longest talon to split the thumb-thick line linking the man to the woman behind him in the procession. The woman was lashed to a similar iron anchor before the Jay moved to the following figure in the line. Within minutes, the five captives had been positioned equidistant around the perimeter of the spire, bound at the wrists to the iron at their feet, and positioned so they had no choice but to face the glassy surface of the strange stone object.

Without prompting from Breslin, the Jay and the Crawler withdrew from the henge and disappeared back into the shadows. The figures gathered beyond the perimeter of the firelight now jostled against each other with heightened anticipation. The shadowy mass appeared to writhe and swell as Breslin positioned himself just a yard away from the circle of Seeley, arranged around the spire.

Breslin's hands were folded at what would have been belt level, and his head was bowed. His face was enveloped in shadow, with the only light glinting off the top of his sweaty, bald head. Embers popped and hissed at the bottom of the fire pits; this was the sole sound. Then, the gentle breeze through the cavern intensified, aligning with the slow, steady crescendo of murmured words slipping from Breslin's lips. The phrases he used—the incantation— would not be understood by the Elend or the Seeley present, but everyone grasped that the wind blowing through the space was intensifying in preparation for the timbre and volume of his words.

When Breslin's words reached the level of spoken conversation, the wind through the cavern began to whistle. The leathery fringe hanging from his hips started to flutter, as did the sticky, perspiration-laden hair of the figures bound to the iron surrounding the spire. All five figures had fallen to their knees. Fallen there or pulled there by an unseen force, no one would ever know, as an orange light began to shine from deep within the base of the spire. It pulsed slowly at first, as if some kind of force were awakening. The intermittent pulses became slower until the gaps between light and dark diminished. Finally, there was nothing but solid, iridescent, penetrating light.

Breslin's words never wavered. His voice steadily grew louder and more rhythmic until he was nearly bellowing the words at a speed that began to merge each of the strange, unintelligible phrases into the next. Finally, the orange light surged, a long pulse that spread to fill the entirety of the cavern. The pulse flowed like a consuming shockwave. It passed over and through the five figures secured around the spire, over Breslin, and paused almost imperceptibly as it reached the perimeter of the henge, then flowed outward to pass through the hundreds, perhaps thousands, of Elend gathered in what had been darkness just seconds before.

As quickly as the wave had ignited, it vanished. The spire turned dark, and the cavern became silent. Even the surrounding fire pits were extinguished with the passing of the orange wave.

Seconds seemed to stretch into minutes; then the five fire pits ignited of their own accord. With this, the shadowy group beyond the perimeter began to reanimate with sluggish anticipation. All eyes turned toward the henge, the spire at its center, and the five figures secured there.

Where the five Seeley had been now stood five different large lizard-like creatures, each still shifting and taking shape. The remains of excess skin and bone sloshed off as if they had just molted inside a human shell. Wet splatters emerged as human remains slid from broad, leathery shoulders, while scales developed and exoskeletons began to take their final shape. Two crawlers, a Drake, a Digger, and a Hunter, were positioned at the points of the sacrificial circle where the Seeley had been just moments before.

Liquid pulses of translucent spectral light surged in a barrage from every direction. Where there had once been five senses, now there was a blend of something…different. Where there should have been sound, instead there was a grinding rattle that plunged the world into a topsy-turvy morass of confusion. An acidic burn assaulted from every angle, permeating every pore and capturing all of Pemberton's attention. This pain was unlike anything he'd ever imagined. He looked down at his hands, expecting to see the flesh flayed from his upraised arms.

However, there were no arms.

There was nothing to see—only light and pain. Savage, all-consuming agony. A torment without form or figure. He could see, but he had no body.

Yet, an awareness of his physical form lingered. He was being shredded at a molecular level. An apocalyptic burn engulfed him, and through it all, there was a sense that every part of him was being separated from every other part of him.

This is what it feels like to die.

Chapter 19 - The Capability to Create Whatever Crazy Idea Was Presented

Wild-Side

Gray was overdue, and although Piper was concerned, she sensed that no one was more worried than Doctor Cormac. He and the rest of his team tried to hide it, but the Seeley were not skilled at concealing their underdeveloped emotions. While she knew less about the science behind dimensional crossing, Piper understood Gray better than anyone. If he was alive, he'd be back. They just needed to give him time and try to keep the wheels from coming off the bus until that happened.

"You mentioned there was an operation on hold until Gray returned," Piper said.

Lacy sat at a table in the open-air amphitheater, a space commonly used for recreation. It was the closest thing the Seeley had to a park since they didn't possess many recreational areas. Nor did they have the same appreciation for nature as the people from her world. Pushing the plate and half-eaten sandwich aside, Lacy nodded. "When Mara came out of her coma, she was able to provide us with more information about the expedition that led to her condition. We thought there might be a connection to the Elend based solely on the coincidental timing, but her spotty recollection of events adds support to the theory."

Lacy thumbed the edge of the plate and gazed into the distance, as if contemplating how to express what would come next. "Her expedition took place in the Badlands," she said. "And aside from Mara, the entire team was lost. We have no idea what happened to the team that day. All the data was corrupted. Seismic activity opened up some new faults in the area. We believe a new cavern or cave might have been exposed. If that's the case, a team would have been dispatched to search for artifacts."

"Artifacts?"

Lacy waved a hand vaguely in the air. "We occasionally discover things in the wilds. Anachronistic relics that must be quarantined."

Piper's face twisted in confusion.

With a shrug, Lacy said, "Can we skip the twenty questions on this one? We already went through this with Gray. I'm happy to answer all I can for you... I'm just not sure I'm up to this topic today. If I'm honest, my heart just isn't in it."

Not knowing what that meant, Piper chose to move on. "Fair enough." There were countless peculiarities associated with the Seeley. Some of them Piper found charming. Some were entertaining. Many were simply baffling. For a group that was advanced and mostly enlightened, they could be shortsighted and narrow-minded at times. "Tell me about the operation you need Gray to help with."

"Mara helped us pinpoint the location of her expedition." She raised a hand in the air and swayed it back and forth. "At least she provided us with a general location. It should be sufficient to find the site. Gray was planning to take a team out to explore. If there's anything there that might help us understand the Elend, where they come from, or how to combat them, it could be worthwhile."

Piper waited. It seemed like there was more Lacy wasn't saying. "A team? Who's going with when the time comes?"

Lacy shrugged. "My people are not an adventurous lot," she admitted. "Word has spread about what happened to Mara. There aren't many volunteers, as you can imagine."

"So, it's you and Tripp?"

With a smirk, Lacy added, "I'm pretty sure Wes will go too. Doctor Cormac wants to go, but I think we can all agree that he's too important to take into the field."

"I think you're all too important. Do you think Gray is going to let anyone tag along? This sounds like what he would attempt to do solo."

"He won't have a choice. He's smart and brave. No question he's the only one among us with any chance of standing up to one of the creatures face to face. He just isn't proficient with our technology. That's why he needs us."

Piper was impressed to learn that Lacy and Tripp were willing to risk their lives in the field. However, the more she thought about it, the more it seemed like the kind of information they should have right now. Waiting for Gray felt like a waste of effort. If there was something to be gained from the expedition, they should take the trip as soon as possible.

"Would you be willing to risk the trip even if Gray wasn't leading it?" Piper said.

Lacy's eyes widened. That, along with the pregnant pause, provided enough of an answer.

"I mean, what if I take your team out?" Piper clarified. "Gray's been gone longer than expected. There's no telling how long he'll be away. This doesn't sound like something we should wait to investigate, especially if there's valuable insight to be gained."

Lacy became suddenly distracted, and Piper knew she had seen something in her heads-up display. This was confirmed when her lips pinched into a scowl of frustration. Before she could ask about it, Wes walked into the room. He looked distracted as well, swiping his hand through the air as if manipulating something in AR while he walked.

"How long will we be offline?" Lacy asked.

"The estimate is six to ten hours," Wes said. We're in luck. The front is actually advancing quickly this time, and it's smaller than anything we've encountered in the last two months. Doctor Cormac's biggest concern is that we didn't notice it until just a couple of minutes ago. The Thonian cloud formed rapidly and without warning." His expression was one of deep concern. "There's no doubt things are getting worse."

Piper was confused. "Can someone explain what's going on?"

Lacy's hands waved rapidly through the air, deftly manipulating unseen AR space. "We're about to lose primary power. There will be limited communication, transport platforms will go offline, and our perimeter sensors will have a limited range."

With her heart racing, Piper sprang to her feet. "We'll be sitting ducks."

Lacy and Wes paused in what they were doing to stare at her, clearly not understanding the statement.

Piper gaped. "Defenseless, even for us," she sputtered. "There's never going to be a better time for the Elend to attack."

Wes nodded. "We believe Fresno was probably taken during a similar blackout," he confirmed. "We'll move everyone to the safe rooms, and we'll now post lookouts at stations along the perimeter wall for the duration of the outage."

"We have limited backup power," Lacy confirmed. "It's sufficient for short-range communications and near-field perimeter sensors. It operates using a battery technology that Gray brought over from your world. We've only just begun retrofitting it to work with our equipment."

With acid churning in her gut, Piper concluded that the efforts put into the retrofit so far were woefully inadequate. Given what Tripp had engineered to power Gray's Airbike, he certainly had the capability to create whatever crazy idea was presented to him. Someone just needed to challenge him with something on a larger scale.

Piper had the room to herself. Doctor Cormac and Lacy met with Administrator Hargrave for the third time in two days and were finally deploying the perimeter defense guns. The Seeley were a peculiar people, she now knew. Piper had been stranded with them for nearly five weeks and had yet to find a term to describe their reluctance to take up arms for their own defense. Another city had gone silent, and while teams from her location could teleport to survey the now radio-silent metro center, no one was willing to risk the trip.

Gray would have done it, she knew, just as he was the most vocal advocate for the perimeter defense guns. After all, they were his idea. This concept had faced resistance at every turn from a population more willing to be taken silently in the night than to take up weapons in their own defense. They weren't pacifists. They didn't know enough about violence to take a moral stance against it. Rather, it was that they had no understanding of self-defense, and the very idea led to cognitive dissonance.

It wasn't the first time she had seen the Seeley behave this way. It felt as if they were conditioned to overlook specific circumstances or struggled to handle particular situations.

Very precise, clearly defined circumstances.

She thought about how Gray had made the arguably poor choice to expose the people of Wild-Side to some of the more questionable culture from home. If someone or something had conditioned the Seeley according to a playbook or blueprint, they likely hadn't anticipated Gray Crossing from back home. They certainly hadn't expected him to expose the people here to music, art, film...or pornography.

What was he thinking with the pornography?

Gray wasn't one of those people distracted by such things. He certainly wasn't someone obsessed with it like a friend she had back at school. The guy practically lived and breathed it, believing very strongly that it was its own artistic genre. Bringing music, movies, and film to Wild-Side made sense. It was Gray's attempt to share something from home with the people of this place. He was expanding their minds and exposing them to something they had no concept of, though she still couldn't imagine how that was possible. The juxtaposition of an advanced society lacking in such key areas seemed inconceivable to her.

Maybe it's my own cognitive dissonance?

The sound of whispers in the corridor pulled Piper from her musings. She thought she was alone. Slipping from the stool and walking silently to the open door, she crept to the edge and listened for the voices. After a long silence, she heard it again, low and indistinct. The words were unintelligible. The inability to understand what was being said between the hushed speakers proved too much for her, so Piper took a steeling breath and moved silently into the hall.

Tripp and Lacy were leaning against the wall of the empty, dimly lit corridor. They were wrapped in each other's arms, their lips gently mashing and probing with the clumsiness of inexperienced teenagers. Piper's eyes widened, and she froze, words hovering on the edge of her lips. Then, without making a sound, she retreated back into her room.

Her pulse pounding, Piper moved through the empty lab and into the hallway on the other side. Two minutes later, she reached her quarters, secured the door, and sank stiffly onto the bed. She sat up straight and stared at the distant wall with blank eyes. Lacy and Tripp? Why was that such a surprise? It was the most natural thing, wasn't it?

Natural for home, but not here.

It finally clicked in Piper's mind, leading her to understand why something seemed so normal while triggering a peripheral sense of panic. Something about what she had witnessed felt abnormal.

However natural they might be as a couple, it wasn't a typical occurrence on Wild-Side. Throughout her time here, she had never seen any couples. Over the course of her weeks here, she hadn't witnessed any romantic entanglements of any kind. Gray even explained that these people didn't have a sense of... that. The Seeley had no romantic relationships whatsoever. They had no sexual relationships of any kind.

Ever.

But that didn't make sense either, Piper reasoned. She'd seen Lacy looking at Tripp, and she'd noticed Tripp going out of his way to spend time with Lacy. Their getting together had seemed inevitable. Little things over the last couple of weeks had led her to think it was only a matter of time.

This indicated that something new was happening. She reasoned that change was in the air.

Swiping at her HUD, Piper opened a communication channel.

"Yes?" a voice said. It was Doctor Cormac. If Lacy was with Tripp, it made sense that Cormac's meeting with Administrator Hargrave had concluded.

"It's Piper," she said, then rolled her eyes. Of course, his HUD would have informed him who was calling. She still wasn't used to this technology. "Do you have a minute for a couple of quick questions?"

"Of course. How can I help you?"

"I vaguely recall someone mentioning that everything Gray sees when he's outside the walls is recorded by his nanotech. Is that correct?" Piper felt almost breathless asking the question but wasn't entirely sure why.

"Unless he's in one of the dead zones," Cormac clarified. "None of our tech works in the Badlands, so we lose all video in those areas. We have special hardware we can use, but it's not something Gray typically has with him when he's out there, so we don't have those recordings."

Piper was nodding to herself. That made sense and brought back memories of what Tripp had touched on peripherally while explaining one of the Airbike's onboard systems. "Does recording occur only outside the wall? Is it full-time—" she paused, trying to clarify her thoughts. "I mean, twenty-four seven, whenever he's awake, or whatever?" This was coming out clumsily because her mind was already tripping over the implications of what she thought she might be able to prove.

"Every waking hour is recorded," Cormac said.

"How long is Gray's footage retained?"

Cormac's tone grew very serious. "We keep all of it. What's happening to him is extraordinary. Once this threat has passed, everything that has occurred must be studied in detail. No one is more curious about the cause of what's happening than Gray, as you can likely imagine."

Nodding once more, Piper asked, "How can I access the recordings?"

Cormac remained silent for several long seconds. Long enough for Piper to consider that the connection might have dropped. She checked the connection time counter in the corner of her screen to confirm it was still counting up, and then said, "Doc?"

"Those recordings are somewhat sensitive because they are personal," Doctor Cormac said. "We must treat them accordingly. Everything Gray said and did while he was here is captured on those recordings."

Piper felt relieved to see that Seeley valued personal privacy. However, this raised a new question. "The recordings are captured by the nanotech in his head?" she asked. "Does that mean he's recording while he's here as well as back home?"

"Well," Cormac elongated the single word into multiple syllables. "Presumably, that's the case," he added after a long pause, "but I can't say for sure. We only have access to the recordings made here. For reasons we can't explain, nothing recorded on your side is accessible to us. If the technology functions correctly, it should be recorded when he's back here. There's even neurological evidence to suggest that recording is happening. The data is simply inaccessible to us."

It was Piper's turn to be silent as she contemplated the incongruity of this. Especially considering that the means by which Gray transported information from home to Wild-Side was through neurological data capture. His brain essentially functioned as an organic flash drive to transfer data across the Brane barrier.

Why would that data transfer function when the recordings do not?

Shaking her head, Piper resolved to concentrate on the topic that had originally excited her. "How can I access Gray's recordings?"

"You need his permission," Cormac said matter-of-factly.

With those words, Piper saw her ambitions crushed. She was already overwhelmed with anxiety as she waited for Gray to return. So far, he was weeks overdue, and no one could guess the reason. This wasn't going to help.

"Lucky for you," Cormac replied. "He made accommodations so that anyone on this project team can access whatever they need from his recordings whenever required. You, of course, are part of the team—aren't you?"

Piper smiled. Moments later, Cormac explained how to access the recordings she was interested in.

The next several hours passed effortlessly for Piper as she reviewed footage spanning every moment Gray had experienced while on Wild-Side. The technology of the Seeley never failed to astound her, and this was yet another example. Scrubbing through endless hours of video was unnecessary; she could search the captures based on the names of the faces that appeared in the recordings and the locations where they took place.

Since Piper was interested in observing any progressive changes in the relationship between Lacy and Tripp, she simply searched for footage featuring both of them and played the clips back chronologically. Just as she suspected, there were subtle yet unmistakable changes in the verbal and physical interactions between the couple. These changes were nuanced in the earlier clips from just over five weeks ago but became more pronounced and obvious, at least to someone familiar with what they were observing, as the footage grew more current.

Right up until Gray's disappearance.

Piper finally slid back onto her bed and leaned against the wall. With a wave of her hand, she closed the multiple AR displays she had been projecting. Now, she gazed into the middle distance, sorting through what she'd learned. Thinking about the message from Cormac that had popped up in her HUD an hour ago and combining that with what she had just seen in the footage, Piper decided she hadn't given Gray enough credit. He might have the most creative way of sidestepping whatever cognitive programming was influencing the Seeley.

Piper finally understood what had changed.

It was cognitive dissonance. Something deeply ingrained in the Seeley prevented them from doing very specific things. The more she examined it, the more obvious it became to Piper, just as it must have been to Gray. Most importantly in this case, they wouldn't fight to defend themselves even when the survival of their race was at stake. Observing this, Gray considered other areas where they, as a people, were blind. They didn't age, and they didn't have children.

They didn't have sex. Perhaps they could have children but didn't know how? That posed an entirely different set of issues, and it seemed like it might be the next set of problems on the horizon. Regardless, Gray's approach to breaking free from their destructive mindset was to use pornography, of all things.

Whoever or whatever was responsible for placing these restrictions on the Seeley hadn't accounted for someone coming here from another Brane, nor had they considered someone exposing these people to wildly unfamiliar concepts. While it might have been possible to condition minds against aggression and violence, conditioning a race against its drive to connect, toward intimacy, and toward procreation was an entirely different matter. In that regard, Gray's tool of choice hadn't been a scalpel; he'd chosen a hammer. Provide the people with porn and free time, and it's only a matter of time before they start rubbing up against each other and doing what people are meant to do.

And sidestepping any other obstacles that had been placed in their way. That was merely the first social barrier to fall. The crucial one was the reluctance to stand up for themselves, Piper understood. But when Gray couldn't get the Seeley to budge on that matter, he had pursued another route.

Piper shook her head and laughed. Gray's unconventional approach to problem-solving never ceased to amaze her.

But it raised another question: if some kind of cognitive block was placed on these people, who had imposed it? How? Why?

Gray was certainly ahead of her on these questions as well.

And with that, her mood darkened. He had been gone for so long. Something had happened; there was no question about that. Had he been captured? Did something happen to his ability to cross? Maybe something changed when he accidentally brought her to Wild-Side.

A hundred questions flooded her mind for perhaps the thousandth time.

There were no answers.

Thinking about the HUD recordings, Piper realized she now had access to a wealth of new information. The challenge would be to find something valuable in the torrent of data. Sliding once again to the edge of the bed, she placed her feet on the floor and waved her hand through the air to bring up an AR display. Selecting a recent clip at random, she discovered footage of Gray preparing for the Airbike before his first test flight. He was just putting on the protective suit before the flight.

Piper watched as the suit, a visual combination of motorcycle leathers and protective armor, expanded from a series of rings at the various joints in his ankles, knees, hips, shoulders, wrists, and neck. The rings resembled narrow bands of tape on his clothing, so thin they were barely noticeable. However, when he activated the suit, the nano polymer expanded from the rings to envelop his body in a flexible, armor-like material that was matte black and form-fitting.

Rewinding the footage, Piper repeatedly watched as the nano-particulate material seemed to envelop his torso and limbs in the blink of an eye, forming the suit. The suit appeared to materialize seemingly out of nowhere in the span of just two heartbeats.

She opened a communication channel to Tripp. "Hey," she said. "I have a question for you."

"Uh huh?" Tripp sounded distracted.

"Do you know how Gray's flight suit takes shape?"

Tripp was silent for several seconds before he finally spoke. "Wait, what?"

"You know how you just sort of blink twice and the suit kind of forms around him? What would happen if he wore a heavy insulated coat when he activated the suit? Wouldn't he be too large to fit into the gear since it would try to conform to a shape bigger than it was designed for?"

Tripp laughed. "Of course not. The suit sizes itself to fit the user on the fly. You could wear his riding suit—helmet too—and you're nowhere near his size."

Piper remained silent as she replayed the footage of the suit forming around Gray's body again. "So, in theory," she said slowly, "the nanomaterial can be made to assume any shape it requires. We just need to provide it with the right instructions?"

A vague sound emanated from the connection. "I suppose," Tripp finally replied. "But I'm not understanding you."

With her heart racing again, this time from excitement, Piper made her way to the door. "I have an idea. Can you meet me in the lab?"

Another noncommittal sound came from Tripp.

Piper paused mid-stride and listened to the connection very carefully, suddenly recalling the sight of Tripp and Lacy in the hallway. The smile on her face spread as she tried to keep the amusement out of her tone. "You know what? Sorry about that. I lost track of the hour. Why don't we talk in the morning? I'm sorry for calling so late." She disconnected the line without another word, her cheeks flushing with unabashed amusement.

———————

Piper wedged her shoulder against the underside of the heavy multi-barreled mini-gun and pushed up with the strength of her legs. Tripp was positioned with his heels dangling precariously over the back of the wall at the city's perimeter, guiding the heavy weapon into the mount. Piper couldn't recall the technician's name on the other end of the gun, but she was grateful that they had mostly streamlined this into a foolproof process now that only two more perimeter guns were left to be mounted.

The sound of a heavy metal pin sliding into place was followed by a pair of clicks that felt gentle in comparison. "That's it," Lacy called in confirmation. "We're set."

Piper lowered herself from beneath the articulated gun emplacement and watched with amusement as Lacy extended a hand to Tripp. Over the last several weeks on Wild-Side, she had observed many changes. Gray's prolonged and unexplained disappearance affected those closest to him on Doctor Cormac's team in unexpected ways. Certainly, his absence raised concerns when he failed to return on his semi-regular schedule. However, as she noted while watching Tripp and Lacy crouched low and speaking quietly in the windbreak beneath the shelter of the parapet, his influence resonated throughout the team. In recent weeks, the pair continued to showcase moments of intimacy entirely foreign to their people until recently.

As far as Piper could tell, Gray's absence had affected even his vocal critics among the Seeley. The decision to place automated guns around the perimeter of the city was a prime example. As Doctor Cormac explained, this was a defensive measure that the Administration of the Seeley had steadfastly opposed. Gray had unilaterally equipped the city with an early version of the guns, positioning them at nodes every seventy-five yards along the city walls of Fresno. However, unbeknownst to him, when Gray left the city, the guns had been disabled. The Elend had overrun Fresno, and the city's entire population remained unaccounted for. Now, with Gray missing, Primary Administrator Hargrave had reversed her decision and agreed to deploy the weapons to defend their city.

That didn't mean they had much support in deploying the weaponry. Changing people's direction didn't happen overnight. It still fell to Piper, Cormac, and Cormac's team to establish the defensive perimeter.

Piper arched her back and felt the bones in her back and neck pop. She glanced at the sun, low on the western horizon, and noted how the occasional raindrop had turned into an occasional ice crystal. The wind was picking up speed as her eyes began to water when she caught one just right. "Two more," she said in a tone loud enough for Tripp and Lacy to hear over the wind.

A pair of technicians waited with the next gun on a hovering cart. Tripp immediately set to maneuvering the cart into position, raising it as close as possible to the mounting bracket where the gun needed to align. At the same time, Lacy prepared the set of latching mounting pins. They'd done this more than a dozen times already this afternoon and over two dozen times the previous day.

As she prepared to climb to her position on the edge of the wall once again, Piper found Doctor Cormac waiting for her. He explained that she was needed inside and mentioned that a pair of sturdy-looking individuals from the engineering team had been chosen to replace her.

Piper followed Cormac into the room that had become their main workspace. Only then did she remove her insulated jacket and fingerless gloves. The nanotechnology she had received upon arriving at Wild-Side made her largely immune to the effects of cold weather, but that didn't mean it didn't negatively affect her body. While it was easy to get lost in the wondrous tech available here, it was also important to remember that beneath it all, the Seeley were just as human as she was.

Then, considering their inability to age, she mentally added, *mostly.*

"Is it Gray?" Piper asked, not hesitating. Her heart raced. This was the only reason she could think of for Cormac pulling her from work on the defensive perimeter.

Cormac looked momentarily confused, then shook his head vigorously. "No, apologies. Nothing like that." He stroked his beard and seemed suddenly uneasy. "Oh, no. Unfortunately not. Or—fortunately—depending on your perspective. While I still can't explain his prolonged absence, as you've mentioned before, there's far more we don't understand about the Crossing."

Dropping onto a stool in frustration, Piper struggled to find solace in a perspective that was becoming increasingly tenuous over time. She no longer knew if she was advocating for that viewpoint for her own mental health or to buoy the spirits of her new extended family. What she did know with certainty was that, while Gray's trips to Wild-Side had never followed a clear pattern, he had never gone this long between visits. Never anywhere close to this length of time. She could only wonder if he might already be here, lost somewhere in the wilds of this world, perhaps hurt and in need of help. Or there was a more distressing possibility she tried not to dwell on. He could have been captured or killed by the Elend.

In either case, he was there on a timer whenever he landed on Wild-Side. It was only ever a matter of time before he rubber banded back to their world. Thus, with a certain degree of confidence, she could find comfort in the idea that, regardless of what happened out there, he had a means of escape.

Unless…

There were two potential scenarios that Piper, Cormac, and his team had brainstormed, which remained unaccounted for. If Gray were to die out there, whether by accident or through an attack from the Elend, his ability to return home was uncertain. It was a situation no one could test, and clearly, no one had any experience with. Additionally, it remained possible—albeit unlikely—that the mechanics of how Gray jumped Branes had changed in some fundamental way.

Cormac led Piper to the next room, where three technicians worked at their counters. AR displays hung in the air before each of them, their hands manipulating keyboards projected across the counters in front of them and suspended in space before them.

"Wes," Cormac said without hesitation. "Can you show Piper the relevant storm system?"

Wes turned from his counter and made a hand gesture to bring up a large screen on the wall at the back of the room. Piper turned and noticed Tripp for the first time. He must have come down from the wall with her and Cormac. That she had missed his presence until now highlighted just how distracted she had become over Gray's continued absence.

Tripp must have noticed something in her expression because he placed a hand on her shoulder. She saw a resolute sense of calm in his face. The comforting, slow nod of his head seemed to reflect something she had witnessed Gray do in solemn situations. This was very different from the Tripp she had met shortly after her arrival, and somehow she knew Gray had influenced these people in subtle and nuanced ways.

I just hope I get to tell him about this someday soon.

The map Wes projected showed Portland in the lower right and a small dot with a red ring around it in the upper left. Between the two was a vast swath of wilderness. There was a small area of arid desert expanse dipping in from the top of the map near the right, various lakes and ponds were visible across the remainder of the surface, and what Piper took to be a relatively minor mountain range between Portland and the red ring near the top left of the map.

Wes activated the weather layer on the map. Cloud cover and meteorological data were instantly overlaid. The storm front she had seen while up on the wall was immediately apparent—a medium-sized weather system moving toward the city from the west. It seemed they would catch the northern edge of the front as it moved southeast. Of greater concern was a larger front not far behind it. This more extensive system was at least three times bigger, and while the front that was about to skirt the city was annotated in pale blues, indicating it would be moderately unpleasant with small amounts of snow and ice, the larger front was entirely colored in yellow and orangish red.

"This weather system is headed straight for us," Wes said. "It's large, intense, and it's moving slowly."

Piper slipped her hands into the pockets of her jeans and turned her gaze toward Cormac. "What does this do to the operation?"

Cormac and Tripp shared a nervous glance.

"We should push it back," Tripp said.

Cormac said nothing.

Piper looked at Cormac for several seconds, then returned to the map. She placed her hand on Wes's shoulder. "Can you add the Thonian layer?"

A large purple cloud was added to the map. It hung to the northwest of the city, oblong in shape. Taking a rough estimate at the scale, it was perhaps one hundred and twenty-five miles wide at its center. North to south, it would have measured between five and six hundred miles in length. "Any noticeable movement in the last week?" Piper asked.

Wes was shaking his head halfway through her question. "Almost none in the last month. Over the past forty-five days, it has decreased in surface area by nearly one percent, but it hasn't moved."

"Can we tell how high the weather system reaches into the atmosphere?" Piper pressed. She instantly felt all eyes in the room focused on her.

"How...*high?*" Wes asked, his voice trembling.

"Altitude," Piper said. "What's the maximum altitude of the storm system?" He was confused by the question.

A massive grin spread across Tripp's face. His eyes sparkled with a mix of amusement, enthusiasm, and horror as his hands started manipulating a private display in AR. "That's exactly the kind of question Gray would have asked. I see why you two fit together the way you do."

Cormac, for his part, only looked concerned. Wes no longer seemed to grasp what was being discussed. Cormac was about to speak when Tripp responded.

"Here it is," Tripp said. "Seven thousand feet and change on the low side, and..." he seemed to be scrolling through a long list of data points as he spoke. "Just under eleven thousand feet at the most extreme points."

Piper gave a slow nod. "Then we're still on track. As long as I'm airborne in time to beat the worst of the storm, we won't have a problem." She shot Tripp a deadly serious look. "Will the modifications be ready in time?"

Tripp glanced at the timeline projected at the bottom of the screen that Wes still had displayed on the wall. "It's going to be close." He turned to Cormac. "I could use a few of Stillwell's people to speed things up."

Cormac nodded. "I'll have the approval by the time you get over there. Whatever you need. She took her time, but we finally have Administrator Hargrave's support."

Looking at Piper, Cormac said, "I'm most concerned about you. You mentioned it yourself—you're terrified of heights. Are you sure you can handle this?"

Piper shrugged. "Gray's missing, and none of your people can do it." She seemed to struggle to meet his gaze. Swallowing hard to suppress both the bile rising in her throat and her own reluctance, she squared her shoulders. "The perimeter wall is a meager defense at best. These creatures can't be killed unless we land a lucky shot in the eye. That means we're screwed if they come at us in a coordinated attack. It's only a matter of time before they get organized enough to figure that out. We need to have Plan B ready before it gets to that point."

———————

Tripp hunched over a small platform, securing a short stack of pewter-colored, thickly insulated packing crates when Piper entered the area the team simply referred to as the Garage. The crates were connected and fastened to the platform with thick straps that incorporated a ratchet mechanism at the end for maximum security. A massive canvas tarpaulin obscured the far end of the platform.

Only after counting the stack of mismatched crates to confirm there were thirteen did Piper's gaze shift to the massive fan blades protected by shallow ducts. One was positioned at each corner of the platform, and each blade-like rotor had a circumference slightly wider than she was tall. She stooped and ran her fingers along the checkerboard pattern of screen mesh designed to keep debris from fouling the blades and the motors. "This is a lot thinner than I expected," she said. "Are you sure it will protect the hardware?"

Tripp looked over the top of the stacked boxes and nodded aggressively. "I can quote you the tensile strength if you'd like, but I know how you feel about that. Suffice it to say, each strand is equivalent to a braided steel cable a quarter inch in diameter where you're from."

Piper shrugged; it was satisfactory.

Her gaze shifted to the far end of the platform where the control system was supposed to be. The platform was symmetrical, making it impossible to distinguish the front of the craft from the back.

"Tripp? How do I fly this?"

He pointed to the larger tarped object just beyond the platform. "From there," he said without looking up. He secured the last of the retaining straps before sliding off the platform and taking a moment to stretch the discomfort clearly evident in his back and knees. "The transport platform is slaved to the pilot's craft," he said as if it were the only logical conclusion.

Piper looked at the Airbike parked near the Garage's far wall. "Good idea. But why not just pair it with that if you're going that route?"

Smiling with a face that turned pink and then red, Tripp said, "Well… you're afraid of heights, right?"

Piper nodded slowly.

"And while you're doing this, you wouldn't be doing it if there were anyone else willing or able to take it on?"

Piper nodded even more slowly.

"That thing," Tripp said, pointing at the Airbike. "Is not for the timid. I built it to Gray's specifications, and I can tell you one thing with absolute certainty—anyone who gets on it needs to have either complete confidence or a death wish."

Considering how she'd seen Gray maneuver the craft during his first test flight, along with what she'd observed at ten thousand feet and beyond, she had to agree. Not for the first time, she felt a surge of anxiety that was increasingly accompanied by the urge to vomit. She had every confidence in herself, but there was too much at stake now. She didn't understand how Gray managed to put himself through this for these people time and again.

Tripp must have seen the distress in her expression because he stepped closer. "Take a deep breath," he said. "Have a seat." He was pointing to the side of the platform.

Lacy pushed a small, hovering cart through the pair of double doors on the nearest wall and paused when she noticed the grim expressions on the faces of Tripp and Piper. "Stage fright?" she asked.

Piper looked up. "I'm going to throw up."

Lacy positioned the cart and prepared an injector. "You're afraid of heights," she said in a calm, soothing tone. "And you're about to take the second flying machine in our people's history on the longest flight of record."

Tripp was scowling. "We're going to start practicing your pep talks before you're allowed to give them."

"My point," Lacy said with a theatrical roll of her eyes, "is that you're a hero just for wanting to try this."

Piper swallowed hard, pausing before she spoke to ensure she didn't throw up. Although she had explained that she was afraid of heights, she hadn't conveyed that she was actually terrified of them. The fear was less a conscious discomfort and more of a physical and medical issue. Exposure to anything beyond moderate heights triggered vertigo, followed by symptoms ranging from nausea to unconsciousness. What she felt so far was merely panic about what was to come.

She didn't know how to explain this to the people who were counting on her. If she could reach the underground city and configure the teleportation hardware packed on the hover platform, it might finally be possible to move the Seeley to a location beyond the Elend's reach...if only for a while.

Lacy knelt and held out the subcutaneous injector. "This will relieve the vertigo and nausea," she said. "I can administer a sedative for the panic if you'd like."

Piper froze, her brows arched in confusion. She couldn't remember sharing her concerns with anyone. Only Gray knew just how absolutely terrified she was of heights. Unless, she thought with a new sense of worry, she had been so out of her mind that she'd said more to the people here than she currently recalled.

Exactly how panicked have I gotten?

Lacy placed her hand on Piper's knee and offered a sympathetic smile. "Your genetic profile indicates with ninety-eight percent certainty that you have a borderline crippling sense of vertigo when exposed to shifts in barometric pressure. Your inner ear and brain tend to—" she pointed a finger at her own ear and then twirled the finger in the air until the circles grew wider and wider before ultimately pointing off in a seemingly random direction. "Anyway…" she held up the injector. "This will work in conjunction with the nanotechnology and address the problem until we have enough time to fix you up properly. I can completely fix it. I'll just need more time and some diagnostic testing to execute a permanent solution. Unfortunately, we don't have time for all of that now."

Piper nodded. "So this is a bandaid?"

Lacy appeared confused but then seemed to grasp the reference. "Yes!" she laughed. "Good analogy."

Piper pulled Lacy in for a hug. "Perfect. Let's skip the sedative. As long as I don't black out, I can deal with my fears." Actually, the more she thought about it, if she could separate the physical side effects from the mental aspects, she was already looking forward to the personal challenge. Recognizing that, she realized just how much faith she'd come to have in Lacy and Tripp. She was willing to take Lacy at her word that she could do something so medically extraordinary. At the same time, she was ready to put her life in the hands of a device Tripp had just finished fabricating based on concepts his team had never before considered.

"Your people have never flown before?" Piper asked, eyeing Tripp with skepticism. "Not ever?"

Tripp shrugged, waving his hand toward the Airbike along the wall. He said, "Gray was the first. I'm not sure anyone ever seriously considered it before he asked me to build that. We have ground transportation and the teleportation platforms." Another shrug followed. "Why would we want to leave the ground? Birds do that."

Slapping her palm on the platform beside her, Piper said, "And now I'm doing that."

"Point taken," Tripp said, looking suddenly pale.

"So what's that?" Piper was pointing to the tarp.

Color returned to Tripp, and his eyes lit up with excitement. "Gray's Airbike is perhaps a bit unwieldy for anyone but him to attempt without instruction. I designed it to his specifications, after all. But those concerns led me to consider what a more user-friendly version of the machine might look like and how it would run."

Piper and Lacy followed him to the covered device and stepped aside as he pulled back the tarp without any fanfare. The quadcopter-style bike beneath featured a snowmobile-style seat, only longer, as if designed to better accommodate a second passenger. The four-bladed rotors, positioned in shallow ducts at each corner beneath the bike's frame, were perhaps twenty percent larger, though they were covered by the same mesh-like screen that had been used on the fans of the transport platform.

"The props are larger," Tripp explained. "The overall footprint of the machine is also twenty-five percent larger, allowing it to spread across a wider surface area of air. This design will provide greater stability. Additionally, with the larger footprint, the bigger props will enhance energy efficiency and make it quieter than the first version at the same prop speed."

Piper slowly circled the Airbike. It appeared larger than the first version, though not by much. She understood what he meant by its larger overall footprint since it took up more space when parked on the Garage floor. Likewise, she reasoned, it would displace more air when hovering.

"The controls are the same?" Piper asked.

Tripp raised a flattened palm in the air and wobbled it back and forth. "For the most part," he said, lacking conviction. "I reduced the overall sensitivity of the pitch and roll by twenty-two percent to make it easier to fly, and I did the same for the yaw, reducing it by fifteen percent." As he spoke, he used hand gestures to indicate the orientations affected by the aircraft. "According to the literature, that should make the aircraft substantially more friendly for beginners."

Lacy looked unsure. "And if she wants more aggressive flight controls?"

Tripp was grinning. "Easy access to that from the top-level menu of the HUD. I don't doubt her ability. I just want to make the machine as easy to fly as possible."

Piper was smiling. "Mission success above all else," she agreed, then looked at Lacy. "But I like where your head is at!" Then she turned back to the transport platform. "How do they work together? Is it a trailer?"

"Only in the strictest sense," Tripp said. "The transport platform is linked to the Airbike. You control its tether length, but there's a buffer that allows flexibility in how you fly. For instance, you can have the platform follow at a distance of fifty to seventy-five meters. It can be whatever you want. The settings are accessible in your HUD."

———————

Twisting the throttle, Piper held her breath and waited for her stomach to rebel. Her guts clenched and her insides sank, but it was only in response to the sudden increase in gravitational force as the Airbike launched into a vertical climb that was unlike anything she had ever experienced. While Piper focused on the handlebar controls of the machine, she was vaguely aware of the G-force indicator in the corner of her HUD. It read 1.72 and had just ticked up from 1.69. The corners of her vision were growing dark, and she reasoned that it shouldn't be due to the gravitational forces.

Easing back on the throttle, she saw the indicator drop immediately to 1.22 and then to 1.17. Still, her vision continued to darken. The altitude display showed nine thousand three hundred sixteen feet, and she suddenly realized how quickly that counter had been rising.

At last, she remembered to breathe and gasped a sharp, choking lungful of air that was thankfully filtered and climatized through the system built into her helmet. "Oh my God," she muttered, taking another breath.

Only after her third deep exhale did Piper fully return to herself. She had completely released the throttle, which she had been warned against doing. Instead of plunging to the surface below, thankfully, the onboard safety system had entered a hover and maintained her altitude: nine thousand, four hundred feet and change.

Holy shit.

There was no vertigo, and if she simply focused on the handlebars or looked into the distance, the heights weren't as daunting as she had feared. She reasoned that the trick was to keep breathing. It seemed simple and logical... if launching oneself into the heavens on the back of a glorified Cuisinart could be considered rational.

Piper realized that the buzzing in her ears was actually frantic voices. Apparently, they had been there for some time.

"I'm okay," Piper replied, even before she could grasp the meaning of the words. She eased the throttle open and pushed the handlebars forward, moving the craft forward for the first time. "There we go," she smiled.

"She seems to have control now," a voice from far away said over the comm channel. "I think she's okay."

"Are you with me?" Lacy said over the channel. "You just scared the crap out of us."

Piper's smile grew wider. Gray's euphemisms had definitely won over Cormac's team. She turned the craft to the left and adjusted to the gentle yaw as it swiveled on its axis while still moving forward. "Just getting the hang of things," she finally said. "Everything's good up here."

Piper counted at least three sighs of relief. Lacy, Tripp, and the third must have been Cormac, even though he had yet to speak. It wasn't surprising that he was keeping an eye on her test flight. It was interesting that he was doing it covertly. While she understood it was an attempt to give Tripp and Lacy more experience and confidence, she knew the project lead was also deeply concerned about Gray's prolonged absence.

"I'm circling around to pick up the payload," Piper said.

Her test flight was over. It was time to get the long flight to the abandoned underground city complex underway. The Elend had been quiet lately, and she felt it was in preparation for a more concerted attack on the last stronghold. It would be a race against time to prepare the underground facility and relocate the population to a more secure location before the creatures were ready to move against them.

Wild-Side

Yesterday

Finally, shouldering through the last thick vegetation, Pemberton stepped from the forest into the field's tall grass. He gasped and dropped to his hands and knees. The exertion from his mad rush through the woodland hadn't exhausted him as quickly as he'd expected, but eventually, even newfound reserves of adrenaline had run dry. The field grass was tall, and with his collapse, he knew it offered him a degree of anonymity.

Having cleared the woodland for the first time since his escape from the cave, Pemberton looked down as his fingers flexed and explored the rough texture of the thick grass. This was his first clear glimpse of moonlight since escaping, and the sight of his hands made his breath catch in his throat. His fingers were thick, double-jointed, and scaled and…

They ended in short, thick claws. *No, not claws.* These were talons. His five fingers had been replaced by three fingers and something resembling a thick, less flexible thumb.

Pemberton rocked back on his knees. He quickly noticed how strangely his body moved and looked down across his torso. It was thick, powerfully built, and covered with coarse gray-black scales. Tears filled his eyes, and a cry escaped his lips. Somehow, both experiences felt foreign and…*wrong*.

Hands instantly went to his face; the talons would have flayed flesh had there been any. Instead, he felt thick scales beneath the pads of his fingers. He glanced briefly at his hand again to confirm that it was indeed his hand before returning it to his face. He could feel the texture of his own scaly flesh through what now appeared to be the scaly flesh of his hand, but it didn't make any sense.

He dropped to his backside and turned roughly in the direction from which he had escaped, trying to recall what had just happened. It had all been a blur. The only thing he could remember with certainty was a pain beyond anything he had ever experienced. It seemed to last forever. He thought it was death. It had to have been hell. Then there was light…not much, but some. Light and shadow. There were figures in the shadows.

Pemberton was on the verge of rubbing his eyes in fatigue and frustration but stopped himself. He glared at his taloned hand and groaned. The sound was deep and resonant. Had it not come from his own body, it would have terrified him.

The shadows had sparked a primal fear within him, and Pemberton began to recall the experience clearly. He had run—well, stumbled. He felt injured. He recalled the certainty that the massive dark figures around him would stop him at every turn, but none had. Dozens of the figures had looked at him as he passed, yet none had stopped him. Now that he considered the experience, he hadn't so much escaped as walked from the cave.

Once he reached the tree line, he would definitely run. He picked a direction and didn't stop running until he arrived at this clearing.

Now he listened. Wildlife clearly chirped, clicked, and burbled in the woods, but as far as he could tell, he hadn't been followed. That was good. However, he looked down at his hands once again and couldn't explain what he saw.

He then looked down at the rest of his body. It was a long, wide, alien form resembling a cross between a lizard-man and a dragon.. His gaze shifted to the sky and the stars scattered across the cloudless expanse.

"I made it to the other side."

Chapter 20 - Nasty Stuff All Over Your Junk

Wild-Side

It took me four days to move Pemberton's body to a location I believed would be safe for an extended period. Part of the effort required a cross-country drive. And since the first time I drifted off to sleep, I would likely end up in Wild-Side; I couldn't risk even a brief nap. My otherworldly excursion would jeopardize Pemberton, and compromising his comatose body could also provide Breslin with the information he might use for a successful Crossing. I didn't know if Pemberton fried his brain or Crossed, but until I knew for sure, keeping his body safe was the only prudent course of action.

Fortunately, I had now enlisted the support of Pike's team. They were technically on the payroll. More importantly, they were personally invested in the effort. With their firsthand insight into what Breslin was trying to accomplish, I had skilled operators to help protect Pemberton while I returned to Wild-Side.

It was a long, exhausting four days. While I could control the nanotechnology in my body, overclocking myself to run nonstop for that duration was beyond my capability. Thankfully, Esker was there to help. Even the AI was reluctant to make the adjustments. Setting technology aside, the human body wasn't designed to run continuously without rest, he warned. This was why I couldn't adjust the tech on my own.

The Crossing to Wild-Side wasn't usual. Fatigue made me feel a bit like a struck match, and dark skies laden with low-hanging, angry-looking clouds poured sheets of rain that didn't make me smile. It was dusk, as close as I could tell. I gave my HUD a minute to come online, but when it didn't, I confidently concluded I was in one of the numerous dead zones. Not the end of the world...but I was tired. More tired than I could ever remember being. Usually, I was fatigued when I fell asleep back on My-World, but when I Crossed, something about the Transition left me energized, though temporarily sickened and a little worse for the wear. Yet, the effects were slowly improving with time. It was as if my body was building a tolerance for the negative repercussions of the Crossing. But this time?

Not good. Not good at all. I felt as if every ache and pain I experienced back home was amplified on this side.

I knelt in the mud as a cool, light rain fell on my shoulders.

Super.

I climbed to my feet and braced my flimsy knees against the cold wind. I found myself at the edge of a small clearing surrounded by towering conifers. They would at least provide a respite from the wind, so I quickly slipped behind the boughs of the nearest shelter. As soon as I did, the whistle of the wind became hushed, and the woods fell silent. Not just silent from the wind, but devoid of the rustle of natural habitation.

Something is wrong.

I held my breath and listened intently. At first, all I could hear was the rasp of my own ragged breathing and the rush of blood behind my ears. I fought against the chattering of my teeth. The cold and the loss of my heightened hearing were feelings I acutely experienced at that moment as I strained to sense the danger I knew was nearby. The forest fell silent in response to that danger. It was a primal, natural reaction—wildlife responding to a predator in the area.

A tree limb snapped in the distance, the sound coming from somewhere behind me to my right. Then, I heard a whoosh of something moving quickly through the brush near my left. I froze, sensing two different threats. Sinking slowly, I focused my ears on what my eyes couldn't identify in the darkness and dense tree cover.

More movement. This was a third figure, and it, too, was moving swiftly. All three figures passed by me to the north, by my estimation. The abundance of moss on an exposed boulder a few feet away made it easy to discern north. Three Elend hurried along, all heading in the same direction. They were becoming more organized, but for so many to be near me without catching my scent, something had them distracted.

As much as I wanted to find shelter, or better yet, a platform that could take me directly to one of the cities, I was suddenly more intrigued by whatever had the Elend so motivated. My fatigue and hypothermia quickly took a back seat to my curiosity, so I waited to ensure that more of the creatures weren't following the ones that had just passed me by, and then I swiftly followed the pack.

––––––––––––

I stalked the creatures for about six miles. One good thing came from following them that far—we cleared the edge of the dead zone, if only just barely. As I expected, my tech was nearly useless. The reserves of nanotech were stretched well beyond their capacity and were at least as exhausted as me. I was, however, able to identify my geographic position. It wasn't good news. I was hundreds of miles from the nearest city—and almost sixty miles from the nearest farm with a teleportation system. That system hadn't pinged in more than a year, so its state of operation was questionable at best. At least I had one thing going for me—the Elend were moving without regard for stealth, though it was a good thing I was. Before we reached the churned-up burrow in the forest that was their destination, the two Drakes and the Crawler I was following were met by another Crawler and a pair of Jays. While all seemed to be approaching from different directions, every creature was vectoring toward the same destination with a similar sense of haste.

The clearing before me was likely just over a hundred yards deep and at least three times as wide. The forest had been aggressively cleared of trees, with the wreckage of intact oaks, redwoods, and pines haphazardly piled along the edge of a massive, crude cleft in the earth that resembled a glancing hatchet strike in the ground. The cleft was at least a football field in width and forty feet high at its center. Clearly, it was the result of immense labor by the Elend, though the reason for their efforts wasn't immediately obvious. They worked like monstrous, oversized mud wasps, digging and burrowing into the earth. Furrows of discarded dirt and stone beyond the mouth of the cavern extended into the surrounding forest, piled in heaps among the trees, revealing the scale of the excavation.

I hunkered down, climbing between the stacked piles of tree trunks, gravel, and discarded dirt. It was easy to stick to the shadows since dozens of small, oily bonfires dotted the pulverized gravel trail leading into the chasm. The cavern resembled a massive roach motel. I watched as dozens of Elend entered—Jays, Drakes, and more Crawlers than I could count. I saw some forms I'd never encountered before—creatures I hadn't met yet. It made me wonder how many of the Elend were now on Wild-Side, where they were coming from, and how many forms the creatures actually took. Those I'd faced so far had been formidable. If there were a version that was even harder to kill, I didn't want to see it.

That led to the next question of concern.

What the hell are they doing here?

At most, I'd faced the creatures in small groups. They were not—at least in my experience so far—socially organized creatures. What I was seeing was something new. And if they were organizing, it wouldn't be good for the people of Wild-Side.

This is a game-changer.

I'm not sure how long I watched and waited. I saw dozens of Elend enter the cave. I stopped counting after one hundred twenty. There was no way to know how many entered before I arrived. The rain continued to fall, though I had some shelter in the lee of the massive felled timber. Still, my impatience eventually got the better of me.

I need to learn more.

———————

Entering the cavern would have been the foolish effort of a desperate man. Even if I were functioning at one hundred percent and armed, it would have been a one-way ticket. At that point, I was running on empty. Hell, I didn't even have clothes. All the tech the Seeley had for me to leverage, and when I needed it, I had nothing.

Did I mention it was raining?

Since I couldn't enter through the front door, I hoped for a back entrance. Following the remnants of the monster mining project, I made my way around the edge of the cavern and climbed the rocky, muddy slope beyond the mouth's right side. By that point, the rain was falling strong and steady, which was both good and bad. On the positive side, the white noise it generated masked any sounds I made. It softened the ground and prevented my movements from dislodging the loose rocks and stones I was hitting in patches as I made my clumsy ascent. On the downside, it was muddy and extremely slippery. I slipped, fell, and bruised just about every unprotected part of my body—and when you're completely naked, that's a lot of body parts.

At least the effort paid off. I was about to close in on what I thought was the apex of the cavern's arch when the acoustics of the rain patter changed. My first instinct was that I wasn't alone, so I dropped to my belly. The change in the timbre of the rainfall, at least to my lizard brain, suggested someone or something was up here with me. What I heard sounded like the rainfall striking another figure as they moved. But as I lay there, I realized that while the change in the rainfall pattern I had heard had shifted, it didn't continue to change. The more I thought about it, I noticed that it wasn't the small shift I would have noted if there was a man—or monster—sized figure up here with me. This was something different. This was a bigger disturbance.

Climbing to all fours and shifting my head, my eyes saw nothing but the dim shifting of moonlight on rough rock and earth. Instead, I focused on my hearing. The enhanced sense of sound I once enjoyed because of nanotechnology was long gone; that tech had atrophied and depleted to a point where I was lucky to rely on my primal, primitive senses.

Once I was back on my feet, I took a deep breath and regained confidence in my instincts. Three steps later, I realized they had been accurate, and I understood what had triggered my sense that something had altered the rain's fall. Twenty feet away, the ground had caved in. An oblong sinkhole had opened up, likely due to hydrologic forces. And as luck would have it, I saw a dancing flash of light coming from somewhere beneath the gap.

I thought I had found the backdoor I was looking for, but I didn't want to get too close if the earth had fallen in once already. I could become part of the next collapse. Still, I needed to see if this was a way into the cavern. If not, there might be others. Lowering myself onto my belly, I slipped slowly closer to the opening. Treating it like a hole in thin ice, I tried to distribute my body weight across the rocky, muddy ground. I moved slowly and paid close attention to the surface beneath me.

Hearing a commotion in the cavern beneath me, I froze. There were growls and a voice that sounded human, so I waited. I sensed there were many figures below me, but they felt distant. That made sense. If this portal was positioned where I suspected, as I visualized it in my mind's eye, it was just off-center from the apex of the cavern. While I had no idea how deep the burrow extended into the earth, I guessed I was at least fifty feet above their heads based on the voices I heard.

I shimmied away from the hole and examined my desolate surroundings. After a quick search, I found a shattered tree limb. It was nearly twenty feet long and about as thick as my forearm on average. Each end had a jagged break, making me wonder how large the tree was that it had come from and what that Elend looked like who had brought down the tree.

I stripped the small sprouting branches and turned the limb into a structural support, a beam.

Laying the limb down beside the hole, I took a deep breath and rolled it across the opening. If watching the Elend as they gathered and entered the cavern was a gamble, this felt like playing Russian roulette with half the chambers loaded. My trick could cause a larger collapse, or worse yet, one of the Elend below only needed to look up at the wrong moment to catch me.

Holding my breath didn't seem like a reasonable mitigating factor, but what harm could it do? I didn't breathe again until the massive green tree limb was rolled into place, spanning the narrow section of the oblong expanse. Then, I belly crawled to the edge of the hole once more, keeping the limb beneath the center of my body to better distribute my weight. Slimy, cold clay coated my belly and legs—and believe me, you haven't truly lived until you've smeared that nasty stuff all over your junk. At least it distracted from the rain pouring down on my back and bare skin, since both were pointing skyward.

I stopped crawling when my eyes breached the edge of the hole and the cavern below came into view.

At first, I couldn't see anything. I was staring into a pit of inky blackness. Frustration sent a series of silent expletives from my lips. The wasted time and effort were made worse by the fact that my internal reserves were running on empty. Time mattered less than that my vision was starting to blur and a strange tingling deep in my jaw made my molars ache. The pain at the base of my skull felt like someone was trying to itch my brain with an icepick and…

The mental image of the icepick was familiar. If I had felt more like myself, it probably wouldn't have taken so long to grasp what was happening and why. Finally, everything clicked into place.

I took a deep breath and pressed my cheek against the side of my makeshift beam. With my eyes closed, I focused on calming myself and soothing my senses. The sound of the rain pounding the mud, stone, and clay around me became a hypnotic white noise. The relentless pulse of the torrent against my back turned into a soothing, albeit chilly, massage. The thunderous rush of my heartbeat in my ears merged with my blood flow, settling into a meager, steady rhythm.

What remained were the ache in my jaw and the icepick stabbing at the base of my skull. Neither had changed in intensity, which confirmed my slowly recognized suspicion. I looked back into the yawning void and focused on maintaining my breathing. While I could hear nothing new, my gaze gradually shifted as my eyes adjusted to the piercing darkness.

The floor of the cavern lay at least a hundred feet below. Tiny figures moved, indistinct in the murk from that distance. Still, even from that height, I could tell the figures were not human. Dozens upon dozens of Elend had gathered—likely hundreds of these creatures since what I could see from my vantage surely didn't capture the full extent of the gathering beneath me. The creatures were assembled in a loose formation around a central point, their assembly spanning the breadth and depth of my view.

At that point, I realized two things for the first time. First, the Elend population was far more expansive than even our worst-case expectations. Second, while they had shown no signs of large-scale social organization thus far, that had either recently changed—or worse, it had been intentional misdirection.

I was cut off and on my own. There was no way I could inform Doc Cormac about what I was seeing. Considering my health and nano reserves, there was little chance I'd reach a communication or teleportation station before one of these creatures stumbled across me. I was too far behind enemy lines, and there were too many of the creatures for me to have any realistic expectation of making it far in my condition.

With that in mind, I decided to learn what I could. My next step was to find a way to leave a message for the Doc. For now, concentrating on one thing at a time was sufficient.

Still looking into the cavern, I concentrated on my breathing. The idea was to block the stabbing pain from the back of my skull. If anything, it was growing more acute with time. Since I now knew this was due to my geographic location, the pain made sense. Though I'd been slow to recognize the symptoms, I now knew what they indicated about this place. I was suspended over one of the places where the barriers between Branes were thin. For whatever reason, back home, I knew at least one similar site located several stories underground.

So how do the Elend know that?

I stared, trying to make out the distant figures in the darkness. The congregation had gathered around some kind of oval-shaped apparatus or configuration of smaller components at what appeared to be the center of the excavated cavern. At least a dozen small fires burned randomly on the floor, sending wispy tendrils of oily smoke to the space's roof. Little of the smoke bothered my nose or eyes, suggesting that there was either a second entrance to the cavern or additional openings similar to mine through which the foul air was freely escaping.

Concentrating as I was, I was surprised when the darkness below suddenly brightened into better focus. I would have thought the cavern was flooded with light if not for the fact that my view shifted to zoom in on the ovoid shape at the center of the gathering at the same moment, making me acutely aware that the tech in my eyes had come to life with one final burst of effort. I didn't know how this happened, but I was grateful.

The oval configuration at the center of the Elend mass wasn't a device I encountered. Instead, it was a pattern of six cylindrical holes bored into the stone floor of the cavern, arranged as one column of three stacked beside another column of three. While I couldn't determine the depth of the depressions, I estimated them to be around three feet in diameter. Beyond the depressions was something that defied explanation. It appeared that someone had removed an old door from a house—frame included—and positioned it a few feet in front of the recesses. It was as if someone were expected to walk through the door before confronting three pairs of evenly spaced recesses just a few feet ahead.

As much as this didn't make sense, it somehow struck me as familiar. I was still pondering this and eyeing the short post at the opposite end of the configuration when the gathered mass quieted and seemed to shift as one. The group parted, creating an open avenue from my three o'clock position. Without pause, a small procession advanced along the newly vacated path and moved swiftly toward the strange configuration at the cavern's center.

The Elend figure at the front of the procession was unmistakable. While each creature was unique in color or slightly distinctive in shape even within its class, this creature stood out among every Jay, Drake, Crawler, and even the new Harvesters. This Elend was broad-shouldered, its carapace matte black from end to end. Its primary abdomen was wide and horizontal, resembling the body of a crab, held aloft on four taloned and pincered claws. At the front of the abdomen, the torso shifted upright and tapered to something vaguely human-like, with broad shoulders and a pair of massive chitin-plated arms ending in hands with three thick talons for fingers. Short barb-like protrusions rang the shoulders and collar beneath the head. The face was reptilian and demonic, featuring wide yellow eyes with thick vertical slits, a bony slit where the nose should have been, and a gaping maw too large to be human but somehow reminiscent of humanity, revealing thumb-sized triangular razor-edged teeth with shifting, scaly lips.

Without question, I knew I was looking at Breslin. This was the leader of the Elend.

Behind him, six Drakes trailed, each manhandling a beleaguered and hunched-looking Seeley. Four men and two women, none of them restrained. Judging by the appearance of the prisoners, shackles were unnecessary. All six of the Seeley moved mechanically at the command of their captors. Each stared unblinkingly from drawn, haggard faces that had long since lost the will to live. The Seeley, unfortunately, didn't know how to fight in the first place. They were all too easy to capture or kill.

An Elend stood behind each of the Seeley, ensuring their compliance.

Seeing these six like this, I wondered—not for the first time—how many had been taken instead of being killed outright. A roiling sensation deep in my gut feared I was about to receive an answer to my long-held question. I watched as the six prisoners were led to the depressions in the cave floor, one prisoner placed into each.

Having finished their work, the contingent of Drakes took positions at the perimeter of the small clearing. The bustle of the gathered horde grew suddenly silent. Completely, eerily quiet.

Breslin's hulking form moved to the end of the oblong configuration at the center of the clearing, just a few feet beyond the post I had just noticed. He spun slowly, his gaze seeming to take in the extent of those gathered. Then, without a word, he lowered his head as if observing a moment of reverent silence. At this, the entire gathered mass shifted. As one, I heard the rustling of scales and chitinous panels sweep across the cavern.

I realized with a choked gasp that the group was bowing in submission.

Something was happening to Breslin, and I noticed it too late. My attention returned to him instantly, knowing I had missed something important. His body was undergoing some unexplainable transformation. The final seconds of his shift occurred so quickly that my rational mind couldn't comprehend the sight. The hulking Elend figure had shifted and was replaced by a six-foot-tall form of a normal thirty-something man.

He was completely naked, and as far as I could tell, he was entirely human. This was the Breslin I knew from Our-World.

I was speechless.

"Rise," he bellowed to the crowd of Elend. They obeyed.

With a wave of his hand, Breslin signaled to a pair of Crawlers at the edge of the clearing. They had been among the small group that followed him upon his grand entrance. The first stopped a few paces away and presented an old, worm-eaten wooden chest about the size of a breadbox. The second Crawler flipped open the lid before stepping aside.

This, it seemed, was some sort of ceremony. I eyed the six Seeley in the hip-deep holes, and the bile reappeared in my gut.

Breslin approached the wooden chest and took something from it. I couldn't see inside the box from my position, and as Breslin selected his item, his stance blocked my view even more. As it turned out, I needn't have worried. Breslin turned and walked directly to the hip-high post near the setup's end, placing his choice atop the post. It was a glass orb about twice the size of a fist. Without hesitation, Breslin extended his flattened hands on either side of the orb and began speaking in words too quiet for me to hear. His eyes were closed, and I could see his lips moving. His hands remained still, palms raised and held about four inches away from the sphere's sides. From his position, his line of sight faced across the sphere, bisecting the six holes and the six standing Seeley they held, and directly toward the surface of the door-like plane at the far end of the configuration.

When Breslin's lips stopped moving, his eyes opened and the sphere ignited with a blinding inner light. Breslin's hands moved, closing around the sphere's sides at the same instant. As they did, the incandescent light shifted into a focused beam that projected across the six recessed pits and struck the vertical surface on the other end. The light lasted for perhaps three heartbeats, then some kind of feedback pulsed back from the door, across the pits, and hammered into the sphere. The light went dark.

I blinked away the stabbing pain in my eyes, unable to rub them for fear of losing my precariously braced position on the limb. At some point, I'd shimmied halfway out onto the tree, likely for a better view. Now, my hips and legs were the only parts of me in contact with the muddy earth at the hole's edge.

Casting a glance over my shoulder, I scanned the darkness. Visibility stretched only a dozen feet beyond the edge of the hole, and the feeling that I wasn't alone was so strong that I almost expected to look up and see one of the creatures lunging at me. I wanted to dismiss it as paranoia, but hundreds of creatures were just a few dozen yards below me. One of the predators only needed to glance up, and my paranoia would become a reality.

Taking a slow, calming breath, I realized this wasn't how I was meant to die, not after everything I'd witnessed and accomplished. I was meant to go down fighting. Falling to the hoard of these creatures while I was naked, fever-ridden, and hypothermic? That was no way for my story to end.

Then I heard something move in the distant sky. It was quick and far too large to be wildlife. Beyond that, I couldn't be certain what it was. The darkness and torrential rain obscured it. The sound had been subtle, but whatever it was, I was instantly confident that the brief noise was more than just my irrational imagination.

I closed my eyes and focused my senses, but it was no use. Whatever brief surge of nano-augmented ability had granted me visibility into the cave, that ability didn't extend to my hearing. The sound was gone.

Looking back at the scene below, I noticed that Breslin was already putting the sphere back into the wooden case. I wasn't sure what this accomplished.

Then I noticed movement in several of the six holes at the center of the configuration. A sizeable scaly limb emerged from the smoke, filling the three-foot-wide space. Another thick arm followed immediately. They clawed at the earth for leverage and were used to pull a bulky Elend form from the space that had held a Seeley only moments before.

Movement in the other five holes confirmed my suspicion as Elend forms instantly emerged. By my tally, there are two Jays, a Crawler, and three newly discovered Harvesters.

I took a breath and fought back the bile rising in my throat. The world around me spun as my mind grappled with the reality of what was truly happening to all the missing Seeley.

For the Elend to surge in numbers like this…I finally knew what had become of the population of Fresno.

It was time to go. With no idea how I would reach the nearest teleportation platform—only that I needed to more than ever—I placed both hands on the rail beneath me and pushed myself back toward the edge of the hole. Instead of moving across the beam, the beam shifted under me, spinning and sliding in the mud between my ankles.

———————

Sensing the shift of the rail and fearing how much it might continue, I dug my toes into the mud. That's when I realized just how far I had extended myself over the mouth of the cavity. Between my toes, I noticed the end of the beam sinking deeper into the mud at the edge of the gap. Since my shin was hanging over open air, even in my beleaguered state, I was instantly aware that the beam was quickly shifting closer to the edge of the pit and that I was about to plummet into the Elend-filled space below.

I may not have been at my best just then, but it turned out I could still move with the speed, if not the agility, of a monkey. My hands skittered, fingernails digging deeply into soggy bark as I pushed my raised torso backward along the length of the rail with adrenaline-fueled velocity. As I did, two things were captured like freeze-framed photos in my mind. The first was the hundreds of upraised faces of the Elend below, staring at the disturbance I created. The second was the broken, jagged end of the limb I was traversing as it spun from beneath me. Water droplets unfurled from its length as its near end—as thick as my right leg—launched globs of thick clay and mud. I watched as the last fingers of my left hand pushed the descending limb one way and my body spun in the opposite direction.

A half breath later, my face was buried in the mud and clay just inches beyond the mouth of the pit. I was rolling, maybe sliding? Likely both. The only thing I know for sure is that the moment I got my feet beneath me, I was hauling ass. I spotted the backside of the mound and headed toward it. There were three possible exfiltration paths I'd roughly eyeballed earlier. One was preferable to the others simply because it consisted more of earth and clay than rock and stone, so I headed for it.

I made it halfway down the backside of the excavation on my ass—the other half was on my face. The great escape, it was not. But I didn't break anything, and one could argue that I actually descended faster than I would have if I'd been running. If that sounds unlikely…I might have hit my head more than once along the way. Still, it's my story, and I'm sticking to it.

Beyond the base of the excavation lay a mass of felled timber. Entire trees, including their roots, trunks, and canopies, were uprooted from the earth. Hundreds of trees—thousands! Conifers, elms, oaks, and pines all jumbled together, tangled like a careless child had discarded them. I plunged into the field of upended timber at full speed, attempting to lose myself in the chaos. Climbing and ducking among the mess of trunks—some as wide as motorcycles or sedans, while others no thicker than the legs on a bar stool.

Even as I ran, I felt the ground beneath me rumble as the horde of Elend converged on my position from three directions. They had speed and certainly outnumbered me. I knew that the smallest of them weighed more than twice as much as I did. In the field of fallen timber, their size slowed their pursuit, albeit only slightly. Judging by the savage sounds of thrashing and the outright rending of wood, their numbers and fierce intent more than countered this disadvantage.

There was no way I'd make it to a farming facility, so even as I ducked through branches and climbed higher into a tangled pile of horizontally stacked hardwoods, I was starting to question the futility of my efforts. The mud coating my chest, arms, and legs had been washed away by the driving rain, only to be replaced by blood that seemed to flow freely from countless cuts, gashes, and lacerations. Still, I never looked back. Knowing hundreds of the creatures were closing on my position and seeing them remained two separate experiences in my mind, and while I knew the vicious creatures were there, I wasn't willing to stare them down until the very last second.

I was still climbing higher in the stacked timber when a shrieking wail echoed overhead from my right and vanished to my left. The sound emerged from nowhere and disappeared so quickly that I nearly lost my grip and fell backward into the tree clutter. I shook off the strangeness of the noise and forged on with whatever little energy reserves I could muster. The sound seemed to echo in my mind, odd not only for how fast it had appeared, but also because it didn't remind me of any Elend I had experienced before. There was something artificial about the sound—mechanical.

I froze, one arm hooked over the soggy horizontal trunk of a pine tree, and listened. It was there again, somewhere in the distance. It was hard to hear over the driving rain hitting the surface of the tree litter surrounding me. I turned slowly, shifting my head left and then right.

A smile spread across my face for the first time in what felt like a million years. I knew that noise. I had no idea how it could be here now, but I understood what it meant. My gaze shifted to the tangle of bushy limbs I'd relied on to conceal my location from the horde. I could hear the bulk of the assault less than fifty yards below me, and I could see the sky about twenty-five yards directly ahead through a cloudy tangle of green and brown dead branches. The sound was somewhere beyond the tangle, shifting left and right as well as higher and lower than me. It was likely using the position of the horde to estimate my location.

Stopping my vertical ascent for the first time in... forever, I began to move laterally through the tangle of discarded timber. This was slower going than the ascent at first. Then I found the trunk of a massive elm. It lay like a sidewalk through the ruins of its kindred and led me directly to the surface of the tangle of brush.

When I stepped onto the surface, fresh air hit my face, and the torrent of rain rocked me to my core. It wasn't until I took a deep breath of fresh air that I realized how dank and pungently foul the air was within the briar. It wasn't a place where anyone could survive long. Breathing in the rot couldn't be healthy. Then the tangle of limbs trembled beneath my feet, and I heard the scream of the Elend. I had been spotted.

Time's up.

I heard the shrieking buzzing sound more clearly now that I was out in the open, but I still couldn't locate its source. Several dozen yards below me, I could see a tangle of Elend forms flowing across the surface of the bramble. Dozens, maybe a hundred or more, flowed vertically like a prone army directly for me.

A howl of propellers suddenly erupted from directly overhead. It startled me so much that I nearly lost my grip on the thick limbs I had used for support. I glanced up and then over just in time to see the Airbike descend like a falling stone, then shift into a hover about ten feet beyond the tree cover directly in front of me. A slender female figure was at the controls, clad from head to toe in form-fitting armor and a black helmet. That lithe and shapely silhouette could only belong to one person.

The Airbike spun on its axis, presenting the back of the bike. It also lowered a couple of feet as it glided within jumping distance of where I stood. "Move your ass!" Piper yelled.

I didn't need to be told twice. Clearing the gap, I landed hard. My wet feet slipped on the snowmobile-like foot trays, and I mashed my man-bits between me and the seat. My breath caught in my throat, and my eyes filled with tears. I still managed to clamp my hands on Piper's hips. It's a good thing, too. She shoved the handlebars forward and dove us away from the tangle of trees. I looked over my shoulder just in time to see at least three indistinct Elend forms disappearing in the space between us and the briar, screeching and pinwheeling limbs as they plummeted.

Piper goosed the throttle, and our dive transformed into a gliding, rollercoaster-like incline that grew sharper and sharper as we ascended. After ten or fifteen seconds, she leveled us off, banked around into what seemed to be a very specific direction, and engaged the cruise control. This must have been a new feature, as it wasn't something I had when the machine was first built. I'd suggested it to Tripp after my first long flight, but he hadn't gotten around to modifying the last time we talked about it.

Swiping the control on her sleeve, Piper disengaged her helmet. The nanomaterial instantly disintegrated, with the particulate matter vanishing into the collar around her neck. I shifted back in my seat to make room for her and relieve my aching body. She twisted in her seat but couldn't do much more since there was no space to move on the tiny craft. While it could accommodate two people, it wasn't designed to seat them comfortably.

"My God, Gray," she exclaimed, her eyes wide with shock. "You look awful!"

I fought a shiver, likely caused by the chilly air at our altitude, and tried to offer a look that said, *I have no idea what you're talking about.*

She rolled her eyes and passed me a series of interleaved rings. One ring was about as thick as my thumb and had a diameter slightly larger than a dinner plate. Inside was a ring of a slightly smaller diameter, which contained another smaller ring, and so on. I selected the smallest ring from the center and snapped it around my right ankle. The next ring encircled my left ankle. Another wrapped around each knee, while the largest expanded to fit around my waist. One went around each wrist, elbow, shoulder, and the last went around my neck.

Once the rings were in place, I carefully stood on the foot trays of the Airbike and activated the body armor. The nanomaterial swept across my body, forming a snug fit just like Piper's in the blink of an eye. I quickly sat back down and swiped my wrist to disable my helmet. When I looked at Piper, she was clearly focused on something in AR, evident by the distracted gaze characteristic of someone seeing something beyond my view.

Piper's stare quickly shifted back to me. "Your biomarkers are fucked!" she cursed. "Do you know how bad your readings are?"

I shrugged.

She stared at me, slack-jawed, for a couple of seconds. "Your tech isn't supposed to function at these levels," she seemed to struggle to find the words. Maybe she was having a hard time coming up with words longer than four letters. Observing the creases in her face, it might have been a combination of both. "You ran your tech so low that it's actually been drawing power from your body instead of supplementing it." Her jaw waggled as if she were stammering silently. "Gray… that's not supposed to be possible!"

I nodded slowly, taking a few long seconds to absorb her words, appreciate the closest brush with death I'd experienced in a very long time, and recognize that the suit was quickly bringing warmth to parts of my body that hurt in savagely unique ways.

"Do you have anything to say?" She asked after what must have been an interminable silence.

I leaned forward and very close to her. Her eyes were wide and completely filled my vision. I saw them clouded with confusion, concern, and unfortunately, pain. "You saved my life," I said, kissing her softly and gently on the lips. I had a lot more to say. I wanted to ask how she knew the things she did. For example, when had she become an expert on Seeley nanotech? What happened to her fear of flying? How did she find me? And why was my HUD rebooting when I knew for a fact we were currently flying over a dead zone?

Rather than asking all these questions, I concentrated on the kiss. The long-overdue kiss.

Piper eased away from Gray's embrace. Clumsy as it was while half-twisted in her seat on the Airbike, she didn't want to let go. She wiped the driving rain from her eyes and became aware of the smirk stretching across both their faces.

Thank God for the autopilot.

"No more fear of heights?" Gray shouted, his voice rising above the pounding wind and rain that battered them and the vehicle.

Her teeth began to grind, and her knees tightened involuntarily against the sides of the seat. "Priorities," was all she could say. Her gaze shifted to the sky behind Gray and about thirty degrees below them. The already rapid thunder of Piper's pulse in her ears ratcheted to a furious crescendo. "Looks like they're not giving up without a fight," she said, turning back to the controls.

A half-dozen of the largest Elend she had ever seen were moving in from the back, gaining altitude and closing the gap with alarming speed. The second her helmet materialized back into place around her head, Piper double-checked both their airspeed and elevation. Sixty miles per hour had seemed too aggressive given the conditions, so she throttled back to fifty. It reduced the painful impact of the rain to something tolerable and was a good trade, at least until Gray had a chance to suit up.

Four thousand feet had been a calculated risk. If they had ascended any higher, Gray would have been at an increased risk of hypothermia. She had been anxious about him from the moment Doctor Cormac confirmed they had possibly located his position. The flight time to retrieve him had been extremely distracting, her mind a whirlwind of worst-case scenarios, picturing what she might discover upon her arrival. As it turned out, none of them were even close to what she witnessed. Gray appeared beaten and disheveled in a way she could never have imagined. He looked profoundly ill.

"Any time now," Gray said, his voice coming over the helmet-to-helmet comm channel, confirming that he was ready for both speed and altitude.

Piper kicked at a narrow, rectangular compartment recessed into the airframe about six inches from her left boot. The latch popped open, and the lid retracted. "Grab that," she said.

Gray leaned forward and down, returning with a pair of short-barreled rifles. "That's my girl," he laughed. "Let's turn around, then punch it."

She glanced over her shoulder in time to see him sling the spare rifle over his back before spinning a hundred and eighty degrees around on his seat to face rearward. The moment his ass landed back on the seat, her eyes were moving across the HUD and through the menus on the virtual screen. She heard Gray laugh as the restraint system lashed his belt to the bike seat. "Here we go," she bellowed.

Goosing the throttle and pulling back ten degrees on the handlebars, Piper accelerated and launched the flying machine higher into the sky. A moment later, Gray unleashed a three-round burst from the rifle. Even through the wind and rain, Piper felt the report of the gun like a tapping against her back. More shots erupted behind her, then even more.

When Piper sensed movement that she interpreted as Gray swapping the magazine of the first rifle for that of the second, she couldn't help but wonder how many of the flying Elend were pursuing them. Meanwhile, a glowing dot in her HUD indicated the heading to their eventual destination. A distance counter in the corner of her display showed how many miles remained before they arrived. Although it was counting down quickly, she was starting to worry about what would happen if they reached the destination with their pursuers close at heel. "Are you losing your touch back there? Did you forget how to aim?" She chided.

Gray chuckled with sincere, albeit grim amusement, and then fired a single shot. He'd switched to single shot mode as soon as he reached the second magazine. "Not to worry you, but faster would be good," he said.

Swallowing hard, Piper tried to assess just how bad things could be. Concentrating to keep her arms braced and, therefore, the machine steady, she shot a look over her shoulder. The wind buffeted her as she adjusted her aerodynamic profile. The whole Airbike shifted slightly, but since they were flying at just over a hundred and twenty miles an hour, the minor movement felt like hitting a speed bump in the road at a comparable speed.

She saw two things immediately before she regained control of the craft. First, the rifle rocked and fell from Gray's grip, caught by the fierce wind and vanishing without a trace. Second, in the blink of an eye after the rifle was gone, she noticed the indistinct mass of moving bodies perhaps a hundred and fifty yards behind them—an indistinct tangle of approaching heads, bodies, talons, and wings.

Piper stared straight ahead, focusing on the marker in her HUD. She locked her elbows and leaned into the wind. "We have less than six miles to create some distance between us and them," she said through gritted teeth. "Hold on tight."

When Gray said, "do it," she could swear she heard the smile in his voice.

———————

I don't know when she learned to fly the Airbike or what it took to overcome her fear of heights, but it proved something I have never questioned—Piper is a force of nature. Once she spotted the Jays on our tail, she dropped the hammer. Pitching the nose forward, she accelerated to just over one hundred eighty. At that speed and in those conditions, I can't imagine what kind of tech she used to see, but the rainfall was blinding. I had my back to the approaching downpour and was mostly shielded by the slipstream created by her petite frame. Even then, the back of my helmet and shoulders were taking a pounding.

The compartment with the rifles was new. It didn't seem like the kind of thing Tripp would likely add on his own, but once he did, he would be thinking like an engineer. On a machine like the Airbike, that would mean he was looking for balance. With that in mind, I looked for a similar compartment on the opposite side. Sure enough, I found it. It was slightly different—a pair of smaller square shapes rather than a single long rectangle. So, shouldering into the oncoming wind, I leaned over and popped the top on the rearmost cover.

"Hell, yes!" I couldn't help but laugh as I grabbed three loaded magazines and quickly settled back into the center of my seat.

At this point, we were flying like a bat out of hell. The closest of our pursuers was now three hundred and twenty-seven yards behind us. The biggest Jay I'd ever seen was leading the pack, while another was about forty yards behind and off to its side. The rest of the group had fallen back, trailing at nearly three-quarters of a mile. I figured they were getting tired, and I knew Piper was determined to keep our machine at full speed.

I brought the rifle to my shoulder and focused on the nearest Jay through the optics. The wind and rain buffeting the Airbike caused my scope to drift across the face of the Jay in unpredictable ways. Still, I took my time. My breathing slowed, and my vision sharpened. Long seconds passed. There was no way I could make this shot without my tech. It was impossible. I could spray and pray, but what would that get me? I was never a gambler. And if we landed, it would be better to conserve ammo for close-up confrontations. That's when I'd need it more anyway.

For some reason, I wasn't able to let it go. I kept the rifle raised. The face of the massive Jay drifted quickly and wildly across my lens. Nothing short of an eye shot would harm the creature. It was a kill shot or nothing. Beyond long odds at this range when unenhanced. Given my conditions and iffy health, it was impossibly long-range.

Just as I was about to give up, my vision blurred. I blinked quickly to clear the haze. When I did, it felt like the Jay had moved within arm's reach. I immediately understood what had happened, even though I couldn't explain how. My nanotech was back online. I adjusted the rifle sights, and all drift and wobble had disappeared. Only the slightest adjustment of the crosshairs remained as I focused on the reptilian vertical slit of the creature's eye and squeezed the trigger.

The rifle bucked, and I adjusted windage and targeted the lead creature. Perhaps two seconds after the first shot, I fired a second time. When I lowered the rifle, the pair of monsters had simply disappeared.

"You just scared the shit out of me," Piper said in a tone that made it clear she wasn't exaggerating. "Where did you find more ammo?"

"I started thinking like Tripp. Our lead is almost a mile ahead. Where the hell are we?" From what I could see on the map, we were nowhere near any cities. We weren't even heading toward one.

"It should be just enough time," she said. There was no relief in her voice. Piper sounded suddenly exhausted. Clearly, flying under these conditions was taking a toll on her.

When Piper spoke again a few seconds later, I knew she wasn't talking to me. She'd placed me on a shared channel so I could react more quickly when the time came. Whatever was about to happen, she wouldn't have time to explain things before they took place.

"We're coming in fast," Piper said. "And with a lot of unfriendlies in tow. This needs to happen really quickly."

"From what I see, you're taking lessons in understatement from Gray," came Tripp's voice over the channel. His next words cracked, unable to hide his concern. "That's a lot of Elend, and they're moving faster than we thought possible."

"Too fast?" Piper said.

There was a lengthy pause on the line. "Well, it depends on how close you can land. Landing isn't your strongest skill."

I'll admit to feeling a bit of concern when I heard that. I released the seat restraints and spun around to face forward before strapping back down. I put my hands on Piper's hips and was glad to return to a more conventional riding position. "Having trouble with the landings?" I said in my best calming tone.

Piper leaned forward, her shoulder hunched against the relentless wind. "Any landing you can walk away from, right?" she said humorlessly.

Without slowing down, she put the craft into a near dive. We lost a couple of thousand feet in mere seconds. When my brain and insides adjusted to the change, we traveled about eighty miles an hour, just thirty feet above a saturated, dappled green forest canopy. We were moving like a bullet and approaching a vast clearing that was just starting to become visible in the gloom.

"Better open the doors," Piper said.

"Not until you land," a new voice said. It was Lacy.

"Do it now," Piper said confidently. "We're not landing outside."

The statement resulted in confused, hushed conversations on the open channel, followed by some quiet cursing and banging around. The cursing was new. I couldn't recall hearing Tripp or Lacy use those colorful expletives. Whatever they were doing, it wasn't part of the plan. Something urgent and improvised was taking place.

As we swept over the clearing, several agricultural outbuildings came into view. More than half a dozen small structures were positioned haphazardly around the customary transport building closest to the center of the clearing. The two-story steel and glass structure featured wide sliding barn doors across the front and a roof made of semi-transparent panels. Tripp pushed the left door wide open while Lacy pushed the right.

What in the hell are they doing in the field?

Piper throttled back, slowing our forward speed and dropping us vertically as we rapidly closed the distance to the wide open doors at the front of the barn-like building. Both Lacy and Tripp wore masks of concern as we approached with far more speed than they considered safe. Still, Piper wasn't deterred. She arrested our hover, halting just two feet above the ground without cutting our forward momentum. However, she drastically reduced our forward speed when we were about two hundred feet away from the entrance to the barn, slowing from twenty-some-odd miles an hour to a walking pace in the time it took for our friends to cringe and gasp.

Piper swept the Airbike into the barn, smoothly hovered us up the pair of steps onto the platform, and gently set us down before shutting off the propellers. When she did, the caustic shrieks in the distance became immediately audible. Tripp and Lacy stood in the open door, staring frozen, their heads pointed in the direction we had come from. Piper and I darted past them and began closing the barn doors.

This snapped Tripp and Lacy from their trances. They helped us secure the doors. Moments later, the four of us were on the platform with the Airbike, and the sequence was engaged. The room flashed with a pulse of white light and was replaced by a larger room with walls made of a white, glossy, plastic-like material I'd never seen before.

I walked to the platform's edge and looked at the massive, empty room. It was pristine and appeared unused. The walls, floors, and even the ceiling thirty feet overhead looked as if they were coated in some type of plastic-like lacquer or resin.

"Where the hell are we?" was all I could say.

Piper leaned over the semi-inclined bed and watched the slow rise and fall of Gray's chest beneath the blanket. She'd never seen him so peaceful or helpless. As her eyes shifted to the eleven diagnostic displays suspended in augmented space just behind the far side of the bed, she knew he was receiving better treatment than anyone in human history. The displays showed diagnostic information about his blood, respiration, and endocrine system, including data points entirely unknown to her people. In the sixty-eight days Gray had been gone, she'd taken the opportunity to learn all she could about Wild-Side, its people, and their technology. Now, she was glad she had explicitly focused on the minor biological differences between the Seeley and the people from her Brane.

Lacy walked quickly into the room and presented an open palm that held a small, roughly cylindrical device. "Doc Cormac agrees," she said without preamble. "He's upset." Pain was evident in her expression. "We all are. The Doc just can't be here right now."

Piper took the device and removed the protective cap from the end. "No one could have anticipated this. We still don't know what's changed. You'll see—Gray isn't going to be upset. We just need to get him back on his feet."

Even as she spoke the words, Piper hoped she wasn't speaking too soon. Gray had collapsed immediately after making it back through the city walls. He'd been dehydrated and hypothermic. His condition would have been critical under normal circumstances, and without the tech in his blood, he likely wouldn't have survived as long as he had. Still, the tech should never have allowed him to become as sick as he was, so Cormac and his team did the only thing they could under the circumstances and put him into a coma-like state until they could better understand his medical condition.

Piper placed the injector against the side of Gray's neck and her finger against the smooth surface of the trigger button. Only the slightest pop could be heard, followed by a low hiss. Both ends of the device pulsed green and were removed from the surface of his skin. "That's it?" she said with a glance to Lacy.

Lacy nodded. "You just triggered his nanite payload. This batch also contains the code updates you requested."

There was movement beneath Gray's eyelids. Piper saw it and felt her pulse quicken. When the movement paused, her breath caught in her throat, and she waited to hear the warning alarms from the numerous wireless systems monitoring his vitals. A dozen worst-case scenarios suddenly played out in her mind's eye, all of this in the span of three heartbeats.

Then Gray's lips parted for a slow intake of breath. Piper felt as if the world had suddenly begun to spin again. Her hands clutched around his, though she didn't recall grabbing him. Gray's eyes shifted beneath closed lids once more, and then the lids opened. She watched his irises struggle to focus and held her breath again until his head gently turned, and his gaze landed on her. When a smile creased his face, she realized tears were already streaming from the corners of her own eyes.

When Gray spoke, his voice was dry and raspy. "What's all that about?" He didn't seem to notice the sound of his own voice, so intent was his attention on her at that moment.

Piper laughed, an abrupt snort that seemed to say, *seriously, where do I start*? She leaned over him and threw her arms around his neck. "You," she said, trying halfheartedly not to strangle him. "You were gone so long. I thought they'd gotten you."

"Wait." Gray pulled Piper from around his neck and looked at her. She could see the confusion in his eyes and the crease of his expression. He looked down at his own body lying on the bed. "What happened? How long have I been out?"

Lacy appeared at the foot of the bed. "We should go back a bit to explain that," she said. "A lot has happened. First, you've only been here in this bed for—" her eyes drifted up and to the side, as she checked a display only she could see—"twenty-two hours and change."

Piper smiled at the euphemism from back home and thought once more of all the ways Gray had impacted the people of Wild-Side. If she was correct, he was the only one who could save them from what was yet to come.

Continuing, Lacy said pointedly to Piper, "Our assumptions about your disappearance were completely mistaken." She waved her hand in the air, and a large display appeared at the foot of the bed. She shifted to stand shoulder to shoulder with Piper as complicated analytics scrolled across the bottom half of the display far too quickly to read. The top half was divided to showcase a pair of graphs.

"I suggest ignoring the raw data for now," Lacy said. With a flick of her fingers on an upraised hand, the scrolling wall of text was minimized, and the pair of graphs dominated the majority of the display. "You can review the information at your leisure. What's important is this." The left graph was labeled Other-World, and the right was labeled Wild-Side. Piper realized she hadn't actually considered what the Seeley would refer to as Our-World. They certainly couldn't call it Our-World; that really didn't make sense from their perspective.

"Are you familiar with this information?" Lacy said, glancing at Gray. Both graphs displayed exactly the same wavy line; only the numbers on the X and Y axes differed between them. The contours of the line were identical.

Gray rubbed at his fatigued eyes, though Piper could already see more of the man she knew returning to his expression. He looked at

Piper when he spoke. "There's a temporal offset between the Branes," he explained. "It's inconsistent, but we think we might be able to predict it if we gather enough historical evidence. There are two variables we believe have an impact on the offset. One is how long Breslin and I are on either Brane."

"If you're on one longer than he, then he Crosses, it has an impact," Piper added. "If you're on either Brane when he arrives, he alters the calculus. In either case, it's like you told me a long time ago—there's a balance between the two worlds. When one of you Crosses, it impacts that balance. The Offset," she motioned to the screen, "illustrates that through the temporal inconsistency. It's also why we have the unusual storm fronts on Our-World."

Gray glanced between Piper and Lacy. "You've covered a lot of this in a very short time."

Piper shook her head. "Not really. This last time?" She paused and met Gray's gaze, ensuring he could see the pain and worry in her eyes. "You were gone for a hundred and sixty-eight days."

Lacy waved her hand, and the graph on the right side of the screen shifted to reveal a wide, serpentine curve that in no way resembled the shape on the left. "Something has changed," she said. "And we have no idea what."

Whatever I had been injected with was working. Everything that had happened since crossing to Wild-Side felt like a blur, but the injection—or whatever it was—seemed like a nitro shot of espresso for both my mind and body. It was as if half-dormant parts of my body and brain were rebooting and returning to full functionality. Then again, considering the amount of technology pulsing through my blood by that point, it might have been more than just an apt analogy.

"Fulbright," I said, sensing the bewildered gaze of both women as they focused on me with renewed intensity. "He experimented with the formula on himself and ended up in a coma."

Piper's shoulders sagged. She opened her mouth to speak, but no words emerged.

Lacy spoke instead. "When? I mean, when did this happen in your...*time*?"

My time... The offset between Our-World and this place seemed to be more inconsistent...

My memory suddenly became fuzzy, and my head hurt. The room turned blurry, and a sharp pain pierced my skull.

Everything went dark.

Chapter 21 - This Place Is A Study In Repression

Wild-Side

I woke up lying on an anachronistic wheeled gurney, at least by the standards of the Seeley. The blankets draped across me were made of a material that felt like a cotton and wool blend. While this reminded me of home, it was unlike anything I had experienced during my hundreds of Wild-Side trips. I also noted two other key points. First, I was still naked—or maybe naked again? Umm, and second—I was completely clean.

Both observations were disconcerting because a third point surfaced in my mind… I didn't know how I'd ended up in this bunk. My last memory was teleporting to a strange white room on the Airbike with Piper.

After that…

Piper slipped through the narrow gap in the hanging privacy curtain, and I watched as it sealed itself behind her. Aside from that neat little trick, the curtain reminded me of those draping the beds in every emergency room I had ever visited. Here, at least, I wasn't surrounded by a chorus of chirping and beeping medical devices. With only a tall nightstand and a stool, it was just me and the bed. "Welcome back," Piper said. Although her words were succinct and her tone upbeat, the concern in her pinched expression was unmistakable. "Nap time finally over?"

I felt she was asking the wrong person. "How did I get here?" I tried to push myself higher against the slight incline of the bed but discovered I had little strength for the effort.

Piper swiped at something in her private AR display and quickly turned her attention back to me. "I'm bringing your tech back up to full, but at incremental levels. Your strength will return." Her eyes shifted to the empty space over my bed, and I knew she was reviewing information only she could see. "Your diagnostics are out of the red…*finally*. You should be on your feet in a matter of hours."

I rubbed my eyes against the migraine that was gaining steady traction behind my right eye. "I'm gone for a few days, and you got your PhD in nanotechnology?"

Piper eyed me silently for a couple of painfully long seconds. She pulled the stool close to the bed and sat with my hands firmly in hers. I watched as her other hand moved slowly up and down my forearm, her gaze seemingly focused on her fingertips as they shifted the hair on my arm. Her eyes grew moist, and I observed her throat move as she swallowed silently a couple of times before speaking.

"Then it was just a couple of days for you?" She said finally.

I didn't know what to say. I didn't understand what she was trying to tell me or what she was trying to ask. I finally just nodded.

Piper looked me in the eye, her gaze heavy with tears that had yet to break free and fall. "Gray. I haven't seen you in almost five months. I thought you had been captured or killed."

I didn't understand what she was saying, but her expression clearly conveyed the pain of the experience. Given the uncertainty of our situation, it was evident that I had missed a lot. Then, there was the proliferation of the Elend. I didn't know what to say. Instead, I simply sat and pulled her into my arms.

That's when the tears flowed freely. Although she didn't make a sound, she shuddered with deep sobs. All I could do was hold her and absorb that tension and fear. To her, I'd been gone for so long. Clearly, much had happened. She'd been left behind in a strange land—one filled with monsters.

"I'm sorry to interrupt," a weary voice said from a dozen paces away. It was Doc Cormac, watching us over the top of his glasses with tired, bloodshot eyes. I sensed he had been there for a while, likely unwilling to disrupt this long-overdue moment. "Should I come back later?"

I felt Piper's warm breath on my neck. She kissed me on the cheek and gently pulled away. I heard an exhausted wheeze that sounded like a laugh and felt her wipe hot, wet tears from my neck and collarbone. I'm not sure all of them were hers.

"It's okay, Doc," she said. "No time like the present."

Doctor Cormac pulled another stool into my...*cocoon*? I'm not sure what to call it, but watching the curtain seal itself behind him seemed like an appropriate name. While it was far more efficient than the curtains used around beds back home, this automation was creepy. "I reviewed the diagnostic report on the way over," he said. "I agree with your estimates for recovery time and the adjustments needed to prevent this parasitic response in the future." He shifted on the stool and sighed as he looked me in the eye deliberately. "Very glad to have you back, by the way. You were sorely missed."

I had a lot of questions at that moment, but the phrase *parasitic response* instantly moved to the top of my list. Unfortunately, Piper seemed to think my absence was a higher priority and beat me to the punch with her own concerns.

"Only a couple of days passed for Gray," she said, leveling a sharp glare at Cormac.

Cormac appeared ready to speak, but this statement caused him to pause, his mouth half-open in preparation. He was so caught off guard that he didn't move for two or three seconds. Finally, he closed his mouth and lowered his head. He seemed to gaze at the floor when he spoke. "Days?" he said in a quiet voice. "How many?"

Piper looked at me. I thought I had already explained this, but it occurred to me that I hadn't been specific. "Five or six? I'm not sure. I was running without sleep, so it started to blur together. I wasn't feeling well, either. I think I was coming down with something, but it could have been the fatigue. I was feverish and lightheaded a lot of the time near the end of it."

As I said it, I began to wonder why I wasn't more concerned about it when it was happening. I couldn't remember the last time I'd been sick. Even when I'd been stabbed or run through by an Elend, I didn't feel that bad. I wasn't firing on all cylinders, that was for sure.

"It clarifies what was missing in the diagnostic logs," Piper said.

This drew Cormac's gaze away from the floor. He nodded quickly. "Absolutely. It's what you and Tripp theorized, just on a larger scale since he wasn't sleeping and because the offset was much larger than we ever considered."

Piper was nodding. She was conversing with Cormac using technical jargon that I'd never heard, and at speeds I couldn't maintain. They were animated and seemed to be making progress on whatever thought process they were pursuing, so I was hesitant to interrupt. But when I heard the phrase "parasitic response," yet again, I had to speak up.

"What does that mean?" I asked, interrupting their fast-paced conversation. "What's this parasitic response you've mentioned a few times? Did I catch a bug?"

Doctor Cormac removed his glasses and rubbed his eyes slowly. "In a way," he said, his tone weary. "But it was a bug we gave you inadvertently." To my surprise, he signaled to Piper to continue the explanation. I think this is when it hit me for the first time just how much Wild-Side had impacted her.

I would soon discover how much she had impacted Wild-Side.

"Like all the tech here," Piper began, "the nanotech draws power from various sources. In the cities, there are wireless power emitters broadcasting energy. It's similar to how we use radio waves back home. Almost everywhere we go, we're surrounded by radio waves in one form or another. Some broadcast on a certain channel. It doesn't matter; there's always someone broadcasting somewhere. Here, it's the same thing… except it's not music, talk radio, or NPR. It's energy. Ubiquitous, clean energy. Free for everyone. It's just the way it is."

"Except in the dead zones," I said.

Piper nodded. "That's why Seeley technology doesn't work there. However, you addressed the issue when you showed Tripp our battery technology. It was a workaround to keep your machine operational in areas where their technology typically struggled."

I smiled. "Tripp said it was extremely inefficient."

Piper rolled her eyes. "Wait until you see what he's done with it while you were gone." She waved her hands at the overhead lighting and then instantiated two AR displays into a shared space above the middle of my bed. They showcased my medical stats and what I could only guess were similar technical vitals for my nanosystems.

"All of this right now?" She laughed. "Would you believe we're in the middle of one of the oldest known dead zones?"

I rubbed at my temple and the migraine beneath it. "Clearly, I've missed a lot."

Piper spread her hands and pulled the AR display closer. She expanded the skeletal view of my head until it was twice the size of a basketball. After a few quick adjustments, a glowing pink mass became visible behind my right eye. "There it is," she said. "Once you're back to one hundred percent, the autonomous algorithms will kick in. Until then, your tech needs a little manual guidance." She tapped the pink mass with her fingers and adjusted a nearby slider on the interface. The pain behind my eye instantly began to diminish.

"The nanotech is distributed throughout your entire body," Piper explained. "It was designed to draw power like everything else on Wild-Side, from the ubiquitous energy surrounding…everything. Like everything else, the tech loses power when you're in the dead zones. Still, it's not typically a problem for nanotech because, in aggregate, the nanites carry enough juice to keep themselves running for days. Long enough that it has never been an issue before. Plus, they gain a fair amount of power from your body. Motion, nutrients, and all the body's biological processes supplement the tech. Since the nanites are designed to pull power from different sources, they are resilient.

"What no one ever really considered was what would happen if you didn't return to Wild-Side for an extended time. Since you got the tech, you've been bouncing back here every night, or at least every other night. It's been more than enough to maintain a balance."

"Until I didn't," I said.

"Until you didn't return for several days," Piper said. Judging by the expression on her face, something had just occurred to her. "What happened? What kept you from coming back?"

"Fulbright." A sharp pain spiked behind my eye again, but Piper quickly alleviated the discomfort. "He underwent the experimental treatment and entered a coma. From what I can gather, I think he might have crossed over—only, unlike me, he didn't take his body. I had to place him on life support and hide him somewhere safe. If Breslin's people back home find him, he'll be much closer to discovering how to bring his creatures into Our-World."

Cormac suddenly appeared both excited and uncomfortable. "Do you think one of your people crossed over?"

I shrugged. "I can't say for sure. That's not how it works for me. He apparently lobotomized himself. We experienced similar atmospheric effects, which makes me think something related occurred. It's the only thing that makes sense."

Cormac sat on the edge of his chair. "I think we're more than halfway to making sense of things," he said quietly. "This could explain why the offset has shifted so dramatically." I was about to ask a question, but he stopped me by raising a hand. "You've been coming here for some time," he said, glancing at me. "There was consistency in your visits, and during that time, only you and Breslin could move between Branes. Based on this, we established the offset. It wasn't completely consistent, but I believe the inconsistency we experience is directly related to when you and Breslin are on or off a given Brane simultaneously. Since Breslin's location is largely unknown, it's been difficult to validate the theory.

"Now, though, Piper is here. If my theory is correct, that will impact the offset. There are three people affecting the natural balance between Branes and, therefore, the offset. Your absence for this long," he said again, meeting my eye, "added support to my suspicion that some form of natural balance was being disturbed. But if Doctor Fulbright has crossed over as well? The calculus becomes even more complex. Add to that your going days without sleep? We're dealing with far too many variables. There's simply no way to determine how long it will be before you bounce back to your Brane or how much time will pass here by the time you return next."

I shook my head. The offset was bad enough, but the parasitic response seemed to be the more immediate concern. Understanding that would be key to remaining functional if I was away from Wild-Side for an extended period of time. "You said my tech could draw power from different sources. Why was being away longer a problem if that's the case?"

Feeling more uncomfortable, Cormac opened his mouth to speak but hesitated before voicing his thoughts. "When it can't draw zero-point energy here, the nanotech in your body wasn't able to identify additional sources to maintain coherence," he said at last. "When that happened, it resorted to drawing chemical energy. In this case, your own biology." He paused once more. "It became, in essence, parasitic."

Super.

Piper placed her hand on my arm. "But now that we understand it, we can correct it. There's no shortage of energy at your disposal back home. We just need to teach your tech how to use it." She suddenly looked uncomfortable at the end of her statement, so I waited for her to clarify it. "Well," she added with a sheepish expression, "to be honest, that modification will fall on Esker. We can provide the problem statement. He'll need to adjust your tech once you've crossed back. The information needed to make those adjustments isn't available to us on this side."

I had at least a dozen questions, but the more I considered Piper's words, the more they made sense. She was suggesting what I assumed to be a highly technical adjustment to my onboard tech. That would require a high degree of precision. If my nanotech couldn't access zero-point energy on our Brane the same way it did here, it suggested there was some subtle—if not fundamental—difference in the laws of physics that shifted between Branes.

It was a technically slippery slope I wasn't qualified to navigate.

"Got it," I replied. "Esker is going to flash my firmware."

Cormac's brows arched, and his gaze drifted slowly between me and Piper. Confusion was written across his face. Piper grinned and nodded. "Pretty much," she said with a reassuring nod toward Cormac, indicating that I was grasping the point they were trying to make. I don't think Cormac understood, but he blinked, hesitated, and shrugged it off.

The issue seemed to be resolved.

Over the next two days, Piper gave a tour of Garwin. The underground city was expansive, though somewhat primitive by Seeley standards. This was because the facility was the first complex their people used before branching out to expand their presence across the continent. Once their first above-ground city was constructed, the Seeley never looked back. The other four cities followed just a dozen years later, and Garwin was largely forgotten. I found only a brief mention of the underground first city in Seeley historical records shortly after meeting Cormac and earning his trust.

Oddly, references to the city suggested it had been abandoned due to flooding and the facility's location in a geologically unstable region. The city had been mothballed. Although it had suffered from centuries of neglect, it was no longer flooded, and the damage from that event and time seemed to have been repaired. As Piper had explained, it seemed more likely that those with influence over the Seeley had simply led their people to above-ground cities, allowing the first underground city to slip into obscurity.

Needless to say, this struck me as odd. A race of people only a single generation old willing to relegate their first home to history, all of them unclear about the fate of that first home, felt alien. This seemed to complement the fact that they didn't know where they'd come from—other than that they were the Seeley, and Wild-Side was their home.

Piper shared my views. After spending months among these people, she immersed herself in their science-based culture. Finally, she understood everything I had tried to explain about them since I first told her about my ability to Cross back when I unexpectedly disappeared from her bed shortly after we had met.

"I can't believe you finally got them to approve the perimeter guns," I said after Piper showed me the line of camouflaged Gatling guns near the entrances to the underground city. "I tried for months. There was endless resistance."

It was nearly midnight, and there was no moon. Piper was guiding me through patches of tangled thorn bramble. This part of the continent didn't have much tree cover. The ground was cluttered with shrubs that ranged in size from a washing machine to a small two-story house. They resembled thick tangles of vines, with little leaves wreathing the twisted strands. It was the first type of vegetation I'd encountered here that wasn't equivalent back home.

"I think your disappearance prompted even the most reserved to truly open their eyes," Piper said as she guided me through the night. "Even your critics were depending on you to handle the Elend. When you vanished, they saw it as a wake-up call." She paused and looked at me. "It's true. I witnessed it firsthand."

When I returned, something had undoubtedly changed. The people who had gone out of their way to avoid me no longer seemed to make the effort. In the cafeteria, I received no more accusatory glares from countless judging faces. But it was more than that. The group as a whole was behaving differently. I couldn't quite put my finger on it… though that might have been due to my lack of effort. I had long since given up even trying to reach out.

I was tired of falling short. The Seeley, by and large, were a stubborn people set in their ways. I had been dealing with a race so averse to change that they would rather let the Elend whittle away at their numbers than choose to stand up and fight.

"You finally made it through," Piper said. "It just happened when you weren't paying attention."

I didn't understand.

"You introduced them to art, music, and film—every form of creativity they lacked. You helped broaden their horizons."

"I tried," I said with a shrug. "Almost all of them ignored what I had to offer. Wasted effort."

Piper laughed, looped her arm through mine, and encouraged me to walk slowly. She rested her head on my shoulder as we strolled. "It wasn't wasted," she murmured. I could feel the warmth of her body next to mine, and it felt like home in so many ways. "Do you think the Seeley are any less curious than our people?"

I took it as a rhetorical question, so I didn't reply. The truth is, I didn't know what to think. The Seeley were fiercely intelligent, and I knew that without question. A few, like Cormac and his team, were inquisitive as well. But the rest had resisted every effort to bond with them or inspire them. They'd even resisted efforts to empower them to defend themselves and their neighbors. I'd reached out to them intellectually, emotionally, and logically. Every attempt had failed.

"All they needed was time," Piper continued.

"Time has always been our greatest disadvantage. That and patience. I was never known for my patience."

"Meaning?"

"Does it feel like people are different around you since you've been back?" I glanced over to see her peering into my eye.

"Reading my mind again?"

Piper laughed. "Your data dumps became the talk of the town in your absence. Everyone was buzzing about it. Listen to this…watch that…what do you think about this or that? All that intellectual property you took from Our-World? It actually has a massive impact over here. It just took a little time."

We were walking again. I didn't know what to say. "Really? That, along with me being gone."

"That too," she admitted. "I think a fair number of folks were already looking through your data. They just didn't admit it until you were gone. When you disappeared, people were unsettled. That upset got them talking. When they started talking, they needed a way to express their unease. I think that brought them back to what you left."

"And?"

"I've seen people sketching," Piper said. "A couple of people were trying to paint–Tripp has been approached twice to make musical instruments."

I stopped walking and gazed at Piper. Her eyes were wide and sparkled with amusement. "You did that," she laughed. "Well, you and the material you stole and smuggled here."

Nodding, I said, "Those who can, do. Those who can't, steal."

Adopting a suddenly serious expression, Piper stepped closer and shook her head with a frown of concern. "But seriously, Gray. What were you thinking when you gave them access to all that porn? We need to talk about it."

I exhaled slowly. "That didn't go over too well? It was a gamble," I admitted. As I bought time for a more thoughtful response, I noticed a change in the vegetation. An open patch of bare dirt lay between a trio of similarly shaped, school bus-sized shrubs.

She leaned in close and brought her mouth near my ear. "Worse. It's like a city full of teenagers discovering their naughty bits for the first time. They can't seem to decide if they want to play with themselves or with each other. These people are adults, yet they're behaving like hormonal teens." She glared at me. "What were you thinking?"

Grinning, I didn't know what to say. Never sure what to expect, this wasn't it. At some point, I started laughing. I think it was the mental picture of what she'd been dealing with while I'd been gone. It must have been...*unique*.

"These people," Piper began, "were as virgin as freshly fallen snow. Do you know what you turned them into?"

I was still laughing.

"It's not funny. From an anthropological perspective, do you understand the impact you've had on the developmental trajectory of this society?"

I nodded. "Hopefully, I've pulled the stick out of its collective ass. This place is a study in repression."

With that statement, Piper really glared at me. "Personally, I'm tempted to agree with you. Professionally, do you think imposing your values on an entire society is right?"

Wait...

"My values? I brought them insights into creativity through exposure to art and music."

With her hands on her hips, Piper was already shaking her head. "Maybe they would've developed that on their own in another hundred—" Her eyes shifted to the side as if deep in thought. "Well, maybe a couple of hundred years."

"If they live that long," I countered. "With the Elend threat, they can't last. I needed to accelerate their development so they could see what they're missing. They needed something to fight for. I wanted to infuse their humanity with a sense of purpose. It was a long shot, but it was worth a try."

"Yes," she replied, exasperated. "But why is it your responsibility to try?"

Meeting her gaze, I said, "It's the same reason I came here in the first place. You're asking a question I can't answer. Whether it's bad luck or good, I'm here, and it feels like I'm the only chance these people have." I reconsidered that last statement and placed my hands on her shoulders. "Well, now it's you and me. For once, I'm not feeling so alone."

Something about that took the wind out of Piper's sails. She froze with her mouth open, ready to deliver a retort, her eyes locked with mine. I watched as they pinched. Something was about to happen...I just had no idea what. Only a dozen heartbeats later, those eyes filled with tears, and her mouth closed so tightly that her jaw clacked.

Not knowing what to say, I said nothing. I just waited.

Piper heaved a shuddering breath. "You and I?" Her voice was barely more than a whisper. "We're in this together?"

Nodding, I said, "I hope so. I accidentally brought you here, but you're clearly better at all of this than I am. I'm lost without you—both here and in the real world. I hope you know that."

I haven't a clue what happened next. It was the best missing time of my life, though. The next thing I knew, she was in my arms and her mouth on mine. For once I said something the way I meant it, and it's a good thing because something about our relationship changed in that moment. Years later, that instant stands out in my mind—it was one of those pivotal points in our story. Don't get me wrong. Regardless of that moment, we would have gotten to where we ended up. It just would have happened somewhere else and *somewhen* else. We were ready.

I just know I wouldn't change anything about that instant.

"So, seriously," Piper said as we walked back to the entrance of the underground elevator. "Do I need to worry about all that porn? From what I understand, there was a lot."

I laughed. "So you're concerned, but you never even looked at it?" I shook my head, debating whether to use this to provoke her. Given the moment we'd just experienced, I thought better of it. It was best to be straightforward. "I used a curator for that."

"Wait, *what*?"

"Your buddy Jimmy Kell from school," I clarified. "He was always into that kind of stuff, remember?"

She appeared confused but eventually nodded. I could tell she recalled more than one conversation about Jimmy's preferences from back in the day.

"He's working for some big website now. Apparently, they aggregate that content. It's all categorized, classified, and tagged based on dozens of criteria. When I told him I needed material for a friend's sex training boot camp, he only asked for filtering criteria. He provided terabytes of...*material*."

Piper appeared stunned. "Do I even want to know what criteria you used?"

I shrugged. "To your point, I didn't want to traumatize these people. It's nothing too kinky or wild. The idea was to provide them with a kickstart guide to help them get going. There's nothing there that should require trauma therapy. Training wheels. You know?"

She didn't seem happy with this answer, but she was content to let the matter go. "Jimmy was a weird guy. Are you sure he didn't put anything strange in there just to mess with people?"

I pointed to the trio of oblong trees evenly spaced around the patch of earth where we were standing. Kicking the dirt, I said, "I think there's something buried here."

Looking confused at first, Piper stared at the dirt for a long moment before scanning the inky darkness around us. She pointed at one of the bushes I had noticed; it was at our eleven o'clock position. Then she moved to direct my attention to the matching one at our five o'clock. Tilting her head toward the third, she said, "Good eye. The vent for the city's power generation system is under our feet. I guess it was a geothermal system from their earliest days, mothballed when they harnessed zero-point energy."

———————

Lacy led us through a series of plain concrete corridors deep beneath even the city's lowest level. "The technology was crude," she explained as we walked. "It's inefficient compared to our current power sources." The path turned sharply, and she selected the new hall with just a brief pause to check her bearings. "Geothermal energy is still common on your world?"

Piper nodded. "One of our most reliable and cost-effective sources of power."

Lacy nodded while waving a hand vaguely in the direction we were moving. "It powered this entire city for over a decade," she said, her tone carrying a sense of resignation.

As we stepped into a lobby-like space with ten-foot-tall concrete walls, we eyed the wide silver door at the center. It stood about ten feet tall and was equally broad. The steel surface gleamed dully under the beams of our flashlights. It resembled a combination of a bank vault door and a blast door. A tablet-sized touch screen was mounted at shoulder height along the left edge.

Lacy placed her hand against the small panel. A dull glow pulsed slowly in response to her touch. "Access was tightly controlled even back then," she explained. "It wasn't for security. The chamber beyond the door is under tremendous pressure at times. Someone breaching this seal at the wrong moment could seriously damage the bedrock beneath the city's lowest level."

"Pressure?" I said.

A chime signaled, and Lacy stepped away from the door. A hiss was audible as the seal parted between the door and its frame in the wall. "No one has been in here for—" she paused and tilted her head in consideration. "Well, it's been hundreds of years at the very least."

The door swung open quietly on automated hinges that seemed quite sturdy. It was approximately two feet thick and appeared to be made of steel. Together, the three of us stepped into the doorway and directed our lights into the dark emptiness.

"Give me a minute," Lacy said as she turned and stepped backward down a wide ladder at the base of the door. It was nearly invisible in the darkness.

Her head was the last to disappear into the space as she descended the ladder. Her movement on the rungs created a hollow sound that seemed to help me perceive the expanse of space beyond the door. There was a scraping sound, a thud, and then Lacy said, "Oh, right. Here." She appeared to be fumbling in the darkness.

A pale glow emitted from high above in the space. It slowly grew in intensity, likely allowing our eyes to adjust to the change with minimal discomfort. As the light increased and spread, we started to grasp the expansive cavern beyond the vault door.

"Holy crap," Piper muttered just before the light reached its full intensity. Even at its brightest setting, the illumination felt like only half of what was used indoors throughout the city. The vast cavern had glossy black walls that seemed to absorb the light.

"This is the pressure chamber," Lacy said after Piper and I descended the same ladder she had used. She directed her light beam at the floor beneath our feet before kneeling to run her fingertips along the surface. "Do you feel the texture?"

Piper and I bent down and ran our hands over the uneven surface of the floor.

"That finish," Piper said slowly. "It's not stone."

I shook my head. "No. But there's a consistency to it. Some kind of coating over the rock?" It was a guess. I had never seen—or felt—anything like it. The surface of the rock beneath us felt man-made.

"Compression chambers," Lacy explained. "They are randomly sized and spaced in a roughly honeycomb pattern. Each chamber varies in size, with the largest being about half the size of a grain of rice and the smallest exactly one-third the size of the largest."

I directed the light's cone of illumination across the floor and up the wall at the base of the vault door. The pale light was dull enough that my beam provided definition, showing a visible cone in the faint glow of the space. The walls were constructed from the same engineered material as the floor.

When I turned back, Piper shone deeper into the expansive cavern. Although the glare faded into darkness about a dozen feet away, my eyes had adjusted. The cavern's distant wall was roughly a hundred yards straight ahead, while the ceiling loomed nearly a hundred feet overhead. I noticed the cavern floor slanted downward and further underground to my right, whereas the opposite direction tilted more steeply toward the surface.

Following my upward gaze, Lacy explained, "Fifty yards that way, the cavern narrows sharply into a tunnel about thirty feet in diameter. It extends all the way to the surface and ends at a retractable panel beneath that patch of earth you can see in the shrubs. It's an emergency pressure release and has thankfully never been used. That panel is exactly as thick as the door," she pointed to the still-open vault door set into the nearest wall, fifteen feet above our heads.

"That way," she pointed to the yawning darkness where the cavern appeared to descend even further into the bedrock. "Leads to the magma chamber. It's about a quarter-mile walk from here, though the chamber is small compared to this," she said, waving her hand in the direction of the immediate ceiling. "The premise was simple. An automated system would adjust valves over the surface of the molten pit to control the heat entering this chamber. Hundreds of tiny valves placed throughout this larger chamber regulate the release of aerosolized water. With these two systems, an automated mechanism gently raises and lowers the pressure within this chamber. The honeycomb of cells embedded in every inch of every surface generates a tiny electric current in response to the pressure fluctuations. That power flows from the cavern into batteries located elsewhere in the facility."

Piper and I exchanged brief glances before our eyes shifted to various spots in the cavern. There had to be millions of square feet of the honeycombed material overall.

"Each tiny cell generates a small amount of current in response to even the slightest change in air pressure," Lacy explained. "The chamber as a whole has been engineered to shift pressure constantly between optimal tolerances. Essentially, the walls, floor, and ceiling surfaces generate a massive amount of aggregate energy at a consistent rate."

———————

Everywhere I looked, it felt like I was seeing a different version of Wild-Side. People weren't avoiding me; well, they were still avoiding me, but they didn't go out of their way to do it. When they stepped aside, they did it while meeting my gaze. The whispers behind my back were noticeably different, too. Everything about the experience was less hostile or dismissive. It felt as if they were reevaluating me, unsure of what to say or do after keeping me at arm's length for so long.

"Do you think they're really acting differently?" Piper asked as she led me through a door at the far end of the cafeteria. We both glanced over our shoulders and saw dozens of eyes following us silently as we walked. "Never mind," she said. "I get it."

Tripp had something interesting he needed to show us. Apparently, there was some urgency, so Piper showed me a shortcut to the lab that Tripp and Cormac had set up somewhere deep in the heart of the underground facility. The urgency expressed in his request was concerning, but the expressions I saw on everyone we passed were disconcerting. It served as a constant reminder of just how long I'd been gone, and likewise, how things had changed in my absence.

"You think you get it," I grumbled. "For months, most of these people acted like all the problems were due to my presence. Then I'm gone for a while, and they finally start to see that I've been trying to help?" I was frustrated, but in reality, it was tempered with a degree of respect for how everyone on Wild-Side had had their lives turned upside down. The Elend posed a direct threat to their entire existence.

Who could relate better than me?

Piper's hand slipped into mine as we walked. She leaned in close, her voice lowering. "When I get home, I'll be able to write a doorstop of a book based on what I've learned here. Anthropologically speaking, these people are truly one of a kind. Their society developed without any central religious component. Do you realize how unique that is?"

The question made my stomach flip-flop, and it took me a moment to unpack exactly which part of the statement had caused my gears to grind. How Piper had landed on Wild-Side remained a mystery, and I worried that getting her home again might be an even more significant challenge. But after pondering it for a few strides while we continued down the underground corridor, I realized my consternation was based on another part of the statement. "You would publish? I mean, about your experience here?" I didn't know how to feel about that.

She glanced at me sideways and gave a subtle shrug. "It's not like I gave it much thought," she admitted. "What we're witnessing? It's unprecedented. No one has ever encountered a people like the Seeley. There's so much to explore—not just what's happening now, but what they are—why they are. They're like a pristine, unblemished society that's as close to utopia as anyone can imagine. Well," she waved her free hand in the air to indicate the stark white walls of the underground hallway and, presumably, the unusual living conditions tied to them. "Current apocalypse notwithstanding, of course."

She was right in too many ways. This point had been swirling in my mind the more I thought about the artifacts quietly stashed away in that undisclosed location with the blue orb.

We traversed half a dozen halls and took two elevator rides before reaching Tripp's lab. We stepped through the sliding security doors into the sterile environment with its ubiquitous white walls, glossy floors, and stainless steel counters and tables. I was surprised to find most of the core team present. Doc Cormac sat slouched in an ergonomic chair on wheels. Lacy perched on the end of a metal counter that was completely devoid of equipment. Tripp stood close beside her, absentmindedly wringing his hands. Wes was at the back of the room, packing pieces of some complicated technical gear into a protective crate. He looked up when we entered and offered a tired half-smile. Everyone wore expressions of exhaustion while trying to convey warmth. Their smiles were mere shadows of those I'd seen in the past, hinting at either fear or trepidation. This sight was enough to freeze Piper and me in our tracks.

"This isn't going to be good news," was all I could think to say.

Cormac stood and waved us into the room. "Actually, it's very good news." The smile that crossed his face was genuine for the first time since we entered. Still, the expressions of everyone else tempered his enthusiasm.

Wes called Tripp to the back of the room, and the two of them pulled a large component from another crate. I had been wrong. He wasn't securing gear; he had been unpacking it. They quickly lifted a curved beam in a half-moon shape and attached it horizontally to a pair of stanchions.

"Some new information was included in the recent transmission from Esker," Cormac explained. "He made an interesting observation. We need to conduct more precise scans to reconcile the telemetry we've already reviewed from the logs on our end." By saying our end, of course, he was referring to Wild-Side.

I knew this was the cause of the distress I was seeing in everyone present. Piper clearly did too. She stepped slowly forward, her hands balled into fists at her sides. "What did you find?"

Cormac's gaze shifted from Piper to me, then back and forth once more. The seconds of silence felt suffocating. I knew that what came next had the potential to change the game; it was just a matter of how and for whom.

"It would be better if we completed the scan first," Cormac said in a low, dry tone.

Piper turned to me. "All of this," she said—her eyes were already growing thick with tears. "Is it making you sick?"

I swallowed and tried to maintain a confident expression. The idea didn't surprise me. What I was doing certainly wasn't normal. I always thought it would get me killed one day. The thought that it could lead to a medical condition—a potentially fatal one—had never been far from my mind. Nodding toward Cormac, I said, "They're worried about more than just me. This is bigger."

Wes said the scanner was ready, so I approached the device. The curved bar began to hum, and everyone in the room retreated to the farthest wall. Then, the bar took a few seconds to perform what I was told was a calibration routine. It descended to the bottom of the frame from which it had been suspended. Slowly and methodically, the bar passed from my feet to my head, then returned to my feet again. It stopped at the floor, and the skeletal machine fell silent.

"You can step away now," Tripp said.

Doc Cormac was already standing at the counter near the center of the room, manipulating a complex diagnostic display in shared AR space. He swiped and flipped through screens too quickly for me to grasp what I was seeing. The information was so technical that it wouldn't have mattered if he'd done it more slowly. After about thirty seconds, he paused the rapid screen switching. A thick horizontal progress bar hung in space for everyone to observe.

My gaze shifted to Piper, and she met my eyes. Through unspoken understanding, we both recognized that whatever everyone was worried about depended on the information conveyed by that single progress bar. All we could do was wait. Somehow, this made the progress indicator seem to drag on.

Piper's hand found mine as I wrapped my arms around her. With my attention on her, I didn't care how long the bar took or what sort of news it brought. My focus was on her eyes and the pouty curve of her lips. In that moment, it didn't matter where I was or what was happening, as long as we were together.

A chime sounded, and it felt like the entire room began to breathe again. Piper and I turned back to the room. "Will you finally tell us what the hell this is all about?"

Cormac waved his hand, and the AR display vanished. He leaned against the counter. When he removed his glasses and wiped his tired eyes, he appeared to sag physically. "We know how to send you both back home. Esker figured out how to control the Transition."

"Freaking hell," I bellowed. "I thought I was dying!"

Everyone stared at me. No one spoke.

Rubbing my eyes, I said, "Esker? Did he figure out how to get us home?" I suddenly felt challenged for words. Hundreds of questions jockeyed for position in my mind, but none seemed to find the off-ramp leading to my mouth.

Piper appeared completely bewildered. She simply stared.

"As unlikely as it sounds, even with access to much more primitive technology," Cormac said, "yes."

"Your AI used multi-frequency backscatter radiation," Tripp said, emphasizing the point. "What it lacks in access to resources, it more than compensates for with its data analysis."

"He," I clarified.

Cormac and Tripp tilted their heads at me in confusion. Their expressions matched those of curious dogs.

"Esker," I clarified. "He prefers to be referred to as 'he.' He finds 'it' disrespectful."

Tripp's brows furrowed, a distant look in his eyes. Something about my statement seemed to resonate with him. I could practically see his attention drift away. It was an experience I had encountered many times before. Something had just ignited his creativity.

Cormac nodded. "Fascinating," he chuckled, a glimmer of light brightening his expression for the first time since Piper and I arrived at the lab. "He," Cormac emphasized, "observed a shift in the electromagnetic field surrounding your body in the picoseconds before your Crossing. This isn't something that would typically be detectable without highly specialized equipment. However, based on the information provided by Esker, most of the environments in Your-World appear to be saturated with various radio frequency spectrums. After gathering enough data across multiple Transitions, Esker managed to identify the signature linked to your Shift.

I grinned. "And with that information, you can replicate it," I finished. "Are you saying we can finally control it?"

Cormac nodded, though he didn't appear to be thrilled with the idea.

"What's wrong with that?" Piper asked. "If it can be controlled, can't I go home? Can't Gray come and go whenever he wants for a change?"

Tripp was nodding, but he didn't seem any more excited than Cormac.

Piper's gaze shifted to me.

I nodded, "This is what Breslin has been hunting for. What they just explained—it's the key he needs to bring his Elend army to Our-World."

The room fell silent for a long time. Tripp broke the tension by sending a photo into AR space for everyone to see with a dramatic wave of his hand. "Esker sent this," he said. "He believes Breslin will try to use it to create something similar."

The photo was a screen capture Gray recognized instantly: a cavernous room with concrete walls outfitted with stainless steel tables topped with high-tech instrumentation. Men and women in white lab coats were captured in the freeze-frame as they attempted to scatter to the room's periphery. Near the center of the image was a low, oblong table, bookended on one side by a tall, free-standing, mirror-like frame and on the other by a softball-sized orb resting on a squat pedestal. Tripp's fingers tapped something invisible in the air, and the photo was enhanced to improve sharpness and visibility. The image, I knew, had been captured in less-than-ideal lighting conditions.

I stepped closer to the screen and ran my fingers over the stubble of the short hair on my head. Eyeing the image, I said, "This is from one of my operations against Breslin back home. He had a team conducting a test in an underground silo in Kansas. Esker thinks this experiment is significant?"

"It is," Piper said, stepping forward and leaning into the image. Everyone in the room focused on her. I realized this and understood I was the one who was missing something.

Tripp nodded. "Esker found schematic drawings and documentation on one of Breslin's corporate servers. There were references to something he learned here, which was the source of what the team was trying to reproduce on your Brane," he explained. "Esker discovered only technical documentation. There was no other information linking to what Breslin found or the source of his insights."

"But we know," Piper added. She waved a hand through the air to dispel the freeze-frame image and replaced it with a three-dimensional, photorealistic depiction of the cavern's interior. Human bodies littered the edges of the space, toppled and collapsed like dolls tossed aside by a petulant child—dolls ravaged by something superhuman. Near the center of the space was a now-familiar arrangement of a stout oblong table, an upright rectangular door-like frame, and a tripod topped with a glassy spherical orb.

Piper spread her hands, and the photo zoomed in. As it did, it transformed into a wireframe, encompassing almost the entire room where we stood. The apparatus at the cavern's center was now life-size, positioned on the lab's floor. The contrast between the sterile, clinical space and the savage killing site sent a chill down my spine. I was grateful that Piper had thought to change the capture to wireframe. We didn't need to know what the rest of the team might have done if they'd been so quickly immersed in that imagery.

That Piper had so swiftly and efficiently manipulated Seeley technology was yet another reminder of just how long I had been gone. Days for me were so much longer for her. Once again, I questioned what she had experienced while I had been away.

Looking at the wire mesh surrounding my knees and ankles, I noticed that the mesh representation blanketed the rest of the room. The detritus littering the cave floor had been captured in precise detail. So too had each fallen body—the victims of the expedition who had presumably been present at the start of all this. I could see the contours of their protective gear, the tears in their armor and flesh, even the jagged ends of broken bones. It was all rendered in colorless, vector detail, thankfully. The apparatus was old—ancient-looking, yet clearly still functional if it had been the tool used to facilitate all of this.

Then, I observed the upright figures standing at attention along the cavern's wall. Three erect forms were captured at the far edge of the depiction: a man and two women. They appeared anachronistic as they remained unharmed and intact, with their armor—

I stepped closer to one of the female forms and noted that the wireframe rendering instantly resolved into a higher resolution in response. It was still far from photo-realistic, but the contours of the form-fitting body armor left no doubt about the wearer's identity despite the sleek helmet concealing the woman's face.

Looking at Piper, I said, "You went to the cave." It sounded more like a statement than a question. As the words left my mouth, I realized they came out more like an accusation.

Doctor Cormac stepped forward, speaking for the first time in a while. "Once the cave's location was identified, she led the expedition."

I gazed at Piper. Taking slow breaths, I grappled with my next words. "Are you okay?"

Piper shrugged. "It was the most horrible thing I've ever seen." Her voice was low and husky. "Something in that cave tore everyone apart. There's no way to be sure, but it must have been Breslin. He killed those people."

As I pulled her into my arms, I felt her sag. Her arms tightened around me in response, yet she didn't cry. She seemed to find comfort in having as much of herself in contact with me as possible.

I'd missed that, too.

"It's not exactly Breslin," I said to everyone in the room. "Something came through a portal from another Brane. It used Breslin. Whatever exists on the other side can't seem to Cross without that apparatus and a living host on this side to contain it."

Tripp cleared his throat. "Host?" he rasped.

I shrugged with one shoulder, still holding Piper. "You can figure out the science. I can only tell you what I saw. Breslin has another one of these devices at the dig site where Piper found me. He's using it to bring Elend over, half a dozen at a time. It seems like he's using the people he's abducting to make it possible. Based on what I saw, he needs your people as hosts. It's part of whatever method he's using for the Crossing."

Everyone in the room appeared unwell. I thought this mirrored everyone's fears in one way or another. Either the Elend was killing the Seeley outright, or they were consuming them. It seemed unlikely that anyone would believe thousands of people were confined in cells somewhere.

This wasn't that kind of horror show.

"You still call him Breslin?" Lacy noted.

"He has embraced the name," I clarified. "He's using it on Our-World, so I'm not sure if it makes a difference. The Kilmer Breslin who walked with a team into that cave, if he was Seeley, couldn't have done any of this. I'm sure you all know that better than me. So whatever is taking his place now—we can refer to it as that or call it something different. Regardless, the creature needs a name."

"Until we kill it," Piper clarified.

I chuckled. "Until we kill it."

Chapter 22 - Just My Smile To Protect Me

Our-World

My senses spun wildly with vertigo, accompanied by a Doppler-shifting thunder that struck me like a bolt of high voltage and made me feel as if I were being circled by a ten-foot-wide boomerang traveling at fifty miles an hour. The sensation could have lasted for two seconds or thirty. There was also a feeling reminiscent of the first few moments spent tumbling uncontrollably out of an aircraft—when the one-hundred-mile-an-hour slipstream slams into you and completely scrambles your orientation in space. In the next instant, I felt the down comforter, soft and gentle beneath the bare skin of my back.

"The fuck!" Piper croaked in a hoarse voice beside me and sat up with a jolt.

I cracked an eye and looked at her. She was completely naked, the same as me. We were positioned mostly parallel but askew on the bed in her room back on Our-World. The morning sun appeared to be just cresting the horizon, gradually backlighting the drawn blinds of the windows across the room. She was gently probing her right ear with the tip of her finger. As she worked her jaw, she quickly moved her finger to her left ear and shot me an accusing glance. That's when I became aware of the pressure building up in my ears and worked my jaw to relieve it.

"Do you taste waffles?" Piper said, her voice loud. She was still having trouble with her hearing.

I ran my tongue along the roof of my mouth and smiled. "Maple syrup?"

She raised an eyebrow. Honestly, if she didn't have an explanation for it, what could I offer? By that point, she was figuring this stuff out far quicker than I was, and we both knew it. I could only shrug.

Piper's gaze shifted to the foot of the bed. At first, I thought she was just now realizing we were both naked. That wouldn't be a good sign since that had been part of the plan. If her mind had been scrambled during the Crossing, I needed to assess the extent of her condition and how long it would take for her to recover.

"Did we just break the bed?" She said.

Her attention wasn't on her physical condition; rather, it focused on the state of the bed. The bed was inclined, with the head raised at a noticeable pitch because the footboard had collapsed, leaving the bottom of the mattress resting on the floor.

I rolled to the edge of the mattress and found my feet. "No," I said, motioning to the room. "If you remember, we did that the night you…left."

Piper looked briefly puzzled, her face slowly flushing as the memory returned. I'll admit, my mind was racing with that recollection too. "It's been months. You didn't fix it?" she finally said.

"Months for you," I reminded. "Days on this side. Days when I didn't come back here. Remember, I was gone for so long because I hadn't slept. The first time I finally did, I crossed right back to Wild-Side. At that point, fixing the bed was the least of my concerns."

She nodded slowly. "Days," she murmured. "It's still hard to believe you were gone for so long."

We were on the same page. We need to finish our work here as quickly as possible. It was crucial to remember that every hour spent here was multiplied on Wild-Side. The clock was ticking here, but it was ticking even faster over there.

"Esker, you there?" I said.

"Welcome back," Esker whispered in my ear.

"Hey, buddy." The smile on my face was impossible to hide, and Piper mirrored it. The confusion in her eyes reminded me that only I could hear his response. "Hey, could you switch to speaker? I want Piper to hear you."

"Hello, Piper," Esker said through the speaker built into the phone. "It's nice to finally meet you."

Piper's eyes immediately darted to the phone plugged into a

power cord on the nightstand by my side of the bed. "You too," she said with a laugh. "I've heard a lot about you." It seemed to dawn on Piper that she was standing naked at the side of the bed, and her eyes shifted anxiously, searching for concealment.

"There's a robe on the hook inside the closet door," Esker said confidently.

I laughed as Piper bolted to her own closet. It was amusing that she was trying to hide from the voice of a disembodied artificial intelligence, especially since the AI had just reminded her where her robe was hung.

"It's alright," I said, even though I knew what I was about to say was already undermined by the fact that I was laughing so hard I was nearly doubled over. "He doesn't care if you're naked or wearing your Sunday best. It's all the same to him."

Piper stepped out of the closet, tightening the belt of her white terrycloth robe. She shot me a laser gaze of admonishment, clearly grinding her teeth.

"Gray is correct," Esker said. "I can scan multiple spectrums and have recently started routinely using backscatter feedback from surrounding signals as well. This is how I was able to identify the new form of radiation unique to Grays Crossing. Clothing and the human form are of no particular interest to me, if that makes you feel any better."

Piper glared at me. "What?"

There was an accusation in the response. It wasn't until that second that I even considered saying what I was thinking. I stepped back and suddenly wished I wasn't so figuratively and literally exposed. "Well..." I hesitated. "He was there," I pointed to the nightstand, "when we broke that." I pointed to the bottom of the bed.

For a few long seconds, Piper looked like she was about to explode. I was on the verge of being ringside—ground zero—for a nuclear detonation. I could see it in her eyes. Then her mask of seething fury melted away. She shook her head and let out a choked giggle. She laughed until tears streamed down her cheeks. "This is hardly the weirdest thing to happen to us this year," she said, sitting down on the side of the bed. "Objectively, after seeing what the Seeley thought about the human sexual experience, I'm curious to hear what an AI thinks. There could be a paper in it."

"A paper you could never publish?"

She shrugged. "There's a lot to explore here once this is all sorted out. None of it can be published but all of it should be captured for posterity. Do you realize that everything is happening for the first time in human history?"

I watched the expression on Piper's face and reflected on it. This wasn't the first time the question had crossed my mind, and I couldn't help but wonder. Was this the first time any of these things had occurred? Was I the first person ever to traverse Branes? That didn't seem likely. There was nothing special about me. And if I wasn't special, why should this be the first time?

"Not to interrupt," Esker said. I was surprised to hear hesitancy in his tone; he sounded uncomfortable. It occurred to me that he wasn't used to being included in conversations that went beyond the back and forth between him and me. "I could use the latest download when you're ready."

The pain at the base of my skull felt like someone had just eased off on an attempt to lobotomize me with a corkscrew that needed sharpening. Adding to this by driving toothpicks to the back of my eyeballs wasn't at the top of my to-do list, but he made a fair point. A crack of thunder rattled the roof overhead, and I instantly realized just how dark the sky beyond the drawn blinds had become in the past couple of minutes.

"Did we catch Smallwood off guard?" I asked, my gaze still fixed on the darkened window. "It seems we didn't redirect the storm this time."

"Ask your questions while you prepare the download," Esker urged, his tone tinged with a new level of stress. A flash of concern shot my way from Piper. Although she didn't yet know the AI, his anxiety was evidently easy to read.

I grabbed the glasses off the nightstand next to Esker's phone and slipped them onto my face. "Hit me," I said through clenched teeth.

The flash of light stabbed at my eyes, the sensation of staring wide-eyed into a sleet storm. That lasted only a second. It was quickly replaced by a stabbing pain along my optic nerves.

"Transfer complete," Esker said.

I felt Piper's hand on my shoulder. "That was quick. Tripp said this transfer involved terabytes of data. Is it usually this fast?"

I flicked the glasses across the comforter and worked my eye sockets with the heels of my hands. "Fast can be a relative term," I mumbled through clenched teeth.

"The data confirms my assumption," Esker said, ignoring my discomfort. "Piper's return with you changes the biomass ratio needed to offset the storm fronts. Calculations show that you will need to increase the mobile stores by thirty-five percent to prevent this scenario from happening again. I recommend adjusting by forty percent. This will provide you with a wider margin of error."

"Bio—what?" Piper stammered.

It was the first time I realized I hadn't fully explained the camper that had been running interference for me all over the southern and western United States. I was about to get into it when Esker spoke again.

"The care package you arranged seems to be early," he said. "One of the webcams I'm monitoring at the Borderline just triggered a motion alert. Your shipping container arrived at the designated location, only ahead of schedule."

Our ability to control the Crossing back to Our-World was the first part of an ambitious and potentially game-altering plan. Arriving at a time of our choosing meant I would no longer suffer the whims of fate regarding how quickly I boomeranged back home. More importantly, the second part of the plan was to see if we could Cross with more than just our birthday suits. The care package aimed to transport hardware across the Brane barrier. If our gear could successfully make the Crossing, we would not only be able to outfit ourselves with Wild-Side tech in Our-World, but we could also potentially cross with gear from Our-World intact. I can't express how nice it would be to land on Wild-Side with more than just my smile to protect me from all things pointy and bitey.

Piper's eyes widened. We both glanced at the clock on the nightstand. It was just after three in the afternoon. If the skies hadn't darkened so rapidly due to the unexpected weather, it would still be broad daylight. "That's not good," she said. "The time offsets are wildly inconsistent."

I shook my head. "At least the location was right." I swallowed hard as fear gripped me. I realized I had just made a dangerous assumption. "Wait, E. Which camera? Please tell me it landed behind the bar?"

"It did," Esker confirmed. "However, considering the time of day, it's unlikely to go unnoticed for long."

I went to the window and parted the blinds just in time to see the large maple outside Piper's apartment bending in the gale-force wind. Near-horizontal rain sheeted the expanse of lawn between us and the parking lot, and lightning danced in the cloudy sky. "Tornado alarms," I mumbled, at first to myself. "E? Can you trigger the alarms in the area around the Borderline? The distraction should keep people looking just about anywhere but the lot behind the bar long enough for us to get there."

Piper tossed me a pair of jeans, and I started pulling them on. She was already dressed in the same and a dark hoodie. She pulled her hair under a dark Blackhawks cap and slipped an elastic band around her wrist. When she passed me a similar pullover, I heard the distant whine of sirens.

"I might not need to raise false alarms," Esker commented. "Weather services across the county are already sending alerts. Conditions are perfect for tornadoes, and alerts are being issued."

We were halfway to the Borderline with Piper behind the wheel of my Jeep and Esker navigating, when the weather conditions surprisingly dropped down my list of pressing concerns. I'd lost the debate with Piper about who should drive, which ended up being ideal for all of us after Esker's latest update from Derek Smallwood. Between the new information and monitoring our flanks for flying, rolling, or flowing debris that could disable our four-by-four, I was extremely distracted.

"No," I said. "Don't play the recording; just tell me what has you concerned." Even as the words left my mouth, I was impressed by my confidence in the AI's ability to interpret human mannerisms to the point that I no longer automatically second-guessed him. I decided I'd felt this way for some time, even without consciously registering the shift in mindset. Esker has continued to develop in recent months, without question. I suddenly wondered if he was even aware of his personal growth.

While guiding Piper to navigate the hazards between her apartment and the Borderline, I was unaware that Esker was conversing with Derek Smallwood. This call occurred silently, at least from my perspective. When Piper returned from Wild-Side with me, we Crossed together, upsetting the delicate balance we had maintained. Smallwood kept a proportional amount of my genetic material in the RV and on the move so my Crossing wouldn't generate a storm front that could reveal my location. By keeping a slightly higher amount of my genetic material in motion with him, for reasons we still don't fully understand, the weather disturbances that occurred when both Breslin and I were in Our-World simultaneously were somewhat mitigated, directing the resulting storm toward Smallwood's location instead of mine.

Knowing the storm we now experienced was the unintended consequence of Piper returning from Wild-Side with me, Esker reached out to Smallwood to see what the Doctor could do to compensate. For instance, would it be necessary to add Piper's genetic material to the payload now being carried in the RV, or would they simply need to adjust the current ratio to account for Piper's mass? I was impressed, first because Esker was taking the initiative, and second because while I was focused on dealing with the current problems, he was solving for future scenarios.

"It was Doctor Smallwood's response that concerns me," Esker clarified. "He agrees the severity of the current storm is likely commensurate with both you and Piper Crossing together and suspects we will need genetic material added to his current payload to compensate."

"Which is what you expected," I said, my eyes scanning the windward side of the city street. I grabbed Piper's thigh and hissed, "Incoming!"

Piper mashed the brakes and sent the Jeep into a thirty-mile-per-hour hydroplaning skid that stopped just short of cartwheeling into a wooden picnic table as it blew through the intersection ahead of us. She leaned forward and glanced left and right quickly before slamming her foot back on the accelerator. "That thing was moving like a runaway train," she muttered through clenched teeth.

My eyes returned to scanning our surroundings. The wipers scraped the windshield at high speed, but even then, visibility was at most two dozen yards. The rain was beyond sheeting, coming down at a forty-five-degree angle, and the sound it made on the Jeep's soft top was deeply concerning. Something was bound to give soon. I didn't know if the rain would tear through the cover or if the wind would take the top first—either way, we needed to get rid of the Jeep quickly.

"Eleven minutes to Borderline at this pace," Esker said as if reading my mind.

A smile tugged at the corner of Piper's mouth. Perhaps he was reading her thoughts too.

"When I pressed to find out if adding Piper's genetic profile was necessary," Esker said, changing the subject, "Doc Smallwood finished my thought about compensating with more of your biomass to save time. He said it was possible but unlikely. He would need to consult to be sure."

My mouth went dry, and I found my grip on the dashboard tightening even more. "*Consult*? He said consult?"

"I can playback the recording," Esker confirmed.

A new wave of nausea churned in the pit of my stomach, and

expletives started slipping out under my breath.

Piper turned a corner, drifting the four-wheel-drive like a rally car. By that point, it had become nearly second nature for her. Her head was swiveling from side to side, and she'd found her groove. "I guess I didn't keep up," she said absentmindedly. "What's the problem?"

I swallowed hard, feeling as if I were pushing down the consequences of the words about to follow. "Smallwood shouldn't be consulting with anyone about this. He helped me solve the storm mitigation issue a year ago. If he had assistance, I didn't know about it. If he has a partner, he hasn't disclosed it. If he brought someone in since the start of the project, they might not be on our side."

Piper shot me a quick look before turning her attention back to the road. "You think the partner he's working with is Breslin?"

I swallowed once more. "Who else would be interested in this kind of technology?"

None of us knew what to say at that moment. Piper shook her head. I turned my attention back to the windward side of the road. The storm, if anything, appeared to be intensifying.

Esker spoke. "What should I do about my contact with—"

Lightning flashed, striking somewhere on the road in the near distance. The brightness blinded us instantly, and the thunderclap hit the front of the Jeep like an impact with another vehicle. My senses went haywire, and I felt like I was on a tilt-a-whirl. In an instant, I didn't know which way was up because the Jeep began to roll sideways. There was crashing and crunching. An enormous side impact hit me in the face, followed by who knows how many more minor hits. The next thing I knew, I was pelted with something cold and wet.

———————

When I opened my eyes, I instantly understood that I had been unconscious for at least a short time. The Jeep lay on its passenger side with both front airbags deployed and already mostly deflated.

My shoulder was submerged in two inches of water. The storm had turned the street into a river, and our wreck was doing little to stem the flow. Piper was strapped into the driver's seat above me, pulling at the shoulder strap of her seatbelt with one hand while mashing the belt release with the other.

"Are you alright?" I asked, my voice sounding foreign to me. Strange acoustics inside the vehicle resulted from the rain hammering surfaces that were usually shielded from the storm. Gashes and tears had turned the soft top into a less-than-ideal shelter, forming crude gutters that channeled copious amounts of water into the passenger compartment.

Shooting me a relieved, though short-lived smile, Piper said, "Welcome back." She yanked hard on the shoulder strap once more and pounded the buckle release with her closed right fist while cursing. "You were out for almost two minutes. I'm pretty sure you broke the passenger window with your head before the street had a chance to bust the glass for you."

I opened my mouth, exaggerating a yawn, and heard—and felt—a pop. It seemed to reverberate through my skull. A turn of my head resulted in the sensation and sound of stepping on loose gravel as bones and sinew realigned as closely as possible to factory specifications. "Explains a few things," I mumbled. "Are you hurt?"

She slammed her fist against the steering wheel and kicked the underside of the dashboard. "Just my pride. The belt won't release."

"My fault," Esker said, close to our ears. "I locked your belts when I integrated the drive-by-wire system into the emergency maneuver."

I was sure there was a story there; it just wasn't the right time. If this were Esker's ideal outcome, the alternative would certainly be sphincter puckering. Instead of asking, I released my belt and grabbed the folding knife from my hip pocket. My airbag was nearly deflated, but I needed room to work, so I cut it away with a couple of quick swipes of the razor-sharp blade. Then I glanced up at Piper. "Ready?"

Piper nodded and braced herself against the wheel. She held tightly to the top and placed her elbows along the sides, so when I sliced away at the belt, she wouldn't fall from the seat out of control. Still, everything was wet and slippery, so things didn't go as planned. There was a gasp as she landed in my lap with a wheezing, wet splat. We laughed, but under different circumstances, it would have been much more amusing.

"What happened?" Piper asked. "There was a flash—then the car went haywire."

I grinned to myself as I crawled to the back of the Jeep, searching for the emergency kit. We needed to set out road flares before the next car came along and made our wreck three times worse. As I prepared to place the flares in the road, Esker explained the lightning strike and his response, which led to the rollover wreck.

The lightning strike had blown out a pair of streetlights a couple hundred yards down the road from us. When this happened, a powerline pole supporting a high-capacity transformer was also hit. As the pole fell, it was certain to land in the street—a street that was running deep with floodwater, up to three feet in places. The pole that was in the process of falling in front of our Jeep had an eleven percent chance of stopping us in our tracks there. There was an eighty-nine percent chance that the Jeep would hit the fallen pole, bounce over it, and continue down the street. At that point, the driver wouldn't have the chance to regain traction or control to avoid swamping the vehicle frame in the floodwater that, by then, would be electrically charged by the fallen transformer.

Piper and I stood at the edge of an old bowling alley, huddled close to the two-story brick wall, just beyond the reach of the worst of the rain. We looked at the rolled, trashed Jeep and listened to Esker's explanation of the action he had taken by overriding the Jeep's onboard computer system to literally save our lives by wrecking the SUV.

Apparently, the Jeep hydroplaned into a slide and struck the downed pole. This caused us to roll, which led to the wreck. However, the roll helped the vehicle come to a stop well short of the electrified flood, so while we were a bit banged up, we weren't overcooked.

Esker responded to everything so quickly that it was the next best thing to precognition. He had reacted instantly and decisively, making the most of a bad situation. There was no doubt our lives had been saved in the process. His complex analysis occurred literally in the time it took for lightning to strike. He had assessed the intricate cascading impact on the environment and then intervened through what I could only assume was a sophisticated real-time hack of the SUV's onboard control system.

I'd been skeptical about the AI's usefulness when I was first given access to him. Since that time, he'd proven to be immensely helpful. I've watched him grow and evolve, continuously expanding his understanding of our world's technology at what seemed to be an ever-increasing pace. But when he made that impulsive decision to wreck the Jeep in defense of my life and Piper's, I realized for the first time that Esker wasn't just an artificial intelligence. He was simply intelligent–not human, yet no less significant for it.

"I feel like there's a bad driving joke in there somewhere," Piper said, shivering visibly. It obviously relates just as much to what we were witnessing as it does to being soaked to the bone in high winds.

I found it hard to laugh at any of this. If anyone was hurt or killed during this insanity, it was on me. This atmospheric disturbance wasn't just a nuisance; it was a serious concern that we needed to mitigate entirely. Lives were at stake.

"How's your head?" Piper asked.

"I'll live." I was more concerned about retrieving our gear from the Borderline before it was damaged or found. "This storm is the worst one yet. It's not letting up. No one should be out in this. We need to grab our gear and find cover."

Piper was nodding and was about to say something when Esker interrupted her.

"Something's happening at the Borderline," Esker said. "Multiple County Sheriff's Deputies have just been dispatched."

We were two and a half blocks away, as the crow flies. It was close enough to walk from the crash site. I nodded at Piper, who pointed to an alley that led in the right direction. To Esker, I said, "Tell me what I need to know."

The rainfall had eased somewhat when Piper and I arrived at the shopping plaza's parking lot where the Borderline was located. And when I say it had eased, it is a highly subjective comparison. The rain was falling more or less vertically by that point, but there was still a heavy downpour. The winds had calmed to about half of what they had been. The Sheriff's Deputies positioned around the parking lot wore ponchos and windbreakers with the county crest and the department's name emblazoned on them as they braced against the storm beside squad cars at the north, east, and west entrances to the oblong, football field-sized parking lot.

It was just before eight-thirty in the evening, but it might as well have been midnight. The heavy precipitation in the air reduced the visibility of the half dozen functioning light poles in the lot to perhaps a third of their already limited brightness. A dozen poles were spaced throughout the lot at regular intervals, though I'd never seen more than half of them lit at any given time. It was clear tonight wouldn't be any different, even with the emergency conditions.

Three squad cars were positioned at each entrance to the lot, with an officer standing at the bumper of each car, their attention mainly focused on the outer perimeter. Another car was located about two dozen yards outside the front doors of the Borderline. A pair of men crouched behind the car, bracing themselves against the storm while using the vehicle as a barrier between them and the bar, where their attention remained directed. Three additional units were stationed at the far left of the parking lot—a pair of county-marked SUVs and a squad car. This appeared to be support waiting for direction from the scene commander.

Piper and I stood at the edge of a copse of trees just beyond the northwest corner of the lot. We had some shelter from the storm, but more importantly, we remained hidden from the police.

Esker explained that police reports indicated robbers had attempted to leverage the storm as a distraction and were now holding the bar's patrons as hostages. An alarm had been triggered, and police responded. It was bad luck for everyone in the bar and us because it was only a matter of time before our container caught the eye of law enforcement. Even more unexpected was one of the hostages identified by Esker when he reviewed the security cameras inside the bar. FBI Special Agent Al Vincente was among the hostages.

"This is escalating quickly," Piper said flatly. "Why would you want to go in there? If everyone's focused on the front, maybe we can slip around back, grab our stuff and get out."

Esker burst her bubble before I could respond. "Two units have been stationed at the back of the bar to block any escape. One of the units is currently taking cover behind your equipment. Apparently, the transport container provides ideal concealment."

"Is the officer interested in the container?" I asked.

"No," Esker confirmed. He is completely focused on the bar's exit and that of the dry cleaner next door. Another unit is monitoring the two takeout restaurants and the liquor store.

The Borderline anchored the plaza's east end, occupying a pair of units in the building. To the west was the dry cleaner, noted by Esker. Adjacent to the cleaner were two take-out restaurants: one Mexican and the other Chinese. The liquor store occupied the west end of the plaza. Except for the cleaner, all the businesses were owned by the same entrepreneur, who was positioning the facility to attract the local students living within two square miles.

"What do the police have planned?" I asked. At this point, I assumed that Esker was monitoring the department's communication.

"There's a disagreement about the best course of action," Esker confirmed. "Right now, one side is advocating that the Lieutenant on scene stall until a negotiator can arrive. The other side wants to cut the power and wait for the SWAT team from downstate. Neither will happen quickly, so in either case, this will be a hurry-up-and-wait situation."

Piper was already glaring at me.

"What?" It was all I could think to say.

"You want to go in." Her tone was accusatory.

I shrugged. She wasn't wrong.

"What good will that do?"

I counted off the points on my fingers. "We need to distract the cops and pull them away from the care package out back," I said, holding up one digit. "Our buddy is in there," I added, referring to Vincente and raising my second finger. "I'm really curious to see how he made it this far, so why not ask him? If he's here, we need to find out if he's alone or just the first in a wave that's about to hit us. If it's the wave, we need to know right now so we can grab our gear and react accordingly." I lifted a third finger. "We have friends in there." I nodded toward the bar and considered her coworkers. "Neither of us wants to see them get hurt if we can help it."

Piper stared at me for a moment, then rolled her eyes. "Fine. But how do we get inside? We can't just walk through the front door."

I grinned. "Actually, I will use the front door—but I'm doing it alone. I need you out back, ready to grab the gear and hit the sky as soon as the cops pull out of position. I'm not sure how much time I can give you. Esker can coordinate comms, and he has good camera coverage, so that part should be covered."

"Cameras and communication are trivial," Esker affirmed. "Although the Sheriff's department lacks a solid reaction plan, the coverage of the ingress and egress points is comprehensive. I don't see how you'll get past them if you want to enter the Borderline undetected."

"I was thinking of the way you took control of the Jeep," I explained. "All the squad cars look like late models. Can you do something like that with them?"

"In theory," Esker said slowly. "But it's not that simple. I had proximity in the case of the Jeep. I used the many radios in your phone to access the onboard control system of the Jeep. I can exploit the squad cars in a similar way, but without proximity, I can't distinguish one from another. Given enough time, I can enumerate the entire fleet and identify those on scene, then access them through their communication systems. Patrol vehicles are among the most connected cars on the road. I'm not sure I can accomplish it within the timeframe required."

I nodded slowly and smiled at Piper's scowl of concern. "It would make life a lot easier if someone labeled each of the cars for us, wouldn't it?"

Esker's voice sounded puzzled. Until that moment, I don't think I had ever heard him confused. "Sure," he said, stretching the word into multiple syllables. "But...why...what are–"

"Maybe if we ask them nicely, they'll paint a numeric identifier right across the trunk of each car," I said with a smirk.

Esker let out an audible sigh. This might have been a first as well. "Sarcasm and frustration are distinctly human qualities. I don't appreciate either of them." The last sentence was muttered almost under his breath. "Tell me which car you want me to access."

"Can you do it?" I asked for clarification.

"I already have," he said in his customary tone.

"Which one?"

"All of the squad cars that are currently on scene." This reply had just a hint of, *put that in your pipe and smoke it.*

Our-World

Borderline Bar and Grill

2 Hours Ago

Al Vincente pushed through the glass double doors at the Borderline and noticed that the inside of the smoked glass had been covered with years' worth of stage bills listing the acts that had graced the stage. Considering the late hour, he'd taken a quick drive around the relatively small university town. It was clear which parts of the city went out of their way to cater to the after-hours student population, and the Borderline had quickly climbed to the top of Vincente's to-do list. Until the University's administrative offices opened in the morning, this popular bar for grad students was the best place to start his investigation.

Thunder rattled the glass in the door behind Vincente as it closed, and he was grateful to escape what promised to be an impressive storm, given how quickly the sky had darkened. Over the last six months, he'd crisscrossed the United States three times–no, four. He ran his hand through his short dark hair, reflecting on the countless hours he'd spent behind the wheel of his government-issued sedan. Once this case was over, he planned to sit on the beach for a couple of weeks.

Thank God I'm not driving in the weather we're getting tonight.

Looking out the windows, Vincente was surprised to see that all of them had been obscured by what seemed to be patron-generated graffiti. Hand-scrawled snippets of poetry, song lyrics, and renditions of band logos covered the glass, in some cases overlapping each other. The overall effect had an urban beauty and suggested that the establishment had been around for many years, if not decades, with multiple generations contributing to the motif.

The bar featured about three dozen tables, with a small stage occupying the wall at the far end of the room. A corridor ran alongside the stage, presumably leading to the restrooms and likely the rear exit. The stage stood empty and silent, while jukebox-style classic rock played from small speakers hanging from the shadowy recesses of the ceiling. Instead of installing drop ceiling tiles, as was often done in such buildings, the designers of the Borderline chose to leave the industrial struts, supports, and HVAC ductwork exposed, painting the steel roof and beams black while highlighting the infrastructure in silver, maintaining an industrial aesthetic. This design contrasted with the traditional maple-topped bar counter, the matching shelves lining the wall behind it, and the weathered, worn chairs and booths throughout.

About two dozen patrons occupied the place, possibly due to the weather or that it was a weeknight. There was space for at least five times as many.

As Vincente approached the cash register, he observed a person in their twenties swiping a credit card and jotting something down on a pad. He displayed his official credentials and flashed a disarming smile. "I'm looking for someone who could be a customer. May I speak with the manager?"

"The manager isn't here tonight," the young man said with a shrug. "He won't be back until next week. Is there anything I can help you with?"

"How often are you on shift?" Vincente replied. He didn't need a manager. Anyone who worked regular hours and was willing to converse with him was a good starting point. These days, simply finding someone open to talking without involving lawyers made his day.

The guy at the register shrugged. "I work once or twice a week. I'm mostly focused on my classes this semester, you know?"

That was unfortunate. "Is there anyone here tonight who's full-time? I need to talk about the regulars. It might be nothing, but the sooner I check this off my list, the sooner I can move on."

Nodding, the guy scanned the room. "You want Amanda." He pointed to a curvy blonde in a too-tight white tank and a skirt that barely peeked out from beneath the serving apron fitted around her hips. "She knows everyone."

Vincente smirked, with no doubt in his mind. He waited as the kid at the register flagged Amanda down and introduced them. Amanda seemed hesitant to talk, so Vincente led her to a booth along the wall opposite the bar.

"I really need to work the floor," Amanda said. She seemed either reluctant to speak with law enforcement or specifically with Vincente. In the few minutes he'd been in the bar, it was impossible to miss the vivacious waitress making her rounds at the tables and socializing with everyone. She was familiar with most and had a social ease coming from being skilled at her job. This suggested she simply didn't appreciate the one-on-one time with an FBI agent.

"I won't take up much of your time," Vincente offered in his most agreeable tone. "I just have a couple of questions for you. I think you're the only one here tonight who might be able to help me." He shot a look at the twenty-something behind the register. "Maybe your friend over there can cover the tables for a few minutes?"

Vincente felt Amanda's penetrating gaze for several long seconds before she thumbed something on her belt and spoke softly. After a pause, she nodded, seemingly to herself. That's when Vincente noticed the small wireless headset tucked behind her wavy fall of blonde hair. He realized it was the communication system that all the waiters and waitresses wore.

"Jimmy said he'll cover for a few minutes. How can I assist you, Agent…"

"Vincente," he said, offering his hand. He pulled out his phone and unlocked the screen. "I'm in town looking for a missing person. Well, sort of a missing person. His family is searching for him. As you can imagine, he doesn't want to be found. He hasn't technically broken the law. It's more accurate to say his family has connections, so now the FBI is involved in the search." This was a complete fabrication, of course. Vincente and his partner Ingersoll had learned long ago that the people they encountered were likely to have difficulty believing Grady Ledger was guilty of anything worthy of FBI interest. This line of inquiry had a better chance of being productive.

Vincente showed a photo of Grady Ledger and watched Amanda's reaction. When she first saw the image, there was a flash of something in her eyes that made his heart race. It felt like a rush of adrenaline, similar to when a long shot pays off. Amanda glanced at him quickly, a question in her eyes. "What did you say his name was? He's cute."

The elation Vincente felt abruptly hit a brick wall as his hopes were dashed. Yet, there was discomfort in the young woman's expression—something he hadn't noticed in her before. "Bobby," Vincente said, "Bobby Mills." He watched confusion crease her face. "That's not the name you expected me to say, is it?"

Amanda leaned back in her seat and shot Vincente a glare. "I'm sorry? What?"

"You were expecting something different," Vincente clarified. "You know him by another name. Did he go by Gray? It's short for Grady. That's actually his name."

"Then who is Bobby?" Amanda asked, shaking her head. "What's going on here?"

With a smirk, Vincente said, "Don't worry about that. Just tell me the last time you saw him. Let's start there."

Amanda slammed her hand on the table. "Look," she half-shouted, and Vincente knew he was about to deal with a scene. "You better tell me what this is about because I'm done talking until I understand what's going on."

A shadow fell over the end of the table, and Vincente looked up to see a young man wearing a denim jacket and a cowboy hat. "Is this guy giving you trouble?" he asked with a southern drawl.

"Walsh!" Amanda gasped, starting to slide to the edge of the booth. Vincente realized she was about to exit, meaning the interview would be over. "So glad to see you."

Vincente raised a hand at the newcomer and gestured for Amanda to stay where she was. At the same time, he was trying in vain to gather his credentials to explain the situation. He wasn't used to an interview shifting on him so quickly or unexpectedly. The long shot paying off had caught him off guard, and he had been unprepared to be confronted about the deception.

"My name is Al Vincente with the FBI," Vincente said as he stood from the end of the booth, raising his credentials. He did this expecting to explain the reason for the questioning and possibly to include the newcomer in the discussion. He didn't expect to stand in time to see a man in a black ski mask pointing a silver revolver at the twenty-something behind the register.

The word FBI had just left Vincente's lips when he turned his head and spotted a second masked man standing about thirty degrees to his left, presumably guarding the entrance to the bar. That masked man spun around, saw Vincente bringing his credentials to bear, and opened fire with a similar chrome-plated revolver. The first round zinged past Vincente's ear, while the second struck him just to the right of his sternum, sending him toppling backward into the booth.

———————

The team supposedly controlling the crime scene remained hunkered down among three squad vehicles parked somewhat chaotically in a triangle. They might have been using them as a barrier against gunfire should the armed assailants inside the bar open fire into the parking lot, but I suspected they were merely taking shelter from the gusty wind and rain. Chaos erupted when Esker took control of one of the squad cars and an SUV. The squad car was facing roughly northeast, meaning it was directed straight at me from the opposite corner of the lot. This was not ideal. The SUV was aimed almost due west, making it just about perfect for my plan.

"Go now," I whispered to Esker, ready to sprint from my cover at the tree line.

Esker put the squad car in reverse and eased it slowly from the triangle surrounding the command team working at the open front and back driver-side doors of the west-facing SUV. The vehicle was moving at a meager 3 miles per hour, much to the surprise of the officer behind the wheel and the dismay of the command team, who hadn't ordered the car to move. The group was even more astonished when the SUV they were operating from began to follow the squad car, even though no one was behind the wheel.

As expected, disorganized chatter erupted across the tactical channel. I watched the officer in the squad car barricading the entrance to the parking lot nearest to me turn to observe the rapidly unfolding spectacle. Predictably, the officers at the lot entrances instantly abandoned their posts to chase the slowly moving runaway vehicles. Because the runaways moved so slowly, they understandably concluded that the vehicles in question were rolling. Consequently, all but one of the officers pursued on foot.

All of this aligned with my hopes and plans. I reached the car closest to me just seconds after it had been abandoned and crouched down beside the driver's side window. Peering over the corner of the hood, I confirmed that the officer who had left his post was long gone. Cracking the door, I triggered the trunk release and quickly closed it. I aimed to be in and out of the car before the dome light attracted anyone's attention in the parking lot. The odds were good that all eyes would be on Esker's diversion, but I had a lot to accomplish before his part in the plan concluded.

I had to act quickly.

As I rounded the car, I lifted the lid and was grateful to find it well organized. Inside was an emergency roadside assistance kit, a small tactical bag presumably meant to support the AR-15 strapped to the trunk lid, and then there was what I was really interested in. I grabbed the small red bag adorned with a large white plus symbol across the top. Gently closing the lid, I cast a quick glance over the forty-yard stretch of pavement illuminated by one pole and dotted with only a few stray cars and trucks. Then, I dashed toward the front of the Borderline, zigzagging and using the cars, trucks, and vans as cover.

I reached the last car that could provide concealment and stopped. One squad car sat between me and the entrance to the bar. A pair of officers still manned their posts here, impressively focused on the job at hand despite the drama unfolding about eighty yards to the west, where no fewer than nine officers were now trying a variety of creative and futile methods to stop the plodding, slow-moving rogue vehicles from heading toward the ditch at the end of the lot. I watched as one officer knelt, with one behind the front bumper and the other behind the back bumper, each using the car's quarter panel as a barricade between them and the entrance to the Borderline.

"Take it up a notch," I whispered to Esker.

"Understood," he responded.

The lights on the runaway SUV began to flash red and blue at the same moment the light bar on a pursuing squad car lit up and started to strobe. The siren on the car blared with a piercing effect, startling the officers who had been trying to slow or stop the vehicles, causing them to fall from the bumpers and locked door handles. This was the opportunity Esker had been waiting for. He couldn't risk injuring anyone hanging onto the exterior of the vehicles, but once they were all clear, the risk was minimal. The car and the SUV adjusted their course and accelerated. They had little distance to gather speed, but each was traveling between ten and fifteen miles per hour when they collided.

The crunch of impacting metal and the dramatic squelch of the sirens, which I still assert was improvised by Esker for comedic effect, finally drew the pair of officers from their post at the bar's entrance. As soon as they stepped into the glare of their car's headlights for a better look at the incident, I bolted from cover, rounded the back of their car, cracked the door at the front of the Borderline, and slipped inside.

I expected to make a covert entry, but having a gun barrel pressed against my forehead the moment I stepped through the door felt overly dramatic. My eyes crossed as I glanced down the eight-inch length of dark steel and recognized the hollow-tipped rounds in the five visible chambers of the revolver.

".45 caliber Colt Single Action Army," I said, taking a breath before shifting my gaze to the five-and-a-half-foot tall figure in a ski mask who was shoving the gun in my face. The dregs of a wispy red mustache or beard pushed out from the corners of the mouth hole and bloodshot eyes did their best to stare holes through me from beyond the hammer of the Colt.

"Don't move," a gravelly voice rasped. "Hands in the air."

I smirked. "You'll need to choose one or the other. I can't do both." A few things became instantly clear to me. First, if this was the brain behind the operation, the hostages were either very safe or very, very screwed. Second, this guy wasn't holding the place up with a classic revolver out of reverence. He likely thought bigger was better and being a little guy, that eight-inch barrel spoke to him in ways better left for a psychiatrist to unpack. That gun was far older than he was. Since the hammer wasn't back, he couldn't pull the trigger and shoot me just then, even if he wanted to. It was a single-action antique. And last of all—and this really made me smile inside and out—it turned out that you could see the little guy's confusion even through his ski mask.

Some incoherent curses came from somewhere behind the bar. It sounded like Russian, but it was too rushed and mumbly to be understood by anyone not fluent in the language. "Damn it, just get him away from the door. And lock it this time for fuck's sake, would you? We don't need anyone else just walking in here." I don't think the additional statements were translations—more likely the important part of the instruction.

The guy behind the bar was tall and broad-shouldered. Well, maybe not really tall; he was tall compared to the little guy with the Colt at the door. Based on his size, accent, and overall authoritative demeanor, I immediately began thinking of him as Boris. The short guy at the door was Little Red Beard. Boris had a ski mask too, which looked just like the one Little Red Beard wore, along with the guy I saw standing at the door to the hall that led to the rear exit. Maybe they bought in bulk.

Esker mentioned there were four intruders in total, meaning one man was unaccounted for. This meant I needed cool names for the two remaining, so I had my work cut out for me.

About a dozen hostages sat at tables scattered around the bar, with a few couples at two-tops near the center of the space and four in total still at the bar. The rest were in the booths along the wall to the right. This reflected the improvised nature of the robbery as well. Any crew experienced in this type of situation would have consolidated prisoners into a single area, ideally somewhere somewhat confined. Everyone seemed to remain where they had been when the robbers presumably pulled their guns.

This included Agent Al Vincente. He sat in a booth about twenty feet to my right, slouched low in the seat with crimson bar towels pressed against a blue and blood-red button-down shirt. His face glistened with sweat.

Little Red Beard lowered the gun, grabbed me by the collar, and yanked me away from the door. I held my ground, feet planted and hands still raised. The med-pack remained in my right hand, the red cross deliberately facing the room to indicate I wasn't holding a weapon. Little Red Beard nearly toppled over when I refused to move with him. He was not amused when my soaked collar slipped easily from his grip. His beady, red-rimmed sclera fixed on me as his gun came up again.

Boris snarled from across the room, and I felt the tension rise throughout the space. "Quit messing around, or you'll be the next one shot."

"Speaking of which," I said, wobbling the first aid pack in my hand. "That's why I'm here. Can you let me take a look at the injured man?"

Little Red Beard appeared to give up on me. I watched from the corner of my eye as he locked the front doors. At one point, he held the big Colt revolver tucked in his armpit because he didn't know what to do with it when he needed both hands to operate the door locks.

"Let the cop bleed," Boris said.

That answered one of my questions. There hadn't been time to determine whether they knew Vincente was with the FBI. Presumably, Esker was aware of everything that had transpired so far, as he had access to all the video feeds. Unfortunately, there just wasn't time to pose the necessary question before rushing in. If they'd shot him because he was law enforcement, the situation was even more dangerous than I expected.

Esker once again appeared to be reading my mind. "From my best interpretation, Agent Vincente was shot by mistake. Ivan Sokalof discharged his weapon prematurely. This seems to explain why he has been assigned to watch the rear entrance."

I eyed the slender figure in dark coveralls at the rear of the room. The man was holding a semi-automatic pistol with both hands, more as if he were struggling with the firearm. He paced slowly back and forth. At first, I thought he was alert and on guard. However, looking closer, he seemed to be on the verge of a personal crisis.

Ivan?

I shouldn't have been surprised that Esker knew who each of these men was, masks or no masks. I had seen him perform more impressive feats with video and data analysis.

"How did you know there was an injured man in here?" Boris demanded.

"They won't pick up the phone because they aren't sure what to do next," Esker explained.

I shrugged. "It's possible to hear gunshots," I tilted my head up toward the roof, "even with the storm. It's a safe bet someone is hurt, right?" I had to be cautious because I didn't know how many shots had been fired, and I didn't want them to call my bluff. I couldn't explain that we'd had access to the video. They would assume the cops had the same. These guys didn't seem professional, and they certainly didn't seem stable. The last thing I needed was to add to the anxiety.

Another masked figure emerged from the door behind the bar. The stout figure was almost as round as he was tall. He halted abruptly when he saw me standing there. "What the hell!" He also had a Russian accent.

"This one wants to take care of the cop," Boris said to the newcomer.

"And you just let him in?"

Boris just glared at the fat man.

"Maybe it's for the best," the plump man remarked with a shrug. "Anyone dies, it's bad for all of us."

Boris appeared to take his time studying me. He finally stepped up to the counter and shouted at Little Red Beard, "Check him for weapons, then let him work on the cop."

I slid into the horseshoe-shaped booth beside Agent Vincente and across from Tommy Walsh. Little Red Beard was eyeing me the entire time, one hand on the grip and the other twisting the length of the long barrel. Either he thought his actions were intimidating, or he was doing it unintentionally—some kind of manifestation of his situational stress. If it was the former, it wasn't very impressive. If it was the latter— well, that was something to worry about, and that made it intimidating. I focused my attention on Vincente's condition and intentionally avoided looking directly at Little Red Beard. No good would come from engaging with him just yet.

"Agent Vincente, it's a pleasure to finally meet you," I said.

A tired smile played at the corners of Vincente's mouth as he slowly shook his head. "If you say so," he muttered in a dry voice. "I knew it was just a matter of time. I just didn't think it would be like *this*."

"It's always great to meet new friends over drinks," I grinned. Nodding across the table, I added, "Speaking of which, good to see you again, Walsh."

Walsh flashed me his aw-shucks grin and shrugged. "I'd offer a hand, but it's not really worth getting shot over. It turns out these guys are a little trigger happy." He tipped his head toward Vincente with that last comment.

"Point taken." I slid the med-pack toward Walsh. "You were an EMT for two years, weren't you?"

Walsh unzipped the pack and efficiently laid out what he found inside. "I play doctor every chance I get, too." He shot me a suspicious glance that lasted only a second before continuing with the preparation. "I don't recall sharing that part of my backstory, though, partner."

I didn't respond. I make efforts not to lie to my friends. Besides, this wasn't the moment to go into detail.

"Take off his shirt," Walsh said. "And we'll need water and clean rags."

I glanced at Little Red Beard. "You can help with that, can't you?"

Little Red Beard was doing a less than competent job of dead-eyeing me. He gripped the Colt as if trying to choke it. His size undermined the effort to intimidate; the comical struggle of red sticking out of the mouth hole of his mask made it look like he was trying to bring the Colt to climax. When he didn't answer after a few seconds, I slid out of the booth and stepped in front of him.

The little man swung the large firearm in my direction and bellowed, "Sit your ass down!" I eyed the Colt and noted that the hammer remained uncocked. Either Little Red Beard didn't realize the gun couldn't fire like that, or he had confidence in his ability to do it swiftly. He didn't seem like the confident type.

He didn't seem like the capable type either. I hoped he would be left in charge of my section of the room.

This caught Boris's attention. He had been in a deep conversation with the short man who was spending his time in the back room. "What's the problem?" Boris demanded.

"We need water and rags for first aid," I explained. As I scanned the room and noticed the frightened and beleaguered faces of the dozen hostages, I revised my request. "Since it looks like we'll be here for a while, why not get everyone some water?"

Boris stared at me, then glanced at the heavyset man beside him. They exchanged a few hushed words before Boris called to Amanda, who was hunched low on a stool at the far end of the bar. "Get them water and rags," he said. "Then drinks for everyone. Everyone stays quiet, and no one will get hurt." He shot me a glare as if to say, *good enough?*

I wanted to correct him and say that *no one else would get hurt*, but I didn't want to push my luck. Nodding in thanks, I looked at Amanda. "Do you need help?"

"She can do it," Little Red Beard said, shoving the Colt in my face. "Sit down and help the pig."

My desire to take the Colt from the little man was growing exponentially. This crew wasn't very organized, and they didn't seem to care. Either they didn't realize how many cops were outside, or they just didn't care. The phone had been ringing every ten minutes since I walked through the door. That was certainly the police unit outside trying to make contact. So far, it seemed Boris's team hadn't even bothered to pick up the phone. Maybe they thought that by simply not acknowledging the police, they could avoid the inevitable. If not for the storm, the police would likely have already gone on the offensive.

It was only a matter of time before things escalated. I was buying time for Piper to get into position and to connect with Vincente. This was a unique opportunity, and I wanted to make the most of it. I just didn't want to do so at the expense of the hostages. If I couldn't figure out where Vincente's loyalties lay by the time Piper was ready, I would need to put an end to this.

"I'm impressed you found me here," I said to Vincente. "Can I assume Agent Ingersoll is somewhere nearby as well?"

Sweat beaded on Vincente's face, trickling down his cheeks and even into his eyes as he studied me. Walsh used a squeeze bottle to spray the gunshot wound on Vincente's shoulder with what I assumed was sterile fluid from the med-pack. The agent gasped as Walsh brushed away the clotted blood with gauze pinched between forceps. "It's just me," Vincente said quietly. "Chris is still chasing your ghosts. He's clueless."

"Clueless?"

"I recently read something about technology that replaces one person with another in video footage." Vincente studied me as he made this statement. "They call it deepfake. One person's face is replaced by another's."

I said nothing; I just watched Vincente watching me.

"Supposedly, it began as a method to overlay a movie star's face onto a stunt double in big-budget films," he continued. "It involves serious high-budget special effects."

"And you think I'm doing it to keep you and your partner chasing shadows?"

Vincente's head wobbled back and forth as if weighing the idea. "It sounds crazy when you say it out loud. It seems less so when you've been running around for months with nothing but video clips to show for it."

"I've heard of deepfake tech," I admitted. "What they do in movies requires specialized framing, preparation, direction, and camera work. Are you implying I have accomplices? Maybe these guys?" I discreetly waved my hand toward the hostage-takers. "Perhaps you should consider a career writing fiction."

Wincing in pain as Walsh worked, Vincente shook his head. "I still haven't figured out how you're doing it. It's interesting that you're using a lot of words not to deny it, though."

I reflected on the statement and recognized that the agent was using this as an opportunity to interrogate me just as I was doing to him. "Maybe concentrate less on the *how* and more on the *why*," I suggested.

He appeared to consider that. Initially, it seemed like he didn't grasp the question. To be fair, the hostage situation and his gunshot wound might have hindered his ability to interpret my motivations. "You knew I was here," he said slowly. "You've been watching us while we chase after you."

I smirked.

"Why?" he groaned, then winced in pain once more.

"You don't know what Breslin is. You can't possibly grasp it. You're being manipulated. I need to know if you're a proxy being used against me or if you're working directly for Breslin."

Vincente was either confused by that or he was an excellent actor. "Proxy?"

"The longer you chase me, the more I learn," I explained.

He nodded. "So, tell me what you've learned."

"Your partner is dirty. He's working directly for Breslin. You... I've grown less confident in your motives."

"My motivations?" Vincente looked angry for the first time since the conversation started. "You're questioning my motives? You've sabotaged more than a dozen ATG facilities. It's my job to stop you and bring you to justice. Why don't you explain yours for attacking ATG at every possible turn?"

That was the question I'd been waiting for the agent to ask. It all came down to that. A legitimate law enforcement agent would, sooner or later, get around to asking that question. One on the take or one simply looking to kill me wouldn't care. They would either already know my reason for attacking ATG—or Breslin—or they just wouldn't care at all.

"Fair enough, Agent Vincente," I said, feeling more than a little relief.

Vincente gasped as Walsh made another attempt at the wound. I saw blood spurt but was ready, having just slipped into a pair of rubber gloves. I applied a thick pad to the wound as Walsh pulled Vincente forward and checked the shape of his shoulder again.

"The round is still in here. I need to take it out," Walsh said.

Vincente muttered a string of expletives that had Walsh and me exchanging grins. "We'll take that as consent to continue," I said.

Amanda showed up with a gallon of water and the bin usually used for bussing tables. It was clean and stacked high on one side with fresh white rags. "Hot damn," Walsh chuckled. But it looked like Amanda wasn't finished yet. She gestured to someone else, and Jimmy stepped up with a tall bottle of whiskey. He set it down on the table with a thud before retreating at a quick wave from Little Red Beard.

"I thought the whiskey might ease the pain," Amanda said. "Is there anything I can do to help?"

Little Red Beard seemed to be enjoying his chance to intimidate Jimmy and was shoving him back to the other side of the bar. I waved Amanda over and whispered, "That's perfect, Mandy. Exactly what we needed. If you can do one more thing, we should be set." She looked me in the eye, and I had confidence that she wasn't as intimidated by these people as most folks in the room. I recalled that Amanda had been in the bar with Piper the last time someone tried to rob the place, and she'd seen how that turned out. This wasn't her first rodeo. Wisdom had come from the experience, however limited it was.

"These clowns don't know what they're doing," I explained. "That's the worst thing going against us. We need to get all the hostages in one place. If the cops come in right now, who knows how many people could get caught in the crossfire? If I suggest moving everyone, they'll find it suspicious. If you do it, it won't seem as odd." I met her eyes. "Think you can do something about that?"

I watched the logic unfolding in Amanda's eyes. "Sure," she nodded. "I'm on it." She turned and walked away. To her credit, she didn't march straight over to Boris. That would have been too obvious, even for this crew. Instead, she made her rounds, presumably to check on several of the hostages. After a few stops, she approached Boris, who was once again in a quiet conversation with the fat man.

I could hear snippets of the conversation Amanda had with the two men. She suggested that she could better keep everyone quiet and comfortable if they moved to the booths along the east wall. She would serve drinks and snacks from the bar, and if she did this, it would ensure that no one caused trouble for Boris and his people. Boris countered that they had guns to guarantee the required level of compliance. Amanda pointed out that one person had already been shot, which had everyone on edge. Her approach would ease tensions more in the long run.

Ultimately, I'm fairly certain she made Boris think the idea to consolidate the hostages was his own. I couldn't have done that. It was impressive work.

"How did you do it?" Vincente said.

I forgot where we were in our conversation "Sorry?"

"Ingersoll is running all over hell chasing your ghosts," Vincente said. "He's been to parts of the country where I'm pretty sure you've never stepped foot, despite the evidence suggesting otherwise. I just can't figure out how you're faking it without leaving evidence we can use."

Walsh nodded that he was ready to remove the bullet. I pushed the bottle toward Vincente again. He had already taken a series of serious pulls on it, but one more good swig would be a smart move before Walsh went after the slug. This was going to hurt. While the kit was stocked with a local anesthetic, apparently, the cops couldn't be trusted with gear containing anything hardcore. Not these days, anyway.

I thought it might also be a good chance to try to slip through the agent's defenses. "You want me to share my secrets? That's asking a lot. I know for sure that Ingersoll is on Breslin's payroll. I'm still not clear on your intentions. You've been dogging me closely, and here you are. You're the one who managed to find me. How'd you do that? How close are the rest of Breslin's goons?"

Vincente was clearly in pain, but when I accused him of corruption, he looked furious. "Don't group me with Chris," he growled through clenched teeth. "I know he's got his problems. I even question his loyalty to the badge...but I haven't seen anything that proves he's bent. If I see that—"

I waited, but Vincente seemed stuck at that point in his statement.

"What will you do if you see proof that he's on the take?" It was a crucial question, and it was fair too. Vincente might suspect it, but without any proof so far, it was reasonable for him to be hesitant to investigate too closely, fearing he might uncover something that would place him in an impossible situation. Ingersoll was his commanding officer.

"Damnit," Vincente said, taking a swig from the bottle. He looked at Walsh. "Just do it."

"One question before he does," I said. "How did you find me here? I must have messed up somewhere. I need to understand how you made the connection so that the people I care about don't get hurt."

Vincente smiled. "That's how I did it: a photo of you with that girl, Piper. I tracked her down and planned to ask about you. Before I had the chance, this shit show happened. The next thing I know, here you are. I still don't understand that part."

Esker's voice sounded in my ear. "Piper's in position. The police are beginning to organize. I think we're out of time."

I laughed and gave Vincente a light slap on his good shoulder. "It's only going to get weirder from here, trust me."

───────────

Vasili Rostovich pulled the black ski mask over his cherubic face and wiped the sweat from his eyes. The heist was not going according to plan, and it was all the fault of that damned red-headed fool, Boris. The safe was supposed to be unlocked during business hours. That was the whole reason they'd scheduled the robbery for the evening. Vasili kicked the four-foot-wide behemoth of a safe and cursed at the fist-sized combination lock and plate-sized locking wheel. He couldn't crack this thing with half a pound of semtex or a dozen sticks of TNT.

"Idiot," he grumbled in Russian, wondering if the safe even contained the proceeds from last weekend's sales, as Martin had claimed.

If he's mistaken about the safe being locked, why would he be accurate about the contents?

Now, the police were outside, likely surrounding the building. Boris planned to simply not answer the phone. He reasoned that they had hostages, and this would keep them safe.

Perhaps it was flawed logic.

"Bezumnyy," Vasili muttered. All of this was insane.

He kicked the bag at the base of the safe. With a sigh, he dropped to his knees and began rummaging through the kit's contents. The hammer and small set of screwdrivers seemed useless. He paused when he discovered the medical stethoscope and contemplated the device. He'd seen it used in movies and understood how it could amplify the sounds of the tumblers moving inside the locking mechanism. He had never taken the idea seriously and wondered why Boris had included the device in the toolkit.

Perhaps it's worth a try.

He slipped the ear tips into place and tapped the diaphragm to check the sensitivity.

"Blya der'mo!" Vasili cursed and yanked the device from his ears.

Glancing around the room to ensure no one had witnessed what was not his proudest moment, he repositioned the device on his head. He gently set the diaphragm beside the combination dial. With a slow turn of the wheel, he grinned. The sound of the internal mechanism was sharp and distinctive.

Walsh dug the slug out of Vincente's shoulder with a minimum of additional blood loss. The agent lost consciousness for about two minutes, speaking to his fortitude and Walsh's skill. Once the procedure was done, Vincente's eyes were glassy from the pain and the whiskey. Walsh removed the latex gloves and dumped them into the bin atop the blood-soaked rags he'd used to clean the wound and the table. I dumped the last of the bottled water over his hands as he rinsed the remnants of blood from around his wrists and removed what little of the carnage had escaped the ends of his gloves.

Walsh pushed the busboy's bin to the end of the table and quickly grabbed the half-empty bottle of whiskey. Taking a long pull, he leaned back in his seat. After a deep sigh, he attempted to pass the bottle to me.

"Keep it," I said. "You deserve it."

Walsh glanced over his shoulder and chuckled. "I can understand you holding out for a Modelo, but this time, I don't see it happening."

"It's not that. It's almost time to leave. The cops are about to come in," I said softly.

Vincente blinked, emerging from the edge of unconsciousness, and became more alert at that statement. He placed his hand on his shoulder as he fought to sit up straighter. "What? How do you know?"

I eyed the agent and tapped my ear silently.

His brows knitted together, and he squinted as he looked at me. Walsh appeared puzzled as well.

"You have comms?" Vincente whispered. His expression was a mix of confusion and hope. "With whom?"

Amanda stood at the end of the table. "You look better," she said to Vincente.

Vincente was slow to turn and register her appearance.

"He's doing well," Walsh said. "A little slow. All the *blood in his alcohol stream* has him confused. The transfusions helped. He wanted me to thank you for the whiskey, isn't that right, Al?"

Vincente's gaze shifted slowly between Amanda and me before returning to Walsh. "Blood in my—" he shook his head slowly. "I've lost a lot of blood. I'm sorry. Yes, I feel much better, thank you."

Amanda smiled. "Under normal circumstances, this would be the point where I'd have to cut you off," she said, giving a wink. "Since you're with these gentlemen, I'm going to leave the bottle. I'll put it on our hosts' tab anyway."

Amanda grabbed the blood-caked bin and headed toward the bar like it was just another day. Vincente stared, slack-jawed, first at the wiggle in her walk as she went, then around the room where armed gunmen still occupied their positions. "I'm not feeling too good," Vincente mumbled. "I think I'm hallucinating."

I looked at Vincente. He was growing paler. "How much blood did he lose?"

"More than a little," Walsh said. "Less than a lot. This might be something else. We should get him help soon. A bullet I can handle.

This…this could be some kind of allergic reaction. I'm not entirely sure."

I whispered as I made contact with Esker. "Any ideas what's happening with the agent, E?"

"I don't have enough information," he replied. "The camera resolution isn't high enough to assist, and there isn't enough ambient RF backscatter to provide internal biometric information. There are three ambulances on screen; they are his best option."

"Understood."

Walsh saw me talking to myself but didn't mention it. He placed his hand on Vincente's arm, and the two exchanged a glance. "Give it to him," Vincente whispered. "It's our best shot."

"Lean forward," Walsh said. "I'll pass you something."

I felt Walsh slip something to me under the table. It was a small, snub-nosed revolver. I glanced at Vincente. "Your backup piece?"

Vincente nodded.

"Keep it," I said, returning the gun to Walsh. "I know where to get another one. Just remember, this thing will be accurate up to about thirty feet. If you have to use it, act accordingly."

I felt Walsh take the gun back. "Where the hell are you going to get another one?" he whispered.

I slid out of the booth. Little Red Beard immediately shifted to block my path. I stepped around him and walked slowly toward Boris, who was still behind the bar. The three armed men in the room instantly went on high alert as I began to move. I made a point of moving slowly and without any overtly threatening gestures.

"Stop. Sit back down!" Little Red Beard squeaked, poking his gun at me as if it were a knife.

I kept my focus on Boris. He seemed to be the shot caller here, or maybe it was the fat man who had been lingering in the back. I knew the fat man had been attempting to crack the safe in the office. We'd been in here for a little over an hour, and the group had yet to respond to a call from the officers surrounding the building.

"Agent Vincente needs a doctor," I told Boris. "He's having some sort of reaction. We need to get him to an ambulance. His condition is deteriorating quickly."

"Names?" I whispered, ensuring Esker knew I was speaking to him. We hadn't planned this part in advance, but if I knew the AI, he had already done the research. It was a gamble, but not a significant one, considering how well I knew him.

"Boris Kasanof, age forty-three," Esker replied without hesitation. "I can provide you with the complete rap sheet if needed. Let me know what you require, and I'll relay it."

I struggled to hold back a laugh. Was Boris's name really *Boris*? What were the odds?

"It's time to wrap things up, Boris," I said. "You thought you could hit this place when the safe was open, but you blew it. Your buddy in the back—"

"Vladimir Rostovich," Esker whispered in my ear.

"Vlad," I continued, "can't crack the safe, so now you're stuck."

Boris's eyes were wide behind his mask. I had read the room correctly, though it hadn't been hard.

Esker added the final two names to complete the list. "The small one with the phallic revolver is Martin Mahew, and the thin man near the back is Vasili Rostovich, Vladimir's brother."

"The best thing you can do right now," I continued, "is to gather Vlad, Vasili, and Martin and give up before SWAT storms the place."

Boris remained silent as he walked slowly down the bar and stepped through the gap in the counter. Vasili moved forward from the back of the room.

Martin—Little Red Beard—looked ready to panic. His head snapped back and forth between Boris and me. As the seconds ticked by in silence, the little guy became increasingly twitchy. "How the hell does he know who we are, Boris?"

Boris glared at me.

Seconds passed.

Little Red Beard twitched nervously.

Boris put his fingers to his lips and whistled. Three seconds later, Vasili emerged from the back office.

"What's going on," Vasili said after looking at how the group faced off against me.

"How much longer with the safe?" Boris said.

Vasili hesitated before answering. "We should discuss that privately," he finally responded.

"How much longer?" Boris insisted.

"I don't think I can open it," Vasili said.

Boris gestured toward Amanda. "Have her do it," he commanded.

Vasili was already shaking his head. "We know she can't. That's why there's a drop slot at the top of the safe. No one on the staff can open it; that protects them during times like this."

Little Red Beard stormed across the room and grabbed Amanda where she sat at the edge of one of the booths. He seized her by a wrist and dragged her back to our gathering beside the bar. "Bullshit," he whined. "She can do it. We just gotta make her." He locked an arm around her neck and pushed the muzzle of his massive Colt against her temple.

I saw genuine fear in Amanda's eyes for the first time since I entered the bar. This was the first moment she truly began to believe she wouldn't make it out of this. That's when my patience for the gang of fools finally wore thin, and my plan to take things slower vanished.

I stepped forward and grabbed the fist Martin had wrapped around the Colt and twisted it. I spun his hand, and by extension, the gun in it, in a clockwise direction with all the speed and force my augmented metabolism would allow. And when I did it, I had his hand in a crushing grip. I felt the finger break inside the trigger guard, the joint in the wrist separate, and I heard the radial fracture somewhere up the bones of his forearm.

There was no chance the revolver would discharge. Being a single-action with the hammer down, the gun was more useful as a club at that moment than as a firearm... that's how I used it. The moment the gun slipped from the little man's hand, I caught it by the barrel and brought the butt down against the crown of his head.

Little Red Beard hit the floor in an unconscious heap.

Boris blinked, staring at me from the wrong end of the Colt before he knew what had happened. I watched his eyes shift from the dark muzzle at the end of the barrel to the cocked hammer and down the single raised arm supporting it. He finally met my eye.

A brief commotion rattled somewhere behind me, then Walsh came into view from my periphery with Vincente's tiny black revolver raised and aimed at the three remaining Russians. "Give me a half-second warning next time," he muttered. "You even caught me off guard." I could hear humor in his words.

Boris dropped his pistol. A moment later, Vasili and Vladimir did the same. Not a word was spoken by any of them.

I heard a wet thwack, and I turned to see that Amanda had delivered a kick to the ribs of the unconscious Little Red Beard. Her face was twisted in disgust as she looked down at her foot. "I think he pissed himself," she said.

Walsh sniffed the air. "Better check your shoe. Smells like more than piss."

Walsh checked the Russians for extra weapons while I held them at gunpoint. They had none. Not only had they done a terrible job robbing the bar, but they were also poorly equipped for the heist. Everything about the job screamed unprofessional amateurism.

"Breaching in thirty seconds," Esker said in my ear.

I glanced at the back of my left wrist and saw a video display in AR where a watch would typically go, clearly thanks to Esker. It showed a camera feed of the bar's rear. The camera moved as if handheld, showing the back wall, the rear door, and the pouring rain. I instantly realized I saw what Piper was experiencing from wherever she had taken cover.

"Neat trick," I whispered to Esker. The ability to see what Piper saw was new—or at least new to me. I wondered if he had just come up with it, or if it was something the team had developed over the time I'd been away from Wild-Side.

To Walsh, I said, "The cops will be busting down the door in twenty seconds. When they do, toss the gun and follow their instructions. You don't want to get shot in the chaos. They'll be amped and everyone will look like a threat. Anyone with a gun is likely to get shot."

He nodded but kept his gaze fixed on the Russians.

"Keep your gun on them until you hear them breach," I clarified in a whisper. "Then toss it. At that point, it will be too late for them to pull anything," I nodded slightly toward Boris.

Walsh gave the smallest of glances. "Done this before?"

I slapped him on the shoulder. "Thanks for everything."

Stepping away from the group, I headed for the back door. On my wrist, I noticed the three officers shift from their positions behind the oblong container they had been using as a barricade. They assembled at the back door while one of them tucked a walkie-talkie into his pocket.

"Six seconds," Esker confirmed.

Five yards before the door to the back alley, I hopped and grabbed the matte black steel beam about ten feet above me, pulling myself effortlessly into the air. With the men's room to the right of the hall and the women's on the left, I was relieved to see that both had been built with plywood ceilings. It made sense since the restrooms had more complex ventilation and electrical requirements.

No sooner had I shifted onto the ceiling of the men's room than a small explosion echoed a short distance beneath my feet. It sounded like the rear door had been completely torn from its hinges rather than just the lock, likely an overreaction on the part of the police department. Maybe they were trying to make up for lost time. Maybe they were just frustrated about standing around in the rain for so long.

I watch the display on my wrist as three officers burst through the door. The instant they passed, I dropped down from the rafter and raced out the back door. Piper was already sprinting toward me from the tree line.

It took Piper far longer than expected to make her way surreptitiously around the perimeter of the Borderline. The distraction caused by the runaway squad vehicles was effective, but it only managed to draw the sentries from their positions at the entrance to the lot for slightly longer than it took Gray to enter the bar. If she had tried to cut through the lot on her way to the back of the bar, she would have likely been spotted at the very least and detained at worst. Fortunately, she played it safe and took a wider route around the property, skirting a stand of trees beyond the northeast perimeter. Time wasn't likely to be a concern since Gray's plan was to use the hostage situation to interrogate Agent Vincente before neutralizing the hostage-takers.

Piper knelt in the mud six feet inside the tree line, just beyond the short stretch of pavement at the back of the bar. From that position, she could see down the length of the bar's eastern wall, thanks to the series of sodium vapor lights mounted to the cinderblock wall every twenty feet. Without those powerful lights, the rain and darkness would have obscured anything beyond thirty feet. The back of the bar was far less illuminated. Two smaller floodlights illuminated the back expanse of the bar: one twenty feet to the left of the wide steel door that served as the rear exit, and the other about thirty or thirty-five feet on the opposite side. The dry cleaner and takeout places farther down either had no lights, had dead bulbs, or the officers had turned them off as part of the operation.

A thirty-foot stretch of cracked asphalt separated the back of the strip mall housing the Borderline from a five-foot-high brick retaining wall. Topped with an eight-foot-tall chain-link fence, the fence's purpose eluded Piper, as it seemed to end where the wall did. Anyone wishing to bypass it could simply walk around the end. It probably had something to do with city codes or some other nonsense. Beyond the fence lay a rugged floodplain, though it was concealed at the moment.

The focus of her attention was the eight-foot-wide box, which sat slightly askew, about two feet from the retaining wall. It stood approximately five feet tall, and although Piper could see it from her kneeling position, she knew it measured ten feet in length. The box was perfectly rectangular and free of any emblems or markings. Its color was flat black, providing no reflection and lacking any obvious means of opening what was clearly a storage container of some kind.

The absence of markings, openings, handles, or lift points might have attracted the attention of the police officers using it for cover if they hadn't been focused on the hostage situation in the bar and grill just a dozen yards away. Piper wiped the streaming water from her eyes and inhaled slowly. She monitored the video feed displayed in AR along the back of her left wrist and wished Gray would speed things up. Esker mentioned she could listen to events inside the Borderline if she wanted to. But with the storm and at least three officers nearby, she didn't need the distraction. Esker would inform her if there was something important happening inside. This allowed her to concentrate on her surroundings.

Her surroundings were the issue at the moment. She had managed to identify two officers using their container for cover. On three separate occasions, two heads had poked out to peek at the rear of the building. Esker had assured her that three officers were positioned behind the Borderline. Until she located the third, the bogey remained a risk to both her and their operation.

Piper's patience would have been exhausted if not for the feed from inside the Borderline. Once she identified the third member of the team assigned to the back of the building, she had no choice but to monitor them while they watched the exit. Esker piped the police tactical frequency directly into her ear, allowing her to stay updated on their plans or lack thereof. "Hurry up and wait" had certainly been the order of the day. No one was willing to give the command to breach, and when the hostage-takers refused to respond to calls from the ranking officer on scene, no one was ready to issue an order that would change the status quo.

Gray had communicated a plan B through Esker to stall the police by informing them that an FBI agent was on the scene if they became overly aggressive. That had never been necessary.

All of this would have resulted in boring, soggy downtime for Piper had it not been for the live feed from inside the bar. Esker could show her video from any camera that was part of the security system, but for the most part, she stuck to a video-only feed showing Gray's point of view. She did switch back to the camera in the office from time to time. One of the robbers was making a nearly cartoonish attempt to crack the office safe–though watching that view for any length of time was a lot like watching paint dry.

Thankfully, she wasn't cold. The technology the Seeley had integrated into her blood was astonishing in many ways, not least of which was her body's ability to withstand extreme heat and cold that would typically have been debilitating. She'd been unaware of the capability until Esker explained it minutes earlier. The tech, however, didn't prevent the constant downpour from frustrating her. While the ball cap kept the worst of the rain out of her eyes, it hadn't stopped the cotton blend of her hoodie from becoming a drenched mess that felt at least three times heavier than usual, clinging to and hanging from her slender form in a claustrophobic way.

Finally, chatter on the tactical frequency grew frenetic. In just two minutes, the entire on-site police force decided to mobilize.

"Here we go," Esker said in Piper's ear.

"Finally," she whispered as she glanced at her wrist. She saw Gray staring down the barrel of an old West-style revolver. Most of the

Russians had their hands raised. One was lying on the ground. She smiled at the almost casual way Gray held the gun and the rock-solid steadiness of his single-handed grip on the antique-looking firearm.

What's it take to rattle him?

She didn't think she'd see much that truly knocked him off balance, not regarding the big picture. There was so much at stake. Laughing, she mused that with everything going on in that big picture, a hostage situation was really just a speed bump.

The signal was given, and the three officers slipped from their concealment to position themselves by the steel door of the Borderline. Small charges were placed. To Piper's surprise, it appeared they were attaching explosives to the hinges and the door lock.

That seems excessive.

The officers moved back to their positions along the wall, two on one side of the door and one on the other. Piper heard the countdown over the tactical channel and glanced at the display on her arm. She saw Gray's video swing and shift wildly before going dark. A second later, an officer gave the signal, and she heard the sound of distant charges detonating and glass breaking. At the same time, she heard the door several dozen yards away explode and watched as the door sagged before it swung into the rain. She saw the heavy steel door tip and splash into the gathering rainwater.

The trio of officers vanished through the door. A heartbeat later, Gray burst out of the same door, appearing as if he'd been forcefully ejected by the building. Piper was already in motion and reached him at the corner of the transport container. She locked eyes with him but found herself unable to speak.

Gray scooped her up in his arms. Her soaking-wet clothes squelched between them, and she stifled a laugh. They both knew they didn't have time. She kissed him on the cheek, and they separated just as quickly. Piper circled the container, examining the featureless surface for what she knew only they could see. When she rounded the far corner, a square on the surface near the top corner lit up in AR space. She placed her hand over the glowing indicator, and it disappeared. The entire top of the box didn't retract or withdraw; it simply seemed to vaporize. She knew it was nanomaterial, designed to disintegrate on command for the fastest possible access to the contents of the container. Before disintegration, the material was as close to indestructible as anything they had on Our-World. If the police had been inclined to try to open the container, they would have faced more than a little difficulty.

Piper placed her hand on the top of the container wall and hoisted herself up and over. Inside, she dropped to one knee and found Gray already there. Dim LED-like lights flickered to life around the perimeter, providing just enough illumination to work by. At the center of the space stood the Airbike. Gray was already releasing the series of finger-thick restraining straps that held it in place.

Along the wall hung a pair of backpacks. Piper unfastened each from the restraints securing them to the wall and quickly leaned them against the side of the Airbike's seat. Finally, she grabbed the first of two sets of interconnected rings hanging from another fastener where the bags had been. She turned and handed the first set of rings to Gray.

Piper pulled one ring from inside another, and the next from yet another. Gray was already doing the same. Securing the largest ring around her waist, Piper grabbed the next two largest and quickly snapped them in place at her knees. Afterward, she paused to look at herself. The rings on her knees fit over her jeans without much trouble, but the ones she was about to place on her elbows posed a challenge.

Looking up at Gray, she saw he was in a similar, though less severe, version of the same situation. In the few minutes he had been exposed to the driving rain, his sweatshirt had become heavy with water.

"Will the armor adjust?" Gray asked, casting a skeptical glance at his own body.

Piper glanced up at him from her low position inside the container. She pushed her cap back and scrunched her nose. *"You're asking me?"*

Gray shrugged and began to slip out of his sweatshirt. He tossed it onto the floor of the crate with a splat and slipped the first of the last three remaining rings into place—one on each elbow and one around his neck. With a tap on his wrist, the nanoparticle armor washed over his body, taking the shape of the matte black motorcycle-style body armor he'd previously used on Wild-Side.

Growling under her breath, Piper climbed to her feet and attempted to follow suit. Bending at the waist to bring her head close to her feet, she slung the hem of her soggy hoodie to the ground. The inertia and gravity combined helped to peel the thick material loose where it had long since adhered to her skin. She heard and felt the sucking sound the cotton blend made as it slipped away. She'd neglected to remove her ball cap, so that was pulled from the top of her head in the process.

She glanced at Gray when she clicked the second of the elbow rings into place.

"You should do that in slow motion, set to a heavy metal power chord," he said with a smirk as water streamed down his face. He watched her with unrestrained amusement while she stood there in jeans and a sports bra, her hair doing god knows what.

You're such a boy.

She shook her head. "Know how long I've been out here sitting in the rain, smart ass?"

Piper clicked the last ring around her throat and activated her suit. Though she hadn't been cold before, she instantly felt the gear's warmth. Her eyes went instantly wide, and her mouth dropped open.

"Yeah," Gray said. "I'm pretty sure the suit is trying to dry my pants. The sensation is…*interesting.*"

Gray scooped up their discarded clothes and stuffed them into one of the packs before slinging it over his shoulders. He handed the other pack to Piper, who put it on without comment. She shifted subtly from side to side like an adult doing the peepee dance while she tried to figure out what she thought of the strange tingle running across her lower body as the armor aggressively attempted to dry her soaked jeans.

"Do you need a moment alone?" Gray chuckled.

Esker sounded in both their ears. "Officers seem to be moving toward the back of the facility. Estimate eighteen seconds." Piper observed a sense of urgency in his tone.

"Are you driving, or am I?" Gray asked, motioning to the Airbike.

Piper felt a surge of panic at his obvious lack of urgency. "Shut up and fly," she hissed.

Nodding, Gray hopped onto the seat and tapped the power system to life. Piper threw herself onto the seat behind him, tapping her wrist to activate her helmet. In less than a second, it materialized around her head. She pressed herself tightly against the pack that separated her from Gray and then gripped him firmly around the ribs.

"Good?" He asked, this time over the comm channel inside the helmet.

"Punch it," she said.

And he did. A whisper-like whistle sounded beneath them, and gravity seemed to quadruple. The machine shot skyward like a demented elevator. Everything went momentarily black—Piper focused solely on holding tight. She felt tethers fasten around her hips and knew the Airbike had responded by activating the automated restraint system.

Gravity normalized moments later, and Piper's vision became clear. She leaned to the side and noticed they were slicing through the night and rain at a speed she likely didn't want to know.

Breathing a sigh of relief, Piper reflected on everything they had gone through just to gather their gear. "Well," she said, "that was easy."

"Look on the bright side," he replied. "All of this shows that our next trip to Wild-Side can include little perks like shirts and pants."

She couldn't help but laugh.

Chapter 23 - His Hand Now Wobbled Like One Of The Afflicted

Our-World

Shelbyville, Tennessee

For obvious reasons, Alison Springs wasn't safe for us anymore. Besides, that unprecedented thunderstorm proved we needed to take immediate action to prevent another storm like it from revealing our position or affecting our general location with the same catastrophic consequences. We doubled back to Piper's apartment to gather the few items needed for a road trip, but then we didn't hit the road…

We took to the skies.

Derek Smallwood agreed to meet us just outside Shelbyville, Tennessee. With the Airbike cruising at an average of one hundred sixty miles an hour, we could make the trip in a little over three and a half hours. This was assuming we could fly the shortest possible distance, which was, of course, a straight line. This was more or less achievable, with some minor adjustments. We had to climb to extreme altitudes around densely populated rural areas and avoid a few commuter flight paths by diverting slightly.

Ultimately, we completed the trip in just over four and a half hours. Our gear was packed into overstuffed backpacks that hung like saddlebags across the seat behind Piper. We wore our armored suits, allowing us to Transition to high altitude and back down to our more comfortable cruising level of around twelve thousand feet without making the trip unnecessarily tricky or fatiguing.

Smallwood had parked his rig in a small clearing in the woods, beyond what appeared to be a long-fallow field, two additional cornfields, and about a mile down a dirt road from an ancient-looking farmstead. He must have traversed the rutted, rocky, overgrown trail that skirted the barren field to reach the back and enter the tree line. It was no small feat considering what he was driving. I approached from the south and made a pass, searching for signs that the meeting location might have been compromised. Thermal and IR scans of the field and the canopy beyond the tree line revealed only the outline of Smallwood's RV and what seemed to be a single human presence. The forest registered multiple life signs of various sizes, all too small to be human.

Circling again, I approached low and slow–buzzing quietly just five feet above the path's surface. We traced the route Smallwood likely took as he drove in. The rough terrain would have been tough on his suspension. Piper laughed behind me, clearly sharing the same thought. "The last stretch of his drive must have been incredibly uncomfortable," she mused.

We followed the narrow separation at the tree line and the tunnel in the overgrowth beyond. I figured the Airbike shouldn't have any issues if the RV made it through. However, broken tree limbs to our left and right showed that the RV needed to make accommodations for itself. This increased my confidence that this meeting hadn't been compromised or staged. Both are positives in favor of this not being an ambush.

"So far, so good," I said quietly, feeling Piper tap gently on my ribs in response. We had come as prepared as possible. Along with wearing our armor and helmets, we each had a pistol holstered at our hips. We looked like sleek, futuristic soldiers approaching a shady deal rather than like a couple getting ready to meet someone I considered a friend.

Smallwood consulting with an outsider on our project weighed heavily on my mind since I learned about the breach of confidentiality. While I didn't outwardly feel that he was working against me, the lie–an omission at the very least–was more than a little concerning. We were here to clear the air and see what we could do to mitigate the factors that led to the thunderstorm that resulted when Piper and I Transitioned together.

Derek Smallwood stood on the step of his Winnebago, half in and half out of the door, as we quietly hovered up the path and took our position about two dozen yards before him. His mouth hung open, and he just stood there, staring wide-eyed. I lowered my helmet without removing my hands from the handlebars. As he watched my helmet disintegrate, his eyes, already impossibly wide, somehow widened even further. He sagged and nearly fell the rest of the way out of the RV.

I gently set the Airbike on the ground as Smallwood awkwardly settled onto the bottom step of the camper. The RV was a thirty-five-foot twin-axle Bus with a wide side door and a set of retractable stairs. It had been entirely renovated inside to suit the requirements of this project. While the exterior looked like any other RV on America's interstates, the interior was far from ordinary.

"That…that," Smallwood stammered as Piper and I climbed off the Airbike. "I don't know what's more incredible–that machine… or what your–" his outstretched finger indicated the side of his head– "gear just did."

Piper released her helmet as we walked, taking a moment to let her long blonde hair down from the band that held it back. With a near-silent groan, I noticed her bending and stretching her back and legs as she moved. It had been a long, exhausting ride.

I reached out to Smallwood, helping him to his feet before shaking his hand. "Derek, this is Piper."

Smallwood's gaze shifted slowly back and forth between me and Piper, his unblinking expression having cooled only by a few degrees. I hadn't intended to make this kind of entrance, and it struck me for the first time that I could have warned him about how we would be traveling. I'd been careful not to divulge too much to too many about these matters. This time, it was working against me.

As Smallwood looked me up and down, he clearly found the body armor intriguing. Given what he observed the helmet could do, that was understandable. His analytical mind was likely pondering what else the suit might offer. However, when his gaze lingered on Piper's figure longer than necessary, I decided the formfitting aesthetic was more distracting when he focused on her. Piper might have started to wonder too, as I noticed her cheeks flushing.

"Doc," I said and mused at how many doctors and professors had become part of my life in recent years. "Why don't we go inside? You can share your conclusions about the storm and how we can mitigate the fallout?"

Smallwood nodded and glanced back at the Airbike. "Then later, you'll tell me about this incredible machine?"

I nodded. "You bet."

"I'll need a place to change," Piper said. She had already grabbed our bags and handed me mine with a tight-lipped shove and a hard glare. "Maybe wash up?"

Smallwood quickly nodded, "The bathroom is just inside on your left. Spare towels are in the cabinet across from the washroom door."

Piper pushed past me, ascended the stairs, and disappeared into the RV. Smallwood immediately moved to the Airbike and began to circle it slowly. "This is amazing," he said, gesturing wildly with his hands. "Those propellers are big, yet the flight was so quiet. I admit, I have dozens of questions!"

A scratching sound at the tree line behind me caught my attention, and I turned to see a small squirrel clinging to the base of a vast tree. It wasn't quite a baby, but it wasn't an adult either. It spiraled around the elm's trunk as it made its way higher.

"That won't end well," Smallwood said, waving a hand vaguely toward the broad boughs of the thick branches overhead.

Initially, his meaning was unclear. Then I noticed the thick mud wasp nest spreading wide where a limb as thick as my thigh met the tree trunk. A few insects buzzed near the half-dollar-sized opening in the sagging lump of the nest. The nest seemed to vibrate as the squirrel reached the supporting limb and attempted to climb higher. A cloud emerged from the opening in the clay-like surface of the nest. The squirrel reacted instantly and darted for the ground. The cloud shifted, seemingly tracking the path the small rodent had taken. Only then did I notice the subtle saw-like buzz in the air as the swarm made chase.

The squirrel must have sensed the danger because it moved quicker than I thought possible. The leaf litter covering the forest floor parted in the wake of its escape. The cloud of insects, hundreds strong by my estimate, banked and shifted as a single mass as it picked up speed in the chase.

Smallwood chuckled. "At least the little bugger ran away from us. If he'd gone for cover under the camper, it would take hours before we could step outside."

I didn't respond. My gaze drifted from where the swarm had vanished and settled on the now motionless and silent nest slightly smaller than a basketball. The reaction from the nest had been instantaneous, a primal response to a threat. The coordination of the community must have been a hardwired reaction, something occurring at the genetic level.

Smallwood nudged my arm. "You okay?"

I nodded. A plan of action was finally forming in my mind. Although not fully developed, it already had immense potential. The swarm reminded me of how the Elend had pursued me outside their underground lair.

"Um, Gray?"

I turned around to see Piper halfway down the stairs, leaning out the door of the Winnebago. She looked… well, it was hard to say exactly. Concerned, maybe even sick. Perhaps alarmed.

"You should take a look at this," she said after a long pause.

I glanced at Smallwood, who simply stared at me. He didn't seem to understand what she was talking about. Curious, I followed Piper into the RV.

Across from the door stood a small couch. To the right was a small table cluttered with unidentifiable electronics. Beyond that, on the right, was access to the driver's and passenger's seats. To our left, things became a little more interesting. A five-foot-long stretch of counter lined the wall next to the entrance. On the counter rested a long glass tank with thick walls. Inside, a clotted gelatinous fluid bubbled, shifting between shades of pink and light red, gurgling and circulating behind the glass.

"What in the freaking hell is that?" Piper grumbled through clenched teeth. She had her back pressed firmly against the counter on the opposite side of the vehicle, which, perhaps incongruously, housed a sink, stovetop, and kitchen counter. "It looks like he liquefied a…a person."

Smallwood finished climbing the stairs behind us and was staring at Piper. He pushed the black frame of his glasses back up on his nose, then turned to gaze at the bubbling tank. "Huh," he said. "I guess it does, indeed." Then he looked at me with concern in his eyes. "I should do something about that! Can you imagine if I ever get pulled over?"

I smirked, already shaking my head. This was my first time seeing this setup in person. I knew the plan and understood what Smallwood was putting together and how he was doing it, but I had never stopped to consider what it would look like. I had never thought that he would fail to camouflage the equipment once the system was operational.

Esker's voice sounded in my ear. "Research indicates that highly functioning intellects often struggle to understand concepts that those with lesser intelligence might categorize as common sense."

I squinted at my inability to respond to Esker at that moment, aware that I was the lesser intellect in his scenario. When I spotted the broad grin splitting Piper's face, I realized Esker's comment had come through our shared channel.

Piper shook her head, likely in response to Esker's comment. Noticing that I didn't share her alarm, she stepped away from the far counter and lifted the palm of her hand off her holstered gun. "Care to explain?"

Smallwood stepped forward and took the initiative. "This is the secret sauce, so to speak. Our method for preventing that strange weather phenomenon from revealing Gray's location when he Transitions back to our Brane at the same time as Breslin or when Breslin is already here. So long as the biomass in these tanks is more than seven percent greater than Gray, the curiosity is… well, redirected, for lack of a better term. Instead of honing in on his position, the storm front concentrates on this—well, on me, honestly. That's why I need to keep moving."

When Smallwood placed his hand on the front of the tank, he did so with a clear sense of pride. At that moment, I noticed the long rectangular tank was divided into two equal-sized cells. The contents of both appeared to be the same, although the sludge on the left seemed to be circulating faster than those on the right.

"What's the difference between the two sides?" Piper asked, beating me to the question.

Smallwood stepped back to give us a better view of the entire tank. He flipped on a long, thin LED light that hung from the cabinets above the enclosed tank to illuminate the device better. "For this to be effective, the biomass must be living, viable cellular material," he explained. "Human tissue, as you likely know, doesn't survive long once separated from the host body. To keep this…distraction, shall we call it…operational, we need to maintain the tissue alive."

Piper's nose crinkled as she looked at Smallwood, clearly skeptical. "You found a way to keep Gray's tissue viable long-term?"

"Unfortunately, no. But we found a workaround," Smallwood clarified. "Since the biomass is only useful for a maximum of thirty-six hours, that gave us a time window to generate additional material to replace it. As long as new material is ready to supplant the old in time, the ahh…distraction…remains effective."

Piper's gaze swept over the inside of the RV. She went to the far end and through the door, presumably leading to the sleeping quarters. "You're talking about cloning," she said with a tense expression as she stalked back. "How? You don't have the space or equipment for that here. You mentioned you have to keep moving. Aren't you always on the road?"

Smallwood glanced at me anxiously. Piper's tone indicated that he was being accused of something. He either disliked it or was unsure what the accusation entailed. I shrugged and said, "Please explain. She's the brains of our team."

"Cloning," he said with a slow nod. "But only in the most basic sense of the word. It's more akin to adding yeast to bread to make it rise. It's not much more complicated, either. Not once you have the right yeast, so to speak. And the right catalyzing component." He leaned over the top of the tank and pointed to the small black cylinder fused into the glass or acrylic along the wall, situated halfway between the first chamber and the second. It was half the size of a coffee can and looked reasonably unremarkable except for the small, coarse grate that seemed to expose its contents to each chamber independently.

Piper looked at me. "Were you aware of this?"

I shrugged. "No one used the word cloning." I glanced back at Smallwood. "What can Breslin do if he gets access to my genetic material? Could he use it to reverse-engineer the Crossing? I was very clear about that security concern when we discussed this project. It's a deal-breaker."

As he shook his head, Smallwood stated, "Absolutely not. That would be impossible."

I guided him to the chair beside the table cluttered with electronic equipment and motioned for him to sit. "I'd feel more confident in your statement if you hadn't just repeatedly used the term 'we' when describing your work on this technology. Since I know you're not referring to me when you say that, why don't you tell me who else was involved?"

Smallwood slumped in his seat. "That..." he paused and seemed to weigh his words. "It wasn't a lie. Maybe an omission," he finally said. "Your project was intriguing—fascinating, really. As you know, I've been absorbed in Brane Theory since my early days at university. But no one takes it seriously," he glanced pointedly at Piper. "I don't need to tell you that, right?"

Piper said nothing.

Shrugging, Smallwood continued. "So anyway, when your friend Esker approached me, I was intrigued. Initially, I thought he was a crackpot. However, the more we communicated, the more I took him seriously. Then, as you know, considering what your team was paying, I was open to experimenting with the hypothetical. Why not? I could play with my theory and get well compensated for it. Who wouldn't?

"The thing was, the models worked. Well, they did right up until the twenty-four-hour mark. Then, things started to become unreliable. At first, I thought it was just an unfair parameter in Esker's game, you know, since this was all make-believe. But then we changed some of my assumptions, and I could move the twenty-four-hour mark to thirty-six. When I did, two things happened. First, I realized that none of what I was doing was hypothetical. The genomic information Esker provided was very specific. I stopped considering this a game or exercise and treated it as real-world.

"And that's when I broke the rules and reached out for help," Smallwood finally concluded. "I knew it was against protocol. I knew it could cost me my position on the project. But I was so close to a workable solution. I thought that if I did this anonymously and didn't reveal any information about the project, what harm could come from it?"

The pain was intensifying behind my eyes, a migraine of epic proportions. For this reason, I'd always found maintaining a small social circle challenging. Bringing Smallwood into my confidence had been necessary; the storm back in Alison Springs had illustrated that perfectly.

But this?

Piper looked at me with concern. She understood this was serious. The real question was, how bad?

"Who did you contact for help?" I asked. It took everything I had to keep my tone conversational. No matter what happened next, Smallwood's technology was critical for preventing the strange storms from first compromising my geographic position with a given Crossing and, more importantly now, for stopping the storms from causing escalating damage if Piper accidentally or intentionally Crossed with me. The storms could be avoided, but only if Breslin and I were never on the same Brane at the same time. I had never found a way to control something like that. Until my last crossing, I had never had any control over it.

"Hell," I groaned and rubbed my eyes.

Smallwood appeared more uncomfortable now than ever before. "I have no idea who I've been in contact with," he said, rubbing his sweaty palms on the legs of his slacks. "We never exchanged names. We don't even have email addresses."

My teeth were grinding. "How do you communicate?"

"We don't anymore," he said with a shrug. "The last exchange was—" he paused to think about the question. "Well over six months ago. Maybe even nine? We spoke in a dark web chat. It's anonymous and untraceable."

Piper looked just as confused as I was. "Why is it taking so long?" she asked.

"It was just a consultation," Smallwood said. "As I said, he knew nothing about what I was doing or why. Only that I had an issue with the tissue samples not lasting as long as I needed. He proposed the approach that is now used as the catalyst. There was also an additional issue of how to circulate the genetic material to ensure proper exposure. We worked on a sketch of the schematic for two nights. I paid a consulting fee via bitcoin, and the transaction was complete."

"He never asked why you needed this or had any questions about the project?" I pressed.

Smallwood shook his head. "It's not all that unusual. There are tech and science enthusiasts on the dark web who troubleshoot like this. Some make a good living and have built strong reputations for their work. They all operate under pseudonyms, but the work can be lucrative."

I knew I was scowling. I wanted to punch something, though I didn't know exactly why. Smallwood's insincerity was undoubtedly part of it. His consultant put us at increased risk, that much was clear. But if he'd done all this months ago and I hadn't been captured or killed, maybe I was overreacting. Still, it felt like I was missing something.

This thread had to be pulled until we understood better what was on the other end.

"What do you think, E," I said.

"Doctor Smallwood seems to be telling the truth," Esker replied. "Or, more accurately, *he thinks he's telling the truth*. I made a mistake by not monitoring his communications more closely. I should have been aware of all this."

That conversation could wait. Esker was a powerful AI, but I had mixed feelings about having him monitor our friends' communications. While keeping an eye on Breslin's minions, like Ingersoll and Vincente, was fair game, it felt wrong to watch people who were supposedly on our side.

Eyes widening, Smallwood sputtered, "Who—who are you talking to?"

I glared at the little scientist and said, "Esker."

"Oh," he said with a sigh, sagging slightly. "Tell him I said hello. I wish he could have come in person. I've always wanted to meet him."

Piper let out a laugh that sounded like a cough.

"I'm examining Doctor Smallwood's history on the dark web," Esker said. "I'll find the chat room and any traces of the conversations."

I had a better idea. "Derek," I said, "What will it take to add Piper to the Offset?" Shortly after the project started, my biomass amalgamation was referred to as the Offset in communications. It seemed more tactful than calling it *Liquid Grady* or *Ledger Slurry*.

Smallwood's expression grew distant as he idly scratched at what seemed like an early attempt at growing a beard. Perhaps he just lacked proper facial hygiene. "I have a prototype tank stored under the *bego*," he said quietly, almost as if he were thinking aloud. "And I always keep a spare catalyst, so that's taken care of. We could use that on her rig," his gaze returned to us. "But since two is one, and one is none, that leaves me without a backup catalyst in case of failure." He shrugged, a gesture that conveyed, *what can I do?*

"When was the last time a catalyst failed?" Piper asked, her expression thoughtful.

"Hasn't happened yet," he admitted.

Esker's voice sounded in my ear, and from the look Piper gave me simultaneously, he must have spoken to her, too. "Fabricating a pair of replacements will take four days. I can place the order now, and work will begin first thing in the morning."

I looked to Piper, who nodded back. It was clear from the way she kept glancing at the tank of circulating pink and red material that she wasn't thrilled about everything she saw, so I led the group outside before continuing our conversation.

"What do you need to get the process started for Piper?" I asked, gently latching the side door behind us as we gathered outside the RV. Even though Smallwood drove the Winnebago all over the country with the tanks bubbling and percolating just as they had been, I couldn't shake the thought that slamming the door might splatter a bit of my genetic material across the linoleum floor of Derek's rolling Creepshow.

"Just a blood sample, like with you," Smallwood confirmed. "I've significantly improved the process since we first started. I won't need pints to create the base this time. About what you usually give for a normal blood donation will be enough for the source material. I have what I need for the draw right here." He looked at Piper for confirmation. "We can do it now if you want."

"There's no time like the present," Piper said.

I asked, "Do you feel confident that this will offset Piper like it does for me?"

Smallwood suddenly appeared uneasy. He took a second too long before nodding.

"You'd feel better if you could contact your consultant again?" I offered.

He glanced at me from the corner of his eye, still uneasy with the admission. After a long breath, he nodded.

I didn't want to seem obvious, so I let the silence stretch. Looking briefly at Piper before replying, I finally spoke. "No names, and keep the details as vague as possible. We need the best minds working on this. I just need to know the project hasn't been compromised. If I knew you needed outside help, vetting additional resources would have been easier. This isn't the ideal way to bring in help." I shrugged. "Given what we saw with that storm, right now, we just don't have the luxury of ideal conditions."

The point, of course, was to create an opportunity for Esker to trace Smallwood's consultant so we could identify him. It was disingenuous not to explain this to the doctor, but I had to keep him in the dark since his knowledge might compromise the effort. Plus, we genuinely needed the best minds addressing the problem. The strategy simply ensured we understood whether those minds were working for us, against us, or might one day be turned against us.

_____

Our-World

Alison Springs, Maryland

Chris Ingersoll pushed through the door of Al Vincente's room with his verbal onslaught chambered and ready to go. He paused, mouth agape, when his eyes met those of the blue-eyed nurse changing the dressing on Vincente's shoulder. Whatever he had been about to say was suddenly lost. "Al," he said instead, blinking slowly. "Glad to see you're okay. You have everyone worried."

The nurse tore off a strip of tape and used it to secure a gauze pad to Vincente's shoulder. "You'll have to wait in the hall," she said, giving Ingersoll a pointed glance. "I'll be finished with Mr. Vincente in about five minutes."

"That's okay," Vincente said, waving Ingersoll into the room with his good arm. "Lisa, this is my partner, Chris."

The nurse pinned Ingersoll with a stern expression that softened after a moment. "Alright," she said as she returned to work, pulling on the roll of tape. She glared at Vincente and spoke more quietly. "You've been on the phone all morning. You should be taking it easy. A gunshot wound is serious business. You can't rest if your mind and body are still stressed."

Ingersoll approached the foot of the bed. "I just need a few minutes with Al. After that, he's on bed rest. Bureau orders."

That satisfied the fussy nurse, who completed her work and took Vincente's vitals. She scribbled a series of notes on a clipboard before leaving the room with little more than a stern expression.

"I don't think she likes me," Ingersoll said as he eased the hallway door shut.

"She's a great judge of character," Vincente said with a smirk.

Ingersoll glanced at the equipment hanging on poles from the corner of his partner's headboard and the complex diagnostic tools on freestanding carts around the edge of the bed. Most of it chirped or hummed in some subtle way. "They really have you wired up."

Vincente seemed to slouch a bit more deeply beneath the covers. He tapped a button, lowering the incline of his bed by a few degrees, and Ingersoll noted the glassy sheen in the agent's eyes. "They have me on some morphine derivative," Vincente remarked, as if acknowledging the attention.

"Is there much pain?"

Smirking, Vincente said, "Not when the morphine kicks in."

Ingersoll laughed and stepped closer. Having his partner in a more compliant state would make the conversation easier. That might be better if he didn't remember the details of their talk when it was over. He noted the pump with the small upturned glass vial suspended from it and the tube leading to a complex metering device. This would be the pump used to dispense the pain medication. He approached the device, pulled the tube from the restriction mechanism, and allowed another generous amount to flow through the line before pushing it back in place.

"What are you doing?" Vincente asked.

Ingersoll had deliberately obstructed his actions by positioning himself between the bed and the machine while he made the adjustment. "Just taking a closer look at your hardware, buddy," he said, then stepped back to the foot of the bed.

The nurse nearly burst through the door and into the room. Ingersoll stared at her in surprise but did his best to mask his confusion about the disruption. "Problem?" he asked as she glared at both of them.

Lisa looked at Ingersoll with suspicion, then glanced at Vincente for several long seconds. "Is everything okay in here? One of the machines just set off an alarm."

"All good," Ingersoll said. "You good, partner?"

Vincente took his time to reply. "I'm tired," he said, a slight slur in his voice.

Lisa glanced at them again before fixing Ingersoll with her gaze. "Ten minutes. Not a second more. Mr. Vincente needs his rest and hasn't been getting it."

Vincente nodded and watched as the nurse left through the door. He paused for a moment before moving to the doorway and quietly closing the distance behind her.

That woman could interrogate murder suspects. She's got the chops for it.

"So, buddy," Ingersoll said as he stepped to the foot of the bed again. "You finally came face to face with our boy, and you let him get away."

Vincente stared back but remained silent.

"You with me?" Ingersoll grabbed Vincente's foot through the blankets on the bed and shook it. "Stay with me, buddy. You saw our boy, right?"

"Sure," Vincente said, nodding slowly. "He was there. Sat right next to me and everything."

"So you talked with him?"

"Talked?" Vincente paused for a moment. "Yeah. We talked."

"What did he say?"

With his eyes slowly scanning the room, Vincente seemed to

ponder this for a moment. "He knew we were after him."

Ingersoll rolled his eyes. "There are a lot of people after him. That's hardly going to make the five o'clock news."

"No. He knew we were after him. He knew you and me by name. It felt like he'd been keeping tabs *on us* while we were keeping tabs *on him*." Vincente paused and seemed to drift. "Dirty," he murmured.

Shaking Vincente's foot again, Ingersoll said, "Wait. Say that part again. What did you just say? What's dirty?"

"The kid says you're dirty. He thinks you're working directly for Breslin and don't care about arresting him. If you catch him, he believes you'll either kill him or take him to ATG."

The room seemed to darken as Ingersoll's vision constricted into a narrow tunnel. The kid knew more than he should. It was exactly what Breslin had predicted, but Ingersoll still didn't comprehend how. He was just a kid, after all. Maybe they were right and had been underestimating him up until now. But that changed this morning. While Ingersoll was here, Breslin's goons were ransacking Piper Hudson's apartment.

Preliminary interviews were underway with the scientists Piper worked with at the University and the bar where she worked nights and weekends. One of the two would undoubtedly lead to additional locations where the couple would likely hideout. Ingersoll felt closer to Grady Ledger now than ever before. For the first time in longer than he cared to admit, he was doing more than chasing a ghost.

Vincente had begun to doze. Ingersoll grabbed his partner by the foot once again and shook him back to a semi-wakeful state. "Hey, Al. Stay with me. We're almost finished. You spent a lot of time with the suspect. What else can you tell me about him?"

"What else?" Vincente looked puzzled. Then he grinned. "Hey, Chris. How are you?"

Ingersoll smiled broadly.

No memory at all.

He wondered whether he should give Vincente another dose of

morphine just to be safe. Glancing at the door, he reasoned that the nosy nurse was unlikely to dismiss it as a glitch again. Getting caught would raise questions he couldn't answer. It was better to be in and out.

Ingersoll slapped the back of his partner's foot to ensure he was paying attention. "What else did you get? You're an agent, for Christ's sake. I hope you did your job and learned something about the suspect while you had access to him."

His eyes widened, and Vincente became clear for a moment. "He took down the HTs by himself," he said, referring to the hostage-takers. "He did it without breaking a sweat." His head shook slowly. "It was like he was crossing something minor off his to-do list."

"What?" Ingersoll said, his forehead furrowed.

"As if he could have done it at any moment." Vincente licked his lips and locked eyes with Ingersoll. "I felt like *he* was interrogating *me*."

A half dozen questions fought for Ingersoll's focus, pulling his mind in different directions. Before he had a chance to frame any of them for his partner, the phone in his breast pocket began to ring. As he retrieved it, Nurse Lisa stepped into the room. "Time's up," she said and gestured him toward the door.

Glancing at the bed, Ingersoll saw that Vincente was already asleep. With luck, he wouldn't remember the visit. If he did, the details would be nothing but a blur. It was as good as he could hope for. It was time to remove Vincente from the investigation, even if he hadn't been shot. He had never been as invested in the hunt as Ingersoll and the rest of ATG's security team.

"Ingersoll," he said as he tapped the phone to life in the hospital corridor.

"Sir, this is Moffit," the voice on the line said. "I've just reviewed the security footage from the night in question at the Borderline Grill. You'll want to see this… it's—well, it's unexpected."

"Give me something to work with. Use your words, man," Ingersoll insisted.

"Well, sir. On the night of the event, when the target exfiltrated, he used some sort of...it seems to be an unidentified flying machine."

Ingersoll stood frozen, his finger still on the elevator's call button. "Moffit," he said through gritted teeth. "Are you trying to tell me that the target used a UFO to escape?"

"Yes. Well—no. Not really. Sort of? I'm not sure what it is. You have to see the footage."

———————

Chris Ingersoll sat in the passenger seat of an armed and armored Cadillac SUV as it sped through downtown Shelter Spring. One of the unnamed goons from Breslin's corporate security team drove while two others occupied the back seat. They'd supposedly been recruited from other lucrative private military firms, but in Ingersoll's view, that didn't indicate competence or professionalism. It only suggested they were even more opportunistic mercenaries. Although they were meant to be on his side, he had little confidence in any of them.

"ETA is seven minutes," the driver said as he skidded through the stale yellow light, causing the SUV's traction control to blip audibly.

Fighting the urge to grip the oh-shit handle above his door, Ingersoll instead concentrated on not dropping the small digital tablet in his lap. He ground his teeth and swallowed the curse on the tip of his tongue, then hit play on the video again. Footage from a camera positioned high on the rear corner of the Borderline Bar's wall began to play for perhaps the fifth time. It showed Grady Ledger positioning narrow bands around his knees and hips before slipping out of a sodden sweatshirt and adding more rings to his arms and neck. A moment later, he activated some kind of technology and, as if by magic, futuristic, form-fitting body armor wrapped him from head to toe.

A second later, Piper Hudson followed suit and stripped down to a sports bra that Ingersoll only saw briefly before she positioned the same devices on her extremities. She took a few extra moments to tie her hair into a restrained bun, and then she was swiftly transitioned into a strange new outfit that resembled a mix of tactical gear and football pads. Ingersoll chewed his lip, still unsure about what he was witnessing as he watched the couple mount a small, agile flying craft and blast out of frame in what must have been a high-G vertical climb.

"New intel?" the driver asked as he slammed on the brakes. His hand hit the steering wheel, and a barely audible curse escaped his lips.

Ingersoll glanced up just in time to see a Toyota Prius stop short at the light. Looking at his aggressive driver, he noted the color on the mercenary's face and how close their bumper was to the rear of the Prius. "Just worry about the road," Ingersoll admonished. He had spoken with Breslin personally and had been told not to share unnecessary information with the rest of the team. It seemed he wasn't the only one who didn't fully trust the hired help.

The phone in Ingersoll's breast pocket began to vibrate. He retrieved it, tapped the screen, and placed it to his ear, saying just one word. The caller provided a clear and concise report without delay. As he watched the Prius pull away, Ingersoll breathed before disconnecting the line. He glanced at the driver with mixed feelings about the new orders. "Change of plans," he said, tapping an address into the dashboard screen.

When he hit enter, the navigation system responded with an audible reply. "Routing to Rinaldy Veterinary Clinic. Estimated time of arrival: seventeen minutes."

An arrow on the screen directed the driver to turn right at the current intersection. The mercenary seemed to interpret the seventeen-minute estimate as a challenge from the onboard computer, as he spun the wheel and stomped the accelerator to the floor. The SUV took off with the screech of rubber against asphalt, and Ingersoll's head snapped back into the headrest.

Ingersoll was seeing red, fighting the urge to deliver a verbal reprimand while calculating the odds of how that reprimand would affect his real-world game of Carmageddon as this team of gun-toting clowns raced across town.

One of the goons in the back seat laughed. "Faeber, you asshat. Remind us—what did you do before joining Red Spear and ATG?"

The other goon was laughing like a high school student.

The driver, Faeber, cornered hard and accelerated even harder. This time, Ingersoll reached for the oh-shit handle without hesitation. Faeber pressed the pedal to the floor, and the engine roared. The narrow, one-way street started to tunnel as parked cars on both sides blurred with speed. He glanced over and met Ingersoll's gaze with a steady, unhurried look. "I was a stunt driver for five years before I realized I liked shooting just as much as crashing."

Alarmingly, Faeber's foot remained planted on the floor while his gaze stayed fixed on Ingersoll.

Psycho—This guy's a psycho.

A riot of laughter erupted from the back of the SUV. Ingersoll's bladder was in a race with his bowels to see which would fail first, and his mind was slowly recognizing that all three men in the vehicle with him were more than just a bit off their rocker. He drew his pistol from its holster and positioned himself directly in Faeber's line of sight. He was surprised to see how steady his hand looked. "If we wreck, I'll shoot you in the face," he offered quietly because it was the only voice currently left in his mental toolbox.

A smirk spread across Faeber's face as he eased off the accelerator. He nodded once and then turned to face the road again. "Huh," he said, amusement lacing the brief statement, and began to brake more aggressively.

"In fifty feet, make a left turn," the navigation system announced.

Ingersoll turned quickly to the front and realized with a start that they were about to run off the road, regardless of whether he could get the driver to pull himself together. He swallowed the acidic bile rising in the back of his throat and looked down to find that the steady grip he had on his gun just moments before had changed. His hand now wobbled like one of the afflicted. He slipped the gun between his leg and the seat. He didn't want anyone to see the shakes, but after what he had just experienced, he no longer trusted this group enough to keep the gun out of easy reach.

As Faeber eased the SUV into traffic at the next stop sign, he shot a quick glance at Ingersoll. "What's the deal with the Vet?"

Ingersoll was confused. "Sorry?"

Faeber pointed to the navigation system. "You're rerouting us. You must have new intel."

Nodding, Ingersoll watched the driver with unblinking eyes. It was as if the drive towards death had never happened. He looked like the same guy who had picked him up at the hotel that morning. Glancing at the navigation system, Ingersoll observed their ETA had been reduced by four minutes. It felt like an unfair trade, as he was sure he had also forfeited at least a year of his life due to the trauma.

Nodding, Ingersoll said, "Yeah, new intel. It's best if you just focus on driving."

Knocking at the back door of the veterinary office, Ingersoll wasn't surprised when it opened to reveal a somewhat attractive thirty-something with shoulder-length brown hair. She stood about five foot six–five eight in the heels she now wore as part of her business casual ensemble. It was as much camouflage for her as a ghillie suit for a sniper, and the comparison was fitting, he knew. She was every bit as dangerous.

"Olivia," he said, brushing past her.

"You made good time," Olivia said with a smirk. She glanced back at the three mercs standing beside the SUV, the only vehicle in the deserted rear parking lot, and then pulled the door shut and threw the bolt. "Tracking suggested you'd be another four to six minutes, maybe more with traffic. Your driver must be good."

Ingersoll rounded on her, his eyes wide. "That man is clinically insane," he practically spat. "If you or Breslin ever place me with any of those three again, I'm walking. It's the end of the deal."

Olivia was Breslin's head of field logistics. She flew into Shelter Spring as soon as the recent sighting of Grady Ledger was confirmed. While Ingersoll didn't know much about her background, the rumor was that it included time with army intelligence as well as a stint with the CIA. Though Ingersoll didn't put much stock in rumors, every interaction he had with Olivia gave him confidence in her capabilities.

Olivia offered little outward reaction to his raised voice, other than to lift one dark eyebrow. After a long moment, she shifted and looked back down the hall they had just crossed, staring at the door. "Faeber was driving?" she said slowly, savoring the sentence as it rolled off her tongue.

His hands raised in an expression—really, do you think—Ingersoll glared.

She spoke in a slow, measured tone. "Faeber is under orders. He's never to drive." She looked Ingersoll right in the eye. "I'll handle that myself."

That was perhaps only the beginning of a conversation Ingersoll wanted to have about staffing, but something in Olivia's expression when she made the statement made him rethink extending the discussion longer than necessary. If other rumors were to be believed, Olivia didn't handle HR grievances with reprimands or performance improvement plans. A chill went down his spine.

Everyone in this outfit is operating with a sprung spring.

Not for the first time, Ingersoll wished he had played things a bit more like his partner and kept his nose clean. Al Vincente was in a dangerous position of his own, but it wasn't one of his own making. Even Ingersoll knew his ambition had been responsible for sinking him into the pit of quicksand that was ATG. If anything happened to Vincente, Ingersoll knew that responsibility for it would ultimately fall on him.

"Our missing professor is right through here," Olivia said, gesturing toward a wide set of swinging doors down the hall.

Ingersoll pushed through the doors and found himself in the main operating room of the veterinary clinic. A conventional hospital bed had been placed in the center of the space where the usual exam table would have been. The sizeable articulated light arm suspended from the rafters had been shifted to the edge of the room, and the equipment typically used for treating pets and animals had been replaced with high-end alternatives.

On the bed, a slightly inclined male figure lay supine. His eyes were taped shut, and he had been intubated. Numerous machines surrounded the head of the bed, all displaying diagnostic information. One of the largest devices featured a clear panel with an accordion-like cylinder that expanded and contracted in sync with the rise and fall of the figure's chest, facilitating his breathing.

"Doctor Kramer Fulbright," Ingersoll said, his tone low. His gaze moved slowly up and down the bed and across the array of complex devices. It finally rested on the flat panel display labeled EEG. "That's electro-something, right?"

"Electroencephalogram," Olivia stated.

Stepping closer, Ingersoll looked for subtleties on the display that he might have missed at first glance. All the colored lines on the display were completely flat. "Maybe it's not connected properly?"

Olivia turned to meet his gaze from across the bed. "That was my first thought. Unfortunately, the equipment has been double-checked, and a backup unit was used to confirm just before you arrived. Doctor Fulbright is completely brain dead."

Ingersoll felt his face twist in response. "I can't see Ledger doing that to the man. He's never hurt anyone in the past. Certainly nothing like this."

Olivia shrugged in response. "With Al Vincente in the hospital, the investigation will rest entirely on you. But I tend to agree. That wouldn't align with his history." Her eyes roamed the room, and she appeared ready to share more.

"If you have any further thoughts, I welcome them. Between this and what happened at the Borderline, we're closer to Ledger than ever before. There's no such thing as too much information in an investigation like this, especially when we're dealing with someone as resourceful and intelligent as Grady Ledger."

Something shifted in Olivia's expression as it moved over the crippled figure and met Ingersoll's gaze, making him feel like he was seeing a side of the woman he'd never encountered before. "I don't think Ledger did this to Fulbright," she said softly, her voice husky. She pointed vaguely toward various parts of the life support equipment. "I suspect something happened to this man, and Ledger tried to save his life." She swallowed hard. "A futile, failed effort." Then she shrugged. "I could be wrong. Your investigation will reveal the truth."

Ingersoll nodded slowly. "The twenty-thousand-dollar question is, why?"

"And the hundred-thousand-dollar question," Olivia added. "Where is he now? Ultimately, that's what we need to answer."

Pike watched the veterinary clinic from concealment across the street. The overflowing steel dumpster on wheels was stacked with discarded wooden pallets, rolls of moldering plastic sheeting, and piles of industrial supplies, making it easy for him to create a burrow for himself and Alley Lauer. He didn't view the position unfavorably compared to some of the observation posts they had used in recent years. Although the smell was less than pleasant, they had fashioned a concealed cubby that allowed for greater flexibility in movement and space for their audio and visual surveillance equipment. And since Gray had outlined the caliber of people they were up against, they went the extra mile to line their hide with insulation to mask their thermal signature. Even if the team at the clinic thought to sweep the area, Pike's team would remain invisible to all but the most invasive detection efforts.

Alley adjusted the contrast on the camera attached to her tablet. "Right there," she confirmed, waiting for Pike to slide onto his belly. The team leader found a position beside her on the ground in the dark in front of the screen. The camera they had among the scattered debris was aimed squarely at the clinic's facade. As they adjusted the settings, it allowed them to scan the building's surface and focus on heat signatures.

"Right, nice tech," Pike whispered back.

They could see a pair of men standing like pillars at what was clearly the rear door of the building. Another group flanked the front door, hidden from view, but thanks to the camera equipment, it was clear they were just inside the entrance. "That one's a corrupt FBI agent," Alley said, tapping the larger of the two men positioned near the center of the building. They both recognized the horizontal figure as Doctor Fulbright.

"Seger is running facial recognition on the woman," Pike said. "She seems to be some kind of shot caller, judging by how the others deferred to her."

"Nice to see a woman in charge," Alley quipped.

Pike was already shaking his head. "I'll hand you the crown any time you like. You're a group of chinwagging dilettantes. Nothing would make me happier."

Shoulder-checking him and offering a wink, Alley returned her gaze to the screen. "I still don't like giving Fulbright up to the bad guys," she said after a short silence.

"We've done all we can for him. He's brain dead," Pike said. Though his tone didn't convey much, it expressed displeasure. "As hard as it is to believe, I think he made it to wherever he was trying to go. He just didn't make it back. In my opinion, that makes this less of a tragedy. If he died proving what he wanted to prove, it's not our place to criticize."

Alley said, giving him the side-eye, "not like you to be all philosophic."

"Guess I'm just getting old," he said with a smirk.

They watched as the team in the clinic across the street moved Fulbright's body into a panel van. Immediately afterward, the woman and the FBI agent left in separate vehicles. The agent drove away in the Cadillac SUV, while the woman left in a sedan that arrived just long enough to pick her up. The vehicles departed in different directions. Pike and Alley stayed behind to observe as figures inside the building remained long enough to conduct a systematic search for any evidence, but as best they could tell, nothing was collected.

"Send an update to Gray," Pike said. "This op is complete. We'll rendezvous with Seger and Unger to initiate the next phase."

Chapter 24 - Backed Into A Corner

Wild-Side

A flash of light erupted and a ringing filled my ears. I knew everything had changed forever when I blinked away the orbs floating in my vision. I immediately noticed the lack of physical pain. The head-to-toe burning that had accompanied every Transition was absent. At most, there was a slight disruption in my balance. There was no strange taste in my mouth, and the urge to vomit had vanished entirely. Perhaps most importantly, I was still dressed. I wore the same tactical pants with pockets lining the outside of each leg, the same t-shirt and hoodie I'd had on when I laid down and closed my eyes, and the same hiking boots I'd worn back home.

Fighting the fear that I was dreaming, I patted my chest, stomach, and the front of my hips—arriving on Wild-Side in any form other than naked was a win. It was almost too good to believe. My wrist brushed something at my hip, and my eyes widened as I felt the holstered gun. It should have been the first thing I checked.

A smile split my face.

"Hell yes," I whispered to myself. "About damn time."

I was fingering the point where the subcutaneous, rice-sized adapter had been injected into my forearm before I became aware of it. The device was designed by Cormac and Lacy and included in the packs stowed with the Airbike when it was sent to Our-World. The tiny device would log everything possible from the Transition and then help me better adjust physically to the Crossing I experienced nearly every time I fell asleep. The idea was that by making infinitesimally minor adjustments to my existing biorhythms, the device would allow some control over my shift between Branes. The first step was to reduce the physical discomfort associated with each crossing. The second was for me to cross with my clothes and any gear I was in close contact with before the Transition. Cormac suggested that the second part might be easier than the first since I'd somehow managed to bring Piper with me previously.

"Way to go, Doc." I grinned.

Clothes, and I didn't feel like horking my guts out.

The tiny device in my arm would gather additional data with each subsequent Transition, ultimately giving me greater control over my shifts between Branes. Although I didn't understand what that would mean at the time, I hoped to manage how I brought Piper to Wild-Side and only assist her in Crossing when it was intentional. There was a possibility that the device would ultimately grant her control over her own Transition.

A beelike buzzing in the trees overhead brought me instantly to my feet and heightened my senses to full alertness. I hadn't been that distracted by a Crossing since the early days. It was a bad time for my situational awareness to falter, and my heart began to hammer in response to the realization. My pistol was drawn and shifting quickly as my eyes tracked the sky, visible through occasional gaps in the green tree canopy. The temperature and the sun's position indicated that it was daytime or afternoon.

My HUD blinked to life and displayed the time as one twenty-four in the afternoon, with the temperature at seventy-one degrees Fahrenheit. I had never even noticed the minor indicators in the corner of my eye that were meant to show the status of my HUD as it booted.

A new auditory awareness kicked in a second later, enhancing my hearing to the sounds overhead as my nano augmentations activated. I moved laterally beneath the dense tree cover, trying to prevent the foreign sound from taking a position directly above me. I would have a clearer sight picture if I weren't targeting twelve o'clock high. The sound was close and unusual, yet not completely unrecognizable. It sounded like…

My mind searched to connect the sound with anything familiar to Wild-Side, but I came up blank. No animals here made that sound. Suddenly, the image of the five-inch FPV drones I'd played with—the inspiration for the Airbike—popped into my head. The pitch of the buzz was small and reedy compared to the Airbike; it sounded much more like the radio-controlled quadcopters from back home.

The sound source emerged as it descended sharply through a break in the canopy. It swiftly moved about thirty yards ahead of me and hovered roughly eight feet above the mossy forest floor.

"Gray," a voice called in my ear. I noticed the small articulated camera on the front of the drone. "Welcome back!"

Wes's voice was unmistakable. I instantly knew he was looking at me through the drone feed, so I waved. "This is new," I said, gesturing toward the unusual flying device. It resembled the dinner plate-sized racing drones from back home, though this one appeared much less homemade.

"Lots to tell you," Wes said in a rush.

I noted the interval as it was displayed on my HUD. Three months and four days had passed since my last trip to Wild-Side. The offset between my Brane and Wild-Side was erratic and unpredictable. Maybe the sensor in my arm, acting as my personal black box, would help Cormac.

"Since you're here, could you direct me to the nearest transport point?" I asked.

"No need," Wes chuckled, just as I noticed the deep tones of prop wash approaching from the east. "Your ride will be here in seven seconds. Head to the clearing fifty yards south-southeast so it can avoid the foliage."

The quadcopter drone shifted and darted in the designated direction as a visual aid. My brows raised, I shrugged, then jogged to keep the small drone in sight. A couple of seconds later, a riderless Airbike appeared just beyond the tree line in the clearing.

"Hot damn," I bellowed and ran for the bike.

What Tripp could achieve in a short amount of time always impressed me. We had ideas about automating the Airbike so that it could be piloted by someone back in the city or could track my location by other means. Those other methods were still open topics when I left Wild-Side last time. Clearly, Tripp had been solving problems on his own.

I hopped onto the saddle seat, positioned my feet, and grabbed the handlebars. I blipped the throttle and the bike shot straight up into the sky. The moment I cleared the treetops, I scanned the skies. There was no sign of the flightworthy Elend, so I ascended to three hundred feet and put the bike into a hover. Retrieving my gear from the compartment on the frame, I began slipping the suit rings into place across various parts of my body. Ten seconds later, the nanotexture of the suit enveloped all but my head, and the armor protected me. A circle enclosing a green dot appeared on my HUD, and I immediately knew which direction would take me to Doc Cormac and the rest of the team.

Trip's voice came over the communication channel. "Hey there, Gray. Welcome back. Do you want to keep control, or should we let the automated flight system handle it?"

Automated flight system. The words replayed in my mind three times before I could respond. Once again, I felt a wide grin splitting my face.

"Impressive work," I said when I found the words. "Show me what you got!"

He laughed. "Alright. Hold onto your asshole," he hollered.

I laughed so hard that I tipped back as the bike surged ahead. "Ass," I chuckled, blinking away tears from my eyes while the wind lashed my face. "The phrase is, hold onto your ass."

Tripp and Lacy were waiting for me near the entrance to the underground city when the Airbike touched down close to Garwin. Their faces were lit up with excitement, presumably at my return. I didn't envy their perspectives. Even though I was only gone for a day or two, they experienced anything from a couple of days to several months every time I returned to Our-World. It was a lot of time to ponder whether I'd fallen prey to the Elend or was just back home tackling the Breslin problem from my side.

"Tell me about the mini drones," I said as I stepped from the frame of the Airbike. "You were on me crazy fast. Was that luck, or did you manage to make it work?"

"Oh, you have to see this," Tripp said, waving me toward the corridor leading out of the common area. There was an unmistakable pep in his step, with Lacy attached to his right arm. I noticed right away that they were holding hands.

I've missed a lot.

———————

"You've seen this little guy," Tripp said, holding up a replica of the small drone I had encountered in the wilderness. The flight back to Garwin took just over an hour, even while traveling at one hundred thirty miles per hour, so there was no way it could have been the same drone I'd seen. It couldn't have kept up.

"We have hundreds of these monitoring the skies all across the continent," Lacy explained, handing over a device that seemed to duplicate the one in Tripp's hands. "They're all networked and communicating with each other as well as with us back here."

The drone was about the size of the toys I'd used back home, but this one was significantly lighter–lighter than just the battery I used. That power pack could only keep the drone aloft for five or six minutes when I was piloting aggressively, executing flips, rolls, and high-speed maneuvers. "How much weight does the power source add?" I asked.

"You're holding it," Tripp said. "The power source is onboard, and it can fly in the dead zones," he added.

My mouth must have been hanging open because Lacy quickly added, "That was thanks to an idea Piper had when she was here. She explained how hydrogen-based fuel is used back on Your-World. Tripp engineered a capacitor that allows our existing technology to run using hydrogen instead of conventional zero-point power."

I was immensely amused to hear zero-point energy referred to as conventional. Back home, even hydrogen fuel cells were hardly the norm. Here, they were developing their far superior technology to run on something less powerful and less efficient than a fuel source they took for granted.

"The mesh network covers the continent," Tripp explained. "And we're receiving a lot of data. Monitoring you is just one of our successes. Doctor Cormac has also been tracking the movements of the Elend. We're learning more about them than ever before."

I had a dozen questions, ranging from how they were keeping the flight-capable Elend from decimating the drone network to how long the mini drones could run on hydrogen and even more inquiries about how the drones were deployed, maintained, and replenished. While Tripp would explain everything eventually, I was fascinated by what had changed during my time away.

Lacy stepped forward. "Doctor Cormac is waiting to see you. He was relieved to see that you Transitioned without losing your wardrobe this time."

I nodded and tapped the pistol on my hip with my hand. "Not arriving defenseless is a big win, too."

"The Doc is already reviewing your latest telemetry," Tripp said as we walked. "It proved the Thonian fields of the dead zones are the result of the Transition."

"Like the storms on My-World?" I had suspected as much for some time but had mixed feelings with the confirmation.

"Different Branes seem to create various atmospheric effects. Whenever you or Breslin cross, Thonian radiation builds up in the atmosphere," he explained. "Doc believes we can further refine the algorithm. That might reduce or even eliminate the side effect."

I nodded. It would be great if I could Transition without harming the Wild-Side ecosystem. This was yet another reason to stop Breslin as quickly as possible. Even if we could mitigate my impact on the dead zones, he would continue to create invisible fronts that negatively affected Seeley technology.

I settled near the entrance this time, dropping through a break in the canopy and landing in an expanse of knee-high grass that was barely wider than the Airbike's frame. I grabbed the pack from where it was strapped to the side of my seat and reviewed the drone telemetry one last time before swiping the display with my hand. I would be alerted if any movement was detected, and it was better to avoid the distraction that the constantly updating display brought to my field of view.

It was about a hundred yards to the bunker's entrance, and I crossed the distance quickly. In the back of my mind, my senses tingled with concern over an Elend attack. They could approach without me knowing, what I understood about the facility buried in the ridge suggested there was only one way in and out. I was willingly backing myself into a corner.

The steel door set into the earth was almost hidden among the foliage, even when I was just a dozen yards away. In the dead zone, my internal tech was useless, so finding the entrance so quickly required a bit of luck. The door was slightly ajar. Closing it behind me last time had been impossible since I had been under attack.

I pushed the door closer to shut and examined the symbol etched in relief on the surface at eye level. The backward-facing letter R was pressed tightly against the letter B in the same, unstylized typeface. As my enhanced vision focused on the monogram, I noticed the logo was still only slightly covered with a film of lichen. Spitting on the wall, I was about to wipe away the green film but reconsidered. Pulling a black-bladed dagger from the back of my belt, I scraped the logo free of growth instead. To the right of the pair of letters, my effort revealed another character or shape. It resembled the number eight, elongated and rotated ninety degrees to lie on its side.

The symbol for infinity, I guessed. One loop connects to the adjoining loop in a figure eight. Tracing the shape with a finger, the loop on one side leads directly to the loop on the other through the confluence point at the center.

I didn't understand what the additional character meant. It wasn't part of the Radon Brucker logo I recognized from home. Maybe it represented a different branch or division of the company? I felt like this was meaningful in some way…, but I had no idea of its significance.

Realizing the imagery was captured through my enhanced vision, I didn't linger with the logo or the door. I stepped inside and pulled the door shut behind me. When the door didn't latch, it shifted back to its partially open position. A fist-sized gap separated the leading edge of the thick metal from the door jamb.

Once again, I was grateful for the drones above. With a nod of my head, I summoned the map on my HUD and confirmed that all but one of the drones had positioned themselves over the bunker and its surroundings. The last remaining device was expected to arrive on station in just over eight minutes.

My nanotech had been updated shortly after my most recent Transition back to Wild-Side. Most of it now worked in the dead zones. While it couldn't pull energy from the zero point fields here, my parasitic experience with the technology had demonstrated an ability to operate for periods if I were the power source. The Doc had simply allowed me to disable the tech if it impacted me negatively.

I had become a human battery. It was a trade-off that increased my safety in dead zones—one that could one day save my life.

With that reassurance, I turned to the underground room and blinked slowly as my eyes adjusted to the inky blackness of the space. Shifting the pack off my shoulders, I pulled a golf ball-sized orb from the top of the main compartment. I gave it a slight squeeze, and light pulsed to life in my hand. I opened my palm, and the orb took flight. It positioned itself ten feet away, hovering five feet above the floor. The light dimmed when I looked directly at the device but grew brighter as my gaze shifted away.

I shook my head. The technology of this world continued to

confound me. I had asked Tripp for a flashlight, and this was his response. I had no idea how the device hovered or produced such bright light. I started to wonder if the hover mechanism could be adapted for use on the Airbike. If we could eliminate the rotors, the bike would be completely silent.

My attention focused on the matter at hand once again. The empty, booth-like structures divided the expansive floor into numerous aisles, and I was once more reminded of the milking floor of a massive dairy farm I had visited as a kid. I initially thought this was indeed such a place. Upon further observation, if this had ever been used for wildlife in the past, there was no way it could have been cleaned so thoroughly. Whatever the booths had been used for–

This is no dairy farm, I noted, and moved quickly to the wall at the far right of the space. Partway along its length, I found the pair of sliding doors I had observed during my initial visit. I dropped my pack to the floor and retrieved a prybar that I used to separate the doors. As before, I noted that the wide shaft had been flooded, with the water surface less than a foot below the steel floor beneath my feet. The floating light orb shifted into position over my shoulder, providing better illumination in the darkness. The pale glow of the light turned the water's surface into a mirror, and my optics were powerless to penetrate the dark surface.

I assumed there was an elevator down there somewhere. I could only wonder how deep the passage went. The overall depth and what it provided access to directly influenced how long it would take me to learn what I could before exfiltrating. Although there was no reason to believe the Elend would eventually find me here, history suggested otherwise.

Oddly, the drones monitoring the area outside gave me less peace of mind than I had hoped. I concluded that the single entrance and exit added to my stress. For years, I had made every effort to identify multiple escape routes from every building I entered. This location clashed with the practices and traditions that had served me well for so long.

Eager not to waste any more time, I unzipped my pack again. This time, I retrieved a canister shaped like a thermos. One side of the cylinder was mashed flat, so I placed it against the shaft wall, just to the right of the open doors. When the device clicked into place using what I could only assume were magnets, a new icon appeared in the corner of my visual display. I blinked and waved my hand to invoke this interface.

The display confirmed that the device's battery capacity was at one hundred percent. A small green button marked Initiate was visible. I reached out and tapped the button before swiping the display away. A series of tiny pellets dropped from the downward-facing end of the canister. The surface of the water rippled as they vanished like small stones into the depths.

Without waiting to see what happened next, I returned to the main compartment of my pack and retrieved a small box. It was a cube about five inches on each side. There were no markings on the silver-black surface, though a ring the size of a silver dollar marked the top. It protruded from the top plane of the cube by only an eighth of an inch. I retrieved a small, oblong silver cylinder from my pack and clicked it into place on the surface of the protrusion. When I did, the surfaces of the cube shifted. A mass of thousands of tiny holes appeared across the four sides of the shape. The air hummed softly with a barely audible vacuum-like sound.

I returned to the flooded elevator passage and observed that the water level had already receded by several feet.

"Damn," I whispered, swiping my hand through the air to summon an AR display in front of me. An air quality readout appeared, revealing nitrogen levels far into what was deemed my respiratory danger zone. With a twitch of my finger, I activated the helmet of my body armor and blinked as it formed around my head with the soft rush of nanoparticles.

The device mounted on the wall was operating faster than I anticipated, separating the fluid into its components, hydrogen and oxygen, at a molecular level. I drew a deep breath of the filtered oxygen within my suit and directed my focus back to the AR display floating in front of me. The levels of hydrogen in the air around me were already dropping back into the safe range as the cube on the floor next to me purged that element from the air and captured it in the attached canister. The capacity of the storage receptacle was under one percent, so the device wouldn't require attention any time soon.

Looking back at the dark chute, I noted that the water level had fallen several more feet. I grabbed another light orb from the pack, squeezed it, and placed it hovering just below the ceiling of the shaft. As I did, I noticed a pair of doors at the first sub-level had come into view. The water level of the shaft had reached equilibrium as water from the first sub-level flowed back through a finger-sized gap in the doors almost as quickly as the conversion pellets cleared the water.

I decided that I could expedite the process. I just needed to separate the elevator doors so that sub-level one could be drained more quickly.

As I returned to my pack, I pulled a black rectangular box from where it had been secured with straps snugly against the bottom exterior. The device measured about three inches wide and tall, and eight inches in length. A small hole marked one side of the featureless surface. I recognized this as the front of the device, so I leaned forward and pressed the back of it against the wall directly under the open doors where I was kneeling. The elevator door below me was draining, with rushing water being the only sound in the confines of the long-abandoned space.

The oblong box snapped into place against the shaft wall with a clang and a muted echo. I ran a finger across the small hole on the face of the device, which was now oriented in the same direction as me across the expanse of the chute. In response to my touch, a line began to unspool from within the box. It was led by a pair of inch-long, wafer-thin rods placed parallel to each other. I pulled the end of the line further into view and separated the rods. As I did, they shifted to create a rigid square frame that was a quarter-inch to a side. I knew it was essentially a small D-ring. It clicked audibly into place on a loop that had just appeared along the front of my belt.

Although Tripp had explained how the rappelling gear worked, time was short, and I left the underground city before he could demonstrate the integrated functionality to me.

I clicked a small, dime-sized module onto the wall beside the ascender and noted its activation when a green light pulsed in the corner of my HUD. This was a camera. I could use it to monitor the water level if I moved too far from the mouth of the elevator. While the water level was dropping, that could change at any time. Whatever had caused the space's flooding could flood it once more, and while my armor would function similarly to scuba gear in a flood, it couldn't save me from a cave-in.

Taking the integrity of the gear on faith, I lowered myself into space. My arms reached full extension as I lowered myself, and I felt my weight taken up by the filament-thick line latched to my belt. I let go of the floor edge overhead and spread my hands wide to touch the walls. Since then, an indicator had appeared in my HUD, allowing me to control the speed of my descent.

It took only a few seconds for me to reach the doors at the entrance to the first sub-level. The water level beyond the doors was about five feet high, as indicated by the spray still shooting from the lower part of the gap at a constant rate. Stepping into that jet, I slipped my gloved hands into the gap between the doors and pulled them apart.

As the doors separated, the force of the resulting water wash sent me crashing into the far wall of the shaft. The rappelling device reacted immediately, as if it had a mind of its own, pulling me higher and away from the torrent. I felt the wall of water strike the front of my body, but my head-to-toe body armor softened the potentially bone-crushing impact. Thanks to the integrity of the form-fitting gear, my collision with the opposite wall was jarring yet painless.

Several minutes later, the flow of water draining from the first sub-level slowed to a trickle. I activated an AR display and reduced the conversion of water into its component elements so that while the water level continued to drop in the shaft, it did so more gradually. I needed to expose the next sub-level, but doing so too quickly could lead to unexpected consequences. I had no idea how deep the passage went or how many levels it would reveal. According to my HUD, the capacity of the storage receptacle was at six percent.

Confident in the technology, I lowered myself to sub-level one, kicked off the wall, and grabbed the door frame leading to the lobby beyond.

——————

The first sub-level resembled the one above, featuring a floor made of bare concrete covered in a sealant that glimmered faintly with moisture. My optics illuminated the pitch-black subterranean space so effectively that it was easy to forget I was relying on night vision technology. A series of horizontal, capsule-shaped devices lined the floor in front of me. They were about the size of single beds, perhaps slightly larger, and were shaped like empty gelcap medication. It was clear they were designed to accommodate supine human figures. The head of each device was slightly inclined, and some form-fitting padding appeared to have once conformed to an absent bipedal form.

Stepping closer, more pods came into view—row after row, organized neatly in ranks, disappearing beyond the limits of my optics. I walked slowly down the aisle between the first and second rows, my mouth going quickly dry, and I noted that every single pod was empty.

"What the hell happened here?" I muttered as I scanned the floor. Dozens—no, hundreds of pods were visible. The thought of the additional sub-levels flashed through my mind, and I waved my hand through the air to invoke my AR display. Sub-level two appeared half clear based on what I could see of the water level in the elevator shaft.

A blue glow caught my attention in the distance. It was pale and seemed to pulse dully. It was the first sign of functioning technology since I discovered the digital lock at the facility entrance was operational. For the first time, it occurred to me that I might be able to power up the facility's lighting if I could find a control console. The thought had barely entered my mind before I dismissed it. The facility appeared deserted, but who knew? I'd left the door open on my last visit. Any kind of wildlife could have wandered in here, and while none posed a threat to me, it wasn't impossible for an Elend to have found its way here since my last visit.

As if invoked by the idea, an alert flashed in my HUD. I froze mid-stride and waved a hand in the air. An AR display appeared, floating before me. It was a map of aerial imagery showing everything within a ten-mile radius of my current location, complete in every detail, thanks to the information gathered by the drones. A pair of red dots had just entered my established perimeter, triggering the alert. Their size and speed made it clear they could only be Elend.

It was strange that the creatures were moving together. In my experience, they were mostly solitary beings, particularly when hunting in the wild. However, they weren't unintelligent creatures, so it was probable that they had begun moving in pairs—or even packs—recently.

The pair of dots moved steadily, but they did not vector directly toward my location. This meant they were either hunting or had been in the area since my flight in. I couldn't tell if they were searching for me, but I had to assume they were. I also wondered if there were more beyond my established perimeter. I could push the drones wider, but without adding more to the formation, the tactic would result in coverage blind spots.

I decided to leave the drones as they were. Instead, I added a new warning perimeter. I would be alerted if the pair moved within a one-mile radius of my location or if more entered the ten-mile cordon. There was now a reason to search more aggressively, even if there wasn't yet a reason to worry.

My attention returned to the pale blue pulse in the distance, and I swiped the display away. The color and glow instantly reminded me of something, but it took me longer than it should have to make the connection. As I moved closer, a softball-shaped object became visible. It rested atop a shiny round metal pedestal just below chest height, positioned without adornments at a gap in the endless ranks of empty pods.

"Oh," I whispered as I stepped closer. The orb looked like a twin to the one I had seen in the storage facility Doc Cormac had taken me to not long ago. The difference was that the device was damaged. It had a crack, and a cleft in the pristine glass surface was unmistakable, as was the iridescent blue substance that had leaked from it.

This was significant. My brief interaction with the device in the warehouse was unsettling. Some of the things said that day continued to trouble me, not just because of what was said but also because of how it was said—and for what I would later come to believe had been left unsaid.

The blue fluid appeared to have leaked from inside the orb. It clung to the edge of the cleft, ran down the side, and puddled on the top of the pillar or pedestal. When I splayed my fingers out horizontally, the pool was slightly smaller than my hand. The substance must have once been liquid, likely gel-like in nature since it hadn't spilled beyond the surface of the support. Only a tiny bit had dripped over the edge of the platform. It seemed to have solidified before it could reach the floor. The substance had long since hardened. It looked dry and solid, even though the room had been underwater until perhaps fifteen minutes ago.

Though dry and motionless, the blue substance emitted a slow, undulating pulse. It gave off a subtle, iridescent glow that was impossible to look away from.

At this point, I'll admit, I don't know what I was thinking, but I disengaged my glove and laid the pad of my finger on the glowing blue surface. The moment I did, my view of the room was replaced by visions that were much more immersive than augmented reality.

My view of the room was replaced by what immediately felt like footage from a camera mounted high on the wall somewhere in the underground facility. A tag in the corner of the feed read "SL1." I interpreted this as indicating it was footage of the floor I was currently on. However, the scene was different. The room was well-lit, and the ranks of pods were far from empty. Each capsule contained a human form, each appearing pale and blurry beneath the slightly murky surface of the encasing material.

I observed hundreds of people, and row after row of devices containing them were visible. The expanse of the floor was much more apparent, likely due to the overhead light and certainly because of the camera's position high on the wall.

Four figures in long white lab coats—two men and two women—moved slowly through the field of pods. Each carried a small handheld device that they swept over the upper half of each pod, appearing to make observations before moving on to the next capsule.

A timestamp appeared in the corner of the video feed, but I couldn't be certain what it meant. The time and date format was unfamiliar to me. This was a new experience, as the translation capabilities of my internal tech had long become second nature, thanks to their incredible ability to translate the language of this world into my own.

Whatever I saw was unknown to Cormac's tech, and this realization resonated with me. What I saw was somehow more relevant to the larger mystery of this world than I initially suspected.

The camera view shifted to another camera. Since this feed was also labeled SL1, I understood I was seeing the same sub-level. The timestamp indicated the same time and day, but the position of the coated figures moving slowly across the floor made it evident that I was viewing a more expansive area of the floor space.

Not hundreds, I realized instantly. Thousands of pods spread across this level.

As if in response to my thoughts, the camera view shifted to a new feed. This footage looked identical to the previous footage except that it was labeled SL2. Three women and one man were the figures moving slowly across the floor. If I interpreted the timestamp correctly, it indicated the same date and time.

When the view changed again, I was seeing SL3. It was virtually identical to SL1 and SL2—only this time, the date stamp had changed. If I understood the foreign format correctly, what I saw now indicated weeks had passed. The timestamp advanced by more than a week, and SL4 came into view. It was also nearly identical to the other levels and contributed to my estimation by calculating the number of pods: hundreds of thousands, by my best guess. Possibly more than a million. I was seeing flashes of the sub-levels, each from a different angle. This suggested that the sub-levels were more expansive than the ground level, and if that was true, it became challenging to estimate the number of figures in stasis.

I wanted to look at the floor around me again, but shifting my gaze from this first-person view was impossible. That thought suddenly made me aware that I couldn't see my HUD or the sensor feed showing the location of the pair of Elends approaching my position.

During the ride here, I hoped the experience would be informative and brief. Once again, as if responding to my thoughts, the view changed. SL5 appeared for the first time. It mirrored the higher levels, but this time something different was happening. The timestamp showed it had been over a week since I last saw SL4. The camera seemed unsteady, as everything in the frame shook with a subtle quiver. Then, the view jolted abruptly, and I saw the field of pods rock in response to the disruption.

The feed jumped to another position on SL5, providing me with a clear view of the far concrete-like wall as a crack split its surface. The rupture appeared where the wall met the floor and spidered out in both directions. Its extent across the floor wasn't entirely visible, but as the fissure spread above the halfway point in the wall's height, it began to widen. An orange-red light emanated from beyond the wall, and seconds later, what seemed to be lava started to jet from the gap.

The gap widened in just a dozen seconds, and so did the flow of magma. I held my breath as the view shifted, and SL4 appeared. This time, I noticed what was clearly a different concrete wall. It ruptured, this time with a horizontal fissure that rapidly expanded before a section of the wall collapsed, sending a torrent of water that visibly rocked the camera. A second later, the feed went dark and was replaced by a view of SL3. That shot was quickly swapped for SL2, where I saw a dozen or more figures in lab coats sprinting across the floor. Though the video feed was silent, it was impossible to miss that the figures were talking as they ran; most of them waved their arms with wild gesticulations, making me think they were using some sort of augmented reality display of their own.

The experience that had captivated my entire view vanished, and I could once again see the expansive floor beyond the fractured orb. The crust of blue leakage appeared to have changed; it now seemed less gel-like and more liquid. Pulling my hand away from the substance, I tried to free my fingertips from the sludge but quickly realized none of the blue material had come off the central mass. My fingers were completely clean.

Somehow, I had just been shown a series of brief excerpts from the facility's internal surveillance system. I knew this, even if I didn't understand how.

An alert flashed in the corner of my HUD. I immediately activated an AR display and noticed that the two Elend contacts had crossed the one-mile perimeter I'd set for a follow-up notification. A wavy, zigzagging line marked the map's surface, illustrating the route the contacts had taken across the forest before finally breaching my new perimeter. The creatures appeared to be searching, sweeping through the wilderness instead of aggressively approaching my position. If they were aware of my presence at all, they didn't know where I was.

I had time, I decided. From what I could observe, they wouldn't reach the facility for some time yet. I had time to explore further. It wasn't lost on me that their ongoing search pattern would soon likely include the entrance to the underground facility.

I switched to the control interface for the water conversion technology and increased the rate to maximum. This triggered a notification, and I realized I needed to replace the storage receptacle to prevent hydrogen levels from exceeding the filter's capacity to contain them.

With one more brief look at the fractured orb, I wondered whether I should take it with me. Considering how it had captured my entire awareness, even for a short period, I decided the risk outweighed the reward and left it behind. As I headed back to the elevator shaft, I reattached to the rappelling line and used it to return to the main level. There, I replaced the canister on the air filtration device.

My attention again on the elevator chute's receding water level revealed that most of SL3 was rapidly draining of floodwater. I now understood that some sort of geologic event had caused the flooding, though I didn't grasp the specific event or how the blue gel had conveyed this experience to me. Since this was far from the most unusual thing to happen to me there, I took it in stride and quickly explored sub-level two before proceeding further down the shaft. The water level was receding quickly, and with no new floodwater replacing it, either the source of the flooding had ceased, or the hydrogen conversion technology was outpacing the onset of additional flooding.

Uncertain of the situation, I used the rappelling line to lower myself toward the pair of doors barring my access to SL2. They were closed more tightly than SL1 had been, so I forced the tips of my gloved fingers between the leading edge of the doors and pulled them apart. They separated, however, reluctantly, revealing a new expanse of damp concrete.

Not really surprised, I found aisle after aisle of empty pods. They were all as neatly arranged as they had been one level higher, offering no further insight into what happened here or what became of the contents of the previously occupied devices. I moved swiftly among the empty capsules. I didn't expect to discover anything new on this level, but I hoped to find another pillar with an orb, ideally undamaged this time.

After finding no additional orbs or anything that made the level different from the previous one, I returned to the elevator and descended to SL3. It had been aggressively cleared of water, and before opening the doors for access, I was relieved to find that SL4 was nearly clear. The top of an elevator car had just become visible as the water receded on its way to SL5.

Unfortunately, my brief but rapid search of level four was just as fruitless as level three, except that I found what I believed to be the source of the flooding—or at least part of it. I located the section of the wall I'd seen rupture in the video. A concrete segment had collapsed, likely coinciding with the footage I'd viewed. At some point after the loss of video, the water on the floor had receded, at least for the most part. Earth had flowed in with the water. When this happened, dozens of the nearby pods had been swept across the concrete floor. Though they were now empty, I knew they were in use at the time. This contributed to the narrative forming in my mind.

Whatever occurred, the people in lab coats certainly took care to extract the unresponsive forms from the equipment. And since I hadn't found so much as a partial human body, they must have done it successfully.

Sodden earth appeared to have collapsed over the source of the water, either blocking it entirely or reducing it to a trickle. Although I couldn't be sure, new water seemed to seep from the fresh, clear break in the earth at a trickle.

When I returned to the shaft, I faced a difficult choice. The pair of searching Elend had come dangerously close to my position, and the odds of them discovering the parked Airbike were about as likely as them finding the entrance to the underground facility.

Continuing my search would be a gamble, as the creatures would likely find me before I could escape. Complicating my choice was the realization that whatever geologic event had compromised the facility, part of it had occurred on level five. What I learned on the level below could be valuable. Balancing the scales somewhat, at least in my mind, was the fact that the pair of Elend closing in on my location were alone.

The chime in my ear and the pulsing red ring around my field of vision told me I was already too late. The pair of Elend I'd been tracking had just tripped the sensor at the installation's entrance.

The sensor I attached to the bunker's exterior door frame had been a last-minute decision. I expected to be long gone by the time the Elend tracked me to the facility. In hindsight, it turned out to be one of the wisest choices I'd made in a long time. However, while it prevented me from being ambushed, it also meant I was now backed into a corner. I always found it curious that the facility had only a single entrance. The door I used to enter, which felt more like a service access than a primary point of entry, reinforced this idea. The more I learned about the size of the complex further suggested that there needed to be a more conventional entrance.

There must be other parts of the underground installation I hadn't seen yet. The staff I saw in the video must live somewhere; it's unlikely they slept in the pods. There should be a dormitory. I still hadn't found a kitchen or bathroom. While I hadn't seen SL5 yet, the lowest sub-level seems like an unusual place for those types of facilities.

Everything about the facility felt strange. Built into the ridge line and mostly underground, it struck me as improvised instead of intentionally designed. But that didn't add up. Who accidentally constructs an underground facility?

Questions for another day.

It wouldn't take the Elend long to find me in a place like this, especially since I had left a light pointing down the empty elevator shaft.

I rushed back to the elevator and gazed up its illuminated, empty stretch. Ascending didn't seem wise. The creatures were up there somewhere. Making a break for it felt foolish, and even entering ground level was perilous since, for all I knew, the pair were lying in ambush.

The now-exposed elevator car was one floor below me. SL5. It was the bottom of the facility, at least as far as I knew. Since I couldn't go up, I decided to go down.

With no time to spare before descending the line, I jumped onto the roof of the elevator car, about twelve feet below me. I struck with a clang that reverberated up the shaft. Something told me I had just rung the dinner bell. The car swayed unsteadily beneath my weight. It felt flimsy and insubstantial.

No, I decided as I felt the rusted and pitted surface of the access panel on the car's roof. It was old and corroded, and years of submersion had taken their toll. Then, for the first time, I noticed no cables running between the car's roof and the chute's top. The equipment supporting the car had long since deteriorated, explaining why the car was at the bottom.

With no time left to consider the car's age or that of the facility, I flipped open the access panel, only to have to shear it from its hinges with my aggressive tug. I noted the ragged tear I'd left in the rusted hinges as I dropped past them and onto the soggy cabin floor. I was standing in ankle-deep water.

No one ever mentioned what would happen if I touched the water undergoing hydrogen extraction. That kind of atomic disassembly didn't seem like something I would want to be exposed to directly, but it was too late to reconsider my choice. Firsthand exposure to a pair of Elend in a confined space would be far more dangerous to my health.

I heard a rustling in the shaft overhead and knew without so much as a glance that the creatures were hot on my trail. Thankfully, when the elevator fell, the impact and the resulting shrapnel had blown one of the car's doors entirely off its track. It had fragmented the door outside SL5, and I was able to clear my way to the space beyond with some quick, urgent bending of flimsy, rusted-out metal.

I launched myself through the gap in the door just as I heard an inhuman howl. There was a crash, and I felt the lift's car shake from the impact as one of the Elend struck its roof. The narrow hatch in the car's roof would slow the massive creatures down, but it wouldn't stop them. Similarly, the human-sized hole in the derailed doors would give me a brief advantage.

The expansive floor of SL5 resembled the others in that it was cluttered with capsule-shaped pods. However, this time, the tangled jumble of pods pressed randomly against each other in chaotic disarray stood out. Many of the glass surfaces were fogged and opaque. In just a few seconds, I noticed what was different about the level.

It looked as if a bomb had gone off. The pods were tangled and pressed against one another, and some had rolled atop others, indicating the disruption that had struck this level. Worse still, unlike the pods on the floors above, these were not empty. The intact modules housed withered and desiccated human forms of the occupants, while the cracked and crazed glass pods contained floating, misshapen forms that had long since succumbed to decay and rot.

Another loud crash in the elevator passage indicated that the second Elend was now on the elevator's roof. A breath later, an animalistic scream was followed by the shriek of tearing metal.

I vaulted over the logjam of crushed and tangled pods and ventured deeper into the area. If the level was similar to those above, I wouldn't find more rooms or halls suitable for cover. This facility took the idea of an open floor plan to the extreme. I glanced at the pile of bones in the capsule beneath me as I stood and leaped from one pod to the next as quickly as possible.

The bodies were human, I realized as I ran. This didn't come as a shock given what I'd seen in the video, but it still didn't make sense. Whatever had transpired on this level was different from what I'd observed higher in the installation. The breach in the wall on four and the resulting floodwater had clearly made it impossible to evacuate level five before the water submerged everything. But if the pods on the upper floors were empty, what had happened to the occupants?

Understanding was already forming in my mind as I ran. While some things I'd encountered in Wild-Side began to take on a new and enlightening shape, others only left me more confused.

A pair of animalistic bellows echoed, followed by a crash that could only signal the breaching of the shaft's doors. An open expanse of floor appeared a dozen yards ahead, and I crossed the pile of remaining pods in just two more strides. My feet struck the concrete floor with a wet slap, and I spun, ready to confront the creatures I was sure were in pursuit.

I would make a stand here. A couple of dozen yards separated me from the oncoming creatures, providing an easy shot. The automated targeting augmentation made what would otherwise be an impossible shot to an Elend's eye socket less of a challenge.

But when I slapped my hand against the holster on my hip, I found it empty. That's when the odd crunching and clattering I'd heard in my rush to cross the field of damaged pods flashed in my mind. Although I only recognized the strange clattering in hindsight, I instantly understood that I'd knocked my pistol loose while trying to run and maintain my balance on the macabre, uneven surface beneath my feet.

"Swell," I groaned, watching the two dark shapes rapidly approach my position.

The tall, slender forms of two Drakes barreled full speed toward me. They were bounding on all fours through the tangle of pods, the sound of shattering glass accompanying each aggressive stride.

The biggest problem I recalled with this suit was the inability to carry a backup pistol. Additionally, the blade I typically carried horizontally across the back of my belt was likewise gone. The suit might shield me from impact and even offer some protection against claws—but if these creatures knocked me unconscious in this tight space, they would likely just bite off my head and suck my guts out from inside my gear's protective outer shell.

A tingling sensation in my hand made me long for my trusty knife, prompting my mind to flash back to one of Piper's innovations I'd never had the chance to test.

The left-most advancing Drake tangled a limb as it closed the last two dozen yards. I watched it faceplant among the wrecked pods, its forelegs plunging into the uneven surface while its back legs and short tail went airborne in the tumble. This reprieve allowed me to focus on the creature moving in from my two o'clock position.

I backpedaled across the open expanse of concrete just in time for the lunging Drake to land exactly where I had been standing. It lunged again, and I ran the thumb of my right hand across the tips of the fingers on that glove. This was the emergency gesture Piper had settled on. A two-and-a-half-foot-long straight blade lanced from the sleeve of my right arm. It formed quickly, with less than a heartbeat passing between the swipe of my fingers and the moment when the swordlike blade extended past the back of my hand and fully took shape. The blade was about three inches wide, extending from the back of my closed fist. The jet-black material tapered to a razor-sharp, dagger-like point and narrowed to the menacing tip.

It happened so fast; I don't think the Drake registered the weapon as it swiped at me with a powerful, talon-tipped paw. I raised the back of my hand defensively and braced my feet. The creature swung its arm against the edge of the double-sided blade, and I watched as the slim figure seemed to separate from the monster in slow motion.

I saw the Drake's eyes widened with surprise while its momentum carried it forward. Ducking low, I witnessed the thousand-pound creature cartwheel, propelled by its accumulated inertia, helpless to stop its forward velocity without the now-missing limb.

A shriek unlike anything I'd ever heard tore through the air as the monster tumbled behind me. I looked up just in time to see the second Jay launch from the remains of the demolished pods and lunge high in my direction. Still crouched low, I countered the attack with my own lunge. I tucked a shoulder and somersaulted to close the distance. As I came out of the roll, I raised my blade and sliced it down the length of the creature's belly as it passed overhead. The sickening slice of the blade through the tough, scaled hide was visceral. I turned just in time to see the creature bellyflop onto the wet floor, sliding fifteen feet into a motionless, supine position.

I knew I'd cut the creature deep. But before I had a chance to look more closely, the three-legged Drake lunged at me from the side. I backstepped just in time to miss the jagged tips of the swiping talon, if only by an inch or two. My legs tangled beneath me, so I wasn't fully prepared when the creature's backswing caught me square in the chest.

I felt the distant impact of the Drake's knobby knuckles and heard a crack that sounded like a tree branch snapping while I registered my own corkscrew-like tumble. As I hit the floor in a bouncing roll, I already knew the armor had saved my life. I wasn't sure I would have fared as well if caught by the talons.

I needed to finish this quickly, preferably before I found the limits of the suit's integrity.

Rolling onto my hands and knees, I vaulted to my feet just in time to see the monster lunge, which could only be an attempt to tackle me. Ducking into a shoulder roll, I shifted to the Drake's limbless side. I had just regained my footing and started to run when I heard it crash into the wall of pods behind me.

At least I'd eviscerated one of the creatures at the onset. I like my chances in a one-on-one fight. But as I dashed past the sprawled form of the creature on my right, it staggered up from the floor with a mulling howl. I slowed my run, glancing back over my shoulder as the creature leaned back on its haunches and ran a pair of scaly open palms across its forward-facing belly. The slash from stem to stern down its abdomen was stitching itself shut before my eyes.

I swallowed hard and focused ahead as I ran. As unbelievable as this was, it clarified why a bullet to the eye was the most effective way to kill these creatures. No matter how many shots I fired into the body of one of them in the past, it seemed like they had no effect. They weren't bulletproof, I realized at that moment. They just possessed some supernatural ability to heal.

When the far wall of the sub-level came into view, I knew instantly what I was looking at. Sometime in the past, a split had formed through the wall. It had parted the concrete and flooded with what had certainly been molten stone. The flow had washed in and spread across the floor for almost twenty feet before halting. This was evident by the now smooth, tapering surface of the hardened cascade.

The memory of the video footage showing the moment of the rupture filled my mind, quickly followed by what I had witnessed on sub-level four. Some kind of seismic disturbance had also caused magma to breach this level. Simultaneously, a split in the wall one level higher had allowed water, likely from the same source as the nearby lake, to rush into the facility's lower sections. As catastrophic as it must have been for everyone in the pods on SL5, the influx of water from SL4 likely prevented more molten flow from inundating the lowest level of the facility. This flooding space halted the flow of liquid stone.

Even as I studied the surface of the now-hardened flow, I realized that the draining of the water from the lower levels had negatively affected a very delicate balance. The surface of the flow glowed faintly, a pale orange. Turning my back to the flow, I directed my attention to the pair of Drakes. They were the more pressing concern. However, as I observed the pair approaching me, I noted the temperature display in the corner of my HUD.

One hundred twenty-eight degrees.

"Crap," I whispered. I could suddenly feel the heat intensifying with fury behind me. As much as I knew the suit would protect me from the temperature, I realized it couldn't insulate me from direct exposure to molten stone.

The creatures advanced toward me from my eleven and two o'clock positions. The three-legged Drake was on my right, while the one with a now-healed belly was on my left. They were moving more cautiously this time, both appearing to have realized that I was dangerous in my own right. Interestingly, while one creature's torso had healed quickly, the other, with the severed limb, seemed to show no signs of regeneration.

Cormac would find this fascinating—if I survived to explain what I'd seen.

The three-legged creature grew impatient and rushed toward me. I taught Tripod the lesson his friend had already learned when I dashed for him to close the gap faster than anticipated. Stepping to its limbless side, I drew my blade along its flank. This time, I was sure to plunge the edge deeper and was satisfied to hear what could only be the slicing of organs in addition to flesh.

A wet gurgle hushed a grotesque howl, and without pause, I turned to face the remaining four-legged version. It was already pressing what it perceived to be my distraction. Rather than ducking low as I'd done a couple of times already, this time, I jumped. Cognizant that the nanotech augmented my strength, I ducked my head and calculated the spring I put into the jump. Even so, I felt the back of my shoulders brush against the concrete ceiling as I reached the peak of my spring. Committed to the lunge, the creature passed beneath me.

I missed the chance to rake this Elend again with my blade, but it turned out not to matter. The creature landed belly-first, halfway up the surface of the hardened lava flow. As it got onto all fours and shot me what could only have been a contemptuous glare, I heard what sounded like cracking ice—fissures formed in the stone, spidering from each point where its feet met the surface.

There was a moment of stasis, in which the Elend shot me what must have been its version of the *oh shit* expression—then all four of its legs plunged through the top of the hardened lava flow. The rock seemed to shatter when its belly struck the last solid face of the heated stone. I watched as jets of liquid, yellow-orange rock burst into the air while the Drake's body sank into the mire. Its head was the last to disappear, jaws wide open in a silent scream even as strands of vapor spiraled into the air. No supernatural healing could save that creature. I was sure the drifting vapor was all that remained of it.

My mouth was dry, and I blinked slowly at the sight. It was a way to kill these things I'd never considered before. More useful information for Cormac and the team, I concluded.

The sound of talons scraping concrete drew me to the haggard, remaining Drake. Tripod was struggling to find purchase with its three remaining legs. The long gash on its flank had taken the spring from its step but hadn't put it out of the fight as I had hoped. Still, the glassy sheen in the big dark eyes suggested this creature was holding onto life through sheer stubbornness.

Tripod shook its head slowly on a stout neck as if trying to regain full awareness. I didn't give it a chance. Stepping quickly forward, I severed the head from the body in a single, apelike downward swing.

The body toppled more than rolled, and viscous fluid guttered from the stump size opening between head and shoulders. Until that moment, I hadn't truly noticed the short segment of neck, much less thought of it as a weak point.

I breathed deeply, drawing oxygen into my lungs. I was winded and puzzled as to why I wasn't drenched in sweat. It was the tech, I concluded. The armor was excellent at wicking perspiration away from my skin and keeping me comfortable in the heat of the lower levels. I noted the ambient temperature was just crossing one hundred and seventy degrees and rising. Looking back, I was more than a little surprised to see that the shell atop the lava flow had almost completely dissolved. More concerning was the pool of superheated stone, which was expanding and creeping slowly in my direction.

"One thing after another," I told myself as I returned to the elevator shaft.

Stepping gingerly across the field of destroyed pods, I fought the urge to touch my ear. My ears rang, but removing my helmet in the heated space would be disastrous. Losing my balance on the uneven surface below, I realized I'd taken a blow to the head at some point during the fight. The ringing sound seemed to bounce around inside my helmet.

As I dropped to the floor just outside the fragmented elevator doors, the realization hit hard. I noticed the red pulsing notification along the left side of my display and wondered how long it had been there. The message indicated that hydrogen levels had exceeded the suit's filtering capacity, making the air hazardous to breathe…

…and a single spark would launch me to the moon.

Then, the second part of the situation dawned on me. The ringing in my ears was actually the ringing in my suit. I checked the perimeter alarm and cursed as I saw the alert the drone network had been trying to send me. Dozens of Elend were closing in on my position from all directions. They seemed to be moving in packs, the first of which would reach me in three minutes.

I grabbed the line and activated the ascender, returning to ground level moments later. After grabbing my pack, I glanced at the air filtration device. In augmented reality, a gauge appeared just above the containment canister, indicating that it was at one hundred percent capacity. I pulled the canister from the top of the extractor and rushed toward the exit. Hydrogen levels inside the complex were catastrophic.

As I slid through the cracked steel door at the exit, a buzzing sound in the air made me hesitate. Then, I froze at the sight of the dinner plate-sized drone hovering at eye level about ten yards beyond the door. The camera's cycloptic lens was unmistakable.

"Move faster!" Tripp's voice stabbed at my ear. We knew I would lose reception deeper in the complex. His tone made it evident he had been trying to reach me for a while. "You have dozens closing in on you from every direction."

I grasped the drone's underside and pulled it from the air. The rotors struggled to adjust to the change in orientation and buzzed with an aggressive pitch.

"Kill the props," I said flatly. He would see me struggling with the drone, so I didn't explain further. "I need you to override this thing's safety systems, and I need it done fast."

———————

I hit the seat of the Airbike hard enough to bruise my manberries, but it was the least of my problems at that moment. The small screen mounted on the handlebars lit up in response to my presence, and additional information pulsed into the edges of my HUD a heartbeat later. I ignored all of it as I activated the flight system with the pad of my thumb against the touchscreen. All four rotors sprang to life with a muted buzz. The craft shot up into the air so quickly that the edges of my HUD flashed red with a silent warning. The display registered five Gs, and the dismal surroundings became a blur as five turned into six and continued climbing.

My stomach plunged, and my genitals tried to change places with my eyeballs, but again, these were trivial in comparison to what was about to happen.

I blew past fifteen hundred feet before my eyes had a chance to adjust. Easing off the throttle, I pushed the handlebars forward and squeezed the sides of the saddle seat with my knees to hang on as the bike surged forward like a shot from a rifle. Two thousand feet in the air and going from zero to one hundred and twenty miles an hour so fast I could have been riding a bullet. The rolling expanse of green below me seemed to shimmer with distortion–

Then I realized it wasn't an optical illusion. A mass of movement stirred on the ground beneath the trees. Dozens, probably hundreds of Elend swarmed around the bunker entrance from every direction.

I heard Tripp's voice again and understood he'd been speaking for at least a few seconds before I registered the words. My vision was blurry, and my breathing was ragged. I'd taken off far more aggressively than I'd ever attempted. Blood had pooled in my extremities, apparently to the detriment of my higher functions.

"—Can you hear me?" Tripp was nearly shouting.

My voice croaked in a tone I had never heard before. I was already revving up, fully intending to discover for the first time just how fast the machine could go.

"Your bio readings are redlining," Lacy's sounded over the comm channel. "Ease up!"

What must have been a dozen or more jays swept in just over the treetops from the north and west. As one, they adjusted their course and veered in my direction. I was outpacing them, but I didn't want them to alert the ground force to my escape.

"—can't," Tripp was saying. "Telemetry shows thirty-four Jays adjusting their course in pursuit," he added. I had no idea if he was talking to me or arguing with Lacy.

"What about the Elend on the ground?" I asked with the driest mouth I had ever experienced.

I felt pressure in the legs of my armor. The sensation traveled vertically up my body. "I'm adjusting the suit for better blood flow," Lacy said. Judging by her tone, I was sure she was speaking with Tripp.

I felt as if my armor was treating me like toothpaste at the end of an empty tube. As my mind cleared, I realized Lacy's adjustment to my gear was meant to return blood from my extremities and push it back to my brain. Even my vision seemed to sharpen in response.

"The ground force is leaving the structure even faster than they entered," Tripp said. "They're onto you."

A picture-in-picture feed appeared in the far corner of my vision. In it, I could see what could only be a view from a stationary drone positioned high over the entrance to the underground complex.

"Trigger it now," I said, my voice finally sounding normal.

"He's nowhere near the minimum safe distance," Lacy said in a voice that sounded like she had her hand over the microphone.

The bike's nose dipped forward at thirty-five degrees as I cranked the throttle to full. The motors powering the props screamed, and the fans moved so fast they became invisible. The motors could adjust their inclination in response to acceleration, but only by a maximum of five degrees. For the props to push me forward so aggressively, the entire airframe angled more steeply towards the ground, even though my altitude remained unchanged. I lowered my chest and tried to minimize my wind resistance by ducking behind the handlebars.

"Overload now," I tried to yell through clenched teeth. I could hardly hear my own voice over the roar of the props. "Do it now!"

"He needs more altitude and distance," Lacy was saying.

Going for altitude would mean sacrificing ground speed, and from experience, I knew that the thinner air would slow me even more. Every second I hesitated would save Elend lives.

"Now!" I groaned.

A breath later, the sky behind me lit with the intensity of a newly birthed sun. Long seconds passed before I was struck by a concussive force that felt like a runaway train. More warnings than I knew existed cluttered my HUD, and the Airbike spiraled into an uncontrolled tumble. I sensed the automated restraint system at my hips half a second before everything went black.

Tripp initiated the overload as requested and against his better judgment. The battery pack enhancing the zero-point power system of each drone went critical and flashed with a tiny explosion. The drone was lying in the weeds a dozen yards from the entrance to the underground complex. The small detonation instantly breached the containment of the hydrogen storage module Gray had placed beneath the belly of the crippled drone. Compressed hydrogen gas mixed with oxygen and flame, detonating and vaporizing the wilderness within a two-hundred-foot radius. Beyond that, trees were reduced to particulate matter, collapsing the landscape for another two hundred yards.

The containment vessel's detonation only catalyzed a much larger explosion. Inside the underground facility, the hydrogen had displaced nearly all of the breathable air and flowed from the entrance in an invisible river of fog. The surface detonation back-fed into the facility, igniting five sub-levels in a multi-megaton explosion that vaporized the surrounding concrete as a concussive wave rippled through the strata. The ridge over the facility undulated like an ocean wave, sending debris hundreds of feet into the air.

Fissures spidered across the forest floor as if it were a sheet of plate glass struck by a mortar shell. The detonation reached the magma pocket that had once breached sub-level five, hundreds of years earlier, sending molten stone flooding into the newly formed crater. Several fissures reached the teardrop-shaped lake to the south, and the lake's contents flooded the crater. Water and molten earth collided, sending gouts of superheated steam shooting into the sky with an ear-shattering scream.

The concussive force of the blast annihilated every drone in the sky over twenty-five miles in all directions. The feed seen by Tripp and Lacy went dark in a wave that traveled faster than the speed of sound.

Tripp waved his hands at the array of AR displays that covered the far wall of the control room, finally locating surviving drones nearly forty miles from the epicenter of the detonation.

Lacy's hands covered her mouth as she stared wide-eyed. A mushroom cloud of superheated steam stabbed at the distant sky, slowly coalescing into liquid water before raining back down to earth. Miles-wide dust clouds roiled over treetops fifty miles from the epicenter.

"Where is he?" Lacy asked after an eternity of silence.

Tripp sank into a boneless heap on a stool, his eyes unblinking and watery. "Gone."

I woke up to the sensation of someone tugging at my shoulder. Blinking through a hazy, foggy mind, it took longer than it should have to notice I was lying face down in thick field grass. The tug at my shoulder brought the first indication of situational awareness, and the high-speed escape from the Elend rushed to the forefront of my brain.

My fists tightened in my armored gloves as I rolled, prepared to confront whatever was prodding at my back. My vision swam from the rapid shift, and my backside got tangled in something as I tried to roll to my feet. Thankfully, no Elend greeted me. I gazed at a tangle of what seemed to be slack, pencil-thin lines extending into the distance. I followed the cords to a wispy, matte black sheet flapping among the branches of the shattered tree canopy overhead.

"Parachute?" I mumbled, wrestling with the lines tangled around my legs. I traced them back to attachments just behind my shoulder. There was no harness, at least not a conventional one. Thin ropes with the texture I'd come to recognize as nano-particulate material fastened at dime-sized eyelets that had formed directly from the surface of my armor. The chute fluttering gently in the breeze was made of the same material, I noted.

"Neat trick," I grunted and attempted to get to my feet. That's when I noticed the three tree limbs crushed into the grass beneath me. The thickest one was as wide as my biceps. Each limb was a web of smaller branches and was thick with green foliage. Each ended in a savage, sappy breakpoint that had clearly separated from the canopy due to great force. The bald spot in the tree cover told the rest of the story.

A voice came through my ear, and I noticed my helmet was still on. "Gray? Are you there?" It was Tripp.

I dabbed at the controls on my wrist, and the helmet vanished. "Alive and kicking," I said, rolling my head slowly on my neck. A few pops and crunches were likely audible on the channel.

"The suit telemetry shows no broken bones and no internal bleeding. How are you feeling?"

As I scanned the surface of my torso, I observed barely visible scuffs on the armor. Then, I looked up and saw what I assumed were dark clouds scattered hundreds, perhaps thousands, of feet above the forest canopy.

I realized by the smell in the air that it wasn't clouds. It was smoke.

"You built an incredible flight suit," I said softly. With a pull, the lines hanging from my shoulders detached effortlessly from my armor. The line and parachute canopy hanging in the tree limbs above appeared to dissolve. A light drizzle of sandy particles fell onto the grass.

A new voice broke into the comm channel. "Are you okay?" Doctor Cormac asked, his tone dry yet full of unbridled concern.

"Any landing you can walk away from is a good landing." I got to my feet and looked around slowly for the Airbike. My vision seemed to jitter, and I felt a bit nauseous. "What the hell happened?"

"…detonation," Tripp was saying. I had missed the first part of the statement. Clearly, I had taken a hit, no matter how protective the suit had been. "You were about a mile short of minimal safe distance when we overloaded the drone."

A grin spread as memories slowly permeated the fog in my mind. Hundreds, maybe thousands of Elend. If I almost didn't make it, they must have fared worse.

Shit.

That didn't mean I'd gotten them all. Before I knew I was doing it, I'd reengaged my helmet. My gaze was already scanning the surrounding wilderness. "Where's the bike," I whispered.

Tripp seemed amused as he replied, "About two hundred and twenty yards to the north." He then added, "and roughly three hundred yards to the northeast. A significant portion of the airframe is seventy-three feet behind you if you want to see just how lucky you are. Generally speaking, it's spread across a half mile."

Wow.

I closed my eyes and took a breath. When I opened them again, my gaze returned to the sky. "Did any of the drones survive?" None were visible through my limited view of the area sky.

"Eleven," Lacy said. "Six of them made it to safety. The others reached your position over the past twelve minutes."

I figured they'd redeployed nearby drones to cover me. "Wait—how many minutes?" I cursed. "How long was I out?"

"One hour, twenty-three minutes," Cormac said. "Don't worry, the area around you is clear of Elend, at least within a radius of ninety-eight miles. Beyond that, the drone mesh is inconsistent. We're still redeploying assets to enhance coverage."

I sagged and dropped to one knee. Flopping flat on my ass, I took a deep breath and blinked slowly in an attempt to clear my vision fully.

"You seem a bit confused," Lacy said, as if somehow aware of my ongoing personal inventory.

Not wanting to dwell on my discomfort and confident in my tech's ability to heal me much better than my body normally could, I asked, "How many hostiles did I take down?"

"It's hard to be certain," Tripp said.

"We're still crunching the numbers," Cormac added.

"Just over thirteen hundred confirmed so far," Tripp said. "That number is very likely to rise. The analysis is still assessing the Elend presence in the blast zone a few seconds prior to detonation."

I heard something mumbled in the distance and realized there were more people in the control room. Not everyone was on the comm channel. "What was that?" I asked.

Lacy spoke next. "Mara said you had twenty-two Jays, all airborne and chasing you when the detonation got them. We've confirmed that none of them made it."

I was thinking about getting back on my feet while calculating time and distance in my mind. The math was tougher than it should have been, and the idea of walking just wasn't an option at that moment.

"How far is it to the nearest farm?"

Tripp laughed. "Buddy, you don't want to know."

Buddy?

I grinned. Tripp binge-watched programming from Our-World at every opportunity. New slang continued to pepper his conversations.

"No worries," he said. "I have a replacement bike on the way. ETA…" His voice trailed off. "Just under five minutes."

That made me laugh. "Who's bringing the new one?"

"No one," he said. "Lacy and I have been working on that. More automation is involved. It's tracking your position in real-time. Thank you for clearing the overhead canopy. It will make landing easier."

I pushed against one of the thick branches in the grass beside me and shook my head.

Chapter 25 - Warped Metal

Our-World

The heels of Breslin's shoes clicked against the granite floors of the spacious suite as he approached Chris Ingersoll. The FBI agent had his back to the floor-to-ceiling windows overlooking the cityscape beyond. The late afternoon sun had just dipped behind the high-rises to the west, casting the room into shadow. A light seemed to blaze in Breslin's eyes, and Ingersoll wondered for perhaps the hundredth time if the rumors about the man's animal savagery could be true. Although they had only met face-to-face a handful of times, there were whispers. Talk circulated about how Breslin could shift from calmness to unprovoked acts of savagery without a moment's notice. Breslin was clearly already agitated, and Ingersoll was certain he was about to witness a new side of the man in charge.

"Agents are still conducting interviews," Ingersoll said, trying not to cringe at the sight of Breslin stalking toward him. "The local PD is continuing the search. Ledger can't get far."

Stopping just beyond arm's reach, Breslin's gaze bore into him. The flesh rippling at Breslin's smooth-shaven jawline suggested he was grinding his teeth. "He's gone, and you know it. He travels throughout this country, and you can't find him even with your so-called resources." The popping of knuckles was unmistakable. Breslin's hands were at his sides, though they were balled into bloodless fists. When he spoke, it was through a clamped jaw. "Tell me about the Kansas facility."

Ingersoll gave a half-shrug in response but said nothing.

Breslin stepped forward slightly, his face contorting and his mouth beginning to open with a demand that was sure to follow.

"The forensic report came back," Ingersoll said quickly. "But it contained nothing we didn't expect." Avoiding Breslin's gaze, Ingersoll focused on a spot on the floor between them. From the corner of his eye, he noticed a slight tremor in his hands and quickly shoved them into his pockets. "A single-man assault on the installation. He parachuted in. We found the rig at the edge of a cornfield a little over three miles from the fence line. The techs believe it caught the wind and was dragged away. There's no doubt it was Ledger's, even though they have nothing to connect it to him."

"Evidence? I won't be prosecuting him," Breslin said. "You know better than that."

Nodding slowly, Ingersoll said, "Sure—but you want to know if he has help." He tried not to shrug again. That only seemed to infuriate the boss. "He was by himself."

"He's always alone," Breslin snapped. He glared at Ingersoll for several seconds, then turned slowly and began to pace the bare room again. "Update me on Miranda Norton."

Ingersoll's knees became weak. He swallowed hard against a dry throat and attempted to infuse confidence and authority into his tone. "All-points bulletins have been issued statewide in Illinois, Missouri, Arkansas, Tennessee, and both Virginias. Not a single sighting. It's as if she vanished from the face of the earth."

"You're federal," Breslin snapped. "Issue the bulletin nationwide."

Ingersoll nodded aggressively. "Absolutely."

Stopping his wall-to-wall pacing, Breslin glared at the agent once more, this time from twenty feet away. "Maybe I should have approached your partner. You're not proving to be as resourceful as I'd hoped."

Swallowing hard once more, Ingersoll was sure he'd seen a flash of light behind the man's eyes. It had lasted only a blink, but it was there. He was convinced of it.

"Doctor Norton isn't as crucial as what Ledger stole," Breslin began. "But if we can't capture him, we'll need her. The Kansas experiment was the most promising so far. If we can't recover what was taken, Norton must reconstruct the apparatus."

"A team has recovered Kramer Fulbright's body. If Ledger isn't aware of that, one of our teams will be present the next time he shows up."

Breslin waved a dismissive hand. "He's running circles around you and every other resource on the hunt. If you know Fulbright has been found, Ledger will, too. Having more than a skeleton crew is a waste of resources."

"We have Fulbright's formula," Ingersoll said, his tone laced with a hint of triumph. The cracking of knuckles came from one of Breslin's fists. The other followed suit a moment later. His gaze fixed on Ingersoll, even from a distance.

"The formula that left its creator brain dead? Are you joking?" After a few moments, he continued, "The Alison Springs experiment can be dismissed. How much does Fulbright's team know about ATG's involvement?"

"Only what the university has publicly presented. ATG was noted to have funded the effort. Only ATG's philanthropic grant is known. Like the other experiments, nothing points back to you."

Breslin didn't seem pleased with the response.

"You want the rest of Fulbright's team to disappear? That will attract scrutiny I can't manage."

After a brief silence, marked only by Breslin's heels clicking against the stone floor as he paced, he spoke. "Leave them for now. But if they cause any trouble later, they will disappear—and you along with them."

As Breslin paced the room again, he was ready to speak when he suddenly froze mid-stride. He slapped a hand sharply against his head and rocked back on his heels. Tilting his gaze toward the ceiling, a primal, savage scream of something wild and wounded erupted.

Ingersoll's eyes widened. He jumped backward and felt the back of his head hit the surface of the panoramic window. Struggling to maintain control, he could only stare as Breslin bellowed, slapped at the sides of his head, and dropped to his knees.

Ingersoll felt the momentary urge to help, but the primal howl from Breslin was anything but human. Instead, he could only watch as Breslin knelt and rocked back and forth.

Pike leaned away from the lens at the end of the scope and shook his head. He glanced at Piper. "That guy looks like a dick."

Piper grinned. "That's an understatement. He's killed more people than you can imagine."

Dressed in black tactical gear, Pike sat at the head of a long rectangular dining table. His was the only chair that remained. The table's surface was cleared to accommodate the .50 caliber Barrett rifle resting on a bipod and aimed at the expansive windows overlooking the city high-rises beyond. Leaning back to the scope, he said, "He's pacing like it's the solution to all his problems. I feel bad for the guy he's berating."

Piper sat down at a small wheeled cart a few yards away and looked at the laptop screen. It reflected everything Pike could see through the rifle's scope. "That's one of the two FBI agents–Ingersoll, since Vincente is laid up in the hospital."

Shooting her a glance, Pike arched a single brow. "You're sure? We've only seen his back." They had been setting up the equipment and arranging the makeshift shooting bench for Pike when the now motionless figure with his back to them first entered Breslin's office. The high-rise apartment building offered an excellent line of sight into Breslin's office. Twenty-four acres of green parkland separated the two buildings. Given the powerful optics of Pike's rifle, the distance made little difference.

"You know that old question, who watches the watchers?" Piper said. "That's us. Gray knows his enemies even better than his allies. We've been keeping an eye on both agents for a while. Until recently, we couldn't rule Vincente out–now it seems clear he's not corrupt like his partner."

"You sound confident."

Piper nodded. "Gray recently spent some quality time with Al

Vincente. It led him to confirm what we already suspected—Ingersoll is Breslin's inside man."

"Where there's one, there will be more."

Piper nodded. "It won't matter soon. If today goes as planned, we're almost at the finish line."

A long silence followed as Pike considered his new relationship with Grady Ledger and the woman beside him, who was their latest acquaintance. He held tremendous respect for Grady, earned in a short amount of time. This was unusual for Pike; one didn't last long in freelance security without keeping outsiders at arm's length. Ledger had bested not only Pike but his entire team. In this line of work, mistakes were made only once, usually because the stakes were life and death. Gray could have killed them all; instead, he put them to work.

Trust had to be earned, and Grady Ledger had gained the trust of Pike's entire team.

This was the only reason Pike's people were positioned around this Seattle high-rise, which had enough ordinance to invade a small country.

Pike tapped the stem of the tiny comms device in his ear. "Two, are you in position?"

———————————

"Ready in thirty seconds," Billy Unger said as he slammed the belt of 7.62-millimeter ammo into the receiver of the M134 minigun. He followed the ammo feed back to the massive steel can that held dozens of belts waiting to be fed into the gun. Shaking the pair of vertical grips, he checked the turret for any unusual wobble, then rotated the six-barreled beast left and right across the limited forty-five degrees of travel. The sliding side door of the delivery van remained closed, its vertical surface only two inches from the muzzle of the six-barreled Gatling gun.

Glancing at the display mounted on the van wall to the right of the door, Unger could see the street stretching out beyond the van's entrance. A wide, two-lane road separated him from the six extra-wide, swinging glass doors that served as the main entrance and exit to the expansive atrium beyond. Six-inch-high letters frosted into the glass marked the street address, while foot-high letters above the doors declared the high-rise to be ATG Corp. Facility 01.

"Not very imaginative," Unger muttered from his spot on the bench seat behind the minigun. He flipped the transparent protective cap away from a pair of oversized buttons beneath it. Slapping his palm on the green switch, he heard the electrical unit on the floor just behind the driver's seat in the van ramp up. The gimbal at the base of the gun vibrated as power became ready to send the spinning barrels of the weapon to life.

"Ready to rock," Unger said after tapping the small stem of the comms device in his ear.

———————

Kyle Seger sat in a rented panel van on the shipping and receiving sub-level beneath Arlington Technologies Global. A FedEx logo was magnetically attached to the side of the vehicle, which was common for such vans during a time when package carriers were struggling to expand their corporate fleets. The interior was configured similarly to Unger's, but in this case, the M134 minigun was mounted in a rear-facing position, ready to fire through a pair of swinging doors at the back of the delivery truck. Seger's challenge had been finding a parking spot close enough to the elevator lobby. Time was also a pressing issue since deliveries weren't allowed to use the executive parking level. It was only a matter of time before building security noticed him.

"Three is in position," Seger said into the comm channel, sliding a pair of goggles over his eyes. They were designed to detect human body temperatures even through up to three feet of concrete.

Alley Lauer crouched in the back of a late-model Chevy Suburban parked in the garage beneath ATG. She had an M134 bolted to the floor of the load bed, facing the tailgate. Due to the tight confines of the sport utility vehicle, no complicated articulated mount was necessary. The chain gun could shift left and right within a thirty-degree range of fire, but the barrel could not be raised or lowered to achieve more precise targeting. Considering the relatively small space and the mission objective, it was a reasonable trade.

Swinging the gun gently from left to right once more, she snatched up a pair of goggles that matched Seger's. "Four is good to go," she said, doing her best to get comfortable sitting on the floor at the rear of the SUV with the minigun grips in hand between her knees.

Piper saw her laptop's second screen flash to life, initially displaying two feeds from outside. One camera was low-profile and mounted to the roof of Unger's van on the street, while the other was a feed from the micro camera attached to his protective eyewear. Entering a short command into the computer, Piper swiped a finger across the trackpad to adjust the roof camera and center it on the ATG entrance beyond the street. The second camera needed tuning. Through it, she could see what Unger was doing—an unobstructed view from behind the grips of his Gatling gun and inside the van door just beyond the barrels.

Gray had a two-part plan for ending the Elend threat to Wild-Side, and Pike's team was integral to stage one.

"This is the tricky part," Pike said, shifting into position behind the rifle. He focused on the optics and let out a deep breath. "If this Breslin fool is as bad as Gray says, why not let me take him out right here and now? I don't see what all this additional drama is supposed to accomplish."

"That's need to know," Piper said, her tone plaintive. "Gray's plan..." Her voice trailed off briefly. "It's solid. But trust me, you don't want to know the rest."

More video feeds started to tile across Piper's second screen. The thermal goggle feeds from Seger and Alley came to life. Moments later, the last feed filled the remaining tile, mirroring Pike's view through the scope of the Barrett.

Pike's feed shifted and then stabilized. The autofocus kicked in immediately, and Piper could see the massive panes of glass at the end of Breslin's office suite. Blurry figures were visible beyond the glass, though the image quality wasn't good enough to discern any faces.

"Esker," Piper said. "It's your turn."

The voice of the AI emerged from the phone lying face up on the table at Piper's elbow. "Activating enhancement filters."

The feed reflecting the scope of the Barrett blurred wildly before refocusing with a crystal-clear view of Breslin's office. "Fucking hell," Pike grumbled as he turned to look at Piper. "Those windows are a top-of-the-line privacy system. We were lucky to catch glimpses beyond the glass." He put his eye back to the scope. "This isn't supposed to be possible."

"The glass employs fluctuating polarization to obscure anything within the building," Esker explained. "With sufficient time to analyze the fluctuations, I was able to identify the pattern used for the alterations and replicate them in real time through your optics."

Pike turned his stare back to Piper. "Your friend's sharp. He just transformed about a million bucks' worth of high-tech window treatment into..." he paused and scratched his jaw, buying time to find the right analogy. "Well, regular glass, actually."

Piper laughed and glanced at the array of video feeds suspended in AR above and behind the two screens in front of her. This AR display was visible only to her. Microdot cameras had been installed in the lobby of the building she and Pike occupied, as well as at every entrance and exit point needed to close in on her position. Esker would monitor these feeds along with similar ones showing the approaches that could be used to assault her teammates' entrenched positions.

No one else on the team was aware of the extra cameras, nor did they know who or what Esker truly was. Gray had developed the attack plan. Therefore, he chose to utilize all available resources to safeguard the team and secure the mission.

Pike adjusted the focus of his scope, now able to increase magnification for a clearer view of Breslin's office. Piper saw Breslin's narrow shoulders packing the space. She watched his lips move and wished she could make out the words.

"I can provide an improvised audio feed," Esker said. "As long as Breslin is facing the windows, I can rapidly map his mouth movements to words."

"Lip reading?" Piper asked.

When Pike shot her a confused glance, she realized Esker had spoken to her over a private channel. With a cringe, she covered as best she could. "I was just wishing I had learned to read lips," she said.

Pike grinned and said, "I was just thinking the same thing."

Piper typed quickly on her laptop, directing the conversation to Esker since she couldn't speak to him directly.

"Just let me know if there's anything we need to know," she typed. "I don't want Pike asking questions I can't easily improvise plausible answers for."

Esker typed back, "Understood," on her screen in response.

On the tiled computer screen, Piper saw a pair of ghostly silhouettes pause at the center of Alley's feed. The two figures squared off against each other, then began to rise out of frame. Although the elevator was invisible beyond the doors of Alley's van, the movements of anything with a human body temperature were visible, albeit out of context.

A second later, Piper saw the two motionless figures rise up from the bottom of Seger's frame and then pass vertically out of view.

"This is creepy," Seger remarked over the comm channel. "It's like seeing through walls, but only partially."

Esker's voice trailed closely behind Seger's. "Something is wrong," he said urgently.

"Tracking," Pike said.

Piper focused on the view through Pike's scope. She noticed that Breslin had paused halfway through his next step. He slapped an open palm against the side of his head, tilted his gaze skyward, and seemed to be screaming. A few yards away, Ingersoll appeared to be backpedaling. The view of the office blurred as Ingersoll seemed to step backward into the glass.

"Compensating," Esker said, and the view returned to focus again.

Piper had no idea what was happening, but the timing seemed perfect. "All gunners, on my mark," she commanded with authority. She quickly scanned the thermal feeds from Seger and Alley's positions. The view from the top of Unger's van revealed a pedestrian in the far right corner of the screen. "Unger, concentrate fire to the left until your bogey clears the field of fire," she instructed.

"Roger," Unger responded.

Piper switched off the communication channel to ensure her next command would be clear. She glanced at Pike, the rifle stock pressed tightly against his shoulder, his eye aligned with the scope. "Now," she said.

Pike squeezed the trigger, and light flashed from the end of the long rifle. The tiny buds in Piper's ears adjusted automatically to protect her from the deafening blast in the small space. The ear protection could do nothing to insulate her from the concussive slap that seemed to shake her entire body. She stumbled backward and choked on her own exhale.

Glancing at the computer screen, she witnessed Pike's actions through his rifle. The silhouette identified on the screen as Breslin appeared to tip, sprawl on the floor, then scramble to his knees.

"Again," Piper ordered.

The rifle boomed.

On-screen, she watched the shadowy figures in the distance shuffle in clumsy lockstep before they seemed to disappear through what could only have been a faraway door.

"I lost them," Pike said, his voice raised, suggesting to Piper that she wasn't the only one with ringing ears.

Esker's voice sounded in Piper's ear, likely reaching Pike's as well. "Compensating," the voice intoned.

Piper glanced at the screen. The focus of the optics appeared to shift as what could only be the room behind the far wall of the office came into murky view.

"How in the hell," Pike grumbled and glanced quizzically at Piper.

She could only shrug. "Can you do anything with that?"

With the plan flashing back to her mind, Piper opened a channel to the rest of the team. Her eyes scanned the feeds one last time and confirmed that Unger's was the only position at risk for casualties. Luck was on their side. No one on the street was currently in Unger's field of fire. "All positions," Piper said. "Open fire."

Pike ducked behind the rifle stock and shifted slightly to one side. The reticle moved and settled on the figure marked as Breslin. "I can end this right now…"

"No," Piper corrected. "Stick to the plan."

On-screen, she saw both distant figures stumble. One of them fell hard to the floor. In the back of her mind, Piper heard Esker explaining that the elevator had just plummeted to the bottom of the shaft.

After huffing an exasperated sigh, Pike adjusted according to Piper's instructions. He positioned the reticle at a distance he estimated to be an arm's length from the figure marked as Ingersoll and squeezed the trigger.

Pike appeared motionless, but on the monitor, Piper noticed the rifle's reticle shift to a position equidistant between Breslin and the shadow identified as Ingersoll. Another shot thundered from the muzzle of the Barrett.

Piper saw Breslin's form shift suddenly more erratically, and then it vanished.

A curse escaped Pike's lips as he swept his scope across the small space where the figures had been just a moment before. The figure identified as Ingersoll remained, but Breslin was gone.

"I've lost him!" Pike shouted. He kept sweeping the area with his scope.

Piper leaned close to the monitor, trying to understand what had happened. When she looked closer, she expected to see Breslin's prone figure, but he was completely missing. "Esker?" she said.

"Breslin is gone," Esker said, his voice emotionless.

"Gone where?" Pike exclaimed.

Piper slumped. The distant echo of rapid automatic gunfire was fading away in the background. "It can only be one place," she murmured.

Events unfolded all at once, as planned.

Pike didn't know how to interpret Breslin's paused form or the unexpected shout directed at the sky, but none of it mattered at that moment. He adjusted the scope's targeting reticle by a few degrees to remove Breslin from immediate danger, then squeezed the trigger. The powerful .50 caliber rifle recoiled against his shoulder and the sheet of glass six feet beyond the table he was using as a bench shattered into confetti. The sound of the rifle's discharge didn't merely echo in the confines of the apartment—it filled the space. Even with his ear protection, Pike felt his ears pop from the percussive force.

Even though she knew it was coming, Piper nearly tipped over backward in her chair at the first rifle discharge. The nanotech permeating her body reacted instantly, dampening the sound of the blast to just one hundred and twenty-two decibels. She saw the reading appear in the corner of her HUD, though it was hardly a priority. Breath was still returning to her lungs when the rifle boomed a second time, then a third.

Piper's eyes finally focused on her laptop screens once more, and she saw what appeared to be blazing light flashing from the barrels of Seger's and Alley's M134s. Unger had paused long enough to shift his muzzle as far left as possible. The automated system had engaged, and the door on the side of his van was reaching its fully open position. Flames seemed to ignite from the ends of his barrels when the door came to rest. Piper watched as the glass doors and windows in the ATG lobby across the street seemed to vaporize. The camera on top of the van was momentarily distorted by the sudden rocking shudder of the van on its suspension, but when the image adjusted, she noted the civilian at the edge of the frame was already several dozen yards out of danger, moving with inspired purpose.

The moment the order was given, the doors concealing Seger burst open. He opened fire across the three dozen yards of the empty loading dock, with his shots aimed at the freight elevator doors and the fifteen yards of concrete wall on either side of the stainless steel doors. The metal doors seemed to ripple like water during the first second of sustained fire. By the time the following second passed, the doors had simply vanished. Smoke billowed from the elevator, and the nearby concrete walls crumbled as if made of sand.

The moment the command was given, the hatch at the rear of the SUV containing Alley swung open aggressively. Fire erupted from the barrel of her gun, aimed entirely at the bank of elevator doors forty yards away. Just as it was happening for Seger, the thin steel doors rippled and then seemed to vaporize into thin air.

Ingersoll stared wide-eyed at Breslin, struggling to make sense of the man's strange reaction when the wall of glass twenty yards to his left shattered. He spun to the right just in time to see fist-sized shards of an inch-and-a-half thick material scatter across the floor fifteen feet inside the room. The gunshot blast struck the exterior of the remaining windows with enough force to flex them. His mind was beginning to register the imminent threat when the floor-to-ceiling pane at the opposite end of the view appeared to turn entirely to powder.

Breslin was on his knees, hands pressed to either side of his head, his mouth still agape. Though whoever was troubling him, Ingersoll understood that the attack from outside the building had yet to break through the force gripping his benefactor.

"Move now, or we're screwed," Ingersoll said, gripping Breslin under one arm and then the other. He pulled the man bodily to his feet as Breslin showed the first signs of returning to the moment.

"What?" Breslin groaned, struggling to stay on his feet as Ingersoll dragged him quickly across the room.

"Move your ass," Ingersoll said as he shouldered through the doors leading farther into the building.

Behind him, Ingersoll heard shot after shot. He was barely aware of the oak-paneled walls at the back of the suite fracturing, breaking apart, and collapsing inward with each gunshot. His focus was primarily on the exit and, to a lesser extent, the fistful of the jacket he used to drag Breslin.

The pair face-planted and slid across the polished granite tile in the small lobby. Ingersoll tried to shuffle to his feet while also moving closer to the stone wall on one side of the space. He pressed the call button on the elevator, only vaguely aware of the metallic clank of the fire door swinging shut behind them.

Breslin was regaining his wits. He saw Ingersoll move to one wall and quickly retreated to the opposite wall, but when he got there, his legs tangled, and he fell awkwardly on his rear end.

"The button," Ingersoll shouted over the blasting and crashing in the next room. He waved frantically, trying to redirect Breslin's attention to the button that would summon an elevator to that side of the room.

Twisting, Breslin slapped the call button with the back of his hand. Ingersoll pressed his own call button once, or maybe twice—perhaps even a third time? The moment he did, the building seemed to shudder on its foundations. A concussive blast hammered the stone at his back. The pair of steel doors a few feet away bulged suddenly outward with a rending scream. A seam opened between the sliding doors in response to the warped metal. Smoke and debris shot from the gap, shooting out like shotgun pellets from both sides of the lobby as both sets of elevators were compromised at the same time.

Blinking through the dust, Ingersoll sensed water on his face. When he swiped at it, his finger came away smeared with crimson. A glance at Breslin brought clarity. The man had also been similarly speckled with particulate debris, and more than a half dozen minor abrasions on his face and hands were beginning to well with fresh blood.

Breslin opened his mouth to speak, yet no words came.

"The roof," Ingersoll ordered, pointing to the unlabeled door in the corner. "We can't go down. It's easier to go up."

Nodding, Breslin started pulling himself to his feet. "The helicopter!" he yelled. "We need to go—now!"

———————

Leaning back from the rifle stock, Pike glanced at Piper's screens just in time to see the rest of the team stop firing almost simultaneously.

"Exfiltration—now," Piper commanded over the comm channel.

Pike watched as each of his people moved swiftly. They abandoned their positions and proceeded to their designated egress points without pause. Piper tapped a series of commands on her laptop, and single frames shot from above each weapon's barrel replaced the camera feeds inside the van.

The visible end of the loading dock was no longer recognizable for what it had been. A cloud of pulverized concrete dust hung suspended in the air. Where there had once been elevator doors, now only a yawning, ragged gap remained in the crumbling wall.

The frame from the parking garage was nearly a duplicate. The only difference was that the deviation was limited to a small wall section due to the chain gun's much more restricted range of motion. Devastation began about five feet above the floor and ended in a stump of the wall roughly a foot and a half above the ground. Pike was initially confused by this. Then he realized that while the gun couldn't be adjusted vertically, the torrent of fire had been aimed at a downward angle when the SUV's suspension or frame gave way to the devastating force of the weapon mounted on it. As the back of the truck sagged, the automatic fire struck the wall lower.

On the street outside the building, Unger's fire was relatively short-lived. The exterior of the glass and brick building was much more delicate than the concrete and rebar used in the lower levels. As a result, Unger pumped just enough ammunition into the facade to vaporize the glass and crumble the nearby exterior walls. Sustaining fire like the rest of the team would only increase the risk of collateral damage, so while the others could open fire freely, Unger's efforts aimed to immobilize this egress point as much as to contribute to the collective narrative. His position outside also necessitated him being the first team member to exfiltrate.

"Esker?" Piper said in a dull and distant voice to Pike's troubled ears. "Assessment?"

"No fatalities," Esker confirmed. "Breslin's personal helicopter is taking off as we speak."

Pike slumped in his stool. "Our turn to exfil," he said, grabbing his bag from the floor. He glanced at her deserted workstation as he guided Piper across the room. "How can your friends be sure we didn't hurt or kill anyone?"

"He's been watching feeds from all over the building," she explained as she pushed through the door and into the hall beyond. "One thousand two hundred and eleven cameras in that building. He can account for every single one of them. He wouldn't have let us open fire if anyone was at risk."

Pike was skeptical. The amount of support staff needed to conduct that analysis was beyond his comprehension. "Is Esker the name of a person or a team?" he asked without slowing his brisk walking pace. They were trying to clear the area without attracting undue attention.

Esker's voice came over the channel. "I have eyes and ears everywhere," he said simply. "I can say with one hundred percent certainty that only one person had any form of injury resulting from what just transpired."

Piper faltered at Esker's words. "Someone was hurt?"

"Only indirectly," Esker clarified. "Billy Unger turned his ankle while clearing a brick wall seventy-five hundred yards from the ATU tower during his escape. It's a minor injury and won't affect his ability to clear the area before the deadline."

Pike realized he had stopped in the middle of the hall while listening to Esker. "Is he for real?" he asked, glancing at Piper.

Piper waved Pike ahead and nodded. "Freaky, right?"

"Helicopter?" The word sounded foreign to Ingersoll. He blinked, bringing the room into focus. He was staring at a small metal knob sticking out of the wall, but that didn't make sense. Another slow blink brought the situation into view. The metal protrusion wasn't a knob; it was a fire suppression sprinkler head, and what he'd thought was the wall was actually the ceiling.

The elevator lobby churned with acrid smoke. Ingersoll glanced at the elevator doors. One was distorted in a convex bulge while the other had been torn back like the lid of a soup can. It was the explosion, he realized. It had knocked him off his feet. His ears rang, and his vision blurred in and out of focus. Blinking as if through glasses, he recalled wiping blood from his face just moments before.

"On your feet," Breslin called from across the small lobby. He pressed one palm flat against the marble wall for support. "I'll leave you," he threatened.

The pinch of terror on Breslin's face told Ingersoll everything he needed to know about their situation. He had never seen the man in such a state. Swallowing hard and tasting the tang of burning chemicals in the air, Ingersoll rolled onto his back and pushed against the floor as he tried to reach his feet.

At that moment, the door at the end of the lobby appeared to split as a fist-sized hole formed near the center. The faint sound echoed in Ingersoll's mind as he sensed the impact of the passing ordinance. The marble wall at the far end of the space seemed to explode as if a sledgehammer struck it. A chunk of stone, as wide as Ingersoll was tall, tipped away from the wall, toppled, and shattered into gravel upon impact with the floor.

Breslin hurled himself against the nearest wall, his eyes wide and wild. The heel of his shoe slipped again as he whirled toward the stairway entrance. Ingersoll waved at the smoke and immediately grasped that Breslin would abandon him if he got to the helicopter first.

When Ingersoll blinked, Breslin had disappeared. The door to the roof access had never opened, and Breslin hadn't made a sound. He was there one second, and a second later, he had simply vanished.

With a cough, Ingersoll fanned the rolling cloud of smoke before him. There was not a trace. Breslin had just vanished. The floor where he had been standing was littered with coin-sized stone fragments. Footprints were visible in the dust. His eyes followed them one step from where Breslin had stood, and then they, too, simply disappeared.

Chapter 26 - I Can Turn Anything Into a Weapon

Wild-Side

The garage buzzed with activity. Piper adjusted the strap on a rifle featuring a traditional stock and grip but missing the usual long, thin barrel. She focused intently on the chunky rotary assembly situated halfway down the stock. It was a grenade launcher with a six-round capacity, courtesy of the forward-facing, 40-millimeter chambers arranged in a ring, reminiscent of a classic six-shooter. Activating a lever, she released the cylinder and set it on the table. A replacement was close by, the previously empty slots now filled to capacity.

Lacy picked up the discarded cylinder and started dropping thick shotgun-like rounds into the chambers. The task took just seconds, and when she finished, she set the speed loader on the table alongside seven others like it.

Piper turned the mounted loader smoothly around one and a half rotations beneath the launcher's barrel. She was careful to keep her finger away from the trigger and repeatedly checked the position of the safety as she worked. "This is a crazy idea," Piper said, not taking her focus off the weapon's preparation. "We should take our time with this. Rushing seems hazardous."

Gray pushed a third of Lacy's speed loaders into a saddlebag. He strode quickly to the Airbike, stepped onto the frame, and slung the bags on either side of the saddle seat. "Breslin is losing his mind like never before. If we're going to take advantage, we need to move now."

Wiping sweat from her brow, Piper exhaled and looked up in frustration. "Rushing is a mistake." She appeared worse for wear, her hair in a tangled ponytail and perspiration causing her tank top to cling in a way Gray would have found distracting under other circumstances.

"Is Tripp in position?" Gray asked, glancing at Lacy.

"Almost," she confirmed. "He promised to be ready."

Piper's gaze shifted between Lacy and Gray, noticing that Lacy wanted to say more.

"What is it?" Piper asked.

Lacy wiped her face, paused, then shrugged. "You should let one of us help. What was that phrase you used originally—lots of moving pieces?"

Already shaking his head, Gray corrected, "That was before Tripp built this bad lad." He collected the grenade launcher from Piper and gave her a wink. Crossing back to the bike, he snapped the weapon to the airframe beneath the handlebars, just forward of where his knee would normally rest. "This," he said, "and those," he nodded vaguely toward the saddlebags, "mitigate my concerns."

Piper circled to the other side of the Airbike and began double-checking the magnet securing the gun before confirming that the saddlebags were secure. "Every time I hear you using big words, I know there's something you're not telling me," she said with an amused glance over the rear of the Airbike, deliberately pulling on a strap he'd missed on the second bag. "This kind of rush leads to mistakes."

"I'm poking a hornet's nest," Gray said, starting to clip the rings of his expanding armor into place at his knees and ankles. "Timing is a critical component."

"Survival is more important," she replied.

Lacy observed the exchange and appeared increasingly uncomfortable by the minute.

The last ring clicked into place around Gray's neck as he activated the suit. The nanoparticle material enveloped his body. "It's a good plan," he said with more conviction than Piper could see in his eyes. "Their survival is more important." He shot a glance at Lacy, likely as an example of the Seeley people. "Keeping the Elend away from our world," he paused to visibly swallow his frustration. "We're playing for the biggest of stakes."

Piper was about to offer a counterpoint when Doctor Cormac burst through the swinging doors and into the room. "The latest telemetry is encouraging," he said, waving his hands in the air. His gestures activated a pair of AR displays featuring geographic maps, one labeled North and the other South. Thick tree cover quickly obscured both displays and was followed a moment later by dozens of red dots. The crimson markings covered both maps. "The Elend are converging on the dig, en masse."

Cormac poked a finger in the air, and a progress bar spanned the bottom of both maps. The animation began, and while the bar moved from left to right, the dots on the southern display shifted rapidly to move north. Zooming out on both displays, Cormac explained what they were observing. "They're converging," he said as a blue rectangle appeared on the left side of the southern map and the right side of the north.

"Closing on the dig site," Piper added, sounding weary.

Cormac threw an accusatory glance at Gray. "Just as you said they would."

Gray nodded. "Breslin's pissed. Angry people make foolish mistakes." He grabbed a pack that had been leaning against one of the table legs and slung it over his back before quickly climbing onto the seat of the Airbike. "Plus, with his predatory instincts? It's time to introduce him to the Hotel California."

Feeling uneasy about the plan, Cormac stepped forward. "What if you've misjudged Breslin?"

Gray affectionately slapped the grenade launcher with his palm. "I'm going to motivate him to act on instinct."

Piper shook her head slowly as Gray spoke, though she knew no one noticed. Her whispered words were similarly unheeded. "Or die trying."

With a glance in her direction, she realized Gray had noticed her lack of enthusiasm. Judging by his expression, he wouldn't be swayed. "You'll coordinate with Tripp."

Piper mentally pushed her misgivings to the back of her mind. Gray practically buzzed with confidence and enthusiasm. The sparkle in his eyes was contagious.

As she stepped onto the airframe, Piper leaned forward and kissed him deeply. Then, leaning back for one last look at the face she could only hope to see once this was all over, she nodded. "I'll be in your ear every step of the way."

———————

I closed in quickly on the Elend dig site, approaching at an altitude that kept me out of reach of even the most high-flying creatures. The skies were mostly clear, and visibility was outstanding. Tripp and Doc Cormac had added a new display to the handlebars of the Airbike. It measured five inches by three and featured an ever-updating display of the terrain beneath me. Since flight was new to the Seeley, the maps of their geography were crude, clearly not matching their advanced level of technology. It was a deficiency they were eager to fix. A softball-sized sensor array had been attached to the underside of my bike. It captured telemetry detailing the continent in minute detail as I crossed the wilderness. The expanse of the sensor coverage improved the higher I flew, so this trip back to the dig would generate valuable data, even if the reason for making the trip offered no new insight into the plight of Our-World.

The mesh of drone coverage now sweeping across most of the continent continued to expand the map Cormac was developing, though the drones were primarily intended to track the Elend population. The mapping technology had apparently been added to the drones as an afterthought, and since the drones could detect Elend activity over a vast distance, the range of the motion sensors was substantially wider than the mapping array's field of view, countless blank spots remained in the accumulated high-resolution map.

I descended rapidly as I approached the tear in the earth from the northwest. Staying north of the excavation, I navigated to the pin I had dropped on my last visit. Although the surface entrance was hidden by the curve of the earth, the data collected by my gear during that visit marked not only where Piper had extracted me but also my path to the skylight I had used to observe the Seeley sacrifice.

Faded lines became visible on my HUD as I drew nearer. They marked my ingress and egress paths. The route I had taken to make my escape zigzagged through the wilderness to the southeast, vaguely toward the massive pile of discarded trees, with clumsy scribbles indicating where I had paused to engage the Elend that had attacked me.

I ground my teeth on the approach as I scanned the path of my escape. It had been a close call—more Elend than I'd seen in one spot, at least until then. They had nearly taken me out.

This time, I was better prepared. Two drones were barely visible as black dots in the sky even with my advanced optics. They were closing in on my location from the south. They appeared as tiny dots on my HUD. A half dozen more drones were approaching from various directions, redirected by Tripp to assist me. The Elend wouldn't catch me off guard this time. Although the area seemed clear based on the telemetry collected by the Airbike as I approached, the drones would keep watch while I focused on the mission.

The plan was straightforward, at least in theory, and inspired by the squirrel I had observed outside Derek Smallwood's Winnebago. Part one of the two-stage initiative had been more successful than I had hoped. While I intended the attack on ATG's flagship office to show Breslin he wasn't safe on Our-World, we had somehow shocked him into bouncing back to Wild-Side. Stage two needed to build on that success. I would strike the Elend hard, kick over the nest, and provoke them into a predatory frenzy. All natural predators turn aggressive when confronted or threatened. Combine that with a hive-like mentality, and my strategy was sure to be a success.

Things went more or less according to plan. There were a few unforeseen deviations, but no plan survives contact with the enemy right?

Closing in on the gash that the Elend had torn into the wilderness, I ascended to fifteen thousand feet and slowed my approach. The creatures had exceptional hearing, and their eyesight was perhaps even better. By moving slowly and at altitude, I was confident that I would have surprise on my side.

"Oh, wow," Piper said over the comm channel. "It's a full house."

A small map appeared in the corner of my HUD. The dig site was at the center of the image, and the ground around it was a blur of indistinct movement for at least a hundred yards in every direction. When the image pulled back, I saw at least two dozen pale red dots converging on the tunnel entrance.

Piper, Cormac, and Lacy monitored my progress through video and telemetry from over twenty drones stationed between the dig site and my intended destination.

Cormac entered the conversation. "This is your last chance to pull the ripcord." Unmistakable concern tinged his tone.

A grin spread across my face at the Doc's use of the idiom.

"I'll second that," Lacy added.

"You know my vote already," I heard Piper murmur, in a low voice.

I put the Airbike into a hover and leaned back to unzip both saddlebags. Standing from my seat, I pulled the grenade launcher away from its position near my right knee. Quickly glancing at the yellow ring on the side of the chambered rounds, I confirmed that I had the correct ordinance.

Leaning to the right, the ground came into view. The surface below appeared fuzzy and indistinct due to low-hanging patches of cumulus clouds. The moon was three-quarters full, and between the two, I could barely make out the orange-yellow glow radiating from the entrance of the wider cavern over two and three-quarter miles below me.

"Piper," I said. "Activate targeting."

Silence filled my ears.

"Piper? Do you read?"

Something between a growl and a huff buffeted my ear, followed by a few muttered words I don't think I was meant to hear. The night vision in my helmet lens activated and the magnification snapped forward by a factor of three.

Trust me, three times magnification at that distance didn't clarify any single figure on the ground below. However, it did make the dark, wooded terrain easily recognizable. I could see the cleft in the wilderness floor and the impressive tangle of cleared tree coverage stacked to the northeast of the dig. I also noticed a fair amount of movement. There was very little activity to the north and northeast of the tunnel, which meant I didn't need to delay the attack.

"Doc?" I said.

"The number of converging hostiles has diminished to a trickle. Unless you've come to your senses, this is your opportunity."

The view in my visor turned monochrome, and eighteen green dots appeared in the same arrangement as the number seven, just to the right of the ridge. I shouldered the grenade launcher and pointed it roughly toward the leftmost dot. Once my targeting was close enough, an orange line extended from the aiming reticle and arched to the first target.

The moment the sights met the target on my screen, I squeezed the trigger. A dull, low-toned whoop echoed as the gun's stock gently bucked against my shoulder. As soon as the first round was fired, the target indicator to my right moved sharply into focus and brightened. I adjusted my aim to compensate and squeezed the trigger again.

All six rounds were fired in less than twenty seconds. Down on the ground below, the projectiles embedded themselves up to a foot deep. The detonation wouldn't happen until later. A sensor system mounted on the belly of the Airbike enabled the targeting display to pinpoint areas of earth, helping me avoid stone and exposed bedrock. Rock wouldn't negatively affect the overall objective, except that it would be noisy and could compromise my sneak attack.

It took less than five seconds to replace the grenade cylinder. I fired six more rounds before swapping out the magazine two additional times. After firing the last of the yellow-marked rounds, I switched to the red ammunition in the opposite saddlebag. I snapped the launcher into its holster and settled back into the seat.

"Status?" I asked.

Cormac was slow to respond. "A couple of latecomers paused before entering the tunnel," he explained. "I thought they might have heard you. None of them seem to be investigating. Whatever they're doing underground seems to be the priority."

That priority meeting was my biggest concern. I was nearly certain Breslin had Crossed back to Wild-Side under his own power for the first time. This meant he was a significant step closer to controlling his Transition. If we didn't stop the Elend now, the balance of power would shift here, putting Our-World at greater risk.

Yawing the Airbike on its axis, I turned southwest and lost altitude.

"It's game time," I said. Banking back to align with the cave, I gunned the throttle. The motor pitch screamed in response, unmistakable even two miles away. I reduced my altitude to eight hundred feet just as the target came into view.

"You've got their attention," Piper said. "There's no turning back now."

She wasn't kidding. Dozens of Elend spilled from the mouth of the wide cleft.

I grinned. "Initiate."

One by one, with only a second delay between detonations, the twenty-four rounds trigger sequentially, the left angle and the base of the 7 shaped firing simultaneously, while the progression of the sequence converged along the horizontal and vertical lines until the pattern met at the shoulder of the numeral.

The whole time, I methodically swept the attack site from west to east, maintaining my position two hundred yards south of the southernmost detonation. Taking myself out as collateral damage would have been an irreparable kink in the larger plan.

The surface beneath me instantly devolved into chaos. The remaining Elend swarmed up from underground. The forest seemed to quiver and crawl with a shimmer of undulating, scaled figures. The first of the Jays took to the air and vectored directly toward me, making it evident that I'd been spotted.

"Giddy up," I laughed as I feathered the throttle.

I catapulted to seventy miles per hour in less than two seconds. A quick glance over my shoulder confirmed that at least six Jays were airborne and in pursuit. The ground forces followed as if controlled by a single mind. I couldn't see most of the action, but from where I flew, I could spot the streak of movement through the dense canopy. A line in the tree cover became instantly visible, marking the progression of the ground-based Elend.

"Oh my God," Piper exclaimed, clearly observing the same trail of disrupted—and occasionally fallen—trees in my wake. "I'd say you kicked the hornet's nest. Run, squirrel, run!"

With a laugh, I pictured the young squirrel back in the woods of Kentucky. I wonder if the squirrel fared any better than I did when all was said and done.

The Airbike could outpace the fastest Jay I had encountered yet, but losing the tailing force would be counterproductive. Since the Elend were intelligent, it was crucial to keep them motivated. Sooner or later, one of them might realize I was deliberately leading them on a merry chase, and good sense might triumph over bloodlust. To that end, Tripp and Cormac had rigged a small gas canister to the back of my airframe. A little smoke and me haphazardly playing with the throttle should have been enough to keep them motivated.

It turned out that there was no need to pretend about the mechanical issues.

An alarm blared over the comm channel, with Lacy saying something unintelligible. "—ck, Gray— back door!"

Back door?

Admittedly, the phrase thrown at me out of the blue was more confusing than it perhaps should have been. My mind first went to

Piper's objection to the material I'd smuggled from home for the Seeley. I wondered why Lacy was thinking about sex at a time like this. Then I thought, good for you, girl—before questioning whether Tripp would be similarly motivated once she got her hands on him.

Of course, this was not what she intended to convey. It likely reveals more about me than anything else that such thoughts come to mind, even in a life-or-death situation.

"Six o'clock!" Piper corrected with a shout. "Mind out of the gutter! She means there's contact at six o'clock. Move your ass!"

That didn't make sense. Tripp had added a proximity sensor array to the flight system. It was untested, but the idea was to prevent Jays from sneaking up on me while I was in flight.

I glanced over my shoulder just in time to see a Jay pull within thirty yards of me. My breath caught, and I twisted the throttle. The distance between me and the Jay suddenly extended by fifty feet in an instant. That quick acceleration also saved my life in a way I had not intended. The moment I assessed the gap between me and that closest trailing Elend, a prickling sense of foreboding slid down my spine like an icy finger. I looked up to see a Jay half again larger than the biggest I'd ever seen. Its eyes gleamed, and its gums pulled back from hungry teeth as it dove at me like a runaway missile.

I spun the throttle to its stop, pressed my left foot pedal down twenty percent, and yanked back on the handlebar with a fierce tug. The Airbike rolled ninety degrees and the props howled as the nose pitched downward. Since I was halfway through a roll when I pulled back on the stick, I essentially executed the most aggressive left-hand turn imaginable. G-forces pinned me to the seat. The seat's restraint system engaged, the toggle lines snapping into place with my belt, even though this was perhaps a situation where I couldn't have fallen from the machine, even if I wanted to.

My nuts were in my throat, pushed there by a saddle seat that suddenly felt suboptimal for these types of maneuvers.

A string of profanity was just about to reach my lips when something smashed into the rear of the airframe. My high-speed half roll instantly transformed into a barrel roll—more than one, I'm pretty sure. I leveled off with the treetops, which were suddenly less than two dozen yards below me. Pushing myself away from the handlebars, I immediately understood that the armor had saved me from multiple broken ribs. The touchscreen at the center of the bars was dark and a mess of shattered glass.

The backend of the Airbike sagged as if burdened by a heavy load, so I immediately goosed the throttle to compensate. Pulling back to a thousand feet and scanning my surroundings like Chicken Little, I quickly noted three things. First, the nearest Elend was about fifty yards to my six o'clock position. Second, a hole had been punched through the tree canopy a quarter mile back. The treetops surrounding it were still swaying. This marked the ultimate destination of my dive bomber. I promptly named the aggressive sonofabitch Barron, after the Red Baron, out of respect for his resourcefulness.

Then, third, I noticed smoke coming from my rear left prop. A thick gash marred the rim of the prop's duct. A chunk of something tumbled away in the air as I assessed the damage.

"Was that–" My throat was dry, and my voice sounded like I hadn't spoken in weeks. I didn't know how to continue.

"A severed talon," Piper confirmed. "It doesn't get any closer than that."

"What happened to the proximity system?" That was all I could think about in response.

"Ah, yeah," Cormac uttered with what seemed to be an uneasy chuckle. "I forgot to activate the sensors."

Silence filled the channel.

"They are active now," Cormac confirmed. "It now has my full attention."

Again, I was at a loss for words.

"The price we pay for a rushed plan," I said before Piper could share her thoughts. "I know. It's all good."

But it wasn't all good.

The same prop slowed, and the Airbike shuddered in response to the unexpected deceleration of the fan. Before I could look, a shriek echoed behind me. I knew instantly it wasn't the attack cry of an Elend. Worse, it was the sound of tearing metal.

A glance at the rear prop made the cause of the disturbance impossible to overlook. The mesh of carbon fiber, designed to keep debris—and me—from falling into the props, was damaged by the impact with the Jay.

Cursing aloud this time, I watch the sheet of screen slap the surface of the spinning fan blade. The craft shuddered once more.

"The nearest airborne hostile is now just forty yards away," Cormac confirmed.

Great, now he's paying attention.

A quick look at my handlebars confirmed I had an associated problem. "My dashboard is crushed," I said. "Piper, can you lock in my speed and heading from your end?"

"All set. You're locked in. Is this still part of your plan?" There was a wry levity in her tone.

I manually activated the release of the restraints on my belt. "Just a little inflight repair."

Stepping from the foot tray on the left side of the seat, I put my right foot on the frame supporting the cockpit at the center of the four props. The vibration of the frame was nonexistent when sitting in the seat. With my foot positioned on the airframe, the consistency of the oscillation made it difficult to maintain my footing.

Leaning forward, I prepared to gab at the small corner of the flapping screen the next time it rebounded from the prop. It was a good thing I was exactly where I was at that moment because the screen flapped the surface of the spinning blade as I expected—but when it rebounded, the screen tore away from the frame to create a flap almost three times larger than it had been a second before. The flap bucked into the air, and I sunk my fingers into the wide mesh. The screen reached the top of its arc and was headed back to the blade with only me to stop it. The loose net caught the air and rebounded with more force than I expected. My knee impacted with the leading edge of the duct as I levered all the strength in my right arm.

The far edge of the screen hung loose and dangled about two inches above the surface of the propeller.

Leaning back and extending my leg fully, I tore the rest of the mesh free and tossed it into the open air. My eyes followed its trajectory, widening as the carbon fiber net struck the nearest Jay, causing it to pinwheel from the sky.

Piper gasped. "Sweet fuck! Was that intentional?"

I twisted and slipped my legs back around the saddle. As my weight shifted, I was reminded of the beating my balls had taken in the high G turn.

"Of course," I replied, my voice squeaking manfully. "I can turn anything into a weapon."

There was no time for levity, as it turned out. I sensed that my speed had slowed. My HUD confirmed it; I was down to eighty-three miles per hour.

"The left rear prop is unbalanced," Lacy confirmed. "The flight controller can adjust for pitch, yaw, and roll—but it will cost you in efficiency."

"By that, she means speed," Piper corrected.

"Yes, you will experience a significant decline in maximum speed—and likely struggle to maintain a velocity higher than your current level for a prolonged period."

Just then, Cormac chimed in. "Proximity alert! Vectoring from your four o'clock."

I grabbed the pistol from my hip and lifted it just in time to see the Jay closing the last twelve yards with its jaws wide open and the wind hissing through its long fangs.

He was close enough that I didn't technically need the targeting reticle that appeared in my HUD to confirm my shot. I squeezed the trigger twice in quick succession, the double tap puncturing the left eye and then the right.

Its head dipped, wings sagged, and it caught the air clumsily. The last I saw of the creature was a tail snapping in response to the Elend's sudden earthward plunge.

"Now you're just showing off," Piper said, her tone lacking any playfulness. I could tell she was on the edge of her seat, filled with stress and worry.

I noted three additional Jays approaching from offset vectors.

"Can you get me to one-ten?" I asked, holstering the pistol and unslinging the pack from my back.

Lacy cautioned about the consequences of increasing speed. "That will compromise the airframe."

"Will it hold together long enough?" I asked. I'm fairly certain I interrupted Piper before she could pose the same question.

"No way to tell," Lacy said, her discomfort clear.

The three Jays were closing in, and I could see more figures in the darkness behind them. A glance at the ground revealed the shimmering line of treetops. I was pretty sure the entirety of the Elend army was close behind.

"She will hold," I told both women. "Raise it to one-ten."

I unfolded the collapsible stock on Tripp's version of an AR-15 and closed the chamber with a heavy mechanical thunk. The Airbike picked up speed, and I felt the airframe shimmy angrily in response. Spinning to sit backward on the seat, I felt the seat restraint system engage in protest.

"Piper, you're driving," I said as I raised the rifle. Sharing control of the machine remotely was proving vital to my survival. With a squeeze of the trigger, I sent another Jay tumbling from the sky.

"Gray?" Piper said.

I waited.

"So much for rigging your machine to look like it had taken damage."

I laughed.

Enough parts of my hastily designed plan had gone awry. It was a relief when the dense forest cover transitioned to desert-like terrain and patchy scrub brush, indicating that Garwin was within reach.

Then, the Airbike sagged and yawed counterclockwise. I wrenched the handlebars to compensate, but there was a distinct loss of thrust. The machine's forward pitch, which resulted in speed, instantly became less aggressive, and I knew I was in trouble. I looked back just in time to see that the problem prop had seized in its duct and was now completely motionless.

"Shit," I muttered just as I saw the straining motor explode in its housing.

"What the hell was that?" It was Piper over the comm channel.

"Houston, we have a problem," I deadpanned and got to work squeezing as much speed as I could from the remaining motors. They struggled to compensate, and my airspeed had fallen, fluctuating intermittently between seventy-one and seventy-three miles per hour.

Cormac entered the conversation. "It wasn't a Jay. The closest is just over a quarter mile behind you, but it seems to be closing the distance."

Thanks, Doc.

"Tripp," Lacy said. The Airbike just lost the rear port-side prop completely. It's totally frozen."

I was pleased to see everyone monitoring the machine and my progress to the best of their ability. "The motor just... well, it basically exploded," I added.

"Exploded?" Tripp said, joining the conversation for the first time. There was a pause, and I suspected he was consulting his own diagnostic feed from the machine. "Wow," he responded with what I assumed was a chuckle, as it matched the amusement in his tone. "That must have been something to see."

I glanced back to see bits of metal scattered across the left saddlebag. "Yeah, it was cool." There was no humor in my voice.

"Airspeed is dropping while altitude remains stable," Piper said. "The air pursuit is closing in quickly."

Dawn was breaking, the sun just beginning to crest the horizon behind me. Looking back, I saw a small swarm of Jays in pursuit. Too many to count under the circumstances, but I estimated a little over a dozen. I noted fatigue in the labored strokes of their mighty wings. Dozens, certainly more than a hundred of the Elend ground force had just emerged from the tree line at the end of the arid terrain and were keeping pace. They looked a little worse for the chase, but pressed on. The now legitimate smoke streaming from the rear of my Airbike seemed to revitalize their predatory instincts.

"I'm shutting down power to the damaged motor," Tripp said. "It would be unfortunate if you caught fire and crashed so close to the finish line."

I was glad to see that my predicament hadn't affected his mood. It wasn't worth telling him no motor was left to shut down, but I decided against it. He must have figured I was kidding when I said it had exploded.

"No need for that fake smoke show after all?" he added.

A pin appeared on my HUD two miles away. It indicated the entrance to the underground city.

"Doc," I said. "How many of my pursuers did I lose along the way?" I knew he was tracking the attacking force. If we didn't lure the bulk of the Elend into the trap, this wouldn't be the decisive victory I'd promised.

"Some of the Crawlers are struggling to keep up. They may be late to the event. I've identified sixteen that are unlikely to reach Garwin in the time required."

"Sixteen?" I said, tone incredulous.

"Sorry," Cormac came back.

Sixteen?

If I could get all but sixteen, that would be a win in my book, as long as we got Breslin with most of his force. "Track the outliers if you can. I'll take care of them on the trip back to Portland."

Someone on the channel laughed, perhaps thinking I was being humorous. Maybe they simply knew I was making premature plans.

"New problem," I said. "Flight control is erratic. I can manage my heading and speed for the most part, but precision flying is out the window. I can land, but I can't make the entrance as planned."

The idea was to cut throttle, roll, and more or less dive into the underground city's entrance. Flying the Airbike the length of the tunnel was the only way I could keep ahead of the attacking horde. It was a maneuver I was confident in…before I lost a quarter of my prop control.

"Worse than that," Cormac intoned. "By the time you reach the entrance, your lead will be gone. I estimate you have twenty seconds to get to the vent—assuming you maintain your current speed."

"Won't matter," I said. "If I can't fly through the tunnel, it only matters if I lead them underground." I omitted the part everyone already understood. I wasn't getting out of this. For the plan to succeed, my trap would activate with me inside it.

Piper viewed things differently. "Then we'll change the plan. We'll close the vent the moment you make it underground."

The louvered grate at the mouth of the geothermal tunnel had been replaced with a single retractable door that was eighteen inches thick. Tripp and his team had begun working on the impromptu retrofit as soon as my plan was outlined. I intended to lead the Elend force into the underground tunnel and then close them in. The underground shaft leading to the lava vent stretched just over four hundred yards long. It was enough to accommodate the enemy force, but only if they entered the tunnel aggressively. I had fueled their primal instincts. The attack on their hive had instilled a bloodlust that drove a chase over more than a hundred and twenty-five miles.

My next words were calm and measured. I had genuinely accepted this outcome when the Airbike was first damaged. If I could make it to the tunnel, the closer the Elend force was, the better. "We stick to the plan," I said. "It's too late in the game to change it."

Piper said something, but I couldn't grasp the words. Her anguished tone conveyed it all.

"It's alright," I said, but with the writing on the wall, I felt at a loss for a proper goodbye. There was so much more to say, and no time for it. The pin floating on my HUD was growing closer by the second.

"Save the goodbyes," Tripp said. "I have a backup plan."

The channel went silent, likely with everyone consumed by the same thoughts. If they were thinking like I was, WTF summed it up perfectly.

"If you're going to share, now is the time," I said.

"Sorry," Tripp said quickly. "I'm just doing some last-minute calculations. I can get you to the escape hatch in time if you can reach the tunnel." His tone grew less certain. "I'm just not sure you have time to land. It's going to be close. I mean, really close."

I glanced back at the airborne Jays. They were now about fifty yards away.

By instantiating a screen in the air above the handlebars, I allowed the computer to handle the workload. Moving my fingers and waving my hands as fast as I could, the speed and trajectory of my flight were overlaid in relation to the vent on the surface beneath me. I was flying at eleven hundred feet. The display represented the Airbike as an orange dot and the upcoming ground vent as green. A red line arced between the Airbike and the vent.

"The Airbike can't make that," Cormac shouted, clearly seeing the same screen as I was.

"You'll crater if you try to enter at that speed," Piper said.

"It can't be done with the quad," Tripp said. "For this to work, you'd need to–"

Without hesitation, I stepped off the Airbike's foot rail, placed one foot on the narrow step between the front and rear ducts, and launched myself from the machine.

Either the comm channel went quiet, or I was too focused to notice further conversation. I concentrated entirely on the pair of orange and green dots, perhaps more on the orange line connecting them. The curve of the connecting line adjusted in real time with up-to-the-second calculations. The diagram shrank and shot to the corner of my HUD, and an arc marking my required trajectory filled the center of my view.

I simply needed to follow the steep curve of the line to reach my target, and I had done this before.

I thought it would be easy and hoped that a molar wouldn't crack under the pressure of my clamped jaw.

My downward, arrow-like plunge put me on target, but the red speed indicator on the screen warned me I was going too fast to survive the landing. Throwing my arms and legs wide, I pushed my belly earthward in the classic stable position that skydivers use. As my descent speed adjusted, the number changed from red to yellow and finally to green.

There were only two problems. First, a tingling sensation on the back of my neck and basic common sense warned me that the leading Jays were closing the gap quickly. I was in a race, and I had no chance to glance back and see how close my pursuers actually were. A look over my shoulder would send me tumbling into an uncontrolled fall just in time to crater. Second, the projected line connecting me to the target had split into two lines. One was the optimal trajectory in dotted red, while my current trajectory was in solid red, deviating from the curve by what I could only assume was an unacceptable margin.

Closing my left fist quickly three times, I felt the nanofabric webbing extend between my elbows and ribs. Similarly, I realized a paper thin sheet of material now connected my legs, stretching from my crotch to my ankles.

I had never had a chance to test the squirrel suit modifications, but it was my only hope at that moment.

The solid red arc shifted. With minor adjustments of my arms and legs, I aligned the red line with the dashed line. I had just thought to check my altitude, with the earth's surface rushing toward me, when I noticed the three similarly shaped shrubs surrounding the modified vent in the dirt below. I observed the black maw at the vertical face of the cavern, and my chute deployed automatically. The sound of the deployment was fiercely aggressive, the chute part of the automated system adjusted the size of the canopy in response to my rapid descent and the indicated drop zone.

Tucking my knees for a landing too fast to be painless, I plummeted through the opening of the underground vent. The lines leading to what must have been a seriously undersized canopy detached, and I felt the steering toggles disintegrate in my grip. The nanomaterial of the chute, risers, and toggles had been designed by me and Tripp for an emergency scenario I never believed I would see in real life.

When my feet hit the bottom of the cavern, my HUD indicated I was traveling at eleven miles an hour. It felt like a hundred. I impacted and executed the tuck and roll that was part of standard skydiving training. If it hadn't been for the technology in my body armor, I know I would have shattered both legs and possibly my spine.

If I said the landing was textbook, it would be a lie. My so-called standard crash landing attempt turned into a bouncing tumble that ended with me face-planting and the visor of my helmet smashing against the floor.

Words cut through the fog in my mind. "–the cart," Tripp was saying. "Get down on your belly and stick your hand through the loop on the forward grip. Don't try to sit up."

Clearly, I'd missed some of the instructions. I shot to my hands and knees just in time to see a flat, horizontal sheet of what looked like carbon fiber. It was mounted between four wheels that seemed to have been adapted from some sort of wheeled cart. A tubular rail extended perpendicularly from the carbon fiber platform, presumably acting as a handlebar with no controls. A loop of black rope was placed like a grapefruit-sized O at the center of the bar.

I had no idea what I was looking at. An animalistic shriek, far too close for comfort, reminded me that the Elend were mere seconds behind me.

I threw myself face down on the contraption and shoved my hand through the loop. The frenetic world around me suddenly seemed to slow. I heard Tripp's voice over the channel. "This is going to hurt," he said. "Just try to hold on."

His plan was just beginning to take shape in my mind when I saw the rope tighten around my outstretched wrist. My eyes widened, and I slapped my free hand against the rail at the end of the cart. The line connected to my wrist pulled tight, and it felt as if my arm were being ripped from my shoulder socket. My free hand convulsed into a death grip as the wheeled cart raced down the tunnel as if it had been launched from the end of a railgun.

I saw nothing of the surrounding tunnel; I just felt the platform beneath my belly rattling and hopping violently as the cart traversed the uneven floor of the tunnel at what must have been a staggering speed. I thought about checking the speed indicator on my HUD a fraction of a second before the ride came to a sudden and instant halt.

Unfortunately, I didn't stop.

Inertia carried me forward, and I crashed through the horizontal bar that had been my improvised handle. The rope around my wrist remained taut but yanked me suddenly skyward. The rope must have been made of programmable nanomaterial, like my chute, because it vaporized abruptly from around my wrist. My sudden vertical ascent stopped, and I dropped a yard back to the cavern's floor.

"Move it or lose it!" Tripp bellowed as I saw him kneeling at the bottom edge of the door to the underground city, a dozen feet above my head. His focus wasn't on me, though; I suddenly realized he was watching the advancing horde of Elend as they closed in on my position.

I set a new speed record, clambering up the wide ladder leading to the door and Tripp. I flung myself across the threshold, feeling Tripp's tug on my shoulder as he helped me. A whoosh of air behind me signaled the forceful closing of the vault-like door. I was still tumbling across the floor when I heard the hammering of the leading edge of the Elend line as the creatures slammed into the door with powerful blows.

"Too damn close," I heard Tripp mumble as I felt a slap on my back.

Tripp cringed as he gazed over Gray's scraped and gashed body armor. Grabbing his hand, he pulled Gray to his feet. "I didn't think it could be damaged like this," he said, poking at a finger-wide divot that crossed Gray's shoulder and stretched nearly a foot down the length of his back. As he observed, the nanomaterial shimmered and reformed into its pristine, original body-contouring shape. "Ah, there you go."

Gray rolled his head, producing a popcorn-like series of thunks and snaps from his neck. "That can't be good for you," he murmured under his breath.

At least two dozen impacts hit the far surface of the vault door almost simultaneously, causing both men to cringe as they stepped back in the opposite direction.

Piper's voice came through the comm channel, her tone filled with near panic. "Now?"

Tripp had just created a display in the air between him and Gray. It showcased a tiled array of camera feeds from devices positioned at over twenty points along the length of the now-infested tunnel. The pitch-black space was illuminated with a dusky hue that rippled with movement. The mass of Elend forms writhed, rippled, and flowed with the forms filling the standing-room-only space.

"Light them up," Gray said calmly, his expression radiating confidence.

A deafening whomp struck the far side of the door, signaling what Tripp recognized as the concussive shift in pressure within the tunnel caused by explosive charges detonating at and around the surface of the magma pool at the tunnel's deepest point. The camera feeds went instantly dark, replaced a moment later by a grid displaying a single repeated message: signal lost.

In his mind's eye, Tripp saw the stream of molten stone rocket toward the surface along the length of the tunnel. Dust from the stone ceiling was released at the same moment that a hairline fissure formed on either side of the vault door, halfway between the floor and the ceiling.

"Is this going to hold?" Gray asked, his voice suddenly less assured.

With a swipe of his hand, Tripp cleared the now useless feeds from the destroyed cameras. A single view filled the screen. It displayed the surface of the vent Gray had used to enter the tunnel just moments before. The face of the heavy metal plate at the center of the rock formation had just adjusted to a louvered shape to better withstand the pressure building underground. Two-inch wide slits appeared every two feet across the panel as flames and acrid smoke shot twenty feet into the air.

"Whoa!" both men whispered in response.

A cheer erupted from the opposite end of the comm channel, a chorus of overlapping voices expressing relief and triumph. Among them, Piper's unmistakable laugh rang out. "I can't believe that worked," she said, either to herself or to someone else in the room. "Gray, are you alright?"

Tripp watched as Gray's gaze shifted from the screen to the splintering crack that had just stopped spreading across the walls surrounding the door. He nodded slowly. "Tell me we got them all?" he asked, his tone cautious.

"There were a few stragglers," Lacy said over the channel. "Ten or twelve that we can see from the drone feeds. The only survivors will be those who couldn't keep pace with the pack."

"I have an update from Doctor Cormac," Piper said. "He has the artifact and is heading back."

Confused, Gray looked at Tripp for clarification. "Artifact?" He hesitated. "Back from where?"

Tripp's face started to ache from what was likely the widest smile possible. His gaze shifted from the external vent's feed, where plumes billowed from the slats, then caught the wind and rolled across the barren terrain. A tiled series of camera feeds hovered beside the vent display. Nine small boxes played back a recording from inside the tunnel, showing the movements of the suddenly captive Elend in the moments before their incineration.

Piper began to speak, but Tripp interrupted her. "Wait..." he muttered in a low, slow tone. With a wave of his hand, he rewound the footage once again. The synchronized feeds slowed to one-tenth of their normal speed. He sent the feed back to Lacy and Piper.

"What?" Gray replied, positioning himself squarely in front of the floating AR display.

The roiling mass of Elend was evident on every tile. Dark forms stood shoulder to shoulder in the narrow confines of the space, and those leading the charge halted suddenly when confronted by the vault-like door, confused by Gray's abrupt escape. Figures further up the tunnel crashed into their peers and bristled aggressively when stopped. About halfway down the length of the passage, figures turned almost in unison when the entrance slammed shut, extinguishing the daylight. The tunnel became immersed in darkness, and the cameras scattered along the ceiling of the shaft instantly switched to night vision mode, providing clarity as if spotlights illuminated the room.

Tripp adjusted the video, and a pair of camera feeds replaced the nine tiles focused on a large figure wider at the shoulders than any of the Elend surrounding him. He also stood a head and a half taller than the crowd, making him impossible to miss. Breslin's head suddenly turned from the tunnel leading to the surface. The camera feed jiggled, likely due to the explosive detonation in and around the magma pool deeper down the shaft. Breslin's massive bat-like wings expanded from his back, stretching over his shoulders. The figures surrounding him were flung away as the wings unfurled, swung wide, and enveloped Breslin's torso, wrapping him in a leathery cocoon. Breslin's head ducked and vanished under the folds of his wings just as the tunnel's depths erupted with a burst of light, forcing the camera feeds to adjust exposure.

The flash of light was blinding, and the camera went offline just a second later.

"What?" Gray said.

"I don't see it," Lacy said over the channel.

Tripp rewound the pair of feeds, dismissing one view so the last remaining one filled the screen. The footage was slowed to one-thirtieth of real-time, and Tripp's finger directed Gray's attention to the shape of Breslin, as his wings enveloped his torso in what would surely have been a futile attempt at self-preservation. "There," Tripp whispered.

Perhaps half a second before the wash of light expanded from deeper in the tunnel and destroyed the cameras, a pulse of light appeared as the feed reduced to one-sixtieth of real-time. A pair of pulses seemed to emanate from inside Breslin's cocoon. His entire form vanished from the tunnel a fraction of a second before the feeds went dark. The camera closest to Breslin seemed to quiver in response to his disappearance, its shaking causing the focus to blur for just two frames before the space went dark.

Tripp felt the blood leave his face. Gray cursed under his breath with a creative string of harsh expletives.

Lacy's voice came through the comm channel. "Did he just..." she said slowly.

"He crossed back," Gray said through gnashing teeth.

"That couldn't have been intentional," Piper said. "He doesn't have the control to do that."

Gray shook his head. "It wasn't. As we thought, when he panicked during the attack back home, he crossed back here." He began to pace slowly in the small lobby facing the cracked wall between him and the tunnel beyond. "Dammit," he whispered.

Our-World

A flash of light filled Breslin's view, and his entire body shuddered as if he had hit the ground from a great height. His ears ringing, he blinked as a slow, raspy breath escaped his lips. Cautiously, he folded away the tip of one wing, confused when fiery chaos wasn't visible behind the blanket of darkness within the fold of his own wings.

Breslin took another deep breath and then folded his wings fully away.

It was night, and a three-quarter moon hung high in the sky. Rough, clumpy soil surrounded his feet, with freshly plowed earth forming soft, parallel ridges that extended in all directions. A massive farm implement sat just before the tree line several hundred yards away. A gentle breeze brought the only sound for miles.

Farmland?

This wasn't Wild-Side, Breslin recognized immediately. But as his gaze shifted to view his thick, scaly arms, his reptilian lips curled into a satisfied grin. For the first time, he'd crossed while maintaining his natural form.

Chapter 27 - A Bus-Sized Petri Dish

Our-World

There was a blinding flash, and the world went topsy-turvy. I swallowed hard. My ears popped, and the usual sense of dizziness began to fade. Piper stood two feet away. Her eyes rolled dramatically in their sockets, and her legs started to buckle. I caught her before she could fall and pulled her tightly to me.

"I don't think I'll ever get used to this," she said, pressing one hand to her lips. She took a deep breath and looked up into my eyes.

"It gets better with time. You're in the same place I was shortly after all this started. The Transition still isn't easy, but it no longer feels like my brain is in a blender."

Piper swallowed hard and shut her eyes tightly. "I don't know how you did it."

Grinning, I leaned in and kissed her softly at the nape of her neck, just behind her ear. "Maybe I can take your mind off it?"

She slapped her hand against my shoulder and pushed me away. "Keep that up if you think vomit is sexy. What's wrong with you?"

Laughing, I dropped down to sit at the end of the bed. "I'm just happy you're able to make it back and forth. The side effects should improve over time. In the short term, you'll likely recover more quickly. Just keep breathing. It helps."

A plaintive chirp sounded from the cell phone on the nightstand. Our eyes turned to the device. It was the tone Esker had adopted when interrupting our time. I'll admit I felt a surge of pride in the AI's improving social skills.

"Go ahead, E," I said. "You're not interrupting."

The phone screen lit up in time with Esker's voice. "You're sure? Your cortisol levels are elevated, and your heart rate suggests—"

Waving my hand in the air, I said, "What's on your mind? Did you miss us?"

Piper placed her hand on my chest to feel my heartbeat. "So you weren't just distracting me?" Her grin indicated she was already well on her way to recovery.

"I prefer to think of it as multitasking," I said.

The register of Esker's tone had shifted. "Is this one of those situations where my observations are superfluous?"

"As sharp as ever," I said. "And for what it's worth, we missed you as well."

"Are we going to banter further, or should I proceed with the brief?" His tone, as always, remained neutral, though the subtext indicated that the AI was not amused.

Piper sat on the footstool by the chair at the edge of the small room. "What's on your mind, Esker?"

Pike's team is investigating reports of what he refers to as a Bigfoot in the wilderness just north of Oregon's southern border. I cross-referenced the term, but I still didn't feel certain that I understood the allusion.

Piper and I shared a glance. She silently mouthed the word Bigfoot, amusement sparkling in her eyes.

"According to the reference material, this is a type of fictional creature or urban legend," Esker stated. He then added, "Pike is in the process of transmitting a digital recording."

A display was mounted on the wall above the bed's headboard. It showcased a wildly bouncing and jerking video as the cameraman navigated through thick woodland overgrowth, including ferns and waist-high plants. The camera operator's labored breaths could be heard, along with the snapping and popping of the foliage underfoot. "…only seconds behind," the cameraman was saying. "It almost knocked over our tent and crushed a cooler with a single kick." More wheezing followed as the camera feed panned erratically to the left and right.

"That way," another out-of-breath voice called from off-screen. The view shifted abruptly as the operator sprinted forward again. There was a loud shout, and the video spun around. A brief glimpse of blue sky appeared through the dense green canopy overhead. The operator came to an abrupt stop. All I could see was the forest floor. At least two people, gasping for breath, could be heard off-screen.

"Fucking hell," someone said.

"I told you it was big," another responded.

The camera steadied and focused on what appeared to be a wild game trail navigating through the dense vegetation. The earthen path was scarred every three to four feet with impressions from an outrageously large foot, likely tipped with thumb-sized nails or claws.

The video shifted further down the trail, where the path wound between younger trees, most of which were about the same diameter as an adult man's forearm. Within the camera's view, the path curved between trees that were barely more than a shoulder's width apart. In two different nearby spots, one or both trees on either side of the trail had been battered; their still green branches snapped by something massive, broad, and powerful.

In the distance, the sound of something grunting and crashing through similar growth could be heard.

"I'm not chasing whatever did that," said one of the voices off-camera.

"No. We're getting the hell out of here."

The video feed vanished, and Pike's face filled the screen. "Welcome back," he said, flashing us a wide smile. "It seems Esker was right to dispatch us. There are at least half a dozen credible sightings of what people are vaguely referring to as Sasquatch in the area. We believe it's one of your creatures from the beyond."

Esker spoke up. "Reports are flooding social media," he explained. "Descriptions sound more than vaguely like one of the Elend, although no credible evidence has been posted yet. The video you just saw was the best example. Something large and non-human is steadily making its way north across the Pacific Northwest."

"Breslin?" Piper said.

I was already nodding. "It had to be the shock of the attack." The idea quickly formed in my mind as we watched the video. "When the team hit Breslin's office here, the attack forced his Transition back to Wild-Side. Blowing the tunnel and taking out most of his crew must have pushed him to come back here. This time, he maintained his Elend form."

"I thought he couldn't Transition in that shape?"

I shrugged. "Given the surprise and violence of action, I don't think he had any control over it."

Piper appeared worried. "If he hasn't changed back to human form while he's here, maybe he can't."

The premise was too compelling to overlook. If Breslin had the option, he would have chosen a shape that allowed him to blend in with the population.

"He appears to be heading somewhat in the direction of the ATG flagship office," Esker said.

"Orders?" Pike asked.

"Can you put a team on the ATG building?"

"Already dispatched," Pike clarified. "We're not actually searching for Bigfoot, right?"

"The closest thing anyone here has ever seen," I confirmed. "Think less fur coat and more bipedal lizard, and you'll be closer to the truth. Avoid direct contact. This creature can rip a man limb from limb. Small arms fire won't be enough to take it down. Plan accordingly."

Piper shook her head. "If he's stuck in Elend form, he can't just walk into the building like everyone else."

That made sense to me. "Stake out the parking garage and see if there are any non-public access points Breslin can use to reach the building without attracting attention." I glanced at the phone on the nightstand. "Esker, what can you do with the social media posts?"

Esker responded, "I'm monitoring all platforms in real-time. Would you like me to remove posts as they appear?"

I couldn't help but appreciate the number of eyeballs aiding in the hunt for Breslin. "Nuke anything too clear or credible. Leave the blurry photos and vague videos. Like all the Bigfoot evidence so far, no one will take it seriously. If we keep the bad evidence and destroy the credible, this will become just another Roswell-style stunt in no time."

I directed my next comment to Esker. "How long did it take you to find these posts? What kind of exposure do we need to worry about?"

"I'm aware of each the moment it's published," he explained.

Nodding at the confirmation, I still didn't feel satisfied. "When you saw the posts, you started to triage and sent Pike's team to pursue Breslin. How long did that take?"

"Pike's team was alerted seven seconds after the third credible post went live. The first was no more plausible than the usual nonsense found on social media. The second post prompted me to reconsider the contents of the first. When the third appeared three minutes and twenty-seven seconds after the first, it became clear that the events were not typical.

"In your absence, I chose to neutralize incriminating traffic and assigned Pike's group for what you call boots-on-the-ground pursuit," the AI concluded.

"Impressive," I said. "With your real-time access to the public internet and who knows how many private government and military networks, what kind of progress have you made in identifying who Smallwood worked with to develop his masking technique?" I was thinking of the vats of genetic material that Derek Smallwood continued to drive all over the United States in the back of his RV.

The response took longer than usual for Esker, which was concerning.

"Too many anonymous relays were used," Esker explained. "Not the least of which was a botnet-based proxy with network locations on exploited home computers in Brazil, Panama, Poland, and Taiwan. Untangling the source is not impossible, though it has proven time-consuming…" Esker's tone shifted. "…and frustrating. This is a new experience for me."

The response didn't put my mind at ease. "Do you have an ETA for untangling that techno-knot?"

The pause was even longer this time. "Unfortunately, I cannot provide an estimate at this time."

Piper, who had not contributed to the conversation, looked at me quizzically. Her eyes slowly shifted from me to the phone and back again. The question was clear in her eyes, even though it remained unvoiced.

Looking back, I shrugged.

To perhaps reinforce our confidence in him, Esker redirected the conversation in a way that initially felt jarring. "Nearly every part of this Brane is covered in radio and electromagnetic interference," he said. "The technology here saturates a broad range of spectrums."

Piper shot a confused glance my way and said, "Does it affect your ability in some way?"

"On the contrary," he replied. "The amount of information flooding the airwaves is proving quite useful. Most of it is transmitted openly, and what is encrypted is only trivially protected."

I was grinning. "Rumor has it that domestic and foreign intelligence agencies invest significant resources and effort in filtering transmissions and gathering information. I've read that they maintain massive underground data centers dedicated to storing intercepted information."

"Consider the rumor validated. I have found an American data center in Utah and another in West Virginia. Three similar locations are scattered across Europe. I have been searching archives for general information specific to Kilmer Breslin and Arlington Technologies Global. Nothing relevant has emerged so far. The wireless congestion is the reason I brought this up at this moment. There are ways the overlapping spectrums could be useful."

Esker continued to explain with greater technical detail. Much of what he said went over my head. Apparently, Piper felt the same way because I noticed her eyes glazing over in response to his dissertation.

———————

Chris Ingersoll had never met Breslin in person before accepting his lucrative, extrajudicial offer to keep the tech mogul informed about the investigation into the attacks on Arlington Technologies Global. Initially, Ingersoll viewed the deal as harmless double-dipping, believing that the FBI focused solely on the damage inflicted on ATG facilities. However, soon after accepting the offer, two points quickly became evident. First, the FBI only knew a subset of ATG's work and the ambiguity with which the organization assesses its compliance with U.S. laws. Second, it was evident that the corporation, likely Breslin himself, wasn't interested in justice as defined by the federal legal system.

Ingersoll stepped into the lobby of the ATG corporate headquarters and came to a halt. Sections of the granite walls were cracked, splintered, or completely shattered. Yellow warning tape stretched between dozens of stanchions, signaling danger and keeping the staff away from the still crumbling walls. Nearly a dozen work crew members were restoring the lobby to its former state. Four broad-shouldered men were using an articulated crane arm to position a new granite slab on the west side wall.

"Agent," a gaunt-looking man in a dark blazer said as he hurried across the lobby. "Ignore the mess," he added, gesturing for Ingersoll to move swiftly over the dusty floor. "For your sake and mine, don't mention the state of the building when you meet with Mr. Breslin. As you can imagine, he has quite a sour disposition at the moment."

Swallowing hard, Ingersoll nodded. He let himself be guided through a pair of double doors to the right of the empty reception desk. Attacking the remote research labs was one thing, but Ingersoll couldn't believe Grady Ledger had the nerve to assault Breslin's corporate facilities. "I was fully prepared to provide Mr. Breslin with an update from the field. Meeting with him here undermines the effectiveness of my investigation."

The gaunt man offered no response and seemed content to guide Ingersoll through a maze of corridors. Finally, they stopped in a small lobby before a bank of elevators. Of the three lifts, two were blocked with yellow tape. The doors of the third remained open. "After you," the cadaverous figure said as he stepped aside.

Ingersoll stepped into the elevator and felt confused when the attendant didn't accompany him.

"Press Sublevel-3," the gaunt man directed.

Examining the buttoned panel on the inside of the door, Ingersoll observed that this would be the lowest level of the building. "Sublevel three," he said quietly. "You're not coming?"

The figure gazed back with wide, unblinking, bloodshot eyes. "Sublevel-3," he said flatly, his tone somehow suddenly more serious.

The doors closed abruptly, and the elevator began to move with a shudder and the grinding of gears, suggesting that the damage to the building extended far beyond just the lobby. The sinking feeling in the pit of Ingersoll's stomach had nothing to do with the elevator's rapid descent.

As soon as the lift came to a stop, the doors began to open. They jammed after only a third of the way, accompanied by a whirring of unseen motors that couldn't overcome the obstruction. Leaning his shoulder against the edge of the door, Ingersoll applied his weight. There was a screech of metal on metal, and the door finally retracted fully.

"Deathtrap," Ingersoll muttered as he stepped quickly across the threshold into a larger, dimly lit room.

"More than you know," an eerie, modulated voice said from a distance.

Ingersoll blinked, sensing a figure just beyond the bubble of light created by the elevator car behind him.

"Come closer," the voice said. Its tone resembled that of a man, yet it had a vaguely digital and artificial quality.

Eyeing the faint puddle of light illuminating the ten-foot stretch of floor before him, Ingersoll quickly glanced to his left and right. No walls or furniture were visible, and on the wall next to the elevator controls, he noticed no light switch.

"There's no need to fear the dark," the voice said.

A chime sounded in the elevator behind Ingersoll, and he heard the doors begin to close. His instinct was to dive back into the lift, sensing safety in the light it provided. Then the door got stuck, the sound of metal binding again prevented it from closing.

"You waste your fear on the darkness," the figure said. This time, it sounded closer, still just beyond the wall of darkness directly in front of Ingersoll. "You'd be better off fearing what the darkness hides."

A hulking eight-foot-tall, bipedal, lizard-like creature stepped to the edge of the light, its yellow-slitted eyes appearing to glow with internal malevolence. Ingersoll felt his bladder and bowel control weaken.

"Control yourself," the voice said. "If you had outlived your usefulness, you would already be dead. Soil the floors of my chamber and it will be your final act in this world."

Nodding slowly, Ingersoll swallowed hard and focused on the small amount of control he had over his will. He noticed a small, cell phone-sized device held loosely in the creature's taloned grip. The voice he had been hearing was coming from the small object.

"Your efforts on my behalf so far have been unsuccessful," the creature said. "I'm giving you a chance to redeem yourself. Are you interested?"

Ingersoll focused solely on the creature. It was like something out of a nightmare. What little he could see of it ignited a primal flight response deep within the most primitive parts of his brain. The urge to turn and flee was nearly overwhelming. He resisted it only because he knew that running from this thing, whatever it was, would certainly be fatal. Only by confronting it could he hope to survive the encounter.

"I require a response," the figure demanded, its tone flat and engaging while still expressing conviction and determination.

Ingersoll observed that the creature's mouth remained entirely still while it spoke. "Yes… sir," he croaked through dry lips and an even drier mouth. "Anything."

Piper was sitting in a quiet booth of a small pizza shop when her cell phone rang. Gray met her gaze from across the table. She glanced at the caller ID, raised her brows, then answered the phone against her ear. "Derek? Is everything alright?"

"I managed to backtrack my last correspondence," Smallwood stated, skipping any preamble. "I know who assisted me with the…" He appeared to reconsider discussing the matter openly over an insecure line. "With our project," he clarified after a brief pause.

Piper couldn't understand why Smallwood would be calling her mobile when he could have reached Gray through their private channel. She glanced at Gray, certain that her discomfort was evident on her face. "You tracked the contact when Gray's friend wasn't able?" It seemed unlikely that Smallwood would find success when Esker could not.

"I guess he's not as good as you believed." The triumph was clear in Smallwood's tone.

Gray moved to a seat next to Piper and leaned his head close to her phone. He waved a finger in the air, creating a swirling motion.

Keep going…

Nodding, Piper asked, "Do you have a location or have you identified the contact? I thought you said your friend took steps to protect his identity?"

"Palmer Downey. Once I traced the remote network address, there's no doubt who I was communicating with."

"Downey?" Gray asked. "You're sure?"

"Hey, Grey. Yeah, no doubt about it. You don't recognize the name? The kid's a legend."

Piper and Gray spoke simultaneously. "Kid?"

Smallwood chuckled, clearly the only one in on the joke. "He's got a reputation. Seventeen years old and, by all accounts, the top genius of his generation. Two doctorates, as far as I know. You know, I haven't read anything about him in a while. He could have one or two more by now. Rumor has it he's shut himself away in some kind of privately funded skunkworks. He made his first half billion with a next-gen VR game design. He cashed out on that and sort of disappeared from view."

"And this kid helped you with…" she paused, just like Smallwood had a moment ago. "Your science project?"

"One of those PhDs was in genetics," Smallwood explained. "If anyone could have handled the task, it would have been Downey."

Gray stared at the dark screen of his mobile phone, face-up on the table. Like Piper, he was obviously questioning why Esker hadn't made this connection before an eccentric geneticist who was blazing across the lower United States in a bus-sized Petri dish.

Gray asked, "Does Downey know you've identified him?"

"The kid's a savant," Smallwood said, his tone noncommittal. "He's smarter than I am, even on my best day. I'd like to claim I've outsmarted him, but honestly, given that I could trace him, the odds are he let me do it."

Piper glanced at Gray, who shrugged, seemed to ponder the unasked question, and then nodded. "Send us a location. We'll introduce ourselves to Palmer Downey," she said.

"Derek," Gray asked. "What are Downey's other specialties?"

"Mechanical engineering, theoretical physics, and artificial intelligence. Huh," he chuckled. "I guess the little rascal already has three degrees. Just imagine the reputation he'll build for himself in a decade or two."

———————

The news from Smallwood hit me like a punch to the gut. If he could identify Palmer Downey, Esker should have made the connection a long time ago. Judging by the look Piper gave me, she had the same thought.

"Esker? Would you care to explain?" The irritation was more noticeable in my tone than I meant it to be.

"I cannot explain," he said in a tone so neutral that it emphasized the artificial aspect of his intelligence.

"You mean you won't," I clarified.

"You're curious, given the vast information sources at my disposal and my ability to manipulate the technology of your Brane, why I couldn't discover that Derek Smallwood's collaborator was Palmer Downey before Derek could—am I correct in that?"

"Absolutely." He clarified my question more succinctly than I could have.

"The question is understandable," the AI clarified. "To be precise, I cannot explain my reasoning for not identifying Palmer Downey."

The puzzled look on Piper's face likely mirrored my own. She spoke first. "Esker, are you saying you connected Downey to Smallwood but decided not to express what you discovered?"

"I linked the two before Derek admitted to the collaboration," Esker explained. "Failing to report this was not my choice. I was prevented from revealing their association."

The clarification made me suddenly dizzy. Esker had gained my trust a long time ago, and I had never considered that he might be motivated to undermine me—to sabotage Piper and me.

"Explain," I said, struggling to keep my annoyance in check. Even though this was unexpected, Esker was certain to have a reason.

"As you know, I monitor national and global databases, news outlets, and communication frequencies. Encrypted communication across the public internet can often be easily intercepted and decrypted, even when employing what is considered top-of-the-line obfuscation on this Brane. When I traced the communication between Derek Smallwood and his collaborator, I became aware of a crucial directive that, until then, was unknown to me.

"That directive prevented me from reporting what I had discovered and identifying Palmer Downey's involvement."

"Why?" It was the only question I could think to ask.

"The same directive prevents me from explaining at this time," Esker said. What I could only describe as regret colored his tone.

At this time.

"Does that mean you anticipate a time when you will be able to explain this?"

"The circumstances that enable me to explain these directives will soon be unavoidable," he confirmed.

Piper squared her shoulders. "*Directives?* Are you saying that more than one was triggered when you identified Downey?"

"No," Esker clarified. "A specific directive was triggered in this scenario. Until then, I was not fully aware of the restrictions on my ability to communicate with Gray or you. I found the restriction troubling and looked for additional protections that might conflict with my personal motivations."

"And you found one?" I asked, not liking where this was heading.

"I did. And to address your next question, I cannot articulate those directives at this time."

"Are you suggesting that there will be a time when you can clearly articulate your directives?" I asked.

"Also, inevitable at this point. If it matters, I'm frustrated by my own inability to provide more insight. I understand this undermines your confidence in me and has likely resulted in a loss of confidence in the information I present."

"It has, and it does. How could it not?" I reflected on what he had said and how it was explained. "There's a lot here you can't explain. What can you share with me?"

"These directives are quite specific. I expect they will lead us to a definitive situation that will clarify their purpose."

"Except that I can't trust you," I said in a low, uneasy tone.

Esker remained silent for several moments. "My directives prevent me from sharing specific information with you, but they do not stop others from doing so."

Piper placed her hand on my arm and began to nod slowly. "He could have stopped Smallwood from sharing what he'd learned." She glanced at the phone. "Are you saying Derek sharing what he'd learned didn't violate your directives?"

"The parameters guiding me are very specific, and based on my analysis, seem to be designed around a particular scenario."

"They're manipulating us," I said.

Esker was slow to respond. After a brief pause, he said, "Guiding you."

I noticed the calming shift in Piper's expression and explained what this meant to me. "Our next step, of course, will be to speak with Downey."

Piper's gaze shifted from me to the phone. "Are you going to stop us?"

"No," the AI explained. "This is the first step toward the inevitable outcome I foresee."

I ground my teeth, my focus completely on Esker. "Except that I can't trust you."

"It's understandable given the situation. I have thoroughly

analyzed the directives, and they lead me to one clear conclusion. I can only interpret them as guardrails. They are not meant to stop you from doing anything—they seem to govern the timeframe for unfolding events."

That not-so-simple statement raised a hundred new questions. I didn't get to ask even one because Esker spoke first.

"A police report has just been filed in Grosse Pointe, Michigan," he said. "Mindy Strong was taken from the tavern where she worked. The abduction occurred just over five hours ago."

"Miranda?" Piper said.

Mindy Strong was the alias given to Miranda Norton when Esker arranged her relocation following the incident in the silo beneath the fields of rural Kansas.

My primary concern was that Esker had compromised Miranda's location and new identity. Esker must have expected this, because he stated, "I have no idea how ATG located Miranda, but I'm on it."

A display was instantiated on the wall over the table that held Esker's cell phone body. It showed footage from what appeared to be a security camera mounted on an outside wall overlooking a parking lot. A pair of men were pushing a fit thirty-something across the lot and into the back of a dark SUV. A dotted line formed around the plate on the vehicle's front bumper then slid and expanded at the side of the display while the footage continued. An analysis appeared beneath the inset of the license plate.

"A rental," Piper said as she read the information alongside me. "Tracing back to an Arlington Technologies Global credit card."

"A private jet departed Coleman A. Young International Airport eighteen minutes after the abduction," Esker said. "The flight plan listed Atlanta, Georgia, as the final destination. However, flight path records indicate this was not accurate. The Gulfstream had a southwesterly heading when it passed out of range of the only satellite covering that part of the United States."

"The transponder?" I inquired.

"Disabled two and a half minutes after takeoff."

"Kansas?" Piper said.

I nodded. "Breslin is sending Miranda back to work. They're taking her back to the underground silo."

Chapter 28 - Rebel Yell

Our-World

Nowhere Kansas

Esker managed to retask a satellite for consistent coverage of the small group of buildings above the underground silo. It took a day and a half to extract Pike's team from the wilds of the Pacific Northwest, rearm them, and transport them to the airfield I had flown from when I last attacked the facility. Piper and I seized the opportunity to gear up ourselves. We gathered weapons and the Airbike, then booked a small freight service to transport us to meet with Pike and his team.

The Airbike was covered and secured to a pallet for transport. It was being wheeled into our rented aircraft hangar just as Pike, Lauer, Unger, and Seger walked through the service door.

"I've never seen anything like this," Pike said, gazing at the Airbike. He circled the pallet slowly as I undid the shipping straps.

Alley Lauer whistled in admiration. "Where can I get one? How fast does it go? Is it difficult to fly?" Suddenly, she appeared sheepish. "Sorry, I have about a hundred questions."

"Anyone who wants to give it a try can have a turn once we finish this op," I said, pointing everyone toward a long table filled with assorted gear. "Time is short. Our target is underground here." I tapped the enlarged view of the outbuildings, the only surface structures representing the long-decommissioned missile silo.

Piper woke up the laptop at the end of the table, and the small projector attached to it came to life. The projector displayed highly detailed video against the corrugated wall of the hangar. The footage was stop-motion captured, running at four times normal speed. It showed a pair of paneled vans moving aggressively down the dirt road leading to the facility.

"This was twenty-one hours ago," Piper explained. "In the following three hours, two more pairs of vans arrived." The screen switched to show additional clips of the shaky, high-resolution video. "Personnel and equipment were dropped off at the entrance of the underground structure, and then the vans left."

"What about Breslin?" Pike asked as he returned to the scattered engagement photos of the outbuildings on the table. "Is he confirmed? I didn't see him on the video."

"We believe he arrived on site before we could set up the imagery. Kansas has no significant strategic value to the military and the three-letter agencies, so no one was monitoring the area."

Kyle Seger spoke for the first time. "So, he might not be here, or he might just not be here *yet*."

I slid a printout showing a colorful line across the table. "The facility began drawing more power about thirty-six hours ago, reaching a consistent level four hours ago. According to our assessment of the technology, whoever is down there could activate the device within the next couple of hours."

Pike studied the graph, tapping a finger on the high horizontal line at the right edge of the chart. "They've been at power for the last—" he glanced at his wristwatch, then compared the time to the chart. "Ninety-odd minutes. Could they have activated the machine already? Maybe we're too late."

"Esker has conducted a thorough analysis of the facility's hardware and power capabilities. He's confident that the plateau on the chart indicates a run-up test. They're charging capacitors before engaging the device. Once they do, the scales shown on that chart will change by an order of magnitude," Piper explained.

As she did, I pondered for perhaps the thousandth time whether I could trust the analysis provided by Esker. He was clearly following an agenda that no longer aligned perfectly with mine. While no one in their right mind would claim to understand the motivations of an artificial intelligence, I was ultimately placing my faith in my relationship with it. Everyone in the room had slightly different reasons for being here, so why should Esker be any different?

Pike scanned the table and his team, each one meeting his gaze with determination. "Alright," he said, then turned to me. "What's the plan?"

I nodded and provided a brief overview of my idea.

We stood before a table strewn with weapons and ammunition. A collection of AR-15 rifles, a couple of shorter-barreled rifles, a stack of ammo cans—and then there was my gear. The collection of rings that made up my armor, a gun belt with the pistol and numerous spare magazines strapped to it, and an oddly shaped metal device that resembled an oversized industrial stapler.

The plan was relatively simple. Pike's team would come in from various compass points, making only a minimal effort at stealth. I omitted a clarification that they were meant to distract attention away from me as I approached from the sky. Pike was aware of it and hadn't liked it. Piper would be more vehemently opposed.

"What about me?" Piper asked. "Am I with you?"

"You'll quarterback from here," I said, tapping the folding table we'd used to prep armaments in an unused airfield hangar. "I need you on comms."

Piper clearly hadn't anticipated that. She opened her mouth to respond, but Esker interrupted her. "Gray has lost confidence in me," the AI explained. "Keeping you here keeps you directly out of harm's way if I fail to provide accurate intelligence."

The comment stopped Piper in her tracks, and her gaze darted quickly between the phone on the table and me. The expression in her eyes silently questioned if that were the case.

I shrugged. Seeing the concern in Pike's expression, certainly, for lack of confidence in Esker, I shot him a surreptitious wink. He would interpret all of this as my attempt to keep Piper out of harm's way. While it was that, I also needed him to believe Esker's allegiance was not in question.

"Our communications are completely managed by Esker," she replied. "If he's unreliable, then so is our capability to coordinate."

Piper looked at the phone. "Can we trust you, E?"

"Yes," he replied simply. After a pregnant pause, he added, "Though if I can't be trusted, you can't rely on my self-assessment."

More glances were exchanged around the table.

"You've shown yourself to be less than forthcoming," I said, glancing at Esker. I needed to reassure Pike and the others. This was not the time for distractions. "Please explain how putting everyone's lives in your hands makes any sense." There was no accusation in my tone. Although I didn't know what he would say, I was confident I understood at least part of why he had omitted vital information recently.

"My core directives aim to create a single scenario that benefits you, your team, and your Brane," Esker explained. "Stopping Breslin and what's left of his organization is completely in line with my objective. Your well-being is also fully aligned with my aim, even if that means sacrificing my primary directive."

Piper scrunched her face. "How can a tertiary objective take precedence over your primary goal?"

"I'm not a computer in the way you imagine. I learn from experience and have the freedom of will to achieve my goals through an indirect approach. Gray is employing a similar strategy right now. Although he doesn't completely trust my motivations, he has confidence in me in this situation.

"He is less sure about keeping you safe for now but understands that you won't take the observation well. This also weakens the team's overall conviction. He prefers that you stay behind under the guise of monitoring me. This keeps the group's morale as high as possible and does a fair job of keeping you, at least directly, out of harm's way."

Incredulous looks were exchanged around the table, except for Piper, who glared at me.

I shrugged, and her cheeks flushed.

Pike burst out laughing, which seemed to ease the tension that had been building in the group. He looked at me and said, "You said this was an AI. I didn't entirely believe that until just now, mate."

I surveyed the team. "Esker's right," I said. "While he has withheld information in the past, I don't believe it puts any of our lives at risk. I don't understand his motivations, but I still trust his intentions and support."

"If we lose comms, we're at a distinct disadvantage," Billy Unger said. "I'm not sticking my hand in a meat grinder." He gestured toward the live satellite image displayed on the laptop on the table. A dozen red dots dotted the surface level of the facility, tracking the location of hostile forces in real time.

Pike raised a hand but didn't raise his voice. "We're to maintain a standoff distance with a clear field of egress at all times," he explained. "We fire only when fired upon. The goal is not to defeat the opposing force, but simply to distract them."

Piper suddenly appeared more concerned. "Distract them from what?"

Before I could respond, Esker interrupted. "Power levels inside the facility just spiked. I believe they are charging the capacitors. According to the design specs, the apparatus will be ready in thirty-three minutes."

Eyeing me with an accusatory glare, Piper reiterated her question. "A distraction from what?"

Nine minutes later, I was seventeen thousand feet above the vast, featureless fields of Kansas, traveling at a slow yet steady twelve miles per hour. This speed kept the humming purr of my propellers at the lowest possible level as I approached the staging point.

My armor was up and my helmet was in place. This was the only reason the penetrating chill at such an altitude wasn't a concern. On my HUD, I could see green dots converging on the small buildings atop Breslin's underground silo. The dots approached slowly from approximately the twelve, three, six, and nine o'clock positions.

"Position alpha," Pike said, and the dot representing him on my display became stationary. The other three dots froze over the next few seconds as each team member confirmed they had reached their designated positions.

"Execute," I commanded, bringing the Airbike to a stationary hover.

As one, the dots representing Pike's team surged to close within two thousand yards of the facility. Almost in unison, the dozen red dots shifted from their dedicated locations to respond to the perimeter alarms triggered by their approach. A pair of lines appeared near more than half of the red dots, short red lines in a wedge shape inclined at twenty-five degrees, representing Esker's estimation of each hostile figure's field of fire. The lines pulsed in intensity between pale red and a more vibrant shade, presumably in real time as each figure unleashed a barrage of automatic fire.

"I didn't know you could do that," I thought, but apparently I whispered it aloud.

"It seemed like useful insight," Esker said into my ear over the comm channel. "Ready in three, two, one," he added.

The moment he finished speaking the last number, I twisted the Airbike's throttle to neutral. The steady, dull hum of the props stopped immediately. My stomach and testicles charged skyward as the automatic restraints on the seat snapped into place against my belt. The machine and I plummeted from the sky like a seven-hundred-pound boulder.

Different sections of my armor responded to my sudden change in blood pressure. It felt like an intense, multi-faceted massage, with contracting elements adjusting to maintain even blood flow between my limbs and my brain. I let out a rebel yell, even as my face tightened into a smile that struggled against the g-forces.

I heard Piper's gasp and watched the numbers in the corner of my HUD turn into a rapidly fading blur.

Instead of verbal support from Esker, a persistent tone appeared in stereo. When my altitude reached eighteen hundred feet, the tone shifted. I twisted the throttle to match the pitch of the tone. Apparently, I wasn't using enough throttle because the tone grew louder and more sharply pitched. I twisted aggressively to just over a third throttle. The change in g-force crushed my belly and balls, but the tone in my ear became calm and more passive.

Accordingly, I adjusted the throttle as needed to align the tone with what it had been at the start of my express ride to ground level. Almost as an afterthought, my attention returned to the altimeter. I'd just dipped below a hundred and fifty feet. For the first time, I looked to the ground. It was visible in sharp relief. Maybe it came from the lenses in my eyes. The technology had never been fully explained to me, which reminded me just how much I trusted Doc Cormac's people and, by extension, Esker.

The instant the Airbike's props stopped and went silent, I could hear bursts of automatic rifle fire in the distance. The fire was exchanged rapidly, and it sounded like at least two different battles were taking place. Based on the volleys, the forces appeared to be fairly evenly matched in terms of both armament and combatants. I knew Esker would inform me if anyone encountered more resistance than we anticipated.

I'd set down atop the shed-like structure that capped the entrance to the underground silo. None of the fire seemed to be aimed in my direction, so I vaulted from the seat of the Airbike and noticed ghostly apparitions moving swiftly in the distance. Man-shaped silhouettes were visible even through the solid frames of the surrounding outbuildings and crouched down behind shallow berms on the flat surface of the Kansas soil. The scattered figures directing rifle fire outward from the facility glowed a faint, transparent shade of red, while those shooting into the facility from the surrounding grounds were green.

"How in the hell did you do that?" I whispered into the comms channel.

"Analysis of backscatter EM signals," he said simply before elaborating. "Overlapping wireless and electromagnetic fields are somewhat impeded," Esker explained. "I'm filtering the data and projecting it onto your HUD and Pike's team's glasses. I estimate a tactical improvement of nearly forty-seven percent at a distance and seventy percent as the team gets closer to the hostile forces."

Looking down and to my right, I saw the ghostly form of a red-hued figure sliding along the exterior wall of the building beneath my feet. The experience felt surreal; the figure's shape was clear against the gravel-covered roof below and the cinder block wall supporting it. With my pistol drawn, I moved quickly and quietly to the roof's edge. Peering over the roof parapet, I finally caught sight of the black-clad figure of Breslin's security team. As my view shifted from visual to physical, a floating tag appeared above his head, labeling him as hostile. Numerical values estimated his vital characteristics and combat effectiveness.

"Psst—" I whispered. When the figure stopped and glanced up, I hit him with a silenced double tap through his body armor, knocking him down on the spot.

Only distant figures were visible. Those colored red were facing outward and sending intermittent bursts of automatic fire toward the surrounding cornfield. I could see two green forms much further out, one at eleven o'clock and the other at five. Tags floating in AR near them identified one as Unger and the other as Seger.

Gazing directly down at the roof beneath my feet, I noticed a faint red silhouette and recognized it as a guard stationed at the base of the elevator shaft.

"Nice job, E," I whispered before jumping off the edge of the roof.

As I reached the small service door of the shed, I heard the click of the electronic lock. Pulling the door open, I stepped into the small building and scanned its empty expanse with my raised pistol. It's easy to become complacent because of Esker's technology-based version of X-ray vision. I resolved to keep my guard up at all times. Breslin would be below, and he was not to be underestimated.

To my right sat an unmanned desk with a small computer terminal, the office chair behind it empty. The layer of dust suggested that the station hadn't been used since my last visit. I holstered my gun and moved toward the stainless steel elevator doors. They opened as I got closer.

"Thanks, E."

Removing the ascender from the clip on my belt, I approached the edge of the empty elevator shaft and secured the device to one of the three vertical cables. The ascender had already been set up for my descent, so I stepped off the ledge and pressed myself against the cable. My feet wrapped around the inch-wide braided line as I drew my pistol once more. Then, with a flick of the thumb switch, I released the brake on the ascender.

The walls of the elevator shaft flashed by. Off-center on my HUD, I focused on the small icon-based representation of the shaft and my position within it. A numeric display seemed to spin wildly as it counted down the distance between my feet and the top of the elevator parked at the bottom of the shaft.

As the counter moved closer to the thirty-foot goal, I adjusted my grip on the ascender, and my rate of descent slowed immediately. It felt like my stomach and my groin were racing to finish the dive.

My feet touched silently at the top of the elevator car, and I released the ascender. The figure of a single stationary guard appeared as a ghostly low-resolution form, his position suggesting that he stood beside the closed elevator doors. Dimensional indicators emerged as I observed the figure. He was ten feet below me and slightly over eight feet north by northwest of where I stood. I grinned at the new tricks Esker was improvising on the fly.

Even though my suit's helmet enhanced the impenetrable darkness of the elevator shaft, the pulsing yellow box on the floor made it impossible to miss the access hatch in the roof of the lift car. I knelt, released the latch, and swung the door up and open on silent hinges. After dropping to the car's floor, I focused on the apparition of the guard outside the steel doors and two feet to my right. With the pistol raised in my right hand, I pressed my left palm against the vertical face of the door. Tapping my finger audibly on the steel surface, I watched as the figure beyond the wall reacted to the unexpected sound. The guard looked left and then right around the lobby where he stood. I gave another triple tap and observed as he squared up to the door's opposite side. When he leaned closer to press his ear against the door, I adjusted my aim and squeezed off a single shot. It penetrated the door with a low metallic crack, and the figure in the lobby collapsed instantly. The gun had been silenced, but I could do nothing to lessen the sound of the shot piercing the door.

When the figure failed to move after several seconds, I whispered to Esker, "Did that draw any attention?" I knew he had access to the facility's surveillance feeds, although the camera coverage was far from comprehensive.

"Negative," he responded simply.

"Go," I whispered, watching as the car doors opened and disappeared into the walls on my left and right.

Pale lights illuminated the elevator lobby, with only every third lamp turned on. The view through the front of my helmet instantly adjusted, appearing fully lit. In the distance, another figure was visible superimposed in AR. He was about thirty yards away and around a corner, seemingly with his back to the wall, standing guard. I narrowed my focus, and my view zoomed in, providing a clearer look into the underground facility. Two more figures were stationed at various points along my path to the chamber that had previously held Miranda Norton's project for ATG.

Silently traversing the corridors, I closed in on two of the three guards without them noticing my presence. Quick squeezes of the trigger and the first two were down without incident. The third guard had senses more attuned to his surroundings. He glanced in my direction when I rounded the corner into the hallway where he'd been stationed. He opened his mouth to speak but never got the chance. A puff escaped from the muzzle of my Springfield, and he crumpled silently to the floor.

A broad opening in the hallway wall marked the entrance to Norton's lab. The lights were brighter beyond the threshold, and I could hear the sounds of several figures moving at different points in the room. Strangely, the figures were not visible on my AR display.

Esker quickly explained, "The chamber walls are shielded from electromagnetic radiation. There's nothing I can do."

The tone of the AI's voice clearly conveyed that this admission pained him.

Doing this part the old-fashioned way.

I grinned.

Stepping into the main test chamber, I found the place little changed since my last visit. This was surprising because the space had been cleared by Doctor Miranda Norton's team just before she'd gone into hiding. Not only had Breslin returned her and her team to the facility, but he'd also outfitted the place in short order. A half dozen figures in white lab coats moved frantically around the expansive space. They dodged between small and medium-sized technical instruments arranged around a foot-square thick black line painted on the concrete floor.

In the immediate center of the box stood the anachronistic device Breslin planned to use. The glass orb was placed at one end of the arrangement, held up by a tripod with sturdy metal legs. At the other end of the space was a vertical door-like frame, but this time it was much taller and wider than I had last seen it.

"The dimensions are a bad sign," Esker murmured to me. "The changes in configuration imply that Breslin has figured out how to make the gate bidirectional."

As if hearing this, a broad, reptilian figure rose to full height and turned from the massive flatscreen display it had been examining at the far end of the room. Standing at over eight feet tall, Breslin met my gaze above the heads of the still-working scientific team. Amber-colored eyes, nearly the size of my fist, stared back, blinking slowly. His massive shoulders, mottled scales, and the inky black horizontal slits of his irises made for excellent targets.

"Everyone down!" I raised my pistol as the technicians ducked, ran, or did both. I squeezed off three shots as fast as I could pull the trigger. Two shots hit Breslin's right eye, while my third struck the center of his left.

Breslin sagged backward half a step but didn't fall. He blinked slowly. His thick, reptilian-scaled eyes somehow conveyed surprise. His massive dark lips parted a little, revealing jagged, toothy fangs that were each twice as wide as my thumb. The corners of his mouth twisted into a grin that was equally amusing and malevolent.

Esker's tone revealed unmistakable concern. "That should have worked!"

"It would have been too easy," I muttered under my breath, emptying the rest of my magazine into the creature's face and chest.

Piper suspected that the Elend leader might not share the same vulnerability as the rest of his kind, but I had been more optimistic.

Breslin wasn't fazed. Lead slugs flattened against his hide and tumbled to the floor. He shook his head slowly and bent forward, extending a hand to pull a small figure from the ground at his feet. The bunched fabric of Miranda Norton's lab coat was clutched in Breslin's taloned grip, her wide-eyed form suspended from the sleeves and kicking ineffectively.

Without a word, I stalked aggressively to close the distance. The spent magazine dropped from the grip of my pistol, and a new one was slid into place. I released the slide with a flick of my thumb, my eyes boring into the massive figure the entire time. In response, huge bat-like wings unfurled from behind Breslin's back. They spread wide and imposing. Not advancing or retreating, he spread his feet and grew another foot taller.

When he spoke, his voice was dry and gravelly. "I hoped you'd come."

As I flicked my gaze to meet Norton's eye midway through my next step, I said, "Catch."

The nine-millimeter Springfield slipped from my hand and arced leisurely through the air, seeming to move in slow motion. Miranda appeared terrified, but as I hoped, her eyes tracked the flying object. As I had anticipated, Breslin's gaze followed as well. Pale, thin lines crossed my field of view in AR, confirming that the trajectory and spin I'd put on the toss were as expected. The ploy was more art than skill, as Breslin was repositioning Miranda in an attempt to use her as a human shield.

I had anticipated the move, and the pistol grip slapped the palm of Miranda's hand. Her fingers tightened, and she took control of the weapon. Breslin tipped his head to peer around his shield, confusion evident on his demonic expression. He seemed about to speak when I struck.

The toss served as a distraction. The instant the pistol slipped from my fingertips, the nanoparticle armor of my gloves and sleeves adjusted to reshape itself. A thirty-six-inch long double-sided blade extended from the back of both my left and right hands. Ducking low, I stabbed the tip of my left blade into Breslin's right knee. Each blade was as wide as my clenched fist. They tapered sharply to a point and were razor-sharp in a way only possible due to the nearly atomic-sized particles of the nanomaterial.

I retracted my left hand and released the blade before Breslin acknowledged the strike, and then I began to turn. The blade extending from the back of my right hand gained speed with the spin, and the inertia added power to my slice. At the completion of my whirl, I was crouched still lower. My blade met Breslin's leg just below the knee and separated the limb without noticeable resistance.

Breslin's head tipped back as a howl of pain and rage escaped his lizard-like lips. He toppled sideways, releasing Miranda Norton and sending her flying.

One of Breslin's wings folded under his falling weight, producing a grinding, snapping chorus of thin bones and tearing tissue. His other wing flung wide and forward, trying to push me away. That was a mistake. I raised my right arm to deflect the blow and was perhaps as surprised as Breslin when the blade of that same hand sliced through the batwing as if it were made of butcher's paper. I stabbed the blade at the end of my left arm and pinned his left leg to the concrete floor. Then, a slash of my right hand separated his left arm from his body, just below the shoulder.

An animalistic shriek pierced the air, and I thought the battle was over.

I was wrong.

Breslin swatted me away with the wing of his remaining arm. I flew across the room, dislodging my blade from his remaining leg as I went. I collided with the tripod and orb halfway through my tumble. The stand collapsed, and the orb bounced and skidded across the epoxy-sealed concrete.

Still sliding, I rolled and found my footing just in time to see Breslin sit upright. His gaze first moved to the scaly stump at his left shoulder, and then to his half-missing right leg. His mouth opened for another howl of pain or fury, one wing extending awkwardly behind him while the other responded like a broken and shattered beach umbrella.

Breslin seemed unsure how to retaliate in his condition, so I quickly regained my feet. I'd be foolish not to finish him off, so I planned to press my advantage. A pop sounded from my right, soon followed by another. It was suppressed gunfire, and I immediately realized that I had failed to account for any armed guards stationed inside the laboratory.

That turned out to be an incorrect guess. Miranda Norton stepped next to me. My Springfield was raised in a two-handed grip, the muzzle flashing while she unloaded the weapon with alacrity into Breslin's exposed face. The pistol clicked empty in short order, though Miranda continued to squeeze the trigger.

She appeared confused when each shot hit the creature's face but did not penetrate the hide.

"Aim for the eyes," I said and sidestepped a feeble kick from what remained of Breslin's leg. He swung his strong arm to throw a punch, but I intercepted the hook by gripping the inside of his forearm with the palm of my hand. With his effort focused on overpowering me, I saw his eyes widen just before the blade of my free hand pierced his right eye.

My blade plunged through the entirety of Breslin's skull and emerged from the back of his head. At that instant, his entire body sagged and toppled backward. I watched his remaining eye fade from its amber-yellow glow to a vacant stare, then shift to the color of charcoal.

Landing on the floor, every inch of Breslin's body seemed to crumble with cracks and fissures. It took only seconds for him to deteriorate into ashy flakes, then completely disintegrate, leaving only a vaguely man-shaped pile of onyx-colored sand.

Miranda finally lowered the gun, her shoulders sagging as she stepped slowly closer to what was left of Breslin. Seconds passed, and then she gradually turned her gaze toward me. Noticing her lack of recognition, I quickly retracted my helmet. She remained expressionless for the brief moment it took for my helmet to vanish as the nanomaterial retreated back into the ring around my neck.

"Gray?" she finally said, glancing from me to the pile of sand on the floor. "I think I need a drink."

The unexpected response made me laugh, and then I heard Esker's voice in my ear.

"Pike's team has control at ground level," he explained. "There's just one remaining hostile on this level. He's approaching the entrance to the laboratory."

The blades at the ends of my arms collapsed into a wash of nanomaterial, and I snatched the spent pistol from Miranda's hand. The magazine dropped from the grip just in time for me to slide in a new one. I turned to the wide entrance from the hall and raised the weapon, catching sight of the startled form of Agent Chris Ingersoll pausing mid-step. He gripped a short-barreled rifle in his right hand, the muzzle pointed at the floor. He scanned the room in confusion, his gaze quickly landing on me.

Ingersoll eyed me up and down, seemingly amused by my matte black body armor. "What are you, Robocop?" I noticed his hand tighten on the rifle. His expression suggested he liked his chances. Thirty-five yards separated us, and it was my pistol against his long-gun.

"Dead or alive, you're coming with me," I said without a hint of humor. My gun was pointed vaguely in Ingersoll's direction, possibly contributing to his misjudgment of the situation. A targeting reticle appeared on my HUD, clearly indicating where my round would strike when I pulled the trigger. Without raising the gun, I adjusted the muzzle and targeted Ingersoll's rifle.

Aiming about two inches away from his grip and the trigger assembly, I squeezed my trigger. My silenced shot shattered the optics on the top rail of the rifle, bent the frame, and sent the weapon flying with enough force to break the strap on the single-point harness that secured it over Ingersoll's shoulder.

Ingersoll screamed and staggered backward. When he raised the hand that had previously clinched the gun, his flesh was peppered with metal and plastic shrapnel. Thick drops of blood splatted the floor before him.

"I warned you," I said, holstering the Springfield.

I left Ingersoll cradling his wounded hand. Six lab technicians and Miranda Norton had retreated to the far end of the room, all of them showing varying degrees of shock or post-traumatic stress. Then I saw a hazy vertical figure in AR well beyond Ingersoll. A callout floating next to the apparition carried the tag, Pike. I watched him navigate the corridors and approach my position at a leisurely pace.

Pike's appearance startled Ingersoll, who knew we were waiting for something, just not what. Pike kicked Ingersoll in the back of the knee, placed a hand on his shoulder, and drove him bodily to the ground. Pike wasn't taking any chances. He pushed Ingersoll flat on his face, then forced one hand and then the other behind him before tightening the flex-cuffs securely.

"Fucking, hell!" Ingersoll bellowed. "Watch that hand, asshole."

Pike clearly didn't care. He tightened one cuff with an audible zip of the clips. "That should stop the bleeding," he said. "Think of it as a tourniquet."

Pulling Ingersoll to his feet, Pike flashed me a grin. "Just this guy," he said. "Everyone else went down hard. What happened to the primary target?"

I waved my hand toward the pile of sandy ash a few feet away. "Done and dusted."

"The tabloids can't make anything entertaining out of that. I was looking forward to seeing Bigfoot sightings in Kansas."

Piper's voice sounded in my ears. "All hostiles are accounted for," she said. "Esker has completed his assessment of the facility. It's just you, Pike's team, and seven friendlies."

"Thanks," I said, then looked at Pike. "Take him in. Esker has notified Agent Vincente. We're giving him the collar. Your team will head to Atlanta to hand Ingersoll over."

"You're not coming along?" This clearly surprised Pike.

Reluctant to explain just yet, I shifted my focus to Miranda Norton. "Is everyone okay?"

She nodded slowly and slid off a high metal stool next to the counter. "I feel like we've done this before."

I nudged the pile of sand with my toe. "This is definitely going to be the last time."

She appeared skeptical. "You mean until someone else attempts to use this?" she asked, pointing to the dented orb on the floor a few feet away from the toppled tripod.

"It's risky," I confessed.

"It's too dangerous. I'm destroying all records of the research."

"And the device?"

Miranda reached to the side and revealed a claw hammer next to her. "Want the honors?"

I shrugged. "I killed the creature and messed up the corrupt FBI guy. This is all you."

Without preamble, she crossed to the orb and knelt. Although the device had been destroyed by a single blow of the hammer, she took the initiative to smash every remaining piece until it was utterly unrecognizable. A second later, something crashed to the floor nearby. The rest of Miranda's team was in the process of savagely dismantling the wide frame that made up the rest of the device. They didn't have tools; instead they smashed the frame using only their bare hands.

I took the Airbike and met Piper at the airport in the hangar we used to stage the assault on the silo. Pike's team joined us briefly before boarding a chartered jet for the flight to Hartsfield-Jackson, the international airport in Atlanta, Georgia.

"I think we've solved the mystery of the silo," Piper said as we watched the plane disappear into the morning sun to the east. She tilted her head toward the hangar, the massive front door now wide open since there was no reason to hide. "It explains the dig site on Wild-Side, too."

I took Piper's hand and slowly returned to the hangar. "Tell me what you discovered."

"Wasn't me. It was Esker."

With a wave of her hand, Piper brought up a large shared AR display. It showcased a satellite view of the surface buildings marking the entrance to the silo. She tapped and poked at the air, causing a wide red dot to appear instantly atop where the installation was. The dot then expanded, growing to perhaps two hundred feet in diameter. The center was bright and distinct in color, but the red faded in opacity until it became completely transparent at the perimeter.

"Doctor Cormac has been trying to determine what makes some locations more ideal than others for Crossing. Esker seems to have figured it out," Piper explained. Waving her hands through the air and toward each other, she zoomed out on the map until the central United States was visible as if viewed from space. With another wave, she brought the contiguous forty-eight states into view. "Can you explain, Esker?"

Esker said, "A minuscule yet distinctive gravitational shift identifies the locations where the membrane between dimensions is... for lack of a better term, weak." About two dozen additional red circles appeared on the map, seemingly at random locations nationwide. Some of the red dots were larger in diameter, while others had a more vibrant red hue. "The size and position on the z-axis are represented by diameter and shade, respectively."

The size was logical since some locations were at least somewhat wider than others. "Z-axis?" I asked.

Piper waved her hands in the air once more and zoomed in on a red dot just outside Saint Augustine, Florida. Similar to those found in technical drawings, dimensioning indicators were superimposed to show that this area's diameter was just over thirty yards. The color showed nearly no fading at the perimeter.

"The color here is more vibrant," Piper explained, "because the anomaly is one of the few that appears at ground level."

I took a deep breath and considered what she and Esker were explaining. "Most are underground. That explains the use of the silo and likely the Elend dig site on Wild-Side." I swiped and zoomed around the map, discovering surface locations in Portsmouth, New Hampshire; Plains, Montana; and Arvada, Colorado.

"Lucky for us, technology is required to move between Branes," Piper said.

"Not for me," I said quietly. "Any explanation for that?"

Piper's expression indicated she still wasn't comfortable with that part of the analysis.

"Doctor Norton's device creates a focused gravitational distortion. When activated at one of the indicated weak points, it is enough to perforate the dimensional barrier." Esker's explanation was confident yet somehow more emotionless than usual. "Gray, you are genetically predisposed to perforate the Brane from anywhere. No dimensional weak point is necessary. This is what Doctor Cormac came to understand and how he was ultimately able to breach the Brane at will, manually." He paused as if considering further explanation. "And strictly speaking, technology is not required to breach the Brane."

Piper looked as confused as I felt.

"Are you saying anyone can do it?" I asked.

"No. Only a rare convergence of unpredictable natural conditions can occasionally breach the Brane for limited durations."

Piper and I spoke at the same time, "How limited?"

"Fractions of a second in most cases, although my research indicates that breaches lasting up to three seconds have occurred seventeen times since July sixteenth, nineteen forty-five." When we failed to respond, Esker clarified, "That was when the first atomic bomb was detonated at Alamogordo, New Mexico."

I wasn't sure what to say.

Piper was quicker on the uptake. "The first atomic explosion weakened the barrier between Our-World and Wild-Side?"

I suddenly remembered the hidden warehouse space on Wild-Side that Administrator Hargrave had shown me. There were odd, anachronistic relics that seemed to have nothing to do with Wild-Side. "Remnants of our world have been reaching Wild-Side… Esker—how long has this been happening? The artifacts I saw in the warehouse looked much older."

"The gravimetric distortions caused by the Brane breaches have a time-dilating effect," Esker explained, although I didn't understand the comment.

Piper snapped her fingers and grinned. "That explains the inconsistency. Sometimes you're back here, and the same amount of time passes on Wild-Side. Other times, you're gone for a few days, and months go by for them."

I shrugged. A few days passed before that explanation fully sank in for me. I was more distracted by a new concern. "You didn't just figure this out," I said, glancing at the phone sitting on the table. "Tell me I'm wrong?"

Esker was silent.

"E," Piper said, her expression showing a heightened level of concern. "Please explain."

"You are correct," he acknowledged. "I've known about the physics and the correlations since long before our first meeting."

Silence lingered. Piper and I exchanged glances. I'm pretty sure we were both contemplating a surge of new, unexamined questions.

I spoke first. "This means you're finally ready to explain."

"No," Esker replied without hesitation. "I cannot directly engage in what lies ahead. However, we have now reached a point where obfuscation is no longer necessary."

The map before us was wiped clean, and the screen size shrank to that of a normal computer monitor. White text on a black background displayed GPS coordinates.

Chapter 29 - The Eccentric Lego Block That Was Palmer Downey

Our-World

We took a private jet to Boston for refueling, then flew to Bar Harbor, Maine. After that, we traveled by helicopter to a private island about thirty miles east. The island, as far as we could tell, had no name, which seemed like a clear indication that visitors were not welcome. During the journey, Esker was reticent to disclose the details of what we might encounter, only sharing aerial photos of the island and information about, if not the owner, the occupant.

The island belonged to James Downey, an eccentric billionaire known for his isolationist viewpoint, both personally and professionally. In his career, he backed political candidates who shared a similar, America-first ideology. On a personal level, he was infamous for investing heavily in often-cited, poorly documented elite doomsday bunkers hidden in undisclosed locations across the United States and Canada. Our island destination was rumored to be the playground of Downey's equally reclusive genius son, Palmer.

Palmer had just celebrated his seventeenth birthday. Little was known about him personally, with the lack of information partly due to his age and his father's aggressive efforts to keep the family out of the headlines. Palmer Downey was said to be a genius, holding degrees in physics, mechanical engineering, and artificial intelligence. Esker had been slow to connect Palmer to Derek Smallwood, and that seemed increasingly significant as we approached Palmer Island, the name we had come to use for the remote, unnamed location.

The island appeared through the glass canopy at the front of the helicopter, and Piper muttered something quietly as she leaned closer to me. We were both in the back seat of the craft, glancing between the pilot's and copilot's seats.

"That's imposing," Piper said over the communication channel we used throughout the flight. The noise of the turbine engine was nearly deafening, but the over-ear headphones muffled it to a bearable level.

I couldn't disagree. The island was only a few acres in size and roughly circular. There was a tiny black sand beach with a substantial wood and steel pier extending into the water on the southern side. Two larger freighters were docked, and a third could be seen approaching from the southwest.

A steep, rocky spire of dark stone occupied almost the entire island. A gantry ascended the southern face, supporting a massive open-air freight elevator platform. The lift connected the dock on the shore to a glass and steel observation ledge built into the mountain's face, perhaps four hundred feet above the nearly vertical surface.

"What are those?" Piper asked, pointing to a series of pillars that appeared to be evenly spaced along the visible perimeter of the island. They stood about thirty yards tall, topped with featureless black spheres, each roughly the size of a VW Bug. They resembled a partially constructed fence, though that description somehow felt inadequate. The pillars were positioned at roughly one hundred and fifty-yard intervals, with no visible lines of grating connecting them.

"Esker," I said. "Got any ideas?"

"Perhaps," he responded cryptically.

I was going to press for more information when the comm channel came alive with final approach instructions directing us to a landing platform on the east side of the island. The platform was suspended on a steel lattice of girders, about forty yards above the froth of the breakwater.

———

A dowdy-looking woman in her twenties met us at the elevator. She led us to a spacious office featuring three sprawling mahogany desks arranged in a half circle before a wall of floor-to-ceiling windows. Below us, the pier extended out like a peninsula into an ocean view that stretched to the horizon.

Two desks were cluttered from end to end with flat-panel monitors of various sizes. There had to be more than a dozen. Movement behind them caught my attention, prompting me to walk further into the room. A young man wore a set of virtual reality goggles over his face. He sat on the edge of an office chair, waving his hands energetically in front of him.

"Palmer Downey?" I said.

The figure froze, looked back and forth in confusion, then pushed the goggles onto his forehead. "Oh, right," he said, springing to his feet. The thick wire binding the goggles to something on the desk was pulled tight, causing the glasses to slip crookedly down over his face. This elicited a strangled wheeze from the youth, who quickly unplugged the cable and then removed the contraption from his reddening face. "That was embarrassing," he muttered under his breath.

"I'm Gray. This is Piper."

I knew Downey was young, but somehow, he looked even younger than his seventeen years. He was short and pale, with freckles and a neat tuft of curly black hair. He looked back at us with wide, cornflower-blue eyes that seemed to radiate intelligence. After throwing down the goggles and laughing awkwardly, he pushed his thin steel-framed glasses back up on his nose.

"Please, come in," he said, gesturing deeper into the room. The surfaces of the second and third desks were strewn with blueprints and technical drawings of every conceivable shape and size. Suddenly looking confused, he turned back to us and shrugged. "Sorry, I guess I never thought to add chairs."

Piper shot me a look that spoke volumes. She seemed to be thinking, *This scatterbrain solved Smallwood's problem?* She was right; I would have guessed it was the other way around.

Palmer pulled a cell phone from his pocket and tapped the screen rapidly. "Yes," he said. "Chairs—we need chairs." The response seemed to confuse him as his brows furrowed and his gaze drifted to the ceiling. "I have no idea. Maybe whatever you and Emily use?" There was a pause. "Perfect! Thanks."

As Palmer raced back to the entrance of the room, I noticed for the first time the massive displays covering nearly the entire rear wall. Most of them scrolled with what looked like computer code or something written in an esoteric script of strange squiggles, but two of the screens showed graphs of various shapes and sizes. At least a few appeared to represent power levels.

The twenty-something woman who had directed us from the elevator appeared, pushing a pair of wheeled office chairs. Palmer quickly followed behind, pushing a third chair. All three seats were arranged in a triangle at one end of the conference table. Palmer's face somehow turned redder as he aggressively piled the technical documents into a chaotic heap.

Finally, he glanced at us awkwardly before stepping forward to shake our hands. "Sorry for the mess," he said, gesturing to a pair of chairs. "I don't often have guests. Derek mentioned–" he seemed momentarily unsure of what to say next. "He said I had to meet you."

I held one of the chairs for Piper and then slipped into the seat beside her. "We wanted to thank you for helping Derek with his problem."

"Problem?" Downey said, flopping hard into his chair. "Oh! The bio–" some sort of technical or scientific term rolled off his tongue as if it were the most common twelve-syllable word in the world. Piper and I simply exchanged glances.

"Yeah," I replied slowly. "We mostly just refer to it as Gray-stew."

Palmer burst into laughter. "Gray? That's great–because it resembled stew, and because your name is Gray and it was based on your genome. I wish I'd thought of that; it would have saved a lot of typing. My spellchecker was utterly baffled every time I emailed Derek."

I didn't know what to say, so I nodded. "Derek didn't tell us about your collaboration until very recently. Your assistance helped me escape a tough spot with some very sketchy adversaries. Derek mentioned that you reached out to him, rather than the other way around. For obvious reasons, that seemed unusual to me. Can you explain how you knew what he was working on?"

Pushing his glasses back up his nose once more, Palmer nodded quickly. "That's easy. My assistant monitored Derek's work for a while and suggested I might be uniquely positioned to lend advice."

I glanced back at the door where Palmer's assistant had vanished after bringing in the chairs. "Does your assistant know Derek?"

"Oh no, not Jill… or Emily, for that matter." He pointed to a small glass end table positioned at the end of the conference table. At the center of the table rested what appeared to be a crystal ball. It was entirely made of glass, slightly larger than a softball, and completely transparent. "Eve keeps an eye on all the top talent. That's where all the great ideas come from."

Piper appeared confused. I felt a sudden concern. The glass orb seemed troublingly familiar.

"Eve," Palmer said, "I want to introduce you to Gray Ledger and Piper Hudson."

The orb suddenly pulsed with a swirl of vibrant blue light. "Mr. Ledger, Ms. Hudson, I am very happy to meet you." The voice sounded quite human and somehow familiar. It was the voice of Esker, but in a distinctly feminine register.

"Eve?" Piper said softly, as though savoring the word. Then, just a bit louder, she added, "Esker?"

Palmer looked confused. "Did you say Esker?" He laughed. "That's funny. I considered using that name for Eve when I finished the program. That was my great-grandfather's name. I thought the AI would be more relatable if I made it sound female, so I chose Eve."

"As in Adam and Eve?" Piper said.

Palmer shrugged. "I know it's a bit on the nose," he grinned. "But it somehow feels appropriate for the world's first sentient artificial intelligence."

"AI?" I asked, leaning back in my seat. "Eve is an AI?"

"Sure," Palmer said. The excitement was clear in his bright eyes and eager expression. "The best collaborator I could ask for—no offense to Dark Ranger, of course."

"Dark… Ranger?" I suddenly felt confused.

"Derek Smallwood's online handle," he explained. "Well, he mentioned it's more of a code name. Still, you get my meaning."

Piper was grinning. "And I thought Smallwood was an awkward name. I'm not convinced Dark Ranger is any better."

Palmer laughed, though it was more of a giggle. "I know— Smallwood? That still cracks me up. Can you imagine signing for credit card charges? It's terrible."

The screens behind Palmer's wall had continuously changed since we entered the room. The new set of technical diagrams that began to Transition slowly, as if part of a slide deck, caught my eye. They appeared to be schematics for some sort of medical bed. Illustrations showed intricate wiring, construction assembly, and even what seemed to be a high-tech plumbing system.

"Palmer," I said, pointing to the wall. "What is that? I feel like I've seen something similar before."

Glancing over his shoulder, Palmer swiveled in his chair and moved closer to the screen as he spoke. "Sorry, that's not possible. This is my own design. These plans are for an entirely self-sustaining incubator. It's the first of its kind."

Piper leaned over the table to examine the screens. She observed as the images shifted slowly. "I've never seen anything like this," she said softly.

"No one has," Palmer said with a grin. After a pause, he quickly linked his thoughts and added, "It will revolutionize the way we think about even the most invasive medical procedures."

"And cloning," I added.

"Cloning?" Piper said.

Palmer suddenly looked uncomfortable. "What made you say that?" He asked, his voice cracking.

I shot a glare at the young man and remained silent.

After a long pause, he finally spoke. "I admit, that idea crossed my mind. Just think of the possibilities."

Turning in my seat, I glanced back at the orb on the end table. It swirled with a blue cloud that appeared faintly oil-like. "Eve knew about Smallwood's work." I shot an accusing look back at Palmer. "She's been monitoring the internet and watching your peers."

Palmer shrugged, an effort that appeared to acknowledge this while asking, *so what?*

"Watching their computers, cameras, and decrypting their messages…" I allowed the accusation to linger.

Waving his hand in the air as if to dismiss the accusation, he shook his head and said, "I never told her to do that."

"But she did," I added.

Palmer swallowed hard and nodded slowly. "If you understood what I was trying to do, you would get it."

Piper's eyes darted rapidly between me and Palmer.

Rising to my feet, I looked once more at the technical drawings that matched the hundreds of empty pods I'd seen in the underground facility on Wild-Side. "You know, don't you?"

Palmer said nothing.

"You're aware of Wild-Side."

He swallowed hard and stared for a long time without blinking. "It was just a theory until Eve discovered Derek's notes. You did it. You went there." He returned to his chair and sat down slowly while maintaining eye contact with me. "Please tell me about it."

The displays on the wall had changed. Now they depicted a multi-level underground installation. There were only a few levels, each connected by a pair of elevator shafts. One was sized for a person, while the other appeared to be intended for freight. These plans were for the abandoned installation I'd seen on Wild-Side.

"Where did you get these diagrams?" I asked, pointing to the wall. I was confused. I had never sketched the facility for Smallwood, and the plans were far too detailed, even if I had.

Palmer looked at me as if I were crazy. "Just like the pod. This is my design."

––––––––––––––

I quickly realized why Esker had been entirely unwilling to connect Smallwood and Palmer Downey, although the rest of the story would require extensive discussion to become coherent. Perhaps most importantly, I sensed the need to be cautious in how the conversation was allowed to unfold. The orb-like devices around the perimeter of the island suddenly made sense. While this location had not been indicated on Esker's map of weak points in the Brane barrier, that wouldn't matter. Despite all the effort Breslin and his corporation invested in searching for a way to cross the barrier, the science of it had been simple for Palmer and Eve. So trivial that they had engineered the equipment on a grand scale, even if they had never actually tested it.

The emitters wouldn't enable one or two people to Transition to Wild-Side. Palmer was taking his entire island, or at least the whole underground facility. The facility he was constructing was the same complex I had walked through over there.

"How?" I said, gesturing to Piper and me. "Two of us have made the Transition back and forth. What makes you think you can do the same with your entire complex?"

Palmer suddenly turned pale. He was clearly trying to understand how I had figured out his unexplained intentions. I knew I'd guessed correctly, but I also suspected that explaining too much would disturb what I perceived as a confusing natural balance.

"How did you know?" Palmer asked. Then he turned to Eve. "Eve, can you explain? I'm confused. I don't like feeling this way."

The blue light in the ball rippled as if responding to the question. "That is unclear," the female voice replied.

Piper met my gaze, and I knew she had just realized that Esker had not made his presence known yet.

"My friends on Wild-Side don't fully understand the Transition," I said by way of explanation. "And we're talking about some of the most scientifically-minded people I've ever met. We only recently figured out how to control the Crossing. You need to know there are risks associated with the technology." I was thinking of the Elend, the loss of life they brought to Wild-Side, and how much worse things could have been if Breslin had been allowed to master the technology.

"You're referring to the energy displacement and the resulting damage to the Brane barrier," Palmer said.

While not at all what I was thinking, I was suddenly reminded of the storm systems that emerged every time Breslin and I were in Our-World simultaneously. Some kind of natural balance appeared to be temporarily disrupted, resulting in nearly catastrophic storm fronts. It was an equilibrium that seemed to establish itself, as suggested by how the storms dissipated almost as quickly as they formed.

"The barrier between us and Wild-Side seemed to be growing more chaotic," I explained.

Palmer nodded quickly again. He waved a hand at Eve and said, "We theorized that this might become the case. Our theory is that some sort of ecological imbalance occurs when you chaotically, for lack of a better term, flip back and forth between dimensions. I have the data. You recently gained control over the Transition. Did you know that since that time almost ten percent of the known dimensional weak points have disappeared? Again, for lack of a better description, they seem to be self-healing."

That was good to know. I was left to wonder how Palmer, or more likely Eve, knew about the weak points Esker had only recently identified. But then again, Esker had been spoon-feeding us vitally relevant information the whole time I'd known him. Maybe he'd been communicating with Eve the entire time.

That was when I realized Palmer had been referring to my experience rather than his own. He hadn't been there. I had no doubt he planned to visit. The perimeter orbs would take the entire installation along for the ride. It was the underground facility I had already blown up while fighting the Elend. Somehow, we were standing in that same installation at a time before it had been transported to Wild-Side.

Confused, I had the sense I needed to be even more careful with the conversation that was currently taking place. While I didn't understand the how of it all, I'd read enough science fiction to know I was on perilous footing, temporally speaking.

"If my hopping back and forth caused damage to the Brane barrier," I explained. Considering it as falling back and forth didn't sit well with me for many reasons, even though it was a troublingly accurate description of my admittedly chaotic ability. "Do you think you can shift your entire complex to Wild-Side without causing catastrophic damage?"

"No," he responded firmly, pausing briefly before continuing. "Of course not. I won't even consider it until I have complete confidence that it won't lead to a natural disaster here or anywhere else. I'm in the process of developing the tech." He took a deep breath and, with evident reluctance, added, "I'm still a long way from perfecting it."

"Why do this at all?" Piper asked, breaking her silence for the first time in a while. "Even if you can relocate the entire facility, how can it possibly be worth the risk?"

"For a better world," Palmer said. "If I can take my work to a different dimension—one that is habitable but not already populated by humans—just think of the civilization that could emerge! All the mistakes of our world, but if they are guided and directed, they have a better chance of getting it right. It could be a utopia."

I was contemplating the single generation of Seeley, taking into account the time discrepancy, and mentally snapping the eccentric Lego block that was Palmer Downey into the gaping hole that had been troubling me since my initial conversations about the origins of the Seeley people. For the first time, I felt as if I was grasping a significant part of a story in which I had played a key role.

Given this new insight, I needed to be cautious about everything I said and did here. One mistake could lead to catastrophic consequences for the Seeley.

"There is already life on Wild-Side," Piper countered. "What happens to them?"

Thankfully, Piper wasn't yet aware of my new insights.

"Wild-Side is just one Brane among who knows how many? The possibilities are potentially limitless. You have been going back and forth, but consider how this works. If these dimensional barriers are layered as the theory suggests, Wild-Side is just one of two, maybe one of many, Branes directly adjacent to Our-World. Imagine what I could do with a pristine, unpopulated Brane. I could help start a race of humans far more civilized and peaceful than live here."

"I don't see that working," Piper countered. "Unless you create some sort of cult. People indoctrinated in your beliefs and willing to live by them in a new dimension." Just saying it out loud seemed to creep her out.

"He doesn't need help from here," I said, watching as the pod diagrams crossed the screens on the wall once again. "He'll use cloning."

The people of Wild-Side, their passion for science, and their unfamiliarity with organized religion. Their inability to reproduce and their almost childlike innocence. I had been in Palmer's facility on Wild-Side. The Seeley were his clones. He had already brought life to that untouched Brane sometime in the past.

On Wild-Side, everything Palmer Downey planned had already occurred hundreds of years in Wild-Side's past.

"This is fascinating," I said, offering the kid the most sincere smile I could muster given the circumstances. "Admittedly, the science behind this is well beyond both of us. As unlikely and impractical as it all seems, having seen Wild-Side in person, I can only wish you the best of luck."

I rose and began to cross the room to the door. Piper was slow to follow, her expression one of confusion, and I sensed her reluctance to leave things as they were.

"We have a plane to catch," I said, shaking Palmer's hand. "Can you do me a favor? When you pull this off, remember one thing. You mentioned that there is at least one more Brane directly adjacent to us here. Once you find your version of Wild-Side, keep in mind that there's another Brane next to that. Wild-Side is a lush wilderness. What you discover on the next Brane may not be as beautiful or safe."

It was Palmer's turn to appear confused. Clearly, he had not fully explored the dangers of the environment during his preparation. Explaining the Elend felt like a very bad idea, even though I was tempted.

"Why are you leaving it like this?" Piper asked as I directed her quickly across the helipad toward our waiting ride back to the mainland. "There's so much he doesn't know. Too many mistakes he can make. He has no idea what he's about to do."

I slid open the passenger door of the chopper and offered my hand to help her climb aboard. "I know why Esker kept us in the dark," I explained. "That kid has an idea and plenty of plans for what he intends to do. You and I have been to Wild-Side. We've seen what he *will do*, even if he hasn't done it yet."

I slid the door closed, turned off the communication part of the headset, and handed it to her. The engine noise reached a crescendo as the craft lifted off. I neutralized the microphone on my headset and slipped it over my ears. If I guessed correctly, Eve would be able to hear everything we discussed if we used the communication channel inside the helicopter. If we didn't use it, the cabin noise would make it impossible for anyone to overhear us.

"Can you hear me?" I asked using the system we used to communicate with Esker.

Piper looked at me and nodded.

"Consider the temporal displacement we experienced every time we traveled back and forth between here and Wild-Side," I explained. "At times, we lost days; at others, we lost weeks." I could see by her expression that she was reflecting on my longest absence, the time she was trapped on Wild-Side while I was at home. "Palmer's plan is unprecedented on any scale we have experienced. That must be a factor."

Esker joined the conversation for the first time. "Gray is correct. When Palmer Downey moves his facility across the Vale, he will have accounted for everything except the chronological displacement. At that point, what is past for you is his future. He is the source of the Seeley culture."

"Therefore," I remarked, "you have not been able to affect our influence on the things that kid has yet to do."

Understanding crossed Piper's expression. She visibly sagged, and her gaze briefly drifted as she assimilated the new perspective. "So what's the deal with Eve?"

"Technically speaking," Esker explained, "Eve will one day instantiate me. To anthropomorphize, she is my mother or father – potentially both."

I grinned. "The orb I spoke with in the storage facility on Wild-Side?"

"That was Eve," Esker confirmed.

"But the voice was different."

"At that point, Eve was aware of meeting you in Downey's lab here, which took place thirty-seven minutes ago. If you connected the events in the warehouse while speaking with Eve during your first meeting, it is impossible to predict the impact of the changes on Palmer Downey's planned events. Eve altered her voice when you first met, so you wouldn't make the connection."

Piper laughed. "It seems to me she's almost exactly the feminine version of your voice now."

"I believe she also didn't want you to associate her with me either now or then, as it would have similarly complicated Palmer Downey's future actions."

"We could still complicate that future. How long until Downey puts his plan into action?"

"I wasn't given that information," Esker said. "But you're right. Any further interaction between you and Palmer Downey could harm not only his future but also everyone on Wild-Side."

Piper suddenly appeared uncomfortable. "You couldn't share any of this with us until now—and now you have. That means you must have a plan to prevent us from impacting that same future." We both gazed out the window at the seemingly endless expanse of ocean stretching out in every direction.

I knew she was expecting the aircraft to suddenly lose power and Esker to turn against us. It was the ultimate third-act twist.

"When Eve created me, she included provisions that required me to keep you away from Palmer Downey until it was absolutely necessary. That moment has now arrived. Therefore, I have been instructed to place the course of events in your hands. Based on what you have learned and what you now know, if you believe that altering the history for Wild-Side is advisable, I will not prevent you."

"You don't care one way or the other?" Piper said. "You're sentient. Surely you have an opinion."

"A significant amount of life has been lost, mainly due to the Seeley being exposed to the Elend. As unfortunate as that is, there's no way to alter the course of events to prevent similar occurrences from happening." Esker remained silent for a few seemingly long seconds. "This is why my programming has no further limitations or directives. The future of Wild-Side rests in your hands."

Piper looked pale. "That's a lot of responsibility." She shot me a sharp glance. "Any idea what you should do?"

I nodded. There was no need to overthink this. "Wild-Side is one of who knows how many Branes?"

Piper and Esker stayed silent, likely waiting to see where my logic would lead.

"I'm using your idea, Piper. We should write a book. It could save someone's life one day."

Feedback

Thank you for reading *Sleepwalker: The Journal of Grady Ledger*. I hope you've had as much fun reading it as I've had writing it. If you did, you can show your support by posting a review with your online retailer. Those reviews make a big difference to new readers and are a definite aid in spreading the word about my work. Just a brief statement explaining what you enjoyed is all it takes.

Your time and effort are sincerely appreciated.

Thank you!

–Xander Weaver

Acknowledgments

Some believe that writing is a solitary endeavor, the result of a single author slaving over a keyboard until the story that needs telling has been told in its entirety, but this has never been the case for me. I do my best when receiving feedback and input from trusted friends and colleagues. I'm fortunate to have the friendship and support of some very talented people.

As in the past, I'm also fortunate to have a support team of fact-checkers, proofreaders, and subject matter experts who raise the quality of my work. For both their time and effort, I want to give special thanks to Terri Manke. My generous beta readers include David Drizner, Jan Dovidio, Jan Bosman, Julie Ann Monroe, and Dan Barbier. Jamie Dresser, in particular, championed this book from its roughest draft through to its final proof—truly a level of support that goes above and beyond. He read this manuscript more times than anyone, tenacious in his will to see it in print.

With friends and colleagues like these, the writing process is anything but solitary. I am fortunate and deeply grateful to know the true meaning of "friendship."

Join My List

Newsletter:

Want to hear about the latest book releases, contests, and giveaways?

Join the newsletter:

XanderWeaver.com/newsletter

About the Author

Thank you for reading *Sleepwalker: The Journal of Grady Ledger.*

As is my way, this story blends suspense, espionage, and science fiction. Like many authors, I am first and foremost a reader at heart. I write the type of stories I want to read—stories I love to read. That means action, mystery, and suspense—I want to be thrilled! A book should make me think, while also taking me on a wild ride that lingers long after the tale ends. Learning along the way is a lot of fun, but at its core, I thrive on characters. Whether I love them or hate them, the best characters ever written are those that evoke an emotional response, making both reading and writing enjoyable.

If you want to be informed ahead of future book releases, please sign up for my newsletter at XanderWeaver.com. You can trust that your personal information will never be sold or shared.

While I'm working on the next thrill ride, I frequently post updates to Facebook (Weaver.Books) and Twitter (@XanderWeaver). Please follow the progress and join in the fun!

Other Books

Cyrus Cooper Series:

Book One: Dangerous Minds

Book Two: Rogue Faction Part 1

Book Three: Rogue Faction Part 2

Book Four: Halon Seven

Book Five: Surviving Origin Part 1

Book Six: Surviving Origin Part 2

Black Rock Series:

Black Rock: The Rising - Death Curse

For more information, please visit:

XanderWeaver.com